DIARY OF AN ADULTEROUS WOMAN

Library of Modern Jewish Literature

Other novels by Curt Leviant

The Yemenite Girl
Passion in the Desert
The Man Who Thought He Was Messiah
Partita in Venice

Diary of an Adulterous Woman

A NOVEL

---

*Including an ABC Directory that offers
alphabetical tidbits and surprises*

Curt Leviant

Syracuse University Press

The paper used in this publication meets the minimum requirements of American National Standard for Information Sciences—Permanence of Paper for Printer Library Materials, ANSI Z39.48-1984.

Library of Congress Cataloging-in-Publication Data
Leviant, Curt.
    Diary of an adulterous woman : a novel / Curt Leviant.—1st ed.
        p. cm. — (Library of modern Jewish literature)
    "Includes an ABC directory that offers alphabetical tidbits and surprises."
    ISBN 0-8156-0670-2 (alk. paper)
        1. Triangles (Interpersonal relations)—Fiction. 2. Jews—New York (State)—Long Island—Fiction. 3. Long Island (N.Y.)—Fiction. 4. Women musicians—Fiction. 5. Violoncellists—Fictions. 6. Adultery—Fiction. I. Title. II. Series.
    PS3562.E8883 D52 2000
    813'.54—dc21   00-58770

Manufactured in the United States of America

For
Saul Bellow
with friendship and admiration

I lost myself in love.
—*The Two Gentlemen of Verona*

Every time I fall in love I think it's gonna last.
The only time I'm happy is when I'm dreaming in the past.
—*Starlight Express,* lyrics by Richard Stilgoe

Oh blues, when my woman got another man.
Oh blues, when my man got another woman.
—From a 1920's blues song

Give me libertine or give me death.
—Guido Veneziano-Tedesco

Truth can be invented. Fiction, right?
What better truth is there?
—Charlie Perlmutter

What is Leviant? . . . A writer of story-books! What kind of a
business in life may that be? What mode of glorifying God, or
being serviceable to mankind in his day and generation?
—Nathaniel Hawthorne, from the Introductory to *The Scarlet Letter*,
an early draft of *Diary of an Adulterous Woman*

Contents

Author's Note

*I*n order to get the maximum enjoyment from the ABC Directory, first read the novel through without the footnotes (if you can resist the temptation) and then re-read it with footnotes—signed with a ♥ in the text and on the bottom of the page—to see how your perception of the novel and its characters changes.

If you cannot resist, first look up the citation in the Index of words and *only then* seek out the alphabetical entry in the Directory.

Not all entries in the ABC Directory are cross-referenced in the basic text, so be certain to read all entries in the ABC Directory. Be careful to follow the leads suggested in the ABC Index and in the ABC Directory, and you will enjoy the tidbits, jokes, and surprises that will enhance, clarify, change, and sometimes even contradict the basic text.

BOOK ONE

Charlie

I float around Milty Rosen's June-green, tree-lined backyard in up-scale Riverdale, looking at the back of a big two-story brick colonial that exudes a near-Scarsdale elan. I'm euphoric, with maybe even a blissful smile on my face. But it's not the house I see that makes me happy. This does: Thirty years after our eighth-grade day school class of fifteen guys graduated, I get eleven of them to come back for a reunion. And all of them—it's amazing!—alive, well, recognizable, brimming with energy and good cheer. Miraculous, no? if you consider what can happen to ten or fifteen people in thirty years: moves, migrations, failure, air disasters, illness, accidents, depressions, disabilities, even—bite your tongue, like my mother says—death.

Our class, in our small, all boys' private Jewish school in Brooklyn, had been together for eight years, since first grade, and so we had a familiarity that could outlast friendship. Perhaps we were even more intimately bound than we dared to admit. Perhaps that is why I dreamt of the guys in my class, often in a reunion setting, for years before I decided to make the attempt to realize the dream.

But this wasn't the first. Our fifteenth anniversary reunion, when most of us were twenty-eight or -nine, was held in a small meeting room of the old Roosevelt Hotel in New York. Without prompting, as if it were a mythic rite we'd rehearsed, every time a fellow came through the door, a wide grin on his face, he called all his classmates by first and last name, as if we'd separated only for summer vacation. The last to enter got a round of applause when he finished his recitation. We all embraced and kissed, and in our effusive backslapping and handshakes and an occasional factitious touch of gaiety, all the old rivalries, jealousies and enmities seemed to wash away. But only for a little while. For as we sat down at the four tables for the buffet supper, like magnets clicking the guys grouped as in the old days: class leaders and clique pals at one table, the peripherals and hangers-on at the other three.

This time, for our thirtieth, to avoid that hierarchical taxis, clever Milty Rosen—efficiency engineer by profession—arranged one large oval of chairs on the lawn, which were gradually filling up.

Although I was happy to see everyone, the guy I wanted to see most of all was my old friend Guido. He had missed the first reunion—the only one who hadn't attended—because he was on assignment in Europe. Also, as I learned later, he was having personal problems at the time and didn't want to face his old classmates just then.

One way or another Guido always stood out. Among boys called Sid, Barry, David, Isaac, Herbie, Irving, Larry, Morty, Milty, Charlie (that's me), Guido was an anomaly. Among family names like Levy, Oxenfeld, Baumgarten, Ginzburg, Horodensky, Lifschitz, Cohen, Rosen, and Perlmutter (me again), having a classmate with the improbable name of Veneziano-Tedesco sounded like a put-on. How could an Italian be a Jew? we thought. You were either Italian or Jewish. You either listened to the Yiddish radio or the Italian. (Our downstairs neighbor, I was sure, had an Italian radio.) In our school we were taught to love our neighbors. But strangers? So, naturally, we picked on Guido. First, because he was an intruder. He came into our class in the September of our fourth grade and spoiled the homogeneity of our happy family of students who had been at one another's throats for the past three years. Second, because of his goyish name. Third, because he spoke English with an accent. Fourth, because he was slightly cross-eyed. Fifth, because we had a tradition of picking on foreigners who came from enemy countries.

Milty Rosen to Barry "Ox" Oxenfeld, standing near the buffet table, Isaac Baumgarten listening:

"One day I'm eating supper with my wife and several guests. I'm at the head of the table. My friend sits to my right, my wife to my left. I feel my wife rubbing her long leg against mine under the table. So, laughing, to pull her leg so to speak, I whisper to her: 'It's not my leg.' She laughs too and says: 'How do you know?' She's got me on that one. 'I can see,' I lie. Meanwhile, my friend whose leg is the real object of the intended rubbing, smiles. Why is he smiling? Because the queer thinks it's me who's rubbing his leg."

At least we didn't beat Guido up like we did Manfred and Siegfried Frankfurter, survivors, twins (so they claimed), born during the war and hidden as babies in occupied Poland by their fleeing German-Jewish parents. They had lived in Europe, and then, some years after the war, came to America with hardly a word of English. With names like Manfred and Siegfried we thought of them as Germans, not Jews. And the Frankfurter didn't help them survive either, at least not with our class. So we vented our anger against Germany by beating them up. "Yidn, yidn," they pointed to themselves as we pummeled them and explained, Not to fear, we weren't smacking them because they were Jews, God forbid, but because they were Germans. How can anyone who loves frankfurters be anti-Semitic? we told them. The pogroms were led by twins Isaac and David Baumgarten, who resented this intrusion on their uniqueness. If Manfred and Siegfried were indeed twins, they were circus material. Manfred was a short Frankfurter, shifty-eyed, thin-lipped, sly, his oblong head too big for his body, while brother Siegfried was tall, gangly, moronic looking, with big dopey bent ears and blubber lips. He looked about two years older. They were no more twins, those liars, than I was. Another reason to pick on them. To top it off, these Germans befouled the air of our classroom daily with their noise-less effluvia. With a battle cry of "Nazi gas!" Isaac or David ran to open the windows, and even when one of our own native sons let one fly, Baumgarten ran windowward with an accusing glance, holding his nose as he passed the Germans on his way to let in fresh American air. Still another reason to whack 'em.

The twins manqué didn't last too long. Their parents complained to our principal, Rabbi Gordin, that the students here were antisemitn. They didn't survive hiding, forests and death camps, and the hatred of Europe to be beaten up here, in a Jewish school, by Jewish children.

Barry Oxenfeld, Herbie Ginzberg listening:
"Now that's the sort of kinky story one would expect from Herbie Ginzberg, not Milty Rosen. Herbie, who after twenty-five years of driving still has a hang-up about going over the Washington Bridge because he's afraid it will fall down. So to get from Rye to Teaneck where he has his fresh milk run, for which any normal human being would take the GW, Herbie goes down the West Side Highway to the Lincoln Tunnel—that won't collapse on him in his mad world—and then takes the Jersey Turnpike up to Teaneck, by which time all his milk is sour."

No wonder the ground was set for unwelcome when the Italian showed up in the fourth grade.

I remember how we came up to Guido on his first day in school, ready for fun.

"Teacher says you're Italian," Morty Cohen, class president, began.

"Yes." Guido looked us straight in the eye—with his squint he could look *two* of us in the eye—nothing shy or diffident about him. Even then he was taller than the rest of us.

"Last year two Germans came. We got rid of them quick." said Sid Levy.

"So?" he said.

"So speak Dago," said Milty Rosen with a rictus grin.

"Dago?"

"Yeah, you know," said Larry Lifschitz, "Italian. Mafia talka!"

Guido rattled off a few sentences. And he smiled.

"Say fungoo," said Irv Horodensky.

"Fungoo," said Guido, with Italian music. Probably the only kid in school who could say it with conviction.

"What's it mean? Yeah, what's it mean?" said David and Isaac Baumgarten.

"I don't know."

We rolled on the sidewalk with laughter. It was Sicilian slang and this North Italian with jacket and tie *really* didn't know what it meant.

"He's a Dago and don't know fungoo?" Barry Oxenfeld cackled.

"Can you say, *Siamo idioti*?" Guido said.

"Sure," we said. "That's easy. *Siamoidioti*. And we began to chant: "*Siamoidioti, Siamoidioti, Siamoidioti*. See?"

And Guido smiled again.

We also called him Mafia, Macaroni and Spaghetti, Mussolini and pastafazool. We left him out of our games. We ate his lunch. We played saluggi—he didn't even know what *that* meant! Some Italian!—with his hat. But after a few months we grew tired of it. Calm Guido didn't respond. The tall smug bastard. But even then we didn't dare say anything about his slight squint. So we found all kinds of synonyms for his queer-duck schizoid nationality, with Macaroni a close second to Spaghet.

Morty Cohen to Isaac Baumgarten:

"Giovanni Battista Vico, a late seventeenth-century Italian historian and philosopher, believed that man's first language was in song, in imitation of birds, and that this language was in harmony with creation. Perhaps this is why the Torah is chanted, as a continuation of man's first language."

Then I saw a shiny red MG pull into the driveway and out stepped Guido, a camera around his neck.

I remembered him as a tall surly boy with a long aristocratic face, high forehead and straight black hair. Even at eleven or twelve he looked noble. Guido was always different. We took (actually, were given; better yet, had foisted upon us) piano lessons—for a year or two—and cut practice to play ball. He studied cello and stuck with it. We were building model airplanes—he was developing rolls of film. We were Brooklyn born. He, born in Venice, had the patina of Europe. We knew of war and hardship second-hand. He and his family were hidden by kindly Italian villagers during the German occupation, escaping roundup a number of times. Our fathers were small tradesmen or worked for others. His father was a physician, as were his grandfather and great-grandfather. We were Cohens, Rosens, Perlmutters. He was Veneziano-Tedesco.

The family's roots in Venice had tendrils four hundred years long. They had emigrated from Germany, part of the rather large wave of German Jews who went to northern Italy in the late sixteenth and early seventeenth century. In fact, to this day one of the several ornately handsome, centuries-old synagogues in Venice is the German, or Ashkenazic, synagogue, known as the Scuola Tedesca. And hence the Tedesco—the Italian word for *German*—part of his musically-rhythmic, hyphenated name.

The family left Venice because Dr. Abramo Veneziano-Tedesco had been awarded a two-year research fellowship at Brooklyn Jewish Hospital. But two became four, and the four, eight. Then came a turning point in their longish temporary hegira. Guido's father suddenly died of a heart attack when we were seniors in high school. His mother, lost and lonely now, wanted to go back home. She had never liked New York or the cultural niveau of the Brooklyn Jewish ladies, and she wanted to be near her daughter (older than Guido, and married, she had returned on her own) and two grandchildren in Milan. Guido was mature enough to take care of himself, she felt. Still, she decided to wait until Guido graduated college and got a job.

Although Guido's parents had urged him to continue the family tradition of medicine—his grandfather had been made a count by King Victor Emmanuel III for his contributions to medicine in Italy—Guido rebelled. He was an *A* student, but he didn't want to spend twelve years studying and slaving. He was drawn to photography. He loved to see the image of a picture he'd taken that same day slowly materializing before his eyes. A face coming up in developer fascinated him. In his darkroom once—we were in Columbia then—Guido told me: "Photography is a metaphor for me. Life is elusive. With a picture you capture reality forever."

The old cliché "pretty as a picture" is apropos here. As handsome as Guido was in high school, he got better looking in college. And the older he got, the better looking he became. He could have been a model in those supergoyish designer label ads you see nowadays, where unsmiling Nazi types with Germanic straight hair model sweaters, jackets and suits, and horses are never far away. But Guido's deep eyes, perhaps rounder than a WASP's, put off any definitive classification as a goy. At our reunion he looked distinguished. Like an ambassador. Whereas some of us were balding or had the beginnings of grey hair—Ox Oxenfeld was all white, at forty-three!—Guido's full head of hair was black. He was easily the most handsome man in the group. No wrinkles around the eyes, no crevices in the skin. He looked thirty. The old energy, that restless buzzing, like telegraph wires humming, radiated out of him. He never knew what it meant to be tired or sleepy. Even the slight squint in his eye was more modified. The guy I'd known during childhood and adolescence as a slightly conceited chap seemed to have mellowed. But the patrician air was still there.

Larry Lifschitz to Charlie Perlmutter, spearing a couple of Casaba melon slices, one of which Charlie nabs:
    "I wonder if melons and pumpkins and squash are in the same family."
    "Because of the seeds?"
    "Yes."
    "They must be related. I remember my parents saying that in Russia when a melon was bad they called it a squash."

"Then cars and citrus fruits must be in the same family, because when a car is bad they call it a lemon."

Guido was six-foot-one but edged it up to six-two. Indeed, he looked taller because he held himself erect, and his old-roots Venetian face gave him an elegance, an elan which his demeanor did everything to support and encourage. He considered himself an aristocrat, of course; he deigned to speak to everyone, but sooner or later he let you feel his own sense of worth. When he wanted to send you this message he modulated his now unaccented English to one slightly hued with an Italian lilt. The look in his eye alone told you he pronounced his family name with a capital *V*.

I envied Guido on several counts. I envied his entire insouciance toward life. The ease with which he related to girls, how quickly he made them laugh. He regaled them with Italian phrases and proverbs. Often a couple of *cara mias* would do the trick. He told them, Other people hear language, I see it. Verbs have colors and nouns have shape. Later, when I studied psychology, I learned the technical term for this phenomenon: synesthesia. He said he had once seen a Persian column of numbers, called the magic square, that defied mathematical logic: the numbers added up differently if you went from the top down or the bottom up. But he couldn't remember it; he had it at home somewhere. And numbers, he said, reminded him of music. Each was a different note. And the girls, especially those with an intellectual or creative bent, would eat this up. They'd never heard things like that before. Like his zany invention, the flashdark, the daytime equivalent of the flashlight. He wanted to invent something that in bright sunlight would give off a beam of darkness.

Out on a double date once, I heard him tell a girl that as a child he had seen in the Milan Zoo the original panther from Kafka's "A Hunger Artist." Or an off-the-wall remark like: "I've been listening to music all my life and absorbing all those notes. That's why I'm afraid of surgery. They open me up and the o.r. will be flooded by 104 Haydn symphonies. They won't be able to take it. Like an excess of light."

For another guy, a slight squint might have been an impediment. But it didn't make Guido look disabled, dopey, or pathetic. On the contrary, he could watch two girls at the same time.

I also envied his cello playing, his passion for photography. Guido didn't dabble; he was disciplined. Like Monet with the Rouen Cathedral, he would photograph a scene at various times of the day. I remember a photograph of his. It was a New England mountain scene on a cloudy day after a rain. Hills, dotted with houses on an expanse of fields. Bits of mist hung in the air. The hidden sunshine gave the layers of clouds multitudes of grey to white shades. It was a black-and-white photo and one could feel the mist. There's no better color, Guido said, than black and white.

His camera was like a magic wand. In the high school orchestra he met a beautiful cellist, Linda was her name, and photographed her in the nude. He posed her on a chair, bare-breasted, her cello between her legs. She showed this stunning black-and-white art photograph to two girl friends in the orchestra, who said "Me too!" (Guido never invited me to these photo sessions as technical assistant.) "There is nothing more real than a photograph," he said. "Not a mirror image, not a painting, not even a person's face—it's a photograph that best reveals a person's character. A photograph is like a fingerprint. You can't fake it . . . Like the old Italian saying has it: Only three things don't lie—the looking glass, the camera, and your mother-in-law."

I once remarked that a picture of a thing was always nicer than the thing itself. I didn't say it to be ingratiating. I believed it. I haven't seen a coat or a sheet or a sweater or a piece of furniture in a glossy color ad that wasn't nicer than the item itself. Even photographs of paintings and of Persian rugs were invariably nicer than the paintings or the rugs themselves.

"You see," Guido crowed, "how great is photography? I agree with you *cento mille per cento.*"

At Columbia Guido majored in Italian only because there was no major in photography. He had been photo editor of our high school paper and of the *Columbia Spectator* too. In his junior year he sold a couple of news shots to the *Daily News* (he never went anywhere without his camera), and they made him a campus stringer. In his senior year he got a part-time job with the *New York Post* and won first prize in *a Camera Magazine* competition for his nude cellist photo. These achievements gave him the connections he needed to advance his career. Now and for the past several years Guido had been photo editor at the *Long Island Post* and traveled all over the world.

You know what else I envied when we were kids? His stamp collection. He had told me that it had been in his family for more than one hundred years and contained many rare Italian stamps. I would show him my latest first-day covers and plate blocks when he came to our small apartment, and I asked to see his albums the first time I was at his house. But on the few occasions I visited his spacious two-story home, he always found an excuse not to show his stamps. The room it was in is being reorganized; things are in a mess; their housekeeper is sleeping or cleaning there; his mother is resting; his father had taken the albums to a stamp show to get them appraised. Then I stopped asking. And the fact that he rarely invited me to his house always irritated me. But instead of asking Guido why, I complained to my parents.

"So don't invite him here," said my father. "He's been here dozens of times. Did you ever sleep there? Once?"

"Why don't you ask him?" said my mother. "It's always better to be direct." One day I asked.

"Because of my father's research," he explained.

"But your father's not home."

"But he may come home any time, and he can't stand noise. He can't work when there's a tumult. That's why he likes me to go to other people's houses so he can work in peace."

But he had a good streak too. Since we both shared a passion for classical music (we also shared another, but more on that later), during our college years at Columbia we used to go to concerts to which Guido treated me. He belonged to a New York music guild and got tickets at discount prices. If he had an extra ticket, he wouldn't sell it. He looked for older people, who stood waiting to buy a ticket at a bargain, and he gave it away. And you could see how good he felt when he found someone who was dying to get into a concert.

Larry Lifschitz to Herbie Ginzburg:

"Remember Rabbi Pelick? When we were bad he would take our pencils and crack them over his middle finger with his index finger and ring finger. You try that. You gotta have the strength of a gorilla."

"How come you remember such benign events? I remember Rabbi Mishkin cracking me over the knuckles with a ruler for looking out the window. Look, I still have the scar."

In our senior year at Jefferson High I remember Guido saying—and it sounded strange to me because he rarely used foul language; for him it was the tattoo that the lower classes were stamped with—"If a girl is old enough to bleed, she's old enough to fuck . . . You don't know how many sexy thirteen-year-olds there are floating in this world." I don't know how many, if any, thirteen year olds Guido had had, but his remark was emblematic of his erotic center of gravity.

Like an eagle, Guido with his telescopic glance could spot a woman blocks away. Most people couldn't tell if something moving one hundred yards down the block was male, female, or scarecrow, but Guido with his aphroditous palate could taste a hip sway and a bob of hair a mile away. The Romans say, he would quote, *Non c'e musica como la andatura della bella ragazza*; there's no music like the walk of a beautiful girl. What anyone else might have assumed was the slow beating of a big bird's wings—condor, maybe; gull, more likely—Guido at once spotted as belonging to a woman. The guy was so attuned to *das ewige Weibliche*, as Freud would say, that for them he seemed to have ESP or sonar. Hitched to a special wavelength. Gonadotropic.

For instance, on a bus. He sits one row in back of a woman. He can stare at her but she doesn't see him. She has grey blond hair, an almost mannish gray felt hat, tilted Marlene Dietrich-like over one eye. Hard to tell is she's thirty or fifty. There's a blank, perhaps worried, look on her face. Her lips are slightly parted. And Guido can't tear his eyes away. He's hooked, a frisson of delight flooding his receptors. The woman turns, looks straight at him, sensing she's being admired by a confident man.

And, no doubt about it, girls respond to self-confidence. Guido had a self-assured, head high, poised walk, a light springy step, as if he were leading a parade, riding a horse, as if he expected water to part for him. But me, on the contrary, my mother always told me to stand straight, keep my shoulders back, don't hunch over, don't slouch when you sit. Speak up, she ordered. Speak out. Don't be shy. Which is exactly what Guido wasn't. He could look at a girl and expect her to melt. Me, I looked at one and melted.

Irving Horodensky to Milty Rosen, Sid Levy listening:
"What do you mean he performed surgery without a license? I removed my own ingrown toenail last year without a license. Of course I botched it and sued myself for malpractice. But since I hadn't paid up my insurance fees I settled out of court."
"What kind of award did you get?"
"A clubfoot."

I said Guido was serious about music and photography. Let's not forget books. He swallowed them, read sixty pages an hour. He loved biographies, histories, especially about the Jews of Italy. When a grown-up had once asked the ten-year-old Guido what he liked to read, he supposedly replied, "I love biography and biology, but I don't know which is which." Going into a bookstore with him was like entering quicksand. You couldn't extricate yourself. He'd look into baseball nostalgia, color theory, modern sculpture, folklore, origins of words, history of languages, anthropology. He also loved novels from everywhere. Especially European and Russian fiction. (Together we took a couple of Russian literature in translation courses that we loved, and a memorable course called Freud and Fiction.) But if works of the imagination were the reality that transported him beyond time and space, photography was super-reality. You couldn't tear him away from photography books. A book about Stieglitz, for instance—he owned several Stieglitz prints—gave him a high. He also adored black-and-white scenic shots of far-off places. His dream was to photograph the Sinai, the Himalayas, the Alps from the air.

The door to the bright red MG slammed and Guido, followed by a tall blonde woman, walked—that old cocksure, water-parting stride—into the backyard where we were all gathered. I sat at the far side of the lawn, reminiscing about Manfred and Siegfried with the twins, David and Isaac Baumgarten. He approached sort of shyly, then lots of the guys gathered around him. I looked away before Guido spotted me, coy like a courted girl who doesn't want the boy to know she's interested in him. When he greeted some of the other guys by the buffet table, a rat-a-tat of Italian suddenly rang in the air.

"Paisano . . . Dago . . . Benito . . . Spaghetti."

"Say fungoo," said Irv Horodensky.

"Fungoo. Now everybody!" Guido commanded. "Repeat after me: *Siamo idioti.*"

"You know," Sid Levy reminisced. "For years I thought it was one word. We really *were* idiots."

And interspersed with all this was Guido's pleased, rather high-pitched giggle. "You still help old ladies with shopping bags?" Morty Cohen asked. Yes, I could have answered for Guido. I'd often seen him stop his car to offer an old lady a lift. I wondered if I should get up or wait till he came to me. Seeing him again was like chocolate on a cake. Save the best for last—for it was with him that I'd had the longest friendship, the longest rivalry.

"Hey, Charlie . . . Charlie Merlputter!" I felt two hands on my shoulders. "You look like you're off in a dreamworld, Perlmutter."

I was. In fact, I had just dreamed about him last night. We're out on a double date at an all-Mozart concert. After the intermission, when I return from the bathroom, Guido and the two girls are gone. He had come up behind me. I jumped up. We hugged and patted each other on the back, inspected each other's faces. Still that slight squint, but he looked good, handsomer than ever. Maybe one silver hair in his full head of black hair.

"You look super, Charlie. My God! Is it twenty years? *Caro amico,* how are things with you?" he said in that vibrato baritone with the faintest music of Italian in it.

Guido was the only one I needed effort to find. The other classmates had lived at the same address for fifteen years. If one or two had moved, one of their friends knew about it. To find Guido I thought I'd have to write to his mother in Venice (I still had her address). But all I had to do was call up the photography department of a couple of New York newspapers and I found him. We had talked a bit on the phone when I was arranging the reunion, but there still was plenty left to say. It was as if we both, purposely, for our own private reunion, wanted to save it for a face-to-face meeting. Now we asked and answered each other's expected questions. Then, looking over glasses that weren't there, Guido remarked with a quirky little smile:

"Anything new?"

I knew what he meant. "From that point of view, no . . . Just a little snack here and there."

"So you're still . . ." and he finished the sentence by raising his index finger. It almost looked like a warning.

"Still. Maybe I should have my head examined."

"Maybe not," Guido said. "Less problems that way." We now stood at the buffet table. Guido wore a simple white cotton shirt with an offbeat collar and eggshell-white slacks. I don't think I ever saw him in all white, but it accented his suntan and his tiger-green eyes.

"Can you make quick U-turns with that little car?"

A Mona Lisa smile charged out of Guido's eyes. He knew what I meant. Years ago when he used to spot a cute chick with bouncing boobs he'd make a U-turn to have a second look.

"Remember I used to tease you the way you'd crane your neck to watch well-stacked broads? You'd watch women, not traffic or lights. I said you're going to get killed one of these days."

"What a way to go!" Guido said.

I looked down. Gucci loafers. With anyone else I'd have marked the sports car and the three-hundred-dollar loafers as upmanship. But I knew Guido wasn't a show-off. He had always been laid back with clothes and possessions. His excellent taste was genetic.

Not like Greg Lipper, the class dope, who didn't bother to show up this time despite his frantic letter to me months ago asking directions to Milty Rosen's house in Riverdale from a) his home in Livingston, N.J., b) his country home in the Poconos, and c) his condo in Cape Cod, because he didn't know which house he'd be coming from that Sunday in June. Oh, how I cannot resist lambasting Lipper! At forty-two the shmuck still couldn't spell. Thirty years earlier he'd tried his hand at *abominable* in a spelling quiz, and it came out as "a bum's babble." It was Greg's mark of Cain for years. Want another? When asked to use *efficiency* in a sentence, he said with a blissful smile, "A fish in sea is worth a beard in a bush." Now, in his letter, Lipper spelled *direction* with two *e*'s and *coming* with two *m*'s. I told him to call the triple A and couldn't resist spelling it for him. During our first reunion fifteen years ago, before the echoes of our hellos had died away, Greg began telling everyone how many rooms he had in his house and how many phones in each room, because he got very important messages he had to answer immediately (one *m*, two *d*'s, no *e*'s).

By now, most of the guys were seated on the chairs in the oval. I motioned to Guido to sit down too. For a moment, silence. We all looked at one another, as if wondering who's going to get up and do an imitation of Rabbi Gordin. I thought about some of the guys who weren't here and why they didn't come. Could it be because they hadn't made it in this world? I wondered what had happened to Abe Storch, Greg Lipper's rival for class idiot. Storch and Greg Lipper were the only ones who meant it when they said *"Siamo idioti"* to Guido's sly bidding. Storch's contribution to world knowledge was a new branch of science. When Storch was asked by a fifth-grade teacher, What's the capital of France? Storch said straight out, "England." The teacher, trying hard not to catch our infectious laughter, asked him a follow-up question, "And the capital of Italy?" Storch pressed his eyes shut, did some heavy ruminating, and came up with "Moscow?" It's not often that one is privileged to be present at the birth of a science. But at that moment Storchiology was born. It was a game we gleefully played for months. Maybe years. To say that Greenland was in Prospect Park was middlebrow Storchiology. But for the question "Where is Chicago?" an answer like "all around and behind Coney Island, except in the winter when it's in Miami" was Higher Storchiology. Like Manfred and Siegfried, Storch didn't last too long either. Tormented by the science he himself had created but could not master, he was sent to London, Brazil, for graduate work.

Since no one was about to break the silence, I said with mock gravity, "We will now observe a moment of silence for those of us, alas, who aren't here . . . like Davey Feigenbaum."

"Who?"

"Who's Davey Feigenbaum?"

"You don't remember Davey Feigenbaum, who dropped out in second grade?"

"My God! Perlmutter remembers drop-outs from the second grade!" said Ox Oxenfeld.

"Okay," I said, "maybe third grade, and I'll tell you why. It's a late winter's day, because the lights are on. We're in Miss Dobkin's class. Remember Miss Dobkin, the bitch? Who got her Master's in Sadism? Davey waves his hand at Miss Dobkin. What do you want? the bitch says, biting off each word. I gotta go, teacher, says Davey. You stay right here. You can't go now. We're going to have a vocabulary quiz. Later, he waves his hand again. I gotta go. Don't you dare say another word! shrieks Dobkin. Then Davey jumps up and waves his hand wildly, making noises without opening his mouth. Again Dobkin says no. It's not about this, says Davey, it's about vocabulary. Okay, says Dobkin, what is it? Is *urinate* on our vocabulary list? The class breaks up. I thought *I* was going to pee in my pants. Sit down, Dobkin shouts. But I gotta urinate real bad, Davey groans, squirming in his seat. If you don't shut up, Dobkin is hysterical now, I'm going to send you to the principal. So Davey shouts louder and louder, I gotta go. I gotta go real bad. Then Dobkin catches on to his ploy and says, If you don't shut up you're not going to the principal. That fools all of us. We can't figure it out. The double negative is too much for our paltry brains. Around the room one can see left thumbs and fingers moving in one direction and right thumbs and fingers in another, trying to break through the mesh net around the logic. But the bitch solved our problem. You're not leaving this room no matter what you do, she tells Davey. A little later we give a look and there's a drip-drip sound and a puddle around Davey's seat. What's that? says the bitch in surprise. What happened? I told you I gotta go, says Davey, so I went."

"I still don't remember him," said Guido. "Merlputter just made all this up."

"How could you remember him, Spaghetti?" said Herbie Ginzburg. "You came in in fourth grade."

Then I suggested that we each in turn briefly tell what we've been doing with our lives during the past fifteen years. Most of us were in the professions—doctors, lawyers, accountants, engineers—some in business. Married for sixteen to eighteen years, two or three children, the oldest in high school, vacations in Mexico, Europe, or Israel. We flossed, commuted, exercised, saw Broadway shows, watched TV. No one was in the arts: no writers, musicians, actors. Normality, even banality ruled. Nothing, absolutely nothing exciting in our lives.

Occasionally, our narrations were interrupted by the shapely Jamaican waitress bringing tidbits to eat and by the click of cameras as we took candid shots of one another. "Have your rates gone up?" I shouted to Larry Lifschitz. He gave a sickly little smile. I guess he didn't want to be reminded of what he'd done fifteen years ago.

When we finished our confessions, we stood and posed for a class picture. Isaac Baumgarten had brought our original graduation photo and we sat and stood as we did on that thirty-year-old, sepia-toned portrait. The few wives and the waitress were called upon to snap a picture with each guy's camera. Guido brought a tripod from his car, pressed the self-timer, and ran to his place. (Unlike Larry Lifschitz at the last reunion who did a little side business selling prints of the gathering, for this reunion Guido later sent out sets of color pictures to everyone, the formal pose nicely enlarged and four-by-sixes of the candid shots.)

After the class picture we remained standing. It was at that point that it hit me. Like in the comics, a light bulb lit up. The only one who had not told his story was Guido. All along he had been fussing with his camera, going in back of the guys, moving his chair, using it as a support, snapping, telling us, "Just keep talking, don't mind me," maneuvering so that he sat down, jumped up, interwove with the waitress. But he did this so cleverly no one noticed that he'd been skipped over when his turn came. Now we all stood and talked and, like fat globules changing shape in a soup, we joined, broke up, rejoined with others, little fluid knots in haphazard motion.

For a few minutes Guido talked "fungoo" with Irv Horodensky, the East Coast's greatest expert, but know one knew in what. Irv had said he was an accountant but was now "into consulting." Of all the guys at the gathering he looked the most like he had an inner tremble, as if all wasn't well with him. Though he put up a good front, that constant salesman's smile gave him away. I wondered if Irv knew that during our junior year at Jefferson High, when his father fell ill and was out of work for a long time, it was Guido who had organized a campaign to raise money for the family. He then had the funds channeled through a local Jewish agency so that Irv's family would not know where the money had come from.

Guido and I stood together again. He held a knish in his hand. He opened his mouth, took a breath, and closed it over an unsaid thought. I noticed this little thread of hesitation.

"Say it anyway," I said.

"Say what?"

"What you wanted to say before you changed your mind . . . And how come you were the only one who screwed out of telling what he's done?"

"You noticed."

I just looked at him. With maturity. Omniscience. Infinite patience.

"I was too busy taking pictures."

"So what did you want to say?" I asked.

"I'm back at the cello," Guido said. He drew out the words like a sigh as he slowly, admiringly, ate the knish, which he looked at as he spoke to me. "I'm still, still, still, amazed by music. Not this background light rock crap that Milty Rosen set up to create a party atmosphere. Goes to show you the cultural level we've sunk to. Or never had. You know the music I mean. Our music. After years and years of listening, I still can't believe it . . . This music comes to us from another world . . . it brings a message we can sense, but whose essence we still cannot grasp. . . . It's like love, the essential mystery."

I still maintained that silent, skeptical stare. Such untransitional remarks, experience had taught me, were fillers, marking time until a person began to say what he really wanted to say. Guido now took my arm and guided me away from the buffet table to the back of the long lawn. He leaned against an old elm, looked to see if anyone was listening. I saw the blonde he had come in with talking to two other women.

"Remember that question of yours, Guido—it must have been the sixth or seventh grade: Where do dreams go when dreams go away?"

Guido thought for a minute. I saw his face brightening. "Yeah . . . yeah," he said with greater enthusiasm. "Everyone bugged me about it for years . . . But I was serious . . . It really puzzled me . . . Boy, you remember everything."

"It's like photography for you. Memory for me is the ultimate reality." I waited. With silent waves I was encouraging him to speak.

"No joke. I've gone back to the cello," Guido said. "Seriously."

I wondered if he'd remember my own thirty-minute flirtation with the cello. In that first and only lesson at Jefferson High, second week of sophomore year, my palms sweated and my fingers slipped on the strings. That ended my cello career.

"I don't know why I'm so hungry," Guido said, looking toward the buffet. "You want something?" I said no. He came back with a plastic plate full of sliced tongue and four slices of rye. "Half for you."

I shook my head. "Don't you remember? I don't eat meat."

"You still on that?"

"Of course."

"No implied criticism meant. I say this because people change all kinds of ideologies over the years. The only constant is change, goes the Roman expression."

"Your Romans must have read Jung, for he said that everything is subject to change. Only basic principles are unalterable. . . . You still on photography?"

"Photography," said Guido, "isn't a religion."

I raised a finger. "Think!"

Guido laughed. "I guess you're right. With me it is."

"Is stamp collecting a religion?"

Guido shrugged. Maybe he looked apologetic.

"You know," I said. "I didn't realize the put-on till years later. And I could never understand why you did it."

"It was a joke at first, and then by the time I wanted to stop it, I was too ashamed to admit what I had done. . . . Here comes the Jamaican girl. I bet Milty's caterer must do a boobing business." He cocked his camera, focused. She posed. "Excuse my friend's staring," Guido said. "He's not used to movie stars."

Yes, I was looking, but it was Guido who was staring. The laser beam intensity of his glance reminded me of his hungry stares of long ago. As if every pound of his lust were concentrated into his eyes.

Guido took one picture, two, three.

"What's your name?" he asked, still hiding behind his Konica.

"Jennifer." She smiled, lifted her tray of drinks, offering.

"I'll bet you're a model, *signorina*," Guido said, affecting a slight Italian accent. "I can tell . . . And this is your day off to make a few extra bucks."

"He can tell," I said. "He's a pro."

Even as she walked away, her head was turned, looking at Guido.

I wondered when Guido would tell me what he really wanted to say. But he still worked his way in convoluted fashion.

"Still playing guitar?" Guido asked.

"*You* don't forget anything, do you?"

Guido played innocent, spread his hands, "I like to ask questions. You don't ask, you don't learn."

"Every time I hear Segovia I say to myself: I'm going to take lessons again. Maybe next year."

"It must be the age," Guido said. "Oxenfeld also said he started learning flute. I guess it's got something to do with our hands. We're too old to jerk off and too young to knit."

I don't know if he made that up or was casually trying to pass off a remark he'd heard as his own.

"Back to your old level in the cello?"

Guido looked pensive. "Cello . . . That word is like Proust's madeleine for me. Say cello and a flood of memories inundates me *como aqua*."

"So why shlep it out? If you want to talk, talk."

"You always were an amateur psychologist, right?"

I looked him straight in the eye, drummed my fingers impatiently on my sides. "You already owe me," I looked at my watch and smiled, "one hundred thousand lire; or only sixty dollars . . . And now, you want to talk about . . ."

Sex. Girls. Women again. I knew. Could smell it. It hovered in the air, jungle-thick and pervasive, a strong earthy perfume.

Guido gave a knowing smile. His nostrils flared. I understood at once and wondered who the other woman was. The tall blonde who had accompanied him?

"It's about a friend of mine . . ."

The oldest trick in the book. Like the man who approaches a movie star and asks for an autograph for his "son".

" . . . who is having woman trouble," I said. "His name is probably Bill."

"How'd you guess?"

"I'm good at names and exact prices for Italian shoes, American watermelons, and Japanese radios."

"It *is* Bill. And he's a married man involved with a woman." Guido pressed his lips together and took a deep breath. "Here's the story . . . and it's a true one. Not like your pisspoor peeing Feigenbaum-Dobkin anecdote."

I knew some of Guido's stories, and a few rode the border of incredulity. For instance, he had told me ages ago he could see the stars during the daytime. That he had begun reading when he was two years old. A Venetian tradition, he said. Or that once, in the summer, a ladybug perched on each shoulder. "Like epaulettes," he said. "Not mosquitoes or flies. On me *lady*bugs land." Or the one he told me when he returned from his native Italy the summer after we graduated college. He claimed that in Palermo he had met a contessa with a palazzo who put him up for two weeks and made love to him daily on an open veranda that overlooked the sea.

"Why don't you make believe the person is you?" I teased him. "It's more fun to hear a story in the first person."

Guido gave a shy little smile, a reticent look so contrary to the face he presented to the world. "Charlie, I'm involved."

I was about to blurt: But you were so furious when *you*—but I couldn't say it. I didn't know if he knew that I knew.

"I know what you're thinking," Guido said. "Or maybe you're *not* thinking it. But I haven't played around. Fourteen years married and not so much as a kiss—well, maybe a kiss or two—and now, pow! A goner! Like this woman friend says, 'We're like high-school kids.' It's never happened to her before . . . Honest, Charlie, I haven't played around. I'm not like Ava. Remember her?"

I gave him a quizzical, who-you-trying-to-kid look.

"I divorced her, in case you didn't know. Long ago."

"How could I not know? The woman you came with looks nothing like Ava."

I didn't mean anything by that and was sorry I said it as soon as I said it, but the contrast was remarkable. Guido was always attracted to good-looking, well-built girls who exuded sexuality. Ava was like that. But the woman at the far end of the lawn, a tall, thin-shouldered blonde, though attractive, had gloom etched into her features, as if the world had driven her into a corner. And I don't mean it in the positive Thoreauian sense. Of course, it's hard to tell what a woman is like in bed, for some women's sexuality flowers the minute you close the bedroom door. But at least from the outside she was nothing like Ava. Why, I wondered, did I intimate that this woman standing by the buffet table talking to Ox's wife wasn't a knockout?

"Is she the one you want to talk about?"

"No. I'd hardly bring *her* here. That's my wife, Tammy. The other one, the one I'll call Aviva, that's not her real name by the way, that's what Bill calls her to hide Guido's identity."

"Enough!" I said. "I can't follow your loopy syntax."

"Okay, okay. Don't get into a snit. If you had the story to tell that I have to tell, you wouldn't even tell it. And if you would, you'd start slowly. Circumspectly. You have to look into another's person's soul too, you know."

Guido said this with such sincerity, even pain, that I felt sorry for him.

"Is she married?" I asked him.

He nodded.

Isaac Baumgarten to Sid Levy, various listeners:

"This didn't happen to me but to a cousin you don't know. When he was a senior in high school, he went out on a date, necked with a girl, couldn't get very far, and came home with a mean case of blue balls. It was late at night. He came in very quietly so as not to wake anyone and went straight to the john

and began playing with himself. Meanwhile, his father had to move his bowels and, not wanting to wake his wife or anyone else, tiptoed into the bathroom barefoot, didn't put on the light, dropped his pants and sat down. But instead of landing on the seat he landed on his son's lap and was poked in the ass by his son's hard-on. With an unearthly shriek, he sailed into the air as if bounced off a trampoline, and my poor cousin too was scared out of his wits and screamed to high heaven when out of the blue a bare ass descended on him."

"How do you handle it, Guido?" . . . My God, what's so funny over there? Look at the pack of them there in hysterics . . . And isn't it tiring? Sorry! I shouldn't have asked." I laughed. "Knowing your energy."

"The sad part of it is," Guido said, but he didn't look sad at all, "that my appetite hasn't diminished."

I could see he had a problem. A patient of mine had it worse. He told me he had two girl friends in his office, a secretary and her boss and he juggled them around. He saw each of them two times a week and then, as he put it, at home he would see his wife's eyes glittering at him across the room with a kind of sly sensuousness and he'd get stirred up again.

"Don't worry about it," I said. "It's the age. Forty-two and three months. Everyone goes through that period. In another thirty years—for you, fifty, it will wear off . . . The photographer is always the last to know, but you fit the Jungian type almost perfectly. In his discussion of psychic balances and imbalances, Jung writes that successful, well-adjusted men in their forties will often discover that despite a brilliant mind their domestic difficulties are too much for them. I.e., a disturbance of psychic balance . . . But, nevertheless, Jung admits that artists, creative people, are hard to type . . . Do you love her?" I asked him suddenly, hoping to catch him off guard.

"Who?" Guido asked. "This one or that one?"

"Your wife. This one."

"I can't explain it to you. You've never been in love—"

"How do you know?"

"—so you can't understand it." Guido stood with his arms crossed, as if expecting to be challenged.

"One, how can you be so sure? And two, there's always a first time," I said. "Now let's see how you bend syntax with this one: do you love that one?"

"She gets more beautiful the older she gets. I've seen pictures of her, first as a youngster, then as a teenager, then in college, then in her twenties and thirties. Pictures of her when she first became a mother—glowing."

"How old is she?"

Guido licked his lips. "Who, Tammy?"

"You know who I mean. Don't be thick."

"Her upper thirties. Sometimes she looks even younger."

"You with a woman in her late thirties? That's an older woman. Guys at forty-two drop their wives to take twenty-five-year-olds. I thought you were a cradle robber."

Guido shrugged. "That's the way it is."

Years ago he had asked me if a man can love two women at the same time. I responded (as usual) with another question: Can a man love no one? Then I explained: Nature compensates. You love two, I love none. Nature balancing out.

"Who is she, Guido?"

"When can we meet?" he said.

"You mean the three of us?" I asked.

"Nothing doing. She's going to be perfectly hidden. Even disguised."

"But you already told me her name."

"I did? Well, that's not her name."

"Don't worry," I said. "I don't know anyone on Long Island."

"It's a small world," he said and nodded significantly as if to cancel the cliché. "And anyway, who says she lives in Long Island?"

"You do, Dr. Watson. And ratiocination and logic do. Remember, in Jefferson High and Columbia we never used to go out with girls from the Bronx no matter how beautiful they were? The interborough factor. So, knowing you, even if you did start an affair, you wouldn't go for someone outside the South Shore . . ."

"It so happens she lives on the North Shore," my big-mouthed friend blurted. "And anyway, most of the time she comes to visit me. So I don't have to do any traveling."

When I looked at the map later I figured that based on the info he'd given me, Aviva must live somewhere between Hempstead and Freeport.

Barry Oxenfeld to David Baumgarten:

"We were talking about old girl friends and one guy at the office said that the queerest sounds he'd heard a girl make when she was being screwed was crying out: "God! God! Oh God! Oh God, Oh God, God, God!... A real frumie!"

"How long you been married to Tammy?"

"Fourteen years. Exactly same as Aviva. Here's another affinity. We got married in the same month. Seven days apart. It was as if fate wanted us to be married at the same time but mixed up the partners."

"And between you and Tammy . . ." I didn't want to articulate it, so I just made rolling motions with both my hands.

Guido shrugged again. "Sometimes things don't work out—but it's not because of that that I . . ." And he stopped. "You know, at the beginning, when I met Tammy . . ."

"Someone fix you up?"

"No. Tammy took a photography course with me at the New York Graphic Arts School. I taught a couple of night classes there at the time."

"Pupils always fall in love with their teacher," I said.

"Or vice versa," Guido said.

"It's a quote from a Russian novel I read recently."

"Very interesting," he said. But he didn't sound interested at all. And he used to love Russian literature. So now Russian lit is out the window, I thought. Guido wanted to get on with what he was saying. "There was no overlap, in case you're curious. I met Tammy a year after I split up with my first wife."

It was strange, Guido calling my first girlfriend, Ava, his first wife. Here we both shared a secret but neither of us was about to discuss it. We pretended—at least he pretended and I joined in the complicity—that the secret did not exist. Guido offered no details about his divorce, and I wasn't about to press him. No wonder he had squirmed out of the round robin idiobiographic narration. The only guy in the class who was divorced. I knew bits of the story from Ava's friend, Pam, with whom I'd maintained contact over the years. I could have bet Guido was waiting for my reaction—to see if I'd make some nasty comment, like "serves you right." But I just nodded. I knew from Pam that it had happened about fifteen, sixteen years ago, when Guido was in his late twenties, already so well known as a photographer that he was getting foreign assignments. The end of the marriage was messy, and it wasn't roving-eyed Guido's fault either. And as I thought of this, a remark that Pam had once made about Guido popped into my head: the way he looks at you makes you feel attractive.

"Wanna know how I met her?"

"Who? Aviva?"

"If you want to call her that."

I rolled my eyes. "Sure."

In the strangest way, Guido began. Like in films you've seen, a guy walks on the street and a gal bicyclist almost hits him and falls off the bike. He picks her up and so on. In cinema lingo it's called *cute-meet*. Well, it didn't happen to me quite like that. But a coincidence, nevertheless. One day I get a call from Janie Altman, an ex-neighbor, asking if I could do her a big favor. She wasn't feeling well and since she knew I occasionally drive to the *Long Island Post* around four or so, could I take her daughter Jill to her cello lesson. It's only a twenty-minute drive. Sure, I said, but what about the trip back? My husband, says Janie, works in the area. He'll pick her up on his way back from work. So I drove Jill to the cello teacher's house, a big house with a circular drive hemmed in by trees. Either the teacher or her husband must be well off, I thought. I rang the bell, which sounded out the opening notes of the "Ode to Joy" and, listen to this, the door is opened by a very pretty woman. I would have given her the Tchaikovsky Prize for looks alone. Not even so much for looks but for the *look*, if you know what I mean. The sort of face whose eyes draw you in. If you look at photographs, like those of Picasso for instance, they radiate a plosive power; it goes out *from* the picture, from the face. Some pretty faces have that. Some WASP models, for instance, a quality that emanates *from*. But some faces, some pictures, like the eye of a storm, pull you in. Come to me. An insuck of breath is the closest I can come to verbalizing it. That's what Aviva's face radiated. Come to me. I suppose only a photo could do justice to my words. Pretty little Jill ran into the music room and I stood in the entrance foyer. We sort of gaped at each other for a moment or two. I couldn't wait to take her picture.

"You must be Mr. Altman," Aviva said with a smile. "Jill is quite talented. And a lovely girl."

No less lovely than her teacher, almost slipped out of my mouth. "This one isn't mine," I said. "I mean, she's not my child." Believe me, I thought to myself, I would have loved to have a child like that.

Aviva looked puzzled for a moment, as if contemplating the faux pas she'd just made. "Adopted?" she said tentatively, flustered, in that unsure way I'd get to know over the next couple of years.

"I mean, I'm not the father." Then I laughed, realizing the double entendre.

"When did you find out?" she said, laughing brightly like a child who knows she's been witty. She was really pleased with her joke. Her eyes sparkled; she smiled broadly. I must admit I enjoyed the aura of intimacy that such a remark reflected. Meanwhile, I'd taken a good look at her. Not only pretty, but lovely, if you know what I mean. Big gray eyes. Long, loose, reddish-brown hair. Auburn, right? Slim, oh, yes, slim, busty, beautifully built. Full red, naturally red, juicy kissable lips. A head turner. Her glance was melting, velvety, honeyed.

That's right out of *Dead Souls*," I told Guido. "I'm rereading it now. For a moment I thought you lost it with Russian fiction."

"Not at all . . . Since you're still into Russian literature, I was hoping you'd catch the allusion. Gogol must've been thinking of Aviva when he wrote that line."

Her smile (Guido continued), even during that brief encounter, was radiant. It came from within. Nothing phony or expedient about it. Not the salesgirl-trained smile. Not the have-a-nice-day smile. Sort of woman I'd admired for years. Yes. I admit. For years.

"Okay," I told her. "I'll explain. Jill's not mine and she's not adopted. And I'm not the not-father you think I am—or am not. Whew! . . . As the

Neapolitans say: Words are like pasta—they stick to each other. I did Mrs. Altman a favor. She wasn't feeling well, Jill's father . . . presumably the real one . . . will pick her up about five on his way home from work . . . Now, can I ask you a favor? Can I stay and listen to the lesson? I happen to love the cello."

She told me to make myself comfortable in the music room. The lesson began. I listened to something I hadn't listened to in years. I liked the way she taught. I liked the little tinkle of Jill's laughter and Aviva's sensual contralto laugh. I enjoyed Jill's childish way of playing—she was about twelve then—and the occasional demonstration, sure and rich, that Aviva gave on her cello. Those sensual sounds awoke something in me. Why had I neglected that beautiful instrument for years? Another thing, I loved her incisive, imaginative comments: I want a nice clean sound. Each measure makes its own statement. It shouldn't run into another like a flood of water. Think of the inner phrase within the larger phrase. Staccato should be delicate, not like machine-gun shots. Try to make it short, light, and bright. Kind of a scherzo feeling of playfulness. Okay, now let's do the opening again. Don't puncture it with a bayonet. Make it sound like water falling. Keep it tight and focused.

What were you, taking notes?" I interrupted Guido.

"Exactly . . . Yes, I was."

And then, when Jill was done, Aviva played the same page. You saw what a pro she was. Her touch was confident and delicate. With those few notes one heard interpretation and shaping and the liberty with the score that makes a piece of music sing. By demonstrating the phrasing, the dynamics, the rhythm, she made Jill bring out the inner essence of the piece.

At one point in the lesson I took out the mini-camera I always carry in my pocket and looked at Aviva through the viewfinder.

She noticed.

"Are you taking my picture?" she said, not displeased. "My hair's a mess . . ."

"No, signorina," I said. "I just want to see you framed." But I took pictures anyway.

She laughed. It was an inadvertent pun on my part. It wasn't till a few weeks after I got to know her that I saw something that I hadn't noticed before. And that usually happens in photographs. Not until you see a picture can you zero in on something the naked eye has been too distracted to notice. I saw that, like me, Aviva too was slightly, ever so slightly, strabismic.♥

♥See ABC Directory, *Strabismic.*

I got up. "I'm going to ask Milty Rosen for a dictionary."

"Forget it," Guido laughed. "Cross-eyed."

Aha," I said. "I see. Like to like. Kind to kind. The Noah's Ark Syndrome."

"Did you just make that up?"

"On the spot. I confess."

"Well, maybe you're right, Charlie. But, imagine, when I was face to face with her I didn't notice it. Perhaps her long hair deflects attention. I'm sure that's her intent. Only after I saw the picture and later looked through my real eye—my viewfinder—did I see it. Her right eye floated slightly to the right. It wouldn't have been noticeable to anyone else, but it's like a slight foreign accent only another non-native speaker can spot. I saw it at once. She cocked her head just a little bit to focus on a person, and as soon as I saw this, I added another affinity between us that the little computer in my mind had unwittingly been recording on a list."

"You mean you fell for her during that first meeting, and her cross-eyes clinched it?"

"Don't let me get ahead of myself," Guido said.

When I had to leave, we stood at the front door. Jill was still practicing in the other room.

"How come you looked at me through the camera?" Aviva asked.

"I wanted to see if your hair is really auburn." Then I thanked her for letting me listen to the lesson.

"My pleasure," she said, and I would tease her about that remark for months. Then she asked me. "Do you play?"

I had to bite my tongue not to say what I wanted to say. That I imagined playing all kinds of musical games with her.

"You mean cello?" I teased. "I took lessons for a number of years, even played in my high school orchestra—but I haven't touched the instrument since college."

She pursed her lips and twisted her head as if to say: That's too bad.

"But there's one instrument I like even better than the cello."

"What's that?" she said.

"The viola d'amore." But I don't think she got it. Or maybe she did get it and made believe she didn't.

In my wild fantasies I was waiting for her to offer: Then why don't you take lessons? But as I would learn later, Aviva never, or rarely ever, initiated anything. Even if she was dying for me to take lessons, she'd never have suggested it. It wasn't her style. When I'd ask her why, she'd give me her typical response: "That's the way I am."

When I left I heard myself saying, "It was so nice meeting you," which I never say to anyone. "*Grazie mille*! I really appreciated the opportunity to stay for a lesson"—I looked for a nameplate on the door, found none— "Miss . . . Mrs . . ."

A clever little gleam flashed in her big doe eyes. She understood my test but kicked the stool from under me.

"Call me Aviva," she said. "And yours?"

"I'm Guido . . . Guido Veneziano-Tedesco," I said with an Italian pronunciation. Crazy way of making an introduction, no? when you're leaving? Like Groucho Marx in *Animal Crackers*. Hello, I must be going. We shook hands and I held on for a moment longer than one usually would. There was no ring on her finger. But I, not she, was the first to let go.

"Veneziano-Tedesco," she said, imitating the accent perfectly. "It sounds like it could be a bridge."

We both laughed.

"Ciao," I said.

"Ciao," she sang.

Driving home, I wondered if she was married. But could a single woman afford a house like that? So she was either widowed or divorced. Janie Altman hadn't even mentioned her family name. Come to think of it, not even her first name. Then I figured it out. She *was* married but for some reason didn't want to say she was Mrs. So-and-so. That's why she said: Call me Aviva. In fact, all along I never thought of her as having a married name. Maybe because I wanted to wipe away the fact she was married. You figure it out, Charlie. I never even associated her with a name. I just thought of her, pictured her image, and I still do, even now. I see Aviva in two colors, rose and olive. I hear her as a C minor diminished seventh. Lovely and a little dolorous. But with a name? No. Even now I hardly ever call her by her name. Forget my name, goes the Neapolitan saying, but don't forget my face.

The next few days, believe it or not, I couldn't get her out of my mind. And this turmoil lasted for weeks. How, I wondered, could I get to see her again? First, I thought I'd call her and say I'm doing a photo feature on Long Island musicians. But then I dropped the idea. That would be a one-time interview and it would be phony. I thought I would ask for lessons, but then realized it would be ludicrous. She teaches *kids*. Then I was sent to London for ten days—I get these juicy assignments every once in a while, which I protest but really love. Then, for a while, she slipped out of my mind. I forgot about her. At least I thought I forgot about her. But one day I went to a piano and cello recital by Peter Serkin and Ian Plaskow. Listening to and watching Plaskow I photomontage Aviva onto the cellist, and that legerdemain made her float back into my skull.

A musical cover-up for old-fashioned sex appeal," I interrupted Guido. "It's just the animal magnetism that old Guido is so sensitive too."

"No, I tell you. With her it was different. She didn't haunt me. I wasn't smitten. It was something unearthly. Extra-terrestrial. Magical.♥ That word again. Mystical. Fated. I swear. Well, maybe I *was* smitten. But in a way I'd never been smitten before. Aviva is for me what Laura was for Petrarch. Do you know what language her name comes from?"

"Of course," I said. "*Aviv* means 'spring'."

"And it's also linked to Vivaldi. Another Italian connection I like so much. Remember Linda and the cello? Her name too ends with an *a*. Symbolic, right?"

"I thought Aviva isn't her real name."

"Boy, are you a nudnick! It isn't. But that's what they called her in Israel. She was born there. But came here when she was a youngster."

Click. Another little fact that Guido had inadvertently let slip.

I kept thinking of her (Guido continued). One month. Two. She shone in my mind, like springtime. One night I woke around 3 a.m. and pop—there she was, framed like an illuminated photo in my head. And then every time I heard the cello on the radio, in the car, at home, those rich, sonorous melodies shaped her image in my memory. As if the notes drew a picture of her. Also, I imagined myself at the cello again. I wanted to play very badly.

You got your wish," I said. "That's why the conductor invited you to leave the Jefferson High School Orchestra."

"What I mean is, you certified, licensed pedant, is that I wanted very badly to play. And it so happens I dropped out of the orchestra because it took too much time away from photography. How come your total recall doesn't remember that?

"I attended another cello program by Ian Plaskow. To a degree I can say I know him. I'd photographed him years back for a *Long Island Post* interview after he won the Tchaikovsky Prize in Moscow. Remember, the first American cellist to win it? In fact, it was I who took that picture when Plaskow's teacher, Pablo Casals, embraces his star pupil after he steps off the plane. That photo was featured in *Life* magazine. So there was a kind of personal link there. Again, as I watched him play, I thought♥ of Aviva. Maybe that's why I went. Suddenly, I was up there on the stage, in Plaskow's chair, playing instead of him. I wanted to be in his shoes. That's when I decided. When I got back home, I went to the closet where I'd hidden my

♥See ABC Directory, *Backward runs time.*

cello and took it out. Just looked at it. Didn't dare touch it. I began reading music reviews of cello recitals. Listening to cello music on WQXR and WNYC really sent a wave of frustration through me. I felt I wanted to reach out and touch Aviva—but was only grabbing air. Then the crucial moment came. *Basta!* Now or never. You have to begin to begin, as we say in Venice. I'm going to start taking lessons. And my teacher will be Aviva. So let her refuse me. I had to make the attempt. If I didn't I'd never forgive myself. There was a time when I'd let such a fact, such an opportunity, slip by. I know, I know, I'm married. But although I could and did resist others, her I couldn't resist. I said to myself: this boat I'm not going to miss. This comet, like Halley's, comes by only once in seventy-six years. It's destined, mystically. So I called her."

"How did you get her number," I asked, "if you didn't know her name?"

"I could have called Janie Altman and asked, right?"

"You could have, but you wouldn't and you didn't."

"Exactly. But leave it to me. In Aviva's house that first time, I asked if I could use her phone and jotted her number down . . . I took a deep breath, knew I was getting into something, taking a giant step. I picked up the phone and dialed. It was like a point of no return. I wanted to play again."

"Play?" I asked.

"I know. I'm aware of the multidimensional aspect of the word."

"In other words, it *wasn't* just music."

"Of course not. But when I first saw her, I realized that that smile, that face, that womanliness she radiated was a fairy tale for me. And she too was aware of me from that very first day. The day I brought Jill Altman over Aviva did some demonstrating on the cello for my benefit. I had a feeling she was playing for me—and later Aviva confirmed it. About three months passed from the time I met her to the day I called. At first she didn't remember me. Or pretended not to. Can you imagine a woman forgetting me? But when I explained that I'd brought Jill Altman whose father I wasn't and didn't even claim to be, she laughed and said she remembered. I told her I'd been inspired to resume lessons and asked if she had room in her schedule for an adult student. She didn't hesitate. Sure, she said. She had a number of adult students and would be willing to teach me.

"When I first saw her I thought she was thirty-five or -six, a woman at the height of her sexual desire. I'll confess. In my mind, I stripped her♥ and saw her playing naked, like our old friend Linda in Jeff High. But when I came back, she looked even younger, thirty-one or thirty-two . . . Looking at her face, I could see how beautiful she'd been all these years. Later, when she showed me photos, it confirmed what I'd thought. Fine bone structure,

---

♥See ABC Directory, *Breasts, shape and geography of, her.*

the sort of face that never gets old, but with the passing of time increases in sensuality. Pictures of her in her twenties show the early beauty, oriental with its porcelain grace, but it was stiff, almost prim and smug. A look of self-centeredness flowed out of those early photos. That look said: me me me. Yet she claimed to have been kindhearted, good to friends, always ready to help, which help was not always reciprocated. From a cold, model-like beauty she had become womanly, softer-looking, sensual. Despite the difficulties she'd had there was a mellow radiance to her face. Of course, her perky personality and sense of humor helped too. I tell you, she enchanted me."

"That's obvious," I said. "And married."

"Only technically. It's on the rocks. And not because of me. She's married to some Arab."

"What kind of Jewish girl marries an Arab?"

Guido laughed. "He's not really Arab, but that's what we call him. He's a Moroccan who emigrated to Israel."

"How could she have become involved with a guy like that?" I wondered.

"Long story. Who knows? A lot of these North Africans are very good looking, very sexy... Maybe he gave her affection, attention. It's a long story... Not now."

"And you're still married?" It was a rhetorical question. But Guido understood my message, my moralizing, my hint of past events.

For a moment that almost snooty, old-family Italian hauteur swept across his face. He looked unapproachable again. That look you see in films when a rich man turns down a pauper's request for help. Then Guido's face softened, became amenable. I expected him to say: I'm in love—with two women.

"I want to tell you the whole story. Everything."

My glance slid over to the twins, David and Isaac Baumgarten, as if to say: Why don't you tell them?

"No way! They were babies throughout our school years, and they've remained kids. That's why they're *child* psychiatrists. I'm surprised they're not sucking lollipops right now. Uh-uh, nothing doing. And they live on the Island too. I want this private. Look, we've known each other for years—I've got to talk to you."

"Why me?"

"You've got the head *and* the heart. You've always had good understanding. Maybe you can tell me where dreams go when they go away."

"I know I have a good memory. About understanding I don't know."

"And you'll enjoy listening. And I've got to tell this fascinating story to someone. I can't keep it in any longer. Got to share it."

I wondered if it would take hours. Or days. I was interested, but I wasn't going to say yes quite yet. Now Guido wanted *me* to help *him*, but years ago there were times, even though we were friends, when he wouldn't lift a finger for me. And even worse!

I remember working one summer with Guido in a Catskill Mountains hotel in Swan Lake—we were busboys then, probably seventeen. When he found a girl, he took her out, alone. He didn't get a friend for me. I couldn't wow them, charm them, bamboozle them with the magic wands of photography and musical Italian. Or with verbs that had color or numbers that sang. He never thought of fixing me up. On the contrary, once I asked a girl at my table out for an evening stroll and then sneaked into one of the empty ground floor rooms in an old-fashioned wood frame annex. Somehow Guido and his friends discovered this and for fun kept banging on the door and on the windows. Son of a gun, he ruined the evening for me.

"You never shared," I told Guido. Sure it was a reunion, but what better time to let old grudges and remembered slights surface? "Remember, you had those girls coming in to pose naked for you? You never invited me . . . We did double date later, but still you were miserly. Quirky . . . Like your stamp collection." I couldn't help rubbing it in.

Guido made a face, nodded in assent, waved his elegant fingers as if to say: Well, that was years ago. Then he said: "To show you how much I've changed, listen to this. You can believe this or not, but I thought of you. Of all my old friends when this feeling came over me, I thought of you, not anyone else. Did you ever feel that when you like someone very much you want to share them?"

"No, not personally, but it's not uncommon," I said. "In fact, what you're describing is as old as the Greeks. As ancient history. It's called the Candaules Complex. Herodotus writes about a king called Candaules who so loved the beauty of his wife that he arranged for a friend to see her naked."

But the Herodotus parallel can only be carried so far. Art at times imitates nature but, alas, as I was to learn later, both are unpredictable.

"Well, I'm not about to put her on view like my naked cellist photo, but it's a real feeling, believe me. Can you imagine that? Sharing someone you love? No, don't answer that. You think I'm sick. Maybe I am. Like the Greek king. But there comes a time, a queer space zone, that you're so in love with someone that you want others to appreciate her. Now, believe it or not, some time after you called me about the reunion, I told Aviva that I'd like to introduce her to a friend of mine. I told her you were a beautiful, brilliant guy. Of course, I didn't mention your name or describe you in any way. So she says to me, 'You're beautiful and brilliant enough for me. And don't tell me to go out with anyone else.' She was mad at me for days. And was even more furious, in fact, a day later, when she'd had a chance to digest the remark. I actually had to apologize to her. She thought that I wanted you to have her too."

"Well, did you?"

"For a wild moment, yes. Crazy, huh? But I didn't tell her this. But I did say I was sorry. Imagine, *me* apologizing! 'Why did you do that?' she asked, truly hurt. Go explain to a woman the meaning of friendship. But I really didn't know why I said what I said. I told her it was a blaze of enthusiasm of liking her."

"Well, will I meet her?"

"No," Guido said. "Not under the circumstances. She'd be dead against it. But I *will* tell you the story. I promise you'll be enthralled. The symbols, the coincidences, the repetitions, the interweaving in both our lives—it's like out of a novel. I can't believe it's happening. To me! Mister Straight."

"Straight my foot. Straight as a pretzel. You always juggled three or more girls in loveland, for you and your id."

"But not once I was married. Believe me, it's an aberration. Sometimes I wake up and can't believe I'm doing this."

"Then cut."

"No," Guido said. "She's come to me from a different world . . . You want to hear another incredible confluence? My favorite instrument, the camera, has an f-stop, and hers, the cello, has an f-hole."

Guido looked delighted, even ecstatic. His eyes widened and a beatific smile encompassed his face. But this idiotic confluence didn't impress me.

"One day," Guido said, "scientists will discover that certain radiations, surely certain smells, come out of men's and women's bodies, and that's one of the pulls between them. They'll be able to identify it like a blood type. Based on the f-hole on the cello and the f-stop on the camera, this new discovery will be called the F-factor. I may have a F-45—that's relatively high—and so does . . . well, never mind. You probably have an F-11, Merlputter. And all women in the range of F-25 to F-50, the highest recorded F-factor, are attracted to me. My F-45 may be the universal donor. I can donate sperm to anyone. It's always better to give than receive."

Guido was like a little boy again, delighted with his cleverness, his braggadocio.

"Sex. That's what it is. You were a sexagenarian at sixteen and you've remained one for decades. I remember you used to get excited when you saw a Frito-Lay truck."

"Love!" Guido contradicted. Then he dropped his voice. "I never knew what love is . . . It's incredible. *Amore*! Blooming love. At almost forty-three. If you've never felt it, it's comparable to a woman who can't have an orgasm but just reads about it. Until she has it, all the reading in the world does no good. You don't have it till you have it. It's like explaining colors to a man born blind."

I looked at my watch. I didn't believe him. Guido and love! A contradiction in terms. He *thought* he was in love, I concluded. But I still didn't respond to his request. I figured I'd let him hang in suspense a while. "Come on, Guido . . . We've been away from the guys long enough. After all, it *is* a reunion."

"Just one more thing," he said. "Once Aviva said to me: You exude poetry. Me, who hasn't read a poem in years."

"A person can exude poetry without reading it," I said. "Like a musician, an artist, a ballet dancer, a mime. Exuding poetry is just an image. Don't let it go to your head."

"*She's* gone to my head." Then, like a true Italian, Guido took me by the arm, said, "*Avanti* . . . Like the Venetians say, Only a dead man says no to eating," and walked me back to the buffet table where he introduced me to his wife. But though Tammy seemed pleasant enough, I felt uncomfortable talking to her. In the light of what Guido had just told me, I felt like a voyeur, seeing but unseen, so I circulated. After the party, on my way home it hit me: he hadn't even exchanged a word with his wife.

A bit later, talking to Milty Rosen, I looked over his shoulder and watched Guido. So you still see verbs in color? I wanted to ask him. Have you added adverbs to your palette? Even now, at the party, I saw his eye roving. And don't think a few wives at the reunion didn't stare at Guido too. He had been and still was a charmer. He was highly charged. Sexuality flowed out of him. Maybe that's why women went for him. Maybe that's why one, two, who knows, maybe more, women loved him.

"You know what I've learned from all this running around?" he told me later.

I thought I would hear something profound from my incisive friend, something that would synergize all his interests: photography, women, classical music, books.

"Remember that first day in school, when the boys wanted me to speak Dago? Remember what I made them say?"

"Yeh, I remember."

"Well, that's what I learned from all this running around: *Siamo idioti.*"

Guido Veneziano-Tedesco to Irv Horodensky, various listeners:
This little shtetl in White Russia got this amazing cow from Minsk. It just kept on giving an endless supply of milk to everyone in the shtetl and the surrounding regions. The town never lacked for milk. Finally, when the cow got old they decided to see if they could get a calf that would continue the supply. So they got a bull to mate with her. But the cow wouldn't let him near her. The bull approached from the side, the cow moved further away. The bull came from the front, the cow moved back. The bull came toward her from the rear, the cow moved forward. Finally, they decided to consult the rabbi.

"Wise rabbi," they said. "We have this problem with our cow. She won't let the bull near her." And they told him the entire story.

The rabbi mused a while and then said, "Tell me, this cow is from Minsk?"
The congregants were astounded. They said:
"Rabbi, how did you know the cow is from Minsk? We didn't tell you where
she was from."
The rabbi said:♥

Being in the presence of a woman fulfilled Guido. It tipped that off-balance longing in him to the middle of the scale. Calmed him, you might say. Gave him equilibrium. It was interesting to see how Guido's face, how his entire demeanor, changed when he talked to a woman. A fire in back of his retina lit his green eyes. Like the sun coming over a mountain—a new glow there. He was a six-footer but in the presence of a girl he stood taller. He wanted them to look up to him. His lips were parted in a slight smile, showing his teeth, as he listened to them. Once in a while his tongue would flick out to wet his lips. Or he'd casually touch the corner of his eye as if to show that the slight squint was something that could easily be wiped away. He cocked his head, frowned a bit, looked skeptical, detached, even superior. You know the space Americans put between themselves when they talk? But Guido stood close. After a while, as if to test them, he would take a step back and invariably the woman would step forward to maintain that six-to-eight-inch distance. Then he would touch the girl's forearm as he spoke, or casually hold her shoulder. Guido was in his element again. Years ago, I imagined him married, hugging his wife at the beach, let's say, in response to her request for affection. And while doing so, Guido is watching a knockout in a bikini walking by. In my mind, Guido turns his wife around slowly during the embrace so he can keep an eye on the bikini before she leaves his uncameraed field of vision forever.

The spirituality that supposedly inheres in a Jewish education seemed not to have rubbed off on Guido. But he was a good man. Remember the concert tickets? And helping old ladies. Also, there was once an instinctive gesture, giving away a piece of clothing—so perhaps I should erase the spirituality caveat, for what is the essence of Jewish education if not doing good? But the religious life per se had not touched him that much, as indeed it touched few of us. America is materialism; the USA, pleasure. If it is true that sex is an American obsession, then Italian Guido was quintessentially all-American.

Charlie Perlmutter to Milty Rosen, Guido listening:
There's the story about this Jewish American Princess who always has headaches and wants to get out of screwing. So she tells her husband she'll make love to him only on days with an 'n'. The guy is delighted. Sunday and Monday are

♥See ABC Directory, *Minsk.*

fine. Tuesday is a problem, but he tells his wife, "In Yiddish, Tuesday is Dienstik.*"* *"No way," she says. "Tuesday has no 'n'" So he skips a day. Wednesday, he's happy. Comes night, she again says "Uh-uh." "Why?" he asks. "Wednesday has an 'n'." "Yeh," she says, "But in Yiddish it's* Mittwoch. *No 'n'." "It's not logical, one day in English, the other day Yiddish." "Logical doesn't have an 'n' either," the JAP snaps. So now it's two days off. By Thursday he's horny. Since she went for Yiddish last time, he tells her, "Thursday in Yiddish is* Donnershtik. *Two 'n's." "Nothing doing," says she. "Thursday has no 'n'." The next day he's really screwed. Friday in English,* Freitik *in Yiddish. A double no 'n'.*

"Venredi in Italian," shouts Guido. "It's Venus's day. Bellissimo. Go for it!" *But they don't know no Italian. So now he's been a monk for almost four days. Then Saturday,* shabbes, *he's fixed again. But the husband has an idea. On Friday night, when it's already* shabbes, *he comes into bed, wishes his wife, "A* gut shnabbes, *screw you!" And does.*

Guido watched the provocatively proportioned Jamaican waitress. He wasn't the only one. We all watched her. Earlier in the afternoon I'd been chatting, flirting with her, asking her family name, which town she came from, enjoying the calypso lilt of her voice. Then along comes Guido—with his camera. His magic wand. He began taking pictures of her. Naturally, she turned again and smiled. Then he took her by the hand, led her around to the front of the buffet table and posed her in the open lawn. Soon she was giving him her address and phone number so he could send her pictures. It was the old story again—Guido Veneziano-Tedesco swiping a girl from me.

We don't have to multiply examples. It had happened when we were in high school and college too. Despite our friendship, there was a rough edge of tension because of girls, and this later caused a rift between us.

I didn't remind him how once, when we were in our senior year at Columbia, we went out on a double date. Another instance of give and take. Me give, him take. This time I fixed him up. My date, Ava, was a perky blonde with short curly hair and a beautiful body. First time I'd met such a delectable girl with all the qualities I wanted. I didn't meet her at Columbia but at a Jewish mixer at City College. The DJ had put on a hora, and I found myself next to her, holding her hand. Then the DJ abruptly switched to social dancing. She asked if I wanted to dance. Later, the DJ shut the lights and said, "Grab another partner in the dark!" But I didn't let go of her hand. When I told her I was majoring in psychology and literature at Columbia, she said she was a comp lit major at City College and had had some poems published in the school literary magazine. Then someone came up to her and said, "Ah, the cover girl herself!" About that she didn't brag, but she had been on the cover of the college humor magazine as "Girl of the Month."

Next time we went out, I asked Ava to bring a friend for Guido and we went to a chamber music concert at Brooklyn College. I knew that her looks and shape would impress Guido, but I didn't realize how much. He couldn't stop staring at her. The force of his entire will was massed into his eyes. Under the guise of looking at the audience during the concert, he slid his glance over his date's profile and kept returning to my blonde poet's lovely breasts. Then the other side of Guido surfaced. During the intermission we went to the men's room, which was located in the basement. A cold draft blew in from an open outside door, and Guido went to shut it. He saw a man huddled in the alley without a coat. At once he took off his windbreaker and gave it to the man. There was nothing theatrical about his gesture. Unlike politicians, he didn't expect bulbs to flash at his deed or legends to be created. In the car, later, when the girls asked what happened to his jacket he said he forgot it in the men's room. He'll pick it up another day. During the evening, my blonde poet said that as a child she had studied cello. This impressed Guido. "Just say no," I told her. "To what?" she said. "When Guido asks you to pose with the cello." And I told her about the girls in the high school orchestra. We laughed, but in a fit of jealous fantasizing I saw her posing for pictures that Guido would sell to *Playboy.*

Then Guido invited us to his house for a musicale. I would play guitar, he announced, and he the cello. And the girls would sing and dance. Then he announced a riddle. "I'm going to give a quick talk about a famous Italian poet, yet I'm going to talk slowly. What's the one-word title of my speech? . . . Don't tell me now. It's a bilingual pun. Think about it while we drive to my house and tell me later. Hint. Think music."

At his house (he had a private back entrance into his own two-room suite) he took out his cello and offered it to my blonde, but she demurred. He put on some dance music and lowered the lights. Meanwhile, we had forgotten his riddle. We began dancing. Soon we were all on one bed, necking. Then, like worms we squirmed and squinched and rolled around on the bed. Before we knew it, without consulting, without coming to a decision, we switched girls. I had turned my head and found myself face to face with Guido's date. In the relaxed mood we were in, the music playing, transporting us to a different realm, on a kind of a high, it was too tempting not to, so I kissed her. She threw her arms around me. And that's how it began.

But the next week, I took out my blonde poet Ava again and dated her for several months. Then, once when I called her, she was busy. Another time, busy again. It turned out that Guido had called her. I felt it was like breaking an unwritten code. You don't take your friend's girl. Or photograph her. Months later, in an art store I saw a photo poster. A string quartet—male violinist and three young women, all formally dressed from the waist down, but naked from the waist up. And guess who was posing with the cello? But I decided not to bring this matter up now.

But I did ask him about that long forgotten riddle.

"Who was the poet, and what was the title of your slow quick speech? Remember? That bilingual pun?"

"Oh, that? On Dante," he said. "Andante! . . . So, what do you say? We getting together?"

I put my finger on my cheek, made believe I was considering it.

Do people change? Perhaps in some ways. I watched Guido eating. Still eating! What an appetite he had. He ate andante, dreamily. Even at school he'd eat his Italian bread sandwich so slowly he would never have time to play ball in the street during our half-hour lunch break. The rest of us wolfed down our lunch in seven minutes. He ate for twenty, then took a walk around the block, or would join the game for a few minutes. When he ate rye, he would strip the bread of its crust and chuck it. I criticized him for throwing away the best part. I could eat a bread made of crust alone. One of my secret desires (when young, of course; later, those desires changed shape, form, and content) was to buy a rye bread and eat only the crust. The rest Guido could have. Once he offered me the crust, but I was too ashamed to take it. From then on I would watch him throw it away.

Now too I watched him as he made rye deli sandwiches. As he ate, he carefully, still, still, still after thirty years, he still stripped the crust away. People never change.

Never.

I don't know if it was curiosity or his description of beautiful Aviva that whetted my appetite to meet her. I guess I also wanted to verify for myself her existence. Years back I'd had a cuckoo friend who told me about a great gal he'd met in Boston whom he wanted me to meet. For months he kept telling me about her. Each time I wanted to see her, he gave me another story: divorce proceedings; away in Chicago to visit an aunt; traveling in Europe; ill. The old stamp collection routine again. Till one day I told him straight out that she didn't exist. He was half a Pygmalion, I said. In other words, a pig. And he, slightly insane, finally admitted that he'd concocted her. I still remember her name: Judy Swanson. Black hair, porcelain skin, black sweaters and slacks. According to my friend's maniacal fantasy, she was sexy and seductive and loved men. The son of a bitch had warmed me to her for months and then, tease that he was, he withdrew her. No wonder I wanted to make sure that Aviva existed. If Guido's stamp collection was a bluff, maybe Aviva was another Judy Swanson.

"Well?" Guido asked again. He looked a little off balance, even desperate now, with that pleading look in his eye.

I couldn't string him along any longer.

"Yes." I said.

BOOK TWO

Guido

1

*W*hen I stepped into Dr. Charles Perlmutter's waiting room, one of the Haydn quartets from Opus 76 embraced me, constant music to muffle the sounds of confidential outpourings in his office. A moment after I came in—admittedly a rather long moment (had he purposely hesitated there?)—Charlie came out and waved me in.

"Nice office you got, Merlputter," I told him, admiring especially his neat, glasstop mahogany desk. "Beautiful, in fact. And thanks for staying after hours. And a happy new year. *A git yoor! Buon capodanno.*"

"You too, Spaghetti. *Shana tova,*" said Charlie. And we hugged each other. I don't know about him, but I truly felt a wave of love for my old friend.

Charlie's phone began to ring, but he wasn't answering. We both plopped into leather easy chairs. He gazed at me benignly. Rather than look him in the eye at that moment, I stared at the paintings on the walls. "I didn't know you were into American art. Pastoral heartland. Old Schooners . . . Very WASPy. You should try photographs. They're in. Very collectible. Good investment." I took a deep breath. "Well, as the Italians say, a new year, a new start. My God, is it three months already since the reunion? *De ja vu,* I tell you, listening"—I pointed to the speakers near the ceiling—"to the Opus 76. I know it's one of your favorites, Charlie. Here's a story I bet you don't remember . . . We're driving through the Brooklyn Battery Tunnel to pick up some girls in Manhattan, remember?"

Charlie shook his head.

"WQXR was playing this quartet. The tunnel, of course, cut the music. But you kept on singing it for about six or seven minutes till we were in the clear. At one point some notes dribbled in, and you said there was a leak in the tunnel, we better hurry, expecting me to believe it. And then, when we emerged from the tunnel, the music picked up right where you stopped singing, you show off!" I looked at Charlie again. He didn't react to my praise. As if his benign gaze had been turned on by a machine oblivious to emotional configurations. "Do you remember when I made a guitar out of a cardboard box and used rubber bands for strings? How come you never took up an instrument, with your great knowledge of music? You loved the guitar too, I remember. Did you have a good summer?"

"Why don't you relax and begin?" Charlie said softly, with a knowing little smile, like a master encouraging his frightened charge.

"Yeah, I know I sound hyper, but just one more thing before I begin . . . I think it'll be interesting for you . . . Have you read *Partita in Venice?*"

"No. Who's it by?"

"I forget, but the author's name reminded me of a French mineral water."

"Perrier?"

"No . . . maybe Evian . . . I don't know . . . but it's a beautiful love story, a kind of mirror image to *Death in Venice*, full of fun and magic realism and a seven-hundred-year-old rabbi."

"Why do you mention it?"

"For two reasons. First, because the lead character in it—and that's the second reason—mentions my grandfather. The hero comes to a villa in Venice and sees a brass plaque in honor of 'Count Moise Davide Veneziano-Tedesco, Physician to all of Venice.' And now the second reason. Remember Tommy Manning from Dartmouth? He was in one of our lit classes in Columbia as an exchange student?"

"Yes, the organic farmer's son. You used to speak Italian to him. In my presence. And I didn't understand a word."

"Boy! You remember everything. You don't forget a thing, do you?"

"So what about him?" Charlie asked.

"Imagine! He's the hero of that novel, *Partita in Venice*, but that brazen mineral water author didn't have the decency to change Tommy's name."

"I'd love to be in a novel," Charlie mused.

"If anyone should be in a novel about Venice, it's me!" Veneziano-Tedesco said with finality.

"Come. Let's leave fiction," Charlie said. "Let's leave higher truth and get on with our fuzzy reality."

"Okay," I sighed. "I'll expand on what I told you at the reunion. Did you get those pictures I sent out?"

"Of course. Didn't I drop you a note of thanks?"

"Yeah, and the only one in the class who did. Okay, here goes, but please don't interrupt me. As you can see, it's hard for me to get into this. So if you have any questions or comments, jot them down."

"There's a famous Sholom Aleichem story," Charlie said, interrupting already, "that begins the same way. The narrator tells his friend: I'll tell you my story, but I can't stand interruptions . . . Anyway, suppose I can't control myself and must speak out?"

"Suit yourself. I'm no censor. But once I get into the flow of it, I want to let go. So, please, okay? Here goes . . . We'll begin with Ava . . . You remember Ava right? Don't give me that stoneface look. Of course you remember her. I married her. One is always smarter, as the Italian proverb has it, after one falls off the ladder."

"There's a Yiddish one," Charlie said. "Pains go away, but a wife just stays . . . and . . . stays."

"Until she goes . . . But in any case, in retrospect, I still don't know why I married her."

"You liked her poems," Charlie said flatly. Not a hint, oh, no, not a whiff of sarcasm in his voice.

"Yeh," I sniffed. "I guess I got it coming to me . . . She wrote poetry like . . . like . . ."

"You collected stamps."

I laughed and gave a disparaging wave of my hand. Two digs in a row, I thought. "At first I didn't see through the bluff . . . It was a portent of things to come . . . Sure, she was sexy, attractive, photogenic. But she came from a low-class family. It was stamped on her face. You won't argue with me, right?, that breeding is written all over one's face? The low class have cheap faces, the elite aristocratic. It even extends to fingers. The cellist I know, the one I've called Aviva, her fingers are long and slender, the digits of a noble woman. And there's this dumb, gum-chewing receptionist we have who has stubby fingers. Her rings cling to the flesh of her fingers like girdles. The extremities of a peasant. Who says that the body, the limbs, do not bespeak class? And Ava's parents also had that same face, those low class hands and fingers. Junkyard owners. So what to expect? Nobility? Grace? I let myself be blinded. Yes, with her I descended into low class. My mistake. I didn't consider the generations of Veneziano-Tedescos gazing down at me. Snooty? You bet. My mother always said there's no substitute for pedigree and family line. Not very American, yes? Nor democratic. But who says I'm a democrat? At first Ava was lively, fun, a tease. She sparkled. She was satisfying, like good champagne. But after you've drunk it, only thing left is the fizz. That my mother wasn't thrilled with Ava would be the understatement of the century. She'd have preferred someone from the old Italian Jewish families. You know, some us have been there since the times of Caesar. But we'd become partly Americanized, so in America you got to accept the vagaries of matrimonial destiny. Imagine this scene of togetherness. *My* mother and *her* mother with the pink Brooklyn curlers in her hair, mah jong in her skull, and inanities on her lips. Some odd couple, right? About my father and her father I won't even talk. My father had more correct English in one gold filling than American-born Mr. Junkyard had in his entire rather enormous mouth. If my mother's mother, who was living in Venice at the time, and whom my mother was anxious to get back to, had seen Ava, just once seen her, mind you, just merely *glanced* at her, she would have wrinkled the nose on her imperious face, raised one eyebrow ever so slightly—right out of the *Garden of the Finzi Continis*, you bet, to whom by the way we're related but not as assimilated as—and that would have been the end of it. That, in case you didn't know, is aristocratic hauteur. I assure you, I would never have taken Ava to meet *her*. Grand-mother Sacerdote had antennae that measured quality much like your Hasidic rabbis could size up a person with one look. In any case, doc, it was done. We married. I was getting assignments and was away sometimes two or three weeks at a stretch. When I came back I noticed there was less and less sparkle. At first I couldn't measure it, but after eight or nine months I became aware of a gradual erosion. Was it because I was going away? I don't know. I spoke to my boss and asked him to relieve me of travel for a few months. Still, Ava was moody, sad, depressed. We went out, tried to have fun. I did my work. But it was up and down. A yo-yo. That yo-yo image will return, you'll see, in another context. Another affinity between me and the woman we'll call Aviva. At that time my mother, who by the way is well and happy back in Venice, was ready to go back to Italy. She wanted to be near her aging mother, and she also missed my sister and her children who lived in Milan, though I can't see how anyone would choose to live in that polluted city. Since my mother was about to leave, she suggested that Ava take her piano—it was an old European beauty, a Bechstein—and start lessons. Ava agreed. She doodled with the keys a couple of weeks and then decided to begin. It seemed to help. Once her mood had improved, I accepted an overseas assign-ment. And then—bam!—Do you know what caused the split?"

"No," Charlie said.

"Pam didn't tell you?"

"I'm not privy to Pam's mind."

"Only her pussy, right?"

Charlie, old pro that he is, did not blink. He was listening. I don't know why I said that. I certainly did not want to irritate him. Charlie was doing me a favor staying after hours to accommodate me, and I was making an ass out of myself. Like the Sicilians say, I told him, open your mouth wide enough and the donkey within is seen.

"It's no secret that it all began—my God, was it twenty, twenty-two years ago?—the night all four of us ended up in my room after the Brooklyn College concert and we all fooled around on my bed and switched partners. It was exciting, that subtle, unplanned switch. First time it ever happened to me."

"Me too," Charlie said.

"Okay, I admit, I apologize, it wasn't nice of me to start taking Ava out when you were going with her, but believe me, in retrospect, I did you a favor. Why should a nice guy like you have gotten stuck?"

Charlie didn't respond. But his look said: I'll be the judge of that. Who knows? Perhaps he's still sore that I took Ava away. On the other hand, Pam wasn't bad either.

"Okay, so you don't take out another guy's girl, especially if he's your best friend. And she could always have said no. But I couldn't help it. She pulled me. She tugged at me. She attracted me."

"Her poetry, right?"

Now Charlie's third jibe got to me.

"You're really riding that phony poetry ploy of hers. Lay off . . . No, if you want the truth, it *wasn't* her poetry. It was her tits. By the way, she had majored not in literature, but in the phony-ass subject, sociology, where syntax and grammar and clear thinking don't count. That poetry bluff was part of her devious personality, but I didn't discover that till later. I was hot for her. I got hooked, I fell, I got burned . . . Anyway, I was on assignment in Paris at the time, and Ava had already begun to take piano lessons. They seemed to help her, as I said. I was supposed to return on a Thursday but got back a few days earlier. I didn't call. Wanted to surprise her. Who knows why? Maybe I was suspicious. We lived then in one of the old buildings on the West Side, the upper 70s. It was about 4 or 5 p.m., middle of May. I don't remember if Ava was temping at the time. She'd done some social work but got sick of it. She had the temperament for social work, that phony, like I do for driving a steamroller. I let myself in. Seems no one is home. Then I hear noises from the bedroom. My bedroom. My bed. I open the door and guess what? The classic scene. Ava's in bed with a man. So I shoot them . . . Don't look so skeptical, Charlie, I shot them *my* way. I had my loaded camera around my neck as usual and first thing I did was shoot for the record. The guy didn't even have a chance to move I was so quick. My sudden entry and the flash froze them. Then he jumped up, this idiot, this boor, coward, clown, wimp. Up the shmuck jumped, with hard-on wilting, and ran, in my presence, mind you, right in front of my eyes the putz runs into the closet. I pulled him out and—should I punch the bastard? went through my head. The poor prick looks so pathetic, so I aimed for his face but clobbered him in the solar plexus. Meanwhile, Ava is screaming, whimpering, alternating these feral cries. Then she jumps out of bed and wraps herself in a sheet. I'm calm, I'm calm—those were the thoughts that ran through my mind, God, I'm remembering this as though it's happening now, but her I'm going to kill as soon as I get rid of the guy. That two-timing bitch. 'My God,' I yelled at her, 'look!' and I pointed to the ceiling. She looked up and I gave her—everything that I restrained concerning the guy I let out on her—gave her such a slap on the face with the full force of my hand that she fell screaming and sobbing back on the bed. Then I swooped up the bastard's clothing. Everything. Jacket. Pants. Underwear. Shirt. Shoes. He even had a London Fog raincoat, so it must have been raining that day. I ran out into the hall and dumped the works in the garbage chute, right into the incinerator, which they still had at the time in New York. Then I run back into the apartment to pull the bastard out of the closet. And from the closet, his voice muffled by my clothes, my suits, his bare ass touching *my* hanging chinos, the asshole brays, 'Don't get the wrong impression. It's not what you think it is . . .' I laughed so hard I almost forgot my rage. And then the son of a dog finds his tongue again and says, "I didn't come here for that. I promise. I swear. She seduced me . . .' I pulled him out of the closet. As a wet sock so limp was he. About thirty, with a little mustache. Not a bad-looking guy. But naked. Caught naked, everyone looks pathetic. 'Where are my clothes?' yells he. Suddenly he's a boy soprano. Maybe even a castrato, after I get through with him. 'Please. I'm sorry. I'm sorry. Where are my pants?' So I say: 'How the hell should I know? Ava, what did you do with the gentleman's jacket and trousers? Did you chuck them out the window, you spiteful vixen?' Ava, meanwhile, is now face down on the bed, a pillow over her head, moaning and keening. 'My jacket,' the guy is bawling now. 'I just took $5000 cash out of my mother's account. It's my mother's money,' he shrieked. 'It's my mom's money. I swear. It's in my jacket. Where are my clothes? . . . I'll sue you.' So I said, 'Chalk it up to debit, Randall Parker. Now get out of here, you piece of shit.' 'Do you know me?' he says. 'How did you know my name?' Simple, I'd looked into his wallet before I dumped his clothes. 'I know everything about you. I have all the facts. I knew you before you knew yourself. Now disappear, but quick. For you're getting off cheap. Some whores charge more than five g's, and then the pimps slice your balls off.' And I threw him into the hall."

"How did he get home?"

"How should I know? Maybe he called a cab. Maybe a nudist colony. Maybe he dove down the chute, five floors down, to follow his uniform . . . Now who do you think was the guy she took up with?"

"A psychologist . . . treating her for depression."

I chuckled. "Ha! All these psychiatrists pursuing their women patients' pants. Can you imagine the doctor riding naked in the elevator protecting his balls with his hands? Poetic justice. Like out of a novel. The emperor who sees everyone naked is finally revealed."

"You threw him a towel," Charlie said. "If I know you, you threw him a towel."

"Well, you *don't* know me. The only thing I threw him was out. I suppose others would like to have me think that I should have thrown him a sheet and a credit card and watch him maybe redo himself at Zabar's. A layer of lox, then a coating of dried apples and a wreath of garlic or figs for headgear, until he turned into a respectable fruit and vegetable tree. Or perhaps watch him clothe himself, reinvent himself at Bloomingdale's, seeing him go from department to department, gradually accreting clothes until he emerged a fully-dressed gent. But all this is decorative, moronic speculation and entertainment. With absolutely no sympathy whatsoever I threw the bastard out. How would you feel if you came home and found someone screwing your wife?"

"Very surprised," Charlie allowed, "seeing as I'm not married."

"*Molto* funny. Well, pal, it wasn't a doctor. The guy in bed with her was her piano teacher. She'd been taking lessons for four months, and he'd been plucking her strings for three . . . Well, that's one way to get rid of depression. You know the old story. You fall in love with your teacher, your priest, and your psychiatrist."

"But that's *my* line," Charlie said. "At least part of it. Remember, at the reunion I said that pupils always fall in love with their teacher?"

"Yeah. I knew one of us said it, but I forgot which one."

"So, did she marry her piano teacher?"

"Are you kidding? He was married, the shit. And he had the gall to plead with me about the shame, the humiliation for his wife and kids. So I say to him, 'And this isn't humiliation, you adulterated, adulterous, adultering filth?'"

I drew a deep breath and blew it out, as if to get rid of these awful memories. For a moment I lost myself in one of the sea scenes on Charlie's wall. Then I turned to him.

"As for Ava I told her, 'Get your clothes and get out before I throw you out naked like I did him.' But like a cat, before I could move, she dashed into the bathroom, locked the door and began to shower. I opened her chest of drawers—I don't know what I was looking for, maybe explanation, revelation, epiphany—and guess what I found? Her diary. There she kept a meticulous record of her affairs. The *Diary of an Adulterous Woman*. I don't know if it's my title or hers. Or maybe even Aviva's, said in a moment of levity about the journal *she* kept. There were listings, the goddamn slut, with the elevator man, the painter, friends, girl friends' husbands, co-workers. Look at her right and she'd drop her panties. Maybe they'd even fall off of their own accord. Maybe she was a nympho, who knows? But the term has lost its meaning because nowadays everyone over eleven screws. In her diary, next to the name, there was even a check or a plus, rating the guy's performance, and a number with a little *o* next to it, probably how many orgasms she'd had. She really loved that short leg, as the Venetians say. It was disgusting. I couldn't read any more. My own wife! She did everything with men, the lascivious bitch, that I'd wanted to do with women. I mean, is it contagious, like leprosy, flu, gonorrhea, AIDS?"

I went into my jacket pocket to produce the evidence. I held the pages in front of me like a speech. Here, Charlie, I was about to say, listen to this. Then I decided—no, I don't have to share everything with him.

But to myself I read the passages I had copied out from the journal I'd swiped from Ava before I booted her out.

Most men don't look at a woman's body. They look only for one or two or three things, and that's it. If I ever have children, I'm going to teach them to look at themselves naked and appreciate their natural state.

Okay, I thought, that's not so bad. I wonder why I copied *that*? Perhaps to show that she might have raised children in a perverse way. Then I continued scanning:

Once, at a zoo, I saw two lions making love. The majesty of it made me hot, and I felt myself getting wet. It made me wonder if female animals have orgasms . . .

You can screw me very easily, but to make love to me, if you want me, you have to cut through layers . . .

I wanted to get laid every day, twice a day, three times a day. I love fucking, but he was in the mood only on weekends, if he was home on weekends. But the crux came when G. didn't want to go down on me. I told him I wanted it and he said, "You don't know what you want." I resented that, so I started looking around.

Bitch, I thought. Two-timing bitch! Maybe I *should* read this to Charlie. She deserves having her reputation smeared in the mud. But, shit, if I do that, mine too is on the line. Then my eye landed on a gem, a lollapalooza!

I just had my 100th man today. The *hundredth*! Imagine! Most women have only one. Some none. Some nun! as Guido would probably pun. But I've reached the perfect score. One hundred. An A for fucking! Here's to the next hundred!"

I leaned back in the chair, agitated, still clutching the two folded pages, my moral center askew. Suddenly, I felt off balance, as if something were missing. Then I realized the Haydn tape had stopped. No more music. Silence settled like snow on the office. The stillness was perfect. Not even the whirr of an electric clock. I couldn't even hear my friend breathing. Had I bored him to death? A pleasant fatigue came over me, as if I were being rocked to sleep, that pleasant sleepy feeling I used to get riding the subway from Manhattan to Brooklyn, in the days kids could still ride the subways alone. I wanted to close my eyes. How I wanted to sleep just then! But I was holding dynamite. I perked up and read once more:

Screwing is just a release. It's masturbating with someone else. Very Presby-terian . . . Fucking is intense, but basically no emotion. Just tactile . . . Making love is a combination of spirit and emotion in the body. And the orgasm is not just of the body, but something deeper, with exquisite pain . . . I hold back on orgasm very often . . . A vaginal orgasm occurs when your soul is touched, which is rare for me. A clitoral orgasm is just for fucking.

My God, I thought. She could have been the Hite, Masters, and Kinsey of her generation if she'd been a bit smarter and spent less time in bed and more at her desk.

I waved the papers at Charlie. "Here's the evidence, But as you can see, I'm hesitating, decided against it. As I said—but what *did* I say before you fell asleep?"

Charlie laughed. "It wasn't *me*. I thought you'd spaced out."

"Anyway, Ava was the female version of a womanizer, for which a word, as far as I know, at least a semineutral one, does not exist . . . I know what you're thinking, Charlie, but could I be called a womanizer, like those cabinet secretary designees are called by the press just before Senate confirmation hearings? I supposed I wanted to become a womanizer as soon as I heard the word. It's an all-inclusive word, mirroring its meaning into itself. But I still didn't know what a womanizer did. I mean, of course, I knew what he did, but I didn't know the, how shall I put it, the qualitative extent of it. Or perceive its intensity or depth. Is it lust? To screw them daily? Some women want to get laid three times a day. Are they called *man*anizers? What does a womanizer *do*? Run from one affair to another? Undress every attractive girl he sees? But once, when I screwed three girls in one day—one in the morning, another at noon, and a third at night, I knew what the word meant. I could look myself in the eye and without fear of contradiction declare: Today I'm a womanizer.

"Wait! I was talking about Ava, not me, right? Why did you distract me with your question? I should have seen the signs. When things are on a downhill course people sometimes send subtle signals to each other. For instance, she stopped looking into my eyes when she spoke. And there was something else I didn't notice but a friend pointed out to me. Once Ava and I came out of two different rooms and walked toward each other in the narrow hallway. But instead of facing each other my friend saw that we turned our backs to each other. This was the body language unconsciously expressed by our thoughts. So—it was finished with her."

Like an addict, or a drunk, my hand kept yearning to go back to those pieces of paper in my jacket pocket. I had to share some of Ava's remarks with him. I just couldn't keep her notations to myself.

"Here . . . I changed my mind. I copied out some of her diary entries. Judge for yourself what sort of person she was. April 2: 'If I were a man with my sex drive, I'd go crazy. Thank God I'm a woman and I can have a man any time I want. I'm in control. I'm the master (mistress?). Since men always want sex, I can have any man I want.' May 30: 'I love men, I love sex with them, especially good-looking and charming ones. Are there any other kind? I especially love . . .' sorry, Charlie, no more . . ."

But I couldn't help reading it myself. "I especially love that first moment when the cock breaks through the lips and enters. Nuns are crazy. Women who feign headaches and don't sleep with their husbands are nuts. Woman who do it once, or only once a day, are crazy. I love being fucked by different men. It's a wonder I don't spend all my time in bed. Who needs drugs or alcohol for a high? Sex is the greatest invention in the world. Who says there's no God!?"

I shoved the pages back into my jacket pocket with a grimace.

"I thought you came here to talk about Aviva." Charlie said.

"I did. I will. I shall. But first I had to give you some background. Just one more thing. No, forget it." Again that caveat not to tell Charlie everything waved through me. I'm not a patient of his. I don't have to turn myself inside out and upside down like a bottle and pour it all out.

He knew things were wrong with him and Ava when he began paying attention to her sex noises, listening to how they developed musically until their finale. She adored fucking, true. But then so did he. She moaned and sang up the scale in gradual but not predictable increments the hotter she got. When he began listening he knew he was becoming disinvolved. But he had to admit that remembering all this now was delicious. A mental sexual thrill.

I withdrew from my reverie and looked at Charlie. "I can't say things were always bad between Ava and me. Example. When things were good at the beginning, I wondered once why she stopped wearing those big loop earrings. 'Because you said you didn't like them. You said they're too big for me.' And as I looked at this blonde beauty, I thought now that's extending the frontiers of love. Love moving into subtleties of feeling, like a nuanced wrist motion that distinguishes a great cellist from a good one. Those textures that critics are always writing about. So she was giving. Giving in. Like saying nice things to me and wondering if it was really she who said it, 'Me who never said such things before!' So I told her it was her heart talking and not her self-conscious mind."

Guido smiled to himself, remembering something else she had said: "I liked you for your sensitivity. I remember how impressed I was when I saw the tears in your eyes when you told me how your father died of a heart attack giving emergency care to a man trapped under a car... Another reason I fell for you was your energy," Ava said, recalling that double date with Pam and Charlie.

"And Charlie doesn't have energy?"

"Yes. But he's different. Quieter."

"But you didn't know that about me until later."

"Maybe. But I can sense a person's energy even when he's sitting still. And you radiate energy even if you don't move a muscle."

But taking her, winning her, from Charlie wasn't enough. It wasn't just jealousy or salaciousness that made him want to know every detail of her teenage and college years. It was as if by listening, he had known and possessed her too. "I should have gotten to know you when you were a nubile fourteen," he told Ava. "You were my counselor in camp, remember? I peed in and wanted to creep into your bed, but I couldn't." "Why?" she asked. "Was the cot too narrow? "No," he said. "The rest of the bunk was there already." Only later, after he discovered her diary, did he realize how true was his little joke. And it was to her that he said in a surge of romantic feeling: This happens only once to a man in his lifetime. But then she began to resist his questioning. It's old stuff, she said, rolling her eyes in mock desperation (with an expression, however, that said: All right, I know you'll ask more. I'm helpless to resist you. Ask and I'll respond.)

"You know, Ava came to visit me not too long ago. Just dropped in out of the blue." I could see Charlie was skeptical, but I didn't care. I started tapping my index finger on the armrest of my chair. I was disconcerted by the uncurtained window. Instead of light pouring in, a rectangle of blackness just hung there. I got up to stretch, walked to the window to see the view but only saw myself approaching in the glass. I didn't really want to look out the window but sought an excuse to put off the question I wanted to ask Charlie: if he'd seen Pam during the past month. Looking over his head, I asked him.

"I haven't seen her in a long time," was his reply.

"You still in touch?"

"Yeh. Occasionally." But there was neither a smile or a glimmer of interest or warm memory on his face.

"Is she married?"

"Not as far as I can tell," Charlie said. "I stick with the single ones."

I sat down again.

It was in mid-September. Tammy was at the photo shop; Guido hadn't yet left for work. Someone rang the bell. When he opened the door, Ava stood there in a bright red topcoat. The Giorgio perfume spoke before she did. Its essence covered the nervous "Hi," the fetching, tremulous smile. He invited her in. He hadn't seen her—was it fifteen years already? For a moment, as their eyes met, a surge of lust ran through him. I'm going to fuck her, he thought, then throw her out. I'm going to photograph her naked and compare her body with the nude studies I have of Aviva.

"How?" he said.

She understood the question but didn't answer. How had she known he was home alone? For she'd never have come if she suspected someone else was home.

"What beautiful roses!" she said, going up and sniffing. "It makes you heady." She looked around, drew a deep breath. "The Stieglitz print of Venice is missing."

Not here a moment, he thought, and already doing inventory. "It's on loan," he said, but he didn't tell her it's at the Museum of Modern Art nor that the print was worth a fortune now.

She took off her coat, threw it like a paper plane over a chair. With her red coat off, what little bulk she appeared to have vanished. With the coat off, he saw she'd lost a lot of weight, was gaunt, looked like death. With her red coat off, her face seemed pinched and tight. Gone the brightness of fifteen to eighteen years past. Her lips were thin, her nose sharper. In this age, when no woman looked her age, when women at sixty looked forty and women in their thirties looked like college girls, Ava at thirty-nine looked a dozen years older. A dozen bad years older. But then she was never good at numbers. She could never balance a checkbook or remember her license plate or social security number. She added a column of numbers three different times and got three different sums. But after she took off her coat and stood there, vulnerable, he hugged her even before he thought about it, and she gave a little sigh; still, he felt the restraint in his muscles and in his heart. But Ava was grateful for that little hug. Some of the tension seemed to dissipate with that hug. A breath of darkness left her eyes with that little hug. She wore black slacks and a bright green silk blouse, and a tight black belt to show off what bit of bosom she had left. Where had her tits gone?

They sat on the sofa. She tucked her legs under her and sat facing him, then began a nonstop hyper talk, as if to prevent him from asking questions or making comments. An anxious, vibrato flow of words. He can't remember exactly what Ava said, but one remark stood out. "I thought you'd kick me out again when you saw me, but I took the chance," were her pathetic words. He rubbed her shoulders and back as she spoke; he rubbed and rubbed. Then he unbuttoned her blouse. With a practiced gesture he knew so well, she took it off and removed the bra. Her breasts sagged, he saw. She used to have full delectable breasts and now they sagged like an old woman's. She pulled a red rose from the vase, broke the stem, and put the flower in her hair. He told her she'd lost weight. She said she hadn't; she'd always been thin. He didn't want to contradict her. Maybe she was ill; maybe she had STD. Who knows, even AIDS. Freckles, speckles, spots, dotted her pale skin. He didn't want to remember, but on her chest he saw their bedroom and that piano teacher in bed with her. His flash of desire at that moment shut like a light. He stood her up, unbuttoned her slacks coolly. His lips didn't show it, but in his mind's eye danced a cruel little smile. He'll take her clothes off, he thought, and throw her out, just like he threw out her lover. Down her slacks slid, and the black panties followed, to her ankles, but he clamped her foot to the floor with his shoe as she was about to step out of her panties. Wrinkles on her sagging little belly. The thighs were fallen too. The red rose petals floated from her hair to the floor. He couldn't see what interest men would have in her. She was always hot, he remembered, not like Tammy who lately had to be coaxed, but once on the path, zoomed along. He had never met a woman who reveled in touch, loving, lovemaking like Ava. She got hot just looking at him (and at other guys too, as he discovered to his chagrin). Ava would want to make love morning noon and night and in between. He stared at her for a while; she looked at him expectantly, then he told her to get dressed. It seemed to him she whispered, "Take me back!" But it was said so softly it could have been a dozen other phrases, not excluding, "Scratch my back!" But whatever she said she articulated it without passion or insistence. So if there was no passion, if she didn't mean it, why had she come? To see if she could seduce him? She was thin as a scarecrow. Her flesh was starting to go. A scriptwriter nestled in his cerebral cortex was urging him to say, "Get away from me, you whore." But he bit his lips and chased the goblin away. He shook his head, slowly. He thought it would trigger a tear in her eyes. It didn't.

"It wasn't exciting with you any more. The spark was gone," she said.

"That's why one betrays one's husband?"

But she didn't respond directly. "You didn't court me."

"We went out. God, we went out more than normal couples."

"Yes. But you weren't there. You were boring."

"Me? Boring?"

"Yes, Mr. Ego. You. Boring. Bawwwww———rrrring."

He looked up at the ceiling. Why in heaven's name had she come? To insult him? Did she want money? Medicine? A referral?

"For others you turned on the charm. I just listened to you on the phone. To strangers. Salesgirls. Friends. Everyone. To everyone—but me. Me, I was old hat. Taken for granted. To be had. Wake up in the morning with that big hard-on of yours and zhloop—in you go. So no need to be charming any more."

Years back, he thought, she wasn't that way. Then she would grab him and growl, "It's a good thing girls don't get erections."

"Otherwise, you'd be walking around always with a hard-on a mile long, right?"

"Uh-huh," she said. And more, he also remembered Ava singing: "How delicious it is to be made love to by you. It's a good thing other girls don't know or I'd have a problem."

"So that's why you fucked the piano teacher, because it wasn't exciting with me any more?"

"You drove me to it. You and your sexual frenzy. You stimulated my appetite. You kept telling me how my pussy was like an oven. Every time you put your knee or hand there you got burned."

"Once too often," he said.

"Very funny . . . You wanted it morning noon and night. I was never like that before I met you. One Saturday, I remember, you screwed me every hour on the hour. You wanted to get into the Guinness Book of Records. *My God, you were a fucking fucking machine. Waking me up two three times in the middle of the night."*

"I didn't go it alone."

"I liked it, but I wasn't crazy for it like you. You made me crazy for it. You told me I was crazy for your cock and you made me repeat it while you screwed me. You made me say it so often I got to believe it, you pervert."

"Me? You fucked every male in sight while I was away."

"Because of you. You trained me. You pushed me over the top."

"In other words, it's all my fault. All the entries in that Diary of an Adulterous Woman *of yours are all my fault."*

"Yes."

"You're sick. Demented. You're the pervert. Nymphos blame everyone but themselves."

"If so, I'm not the only one. I didn't want to tell you this, but what the hell, you ought to know. Here's a story about your fuddy-duddy buddy that will make your hair stand on end."

And she was almost right, the bitch, he thought. It almost did.

With no shame whatsoever, quoth the slut:

"One night last week Pam and I and Charlie went out. First it was Pam and Charlie, and then Pam says, Mind if I bring Ava? Charlie said no. We had a few drinks and went back to Pam's apartment. She put on some music. Everybody was a bit woozy. They were dancing and I felt left out and horny. Remember when we switched way back? Well, it was fantasy time. I noticed Charlie looking at me all evening. I could see his tongue was hanging out for me, though it wasn't actually hanging out. I said to Pam, I dare you to take out Charlie's cock and suck it. And if you have trouble, I'll help. Pam went right down for the zipper and pushed Charlie onto the couch. I thought Charlie's hand would protect his crotch, but he didn't protest at all. All he said was, Hey! in a kind of surprised voice. What luck! Two women all over him. Pam began and before I knew it I joined her, licking and sucking until Charlie came all over my face and Pam's. By now our clothes were off and Pam says, You take him first and I'll watch. I was on top and she watched us fucking till I screamed my head off with the excitement of being watched, as if I were doing a film and then Pam brought her pussy down on his mouth while I licked her breasts. Excited? I see the bulge in your pants. Wanna hear more?"

"No. I had enough." The goddamn liar, he thought. It's Ava's fantasy. A porn flick she'd seen. Pam wasn't like that at all.

She walked to the door. Only when her back was toward him did she mutter a brittle good-bye.

"You're thinking about Ava, right?" Charlie broke in. "There's this dreamy look in your eye."

"I must have caught it from my mother. Sometimes she just sat there, reading, and drifted off, a happy little smile on her face. It runs in the family . . . I told you Ava popped in on me. Have you seen her?"

Charlie closed his eyes slowly, all the while shaking his head. "Are you kidding? Not since our college days."

One of them is lying, I thought. Maybe both.

"You could have been anything." Ava told him. "A cellist. A conductor. Choreographer. Businessman. Genius. Whatever you touched was great."

Guido's eyes sparkled, looking at her naked body.

"And you remained a photographer. And married again. How boring!"

He didn't want to give her the pleasure of a clever response: Even people who are bored well stay married; or, even people who are married well stay bored.

"I keep wondering what made her come and see me. I think she just wanted me to screw her, but I showed her the door. Maybe it would have given her some perverse satisfaction having me betray my second wife with my first."

"Come on, Spaghetti, get back on track . . . Aviva."

"Did you know that Aviva is a palindrome and if you remove *vi* you get Ava, a smaller palindrome. Or add *vi* for victory to Ava and you get Aviva. Mystical. Coincidental."

"I've never been into mysticism," said Charlie. "Mystical affinities and coincidences is your bag. It's the genes of Sephardic and Italian kabbalists riding in you."

Like a magnet, my hand went for my pocket again. I wanted to prove to Charlie what a bitch Ava had been. Let him know what a favor I did him by preventing her from hurting him. But what was the point of it? It was like rubbing your own nose in the dirt. What would I gain by showing him that it served me right swiping his girl? Masochism wasn't *my* bag. I put away those excerpts from the *Diary of an Adulterous Woman.*

Again, for a while there came that dreamy, relaxing, silence. The Haydn had long finished and now the Mozart *Symphonia Concertante* was on. Then Charlie's voice.

"You know, I never asked you this, and I don't think you mentioned it. Did you, do you have any children?"

I felt as if in sleep a sudden, involuntary twitch of a muscle. Frozen for a moment. I licked my lips and said, "With Ava, thank God, none. But with Tammy I had a son."

Charlie was about to say something. But seeing the noncommittal expression on my face, he stopped.

"I don't talk about him," I said sadly. "But I . . . we . . . do have one child. He has Down's Syndrome, a mongoloid in the old terminology, and he's been at a care center for years. But if you don't mind, I don't want to go into it."

"I understand," said Charlie, and for the first time, he choked up. Tears welled in his eyes. He really felt for me that sweet, lovable man. "Are you finally going to start . . . ?"

I laughed. "I will, but so many things are linked. Let me continue the way I sort of planned it. First, chapter one, Ava. Then chapter two, Tammy, for one story cannot be understood without the other, and there's a . . . how shall I put it, like a curtain over a source of light, a darkness within me, a darkness I can't figure out."

"You're not alone," said Charlie. "No man can clarify all the darkness within us, says Jung."

2

"Chapter Two. My wife, Tammy . . . You saw her," I told Charlie. "Tall, modelly, straight blonde hair. Very goyish looking hair. Only WASPs have hair like that. When I first knew her I used to think she was adopted and no one told her. Or at least no one told *me*. That tall frame, straight nose, narrow shoulders, maybe even the moroseness, all pointed to gentile genes."

Tammy was a pretty woman, he thought. In a fashion magazine sort of way. Cool and detached. Some women aren't photogenic, but Tammy's pictures made her look better. You'd never think that such an almost impersonal beauty could sizzle in private. No one would ever say that Tammy was sexy. Pretty, yes. Handsome, yes. Aristocratic, definitely. But sexy? Never. Except in camera. But yet, early on, before the boy was born, she was on fire always. Hours after lovemaking she would come up to him and say, "My nipples are glowing, my breasts are glowing, I'm glowing. I'm so hot for you," she'd say. "I think of you during work. I think of the down on your cheeks. I play with your balls, I know it's not sexy for you, but I love them. They're so rich. So heavy. I could have an orgasm just thinking about them." Perhaps she didn't say all that at once, but on separate occasions. He wished he could tell Aviva that. For sex she had no imagination. Sex for Aviva was only stimulation, except during that first month of lessons when her imagination ran wild, like a Bosch painting. "Sex is imagination," Tammy once said, "and all the rest, the physical part, is just beautiful decoration." "Interior decoration," Guido added.

"I told you, Charlie, that I met Tammy at a photography course I taught. Here too the old truism, which I once read, I mean, you once read, in a Russian novel—you always fall in love with your teacher—held true. I still don't know why she took the course. Maybe to socialize. She really has no talent, no heart for photography. Maybe even hates it. Once, at home, in the dumps, she cried out. 'All those stupid pictures at the shop. Thank God I don't have to develop them. One day I'm going to put Smith's birthday pictures in Brown's envelope and vice versa. They'll never know the difference. All babies look alike.' Still, she faithfully runs that photo and camera shop we have in Merrick. Works Monday through Saturday, 9 to 6. Except Wednesdays, which she spends with the boy, and then her assistant is there by herself. His name is Adam. The truth is, not all babies look alike. All mongoloids look alike♥ . . ." Then suddenly I felt my head drop. I covered my eyes with my hands and whispered hoarsely, "Maybe it's a punishment."

"For what?" Charlie asked.

"For my lascivious behavior."

"That's absurd. Your son was born years ago and you're doing what you're doing now . . . And how about your wife? Why should she be punished?"

I shrugged. "God makes mistakes too."

Charlie shook his head disdainfully. "You were talking about your wife working at the shop."

"Yeah. She works because she can't stand being at home. Being busy keeps her thoughts away from the kid. It puts a gauze over a wound that won't go away. Wednesdays are bad. That's when her gloom peaks. I tell her, don't go. But she says it's her boy, her child, a child needs love. But he sucks the love out of her, and then anger and depression come in to fill the vacuum. On those days she's especially sensitive, like before, during and after her period. She loses her patience if I didn't do something she asked me to do—of course, I didn't do it; I was too busy doing it with Aviva. Take the chairs for re-caning; pick up the blinds; bring the drapes to the cleaners. 'You do it.' I tell her. 'It's on the way for you. For me it's twenty-eight miles out of the way.'

"Can you imagine someone not liking photography? And she married into it. It's weird. You might say, well, at least she shares another passion of mine: classical music. But she doesn't. She tolerates it, but it's a chore. She has no ear for it. She has ears like fig leaves, as they say in Calabria, big and useless. So on occasion I go off by myself. So then what *is* her passion? Flowers! Roses growing in the backyard. A perfect rose will give her a high. Orgasm, almost. You're the psychologist, you figure it out. And then there's this gloom. The Wednesday gloom syndrome, which finally wears off by the following Tuesday night.

"Example of how fixated she is on that poor kid. In the spare bedroom upstairs, the room that should have been Adam's—he's eleven now—there hangs a calendar, one of those large print tear-off-a-page-a-day calendars, with the date of the child's birth. It has never been removed. That was the day that should have been Tammy's rebirth, but it has become her day of stasis. Frozen in time. Nothing has moved in her since then. Her inner

♥See ABC Directory, *Guido's son.*

clock has stopped. From that day she's no longer been fully alive. "There was a time I could make her laugh. Even hysterically sometimes. But it was a hyper laugh. To cover up her basic malaise."

Once, he remembered, he lifted up her bra to kiss her breasts. He kept popping the bra up and putting it back, alternating with his kisses.
"*Stop it,*" *she said.* "*You're ruining my new bra. It cost twelve-fifty.*"
"*What?*" *he screamed.* "*Twelve-fifty? I just lost all desire.*"
"*Nine-fifty,*" *she said quickly.*
"*With or without tax?*"
"*Six-fifty,*" *she said,* "*without the nipples.*"

"She used to be funny," I told Charlie, "but this bubbly, nimble wit left her once the boy's retardation became evident. The lines around her mouth gave her a mask-like look that raised eyebrows in company. She had a husband—but looked like a widow. She had a son—but looked bereaved. The incurable child had sucked the life out of her. If a child dies you mourn him and then you're gradually restored to life. But if your child dies daily, mourning never stops. Seeing him once a week, loving him and hating him, depleted her strength. Because of Adam she dared not have, she feared having more children. I wanted; she said No. She never even had the faint hope in the morning of seeing an improvement in the afternoon. So she found consolation with roses during her spare time."

And at night, he thought, when her mood was even with the lights out and soothing Beautiful Music in the background, Tammy usually pressed hungrily to him. Once, in the middle of it, she stopped. A switch turned off. She began to cry hysterically.
"*Why are you crying?*"
"*You don't love me any more.*"
It was dark. He couldn't see her. But her tears splashed on his cheek. He didn't say a word. Had he seen a mirror, he knew, it would have shown a stone face, devoid of emotion. Stubborn in his silence, he wasn't going to lie to her or console her with false words or false hope.
"*It's mechanical,*" *Tammy said.* "*You're just going through the motions . . . You're never tender to me,*" *she complained.* "*You pay more attention to your lenses than to me. Why? Why do you stare into your camera or your idiotic enlargements as if I weren't there? Or are you hooked into that lens to avoid looking at me?*"
"*What do you want me to do?*" *he shouted, then at once retreated.* "*Now don't start crying. Crying is out . . . Life isn't a B movie. There aren't always close-ups with the whispered I-love-you's flying like pigeons all over the place*

while orchestral music swells in the background."
"*I'm not talking about movies,*" Tammy insisted. "*I'm talking about real-
ity. Here. Now. Today. About a heart that's breaking . . .*"
That's news to me, he thought.
"*For you pictures are enough. For you a photograph is a million words.
Okay, you don't need words, but I do. It's all I have. Do you realize you haven't
said one word to me today since you came home?*"
*He couldn't believe that this tall blonde who had always looked so collected,
so much a WASP, could be so weepy, so tender, so weak. So Jewish.*

"You want to read symbolism? It dawned on me one day that my house
was full of broken things I didn't have the heart to throw out. I made believe
I was a camera in an Ingmar Bergman film, moving slowly in black and white,
with no music in the background and everything in crystal clear focus. It was
dead silent as it zoomed in on the broken old Czech china teapot, a gift from
Grandmother Sacerdote, which *her* mother had given her, with a linear curve
and grace and subtle colors that one can't find nowadays and which in one
clumsy cleaning swoop my wife broke. But I fixed it. I loved to fix things.
Fixed things were even more precious than new ones because love had been
grafted onto them. Like you loved a sick child all the more."

*Then he withdrew the image. It held for Tammy, not him. And he felt
suddenly awful that he could love the old porcelain teapot more than his own
son. Again the darkness gnawed at him.*

"By fixing things I demonstrated I wasn't part of the throwaway American civilization. So I pick up the pieces of that teapot that she broke in her
carelessness and, like God on Day One, I start anew. Every piece glued
together. Dem bones are gonna rise again, bit by bit ascending until the
teapot was no longer shards. I was furious when it fell. It seemed to me she
had no feelings for antiques, for the past, for she cleaned and swooshed her
little dustmop like a tank. I heard it falling and splitting open and all I could
say was, 'Son of a bitch, my great-grandmother's china, son of a bitch, my
great-grandmother's teapot,' and she in the background smaller and smaller,
repeating in counterpoint, "I'm sorry I'm sorry I'm sorry.' Other broken
things in the house? There were chipped chairs, the cracked scarlet rimmed
service plates from Bohemia in the cabinet, the cabinet itself, the edges of
the two doors chipped, me vowing that I'd have it redone, refinished but
never doing it. The pot from the silver tea service was dented. Pieces
broken off moldings of old frames. Breaks and chips and dents were everywhere. Why? I don't know. I didn't want to analyze. I hadn't the heart to
throw out old things. I would rather mend than buy.

"Does dislike for a woman make you lose patience with her?" I asked Charlie. "Does it make you become picky? Or do little behavior traits that annoy you accrete like barnacles until you end up not liking that person? Rhetorical. Don't even answer. I don't want to know.

"I don't like the way she eats. Quickly. Nervously. Never sits through a meal but jumps up a dozen times. Now for a fork. Now for a drink. Now for a napkin. Now to make a call. Now to get something from the fridge. And then she lingers at the table to nibble on crackers for twenty minutes to read, or seems to read, the gardening column. And her crackling diet rice biscuits drove me up the wall. They sounded like somebody methodically destroying styrofoam cups. She would leave crumbs on the tablecloth and I, muttering, would clean them up later when she left, oblivious to the crumbs she's left behind. Her crumbs irritated me. I hated that word *crumbs* because Aviva always said that *she* got the crumbs while Tammy got the banquet. And lately she's begun to make gulping noises when she drinks. She didn't used to drink that way. When I married Tammy I thought I married a princess, a woman whom Grandmother Sacerdote, peace upon her soul, would have approved of with a glance. But maybe it was me. First comes the disdain, for whatever reason, and then, you find, you hunt out, you nitpick, you revel in the discovery of something that annoys you to buttress the disdain. Maybe it was Tammy's aristocratic look that made me marry her. A sort of unconscious desire to satisfy my family. Maybe that, not love. For after Ava, Tammy was a queen."

The older Tammy got the more sensitive she became. You looked at her crossly, you said a word with the wrong stress, the wrong (for her) tone and she began to cry. Even when he said nothing, she cried.

One night, out of the darkness, she began to speak. They had already shut the light and he was wanting sleep. He was exhausted, looked forward to sleep. He tried not to listen but she was insistent, depriving him of sleep. At least she didn't put the light on.

"You don't see the problem?" Her voice came from somewhere else.

His "No" like a diamond, hard and cutting.

"You who are so sensitive to light and shade, to composition, to color tones, you don't care what's going on with me. To pictures you're sensitive . . . I wish I were a photograph." And she began bawling.

"What's the problem?"

"You don't see the problem? You don't talk to me from within . . . That's why I'm lonely. Can't you see how lonely I am?"

You have the boy, he held back from saying. You have the shop. You see more people in one day than I do in a week.

"I'm married and *lonely. Isn't that absurd? I hear about all these women in their thirties and forties who get divorced after fifteen, twenty, even twenty-five years of marriage. They think they'll find heaven and all they find is loneliness. And me, I'm married and lonely. Because you don't share anything with me. All you think of is your comfort, your peace, your pictures, and that's why your own son doesn't mean a thing to you."*

To shut her up he wanted to quote from the opening of Bach's Coffee Cantata, "Schweig stille, plaudert nicht"—*but it would be a wasted musical allusion. What did she know of Bach, except what she osmosed through him? What did she care about Bach? So he translated it for her: Be still, don't chatter. And when that didn't help, he told it to her straight: Shut up. He was tired of listening to her, tired of her voice, it grated on his ears like twelve-tone music.*

"And off and on," she kept plaudering," *you've blamed me for Adam."*

"That's a lie," he shouted. *"Dead wrong! Not off and on. Constantly. Without a moment's break for station identification. It's your bad genes. There's morons on your side. My healthy genes have yielded doctors and counts . . ."*

"So how come you wanted to have another child so badly?"

"God's not perfect. He may not make the same mistake twice. And don't stick Adam into this. Out of bounds. No go. If you want to rant about us, rant on, but don't hang that nonvisiting guilt trip on me."

"I'm not ranting," she screamed hysterically.

He wished she would stop. He wished he could make her stop. She was getting on his nerves. *"One can shut a light with eyes, goes the Roman proverb, but ears don't have lids, alas."*

And twisted away from her, but she, with a loud, *"Don't turn around,"* pulled him with a force that must have surprised her too. He lay on his back again.

"I already know I can't talk to you after supper. Because I'll disturb your literary reading . . ."

Shut up, Shut up, shut up.

". . . a fat lot of good literature does you. I can't talk to you because the CDs are on and God forbid you'll miss a note of your Mozart . . ."

"Shut up!"

"You shut up! You like music more than you like people. Remember when on that rare occasion I invited a few of my friends, you sat there with your Walkman plugged into your ears, making a point how bored you are?"

"Because I can't stand inane small talk."

"But the fact that you may have insulted my friends didn't bother you. But I'm not talking about that now. I'm talking about how I can't talk to you when I come home. If you're not at work or overseas, then you're listening to your music or judging a photo contest or working in your darkroom. And if I interrupt, you get angry. And so quickly too. Do I deserve that?"

Now that's the right approach, he thought. No, she didn't deserve that, but he wasn't going to tell her that.

"You go down into that darkroom of yours and stay there for what seems days. I feel like a widow."

He thought her speech had ended, but it was only a pause. Even a windmill, Grandmother Sacerdote used to say of a garrulous woman, has to catch its breath.

"You don't even see me any more."

He flicked on the light. Saw tears in her eyes.

"Now I see you."

She shut the light in a rage. As the light went out, through the shutter of his eyes he caught her pressed lips, her eyes distorted in anger.

"Your darkroom you see. Me you don't, Me you don't see. The me of me. You look at me and I'm not there. You look at me and wish I weren't there. But you I see even in the dark. I'm your camera. I see the curve of your fingers, the way you hold a newspaper, the way you tilt your head when you look at someone to compensate for the slight crossed eyes. And you, you never see anything like that. You never see anything in me that pleases you. Because I don't please you."

"Enough with the nevers. You're exaggerating."

"But everything I'm saying is the truth . . . Say something!" *she suddenly shouted. She started shaking him. She took his shoulders and moved him back and forth like a rag doll. He let himself be shaken. There was some pleasure in it.* "Say something! Say something to me," *she pleaded.*

Now he felt sorry for her. He wanted to say something nice. But he couldn't think of what. He gathered slowly the words scattered in the tangled undergrowth of his mind. It felt like working through thorns. "You're an angel," *he said.*

"She used to noodge me," I told Charlie. "It was like mental cruelty. Tell me you love me tell me you love me tell me you love me. The more she sank into gloom with Adam the more emotionally dependent she became on me. She was like a wilted flower, moribund rose, and I could prop her up with a pinkie."

What happened with Aviva, he thought, was really Tammy's fault. Maybe he should tell this to Charlie. Guido looked at him for a moment. Charlie was sitting there, well down in the chair, his hands over his crossed knees. No, he decided. It's not relevant. He had thought about it for a while and concluded, yes, it was Tammy's fault. She loved screwing. You couldn't tell by looking at her. She didn't give a hint of a signal. But she loved it. For her it was a narcotic. She told him how great he was. So often. What a waste of talent, he had thought. What a waste of sexual energy. Before Tammy he'd had so many girls, had spread his gifts far and wide. But with her, for fourteen years he had been monogamous. But it was when he began to montage Ava onto the image of Tammy when he was screwing her until Tammy's image was completely covered that he realized he was already being unfaithful to her. Then other faces joined the montage. But this he wouldn't tell Charlie.

"So it just happened, Charlie. It overwhelmed me. Like I tell Aviva. She came to me from another world. It's mystical. Goes beyond intergalactic norms. Aviva doesn't feel any guilt either. She says: 'I'm only technically married. In practice, I'm not the Arab's wife. So it's not adultery. And anyway, the same God that forbade adultery also sent you to me,' she says.♥

"Before I met her I felt I was on a treadmill. Going nowhere. I did my work, but without passion. A huge lens suddenly rolled in front of my eyes, it dollied up silently, silently like a movie camera, and enlarged everything I did. I was watching myself go through hundreds of routine motions. Daily activities, regular, normal, repetitive activities got to be a pain. Dressing. Tying shoelaces. Into pajamas. Out of pajamas. Bathing. Brushing. Flossing. Every day. Twice or three times a day, that boring five-minute ritual. Thinking that I'd have to brush and floss later made eating a burden. Everything was enlarged, expanded. The floss thread became heavy as lead. Then shaving. That same idiotic routine on one cheek then the other, above the lips, below the lips. Watch under the chin. Clipping nails. Bodily maintenance. Then car maintenance. I had to watch the mileage. Now the oil change, now the brakes, now the spark plugs. If you read the maintenance book and watch the recommended activities like a hawk there wouldn't be time for anything else. The cameras, their batteries. The radio, its batteries. Batteries in watches. Just oiling everything I own, from the furnace to the car to the Cuisinart is a full-time job. Even doors and scissors and lawnmower. Then the fridge, the hot water heater—drain a few buckets of the rusty-looking liquid each month to prevent the damn thing from exploding one mysterious night. Then the car's fuel filter, the air filter, the air conditioning filter, the furnace filter, the vacuum cleaner filter, the washing machine filter, the pure water filter, the lens filter, the coffee filter. You could change filters all day long. There's even a filter in your lung, Or maybe the lung's the filter, I forget. I once thought of writing a little piece which listed the maintenance a man has to do. There would be no time for jobs. Or mischief. Or is mischief a person's destiny if his name calls for it? Don't look so quizzical! You don't know what I'm talking about?

"A person's name is his destiny. You must remember that from our Hebrew classes. How God changes Abram's name to Abraham and thereby changes his destiny. Take Gwendolyn? How much mischief is a Gwendolyn capable of? Or a Shirley? And doesn't a Rupert just encapsulate his name?

♥See ABC Directory, *Adultery, rules of.*

Take mine for instance, How did I get the name Guido? There's a musical reason for it too, but not now. I want to show you how a person's name is his destiny.

"Guido is as close as an Italian name can be to *giudeo*, the Italian word for Jew, and still sound like an Italian name. Since the Jews guided the morality of Western civilization, perhaps the word *guido*, or guide, evolved. But in any case, my Hebrew name, as you no doubt remember from school is Yehuda, Judah. I wasn't named Joseph. Joseph fled from Potiphar's wife when she wanted to seduce him. But I didn't. I'm more like my namesake Judah, Joseph's brother, who doesn't resist temptation on the crossroads when he sees what he assumes is a harlot. She turns out to be Judah's own daughter-in-law, Tamar, in disguise, who, no pun intended, waylaid him. But you know the story. So that's the power of a name. A name makes a person. Take away the name and no man's the same, is my rough rhymed translation of an old Roman saying. If I'd been named Joseph I would have acted differently . . ."

"Bullshit," Charlie said.

"I would have acted like that hero of a great novel I once read, *Passion in the Desert*—did you read it, no?—I'll lend it to you. The hero's name is Joseph and he's married and he doesn't fall for a girl who is after him when he's out on a bus trip in the Sinai desert while his wife is back home. Joseph, like his Biblical namesake, resists temptation. If I'd been named Joseph I too would have fled from Potiphar's wife, from Aviva, the Arab's wife. But my Hebrew name is Yehuda, Judah, and I succumbed to Tamar, Aviva, who waylaid me.

"I told you at the reunion that I mulled over the idea of having cello lessons. Finally, I decided. A big leap—because I knew how attractive Aviva was. It wasn't just any fuddy-duddy librarian-looking teacher with a Presbyterian prim chin and granny glasses, perhaps too thin, perhaps roly-poly. No. She was centerfold stuff. Trouble. But I went anyway.

3

"Don't think that my interest in Aviva was only sex, although that too played a role. It's because she's a woman and I've been interested in women ever since I can remember. I began my career at a very tender age, at six or so, when I first began school in Venice. The classroom had one of those old-fashioned wooden teacher's desks covered from the classroom side that respected a lady teacher's modesty, that is, you couldn't see her legs when she sat down; but you also couldn't see who was hiding in the nave of the desk. When my first love, blonde Signorina Gina Milanese with her beautiful long legs and divine walk, stepped out of class one bright morning, I stepped out of my seat and crouched in the cubby of the dark desk to the giggles of the class. When Signorina Milanese returned and sat down, it was dark in my little cubby; but when she stood to look for me, the dark suddenly became light, and I, on my back now, slid my look right up her calf, past the knee and up the thigh. She was wearing a white dress—it must have been late spring—of frothy material. She seemed to be made out of air. She billowed when she walked. She almost stepped on me. If I'd been made out of Scotch tape I would have adhered to her thigh and just remained there near her puss-puss, like a benign growth, a third leg, until I grew old enough to appreciate that treasure. I think it was you Charlie who said I became a sexagenarian in my late teens and never grew a decade older. But you were off by a dozen years. I became a sexagenarian at six. Pre-six. I got my first whiff of it when I was five-and-a-half and have been enchanted ever since. Call it an extra force. The fifth force. I read in a magazine the other day that a force is anything that can move an object. Magnetism is a force: it can make a compass needle spin. Electricity, too. It gives a shock. Makes hair stand on end. There are four fundamental forces: gravity, electromagnetism, and the weak and strong nuclear forces. Every action—a flower blossoming, the sun shining—can be traced to one or more of these forces.

"But isn't there a fifth force?♥ The extra one? The magnetism of love? Desire? Woman? It can bring one person to another. It can change. It moved me from my darkroom to the phone to Aviva's house for lessons.

"Between some men and women there's a magical, instinctual, chemical cognition. Example. Once I went with Ava—that's Ava now, not Aviva— to a blues concert in a night club. She sat in front of me in the small, crowded club and another woman, about thirty, with a broad pretty face and frizzy black hair and sensual lips sat so close to me that if I pushed my left knee out a bit I could rub her ass. She wore tightfitting white slacks, a yellow short sleeve blouse and a green belt. The slacks were so tight I saw the outline of her panties on her cute ass. And in the semidarkness those tight white slacks made her look naked. The blouse, or maybe it was a tank top, was cut low. I remember her collar bones stuck out, which for me is always a sign of a hungry woman. Despite her smile there was a sadness to her face, as if she hadn't had an easy time of it in this life. When the band came on, she kept beat to the rhythm by turning her head, moving it from left to right and right to left as if in a trance. And in so doing, she caught my eye and smiled at me. I thought of slipping her my card, but was afraid Ava might notice.

"Such chemical cognition between man and woman often happens at first sight. Whether from smell or taste, voice, or wavelength, it's instantaneous, sometime even before names or phone numbers are exchanged.

♥See ABC Directory, *Zing! the fifth force in physics just discovered.*

They know, without a word, that there will be fireworks between them. Some day scientists will isolate that chemical, that electrical pulse, and then maybe you can order a quarter pound of it, Charlie. Which is what happened as soon as I laid eyes on Aviva, soon as her slightly squinted eyes waylaid me.

"Okay, now to Aviva.

"The transition between nihilo and somethingness is often enormous. Like creation. I feel it when I see that image floating up to me in the developer. First, the paper is white and then, magically, the scene or the person you've photographed comes into view like an embryo growing in speeded up time. Or like in writing, from a black page to thoughtful scrawl. My transition was the photographs I took of her the day I watched her give a cello lesson. Remember? A former neighbor called and asked me if I could bring her daughter Jill to Aviva for her cello lesson, since she wasn't feeling well. I sat through a lesson and before I left I bragged to Aviva that I could sing the first note of almost every piece of classical music. It's the second that gives me trouble. Her infectious, flirtatious laugh hummed with electricity. And I was the wire through which that electricity coursed . . . Okay, I told you at the reunion what else happened when I first set foot in Aviva's house. I had made up my mind to start cello lessons again. So when months later I called Aviva for lessons, I told her I had some nice snapshots of her. By the third or fourth lesson, I saw that one of my pictures of her—one that accented her face, hair, hands, and part of the cello—was framed and standing next to a photo of her late father, also at the cello. She asked me if she could use my picture as a publicity photo and I told her, 'With pleasure.' My portrait of her, by the way, completely eliminated any trace of her crossed eyes."

I got up, rubbed my eyes. I couldn't believe I was talking so much. Was that the reticent, close-lipped me? I paced back and forth. I pressed up to the window. Looked down from the third floor.

"I don't know if you know it or not, Charlie, but all my life I've been sensitive about my squint. I always thought of it as a defect, a kind of moral flaw. And all my life I've tried to compensate. And that's probably another reason I fell for Aviva. Here was a gal who had my problem and she looked so great. It didn't bother her at all. And so it made me feel good too. And ever since I met her, I feel more open, more relaxed about my own crossed eyes.

"At first glance I saw her as an innocent, gentle woman. Not that my wife wasn't innocent or gentle, but ever since our son's retardation had become evident, a moroseness suffused Tammy and it showed in the lines about her mouth and eyes. She had become middle-aged practically overnight. The gloom made her look hard. And the look was often perceived by others as the attitude. Aviva, however, had a ready smile. Her eyes radiated a pleasant light. It wasn't till I got home that I realized why Aviva's face pleased me so much. It stuck to the inner lining of my lids, so that whether my eyes were open or shut I saw her face, like a small photograph on the retina. My grandmother Sacerdote! No doubt about it. She resembled my mother's mother in early photographs taken in Venice and Milan, that demure, distinguished oval aristocratic face with that amiable Mona Lisa light shining from the eyes. Those Venetian and Milanese photographers knew their business, their art, in the early days of the century. And she, Aviva, had the same look, the same eyes, a bit sad, smiley, and haughty. Maybe those Venetian photographs set the tone for me. Destined me to my career. I wanted to create pictures like those Italian photographers.

When she smiles you see teeth that show energy and, excuse the pun, bite. Teeth that looked like they had orthodontia that didn't quite succeed, for which you might expect her to lick or pucker her lips the way women with slightly protruding teeth are wont to do to hide the fault. But she had never seen an ortho man. And of course those slightly crossed eyes that sent a mystical message and a shiver through me the first time I saw her. She is a mirror image of me, I thought.

"You sound like you're in love, Spaghetti," Charlie said flatly.

"Can you bottle love? Put it in like a print in developing solution and see the image emerging? Place it on a slide and screen it? Is it visible, tangible, bottleable?" I said. Then stopped.

But Dr. Charles did not tell me to continue. He knew that people who want to tell will tell.

"Aviva is a wonderful teacher. But she refused to take money once I became sick. Lovesick. She stubbornly refused. She taught me what I had forgotten. She was teaching a grown man like a baby. After the third or fourth lesson, I said to her, of course she didn't realize it was tongue-in-cheek: 'I hope it's not boring for you to give such baby lessons to a grownup. I mean, for a famous cellist like you to have to sit–' 'No, noooo,' she cooed. 'Not at all . . .' I said this a number of times and each time got the same response.

"Of course I knew it wasn't boring for her. She loved it. I could tell by the way she extended the lessons. The way she ran up to her room once to bring down a book of musical themes. Months later I would tease her for having said, 'Wait here, I'll be right back,' as if I would follow her upstairs—perhaps that's what she secretly dream-wished—perhaps even carry her up the stairs to her bed. Even the way she smoothed down the score after I turned a page when it wouldn't stay flat, even that I read as a stroke of love."

"Egotist!" Charlie shouted.

I laughed. "Almost what Aviva said—'You reek of ego!'—in another context. But ego is only when you fantasize something that isn't so. I didn't fantasize it. I asked her about smoothing down the pages. Didn't you feel, I asked her, when you smoothed down the pages, it was as though you were stroking me? And she said, yes. Yes, she whispered, like a kiss. But I should have asked, in order to get an answer that wasn't forced: What did you feel when you smoothed down the pages?"

He remembered what she said about those first few weeks. "I wish one could bottle the first six weeks of love. When you left after the lesson, I was so excited I couldn't breathe."
"Literally?"
"Literally. My chest, my throat felt constricted, I had trouble breathing."
"Smitten? Like a teenager."
"Smitten," she agreed. "Like a teenager. I couldn't even drink a glass of water. I looked at the calendar. Seven more days. Fantasized that the days would pass as quickly as I could rip the pages off the calendar. I was so nervous. Not so much when you were there, but as soon as you left. No wonder I lost weight then. I went down to one-hundred-ten."
He remembered that slim, girlish waist.
"It was electricity," he bragged.
"Definitely. Electric charges. Did you know it would lead to this?"
He thought a while.
"You're thinking."
"I'm thinking," he echoed. "No, not from the beginning."
But she said, "I knew from the very first meeting that this, that you, was/were something special."

"Have you ever been in love?" I suddenly asked Charlie. But he didn't reply. He just lifted his chin as if signaling: keep talking. I'll do the asking.

"Love, I discovered, takes various shapes. Here's a curious one. Once I heard her name on the radio. On one of the classical stations they were announcing her concert with one of the community orchestras in Westchester. It was the first time I heard someone else—from the real world—say her name. And it made her more real for me. Another is a simple thing like a phone number. Can you imagine falling in love with a phone number? But it's the association. Say 516 to me and it does nothing. That's my and everyone I know's area code. But if I'm out of state and I see 516, I immediately think of her."

"Meshugge," Charlie said.

"You don't understand because you've never been in love. But train of thought, allusion, association, symbol are all crucial to the emotive process. *Que è il amore?*, the poet Manzini asks in one of his poems. 'What is love?' I once told her. 'Love is the road to your house bringing memories of you. Love is seeing a tan station wagon with a roof rack because I imagine your cello on it. At first I thought it was just the loving that she liked, but now I think it's love. She's after me."

Charlie smiled. "It's nothing new. Remember our Freud and Fiction class? 'A lady's imagination is very rapid; it jumps from admiration to love, from love to matrimony in a moment.' Jane Austen. *Pride and Prejudice.*"

"Humbug! 'Any library that doesn't have books by Jane Austen is an excellent library.' Mark Twain . . . But you may be right."

And so, in appreciation of her extra-long lessons, one day he brought her a dozen yellow roses from his backyard.

"I can't believe it," she said, thanking him. The golden color of the roses reflected on her cheeks. She inhaled their fragrance. "They're beautiful—you shouldn't have." And then quickly, "But I'm glad you did," laughing at her change of pace. She put the flowers in a vase on the coffee table and kept glancing at the bouquet throughout the entire lesson, her face aglow.

4

"You want to know how it began? *When* it began? Before you can know that you have to know how I felt. I know, I know. There's lots of beginnings. But each step a man takes in his lifetime, every move he makes, that's a beginning. Week after week, I would go to lessons with her. Can that be considered a beginning? But didn't it begin the day I brought Jill Altman to Aviva's house for her lesson and I took pictures of Aviva teaching and playing? I would spend thirty, forty, fifty, sometimes even ninety minutes next to this desirable woman, becoming more and more hooked with each passing week. As if the force of the magnet were being turned higher and higher. When I practiced, she crept into each note I played. Sound transmogrified into flesh. And during these lessons each verbal exchange was subliminal love play. I never, believe me, never thought of screwing her. During each lesson I would look at her and long only for her lips. We spoke. We flirted. We courted. We laughed. The weather was always fine when I came. Like the Tuscans say, It never rains when you're in love. But it was all very proper. Like out of the medieval romances. We maintained a respectable distance. All I thought of was kissing those full, luscious lips. One night I woke up, lusting powerfully for her. I was so hot I was feverish. If you'd have taken a color picture of me you'd have seen an orange-red man, so fiery was I. It was then I decided: I can't postpone it any longer. I'm going to act."

He tried to figure out how old she was by various remarks she'd made—travel, education, work. Even though he told himself he didn't care how old she was, still he was curious. Two forces moved within him. It was like—Don't think of apples. All he could do was think of apples. She'd told him she had been born in Israel, had come here as a child and got her education here. After college she'd studied music in Italy for a year. That is, she was supposed to go for a year, but she missed her parents and stayed only six months. "The little chickee missed her mommy and daddy," he teased. "I did," she said, "even though I wasn't such a chickee." "You did this after college?" "Way after," she said. "When?" "More than twenty years ago."

The thirty-nine he'd given her as a maximum age was slowly being eroded. If she was twenty-one when she graduated, plus twenty made her forty-one minimum. Then "way after"—so let's add four. Forty-five already. He couldn't believe it. Aviva, forty-five? "Did you master Italian?" he said, really wanting to ask her how many years after graduating did she go to Italy. "Not really. Just a smattering. I regret not learning it. It's such a beautiful language." He was so excited about the numbers he didn't even pick up on the language. He didn't ask her how many years after graduation did she go to Italy, but spent the next few days trying to make her younger. My God, she's older than me. Me with an older woman! Women tend to exaggerate time, he thought, so if she graduated at twenty, as most girls do, and "way after" was two or three years, and she did this twenty years ago, then she was forty-three maximum, but only if "way after" meant two or three. My God, he thought, suppose "way after" meant seven or eight years. That meant she was forty-eight. But he got a reprieve of sorts when he asked her how old she was when she graduated college and she said, "Nineteen . . . I was precocious!" And then re-hearing in his mind her regrets about not learning Italian gave him an idea. He had origi-nally wanted the teacher to come to his house, but Aviva said she never goes to houses to teach, so now he said to her, "Would you like me to give you Italian lessons?" "I'd like that," she said immediately. Her swift acquiescence, he felt, moved her closer on the chessboard. "But I only give lessons at my house," he said. "I never go to pupils' houses." "That's only fair," she said, not catching his ironic parody of her remarks first time he called for lessons. "When would you like to begin?" he asked. "I'm preparing for a little recital, so not for a couple of weeks." But two weeks later she said nothing, so he assumed she regretted her decision, and so there went his fantasy of giving her a lesson then putting some dance music on the phonograph and asking her to dance and taking her in his arms and kissing her lips, first kissing only those red luscious lips and then slowly, still while dancing, slowly taking her clothes off and making love to her. It still bothered him that she was in her early forties when all along he had thought of her as thirty-five or thirty-seven. Once he asked her if she'd been to Venice and she said, Yes. He said, "That's where I saw you. I knew I'd met you somewhere before." "I visited Venice exactly twenty years ago this month," she said.♥ Then he slyly asked her how many years after college did

♥See ABC Directory, *Venice, why that urge came to her in.*

she go to Italy and she said. "Well, after college I went to the Philadelphia Academy of Musical Arts or PAMA for three years and then I taught several years and then I felt I needed a break from teaching."

His heart fell.

"How long were you teaching?"

"Let's see, I studied three years at PAMA . . ."

"With Ian Plaskow?"

Aviva flushed. "Yes. How'd you know?"

"I know he's connected with that school. I met him years ago at Kennedy when he returned from Moscow with the Tchaikovsky Prize. Snapped a picture of him that appeared on the cover of Life."

"Was that yours? He and Casals embracing?"

Guido nodded.

"And there was also one of Casals," Aviva continued," cane in hand, as he waits for Plaskow to come off the plane."

"Boy, what a memory you have!"

Aviva clapped her hands. "My God, is that your photo, too? It was one of my favorites of the old man. He's standing there, leaning on his cane, a delighted look on his beautiful face. So you met Casals?"

"Yup. And you?"

"To my regret, never."

"Plaskow never introduced you?"

"He wasn't the sort."

But Guido was a steamroller, refusing to be stopped. "You said before you needed a break from teaching. How long were you at it?"

Aviva put a finger to her lips. "Let's see, all told, in public schools and privately . . . about six or seven years."

Tick-tick-tick went the computer in Guido's head—and his heart, phhhtt, it landed on his toes.

"You say you graduated quite young."

"At nineteen." She gave a bright smile. Stood on tiptoes. "A girl genius."

"Including PAMA?"

"No, no, I'm just a genius, not a prodigy. I was in my late twenties when I studied in Philadelphia."

Clomp. A blow on the head. Oh, my God, over fifty! It couldn't be. It had to be a mistake. He was sure of that. And so he tried to bend logic and math to shave a dab off each number. She was closer to nineteen when she graduated and the four was three and the six five and the exactly twenty years was nineteen. That still put her in her late forties. In other words, six or seven years older than he.

"You still interested in Italian lessons?" he asked, with somewhat diminished enthusiasm.

"Of course," she said.

"If you like, we can begin next week."
Which gave him the impetus to act on another brainstorm.

"You see, Charlie, one of the beginnings, one of the possible beginnings, was for me to give her Italian lessons. It would have, so to speak, put the ball in my court. Because I was going to her house every week and suffering from that close contact with her, but it was as if a glass wall were between us. Deep down I knew that that glass wall was really a soft shield of plastic wrap that could be punctured with ease. So my suggestion that she take Italian lessons, especially since she had studied in Italy and never learned the language, was quickly accepted. I suggested we take a nature hike in Eisenhauer Park, which was convenient for both of us. We took that walk and that was the beginning.

"Like a musical motif, that walk kept returning to our conversation. 'Do you remember when you took me out for that walk?' she would say. How could I forget? It was the genesis of what followed. She charged me only for half an hour but the lesson always stretched for an hour or more. 'I didn't want to let you go,' she said. Although I promised myself each time as I left her house and before I entered her house the next time, ringing the bell, heart beating, vowing that this time, *this time* I'll do it, I never made a move. For suppose she would reject me? Or worse—laugh. Are you kidding? I'm your teacher. I'm a married woman. But she said, 'I'd love to.' Now there was no turning back. We had both hitched a ride on a passing cloud. A fall into the abyss? Matter of opinion."

He came in for the lesson and walked across the polished oak floor of her studio, still seeing that welcoming smile on her face. He sees himself driving into the circular driveway, parking at the two o'clock spot and walking up to the rounded brick portico. The two white pillars at the edges are too far apart for him to Samson embrace them and pull the house down. He rings the bell. Through the closed door he hears the gong play the opening notes of the "Ode to Joy." Then she opens the door and he sees her glowing smile. I'm back again, he thinks, as if he never left. It's the only thing he sees, her smile, which has no palpable bounds, but has a metaphysical space all its own. She walks ahead of him, but her smile is behind him, at the outer edges of his peripheral vision.
The lesson is about to begin.

"Did I tell you about the mood during those lessons, Charlie? I loved watching Aviva as she instructed me and I loved that instrument between my legs. Then I immediately transposed the thought to her head and imagined her saying those very same words, and a dark green surge of jealousy invaded me as the implication of the remark burst in my mind. The 50 percent electric current that I sensed flowing between us I didn't have the guts to switch on full force. Never had I had a desire like that. When I came for a lesson, she usually hung up my jacket. One time I came and hung it up myself. Opening the door and entering her closet was like you know what. I had made myself at home. This time I helped myself. I entered her dark closet. When I paid her I never handed her the cash in hand. Delicately, it was in an envelope. Once, I gave her a dollar more, let's say twenty instead of nineteen, and she said that was the first time anyone gave her a raise of their own accord. My excuse was that nineteen was such an awkward number. Twenty is round. Once I had the fantasy: instead of the cash I would put in a note: I love you. And to get the money, she'd have to burrow into the pouch of that envelope, just like I burrowed into the depths of her closet and pressed my jacket between two of hers. Yes, I knew. It was absurd. It made no sense.

Perhaps, he thought, that was the first embrace, his opening the closet and hanging up his coat, making himself at home—there was a possession there, an embracement of a different kind. But this time, as he glided across the sunny floor (strange, it had never rained during the many weeks of lessons; whenever he came it was sunny), he had thought out what he was going to do. Her cello was prepared, leaning against the wall. The student's cello propped in the corner. The two chairs still empty. And this is how it began. From nihilo to somethingness. He remembered how he approaches her as she stands near her cello, that smile still on her face like a sostenuto, and he firmly placed two hands on her shoulders, first time he's touched her, with the same resolve and confidence that he'd opened her closet door and hung his jacket within, first time with the exception of shaking her hand first time he came. A couple of weeks earlier she had lifted his right elbow as he played to show him how to hold his bow hand, how to move it lightly, and how to relax, a nuance he hadn't been able to master. But he did not relax. And that was another reason, she admitted, she had been afraid to make a move.

To a degree he gauged her friendliness by her not watching the clock.♥

Between selections he would impress her. He told her about the panther he'd seen in a zoo in Milan that was the original panther from Kafka's story, "A Hunger Artist." He told about a book he'd seen in a London antiquarian shop—not for sale—that never read the same. Each time one read the story the ending was slightly different. He told her about a Persian set of numbers—the famous Persian number riddle from the Middle Ages—that had a different sum if you added it from the top and a different one if you started from the bottom. He told her he was afraid of surgery because all the music he had listened to would come tumbling out and the notes would flood the operating room.

♥See ABC Directory, *Atmosphere she creates teaching cello.*

You knew where that walk would lead, right?♥ she said later, tilting her head, eyes brightening. Of course, he said. You knew it wasn't just a walk, she said. Of course, he replied. "I had to think up something where we could meet outside of your house. First, I thought of taking you to the Wax Museum in Ronkonkoma . . ." "Wax Museum," she said with a disparaging laugh . . . "But then I thought a walk would be more fun."

Should I wear boots? she asked. Are we going into the woods? Those questions too excited him. ("I always knew we'd be together," she told him later. "From the first or second time I saw you. Maybe the third," she teased. "Even before that walk. Could be I was mistaken, but I felt it.") Her asking him what to wear was exciting. Her asking if he was going to take her into the woods was doubly exciting. As if she expected him to take her deep into the woods, reenacting the subliminal sexual themes of Hansel and Gretel or Little Red Riding Hood, the adult version (i.e., the real version) of kiddie tales, where they could finally be alone outside the formal arena of lessons.

"It was the most beautiful walk in my life," she told him the day after the walk when they lay down naked for the first time, in the room that would have been Adam's room. Even though Aviva was usually sparing of words—for instance, she never called him by name or used any terms of endearment—she had that quality of coming up with a gesture (writing "I love you" with her tongue on his neck) or a word, or even a melting of the eyes. And just before he left her house, the appointment to meet in the park accomplished, he took out a manila envelope from his briefcase and handed it to her. "For me?" As if she didn't know. "No, it's for me, but I'm just mixed up as to who's me and who's you." She looked at the envelope. "Go ahead," he said. "Open it." She took out the 8 × 10 enlargement of his famous photo of Casals. "Oh, is that gorgeous! Is that beautiful! I've always wanted that picture!" And he thought she would lean forward to kiss him, but instead she gently pressed the picture to her heart. It was an involuntary gesture, he knew, but then again, nothing is involuntary. "It's a beautiful composition." she said. Guido smiled and said, "That's what Haydn said when Beethoven showed him his first sonata." Then, touched by her gratitude, spontaneously, without thinking, he leaned forward and gave her a brotherly kiss on the cheek and, without saying another word, went out the door.

Over the weekend a fluke October snowstorm. There goes the walk, he thought. But Monday was bright and clear and sunny. They met at the library and then the two-car caravan proceeded to Eisenhauer Park. He gave her his Italian poet riddle. I'm giving a quick talk on a famous Italian poet, yet I'm going to talk slowly. What's the title of my lecture? Think music! She laughed and said. That's easy. Nice and slow. Andante—On Dante. The only one who ever correctly answered his riddle of the Sphinx.

♥See ABC Directory, *Affair, how it began.*

How long were they in the park? An hour? Two, three? Time was suspended with her, and he felt that all the tension of attraction that had been played out on the cello (for instance, in the ritardo of one piece, he purposely played the last two notes sostenuto, holding back, as a kind of erotic tease, before coming to the coda), all the little jokes and flirtations, had in the park, among the trees, within the magnificent silence and aloneness, blossomed like a dozen yellow roses.

*W*hen he brought his lips to hers—first they walked out in the snowy field; he never did find the alleged nature trail; and he at once put his arm around her waist and she did the same. Weeks earlier their arms had involuntarily criss-crossed on their chairs and neither wanted to move; and now he took her hand and they chatted to break the tension, to make believe their hands weren't really clasped. She complained that a couple of her students were so bad they were actually worse now than when they began. So he suggested that she open the Retrogressive School of Music. It would be a new school for those people who want to withdraw from the addiction of playing, for those who have achieved a high level of musicality but see no point in playing any more but can't cut cold turkey, for those who are afraid of success, for those who are nostalgic and want to recreate a simpler time past—the eminent Frau Director and her staff, one of whom is a professor of decomposition, will take you from Bach to "My Country Tis of Thee" in Ten Easy Lessons. If you don't play worse three months from now, double your money back. And so, laughing, and with hands clasped, they walked toward a little latticework arbor that stood out in the open next to a clump of trees. When we get there, he thought, I'm going to kiss her. There, after the first long kiss—Columbus setting foot on American soil, the astronauts on the moon, fireworks in their dreams—she muttered something and he asked, "What?" and she said, "It's nothing." But later, after the a-b-a rondo of walking kissing walking repeated itself, she said it again and this time he heard her. "What an incredibly sexy man!" She kissed him with passion and abandon, her hands on his face and in his hair. In the woods, after jumping across a little brook, he unzipped her jacket, lifted her blouse, and took out and touched and kissed her full breasts. She stiffened, pressed up against him, and said, "Are we going to make love?"

The question took him by surprise.

"Here?" he said, half-seriously.

"I think we can find a better place," she said.

"My house," he said, and they agreed on a time.

"Are you going to continue lessons?" she asked. Was she concerned about the loss of fees, he wondered, or did she think that the lessons were only a front, and now that he had accomplished what he sought, why bother with music?

"Of course," he said. "Love is love, but business is business. Will you continue to teach me?"

"With pleasure. Of course, I'll teach you, but not for pay."

"We'll talk about that some other time."

The next day she told him she had been dreaming and fantasizing this for weeks. And months later she admitted that at night in her bed, during those first few lessons, she had him making love to her in every conceivable position, she kissing him and licking him all over.

But even as he walked with her he thought about her age, even though he didn't want to think about it; he didn't want to know that she was six, maybe even—ugh!—seven years older than he. Then, as if reading his mind, she said, "I never told you, did I? That I was married when I was very young."

"While you were going to school?" he asked nervously.

"No. Between schools. First I finished college, then I got married. To my first husband. I stayed married seven years and did absolutely nothing, and only then, when I realized my marriage was going, during the last two years of my marriage, did I go to PAMA, and pick up music again."

He bent down for his heart.

"Did you lose something?"

"No, my shoelace is loose." He straightened up. "You're in your late forties?"

"Not quite," she laughed, and he felt better again, vowing to expunge the demon of Aviva's age from his mind.

"And, so, Merlputter," I said, "we had this delicious walk in the park. We drove back from the park in our cars, she behind me, as is only right and proper. But then, as I was about to turn off toward Rockville, she speeded up and pulled up alongside me, and we exchanged glances. Then occurred one of those magic moments that two people remember a lifetime. She sent me a kiss.♥ And if that kiss didn't contain all her love, then I don't know what love is and what kisses are.

When he lay down with her the next day he thinks to himself, I'd like to give her a baby. I'd love to have a baby with her.♥♥ Because from the first and only child he'd had, he can never expect any progeny. It would be the end of the line for him. Hundreds of years of Veneziano-Tedescos and it ends with a Down's syndrome. Finished. Finita la comedia. *But still, this first time, when he stretched out his hand and told her, follow me upstairs, he put on a condom for protection. But she said, "It's not necessary," he thinking that it's near the end of her cycle and a condom isn't needed. But still he was afraid of disease. Who knows who's been banging her and who the banger's been banging? AIDS is all over the place, so he slips it on and then there surfaced her volatility, the erratic, up-and-down graph of her life that would be dis-*

♥See ABC Directory, *Walk, the first, Aviva's version.*

♥♥See ABC Directory, *Baby, supposed.*

played in the coming months. She sat up, electricity turned off. A switch thrown. "What am I doing here?" she said in a granite voice. They had worked so quickly, stripped so quickly, lain down so quickly, the fire that had been burning in him for weeks hadn't had time to ignite. Perhaps the ma-nipulation, with the rubber, all with one hand, did it. Her "What am I doing here?" killed it. Semi-detumescence became flop. Then, seeing what she had wrought, she began to kiss and lick him. The suddenness of her movement, the intimacy of it, surprised the hell out of him. Nevertheless, he was pleased. But it didn't help. It would take months before she did that again, on her own, without being urged.

"That little thing isn't necessary," she said.

"Why?"

"Because I don't need it any more."

"But, you know—"

"Don't worry. Nobody goes near me."

"And, but . . ."

She smiled. "I guess you still, after all that figuring and asking, you still don't know how old I am. You asked me if I was in my late forties."

" 'Not quite,' you said."

"And you seemed to breathe a sigh of relief."

"Who me?"

"Yes. You. But I don't care. I don't hide my age. I'm—"♥

"After the first time we made love, Charlie my boy, our desire was as open as the field we'd trod on the day before. But I was still objective enough to value her as a teacher. 'But not for business,' she said. 'But of course,' I countered. 'For full pay. Otherwise, I'd be screwing my teacher two ways.' 'Why not?' she laughed. 'The more the merrier.' And when I tried to give her the envelope the next time, she refused it. 'Don't,' she said 'You're going to make me feel bad.'

"That's the sort of teacher she was. She put her entire soul and imagi-nation into it. I recalled the first lesson I watched. When it came to showing *sFz*, the sudden fortissimo, she told little Jill Altman, 'It's not a sudden hammer bang over the head but,' and here she made a suggestive little forward movement with her body, as if she were an Indian dancer, 'it's a subtle little wave, like a ballet movement, up and down,' And when it came to showing a staccato, she gave Jill a little pinch. At the end of the lesson, Jill kissed her and Aviva kissed her too. 'Do you always kiss your students?' I teased her. 'Quite a few,' she said. 'One little girl doesn't want to go home unless I kiss her.' 'Me too,' I joked and Aviva laughed. And much later when I reminded her of this, I added, 'Jill Altman you

♥See ABC Directory, *Age, her.*

kiss in the house, but with this student you waited till you got him in the park."

After watching the lesson with Jill Altman, he told Aviva:
"I used to play the cello too."
"Did you really? Do you still play?"
"I gave it up some years ago. But the cello is still my favorite instrument. I used to love it so much as a child that even before my parents gave me lessons, as a kid I made myself a toy cello out of a cardboard box. I cut it into the shape of a cello and strung it with rubber bands. I don't remember if I had a bow or not, so I used—"
"An arrow," Aviva interjected, laughing.
"I probably just plucked it by hand."
"True devotion. Maybe because my father was a cellist, I didn't like the instrument. In fact, as a kid I hated it. But you seem to have true devotion. With a love like that you should continue."
"Maybe some day," Guido said.

"I was so enthralled with her, Charlie, I found myself talking to her even when she wasn't there. When she would come to visit me I told her, 'I don't believe you're here,' and she said, 'Why?' and I replied, 'Because it's like a dream. Your being here is the unreal part. It's when you're *not* here, *that's* the reality.' When she did come, fantasy set in, make-believe entered like an interloper for an hour or two."

"Stop!" Charlie cried. He rose and paced in the office. He picked up a paperweight—was he going to throw it at me?—and put it down. "I'm losing my objectivity. Enough of your pseudo-mysticism and phrenics.♥"

"Phrenics?"

"Yeh. Look it up. I've been listening, silently, carefully, objectively, but this mystical stuff—please!"

"I'm being honest, putter-head. Shouldn't I be telling you what I feel?" He stood over me and I looked up at him like a teacher.

Charlie grimaced, nodded, as if giving me the right. "Sorry. Go ahead. Whatever is real to you is real. Whatever you feel you feel."

"Sounds like an Italian proverb," I said.

"Them's are your specialty," he said. He sat down and clasped his knees.

"So, the long and short of it is that she fell head over heels, but I wonder if it's me she loves or if she latched onto the first man who happened to come along. Just like she latched on to this Moroccan Israeli, with the suave dark good looks, black curly hair and seeming charm and smoothness. After

♥See ABC Directory, *Phrenics.*

all, he's Israeli, one of her own, even though there's a great intellectual and educational gap between them. But hormones talk louder, don't they, and he wins her over until she marries him and then literally overnight the bastard shows his true colors, the old Arab mentality, where the man is boss, the wife is shit, and he's king. You can't whip a woman with pasta, as the Sicilians say. Like an electric current, the Arab switched and it was too late to do anything about it. The guy's personality changed literally overnight. It started the morning after the wedding, when they had flown to some warm island south of Cuba. The hotel was a couple of miles out of town, on the beach, and she wanted to spend a morning in the city. She wanted to take a cab—but no, he's too cheap, so he made her walk in the heat. And then he's too stingy to buy her a cold drink. He goes to the bar and cons the bartender into giving him two glasses of water, with ice, and then, as an afterthought, asks for a couple slices of lemon. But she stuck it out because she always hoped he would change. Even when she had the first baby, the Arab wouldn't hold it. Aviva said, 'He wouldn't even take it from my hands, as if it were mine and not his.' . . . Okay, Charlie, I see by my watch that it's late. We'll continue next time."

"—I'm old," Aviva said, in a tone which her interlocutor is supposed to contradict and say, "No, you're not!" Every once in a while she would draw attention to her maturity—especially her menopause which she was delighted with and which caused her no discernible problems. Most women become menopausal in their forties, he figures. But the culmination was her response to his casual remark that for a while his section at the Post *had a receptionist about thirty who had Aviva's spunky sense of humor. "Do you have a sister?" he asked Aviva. "Yes, but she's not thirty. Maybe it's my long lost daughter," she said. His mouth hung open. "You, with a thirty-year-old child? "Yes," she said. "I could have a thirty-three year old." That was beyond his ability to imagine. Still, today fifteen, even twelve year olds were dropping babies like fruit flies. So a forty-five year old could easily have a thirty year old child. And a fifty year old a daughter of thirty-three. Short of asking her straight out how old she was, he was still frustrated about her age. The worst case scenario was —ugh!— about fifty. Best—forty-five. Whatever, she looked terrific—but his heart still flip-flopped when considering that this lovely, sexy, auburn-haired, busty piece was not only four to eight years older than he, but that he, chaser of chicks, had actually fallen for an older woman who was perhaps fourteen years older than Tammy. He spent hours at his desk reconstructing a flimsy chronology of when she'd gone to Italy, how long she spent at school, what she'd done in the interim. Why didn't he ask her outright? He was afraid of the answer. No matter what, she looked great. No more than thirty-eight. "Is she pretty?" Aviva asked. "Who?" "Your thirty-year-old receptionist?" "Who says it's a she?" "I do. Is she?" Guido*

smiled slyly. "Incest?" Aviva said. "With my long lost daughter?" "For you," he said, "anything." "I see you counting the rings on my trunk . . . Stop breaking your neck." Aviva smiled. "I'm fifty-three."♥

5

"Sometimes I say to myself, isn't it a sin what you're doing? And I reply—phrenics! See, Charlie, I looked it up as soon as I got home the other night. And I say to myself: The Gnostics believed that the only way to avoid sin is to commit it and be rid of it."

"Interesting," Charlie interjected. "The Talmud says the same thing. The continuous thought of sinning is worse than the deed itself."

"You think they influenced each other?" I asked.

"Of course," Perlmutter said. "The rabbis were in touch with the Gnostics. You see, they—"

"Forget philosophy! Sorry, I'm not in the mood for Higher Rabbi Gordinism. *My* problem is that I wanted to get rid of that sin again and again and again. If only she were uglier, I tell myself, I might be able to refrain, to stop. But even her one flaw, her cross eyes, were cute."

"Marry an ugly woman, says the Talmud, and she'll be true to you."

"Fine and dandy, O Mother of Pearl. But how does that solve the husband's roving eye? . . . I made a little study of cross-eyed people. Those whose eyes turned sharply to their nose, poor souls, had a goofy look. They're so nebby their seeing eye dogs are cross-eyed. But the ones whose eyes turned outward, they had a surprised look, as if someone goosed them. Aviva was in this latter group. It wouldn't be an exaggeration to say that I fell in love with her as soon as I saw that left eye that floated slightly outward.

"But the rest of her—well, maybe not the teeth—was okay. She presented a young girl's figure, size 6, with narrow waist and pendulous boobs, breasts that now failed what she once called the 'boob test' and at another time the 'pencil test'.♥♥ She had a straight back and a young girl's neck, smooth from the back of the head, with no hint of the middle-aged hump that women sometimes even in their thirties get.

"I could say with the poetry of the cliché that she walks like a dream, but that would say nothing. The Roman saying that you heard me say years ago captures it beautifully: *Non c'e musica como la andatura della bella ragazza.* There is no music like the walk of a beautiful girl. But in her typical self-putdown mode, she said that she walked like a duck.

♥See ABC Directory, *Discovering how old she is.*
♥♥See ABC Directory, *Boob test.*

"I can't get the Gnostics and sin and punishment out of my head. I keep thinking of Emma Bovary and Anna Karenina, and they fused with Aviva. What's being done was already done in other places, maybe not precisely the same way, and surely not with the same brilliant, high-pitched, diamond-perfect love molecules, erotic electrons, and haphazard atoms of desire. It was done one hundred years ago, three thousand years ago. In France. In Russia. In ancient Israel. In real life and between covers . . . of a book. The players change. The script remains the same. The book, it reads itself.

"What was it that drove me to Aviva, you ask? A Madame Bovary complex? A last chance? What last chance?! Youth recaptured? I'm only forty-two, for God's sake, young and vital. Perhaps my current is on too high. Even now I looked at women, older, younger, no matter, with eyes and heart aflame, with longing and desire. And I noticed how they looked at me. Maybe I too had a magic something that radiated out of me that women sensed, that women wanted. Maybe they sensed and imagined what I sensed and imagined. Women have a much richer fantasy life than we ever imagined. And since knowing Aviva I've become even more charged up, as if she'd infused me with an electric current that sent the transformer into super voltage.

"Once, while practicing, I suddenly smelled her, though she doesn't wear perfume and doesn't really have a particular smell like some women do. With some you can feel their sexuality through their hair. They give off a scent, just like an animal. But the curious thing is—just as I played a two-triplet phrase, her smell came to me. And next morning, brushing my teeth, I tasted her in the back of my throat.

"Once I became involved with her, I began to look at all married couples as oddballs, I go to a party or a concert or a play and see couples sitting together or walking out together and I say to myself, What's wrong with them? Why don't they have some excitement in their lives? Or I look at a couple and I wonder, Who is cheating on whom? That's the sickness that strikes when you have an adulterous affair. Of that the Gnostics never dreamt.

"You know, in folktales there's always a poison apple. Well, that's what adultery is—a poison apple. It's not all honey. It's not the magic fruit in the Garden of Eden. Poison is created. And I must admit there is this poison between us that drives me crazy. Savor the honey, the Italians say, but watch out for the bee. The spiderweb shimmers in the dew, but at the center the black widow sits. What's the poison? She doesn't trust me, for I have an eye out for other women. And she feels I'll eventually leave her."

For someone younger, he didn't say.

"And I don't trust *her* because if she could betray her husband once, she could do it again. On the other hand, the Arab was mean to her. She didn't consider him a husband, so she felt free. On the third hand, she has often said she doesn't want to share me and speaks of the inevitable breakup. But when I say, then let's break up now, I don't want to go for a short ride, I like the long haul, she takes two fingers and clamps my lips shut. At other times she whispers, I'm never going to leave you. But when she's upset, she says we'll break up eventually and she had better start looking for a single man and plan on living a normal life."

I got up, stretched, walked to one of Charlie's pastoral paintings. I set my gaze into it like I used to when I was a child, imagining myself deep in the field, about to enter the woods. I pictured myself in the meadow, but the breath of the fields was not in me. I sighed and sat down. I hesitated to say what I was about to say, lest Charlie think me an egoist—but I said it anyway, because it was pressing within me.

"To mouth her criticisms of our relationship she wasn't shy. But in general she was reticent with words. I wanted her to tell me how nice my skin is, how she loved my body, how—well, you know what I mean. But she didn't. She was silent. All she said is, I love you. I think of you constantly. The thoughts of you shape everything I do. Will you like this, will you approve? Wherever I am, whatever I do, you're in my mind. I feel you in me all the time. Sexy man. Marathon man. My miracle man. You're the best thing that ever happened to me. You know how unique you are. They don't make them like you. When they made you, they broke the mold. You make me so happy, she said, then cocked an eye at me, tilted her head, and added, well, at least, partly. My darling. My love. That's all she said. Not all at once, of course, but over a period of time. As she got to know me she would whisper, again and again, You beautiful man, you beautiful man. That's all she said. She never said how much she liked my straight black hair, how magnificently hard were my thighs, like rocks. How she loved to kiss them. She didn't say, until I told her to, how beautiful were my eyes. Then she said, Your eyes *are* beautiful. But once, as we were kissing, she looked up at me and said, 'You have such beautiful lips.' 'Do you know,' I said, 'that's the first time you ever said anything like that?' 'I did?' she said, big grey eyes purposely fluttering as always. 'Yup. How come you don't say these things of your own accord?' 'I don't?' 'No, never.' 'That's because,' Aviva said, 'I always think it.'

"So I coaxed her, Charlie. I told Aviva to say it anyway. Even if it sounds like a B movie. Nothing *you* say, she said, is like a B movie. It's always an A+ film. Just for that, I said, I'm going to say something nice to you. Your boobies may be size C, but the taste is a solid B-. No, I'm just kidding. *This* is what I wanted to tell you. The other day I imagined for a moment that I wouldn't see you again and suddenly an emptiness swooped over me and I felt a sense of loss. It felt like being in a long tunnel all alone, like sometimes late at night you're the only car in the long tunnel and you get a sense of infinite aloneness."

" 'So you do love me,' she said.

" 'Hmm,' I said.

" 'Well, say it. I like to hear it too,' she said.

"Then she admitted that she became tongue-tied when she spoke to me. 'That's never happened to me before. I mix up words,' she said. 'Idiomatic expressions come out wrong.' Aviva said. 'Like when I said the other day that you're my recrimination when I meant salvation.' 'When I come close to you,' I asked Aviva, 'do you recriminate or salivate?' 'Or,' she continued, 'like when I once asked you, Did you notice that I get a cole slaw on my lip when I get sick?' "

When you're up there in your sixth decade, you start to flirt with senility, he told her.

" 'You know why I get tongue-tied? Because I don't even have an op- portunity to talk to you. We spend so much time in bed. I've never spent so much time in bed with anyone. Not my husband, not anyone else. I seem to spend *all* my time in bed with you. You fill me so completely, I don't need anything. I don't even need the cello.'

"I reprimanded her: 'Don't say that.'

" 'Don't worry. I won't stop playing. I said that to let you know how completely you fill me.' And then, suddenly, this normally reticent Aviva exploded in a torrent of nonstop words. She stood, or lay, there, delivering a speech, a manifesto. She let go a litany of her feelings for me, did prim-lipped Aviva. 'With the exception of my children, I don't want or need anything. When you're away from me, thoughts of you fill me and my feelings come more clearly into focus. I'm keenly aware of how precious you are to me.' She held my face like a rose, sniffed the petals of my skin. 'When you're away, I long for you in every way. I think of you constantly, and even though you're not here, you enrich every moment of my day. I know adul- tery is wrong . . .' and a cloud passed over her face as she said this, 'I've never committed adultery before. But the same God that forbade adultery also brought you to me, right? So I thank the God I don't think I believe in every day for you. Do you think' she suddenly asked me, 'suppose we'd gotten together fifteen years ago would we still be together now?' I said I didn't know how to answer that one. I had heard her say that her husband was a difficult man, and I admitted to her that I'm not so easy myself. 'Okay,' she said, 'everyone has difficult moments, but you're not malicious or cruel.'

Only when I have to be, I thought.

"Her shyness also expressed itself in her fear of performing, a terror that made her physically ill. So I told her, 'if you're scared of playing, why don't you put a recording of Casals in the cello and just go through the motions?' So she said, 'Then I'll have to redo my entire cello, fix it so I won't have to depress the strings.' 'Better the strings than the audience,' I said.

"Okay, so she was afraid of performing. But when it came to teaching, she was super. The cello, Aviva says, is the only instrument where the player totally enwraps herself around her instrument and becomes part of it. It's very sensual. And then she remembered what she had said as a child when her cellist daddy suggested she study cello. 'I don't want to spread my legs for anyone.' Everyone laughed, of course, but she didn't know why. Sex, sex, sex, I said. Aren't those sonorous low notes on the cello sexy?♥ Don't they drive you up a wall with desire? It may happen to others, she said, but not to her. She just didn't have that strong a libido. But I disagree. Sexiness exuded from her as she played. Maybe she just wasn't aware of it, but I was. I loved to watch her play. She bent her head so close to the bridge she seemed to become one with her cello, her hair hanging down, the bridge so close to her mouth she seemed to caress it with her lips. It made me jealous. Maybe I imputed a sexiness to her playing that wasn't there. But in any case, when she played I wanted to possess her most because I knew that at such moments she wasn't thinking of me, and I wanted her to think of me all the time.

"And then suddenly she breaks the mood and stops playing and says she has to clean her house. Charlie, I can't imagine her doing housework. To me she seems so ethereal, so un-earthbound. Cleaning? 'I can't imagine you doing laundry, ironing, cooking,' I tell her. 'I don't,' she laughed. 'That's why my house looks the way it does.' 'I can't see you baking, washing windows, taking out the garbage. I can only see you playing the cello and lying in bed doing you know what.' And then do you know what this darling said in her whispery loving voice? 'And I can imagine you doing anything. Flying. Climbing mountains. Fixing a car. Swinging on a trapeze. Walking on water . . . In fact, that's just what I thought of the last time I was on my hands and knees, washing the kitchen floor for the first time in months.'

'I told her that it would seem to me that living in the sort of house she lived in that she could afford a maid. She looked down and said, 'Of course we can, but he won't let me.' 'What do you mean, he won't let you?' 'I can't fight any more. I could bring one in but the repercussion won't be worth it. I need tranquility, not aggravation. So I'd rather clean myself.'

" 'If I were married to you,' I said, 'under no circumstances would I let you wash the kitchen floor—"

"Really?' she said, looking up gratefully.

" '—alone. I would be there on my hands and knees behind you, while you were on your hands and knees, cupping your breasts so they shouldn't

♥See ABC Directory, *Cello, sexiness of the.*

drag on the floor. Or I'd stand in the doorway, while you were on your hands and knees washing the kitchen floor, watching so that no one comes in until it's ab-so-lute-ly dry.' "

He once told her: "I wish I had twelve hands for you."
"We can arrange that surgically," she said.
"Fine," he said, "I'll cut off your little friend and exchange it for twelve hands."
"Don't you dare! You want to spoil a nice friendship? By the way, do you think your little friend would want to come home with me one night and sleep over?"
At first Guido thought she wanted it to use at home instead of playing with herself. But then the real reason dawned on him. She wanted to kill two birds— one of them a cock that could fly—with one stone. She just didn't want him to use it.

Sitting so long in one place—I wasn't used to such a lengthy sedentary position—made me fidgety. I felt lightheaded. To Merlputter's surprise, I sprang up and did some vigorous toe-touching and deep-knee bends.

"You know, she wasn't only my music teacher. She taught me that women are different. I had thought that all women were passionate and orgasmic. She taught me that desire may or may not come according to mood, degree of fatigue, state of biochemistry, hormones, health, allergies, time of day, foods you've eaten, the weather, the season. And she taught me that not all men are as lively and loving and modest as me. Some just lie there like the proverbial WASP woman or the JAP on the rare day she doesn't have a headache.

"Now listen to this twist. You know someone and you know someone, but when it comes down to it, you don't know them. Like they say in Tuscany, A man knows his walking stick better than his wife. Once, and this must've been a few months into our friendship, I said something about Tammy closing up the camera shop for Rosh Hashanah and Yom Kippur. What? she says tentatively, you're Jewish? Yes, of course, I say, aren't you? Sure, she says, but I thought you were Italian. Especially with a name like Veneziano-Tedesco! 'You never heard of Italian Jews?' "

"Of course," Charlie says, "what's the matter with you?"

"I don't mean you, moron. I'm talking to Aviva, who also says, 'Of course. Boy!' She shakes her head. '*That's* a surprise.' "

He remembered adding that many Italian Jews have names from towns where they lived. That Giorgio Bassani makes an interesting point in his novel, Beyond the Door. *I ask her if she read it. But Aviva says no, looking crestfallen and guilty. She doesn't know a thing about Italian literature. You must've seen the film,* The Garden of the Finzi-Continis. *That she's seen. In Beyond the Door, the narrator has a Christian friend, appropriately named Cattolico, who berates the Jewish narrator for thinking that only Italian Jews have cities for family names. He says that Catholics have them too. Then Aviva said now she understood the Veneziano part of the name. But how about Tedesco? I told her it was the Italian word for "German." It shows that my ancestors were German Jews. They settled, as did many Ashkenazic, that is, German Jews, in Venice in the sixteenth century.*

"So you're Jewish after all. Wow." She looked at him. Her mouth was open. "I didn't know. I would have sworn you were a gentile."

"And here you are, you antisemitt, *in love with a kike. Disappointed?"*

Aviva lowered her head and smiled to herself. "Well, I must tell you. After my experience with this wild Israeli, with this obnoxious Moroccan animal, with this Arab, I didn't really want to seek out a Jew. First of all, I wasn't too anxious to meet anyone. I wanted to be by myself. But, I thought, if I do meet anyone I'd prefer a gentile, a civilized man, the opposite of what he represented. You see, the Arab displayed his Jewishness for his convenience, for societal, for community approval, that hypocrite, and I was sick of it. I had had enough of them."

"So you fell in love with me for my goyishness."

"No, silly, for your gentil-ity."

He liked that turn of phrase.

"And if you had known at the outset that I was Jewish, would that have turned you off?"

She actually had to think for a moment. "No, I don't think so . . . In fact, definitely not . . . You don't like what I'm saying about Jews, right?"

"And you, born in Israel, to parents who were pioneers."

"They weren't pioneers. They came in the mid-thirties, fleeing Hitler . . . It's terrible what I said, right? And I noticed that flicker of impatience when I didn't recognize Busoni's name."

"Busoni is a composer."

"I know."

"The author I mentioned is not Busoni but Bassani."

"I'll read him."

"You'll like him."

"I'd love to read what you read." She hugged him. "Just tell me and I'll read. That's another way of me joining you."

"So remember," he said as her arms were around his neck. "Bassani is a writer, Busoni is a composer, Buitoni is a spaghetti and baloney . . ."

"Is what you're full of," she said, dropping her arms. "Please don't be so smug and sarcastic, Mister Know-it-all."

Sometimes as I talked to Charlie, I stared at the beige rug. Nothing in the room was loud. The doctor didn't want to upset, excite, his patients.

Everything had to be subdued. Fine Baroque or Classical music; paintings that didn't jar the senses or create a sense of dis-ease. Now I looked at Perlmutter. His eyes were closed. But he wasn't sleeping. How do I know? Because when I stopped talking, he sensed me looking at him and, with eyes still closed, said, "I'm not sleeping, I'm concentrating. Continue."

"I mentioned the JAP before with the headache. Listen to this. I once asked her how many times she would make love to her husband, you know, when things were okay between them. She thought a while, then said, as if in exculpation, It's been so long. Maybe three times a week. At least three times a week. And what if he wanted more? Then I didn't feel well, she said. I had a headache. You know how to cure a headache? I asked. Her eyes sparkled naughtily. 'Put an aspirin between your legs,' she said. Then she put a finger to her lips, cocked her head, crossed her eyes even more to give herself a dopey look and asked, 'Duh! But what do you use to push it in?' so I replied, 'My cure dispenses with the aspirin—you just use the pusher, *id est,* the thermometer.' 'I love your thermometer,' Aviva said, 'the only problem is it doesn't have numbers.'

"Yes, she was funny. Good timing. She was particularly talented in double entendres. Her wit shone when it played with sex. But she seemed to like the thought of it more than the actual thing. For instance, I would run my hands over her body. But where other women would moan, she *laughed.* 'Sex for you,' I scolded, 'is one big tickle.' 'But *what* a tickle!' she retorted. We would spend hours in bed. With him, she said, with the Arab, it was always quick. 'In and out, huh?' I said. She nodded, sadly. 'And then he went back to his room, claiming *he* had a headache, the JAP . . . Jewish American Putz."

And Aviva's pleasure in screwing, Guido thought, was always different. Once, he reminded her of her reaction to his comment that it was a perfect fit and she came back with, 'What are you, a tailor?' " Guido shook his head in *mock exasperation. "I could have killed you!" "With your thermometer, I hope,"* she said.

"But strangely, when I told her some months later what she had said to the Arab about having a headache, this time she denied it. She often did that when telling a story a second time. She'd say, you didn't hear me, or I was joking. 'I would never say to the Arab,' she swore, 'that I had a headache. I didn't beat around the bush. I told him straight out: I'm not in the mood, or, I don't want to. I would never use that JAPpy headache excuse.'

"Time for us, I explained, is both expanded and compressed. We've known each other for a year. That's the objective part. Yet these twelve months flew by so quickly. At the same time, we feel we've known each other for years.

That time moves slowly, like on Mars or Saturn, and an hour becomes a day, and a month a year. She finally understood it was a great compliment when I told her that spending five minutes with her felt like an hour.

"Would you believe she's looking at the mirror when I'm having these brilliant insights? She's inspecting her face, doing her hair. Typical woman. Did she look at herself shyly as some women do when they face a mirror—in the same self-conscious way they look when a camera is pointed at them—or did she look at herself boldly, with self-assurance? After all, she had said she'd been painfully shy as a youngster. Well, it turned out that she smiled at herself in the mirror and ran her fingers through her reddish brown hair, then tried to straighten it with a comb. She had just gotten out of bed. 'My God!' she exclaimed with a delightful laugh, paying absolutely no attention to my time phrenicism, my astral comparisons. 'I look like I just been laid,' And then, the sexiness she disclaimed having clustered around her like bees hunting on a wide yellow sunflower.

"But then I look into *my* mirror, the one without the silvered glass, and I want to know if she would have been attracted to me had she seen me at a party and I was at the other end of the room. "Yes, I think so . . . I know so.' And then she explained why. Because I have straight black hair, I'm tall, and I have a very noble, attractive face. 'In fact, I liked you from the time you brought in your not-daughter, Jill Altman. I always liked tall, aristocratic-looking men. They, you, give off a certain confidence, a mastery of the world.' "

"I want to know one thing," Guido asked her the next time they met. "Can you still say 'entirely' when I say to you, 'Are you mine?' or is the life-span of that 'entirely' a week or ten days?"

"You're being cutting again."

"Yes, but you didn't answer the question."

"I don't see the list," she snapped, referring to the dozens of questions he had asked her, an idea he got from a sex book, plus his own endemic curiosity.

Charlie had been pacing and stopped by his desk. Just then the phone rang and he automatically picked it up. "Uh-huh," he said. "Of course, I'll be glad to . . . I have someone in with me now . . . I'll call you later." He jotted down a number. "Sorry for the interruption, Guido . . . Please continue."

I couldn't tell if he'd been speaking to a man or a woman; and it also dawned on me that it was the first time in ages that he had called me Guido.

"You don't mind the fact that I'm older?"

"No." he said. "Not at all. I always wanted to make love to my teachers, beginning with lovely Gina Milanese in Venice in first grade, up whose legs I looked when I hid under her desk."

Guido thought she would hug him for this and say how adorable he was, but—predictably—she never said directly how she felt. However, her comments would pop out at odd moments.

As a joke, once before she came for lunch, he neatly cut in half an eggplant, scooped out some of the flesh, placed an egg in it, and put the two halves together. Later, he made believe he cut it open and showed her that true to its name it was an eggplant. And he began pawing her. "You're crazy, you're fun, you're adorable, I love you . . . And you're also a lech."

"No, actually, I'm a linguist . . . a cunnilinguist." And he lunged.

"Stop it," she screamed and giggled. "Put me down."

"I obey. I am putting you down. I will put you down. I will continue to put you down."

"But of course, along with her calling me adorable on occasion, she also had this terribly strong feeling of possessiveness. An obsessive jealousy that she masked with light humor. 'Remember,' she said before one of my trips, 'don't use that thing for anything, with anyone, anytime, anywhere, except, *maybe*, for peeing.' And then she'd smile a sad little smile, for in truth, she didn't know, she only trusted, hoped, that I would be faithful and love her even when I was away."

6

When I came in next time I gave Charlie a slim package.

"What's this?" he said.

"Open it."

He unwrapped it, eagerly, like a child opening a birthday gift. He held the framed picture at arm's length, admiring it.

"Hey . . . It's your famous photo . . . And . . . my God . . . it's signed too . . . You're giving this to me? Why?"

"Why? you jerk! Why?" he asks. "Because I don't appreciate what you're doing for me."

"Wait a minute. This isn't your only . . . You're not . . ."

"It is. I am."

"No." But he didn't put it down. That much of a psychologist I am. "I'm not taking it," Charlie said.

"You will. You are. You do. You shall. Please don't deny me the pleasure of sharing something of mine with you . . . There's a nice little story attached which you'll appreciate. The next time I saw Casals in New York after a concert, I brought him this eight-by-ten. But instead of taking it, he signed it for me, said, This is for you and you mail me another, is all right?"

"And it's the only signed one you have?"

I nodded. "It's yours, Merlputter," and I threw my arms around him and pressed him close.

"I appreciate it," Charlie said. "I really do. And even more, I appreciate the feelings, especially since I thought of you as being so cerebral."

I laughed and sat down, ready to talk some more. "Imagine! That's her word for me. She often told me, It doesn't pay to be so cerebral. Don't pick things apart, for sometimes you're left with only the pieces. And then suddenly, she said, 'I bet you get a kick out of this adventure, don't you? . . . Don't you?' she repeated, head down, eyes up, in a more questioning tone.

" 'No,' I said.

" 'I think you're gleeful . . . Well, hello! Hello! Are you there? Say something!!'

" 'I'm not gleeful . . . I feel like I'm leading two wives . . . I mean, two lives.' Boy, was that a slip . . . ! Charlie, what would Freud say about that?"

"I'm familiar with his works," Charlie said flatly, "but I'm not a Freudian."

"But I made light of the slip and continued in that key. 'Would you like to come over for dinner?' I asked Aviva, 'and meet my life?'

" 'Okay,' she said, falling into the role.

" 'I think you'll like her.'

" 'I probably would . . . How would you introduce me?'

" 'Ver-y care-ful-ly,' I said slowly.

"But this conversation gave her an opening to ask me something else about Tammy. Once, in the middle of a lesson, she began pounding me gently on the chest. "Why? Why? Why did you do it?' I knew what she meant. She meant this. Us. The adventure. As if I worked alone. As if I had no partner who sent out those sting rays of seduction. As if she were totally and entirely an innocent pussy . . . cat. 'You think?' I asked her, 'I did it out of sexual deprivation?' 'Yes,' she said. I laughed to myself. Me. Sexually deprived! There's a laugh.

" 'Dead wrong. Dead dead wrong,' I told her. 'Not only are you wrong, you're crazy besides. I did it for you. You came to me from the clouds. A UFO. From the moon. From Venus. Another galaxy. A gravity that gravity itself doesn't know about. A magnetic force that physicists haven't yet discovered. Or if discovered, haven't been able to explain. It's the fifth force in physics. We're on a different time zone, you and me. It follows no known space-time continuum. We're the electrons that not even the twenty-mile-long circular super atom smasher under Geneva can split apart. We belong together. Destined.'

" 'But it doesn't fit,' she said.

"So I threw one of her remarks back at her. 'What're you, a tailor?' But she didn't react. She couldn't tie old jokes together. 'Did you hear what I said?' I hissed angrily. She came closer. Kissed me. 'Yes, yes,' she said softly, 'but let me talk. Let me ask. You always ask questions.' She stroked my arms, neck, face, to show she loved me. 'It just doesn't make sense.' She shook her head. 'You're a puzzle.'♥

"Did you ever screw your husband when you had your period?" Guido asked Aviva, quickly changing the subject.

"Which marriage?" she laughed.

"Take your choice."

"No, for the first, because during those seven years I was a professional virgin. didn't I tell you? My husband was impotent."

"Oh, my God," he said. "I didn't know that . . . Seven clean years."

"Very clean." Aviva laughed. "Immaculate. As for the second, I used to have very quick periods. Three days at most. Ever since I began taking vitamins, it cut them down. My periods used to be so awful I would literally stand on my head. No joke. I would prop myself upside down by the closet and when the blood rushed to my head and my kishkes were upside down it helped. My periods were so bad it was like giving birth. For days I was doubled over with pain. For others, menopause is a curse. For me it was a blessing. When it came I was ecstatic. Some women get depressed when they stop bleeding once a month. Me, I said good riddance and hailed the beginning of a new life."

"But I guess Aviva felt those tentative vibrations in me, for the next day, when I was supposed to come over to her house for a lesson, she called. There was an urgent tone to her voice. "I have to talk to you,' she said. Last time she had done this, we hadn't seen each other for a while; she missed me very much, she said, and wanted to come over just for an hour and ended up spending the day. But now her voice sounded edgy. Maybe she had hot pants, I thought. Maybe she has something startling to say. It turned out it *was* startling. She didn't want me to come for a lesson; rather, she would come to see me. No sooner was she through the door than she said, grim-faced, 'What would you say if I told you I slept with my husband last night?' Well, there's an interesting twist, I thought. Inconstancy, thy name is woman! This, after vowing passionately, 'I'm yours entirely.' 'Well, did you?' I asked her. 'But you still didn't tell me your reaction.' I was silent for a while. I shook my head in bedazzlement. Things had been going rotten for Aviva and the Arab for years. She said she couldn't stand the sight of him. And now this! Maybe it was a test. Maybe she wanted to make me jealous. But I was jealous enough as is. She had mentioned this three-and-a-half year relationship with the South African we called Capetown. Then she had told me about another affair she had. Very brief. It bothered me. Those guys filled my head with jealousy. So now she was testing me.

♥See ABC Directory, *Enigma, the, that Guido is.*

Or maybe, quirky woman that she was, she wanted to see, you know, for the sake of comparison, how someone whom she could not abide felt inside of her compared to someone she loved. Maybe all cocks felt the same. Or maybe she wanted to tease me, both with the question and with the fact of the deed. 'I'd be very surprised and upset,' I said. 'Did you?' She purposely said nothing for a while. She didn't smile; she didn't twinkle. There wasn't even a naughty look in her eye. A morose, serious expression settled there. She looked angry. I don't remember if she said, I didn't, or, Of course not, though I would have preferred hearing the latter. 'But now you know how I feel. I don't want to share you. I don't want, I'm tired of crumbs.' 'I'm not giving you crumbs.' I said. But she said it was crumbs. 'That's exactly what it is. Crumbs.' So I thought about it, didn't respond any more this time. But weeks later I came up with a rebuttal. 'What's the best part of a streusel cake? The crumbs. What's the best part of a chocolate cake? The thin icing. What's the best part of chocolate chip ice cream? The chips. In other words: crumbs.' 'Did anyone ever tell you you'd make a good lawyer?' Aviva smiled. 'Only if you're the attorney,' I said. But she didn't keep up with this banter. She turned serious again. 'I don't like the secretiveness of this whole affair.' 'We're locked in by circumstances,' I said. 'Do things ever go smoothly? Nothing ever goes smoothly. Only sleep goes smoothly, goes the Sicilian proverb, and even sleep doesn't go smoothly. There are ups and downs, bumps and warts on what you hope is a smooth ride.' 'I told you I don't like the secrecy of it, the sneaking around. I keep turning around every time I walk up your street.' 'But fortunately,' I said, 'I live in a yuppy neighborhood where husbands and wives and even maids go to work to keep up with mortgage payments, so no one ever sees you."

Charlie interrupted. "Remember that Talmudic expression we learned in Rabbi Pelick's class?"

"I don't remember a thing about Talmud. I closed my mind to it." I crossed and uncrossed my legs; played with the smooth leather of the easy chair.

"It says that even paving stones have eyes and ears," Charlie said.♥

I shrugged. Aviva was on her secretiveness kick and she had plenty of thoughts on the subject. 'For secretiveness like this there's punishment. I know it. I feel it.' And perhaps it was expressed in her dream. She said she never used to dream before, at least couldn't remember her dreams. But since getting to know me she was constantly dreaming. This one she remembered. She had fallen asleep next to me. She was tired and wanted to nap. Lately, she was always tired. So take a nap, I said. I'll watch you sleep. Soon her breathing was even. Then suddenly her head twitched and she shuddered and moaned. I wondered if I should wake her. When she moaned

♥See ABC Directory, *Italian proverb.*

again I gently shook her. 'Aviva, Aviva, what's the matter?' She woke as if from another world. For a moment she didn't know where she was. 'I had a dream,' she said without moving her lips. 'An awful dream.' 'Do you want to tell me?' 'Not now, it's too awful,' she said. 'A nightmare...'

"I knew, I just knew it pertained to another woman. And I thought like in the German concentration camps—no matter what the prisoners dreamt, the reality was always worse. That's why prisoners didn't wake up their bunkmates, no matter how much they moaned. I had a hunch what she dreamed. Here too reality was worse for Aviva. She really had her nightmare, only she didn't know it.

"Only days later did she tell me the dream:

"She's walking along a road and a car comes and knocks her down. She falls, but in falling sees that a woman is driving the car. But once she's down the woman backs up her car and runs over her again and then moves forward and does it again. Again and again the woman with an expressionless face keeps running her over.

"Like in fairy tales, she had dreams for three nights running. The second: A dream where the woman has the man only on a physical plane, but he eludes her spiritually. Also, a nightmare for her. The third: A dream where the strings of the cello are made of men's fingers. And she says in her dream: All throughout history men have played with us, and now for the first time we're going to play with them.

"The dreams opened a portal of complaints. She was on a sliding pond, in more ways than one. Once the slide begins, goes the Italian folk saying— this one is from the Alpine valley where they often have mudslides—even God Himself can't help. Again, the complaints about the secretiveness, the sneaking around. 'In other words,' I said to her, couldn't restrain my sarcasm, 'you want to carry on an adulterous affair in the open. Maybe have Tammy invite you in and then excuse herself for six or seven hours.'

"The crux came the day Aviva's depression hit a low point. Her miserable marriage, stalled career (which obviously was my fault because she was spending so much time with me instead of practicing and following leads for concerts), no opening with . . ."

The Long Island Symphony, Guido almost blurted out, which she occasionally performed with.

". . . any orchestra and just an occasional solo engagement here and there, and worst of all not having as she put it, a refuge, a secure place for herself. The sneaking around, the part-time loving, the guilt about taking another woman's man, the insecurity of being the second wife, the frustration of having to share him, of not having him all to herself, in waves these feelings came and she could not suppress them. Swept them under the rug, as she used to say. Shoved the cork into the bottle. But occasionally the pressure would pop the cork up and the feelings of depression would surface. A couple of weeks could go by and she would enjoy her man, the one who was perfect for her, but then the depression would descend like a heavy blanket and enmesh her, suffocate her. Couldn't he understand that? Couldn't he, just, for one lousy moment, put himself in her place? she would say to me.

"And I, for my part, tried to use all my lawyerly skills to persuade her that if this was the best love of her life, then *it*, this, should supersede, that this should be the axis around which all else revolves.

"While I spoke to her, my head was split in two. My mouth said one thing, my mind another. Two trains running on parallel tracks. Remembering Aviva's Why? Why did you start?, when I looked at it objectively, with make believe lenses through another guy's eyes, or maybe even Aviva's, I would see: Guido has a beautiful woman for a wife, maybe gloomier than Aviva but better in bed, maybe less stable than Aviva but more loyal . . . Why, then, why? It's the old story. The left hand doesn't know what the right hand is doing; the bottom half has a different agenda than the top.

That night he woke in the middle of the night. Aviva's words haunted him: Why did you start? What was he doing? He couldn't think straight. Right wrong. Up down. Left right. Indeed, what was he doing? No more, he decided. He remembered the lesson taught him years ago by a married girl, alone in New York while her husband was on a business trip abroad. What was her name? Miriam. Married Miriam. He slept over at her house and while she was screwing him she rubbed the ring with the diamond on it in his face, to drive the point home—and expiate herself. That's the woman's game: guilt. Enjoy it—but dish out guilt. But maybe Aviva was right. Next time she said stop, he'd accept. And if she left him, would his moral confusion be eased? Suddenly he felt sorry for Tammy, for Aviva, for himself. He even felt sorry for Adam, whose face he forgot. In the midst of the midst of the night, he felt heavy, lugubrious, guilty. His mouth ached, as if all his teeth were infected. His left side felt numb. A stroke? A wave of prickly fear that this might indeed presage the end pulsed in his constricted throat. Slowly he coaxed, rubbed, massaged feeling back into his body.

Only once before had he felt so ill. Years back, alone in Venice in a small hotel, first time he had returned since his childhood. His mother was still in New York, and he didn't want to stay with distant cousins. Perhaps the illness was homesickness. But he had a fever. Couldn't the soul that is affected, touched, upset, also develop a fever? He was delirious in his little room. The design on the old peeling wallpaper disengaged itself and climbed up and down the walls like worms, wriggling like snakes. His mouth was dry and goose bumps traveled jerkily up his arms and down his legs.

The previous day he had seen his old Hebrew tutor. He had made inquiries about Signor Abramo di Rossi and learned that he was now a resident of the Jewish Old Age Home in the Ghetto Vecchio. When di Rossi, who stemmed from one of the oldest Jewish families in Italy, saw Guido, the frail old man hugged and kissed him and could not let go of his hand. Throughout the entire visit, di Rossi clasped Guido's hand in his. Guido was the first of his pupils to visit him in years, he said with tears in his eyes. The old man was kind enough not to recall what a mean rascal Guido had been. Or perhaps he had forgotten. The touching welcome made Guido all the more regret his childish pranks. The tutor would come to Guido's house and drone on about the creation of the world and Guido would think to himself, My God, the world has already been created and here he is still talking about it, and he would drift off to sleep. It's a wonder Signor di Rossi didn't drift off too. Maybe he did. But to keep himself amused, Guido would play with little toys, rolling them around in his hand. Then di Rossi would spot them and whoosh—swoop them out of his hands and fling them to the other side of the room. Wanting revenge, Guido bought little crackles, miniature firecrackers that flashed and popped and created smoke upon contact. He wrapped some in something else, then whoosh, di Rossi swooped it out of his hand and flung it to the wall. A series of little explosions followed. He remembered di Rossi swearing that Guido was the devil.

But by morning he was fine, pulsating for Aviva.

Even though she was older. In another few years Aviva would be, as the Italians say, nonnanese, *grandmotherly. Borderline wrinkled. Over the hill.*

"But her view was: she had to get a job, perhaps as professor of cello, even though she didn't have a doctorate, but weren't performances, an active career, just as good? She might have to go to California. She didn't want to teach kids any more. If she left the Arab he wouldn't give her a penny. As is he only left her a minimal amount of money every week. And where? Would you believe, in the dish closet, in a paper bag? He said his taxi business in New York wasn't doing well. If she left him she'd have to go on welfare, and she didn't want to go on welfare. So hence, it was inevitable that this would come to an end. She had been hurt before, too many times, and didn't want to be hurt again. She didn't want, she said, to be cut up. I told her I felt used. 'So,' I said, 'then the love I've poured into you has been wasted. You said you'd be mine entirely, right?' 'Yes,' she said, 'but you're turning the tables on me. Are *you* entirely *mine?*' Aviva said. I knew she had a point, but I said, hoping that I could convince her: 'Isn't half of me better than none of me? You'll never meet another man like me. Never!' And she knew I was right; she knew I wasn't being smug, otherwise she'd have told me. 'If you ever do decide to leave the Arab,' I said, 'you're going to yearn for me.'"

But that wasn't what Guido told her. For the words he really said he didn't want to share with Charlie. "If you leave him," Guido told her, "You'll behave exactly the way you did after your first divorce. You'll go wild. You'll get into one relationship. And then another. You'll fall into bed with some guy not because you like him but because—why not? And then another, and then another, but you'll always remember and long for me." "You're wrong," she said. "I'm a completely different person now."

"She'll always remember me, I told her. 'Like out of a B- movie,' Aviva said. 'A B- movie.' That old tongue-in-cheek image again.

"Our sparring was serious, but what was unique was the occasionally bizarre humor that popped in, as if we were watching a movie for a second time and could start parodying the actors' lines. Our jokes seemed to say: "This is all absurd." When she said a B- movie, she laughed, but her laugh was sad. I guess I was getting to her. 'And you'll say,' I said, 'I'll always love you.' 'I will,' she said. 'To have had the joy of remembering you will be one of the pleasures of my life.' 'I can't stand the pluperfect voice,' I said. 'You're pluperfect,' she said, hesitated, then added, 'for me. Knowing you *was* the highlight of my life. You're special and you know it.' We were on our goodbye routine again. 'But I don't want to be,' I said, 'part of a B- movie script. I want this to be like out of a fairy tale, where the beloved says: I love you no matter what. I'll give up everything, anything, for your love.' But I could see her shaking her head even as I'm concocting the fairy tale. 'Real life,' she says, 'is not a fairy tale. Time moves on.' Well, I guess it's like the Italian farmers say: A broken watch doesn't stop the seasons."

She's never been able to hold on to the things precious to her, he thought. She always leaves men. But me she won't leave. I won't let her go.

"Your trouble is," he told her, "you give, but you don't give enough. It's the old self-centeredness."

"We're talking about two different things as usual . . . Don't you understand? I want to be with you. Always . . . You go away for weeks—"

"Never weeks . . ."

"It seems like weeks. Soon Iceland for a month."

"Well, it's a summit. Big thing."

"Now Buenos Aires. Now Seattle. Ten, fifteen days each time."

"Suppose you had a concert tour in Europe."

"But I don't. I have two kids to take care of. They're more important. Think I'll leave them with that jerk?"

"I'm going to London for ten days in a couple of months. Want to come with me?"

"Who'll take care of the kids?"

"Bring 'em along."

"Sure," she said.
"And the Arab too. Let him babysit. There's a shortage of Moroccan taxi drivers in London."

"She told me she didn't want to get involved any deeper. I reeled back. Actually felt as if I were pushed. 'I don't believe it,' I said. '*Now* it comes out? After me loving you—for how many years now? Ten, twenty? That really hurts . . ."

She looked gray. Older. What the hell was he doing with an older woman? Even if she did look thirty-five. But only when she was up. Down, she looked sixty. She didn't glow. She showed him some snapshots; good pictures, but she said they made her look too old. Nonsense, he thought. One showed a young seductive woman with a beautiful face. Of course she didn't like the pictures. Any plain woman is jealous of a beautiful one, and today she looked plain, gray, old, like a city in Eastern Europe, like Prague.

"You know, Charlie, one evening her depression hit me. I became her, felt her pain, sensed what it was like to have a boyfriend who was not always available, like normal boyfriends, who had trouble at home, and who didn't quite make it as a musician of promise. So I felt for her. I absorbed her mal, sucked it out of her like poison from a wound. Next time I saw her she looked fresh and young again, glowing again. Just like the pictures she had shown me a few days earlier. But now she asked *me*, 'What's the matter? You all right?' 'And how are you doing?' I asked her. 'Better,' she said. 'Much better. And you?' 'Couldn't sleep,' I said. 'I felt ill, recalling your malaise. I felt split in two and both of my selves were uncomfortable. As if wearing garments far too tight. I wanted to get out of my skin, to step out of myself and leave myself behind. I felt everything you said and I empathize. I was you for a while and I know what it feels like. You're right, You should leave me. I mean I should leave myself, that is, if I were you and you me.' She laughed and hugged me. 'No!' she said. 'Sure you're all right?' I asked her. 'Yes,' she said. 'but it will come back. I know it.' 'And the you'll leave?' 'Yes,' she said.

"So then I told her that if she ever left me and took up with another man, 'I would enter the house and lie down in my, that is, our, your bed, and refuse to leave. I'd invade our bed, possess it, arrogate it.' 'You wouldn't do that,' she said with a slight up-pitch, almost questioning tone, then came an imperceptible caesura in her voice, not as long as those full-of-music silences in a Haydn symphony, but pause enough. Then Aviva added, 'Yes, you would, wouldn't you?' 'And how I would,' I said. 'Because you're mine. If I'd seen you at a party, in a restaurant, on a line at the checkout counter, I'd have gone up to you and, like a Neanderthal, slung you over my shoulder and walked away with you.' I guess she liked that because she came up with one of her unpredictable but nevertheless ego-boosting remarks: 'If I had dreamed of a man in my wildest dream of imagination, I would have dreamt up you.'

"But still I realized that Aviva was a pathetic soul, and in my heart I cried for her. She had the musical talent but never pursued it. Now when she went to cellists' recitals, she saw only her own lack of achievement in comparison to the success of the musician on stage. She was in the audience; they were up there . . . "

So Aviva, he knew, was in a no-win situation. No matter how happy she was with Guido, she knew the hour would come when she would go out the door alone and spend the night by herself. He consoled her by saying, Don't think of the leaving, think of coming back next time. But for her this was wordplay. Specious reasoning. A placebo. Words, words, words, as she said. The truth was that Guido was a pleasant bump of joy on the long, straight, endless line of misery and loneliness of her life.

But. And this bothered him. Beneath the glitz and glitter of her sexiness was her middling level of culture. Unlike European musicians, she wasn't well read. And Aviva's link with music wasn't spiritual, all-encompassing, monomaniacal. She would never talk about music on her own, its effect on her, its emotional, esthetic, intellectual underpinnings, She never talked about her father's career. She never relayed anecdotes about famous musicians (except Ian Plaskow, of course, and then only under Guido's prodding.) She talked about getting her career on track; she mentioned how sleepy she became teaching bad students; how she literally felt her head falling, about to doze off. Sometimes, she said, she may even have fallen asleep. She locked music out of herself. Yet, when he watched her practicing, singing to herself, blinking, looking older, taking those deep-sniff cellist breaths, she fused with her instrument. And if they were in the car or at home together and he had a cello-piano sonata on the stereo, she would often drift away from his remarks and comment on the performance, and he wouldn't realize she hadn't been paying attention to him till the piece was over, and she gave her analysis with a critic's depth and bite.

Still, he felt her links with music were superficial. Her father had started her on the cello because that's the instrument he played. She never really had a choice, and she never used her father's name; she was determined to make it on her own. Perhaps deep down she didn't even like music, Guido mused. In another era, another place, she said, her mother would have given her piano lessons because that's what mothers do. But no, she had to do the cello. When she was feeling ill or gloopy she could stay away from the instrument for weeks. And yet when she taught good students, her knowledge, technique, and imagination soared. But he also didn't picture her as a cogitating animal. She was the perfect example of Richelieu's dictum; intellect doesn't become a woman.

On the other hand, maybe Guido underestimated her. Maybe she just wasn't a talker—she'd once told him long ago: except for her father practicing in his studio, her home was basically silent; no one spoke. They read the newspapers, listened to the radio, later watched TV. That's why it had been so hard for her to articulate her feelings; only lately was she opening up. But there was nothing shy about her once her clothes were off. Yet music had never really melded itself like racial color onto her being. Music for her was more like a suntan. It just looked like it was part of her—but could fade whenever she went out of music's sun. That snapshot she'd once shown him of her standing in her apartment holding the cello with her left hand and in her right a knife about to be thrust into the cello's gut—that was symbolic of her relationship with music. She was never photographed with the instrument in a lover's embrace. Perhaps because she didn't know what love was until she met him.

"So when she was down," I told Charlie, "I tried to perk her up. 'With you and me,' I'd tell Aviva, 'two beautiful elements that might have gone on for years giving off their half-life alone and unfulfilled have combined . . . Two half-lives make one, don't they, doesn't it?' And I told her, and I meant it, I think, that she was beautiful. 'No, I'm not,' she said. 'Not any more. I used to be. But not any more. I looked at the mirror today. I've aged awfully during this past year.' 'No, you haven't. You look super . . . Not a day over sixty . . . okay . . . Maybe a day and a half.'"

But the truth was that she had indeed aged. And don't think he missed the implication of that "this past year" bit. As if it was his fault. He was the anti-Shangri La. Of course, he wouldn't agree with her. When she smiled, was happy, she looked great, beautiful. People still turned to look at her in the street. But when gloom waved over her, her face fell, her lips drooped, the corners of her mouth slanted down, and the fuzz on her face became more noticeable. More than ever the tiny lines above her lips, lines that toothless old ladies had, were etched deeper. In gloom, no doubt about it, she looked like she was climbing over sixty, and not a good sixty at that.♥ In smile, fifteen years younger.

"I wish I were younger for you." She echoed a remark made two or three times before. She kept saying that—until her wish came true. Of course, she didn't know it, but at the Long Island Post *personnel had sent him a lab assistant, twenty-two or twenty-three, who looked like a younger version of Aviva, except her hair was black. He couldn't believe it; Teresa had similar facial lines and generous pouting lips. But she had porcelain skin. A fresh rose, not a fading carnation. And of course, no squint. That would have been too much. But like Aviva she was spunky and flirtatious, and he imagined Aviva at that age, fending off the men. But Guido played coy with her; he restrained*

♥See ABC Directory, *Older, getting; Old, looking.*

himself, was proud he did not respond to her overtures. And anyway, she was
a cultural moron. He didn't need more complications. Not yet, anyway. But
who knows what webs that spider known as destiny could spin?

"Well, at least," Guido said, "there's one remark you can't accuse me of
making."

"What's that? Aviva said, falling neatly into the trap.

"That I love you for your body." And then he added. "Have you ever heard
me complaining about my belly, my chin, my hair? Have you ever heard me
denigrating my slightly cocked eyes?"

"No, but then again, you're more secure, more even, more confident than I
am. And anyway, women are never satisfied with their bodies.'

"You're a kvetch."

"And you're a lech. Lech and Kvetch."

He pointed to her pussy. "Lech, kvetch, and hungry wretch."

"It is hungry," she said, her eyes brightening.

"Remember Charlie, I was once telling you about how we joked around
about her meeting Tammy. Well, one evening I did something strange. I
told you Tammy isn't particularly crazy about classical music. She tolerates
it, but it's not up there on her Things To Do list. Anyway, one evening,
perhaps seven or eight months into our relationship I took Tammy to see
Aviva . . ."

I could see Charlie's eyes widening. "Meshugge?" he said. "You're pulling my leg . . . You took Tammy to see Aviva? Where? How?"

"Simple, Merlputter, I took her to a concert, where Aviva was not a
soloist, but an ad hoc player in the orchestra. Something in me pushed me.
I wanted them to see each other. Surely Tammy would see Aviva, but perhaps
Aviva would look out at the audience—musicians do that sometimes—and
see Tammy. I didn't tell Aviva because I thought she might chicken out and
call in sick. There was, I must admit, a perverse pleasure in seeing them in
the same room at the same time, innocent, not caught in flagrante, like Ava
was. Maybe I would take her backstage to meet Aviva."

"Did you?" Charlie asked.

"You see that almost red-headed cellist?" he whispered to Tammy as the
conductor strode onstage.

"The pretty one? With the long hair?"

"Of course. You don't think I'd look at the other beasties, do you?"

"Well?"

"Doesn't she look like the sort that could be in Playboy *instead of playing*
cello?"

Tammy didn't reply. But he felt a palpable excitement now seeing Aviva
and Tammy at the same time. Once before, at a benefit concert, Guido had

spotted Aviva in the orchestra without her being aware of it. He watched her. Holding her cello, Aviva sat straight with a queenly bearing at the first desk cello section, just to the right of the conductor. The sheen of her fluffed-out, auburn hair could be seen everywhere in the hall. When she played, wearing long, tight-fitting velvet pants and an airy black satin blouse, her ass slightly out and her back concave, which accented the roundness of her tush, no music lover, seeing her slim form and fetching profile, no man with a hearty set of gonads could have resisted jumping onstage and jumping her. Only her doe eyes and bridge of nose were visible above the music stand. The slight squint was hidden, as usual, by a dose of eye makeup and loose long hair. She looked like a still photograph of herself, so immobile was she when she played, except for the imperceptible movement of her eyes following the score. Whereas the conductor had to be tied down lest he soar away with Schubert's Third Symphony, Aviva just ticked her head a teeny bit. Only at the end did she allow herself a little smile, shared with the cellist to her left.

He watched Aviva to see if there was any other-speaking as she looked at the conductor, or for a hint of extra-musical waves flowing between them. None, as far as he could see. When Aviva played, Guido imagined that on a Peter Pan aerial glide another Aviva slid down from the wings, coalesced with the vulnerable, problematic, unsure-of-herself Aviva he knew, and took over. He could never believe or fully understand the switch that took place. She became Aviva the cellist. For him that Aviva was a different person. And at times, as he told her, her womanliness and her marital problems possessed her so that he would forget that the other Aviva, musician and performer, teacher and interpreter, even existed. And then, after her practicing, he would just look at her, run his hands and fingers over her from five feet away, sculpt every curve without touching her and say, "I make love to you with my eyes," and at once she became fifteen years younger. She sucked in her breath each time she heard a beautiful remark from him, just as she sucked in her breath during difficult passages where the concentration almost made her stop breathing. A warmth infused her, her cheeks glowed, the little wrinkles around her eyes vanished.

During intermission, Tammy asked him in the lobby:

"You want to photograph her for a centerfold?" Tried to smile. But there was an undercurrent of hurt in her voice. Knowing the way he looked at other women. Knowing that years ago he had photographed girls in the nude. A huge black and white blow-up of his naked cellist still hung in his darkroom. But Guido did not respond to that. Instead, he said, "On a musician you'd expect an ethereal face, not a self-indulgent one, one that says: Me, me, me. Take me out. Feed me. Entertain me. Dance me. Clothe me. Pamper me. Love me. Screw me."

"Is that what her face says to you?" Tammy said, surprised.

"Not really," Guido replied. "I'm just babbling. Actually, each face has its own individuality, and each musician onstage would make a great photograph."

"Well, anyway, she's too young for you."

"Why, how old do you think she is?"

"She's too far away for me to tell precisely, but probably twenty-eight or thirty. You know, with you, it's the lost-youth syndrome. All these guys in their early forties who go looking for someone younger, something better."

"Not better," Guido told her. "Not better at all. Just different."

"Remember that Longfellow poem?" she said. "My Lost Youth?"

He could feel his jaw falling with surprise. He never believed that Tammy knew Longfellow, or could even remember a poem. He just never connected her with poetry. "The Venetians say: Il mondo e sotto la lingua. *The world is under your tongue. If you know how to speak you have the world by the balls."*

The next day he told Aviva, "I was at your concert last night, watching you like a hawk."

"Really?" She broke into a happy smile. "Why didn't you tell me? Or come backstage?"

"There was a crush of people . . . I didn't know it was possible . . ."

"Oh, come on, you have a Long Island Post *press card."*

"Actually, I took a quick hour off from work just to catch the concert. Why didn't you invite me?"

"Silly, because I know you work . . ."

Charlie leaned forward in his chair. "Well, did you take Tammy backstage?"

"Nah," I said. "Think I'm crazy? . . . But maybe it was a mistake, even taking her to the concert, for a few days later she told me, 'I noticed, don't think I didn't notice, how you couldn't take your eyes off that red-haired cellist. You devoured her with your eyes.' 'Another county heard from! What nonsense,' I said. But Tammy continued: 'You hardly looked at the action onstage. You looked at the cellist, her shoes, her hands, how she tapped her foot. You watched her grimace.' So I said, 'Then you weren't watching anyone else either. You were watching me allegedly watching her. But let me assure you, ladies and gents of the jury, that it wasn't anything personal. I like to watch the little real life dramas that take place while the fake drama is proceeding onstage. Like the trumpeter criticizing the tempo by making Lone Ranger cowboy motions with his right hand. The cellist exchanging a smile with the oboist.' But Tammy countered with: 'Methinks you doth protest too much. I can tell she brings back your fascination with the cello. She's alive for you, while I'm only treading water, trying to survive, wouldn't you say?' 'Dead wrong!' I said. 'Then how come you sniffed each time she sniffed?' 'What are you talking about? . . .' 'You know what I'm talking about. Sniffing. Breathing in unison . . .' 'You know what,

Tammy?' 'What?' she said pleasantly. And then I purposely, maliciously, remained silent, refusing to discuss it."

But with Aviva he was dying to discuss music; he sat open-mouthed as she revealed little nuances in interpretation, and she in turn, sat, or lay, ga-ga-eyed as he told her about camera lighting or how to spin an enlarger lens for fuzz effect. Then she suddenly asked him: "What's the purpose of photography?"

He felt as if he'd been hit below the belt. "I don't want to discuss it," he said. He didn't know what the purpose was. He didn't care. He didn't want to think about it or analyze it. All he knew was that he liked it; he loved it; he was crazy about it. He loved black-and-white pictures, he loved snapping, he loved the click of the camera and the sound of the film forwarding on the spool, the smell of developer and the vinegary odor of the fixer; he loved matting his pictures, loved seeing them framed. What better feeling next to holding a woman than an image slowly materializing ex nihilo from the developer, which he loved best of all?

No, actually he loved holding a woman more. And he loved best of all their screaming. Ava loved it so much she would go off into a different world. She was the first woman in Venus. Aviva loved it too. But she, bless her, in the middle of screwing would come up with a remark like, "I got a ten-pound turkey for five dollars." He was lucky she didn't file her nails. "That's pretty cheap," he told her. "But the magnifying lenses for each person will be expensive." He was so pissed he wanted to pull out. If he told this to Charlie, he'd probably hear a remark like: Doesn't say much for your screwing. Or another time, she came up with: "Do you like tofutti?" To which he said, "Yes, very much . . . and to-fucky too." And once, while she was going at it with eyes closed she popped them open and asked, "Do fish screw?" "No," he said crisply to put an end to it, but she countered with: "No wonder sharks go wild. If I were a mermaid I'd bite too." And that was typical of her. While screwing she was thinking of how she would feel were she deprived of the ability to screw.

"So what's the current situation?" Charlie asked me. "Everything fine or no? Do you mean to keep this up, divorce your wife, and take her?"

A chill ran over me, an inner tremble first, followed by a shaking in my stomach, uncontrollable as on the day my father died.

"I don't know . . . I don't know what to do."

"Well, look at it this way, answer . . . think . . . is everything good between you?"

"Not really. Aviva is a loner. She told me so. Doesn't need friends. She once said: 'Even now, thoughts of what you do to me is more exciting, at times, when I'm alone than being with you.' You see, that's part of her aloneness syndrome. So why does she need me? She's a narcissist. Did you know that fifty percent of the men in this country and forty percent of the women commit adultery? I wonder who takes up the slack on the other ten."

"Don't change the subject," Charlie shouted. "You jerk! You're the narcissist! Did it ever occur to you that her behavior is a kind of psychological protection? An armor against being hurt? And how much she's been hurt by her husband already! Don't you have *any* sympathy? She obviously senses that things won't work out with you, so she's by degrees building armor. Can't you look into her pain, grief, frustration? You egoist, you cry about a couple of affairs she had fifteen, eighteen years ago, and even if she had a couple more, what's the big deal? You're bothered by phantom competitors, ghost lovers about whom she doesn't give a damn, a whit? Or shall I be more blunt and rhyme it? And now she has the agony of knowing that while she pours out all her love to you, just hours later, not twenty years ago, you ass, but hours later, you're going to be with another woman, your wife. Put yourself in her place. How would you feel if she went and slept with her husband after making love to you?"

"I told her," I said without any emotion whatsoever, "that in an adulterous affair, one cannot be jealous of one's husband or wife."

"Such sanctimony reminds me of Swift's "Modest Proposal." Since baby-eating doesn't affect the narrator who is childless, he can be noble and generous with other people's kids. Since you *know* that her husband is out of the sexual picture, you too can be very generous. But wouldn't you climb the walls with rage if you discovered that Aviva had another lover?"

"I told her that I know my jealousy of her previous affairs is no comparison to the unconscionable act of betraying one's wife or husband. In fact, that's her phrase and I immediately agreed."

"But you didn't answer my question?" Charlie insisted.

"I also told Aviva I don't answer every single question."

"You know what?" Charlie said. "You don't deserve her."

Charlie

After I told Guido that he didn't deserve Aviva, I didn't utter the next, the higher, ph(r)ase of the logical postulation.

And with that, I had finished talking with Guido for a while. Soon he would be going abroad and business was taking me to Long Island for a couple of months. During one of my sessions with Guido I had gotten a call from a colleague who had to go back to Israel to care for an ailing father, and he asked me to substitute for him a couple of evenings a week. While listening to Guido I made firm my earlier resolve to see for myself who Aviva was. Was he telling the truth? Or fantasizing? Could such a luscious woman really exist? Or was it his apocryphal stamp collection all over again?

I must also admit that I hadn't forgotten what he told me at the reunion. In fact, it burned its way into my consciousness like a tattoo. He was so enthralled with her that he wanted to share her—with me. I told him I had read an article about this, but I didn't say that I'd written it and given the name Candaulus Complex to this odd but not uncommon psychological phenomenon. He wanted to share her with me? Fine. I'd be glad to play Gyges to his Candaulus, but first I had to find her. But how?

I thought it might be difficult for I had no last name, no real name, although I presumed her name *was* Aviva. It seemed to fit. But I knew the instrument she played. Go find a pretty, auburn-haired cellist in Long Island. The only lead I had was that besides playing the cello she also taught. How many cello teachers could there be on Long Island? And if I did find her, I wondered, should I warn her that Guido could not really love anyone? To watch out for him? Or would that be professionally unethical? On the other hand, Guido wasn't technically a patient. I was seeing him gratis, as a friend. Wouldn't it have been easier to pressure Guido into introducing us? Saying I wanted very much to meet her, couch it in professional terms— that it would, let's say, make our sessions more realistic and perhaps in that way I could *really* help him, instead of him just getting this whole matter off his chest. Perhaps. But now it was too late. I have a hunch he wouldn't have done it anyway. And in any case, I wanted to do things my way.

I confess, Aviva enthralled me. I felt like a play-goer watching a play where onstage everyone talks about a heroine who hasn't yet appeared but for whom enthusiasm and anticipation is high. But before the first act was done she'd be there for me to see.

Some detective work was needed and I went about my way trying to locate Aviva.

BOOK THREE

Aviva

*A*s she drove home from Guido's house the pain in her stomach returned. It wasn't quite a pain as much as an anguish, an emptiness akin to pain. A vague feeling of loss, of the merry-go-round ring, so close, so close, just missed, as the horse bobbed up and down and cantered away. He once told me, she thinks, or did I jokingly tell him?— I can't remember any more—that I should have kept a diary and called it *Diary of an Adulterous Woman,* although I never did commit adultery, well, maybe just a little bit, but I wasn't married then, and Guido and I have different definitions of adultery. Mine is if I'm married; his is if all four partners know. If they don't, it's just cheating. But the truth is, she thought, she did keep a secret journal hidden in her cello scores (where he'd never find them) that recorded her Arab miseries. Although she didn't keep a diary of her various adventures, her current one with Guido was recorded and re-recorded in her mind so vividly that if she were asked she'd be able, in detail, to write an oral history, her own diary of an adulterous woman tattooed with an *A* that branded her heart with Anguish incessant.

Even now when she was seeing her counselor for help with the stress of this no-win situation with Guido, she could not be absolutely open. She did not, could not, tell all her adventures. And she only revealed a few of the hundreds of questions Guido asked to spur her memory and invade her privacy and awaken old wounds and doubts and mistakes. Still, the counselor listened well and was helping her. Partly. For in the very act of soul-baring anguish is relived.

For years she had wanted to suppress her adventures. Some years back, when life with her present husband had become impossible and he went into a jealous rage every time he saw her putting on lipstick and for no reason called her slut and whore ("You going out? Again?"), when she didn't even so much as look at another man, the venom of those epithets seeped into her. She fell into a depression remembering her past, began to believe that indeed she had been promiscuous. And it was him. All because of him. Her husband. The Arab. Rahamim, his mother had named him. For days she didn't want to get out of bed; she felt the ceiling descending on her. Her chest, a dead weight on it. Only sleep, lots of sleep, relieved her. And he, he didn't sympathize. Finally, a friend, seeing that she was on her way to becoming a vegetable, dragged her to a psychiatrist. But the kindly old Jewish shrink, Dr. Gelbauer, with the pale blue shirt and yellow polka-dot bow tie, to whom she revealed almost all her affairs, concluded that she was seeking only love, not sex, and that she wasn't promiscuous at all, not by today's standards, not by yesterday's. Aviva smiled recalling the old man' face lighting up when he saw her. "I'm eighty-two years, Aviva," Dr. Gelbauer said, his ruddy face almost crimson, "and when I see you my heart still goes pitter-patter."

Hi, I'm Marvin, she's forgotten my last name. I think I was the first, though Aviva sometimes mixes me up with the other guy. I got to know her at the Philadelphia Academy of Musical Arts, or PAMA. Like Aviva I studied cello. We started going out for coffee and then, after a couple of dates, I went up to her small apartment. She was separated then from her husband, and I didn't know till later that she was eight years older than me. I thought she was my age, twenty-one, even younger. We lay naked, the lights were off. She had never seen a, in her words, "you know . . . that!" before. I almost rolled off the bed, hysterical, incredulous. Almost lost it. "No, honest," she swore. "Lemme look at it. What a monolith, and in the moonlight too," she said. She couldn't get over it. "How long you been married?" I asked. "Seven years," she said. "And you never . . . ?" "No," she said, and I suddenly felt sorry for her. For years she thought I was the first one who devirginized her until . . .

She remembered, prompted by Guido's relentless questions.

Hi, my name is Al. Actually, I'm the first. And it happened this way. Only once. But it happened. I'd known Aviva and her husband, Paul, in New York and then found out that she was separated from him and living in Philly. And now, since I was driving cross-country to California, I stopped in to see her. I had no intentions of seducing her. I really wasn't that interested in her, or in sex for that matter. But she was so warm; she gave me such a nice welcome as an old friend, before we knew it we were cuddling on the sofa, kissing, and she was saying to me, "I've never made love before." I thought she was pulling my leg. I asked her, "How come?" and she told me about her husband. I invited her to join me on the cross-country drive. It was June, her semester was over. "Don't you want to make love to me?" she asked. Sure, I said, but I wasn't really that sure. Half an hour later, I was the first to penetrate Aviva, but she wasn't that ecstatic about the lovemaking, perhaps because . . .

Al had such a teeny-weenie weenie, she remembered. Maybe that's why she forgot him and always thought that Marvin with the monolith was the first one. When Al went to Europe for the month of June, Aviva moved to Philadelphia alone to continue her studies at PAMA. He sent her one card from Paris. Toward the end of June he came unannounced to her house.

Must have found out from the school where she lived, she thought. It was a total surprise. Why had he come? She'd given him no encouragement, hadn't flirted with him. Except maybe once, during a party in her house, when she still lived with Paul, when she was a bit high, dancing with Al she told him that she loved him. Now, with her prompting, he kissed her and she felt obliged to make love. No wonder her first screwing was a disappointment. The guy had a mini, and minis had been out of fashion for years. Sex, Aviva concluded, was grossly overrated. All this talk and all this excitement, for what? For this? Over the years the Philly memories became muddled, and she couldn't remember the first real screwing she'd had and was mixed up about the first guy who really laid her.

But sex with Marvin taught her—much later of course—that the old hankering for a big cock was just so much hot air. What's the difference if it's a grand piano or a spinet? A Strad or a rented high school cello? It's the player that counts. But sex wasn't that great with him either. In fact, sex wasn't great with anyone. It had a word-of-mouth reputation, but it was vastly overrated. Even the excitement of dropping Marvin months later for Tim—for years she had thought *he* was the first—also didn't prove to be that thrilling.

Hi, I'm Tim. Another first. I was the token goy at PAMA. I have pale blue eyes, as blue as washed out jeans, blond wavy hair, born in Kentucky, rather tall, maybe gawky, but I try to stand straight to counteract that. I'm Timothy for registration but Tim for everyone else, even Timmy. But she never called me Timmy; I was dying for her to call me Timmy, darling, but she never did. Never. And I have a last name, but by now she's forgotten my family name and remembers me only as Tim. Hell, when word spread she was twenty-nine, no one could believe it. She looked and acted like a kid. But when we found out she was married and experienced, we twenty-one-year-olds thought she was hot stuff. Married for seven years, they said, so she must be a woman of great experience, but I didn't notice any of that, not that I was so experienced myself. She'd been going for a month or two with Marvin, but all is fair in love and war and music, though it did cause some friction between me and Marvin, my roommate. We were in a music theory class together—I play violin, she cello—and we'd go to school concerts. Plenty of musicmaking always at PAMA, and sometimes I'd give them kicks with bluegrass which I'm a whiz at. She was beautiful. She looked haughty before you got to know her, but when you got to know her she was lots of fun, always laughing and joking, even if moody sometimes, but the façade of smugness disappeared quickly once you got to talking to her and her softness surfaced and you realized that haughtiness might be self-protection. And I think she liked me too. She surprised me the first time we went out, for I told her I'd like to hear her play sometime and she said,

"Come up, and I'll play for you", but the "for" soon became "with", and as she played, I felt a drive of pure sex and warmth going through me. I put my hands on her shoulders as she played and stroked her neck. She stopped playing. Carefully, she put the cello down into its case and came up to me. I kissed her, she responded, and I threw my arms around her, then picked her up and brought her to the bed. She pressed up against me, and we undressed and quickly made love, but she didn't scream as I thought she would; she never screamed. But Aviva will remember nothing about my sexuality, or our little affair together. Later, she'll even forget the order of the guys. Like a tape erased I'll be wiped out of her memory, our going to bed together in her apartment. I don't even think she closed her eyes; she hardly moved till I was done. Twice a week, for about two months, I'd go up to her apartment where we would screw, and it was a pleasure because I was twenty-one, and she was twenty-nine, which surprised me, for she looked eighteen. But it was me who later was *really* done, for six weeks later, when I thought I was in love with her, in fact, quite sure I loved her, and assumed she had an emotional bond with me, she abruptly took up with my roommate Marvin whom she knew from classes and saw when she visited me in our apartment. He also played the cello. Maybe it was a game of rivalry, maybe she enjoyed the game, but I had always thought it was a code that a roommate didn't take his roommate's girlfriend. But Marvin did. Or maybe I took her away from Marvin. I forget now. Maybe she dropped me for him because he was Jewish, but with a girl like Aviva you never know, you could never get behind that melting-eyed smile of hers which hid so well that fact that she was a bit cross-eyed, because one day Marvin's turn came too, even though he was Jewish. That didn't save him from Aviva's moods, which changed quickly. I asked her, but she wouldn't go out with me any more, so I stopped talking to her. It was like a light switched off. A bow removed from the strings. I couldn't understand it. I'd been going higher and higher with her, and then I was mercilessly kicked off the cliff. I didn't talk to her for months. She never screamed when we screwed, never asked me if it was good. Never asked me how I felt. Always seemed locked into herself. Not even the screwing unlocked her. But she did say once she liked my mild Kentucky accent. Only once did I spend an evening, or part of an evening with Aviva, one more, final, time.

Hello and greetings, Brothers in Freud, I'm Dr. Max Gelbauer, the old psychiatrist who always wore a yellow polka-dot bow tie with a blue shirt, whom Aviva made catch his breath and gave heart palpitations to listening to the stories she told, and especially looking at her lovely face and feminine form. I'm not very tall. When I sit at my desk you can only see my head. But my arms are long and they go under my desk, across the room to where Aviva sits to touch her lovely breasts.

Hi. I'm the elevator operator in Aviva's apartment in Philly whose name she never got to know. Who knows what stories this elevator, older 'n me, could tell if like, Charlie McCarthy, someone made it talk? I took guys up to Aviva's apartment, and boy did I long to be one of them guys, but I didn't know how to approach her. I always seen these guys carrying violins or big cases I coulda fit into, and I once got the nerve up to ask to hear her play. She says, okay. She's a nice friendly gal. I come in and she closed her eyes and played some heavy stuff for me, but I was too chicken to make a move cause she might laugh at an old guy like me, but when she started playing Happy Birthday, and I asked her for who, she said it was for me, whenever my birthday was, I was so happy I coulda cried.

Hi, my name is Peter. Beat it, you ole spittle dribblin skunk of an elevator operator with the wild leer in your eyes. My leer is clear. What she remembers most about me is my nonstop talking. I admired her gutsiness in talking back to her piano accompanist in my class. We're doing the Opus 114, a reading of the Brahms Trio for piano, cello, clarinet, that really sent me racing after her, why, because I like girls with spunk. But like she said, that ruckus was an anomaly for her. She's never really like that. She's more laid back, heh heh, I liked the image. Another thing she remembers about me is once I took her to New York in my car and we sat under my ex-wife's window and it didn't bother her, she didn't have enough sense to ask herself: What am I doing here? That summed up Aviva. What the hell am I doing here? She wants and she does and there was no rhyme or reason for her deeds. During that PAMA period, Aviva said she felt she was a hunk of meat without brains. I thought her desire would be a match for her mouth. In other words, Fireworks! But I was disappointed. You'd think an experienced woman in her twenties would react to a seasoned lover in his forties. But still when I played clarinet and she the cello, we did make good music together.

So, it wasn't that exciting; still, she thought of that period in her life in Philly as her wild period, her way of showing herself that she was attractive, that men fell for her, that she could play the role of a femme fatale. And after making it with Tim and Marvin for half a semester she was attracted to Peter Hollis, the visiting professor of clarinet whom she joined in occasional trios. Usually meek and complacent, once in the Brahms, while Hollis was listening, the pianist lost his temper and began shouting at her, "Are you blind? You keep playing a C natural." Aviva shouted back, "Keep a civil tongue or find yourself another cellist," a totally uncharacteristic response for her. Peter, a big robust man with booming voice, a guy who could talk a blue streak without pausing for breath, took her aside and told her how much he admired her pluck; how he loved gutsy spunky girls. Within a week she had dropped Marvin, or was it Tim, she couldn't quite remember the order, and was seeing Peter, her first older man. Once her took her to New York; he wanted to see if his ex-wife was entertaining other guys. It was fun sitting there, spying on his ex-wife. She remembered Guido asking her if she'd made love to Peter lots of times. And she said; I don't remember, he was too busy talking. How Hollis loved to hear himself talk. And so Peter was number four. And then she moved to New York during that summer and in late June went to a hotel for a singles weekend her mother had recommended, something she'd never done before, and she met a doctor that Friday night whom she fell in love with after dinner. But he turned out to be like her husband. She tried and tried and nothing. She even spent a weekend with him in Richmond where he lived. Still nothing. She began to think perhaps there was something wrong with her, for the next three boyfriends she had during the next few months were also impotent and she was convinced it was her fault. Something in her made them freeze. She killed something in men. Maybe she was too beautiful and zapped their testosterone. Then she got a one-year scholarship to study at the Florence Conservatory, and there, luckily, she met a man who was crazy about her but whom she didn't particularly like—and they would make love and it was okay. But this affair distressed her more each time until she decided she'd had enough and returned to America half a year sooner than she planned, telling everyone she missed her parents and that's why she came back.

Back in the States, she lived at home again, began dating like a high school girl. Each time she thought she met Mr. Right there were problems. If Jewish, they couldn't make up their minds. If gentile, her mother and relatives put up a fuss. She was getting older month by month and her friends, all married with children, couldn't understand how the beautiful and talented Aviva with the full head of tawny hair couldn't land a suitable husband. Then her mom introduced her to—

Sholom aleichem! Hi, I'm Doctor Gershon Kleingeist, actually Rabbi Doctor Gershon Kleingeist and, although I don't show it, I get annoyed when people drop the "l" from my family name, thereby changing the meaning from "small spirituality," "wit," or "intellect" to "no spirituality," "wit," or "intellect." Of course, people don't call me Rabbi Doctor, ha ha, this isn't Germany, you know, where people are so formal that if you have two doctorates they call you Herr Doktor Doktor—thank God we're in America where everyone is on a first-name basis and people slap you familiarly on the back right away. But some people call me rabbi because I have ordination, some doctor, because I'm a psychologist—I took a ten-week pop psych course, but that's a lot of nonsense because there's no substitute for hands-on training—and some call me a writer because I also write a column on counseling for a religiously oriented, Torah true, Anglo-Jewish Queens weekly—which I'm proud to say has circulation *boruch ha-shem* in Jewish cities all over the Northeast and Miami too. But on the side, just for mitzvah sake, like the Torah commands us, I help eligible young men and women to try to find, God willing, their *basherte*, their destined mates. Aviva's mama arranged that she would come over to my home office. She was already past thirty and not married yet and, naturally, the family was concerned. I was about fifty, maybe fifty-five then, with grey in my beard, but no grey in my heart. When she rang, my wife, she should live and be well, admitted her, showed her to my study, and said good-bye. Then I came in. Aviva was—I'll be honest—beautiful. Like right out of the Book of Ruth. Not only beautiful with those big gray eyes and Biblical smile but, like Potiphar's wife, she seems to say, Take me. I began talking to her. In a fatherly, friendly way, like I usually do, and as I speak to her, I stroke her hands and arms and pat her knees. To reassure her, of course. Because people are nervous, worried if they're making a bad impression, God forbid. And she is very friendly and full of laughs. She sits opposite me on the sofa while I sit on a straight-backed wooden chair, I meet lots of young women for whom with God's help I try to arrange *shidduchim*, matches. Few of my clients ever move me. But this one did. Oh, did this one move me! This one seems to have fallen into my lap. I'm available, the message reads. This one, I knew, wasn't, thank God, religious like the rest of them with their long skirts and long sleeves and faces that would stop even a digital clock and heavy makeup that makes a room smell like a Lancôme factory. This one looked like a wanton, with her sweater bulging and overflowing like the basket of fruits the priests offered up at the Holy Temple in Jerusalem, may it speedily be rebuilt in our days, God willing, Amen! And she wore slacks and beautiful wine-colored boots that came almost up to her knees. Oh, God, a blue heat came over me. A fire of desire she ignited. Just by the way she looked. Like Rachel in the Holy Torah filling Jacob's heart with desire. She sat with legs crossed, swinging one leg. I tried not to look at that swinging leg as she spoke to me, but by the way she moved that leg, I couldn't keep my eyes away from that swinging leg that spoke a language of its own. The sheen of the dark leather dazzled me. I'm available, the boots sang to me. Take me. And I thought, what if I would take that boot and run my hand up her thigh and play with her breasts, she wouldn't say a word, while I was telling her all about the fine young men I would arrange for her God willing to meet, and kiss her and take her right here in this study, ah, if only my wife were not at the other end of the house?

Ticktock, ticktock, her biological clock was ticking away and finally she met the South African whose family had come to Capetown, South Africa, fleeing the pogroms and anti-Semitism in Poland, the man whom Guido had nicknamed Capetown so that in time she forgot his real name and herself referred to him only as Capetown, just as she almost forgot her husband's name because Guido had nicknamed him the Arab and that's what she called him, even when the son-of-a-bitch invaded her dreams. Capetown was a sweet man, not terribly exciting, much older, but how she loved to cuddle with him, not necessarily to have sex with, but just to hold him. But like Hamlet he was indecisive, he couldn't make up his mind. As disorganized as she was, he was neat and orderly. He was so precise, that accountant, she could have sworn he lined up the dollars in his wallet according to serial numbers. For three-and-a-half years, a longer relationship than she'd had with anyone else, they shlepped along, until she finally had to tell him she would have to say good-bye. Still, over the long tortuous years with the Arab, Capetown always wrote to her on her birthday and sent a New Year's card—the only one of her old boyfriends who still kept in touch. And now, some fourteen years after she had last seen him, Capetown flew down from Buffalo, still unmarried, an old man in his late sixties, to hear her concert. The Arab, of course, didn't come. Western music was alien to him—and her accomplishments meant nothing to him. His only reaction to her was a smirk and a nasty comment when Aviva herself criticized her playing out loud. No wonder she fell into depression with his constant put-downs and name-callings. "Whore" and "slut" every time she put on lipstick and rouge. Yes, the old yellow polka-dot bow tie psychiatrist with the ruddy face was right, and she agreed—she was not promiscuous. She sought not sex, but warmth; affection, love, not passion. Perhaps Guido was right too. Her father had been too busy with the cello to give her love. So she sought it later again and again with older men. And perhaps to make up for the seven lukewarm years that began in her early twenties, years that got progressively more difficult, living with her impotent husband. Paul's rage at himself spilled over on her; his impotence turned friendship and fun to anger and disdain. He became sullen and, instead of talking to her, played chess with a computer. She sought all kinds of help—they went to a sex therapist, doctor, psychologists, psychiatrists—and the last one was her downfall. All men are alike. Under the guise of helping him—he suggested splitting the sessions, some with Paul, some with her—the Indian shrink, Sambur Patel, tried to help himself to her.

Hi, I'm Sambur Patel, M.D. I became an expert on riding that thin line between medical ethics and self-interest. Between temptation and satisfaction. Looking at Aviva, any divine would forget immediately the words to "Oh, Lord, lead us not into temptation."

Dr. Patel had private talks with her, kept inviting her back, spoke about music and literature with her. She loved listening to him. At least a man talked to her, considered her a human being. And then once, when she wasn't looking, he came up from behind and kissed her. She was surprised, but she liked it. He began calling her at home, but she wouldn't dare do anything more than kiss him. And he, for professional reasons, didn't dare either. But the fool told his wife and the wife in a jealous rage came, dragging the cigar store Indian along, to her house—and told Aviva's husband, news that devastated the poor guy. Paul began bawling like a baby and stormed out of the apartment and the next day, while walking in town, crossing a small street, she saw a car bearing down on her. By a hair she jumped away and saw the face of the driver—Patel's wife. Boy, what a mess she'd made of her life.

And then that marriage to the Arab. At first, when they met in Israel— passion. Fireworks. What a difference from Capetown's mild lovemaking. She wanted a baby. The clock's ticking would soon slow to a stop. In New York, they married quickly. Maybe he married her for the green card. He'd been moonlighting as a taxi driver and soon took their, that is, her money, money she'd saved over the years from private teaching, and money from her parents, and bought into a taxi and limo company. When she had met him, in Tel Aviv, on a visit, he loved music and art, he said, but hardly discussed it. He knew what year the Arc de Triomphe was begun, 1806, what year completed, 1856. He had odd impressive facts like that, a patina of learning, but it turned out to be a patina over a vacuum. She was fooled. Bamboozled by his dark North African good looks, by how nice he was to her parents before they married, for with these Moroccans honor to older parents in pious good deed. But a wife? A wife you treat like shit. For as soon as they married, on the honeymoon in fact, the Arab changed his face. Like a mask slipped on, or off. Stingy, abusive, mean-tempered. A bastard. A dog. Maybe he sniffed her out. She really wanted a baby—that's why she married him—and that's what he complained about for years. All you want me for is to have a baby for you. But she never admitted it. To fulfill herself, to give her mother the joy of a grandchild. For Aviva was a good girl. Her chubby sister had never married. She moved back to Israel in the vain hope of finding a husband—and the tragedy for her mother was to have two empty children. Then Aviva had one child and, two years later another, hoping that at least the children would bind them, but the Arab didn't seem to care for the kids either, would not even hold them when they were babies, and that alone showed her what an un-mentch, as her mother called him privately, he was.

She was ashamed to tell all this to Guido. To Guido she only said that the Arab insulted her and was impatient with her and the children. If he didn't like a piece of meat, she told Guido, his mood would turn foul, and he would fling it sometimes at her, sometimes across the room. And she asked Guido if he would throw food if he lived with her. "You mean if I didn't like it?" "Yes," she said. "Never . . ." he swore, "never directly at you."

When she was a kid in Tel Aviv, when her dad played cello for the Philharmonic, she used to daydream during classes. In kindergarten, for instance, during the music lesson, she was given a triangle and told when to strike it. But off in a world of her own, riding fuzzy, rabbit-shaped clouds, she kept on banging long after the music had stopped. Teacher said, "Stop! Stop!", but little Aviva did not hear. Teacher assumed Aviva was being naughty. Teacher scolded her and wrote a little note home. Teacher's yelling "Stop! Stop!" and her mother's reprimands upset her. She had to be a good girl, Mama said. A good girl, do you hear? You mustn't shame the family. Ever. In kindergarten, she was renamed Aviva, for the teacher had said that her real name was no name for a child in an Israeli kindergarten. Children would make fun of her. Of course, they didn't know that Aviva's father, in love with Vivaldi, had named her Vivalda. Thank God he wasn't influenced by Bach! Imagine being called Bachiana? Or Claviera?

She tried in her own way to be a good girl. To not shame the family. She did not use her recognizable maiden name, Andermann, when she went to PAMA, but registered under her mother's maiden name, Prinsky. And when she went wild with the boys, the Andermann name was not sullied. Did so many name changes have any effect on her personality? she wondered. Now her mother wanted her married again. After all, she was almost thirty-three. Aviva herself wasn't particularly in a rush, but let herself be persuaded to meet other men. Her mother read all kinds of English-Jewish newspapers whose ideology she didn't agree with but liked for their personal and social ads, so, through a common acquaintance, her mother introduced Aviva to a man, a *shadchen*, an informal marriage broker, who ran an introduction service and also wrote a column on counseling and psychological issues for an orthodox Anglo-Jewish paper in Queens jokingly called *The Jewish Stress* for its gloomy tallis-blue-headlined accent on problems Jews had all over the world. It had two mottos: "Bad news for good Jews" and "All the news that (gives 'em) fits, we print." Why her Mama had hooked up with an orthodox Jew, maybe even a rabbi, when her family was not at all observant she could never understand. Maybe her mother felt that a religious Jew would make a good husband. They were honest, loyal, family-oriented, treated their wives with respect, and most of all, kept their hands to themselves. But on the other hand, why should, why would, an orthodox Jew choose her? She'd never be able to present him and his family with blood-stained virginal nuptial sheets, and she had no intention of having nine children. When Aviva came to Mr. Kleingeist's house (sure enough the brass nameplate on the door said, Rabbi Dr. Kleingeist, Gershon) the door was opened by a woman so beautiful that if Aviva had been a man she would have locked the husband up in a closet and gone into the kitchen to court the wife. The woman said a brief hello, led Aviva into a booklined study and, like a good religious housewife, never again showed her face. The marriage-broker, the *shadchen*, was a big, burly man with a brown beard streaked with grey. He wore a large black velvet yarmulke, which during the conversation he kept lifting up and replacing and stroking his hair. She could tell he was very tactile. He loved to touch. Himself. Others. She didn't know it then, but now, thinking about it, she remembered what Dr. Gelbauer had said: a man's gestures give him away. She should have sensed that with Kleingeist from the beginning, that sensuous way he kept lifting his yarmulke and stroking his lush brown wavy hair and teasing his beard. And every other word was "thank God" and "Torah true" and "boruch ha-shem," "God forbid," and "God willing." When he came in to the room, Aviva, flustered, said, "Hello, Mister Keingeist." And he, shaking her hand and then clasping his left hand too over her fingers, said, "That's Kleingeist, with an *L*. But that's all right. You don't have to call me either Doctor, or Rabbi, or Mister. Call me Gershon. Please?" She wanted to know if he was a physician or a Ph.D. "No," he laughed, again taking her hand into his clasped ten fingers, "I'm not a doctor a doctor, God forbid, but a doctor a . . ." And it sounded as if he said Ph.D., but just before the *P* he ran his hand over his mouth as if to cover a cough. Later, she learned why. He did not have a Ph.D. but a doctorate in theology, conning a small mid-western Catholic school—delighted to have its token resident Jew—into accepting all his years of Talmud at yeshiva where they scorned secular learning, considered it a sin against God, as full-fledged graduate credit. So, then, with a cough, a throat rumble and five fingers over the mouth, the Th.D could easily sound like Ph.D. After that welcoming sandwich hand-shake, Kleingeist pulled a plain wooden chair opposite the sofa where he told her to have a seat and began chatting. As Rabbi Doctor Kleingeist asked Aviva questions about what type of men she liked because, God willing, he'd be able to help her, she saw him gazing at her crossed legs. To accent his points, Kleingeist occasionally touched her hands, which were clasped on her knees. She wore slacks, she remembered, and high leather boots which were in fashion then. Seeing the long skirt of Mrs. Kleingeist, she felt a pang of embarrassment. Her mother should have warned her. She should have worn a skirt coming to the house of an orthodox Jew. And she apologized. "No, no," he laughed and patted her knee. "This isn't a yeshiva here, God forbid, and we're not the Board of Rabbis. Actually, many American Jews *are* bored of rabbis. I myself, *boruch hashem*, which means blessed be God, or thank the good Lord, personally have a very liberal outlook which my training in psychology offers me. You're dressed very nicely. Very nicely. You have good, may I say, excellent taste in clothing. I admire that. And these boots! Gucci? Stunning." And he ran a finger over the leather, saying how much he loved fine soft leather and well-crafted boots. "If I wouldn't have become a doctor of counseling and, as part of my calling, help to match young men and women, God willing, to find their life partners and a writer of columns, I would have become a leather craftsman. I love the smell of leather." And he sniffed deeply. "Ahh!" In his nonstop talk she didn't even realize that he had picked up her booted foot and had it on the edge of his chair like a shoe salesman and was stroking the soft leather in obvious admiration, then pulled his chair closer so that the sole of the boot was between his legs. When she saw what he was doing she asked, "What are you doing?" and he said, "Don't worry, it's relaxing." For whom? She wondered. Me it's making nervous, but she was too disoriented to complain. "Relaxing for you and for me too the way a foot slips into a boot so comfortable few people realize the pleasure" and he moved the edge of her boot onto his lap until it pressed into his crotch. She wondered if next he would slip off the boot and run his hands over her bare leg and massage her toes and then press her toes into his crotch. God, maybe he'll even zip down. All this for one lousy fixup. Her mother! God bless her! What had she gotten her into again? She told the rabbi doctor to stop, but not very loudly because she didn't want to embarrass him before his wife, nor did she withdraw her foot demurely or wrench it away in anger or kick him in the balls the way she might have done had this happened to her now. And who would they believe if she created a scene— the bearded rabbi or the woman in sinful slacks and lascivious high boots like the hookers who paraded on New York's Eighth Avenue?

When she told Guido what happened, he couldn't believe that this orthodox Jew was playing a game like that; but Guido was even more incredulous that she permitted the rabbi to do that. She tried to explain that listening to Kleingeist's questions about what kind of guy he should fix her up with and how a prospective candidate would be delighted with her company because, thank God, she was so smart and pretty and personable and what his track record was, she'd just floated off to some dreamworld and simply wasn't paying attention to what he was doing. And he had such a mellifluous, even mesmerizing voice, low-pitched, sonorous, smooth, musical. And she even remembered telling Guido that the *shadchen* was an attractive man. "At sixty? With a beard? Attractive? What kind of taste do you have?" "Eclectic!" She gave her naughty laugh, adding, "And I liked those soft burgundy boots." "And God be praised the pious saint loved them even more." "I guess," Aviva allowed. "As the rabbi stroked the boot, did the leather become hard?" Guido asked. "No, but he did." "Really?" "No, I'm joking . . . I don't know . . . What did he want with me? He had such a gorgeous wife." "He probably did that to all the naïve girls who came to him," Guido said, "raking off prenuptial commission, a Jewish *droit de signeur.*" "You know, I saw that weekly newsrag the other day in a store," Aviva said, "and for the fun of it, I opened it up. Guess what? It's more than twenty years and that clown is still there, with the beard, exuding Jewish holiness. He's still writing his column and the picture hasn't changed."

I shouldn't have told Guido that story, she remembered thinking, and made little sewing motions near her lips, imitating her mother who would also press her lips shut and sew them up when she felt she had spoken too much. As usual, she told the story in stages. First, she told Guido about the *shadchen*. Another time, Guido asked for more details, and she told him he was a very nice man, very helpful, concerned. A third time, she told him he got friendly. That was her undoing. How friendly? Why friendly? *Where* friendly? Be specific friendly, Guido insisted. And that's when the cat came out of the bag and, in Guido's imagination, the foot out of the boot. "I'll bet he was stroking your bare instep, that lecherous monotheist, that God-loving erotomaniac, that pious pervert, praying . . . preying on innocent maidenheads. I'll bet he had the door locked hoping he could screw you." "He did not," Aviva said. "And anyway, he had a beautiful wife." "Since when does that stop a lecher?" Guido said and Aviva gave him one of those quizzical, over-the-glasses looks that said: Gotcha! "You've just put your foot in your mouth—with my boot in it."

But there was one thing she did not tell Guido, seeing how upset he was at the rabbi qua charlatan. And it didn't do much to lessen her antipathy to religious fakers either. When she left the house, Mrs. Kleingeist came to bid her farewell. Aviva shook her hand and then stretched out her hand to say good-bye to the rabbi *shadchen* as well. But quick as a mousetrap he snapped his hands behind his back, and just as quickly his wife explained. "You'll have to forgive him, but religious Jews do not shake hands with women." "Just feet," Aviva purred. But the Mrs. didn't understand it, and the rabbi pretended not to. Guido might have been proud of her retort, but it wasn't worth telling him about that hypocrite's duplicity.

Of course, she never told her mother about the liberties that this man of God took. She never told her anything. With her, she followed her mother's advice and sewed her lips. Only after her divorce were those feelings of constraint and imprisonment unshackled. For the first time a sense of freedom. As a child, as an adolescent, even up to her first marriage, when she was a baby within, although she looked like a young woman without, her mother had kept her under close rein. "I was a baby even during my first marriage," she remembered telling Guido. "And that's why I was ashamed to tell her during the first three years that nothing had happened, that my husband was impotent.♥

♥See ABC Directory, *Impotent men, differences between.*

She remembered what a brilliant insight her little old psychiatrist had, that lovable man. Dr. Gelbauer barely came over the desk even though he sat on two pillows. His finely sculpted head, like the drivers one sees in Florida, noses just barely over the steering wheel, was all she saw. And, of course, that yellow polka-dot bow tie. He pointed out that when her mother told her to sew her lips, she unconsciously meant her other lips. "That's why," Gelbauer said, "she told you to stick it out, when you told her about Paul. It all clicks now: She may have wanted you to stay a little girl a bit longer, her good little girl. You know what Freud said in his famous study of Dora?" And this eighty-two-year-old doctor with the ruddy face, white hair, and yellow polka-dot bow tie quoted from memory:

"No mortal can keep a secret, said Freud. If his lips are silent, he chatters with his fingertips. Betrayal oozes out of every pore. That innocent gesture of your mother's, telling you to be quiet, to sew your lips, was a kind of otherspeaking to keep you a good little girl."

Boy, was he wise, a dear, adorable man. He was probably in love with her too. When Guido asked if she ever thought she was the bad girl her mom didn't want her to be, or that she wasn't a good girl any more, she replied, maybe. And when you had your affairs in Philly, did you think to yourself, I'm like all the other girls now? No, she was not delighted, she said, not pleased with herself. She was confused. Felt lost. Didn't know what she wanted. "Sad, right? I had the talent and the looks and I didn't know what to do. I didn't know what I wanted or needed to make me happy. Of course, my father, who was a cellist, urged me to continue with the cello. Did you ever hear of Gideon Andermann?"

"I think I've run across the name."

"My father was my first teacher. He started me with a small cello, for which I didn't have to spread my legs a lot for." She laughed. "When I was about six or seven, they moved here from Palestine just before the war broke out in Europe. My mother had her entire family here, three brothers and sisters, and she noodged and noodged until my father reluctantly agreed. It was very hard for him to leave the Palestine Philharmonic. After all, he was the principal cellist, one of the charter members, and he helped his friend Bronislaw Huberman found the orchestra. The separation from Huberman was probably the most difficult aspect. They grew up together in Germany, went to the same schools, and fled Nazi Germany and came to Tel Aviv at the same time. My father felt he was betraying his best friend. But he also had health problems and the hot damp climate in Tel Aviv was very hard for him. In fact, soon after coming to New York he had the first of a series of debilitating heart attacks, and he couldn't take the strain of traveling and rehearsing. So he made his living teaching privately. But he still had a formidable reputation."

"And you never capitalized on his name," Guido said.

"No. Never. Uh-uh. Stubborn. I was Aviva. In Israel nobody called me by my original name.♥ Aviva sounded better. Aviva Prinsky. Wanted to make it on my own. In fact, I forbade him—I was too proud—forbade him to use his name in connection with mine. He wanted so much for me to succeed, poor daddy. He wanted me to be like him, maybe even outshine him. But I couldn't do it."

"You mean Plaskow never knew whose daughter you were?"

"Never."

"Naïve."

"Always, In every way. Naïve professionally. Naïve with men . . . Scared . . . A good girl." She laughed sadly.

"And a good girl even during marriage?"

"Yes." Aviva laughed again. "Always a good girl. Seven years of virginous marriage."

"No sex?"

"The ultimate definition of a good girl . . . For seven long years a very good girl . . . A professional virgin.♥♥ . . . No sex."

"Did you know what a hard-on was?"

"Not personally."

Guido leaned back and laughed. She didn't mean it to be funny, but in retrospect, she guessed it was.

Would she choose any of the guys from the past if she had a choice? Guido wanted to know.

Aviva said no. My God, she'd never inventoried them, like Guido. By name, profession, succession. It took Guido to come along to do it. Quite an impressive list, she thought, laughing to herself. But she didn't make strong attachments at that time. Bouncing from one guy to another. Perhaps that was a minus in her personality then. She knew she was inconsistent. Her yearnings went up and down. It came with her moods, her state of well being, if she was tired or not.

And then, after those seven years of slavery, came freedom. Guido's words. It *was* freedom—but a prisony kind. At PAMA, away from home and husband for the first time, she wasn't concerned about respectability. In Philly, she didn't give a damn what people thought of her. In Philly, she did what she pleased. Years earlier she wouldn't have taken up with someone she wanted. Because mother, critical mama, always said it wasn't right. Wasn't proper. She remembered Mama once asking her after a date, "Did you kiss him?" And when Aviva said Yes, mother said: "Ekh! How can you kiss a guy like that?" Her mother's remark made her feel cheap. Mother was always so critical.

♥See ABC Directory, *Palindrome.*
♥♥See ABC Directory, *Virgin, professional.*

It wasn't until way after her first marriage, when she was in her late twenties, that she discovered desire. With Paul there was no desire. Ever. Not even a hint of it. Early twenties, mid-twenties, late twenties, she was still a little girl, the good little girl her mommy wanted her to remain, lips properly sewn. No wonder, she now realized, she wore bobby sox and skirts like a high school girl. Did she tell Dr. Gelbauer this?, she wondered. She and Paul would kiss, but that was all. He never ran his hand over her body. Since she was never fired up, she didn't miss sex. Not for years. During the first night with her husband, she recalls, she wore a beautiful nightgown, which she had kept for years, in fact still owned and wore during the nights she slept alone in her room and thoughts of Guido filled her mind so completely when he took lessons with her she could think of nothing else and her loins actually ached out of desire for him. It cost $49 then, that beautiful nightgown, more than thirty years ago, and her mother got it for her. Only a mother would go and buy something like that for her daughter. But nothing happened. Not on the wedding night, nor for countless nights thereafter. Aviva thought: well, maybe the first night, you know, wedding night syndrome, he's nervous, afraid. But then nothing on the second, fourth, seventh or seventy-seventh night. She was too shy to talk about it: she had no experience, was ashamed to tell her mother. And so it went, for three years. The parents would think it was cute when Paul and she came to visit in Queens, and they would wrestle on the floor like little puppies. That should have been a sign to the parents that it was a substitute for sex, but her mother wasn't that sophisticated. And Father was out of it. Always practicing. Not like me, she laughed. A year later, to Aviva's surprise, her mother's attitude changed. This is no life, she said, completely out of character. Separate for a while. Aviva tried it, but she really didn't want to leave Paul,♥ for she felt comfortable with him. The question was (Guido's, in fact), did he feel comfortable with her? Absolutely not. He thought of her as his albatross. She was the living proof of his incompetence as a man.

So desire for her became not an affair for two, but an affair for one. When alone her desire surged. In company she always felt tense. Am I doing something stupid? Saying something wrong? Am I too fat? Do they notice my cross-eyes? So how could she think of desire? She became hyperself-critical, she recalled. And no wonder. Everyone around her was critical. Especially her mother. When she was twelve, her mother would say, "You still can't do that Bach piece? Your friend, Beatrice, is only ten and she breezes through it." But her father would only softly say, "Very nice, try it again."

When she told Guido that she didn't always have desire, he wanted to know how a woman could spread her legs♥♥ without desire. She shrugged.

♥See ABC Directory, *Curse, her first husband's.*
♥♥See ABC Directory, *Legs spreading.*

She didn't tell him, but she knew there could be hundreds of reasons. Curiosity. Involvement with a man. Wanting to experiment. To see their reactions. To learn technique. To build confidence. But she didn't say it lest he think she was promiscuous. She wasn't, though, never had been. Even Dr. Gelbauer reassured her on that. She wasn't like that. She was a good girl. She never remembered needing it or looking forward to it. Only maybe later on in life. Hungering for it with him. Dreaming about it. Imagining it. With Guido. With him everything was easy. But in the past, why couldn't she relate well to men? she wondered. Every little thing upset her. If she found something disturbing, she would drop the relationship, even after two dates. But to them she would never verbalize or express her feelings. She couldn't put them into words. Flaws were endless. Her impatience swift.

She tried to analyze how she had changed, how she'd remained the same. At seventeen, she was stiff, rigid, unapproachable. She also had a rigid state of mind. But soon she discovered her magic button. And went at it every night. The old story had it that if you masturbated you'd go blind. But she saw quite well, thank you. And, anyway, that old wives tale pertained to boys, not girls. None of her organs were affected, thank God, at least not the important ones, except as she got older, the hearing in her left ear became fuzzy. But then again, Beethoven went deaf too, and he didn't masturbate. Even at seventeen, though she pressed her magic button nightly, she had no desire for a man. The thought alone embarrassed her. It was an immoral act. Even if a man would want to go to bed with her, she imagined he would find her disgusting and that was the greatest deterrent against sex. She'd only learned a year earlier, at sixteen, that men had erections. When she went on a date, which was rare, and the boy tried, surreptitiously, of course, to put, as boys are wont to do, his hand on her breast, she felt tense, and worse— mortified. She wouldn't see that boy again. Later, she remembered seeing plays, opera buffa, where the rich, old, impotent husband's young wife always ran around with men. They needed it, she thought, I don't. And when during the sixth year of her marriage she told a psychologist the story of her incapable husband and he asked her, "Weren't you angry with him? Didn't you want to wring his neck?" she remembered saying, "I felt badly for him. I understood him. It wasn't his fault." And the dope of a psychologist replied, "Wait a minute. You're not supposed to say that. I am. You're supposed to be mad as hell, and wonder what you should have done. I, the psychologist, I'm the one who's supposed to be understanding." "But you're not," she said. "You're not at all. Why should my husband and I have an antagonistic relationship? I like him." "Are you happy?" the psychologist asked her. "I'm content," she said. "Cows are contented," the fool replied. The insensitive bastard. Men, ugh, they're all alike.

And after a while she never even hugged or kissed Paul because she knew that it wouldn't lead anywhere. So gradually these displays of affection ceased. Every time he saw her she was physical evidence of his failure. At some level of consciousness he hated me, she thought, even though she realized it was absurd. And during that period she certainly didn't touch herself. There was no point to it.

Later on, after the divorce, when she got involved several times, it was like setting up a lab. She was intrigued with the idea of the male organ and passion. What it's like, how long it takes to happen, and how it transforms the man. She also wanted to know how they felt about her. Her flaw was that she was curious about other people's attachments—in both senses of the word, she suddenly realized with a laugh—while she herself remained unattached. She didn't share their experience. That's why, she now understood, she remained unmarried for so long. Until she forced herself. Tick, tock.

Of course, after nearly three decades of celibacy, traditional wisdom would aver that the first screwing should be a major event, with trumpet fanfares. And Guido, ever curious, kept wanting to know the circumstances. Shouldn't she recall the first time she got laid after seven years of nothing? She supposed she should, she told Guido, but she can't remember being in bed with any of them. What do you mean any of them? Guido pressed. That was her first mistake, that stupid phrase. That opened the door. Her mother with the lip-sewing motion, how right she was. How right she was, in retrospect, about so many things. Well, Aviva was now obliged to say there were three affairs during that period. I'm not particularly proud of that era in my life. It's not the real me. "Why do I block it out?" she said. "Maybe because of my strict upbringing—I was taught to be so modest, demure. Good girls don't do that." "And when you switched guys?" he asked. "When you went from one man to another?" "That was pretty awful, right?" she said guiltily. "Was it because you were angry at Tim for some reason that you dropped him?" "No," she said, "it was at a party and I sort of began talking—I forget his name now, it will come to me." "Was it hot pants, sex, that made you want another guy?" "No. I don't know. Maybe curiosity. Can you blame me? I was twenty-eight or twenty-nine. Maybe I wanted to play the role of the femme fatale. In Philadelphia, no less! City of Brotherly Love. You know, love your fellow man, says the Bible." "And do you remember thinking how good it is to be with a different man?" "Maybe at the time I did. I just don't remember. You can't help but feel or think that, but I just can't recall." "Did Tim and this other guy know each other?" "They were roommates," she said, smiling down at the floor. He slapped his forehead in dismay, Aviva remembered. But she hadn't been aroused. She just did it. She didn't look forward to it at all. Even the first real encounter with a fellow student wasn't that great. Why she continued she didn't know. Perhaps hope. Hope that it would improve. But with the second or third it was the same. She felt removed, aloof, detached. Distant. It wasn't until after she'd come back from half a year in Italy that she got more of a sense of herself.

What did it?

A suggestion from a friend to use a vibrator.♥ At first she said, "Yek. Ugh." Was disgusted. Nice girls don't do that. But her girlfriend, who could have been sarcastic and said, "Yea, they just use their fingers," spoke gently with her, told her to try it, it would help her become more sexually aware. And her pal was absolutely right. In the vibrator she'd found a friend. One who would never lie to her, cheat on her, compromise her, betray her, let her down. Or knock her up.

I n Philly she was queen. Like moths around a light guys sniffed her out. Once a dean whom she had met briefly at a party popped in on her unannounced, hoping for a tidbit. When she was cool to this intruder, he, embarrassed, said he needed a score. The unintentional pun did not escape her. And once, riding on a train to New York to visit her parents—at this time, Aviva was smoking for a while, in keeping with her femme fatale image—a guy picked her up. How? By asking for a cigarette. But he evidently hadn't smoked before because at once he began coughing his lungs out. But he was a nice guy (as were most guys), and she saw him in New York. He was a grad student in art history, and just as he liked paintings, Aviva had the feeling that he collected beautiful faces. He thought she was the most beautiful girl he'd ever seen. But she didn't have any strong feelings for him. Rafe, yes, that was his name. And he never made any moves. No sparks at all. That's what gave her the feeling that she was just another work of art for his collection. And had he made a move, she imagined Guido asking, would she have gone to bed with him? She couldn't answer that. Couldn't explain why she screwed X and not Y. There was something contradictory in me, she had once told Guido. Only years later, in thinking about it, did she suspect that Rafe might have been gay.

A nd could there be any recall of Philly and PAMA without Ian Plaskow. She wouldn't have thought about him at all if Guido wouldn't constantly be bugging her about him. Here was another instance where she should have listened to her mother and sewn sealed locked her lips positively tight. She should never even have mentioned his name. But no, in the hundreds, maybe thousands, of intrusive, invasive, skin and soul stripping questions that Guido asked—yes, she enjoyed being interviewed, being put on the catbird seat, even though it was uncomfortable at times; it made her feel

♥See ABC Directory, *Vibrator, when first used.*

heroic, like a heroine in a grand play she'd participated in long ago; like holding a press conference—he constantly came back to Ian, perhaps because Guido had photographed him and Casals. Guido felt he knew him and since Ian Plaskow knew her, it bound them together in some screwy triangle. But nothing happened with him, she assured Guido. Nothing. Plaskow had been her teacher for more than two years, and she never considered him anything more than a teacher.

Then a subtle change took place. It happened when she was living in New York during that third year of hers at PAMA and coming to Philly for twice-a-week lessons. She clearly remembered the day, even though for other things, even important events, her memory often failed her. It was an afternoon, in mid-November. The sun was setting, around 4:45. She had just walked through the imposing main hall of PAMA and peeked into the auditorium to see if some activity, rehearsal, class, was taking place there. The auditorium had fake marble pillars on either side of the stage. It was empty but a cello case rested smack in the middle of the stage. She imagined an incredible event. What a stir it would cause if the cello case would stand up, open up its door, and out would march the instrument. She continued down the hall, stopped at the bulletin board where announcements for Position Available and Instruments for Sale were posted. She read a personal note. It wasn't something she would ordinarily have remembered, but she recalled this one not so much for its unique message but for the reaction that the generally impassive Plaskow had to it.

Bob: Why don't you return my bow? Sally.

To which a red pen, perhaps the hand of Bob, maybe not, responded: 1) First of all, you never lent it to me, 2) I didn't think I had to return that broken old saw, and 3) I returned it last week.

With that bit of good cheer bubbling in her, Aviva entered Mr. Plaskow's studio, a big smile on her lips. She told him the story. He laughed and said it sounded like a variant of an old Yiddish joke. Although she knew that Plaskow was Jewish, he had never once in two-and-a-half years made any reference, oblique or direct, pertaining to anything Jewish. Not wishes for the Jewish New Year, not happy Passover, and never even an inquiry as to the meaning of her obviously Hebrew name and how and where she got it.

The golden red sun cast a strange light into the room, and she would remember that light on subsequent afternoons in his studio. That eerie, fleeting, roseate light seemed to cast a spell on the studio, for even the conversation she had with Plaskow after the lesson was unusual. He said: "Did you ever notice how much the cello resembles the shape of a woman?" And said nothing more. Could that question of his have been the overture to his subtle courtship? Aviva didn't remember her response. Didn't recall if she said yes or no. Didn't even know if she smiled prettily.

Next time he said, again casually. "Remember what I said last time about the shape of the cello?" Of course she remembered. She remembered thinking that she had a better shape. And Plaskow added: "Isn't it interesting that besides the womanly shape of the cello, how many parts are named after the woman's body? Ear, neck, fingerboard, belly, back, body. The waist is obvious, no?" Aviva had known that. So what else is new? She wasn't struck by the parallels. And Plaskow surely knew he wasn't giving her information she hadn't known. What did strike her as remarkable was that this basically quiet and serious man, whom she still addressed as Mr. Plaskow, should suddenly bring this up, accent the woman's angle, when he had never even hinted at it before. The only parallel he omitted was the tailpiece. Not that he left it out altogether. But when he got to the southern tip of the cello he just smiled a vague smile. And there was another part she would have been embarrassed to call by name to anyone, even someone close. The f-hole, which every cello had two of. And every woman, one. The third time they met for a lesson another extraordinary thing occurred: he demonstrated on his own instrument. It usually stood in the studio but he never played it. He would use his voice, his arms, gestures, to teach and coach. Only on occasion would he take a student's cello and play a phrase or two. But he rarely demonstrated. This time, however, as soon as the lesson began—Aviva was practicing the opening theme of Tchaikovsky's *Variations on a Rococco Theme*—Plaskow brought his beautiful cello to his chair and held it. A couple of times he put his bow to the strings and teased a few bars.

Was this another beginning to a courtship?

She doesn't recall what she was wearing during the lesson. It was warm in the studio; the radiators working. Perhaps she wore slacks and a short-sleeved sweater. Although she was always cold, the studio was always on the warm side, especially in late autumn and winter. The mid-November sun was setting. The lights weren't on yet. The red sun cast a magic dusk into the room, which seemed to be transported into a Matisse painting. The deep amber color of Plaskow's cello was heightened by the direct sunlight. His instrument gleamed. Was this his Strad? Aviva wanted to get up and watch the sunset; she had a longing to get up and see that red sun setting. But she sat and played. Close of day was always a special time for her. Even back in all-day kindergarten in Israel. A mood of intimacy, closeness enveloped her. The lights weren't on yet, and the daylight—you could just touch its last drops of light. During music lesson she plays the triangle, sails into her own special world. Stop, says teacher. Stop, stop. She was tired. The lush sounds of the *Variations* moved her. It was at this point that Ian Plaskow decided to join her. He played the opening movement with her, note for note. The sound, instead of seeming doubled, was cubed—as if four cellos were playing.

Was it her imagination, her now excited imagination, that saw him embrace his cello in a special way? (All of sudden, she noted, she was referring to him as "him," and not as Mr. Plaskow.) He had never played along with her before. Now her playing sounded better. It reminded her of the time she spent in Tanglewood, two summers earlier, on a scholarship. One of the Boston Symphony Orchestra cellists joined the quartet of student musicians studying Mozart's "Hunting" Quartet. Suddenly, with the infusion of the talented cellist, the four students were lifted up musically, and perhaps even spiritually. What would Plaskow say next, Aviva wondered? Would you like to play with me? Or: May I play with you?

Instead, he said, "Let's do the Bach now," and the light in the room, instead of getting brighter, darkened by two degrees. They played the Cello Sonata no. 1 together, slowly, exchanging glances for tempo and dynamics. Plaskow nodded, pleased. When they finished Aviva gave a little sigh, the only expression of the tension and joy she was feeling.

"Playing together," Plaskow said, paused, and continued, "somehow elevates both players. It's one of the magics of music." If Plaskow intended flirtation, the lackmusic of his words stripped it dry. But still Aviva found it thrilling. Playing together. Until now she had thought of him as a teacher. Up there. Removed. Mr. Plaskow. It never even crossed her mind to imagine what he thought of her, how he regarded her. She never primped, dressed for him, stood before the mirror wondering how she would look. He was a teacher of neuter denomination. Never a fantasy about him as a man, even though she knew that Plaskow was an attractive man. And now a vague strum of excitement ran through her. The reverberation of his cello still echoed. "Playing together." Is this what she'd been wanting to hear for months? Years?

They walked to the elevator together. Was it hot and stuffy in that enclosed slowly moving room, or was excitement opening up her sweat glands?

"It'd be nice," she said, looking not at him but at the elevator button panel, "if you could press a magic button and get an iced tea."

Plaskow laughed. Oh, my God! She blushed, wanted to disappear. Magic button! He must see right through me now. Why do I always make a fool of myself? But he evidently hadn't noticed her discomfort or connected the phrase with any other meaning. Only later did she realize that his laughter was not directed at her remark but at the story he was about to tell. The first time in three years that he had ever told her a personal reminiscence.

"This happened at the Hollywood Bowl," he said, "when I was rehearsing the Schumann with the L.A. Philharmonic. I'll tell you who conducted in a moment; it has a bearing on the story. It was hot. Sweltering. They had put up huge fans on both sides of the stage; you know those specially made silent ones that don't interfere at all with the music? The conductor is giving some instructions to the winds. Suddenly an attendant comes running on stage to the conductor with a pitcher of iced tea and a glass . . . 'Who asked for that?' says the conductor. 'You said open up the iced tea,' says the attendant. The conductor held the podium guard rails, threw his head back, and roared: I said, 'Open up the high C.' It was Zubin Mehta and his accent fooled the attendant, whom all the musicians applauded."

Aviva laughed, laughed harder perhaps than the story warranted. She was so glad to have extricated herself from the elevator and the magic button mortification.

"Playing together was fun," Plaskow added. "Do you know, every time you play you reveal yourself to me?"

Again that phrase. Hardly had she had a chance to digest this new phrase, when Plaskow stopped outside on the steps of PAMA (although she had to go badly to the ladies room, the momentum of Plaskow's walk swept her along with him) and announced—first she heard the words bouncing off his cello case, for he sort of addressed the words down to his instrument, not up at her, "I have to be in New York next week," then in mid-phrase, he turned, lifted his chin, "shall we have dinner together?"

What he did *not* say struck her: Would you like to have dinner with me? Instead, he delivered the rather imperious, superconfident question that left almost no room for a negative response. What should she, what could she, have said to such a declaration, borderline question, borderline summons? No?

It was also at this time, when the November sun was setting through the studio window, that he told her something offbeat. In response to her casual remark that she was looking for a carpet, he said he had a carpet for her. But he lifted a finger as if to indicate he'd discuss it later. Now it was later, but she was so overwhelmed, excited, confused by the turn of events that she completely forgot about the carpet.

"Yes," she said. "That would be very nice."

On her way to the elevator to her New York apartment, Aviva remembers a moment. It's near the end of dinner. Plaskow scans the dessert menu and looks at the goodies on the dessert cart. Aviva either takes or doesn't take a deep breath, taps his hand, wonders if it should linger there a moment, then says, "Let's skip dessert," she's about to say, "Let's go up to my place for coffee," when Plaskow looks at her and there's a moment of warm understanding, as if she's already said what she's afraid to say, and says instead, "Let's walk." And during the walk, heading toward her building, either she says, "Like to come up for coffee?" Or he says: "How about coffee at your place?" She doesn't remember. The gaps in her memory would fill a Bloomingdale's bag. And she still hadn't called him by name, despite salad, appetizer, soup, main course, and a glass or two of wine.

Both knew that "coffee" was just a face-saving device. Because being as shy as she was, even if aroused, she could not simply say, "Let's go up to my place," without adding "coffee" to save face, as if face could be saved, like money, and banked. But as she goes over the scene in her mind, Aviva wonders if that moment of no return had already taken place a week earlier at PAMA when Plaskow announced dinner in New York with that slight uptick interrogatory to a basically declarative remark.

Aviva presses the 7 button in the elevator. Over the years she had no special desire for Plaskow. She didn't dream or fantasize about him or take him to bed in her thoughts as she had Guido during the weeks when he was her student, when in her room her blood surged with thoughts of him as she wore the expensive honeymoon nightgown in her room alone that her mother had gotten for her three decades ago, and Guido traversed every capillary, a miniaturized man in her overheated bloodstream, and she in her wild desire and love for him ran her lips over every inch of his body. It was not the same with Plaskow. Then she wasn't even capable of love or arousal. And the desire of which she was capable was always stronger in imagination. She was more aroused in her room, by herself, without even touching her magic button, than she was with a man. No desire had she at all for Ian Plaskow, and though she enjoyed the lessons with him during the past two-and-a-half years, she forgot about him as soon as the lesson was over.

But now, in the elevator—in an elevator with him again—he standing next to her, and the interminably slow ride and filler conversation (why is the ceiling of elevators so fascinating? she thought) ("You notice," Plaskow said, "how people in elevators always look everywhere but at each other?"), she wondered if desire had been building up over the years and if each of the meetings and conversations and lessons could have been a building block to the desire—if indeed it *was* desire; maybe she *wanted* it to be desire—welling in her. Oh, that interminably slow elevator. There must be a tired old man downstairs—probably the old man from my Philly apartment—operating it manually with a handpulled rope. But then, for a moment, she felt neutral again. Maybe he wouldn't even like her. Maybe he just considers her a toy to play with and discard. What was she doing with this married man? Another aimless encounter which would bring her no closer to fulfillment. And she suddenly felt empty and regretted that she had brought him up. Her skin bristled as she regarded the man standing next to her, and she hoped that he would put his hand on hers, just touch her shoulder or her hair, or even put his hand around her waist, or simply take her hand, to drive these sad, negative thoughts away and bring back the desire. But he stood there looking up at the ceiling of the elevator as if it were the most important thing in the world, as if it contained all knowledge, all music, all secrets and mysteries, and she hoped this slowboat of an elevator would soon, come on already, get to its destination, for the ride was making her feel creepy. That's it. She would make coffee, then say she was tired and send him on his way.

She pressed the magic 7 button again, as if by pressing it she could make this old machine take off like a plane or perhaps serve iced tea, and wondered what had taken Plaskow so long. These past two academic years, and now three months into the third, she had sat next to him at PAMA, taking private lessons, and never a move on his part. This protégé of Casals was as serious and devoted a teacher as she was a determined and serious a student. Determined to get serious with him, she laughed to herself. Of course they always exchanged small talk after the lessons, in the elevator (had he looked up the ceiling then too? No. For it was only a three-floor ride) and in the entrance lobby to the Academy. Over the years he had gotten to know her marital status; a married woman the first year, separated the second, and now, at the beginning of the third, about to be divorced. Once, probably during her second year with him, when—depressed at her separation and imminent divorce—she told him (she didn't know how it came up. Maybe he said, "You don't look too chipper today. Feeling low?") that she would rather feel nothing, he said in a fatherly way that love is a wonderful thing. She shouldn't reject it. That it made one float two inches above the ground. She couldn't recall if she had told Plaskow why she was separating. At that time, she realized, she was naïve enough to say something without realizing what kind of signal it could send a man. She was bitter during the period in Philly and perhaps, she thought, it accounted for her behavior. But, she remembered she wasn't at everyone's disposal. The con guys, the super-seducers, the smoothies, she always said no to. Them she could spot at a glance. In any case, her small talk with Plaskow, was always serious, for he was basically a serious man, intellectual and analytic, not in the broad cultural sense, but in his music. And that made him a superb teacher. But there was little humor in him, though one would have expected some verbal fun to float between male teacher and female student. There was only one joke she could remember. Once, when Aviva remarked that for her next recital she would throw in a few Bach gigues, Plaskow snapped, "Why don't you throw in a few green stamps too?" She laughed with delight as though it were the funniest thing in the world. He laughed too and his normally cold eyes seemed to warm for a moment. Only later did the full import of his sarcasm hit her. For some reason, perhaps because she so much wanted to, Aviva felt that the strings that bound them were tuned even tighter. She saw that joke as a personal little tweak. So many things, she thought, seemed right for something to happen. After all, they sat side by side, week after week, making music together. Shouldn't something happen between a beautiful young woman and a teacher who was her idol? Especially if she was just separated (this he knew) from an impotent husband after seven lean years of virginous marriage (this he probably did not know)? And hadn't she read somewhere, perhaps someone told her, that students always fell in love with their teachers? And didn't Plaskow have trouble and sorrow at home with the tragedy that struck his wife a year before? A brilliant flutist, Victoria Plaskow had been pushed by one of the legions of madmen in New York from an IRT platform on W. 116th Street after a concert at Columbia; she barely survived. Her right hand was severed, but even after microsurgery restored it, she could not play again.

Although Plaskow didn't seem interested in Aviva, she had been attracted to him from the moment she entered his studio at PAMA to audition for him. If she did well, perhaps he would introduce her to his teacher, Pablo Casals, which was probably the hope of every student who studied with Plaskow. And only after she would make her debut at Carnegie Hall in two-three years to rave reviews would she reveal first to Casals and then to others that she was the daughter of Gideon Andermann who cofounded the Israel Philharmonic. Play superbly over the past two years she did, but she never met Casals. It turned out that Plaskow never introduced *any* of his students, no matter how brilliant, to the old man. The old master he jealously, zealously, kept and guarded for himself. And more, she would learn that Plaskow wasn't even helpful to his students. They had to make their own way. Aviva would later wonder how a man with such arctic eyes could play Bach. But perhaps that was why critics said of Plaskow's playing that it was analytical and precise. With him critics never used the words passionate or warm, as they did with Casals. When Casals played Bach, Bach rode on his shoulders. When Plaskow played Bach, Plaskow was on his shoulders. She also could not understand how he could be an excellent teacher and not follow through personally for someone's career. There must be a serious flaw or split in his character, she thought. She remembered her first audition. She swallowed as she approached him. Was she nervous because she would have to play for him, or did that little leap in her heart come because of the big man who stood framed in the doorway waiting for her? She knew the cycles of seven in her life and wondered if another would soon begin. Guido later realized this too but she let him believe it was his discovery. Without even moving or saying a word, Plaskow exuded self-assurance. In him Aviva saw the confidence she had always lacked and the talent she hoped would blossom under his tutelage. At twenty-nine she was still naïve enough not to smile at the last image, but in retrospect (she had learned so much in retrospect she could open a Retrospective University: every stupid move she made in her life taught her something about her past. It was like spinning your life backwards; or inviting someone for dinner yesterday) yes, the image packs a potent wallop—under his tutelage.

For more than two years Plaskow has been a gentleman, that is, neither gentle nor a man. He lost his patience with her when a phrase repeatedly went poorly, and he could be snippety and even harsh. Once, before his wife's accident, Aviva had seen him sitting in his car in front of PAMA with his wife in the driver's seat. Aviva greeted him with a smile, but for some reason he snarled at her, eyes cold, perhaps to show his perpetually jealous wife that he wasn't on cushy terms with the best-looking (at least that's what others said; her mirror never gave her thoughts like that) student in the school. And perhaps it wasn't a snarl after all. Perhaps it had just been a very cool reception. But years later, Aviva, again in retrospect, remembered it as a snarl.

The invitation to come upstairs was a first for Aviva. Her pattern was never to initiate anything. She didn't, wouldn't lift a finger. The boys always came to her. They made the first move. She was not forward or provocative. She'd rather let someone she liked slip away than make a first move and possibly be rejected. And her involvements didn't even come from a wild desire for sex; for her it was just curiosity. But despite her brief flings during the past two years, she was still inwardly shy, heritage of her painfully shy childhood and adolescence, and very self-conscious. She was never sure she was doing anything right. How could guys like her with that awful squint? She still always made love in the dark. Laying men, she realized later, was not so much the ultimate ecstasy as it was an expression of finally, finally, getting her due. Well, now it was her turn. But when finally her turn came, first there was little arousal, and second, no orgasm. She knew the concept existed—in the books. That's the result of seven years of celibate marriage, of nunnish liaison. It kills the ecstasy. Strangely, the *thought* of sex, in her own room, in that ultimate cage of privacy, her own mind, was always more exciting than the real thing. Even her first lay (she realized after Guido's prodding that it wasn't Tim after all), with a guy who knew Paul and her, proved to be a dud. After what's-his-name, it's a wonder she didn't zip up and close up shop forever.

Because of this shyness she would never have dreamt of suggesting to Plaskow, after a lesson, "Let's go down to the coffee shop." For he was her teacher, always Mr. Plaskow, and she held him in awe. And anyway, she thought, he must have been about fifteen years older, in his early forties. (Only recently Guido had told her that Plaskow was only eight years her senior.) Not only was she awed by him, she was intimidated because of his fame and his sharp-tongued criticism when her playing was flawed. But he shaped her manner of playing. During the first year, for instance, they might spend an hour on just four bars. Once, Plaskow played it slow motion on her cello and showed how the fingers, the arm, the bow should move to play the passage correctly. And no doubt, his fame as a soloist and recording star was appealing too. But now, at the beginning of her third year in Philly with him, she felt the atmosphere had changed. It was November and Mr. Plaskow had become friendlier. Flirtatious. Warmer. Less a teacher, more a man. For instance, early in the semester he mentioned that he had to be in New York on occasion. As if testing the ground to see if he could see her there. Overwhelmed, knowing that their professional relationship would have to change—and though in retrospect she regretted her decision—she said yes to dinner.

Aviva was now astonished at this sudden turn of events. Till now, for more than two years she'd called him Mr. Plaskow. What should she call him now? After the invitation she didn't want to say Mister, nor did she dare call him by his first name. And she knew too, with a swiftness that passed through her like a chill wind, that it wouldn't just be dinner. With this invitation, declaration, summons—even if it was a question, it was absolutely rhetorical, one that brooked no response, for the answer was imbedded in the query—she knew that a boundary had been crossed. The hints were slurped all over the lessons like Dali's melted clocks in that famous painting, the title of which she always forgot. Although usually his cello was propped next to him unopened, lately he'd played long passages on it for her. Demonstrating. Demonstrative, she laughed, he's become demonstrative. All the sensuality of the cello seemed to be suddenly compressed into those lessons. And Aviva became more acutely aware of him and his darkly gleaming instrument. She watched his big hand run effortlessly up and down the strings. His bow across the lower register sent vibrations into her. The look on his face as he played was softer, romantically intense, as if posing for her a stage look of the nineteenth-century virtuoso. A couple of times he looked up and smiled at her, something he had never done before. And she felt a special privilege. But still that north wind in his eyes. Perhaps he was purposely playing on the lower register, knowing the effect those vibrations would have. Never in his lessons had he used the words *sensuous* or *sensuality* concerning the cello. But that's what it became. Plaskow was seducing her with his sensuous playing. He leaned closer to the instrument, became one with it. Suddenly, she felt she was the cello he held, and it was across her waist that his bow was drawn. For his cello was shaped like a woman and he embraced this woman, but she could not return his embrace. And as Aviva played, surrounding the cello with her embrace, joining him in the piece, resting her head against the neck of the cello, through closed eyes she saw Plaskow's arched bow. It ran right across his cello into the space between them and into her.

In the elevator, the talk nervously chesslike. A banality like: Nice elevator. Your move. Another banality: They used to have an operator. Your move. Sometimes elevators have mirrors. Now yours. Not this one. Perhaps it had one and they took it away. Perhaps this small slow machine couldn't take the double load, and she laughed. But he looked puzzled and only after mulling over the joke, like a thickheaded Teuton, did he venture a smile.

"Did you ever notice," he said, "people stuck in elevators with strangers have a morbid fascination with the ceiling, as if it's the most interesting thing in the world?" But she'd heard that before. "You said that in the PAMA elevator." "I know," he said, "but this is a different elevator." Now *that* was funny, Plaskow.

Thank God, finally her floor. She opened the door, walked through the long hallway with the closets on both sides into the large room. For a moment the close thick intimate dinner talk surfaced in her mind. It was as if the world around them had been shut away and only they two were in the restaurant. She knew what would happen now, just as she had known when she said yes to his summons. Still, she had a safety valve for a change of heart because other dates had come here for coffee (their suggestion, never hers) and they only had coffee and nothing else.

But as soon as Aviva entered and flipped on the light and said a trifle too loudly, "I'll put up coffee," as if to convince herself that that was the reason she had come here, and filled the kettle with water, and with seeming slow motion, as if in a trance, lowered it to the range and turned on the gas which didn't light because the pilot light was off, and she pushed the kettle aside and her hand trembled as she lit a match that wouldn't light and she tried another and held it to the gas, before the kettle touched down on the flame, she felt his arm around her and wondered, Only one arm? As he spun her to him, while with his other hand he shut the flame and kissed her lips once, deeply, slowly, a fierce kiss which contained the promise of more, at which Aviva opened her lips slightly, for she didn't like deep kissing, but stirred at once by his touch, stirred from the moment she opened the door, stirred when their shoulders touched as they sat next to each other on the soft leather seats in the restaurant, and stirred even more now by thoughts of his touch throughout the dinner, Aviva at once quickly pressed herself to him, as though an electric shock had thrummed through her.

What a mess. She never should have accepted that dinner invitation.♥ That dinner was her downfall. Another of the many messes she'd gotten herself into. Why? Why did she get herself into so many messes? From first marriage to second and in between—a crescendo of messes. That idiotic first marriage. Any normal person would have left in seven months. But no, she had to stick it out for seven years. She could have had it annulled due to impotency. But she was bound up with thoughts of loyalty and consideration. A moron! Naïve!♥♥ Imbecile! Fool, which she remained. She was born a fool and would die a fool. Also part of the problem was her inability

♥See ABC Directory, *Union, Aviva joins carpet workers'*.
♥♥See ABC Directory, *Naïveté*.

to talk about it to her mother. Too embarrassed. She shook her head. That was the way she was raised. In that old-fashioned European tight-assed respectable Jewish way. Even the way she looked then, as her photos revealed, showed her personality. Prim, prissy—pretty, yes—but uptight, with upswept hair and a cold condescending look that was her armor against the insecurity and awful shyness she always felt. A husband impotent? Lord, one doesn't talk about such things. It's a *shandeh*! A terrible shame. Shh.

And the same held true years later with her second marriage to the Arab. She still hadn't grown up. Why did she wait so many years—fourteen—like Jacob working for his two wives, before realizing it was no go? She couldn't explain it. But one thing she did learn, in addition to proper fingering and superb bowing technique: things don't happen to people. They cause their own problems.

Messes don't beckon with a crooked finger. People get themselves into them. Yes, she had made a mess of her life, she thought, and hoped that the nice counselor she was now seeing (Guido would be furious if he knew) would help her. What had she achieved? Nothing. Not in personal, not in family, not in professional life. A balloon. Floating. And she knew what happens to balloons. She laughed to herself, thinking of what Guido said when she described herself as a balloon. It keeps floating until one little prick brings it down to earth. She didn't go from one man to another out of lust but out of searching for something that would fill her life. She felt she was a good person, had a good heart, felt sorry for the helpless, the homeless, the dispossessed of this world. Wouldn't harm a fly. Would literally capture it and send it on its way, outside. She knew she was friendly; she radiated friendliness with her ready smile. Perhaps that was her Achilles heel, that friendly smile. It sent the wrong messages. In a world that was supersensitive to signals and messages. That's why half the population in America from seven to seventy wanted to get their hands on her. And when she was hurt, she was upset inwardly but outwardly calm, never let the other person know she was hurt and hurting. It was love she needed, not anything else. She remembered a neighbor in New York, a spinster, a woman in her mid-forties, quiet as a mouse. Aviva was twenty-nine at the time, just before PAMA. Little did she know how young a woman can feel in her mid-forties—better say, mid-fifties, right? The spinster had the apartment next to hers. She never heard visitors, never heard conversation. If she played the television it was put on so low beyond the threshold of eavesdropping. She seemed to be totally, always, alone. There was something gloomy, really spinsterish about her, in an old reference librarian sort of way. In fact, she was a keeper of rare books in a university library, probably one of those librarians whose sole joy in life is putting obstacles before those who want to use books and whose sole goal is to keep those books eternally behind doors as tightly locked as was her own private portal. ("I'm sorry," said in a soft DAR voice, "this is a noncirculating library; I'm sorry, patrons may not use the rare books; I'm sorry, rare books are rarely used. That's how they stay rare.") When Aviva met her on the floor she said a parchment dry quick hello that seemed to preclude further conversation. She probably thought, Aviva mused, that I wanted to borrow the Gutenberg Bible over the weekend. Her look seemed to say: don't touch me and don't touch my books. Then, suddenly, one day, Aviva began hearing chairs moving, banging, talking, and laughter. The sound of life. What had happened? A man had moved in with her. Aviva never did see the stud but suspected it might have been Gutenberg himself. And when Aviva met her in the hall one day she noticed the Transformation of a Spinster. She'd become younger, happier; she radiated fresh good health. Her look now seemed to say: take me and take my books. Browse to your heart's content. Touch every one of my pages. She seemed to be blooming. That's what love can do.

Nevertheless, love was changeable, depending upon mood, time, and circumstances. She remembered Capetown, her first true sustained love, when she was in her mid-thirties and teaching in New York. First time she met him she didn't particularly like him, didn't think she'd see him again. But she always gave herself a chance. And he turned out to be a fine, sensitive man, even if somewhat reticent and not too enthusiastic in, or about, sex. That is, he was relatively upbeat about it, ideologically, but in the act itself he was rather pedestrian. First time she lay with him she spelled out with her tongue, I love you, on his neck, but he was too thick to realize it. He was like a kid with a new toy. Perhaps this forty-nine-year-old was a virgin. They bought *Joys of Sex* and read it together. It didn't really help, but they did chuckle over the illustrations. Months later, when she spent a weekend with him in his place in Buffalo and she wanted it a second time, he was put off. She could feel his honor falling away like scales. His eyes narrowed, became old, and she saw a tremor at the edge of his lips. Crimson to her navel, she felt she'd sink through the floor in mortification. She never suggested that again. In his book, girls did not take the initiative; he was insulted. He was a Capetown man of European parentage. No wonder her mother loved him.

Aviva remembers that Capetown♥ was uncomfortable with women. Inexperienced. Afraid of them. But she loved him and, although he wasn't sexy, her love made him seem sexy. She like being close to him, cuddling him, hugging him, something she'd never done with the Arab. But best of all she loved talking to him over the phone, getting excited from far away.

Once when Capetown was at her parents' apartment—they had already left for the wedding that all had been invited to—and she and Capetown were alone and she was getting into the dress she was going to wear and

♥See ABC Directory, *Capetown, Aviva's response to.*

he was resting on the sofa, he suddenly said to her: "Let's have a quickie . . ." It was so uncharacteristic, but of course, she agreed at once. As she thinks about it now, she smiles—the smile that Guido said was the shy smile of a fifty-four-year-old ingenue, that smile that Guido said he could have hugged, if one could hug and kiss a smile.

Capetown was old at forty-nine. So imagine him now at sixty-eight! An old man.

At her Town Hall concert♥ there was an interesting turn in her life. Guido asked her afterwards if any former boyfriends had come. She gave one of her self-deprecating snort/laughs that signaled she was about to reveal something.

"You'll never guess who was there?"

"Not Plaskow," he said sadly.

"No."

"One of the Philadelphia cream cheese boys?"

Aviva laughed. "No . . . You'll never guess . . . Capetown."

"You're kidding. It's been how long? Fifteen, sixteen years?"

She nodded.

"How did he know? Of course, you told him. You exchange birthday cards and probably last time around you informed him about the prize and the concert."

"But I didn't think he'd come."

"But deep down you wanted him to. Otherwise you wouldn't have told him."

"Maybe."

"Was it strange seeing him?"

"Very. It put me in a kind of a turmoil."

"Did you screw him?"

"Yes. Onstage. During intermission. To get the audience's attention away from my playing."

"Did he ask you out for dinner?"

"You know everything, don't you? Yes. But I'd made arrangements with my family, so I asked him to come along . . . We rode in my station wagon. Seven of us. A cousin drove. I was too nervous to drive after playing. I sat in the back with my daughter, and he sat in the front with my son on his lap and there came this strange moment when time was suspended, and I remembered the good times I had with him and I felt sorry for this lonely man whom I once loved—he never did marry—that I wanted to stretch my hand out and touch his neck, shoulder, anything."

"Did you?" Guido asked.

♥See ABC Directory, *Bowing.*

"Of course not. The feeling lasted only a few seconds. Then it vanished." For a flash she was overcome by a momentary longing, seeing the man she had loved fifteen years ago who had been kind and loving and gentle to her, just the sort of treatment she needed, but because of Capetown's fear of long-term commitment, because he remembered his parents' own bad marriage, nothing had come of it. And seeing him in the car made those feelings of long ago surface (well, not so long ago, for during her troubled marriage, Aviva had often thought of him and even as she made love to the Arab she sometimes thought of Capetown to somehow make the onerous conjugal duty more palatable). In fact, she had called Capetown once in Buffalo and he'd told her he was flying to Nevada on business and would have a stopover at Kennedy, and she said she'd like to see him, maybe he would check into a hotel, but instead of welcoming this adventure, this opportunity, the foolish toad had said that he couldn't do it because he was afraid he'd lose his luggage. Luggage, rubbish! Aviva concluded. He was just afraid of adultery or starting something he couldn't finish. But now, she thought, it was dead. Or was it? Was that ten-second pulse of warm feeling—she couldn't call it love; but what *could* she call it?— a sign that something still lurked down there in her battered heart? But Guido was not hurt by this admission at all. He said he felt no jealousy. On the contrary. He felt for her and for him too.

At the reception after the concert, speaking to friends and relatives and pupils, she saw him standing there. At first she couldn't believe her eyes. A mirage maybe. Her mouth dropped open. He didn't smile, just nodded as he approached. He hadn't told her he'd be flying down just for the day, How glad she was to see him, she said, what a surprise! as he hugged her and kissed her cheek and told her how beautifully she played and how proud he was of her and how she hadn't changed a bit. But she noticed that he had. He had a rim of white in his hair where before there had been salt and pepper. And as he spoke she saw that the old energy was gone. He had aged. That was the difference between a fifty-two-year-old man and one sixty-eight. Would she want to join him for dinner now? She couldn't, she said. She was going with relatives to a restaurant; would he like to join them? So he squeezed into the car, sat in the front, with her son on his lap, a son who could have been his, while she sat in the back restraining her arm. They couldn't talk much in private, but earlier when the relatives had piled into station wagon and she stood by the rear door packing in her music and the programs—the cello a student had taken home for her—he asked her quickly, "Where's your husband?" First, she hesitated, about to say the truth: she didn't know—then said, "Someone called in sick and he had to go and substitute." The excuse sounded so lame she added, "And he doesn't like classical music anyway." But if he knew she was married, why had he invited her out? she wondered. Was the fact that she'd mentioned the concert months earlier, stating not only that she'd won a prize, but also giving him the exact date, was that a clue that she wanted to see him? And she admitted to Guido that perhaps she did want to see him. Out of curiosity. To see what had happened to him during these fifteen years. "Curiosity," Guido mocked, remembering that that had propelled her years ago from one guy to another. She said it was basically ego to inform him she'd won the prize and would be giving a concert in New York. Because when she'd known him, she was floundering, wasn't playing at all. She had wanted to let Capetown know that she had accomplished something. "Fine," Guido said, "but if you didn't want him to come, you could have . . ."— and she interrupted him, completed the thought for him: "I know . . . left out the date. No," she smiled. "I didn't. I guess I did want him to come, but I never in my wildest dreams thought he'd fly down from Buffalo. I was shocked. My mouth actually dropped open. When I saw him, I was in a kind of turmoil, but it wasn't emotions being churned." "How could it not be?" Guido asked. "You were connected for three years." "Yes," she said, "but it's dead now." "Suppose you didn't know me, would you accept an invitation from him to visit him?" "No," she said. "But I would see him in New York." "Would you call him?" "No." "But if he called you, you'd accept an invitation to see him." "Yes. In New York." And that yes did not bother Guido.

"He asked me to send him a review if it appears and I said yes . . . But now it's a problem. If I send it to him, it's like an invitation to correspond, to open things up again. He'll write, maybe call . . . No, I don't think I'll send it. But then again, I promised."

"So what will you do?"

"As usual, put things off."

"But suppose you did go up."

"But he has such a small apartment."

"Never mind that, you ninny. Suppose you went up. With the kids for vacation, let's say. You know, Buffalo, tourist capital of the cosmos. And you spent some time with him alone. Would you get involved with him again?"

"You mean romantically?" she asked.

"Yes. Of course. What did you think, aesthetically?"

She shook her head. "No. Not at all."

"And suppose I were not in the picture."

"Still not. Not at all. That's finished."

"Remember my wild idea last year about your marrying him and then you coming to visit me? Would you do it?"

"If I married him? No." Then she cocked her head, her eyes widened, and she gave him a mischievous glance. "Well, maybe . . . Would you accept that?"

He was silent.

After the restaurant the relatives took subways home, and she drove Capetown to the Port Authority Bus Terminal where he would take a Carey Transport bus to Kennedy. She would have driven him there, she said, but was invited to a party at her aunt's on the Upper West Side. When she dropped him off, she stepped out of her wagon for a moment and asked him, "Will you find your way back?"

"Of course," he said.

"I forgot," she laughed, "you always did have a good sense of direction."

"Except in life," he said.

"You're not the only one."

And Guido, listening to this, said, "Pathetic. Sad. Pathos."

"That's the word I was looking for," Aviva said. "There was a sense of pathos about him."

Guido said he could have cried for the both of them. She shook her head. One stupid hesitation on Capetown's part years ago and two lives remained empty. Yes, he had become an old man. After she described his slow movements to Guido, he observed, "Where today retirees at sixty-five jog and play tennis, Capetown had the lugubriousness of a sexagenarian sans the sex." But then again she was no spring chicken either, she thought, even though she felt young inside.

Later, the children asked about Capetown.

"Who was that nice man?" David said.

"An old friend."

"He's nice." Yaffa said. "He's so gentle."

"Did you mind sitting on his lap?" Aviva asked David.

"At first yes, but then no. He's cuddly."

"Yes," Aviva said and thought: the fool. He could have been their father.

At home she hugged them both. All three had their arms around one another and she felt the tears welling and running down her cheeks. She cried for him, for herself, for both of them, and for her children too.

"You played beautiful, mommy," David said.

She didn't correct him. It was the best review she could have gotten.

"Why you crying, mommy?" Yaffa looked up at her face.

Aviva wiped the tears away. "Because I'm happy. Because I have such two wonderful children."

Guido thinks I'm so old that I was a counselor for him in camp. Maybe I was, is the thought that runs through her head. I vaguely remember a friend of mine, getting sick once in camp, had to go home for a while, and she asked me to substitute for her. Glens Falls, that's it. And Guido was in camp at the time. Or so he claims. He's probably pulling my leg, like he always does. Camp counselor! Auntie Aviva! What next? He's too much. I could have been arrested for child molestation, he said. He came in to my bed after bedwetting. I hope he at least changed his pajamas first. Naïve! I believe anything. All my life I was naïve, she thinks. Naïve into my forties. But no one could fault her taste, she felt. Or her standards. And she had plenty of them.

She remembered hearing once that it takes a man seven seconds to decide if he likes a woman. Women, however, infinitely more patient, mature and wise, take much longer. But Aviva knew that she was quick like a man. Maybe not seven seconds, but seventy for sure. Maybe that's why she couldn't stay with a man, why she rejected so many. A man's flaws, faults, defects, presumed or real, leaped out at her at once. God! Men were full of them.

If a man sat down too tentatively, as if his ass were made of asparagus—a strike.

If he had hair in his nostrils—finished.

Breath bad—caput.

Walk not vigorous enough—out.

Gentle, sweet men she liked. But if there was a hint of a femininity in voice, gesture, and movement—no go.

The list was endless.

A guy who picked his teeth. Or his ears.

Or had a weak chin, oily skin, or lips noodle thin.

A high-pitched voice; sweated too easily. Dandruff. Combed his hair fussily over a bald spot.

If he didn't shave well under his chin; had hair in his ears; ate sloppily; too high a forehead; guttural voice.

Aviva knew she was picky, picayune, a finicky nitpicker with loads of pet peeves.

But she also couldn't take men who were too short, too gangly, and too scrawny. Of fat men there was no need to elaborate. A fat man could have impeccable manners, no hair in his ears or nose, a mellifluous voice, perfect skin, a full head of dandruffless hair, Einstein's brain, Guido's looks—fatsos still tipped the scale.

She didn't like bulging eyes either.

Or men who kept their wallets in their back pockets. Or who had a little change purse.

Who whistled.

Or jingled coins in their pockets—a sure sign of childhood poverty.

God almighty, she had a laundry list of negative qualities in her head.

If he sneezed not into his handkerchief but sprayed it out at the public like a seltzer bottle or fire hose—the first meeting gave birth to no second.

Or if he cleared his throat too much.

If he repeated certain phrases—thumbs down!

Also, she didn't like men with short necks and high shoulders; and men who cricked their necks or cracked their knuckles annoyed her.

As did guys who bit their nails or picked at the cuticles till they drew blood.

If they had pouches under their eyes—uh-uh.

If they were too nosy she lost respect for them; nay, never had any to begin with.

But give her a guy who was perfect, and hey, with him she had no trouble—although, to be perfectly honest, perfection was a flaw of a kind too. Too good is also no good, she remembered Guido quoting an Italian proverb.

And if he made her laugh, she could overlook one or two of the scores of faults with which men were innately saddled.

Like being too quickly too cuddly-wuddly, like touching her hand or elbow. If they had that sleazy con-man overconfidence that said, I'm gonna bed you tonight, she gave them a cold mask of a face and a return ticket home.

If he tried to impress her too hard with rehearsed jokes—a minus.

My God, how did she even make it with any man, given the metaphysical bumps and excrescences that each man possessed like an extra limb, a chromosome that could not be excised.

If be blinked or had a tic—n.g.

If his eyes were crossed, she looked the other way. After all, she was not intolerant. And by the way, splotchy skin got her goat; and scratching earned him a polite good-bye.

And let's not forget about uneven or stained teeth.

If he talked not to her, but at her.

Or if he smoked. Even if his hair smelled of smoke, not to mention his breath. And more; if he so much as patted his shirt or jacket pocket where the suspect hard or soft pack might be hidden, she bid the loser a mental adieu.

And, oh yes, she almost forgot. Speaking of limbs and protuberances— soft, fleshy ears too old for the head that happened to be on the guy she was dating was bad business.

The list was like strudel dough. It could be stretched ad infinitum.

Sitting in a concert with a guy who inconsiderately turned the program pages too loudly turned her off.

If a guy chomped noisily at dinner or tried to show off his knowledge of wines—his first dinner with her was his last supper.

How about a little elegance and dignity and class like a Haydn symphony? Why can't a man be like the first movement of Mozart's 39th? she wondered. Or one of Vivaldi's cello sonatas?

Why can't a man be more like me? she thought.

Perfect.

Nevertheless, as awful as men were, she still preferred them to women. She'd take a man's company over a woman's any day. Women, she hated to say this, were boring. All they could talk about was recipes and shopping and clothing and lamps, but mostly who said or did what when and where and why to whom. Whether it was true or not.

Her life, she thinks, had only fleeting moments of happiness. She remembered a line from a poem. To help me through this long disease, my life. Alexander Pope. Even her current life, with its shreds and tatters of happiness with Guido, was so full of misery, self-doubt, and pessimism, which the occasional visits to her counselor were partially alleviating. Guido had mentioned *Madame Bovary* and *Anna Karenina* to her—God, she hadn't read a book in ages—and at times she felt like Emma and Anna. There were moments when if not for her children, and not to give satisfaction to the smirking Arab who would possess and ruin those two lovely kids, she would have gladly taken poison like Emma or cast herself under the Long Island Railroad like Anna. Her first and last name began with *A* and so did her mother's first name, Abigail, the same *A* that had adorned her sweater like a family coat of arms which she in her absolute and total naïveté had worn to school thinking it stood for Adorable to the taunts and laughter of her mean classmates that turned the adorable of her imagination to anguish. That novel by Hawthorne, which the class had read the previous semester when she was not yet at that school, was *her* life story remembered. The *Diary of an Adulterous Woman*. No, the *Diary of a Naïve Adulterous Woman*. Again naïveté. Even her marriage to the Arab was an affirmation, confirmation, of her naïveté.

Marrying a man from the Middle East, she thought. Rahamim Ramati from Marakesh. But here he calls himself Roberto and in his taxi business for some reason pretends he's an Italian. But with Jews he says he's an Israeli from Paris. As if ashamed of coming from Morocco. But they were all like that. No one ever admitted to coming from North Africa. It's either from Paris or Barcelona. Marrying a Moroccan with Arab values; entering the macho world of being owned by a male—now wasn't that pure blindness? Naïveté of the first order. In private he was volatile, unpredictable. But if people were present the Arab would be sweet as sugar, even-tempered, hiding his claws and patting his pussycat fur. Typical of his personality. The inner and outer masks. Boy, was he an expert at dissimulation! He joined the local synagogue where he tried to establish a reputation as an honest, God-fearing Jew. Later, she learned that lots of these Israeli Moroccans behaved the same way, ingratiating in public, abusive behind closed doors. In New York, in his taxi business, who knows what kind of rat race he was involved with—she didn't ask, she didn't care. He made money but was stingy in giving it to her. She learned to squirrel away most of the money she made teaching privately. He claimed he had lots of expenses. Who knows? Maybe he had a girlfriend on the side. He had a nice house—to show off his accomplishments in America. But to let her hire help to clean—never. That he refused to do. Once when she paid someone with her own earnings, he sniffed it out—she didn't know how; perhaps the house was too clean—and he flew into a rage and threatened her. She couldn't take the yelling. Rather clean herself, she thought, dreaming, hoping, longing for peace. He would come home late and sleep in a spare bedroom, ostensibly not to wake her. When the spirit moved him, he would come to her and sometimes, after one of his fits, act contrite, make up to her, make love, and then go back at once to "his" room, claiming he had a headache.

"If he could have, he would have put a chastity belt on me," she once told Guido.

"Bravo for that use of the conditional mode. But I'd have picked the lock. Poked through it. Worked around, above, behind it."

"I'll bet you would have too."

"A belt has two functions, the Sicilians say. To keep your pants up and your wife down."

Sometimes, Aviva recalls, the Arab♥ would try to force her, but she thrashed about and he couldn't. It was like threading a moving needle. And the son of a bitch would say to her, "You don't know how to hold on to something precious . . . You said," the Arab whined, "you'd never leave me." "But that was long ago," she replied, "when you were a decent human being for the two or three months you were courting me." And she looked at him with such aversion. If looks could kill, she recalled Guido quoting another Sicilian proverb, only animals would roam the earth. My God, she thinks, what a world of difference Guido is. My miracle man. The best thing that ever happened to me. I never knew they made men like him. He said things she'd never heard before. To her banal, "I missed you so much," he replied; "And I miss you more when I see you because I start thinking of the moment I won't see you but when I see you I miss missing you." Yes, she thinks, the words sounded super, but when she replayed them she heard more wordplay than content. She would ask him to explain and he would say words are like light entering a shutter. They enter once, and only once, and make their impression. Analysis makes words crumble into letters and like Humpty they cannot be restored again.

Once, noting her distress at the progress of the relationship, he said that she seemed to be split in two and that split also cleaved him. Yes, she had been cleaved in two. And it was his darling Tammy who was doing it and that retarded son of hers, his, theirs, that keeps her and Guido locked into a diabolical relationship, bitter and ecstatic.

♥See ABC Directory, *Always disapproves, the Arab*.

All through the years Aviva had always thought that sex was more exciting imagined then real. It didn't involve others. No hassle, no heartbreak. Going it, as usual, alone. But with him it was different. With him sex wasn't better in imagination. Before Guido she had been too shy, too aloof, too detached to ask men if it was good, but with him she had changed. Him she always asked. And wasn't shy to ask for second, third helpings. But she never had to. God, he just never stopped. Because love poured out of him, not like the Arab.

She often thought that for some maniacal reason the Arab withheld love, then realized that if something is withheld it's there. Like money withheld but not given. Which made her conclude that she was being generous in her estimation of the Arab. The truth was that the love just wasn't there, so there was nothing to withhold. Her true feelings about the Arab were once revealed to her in a dream.

She dreamt that she and Guido were visiting a hilltop house that overlooked other houses, hers included. And she saw her children playing in the backyard with her sister and her parents who were long dead. And then she couldn't find Guido; they had been in a room doing some consulting, or rather "guess what?" as she phrased it in her inimitable fashion, and when she came down she couldn't find him. So she gets into her car and goes out looking for him, maybe he's taking a walk on the suburban streets. Just then she sees the Arab sitting in a car. She motions to him but he doesn't see her, or makes believe he doesn't see her. He starts the car; she follows but doesn't know why she wants to make contact with him. She passes him to make him stop his car. As she passes, somehow in the dream she can see down to his seat. He has a long knife there. Next thing she knows he attacks her with the knife, but she's able to get away.

If anyone at that time of stress could have saved her, it was Guido. Incredible, he just walked off the street and into her life. The story she told and retold herself was like a private saga, a myth all her own. Jill Altman's mom was ill and she'd asked Guido to bring her daughter to the lesson. And bam, there he was. He sure made his presence felt, even without saying a word. God, how tall he was—six-one, -two? She remembered the lesson went well; she knew she was showing off for him, hoping somehow she'd see him again. But she would never ever say that outright. She just tried to send him welcome signals. He said he too had played the cello once—how lucky, how fated, how neat—and then called her for lessons. The first day he came he told her that he knew most of the classics by heart. Her mouth dropped open. The smug egoist,♥ she thought. Show off. But as the lessons proceeded, her criticism became muted. He did know lots and he played

♥See ABC Directory, *Ego.*

well. She liked him. He was magnetizing her. Just sitting there at the cello he sent out such powerful sex waves. When he left her house after the lesson she was agitated. Couldn't breathe, Couldn't eat. Lost weight. Her waist became so slim. But you never noticed my state, right? she told him later. I put up a good front, right? He looked at her breasts and nodded.

Why it took him so long to make a move, six or seven weeks, was one of the things they liked to talk about much later.

"How come," he asked her, "if you were so excited by me, why didn't you just drop the cello and throw your arms around me?"

"Because that's the way I am. I'll never act. And besides, I didn't know your home situation. Didn't know if you really liked me. I always feel insecure."

"Rather lose the love of your life."

"And what took you so long?"

"I too didn't know. I thought at first you were thirty-five or so. Especially with an eleven- and a thirteen-year-old. Figured you married at twenty or so and then had two babies. So why should you be interested in a forty-three-year-old guy? I couldn't figure out your friendliness. That puzzled me most of all. Was it the natural chumminess of a teacher palsy-walsy with her pupil, or the special friendliness of a woman for a man she likes?"

"I kept my love for you pretty much under control, right?"

"Uh-huh. I really couldn't tell."

"But when you left I literally couldn't breathe. I couldn't talk. The phone rang, I couldn't say hello. People at the other end said, 'Hello? Hello?' and I couldn't utter a sound so they hung up. My thoughts were totally confused. I didn't know the time, the day, where I was."

"Smitten," Guido said proudly.

"Mmm."

"Say it. Speak it. Utter it," he commanded.

She looked up at him, said it slowly, whispered it lovingly at him: "Smitten!" Chin down, eyes up. Two slow syllables.

A month after this she declared that she began really to love him only after they'd been seeing each other and making love. He almost fell off the bed in astonishment, and she caught him, laughing, before he rolled off. The next day he asked her about it, for as usual, it took him a day to mull over, digest her remarks. She said she never said she didn't love him during the cello lessons. She did, but she wasn't absolutely sure until later.

"But I thought you said you loved me even before I touched you."

"I did. But the more I touched you the more I loved you. I took you to bed with me every night."

"With my competition. Mr. AC/DC."

"Every night."

"I can't believe it took me so long. But I had to think up a neutral way of getting to see you. First I thought of a museum. Then, remember, I offered you Italian lessons. Remember what I told you?"

"No."

"Sure you do. That for Italian lessons you'd have to come to my house." Guido pursed his lips. "Oh, that prim cello teacher. Over the phone she says: it's not my policy to go to students' houses for music lessons. Only screwing lessons."

Aviva giggled. She ran her hand through her long hair, fingering it strand by strand.

"Remember what you said about Italian lessons?" Guido asked.

"Yes. I said it would only be fair to come to your house."

"And you said we could exchange lessons. And I said, No, it wouldn't be ethical because I foisted the lessons on you . . . So, of course, I'd continue to pay you . . . You know, of course, what I would have done as soon as you came into my house for Italiano."

"What?" Her eyes gave out that mischievous gleam.

"This!"

"Fresh," she said, delighted.

"But, of course, that delicious walk preceded it . . . I still can't get over your remark: 'That was the most beautiful walk in my life.' "

"It was. The most beautiful."

She knew she didn't say much, but occasionally, inspired, she did come up with words that remained etched in his memory.

His questions were a kind of leitmotif in their relationship, a kind of driving Baroque theme. It was as though she were being forced to confess, had no choice but. And the range and subtlety of his questions impressed her too. Often, though she enjoyed the questions, she wished he'd cut them short and get into the real purpose of their get-together, But first the ongoing ritual of questions, questions, questions,♥ Suppose, Guido wanted to know, in one of those innumerable "suppose" questions that created a kind of reality in that fantasy atmosphere of theirs. "Suppose that first day I came to your house and we had that nice talk while the Altman girl was still practicing. Suppose I had taken you in my arms and kissed you."

"I'd have been shocked."

"Would you have made love to me?"

"I don't think so."

"Then that would have killed it."

"The way it happened was much better."

♥See ABC Directory, *Questions, questions, questions.*

"Yes. Imagine. One wrong move and I'd have had to have gone—hear that sophisticated grammatical usage I'm learning from you?—away and that would have ended it."

She remembers rolling closer to him as if expunging that thought and holding him tight.

Half their conversations were suppose, half were about her adventures,♥ and half were about things they didn't talk about. Music, for instance. He missed talking music with her, he said. She knew she never spoke much about musical life with him. There were so many anecdotes about composers and conductors, but she rarely remembered them. They passed her by because deep down perhaps she really didn't like music. Leonard Bernstein's song. "I Hate Music," could symbolically have been if not her favorite song then at least among the Top Ten. A feeling perhaps best symbolized by the snapshot her girlfriend had once taken of her holding her cello with one hand and a sharp long kitchen knife with the other, as if about to stab her instrument in the back. She didn't deserve to be a cellist, she knew. She didn't take its nobility seriously enough. She was what a teacher at the Mannes School of Music once said, in a burst of pique and disparagement of a young musician who couldn't make the grade intellectually, superficial. There could be no greater insult than that at the school. That's what, she had to admit, she was. Superficial. What a difference between her attitude to music and Pablo Casals'. It stung her, but she didn't show it, when early on Guido (who seemed to know everything) quoted to her Casals' remark about his Stradivarius: I still work hard to be its equal. That same teacher at Mannes—there was an anecdote to tell Guido—would say to students, "You have the grammar of it, now let's get to the poetry." Guido would appreciate a remark like that. It was something Plaskow could never say because he was too bogged down in the grammar of music, the technique, the composer's supposed intent, The Tradition.

At first, her entire relationship with Guido revolved around music. It was the Maypole, the axis, and the core. But of late that had receded. Her complaints, "Why did I need this recital?" and bemoaning the fact that she didn't practice enough, were the only musical elements in their talk. For performing gave her the quivers. She liked the applause, the elemental silence in the hall just before she began, and that half note of space between her last note, still singing somewhere in the hall, and the rush of applause. But everything in between made her blood freeze. Sure, there was joy in making music, but playing alone onstage took much out of her. Make love, not music, should be her motto, Guido quipped. The jangled nerves, the tight stomach, the headaches weren't worth it. She didn't mind losing

♥See ABC Directory, *Affairs, her.*

herself in an orchestra, but doing solos, thinking of interpretation, squeezed the life and soul out of her. She knew that that Town Hall recital would be her last.

"What's interpretation?" he once asked her.

"Simply put: the relationship between two notes."

She remembers that impressed him. And she was so proud of herself. He usually didn't go into ecstasy at things she said. But for this one he did.

"Wow! What a quotable remark! It almost sounds like an Einsteinian theory. If Beethoven had said this it would have become an epigram."

"Let me expand on it," she said. "It's the kind of character you want the notes to have. The coloration. The mood. Whether you'll take the piece aggressively or tenderly."

"And this genius lies down naked next to *me*. What luck!"♥

"No," she said. "*I'm* the lucky one. Lucky, lucky me."

Guido was still in dithyrambs of rapture at her definition.

"Now you're talking my language. Music. That's what we should be doing more of instead of that dumb fucking fucking all the time. Make music, not love." He shook his head. "I still can't get over it. Your definition is so crisp, so epigrammatic, it sort of condenses everything down to its simplest component, like Picasso's famous line drawing of a bull . . . Didn't Casals say something like that?"

"No . . . it's all mine, but if you want to hear about music—"

"Yes, yes."

"—I heard something very nice about Casals from one of my theory teachers."

"But you never met the old man in person, did you?"

"Well . . ." she hesitated. Her head went down as if swallowing a thought, as if she didn't want to continue.

"Go ahead. Say it. You started it, finish it."

"Once, when Casals was in New York, PAMA arranged for all the cello students to go, and Plaskow and a couple of other cello teachers were there too."

"And he didn't take you backstage to meet him?"

"No."

"Why?"

"I don't know. I guess he kept Casals to himself . . . Anyway, one of my theory teachers spoke about what made Casals unique, what were his special qualities. Here. I'll show you." She rummaged among her scores, found the Bach Cello Sonatas, and opened to the inside back cover. The remarks were taped there and she read: "Casals opened a door in a high wall behind which was the most extraordinary garden imaginable, filled with the great-

♥See ABC Directory, *Lucky, who is?*

est possible variety of colors and scents in wonderful profusion, but with a certain order. This was a garden of unmatched beauty and imagination. Now Casals could show you that this garden existed. But how far you walked into that garden became your own responsibility."

"That's not Plaskow speaking," Guido said. "That's genius filtered through an ethical lens."

Aviva shook her head and grimaced. "Never. I told you it was one of my theory teachers, a wonderful, gentle old man. Plaskow could never talk like that. That would be beyond him. Teacher and pupil are not necessarily alike. In fact, Casals and Plaskow were quite different. Casals gave of himself. He had music and soul, which Plaskow never had. Casals took a stand. Against Franco. Against Hitler. He was an artist who had a moral and political responsibility. For him evil and art could not combine."

"Wagner, Von Karajan." Guido made a face. "The classical oxymoron. Nazi music."

"Right," said Aviva. "We see things the same way."

Now why did Plaskow keep popping into her head? she wondered. There was a time she imagined herself floating with his cello. She imagined him lifting the cello and holding it like a woman and dancing, dancing, whirling deliriously on a cloud. She wanted to feel this dream, wanted to sense this upflow sensation, this heat in her loins spreading like a beneficent elixir through all her limbs, suspended from reality, thrust upward in a crescendo of feeling. But she projected this dream on her imagination; it did not overtake her against her will; she wasn't helpless to counteract it, like a sedative over which one has no control; it didn't overtake her like a dream flight during lovemaking makes the dreamer/lover fly. This flight was forced out of her imagination; it was something she hoped would be, like a fantasy one talks oneself into seeing.

But that was music from the past; now she had—or did she? always doubting—music in the present. But, let's face it, it was jarring music—the very phrase she'd used with her counselor recently—and now that Guido was on an extended trip abroad, this music made her feel good sometimes; and sometimes awful. Casals' magic garden, she thought to herself, you've shown it to me, Guido. You brought me into it. And now I'm lost in the maze.

"When I discuss music with you," he told her, "it gives me such fulfillment I don't even have to touch you anymore."

"Well, then let's stop discussing music," she said. And later, in bed, she said, "My wife, I mean my mother, used to say . . ."

"It's not bad enough that *I* have a wife. Now you have to have one too . . . The Sienese say, When a man is married, his wife also become his mother-in-law."

She didn't know what she was bargaining for when she told him to stop discussing music. They were now into another four-hour marathon in bed.

No wonder she called him My Marathon Man.♥ He would only let her go to pee, no eating no drinking no barefeet please, just screwing.

"Where do you get your energy from?" she asked.

"Practice! Sex is like the cello," he told her. "You have to practice to stay in shape."

"So you practice at home, huh?" she said sadly.

"At home. At the office. At work. At play . . . Again with the wife?"

"No, I mean the cello," she said.

"You like when I screw you."

"Mmm," she said. "I mean, Yes. I love it. You make me feel like I never felt before."

"Then to keep that level, I gotta practice."

"Every night," she said. "I think of you before I go to sleep, and my loins actually ache out of desire for you . . . But . . ." She looked down. She'd said it to him a long time ago. But still there was a but. A big But.

"But what?" he said.

"But what?" she mimicked him. "As if you didn't know."

"I don't."

"You do . . . But some sometimes I hate you. Sometimes I'm so angry with you . . . not so much you . . . as the situation."

"I know," he said softly, commiserating. He was good at that, she thought, just as he was good at that other thing. For hours on end.

"You're gonna kill me," she said, exhausted. "You'll be the death of me—" then quickly, pertly, "but what a way to go . . . What am I going to do with you?" she asked.

He said he liked that young, sad, Pieta-like expression on her face.

"Just love me," he said. "Keep on loving me."

"It's so easy to," she said. "That's the problem. But now that you're on the scene, I play less and less."

"With whom? The Arab?"

"Yuk. I mean the cello. If I only had two basic nonmusical ingredients, security and memory, I could be a remarkable player. Maybe I don't even need security—just memory. If I had memory and just a couple of milligrams of sperm—"

"What?" he said.

Aviva giggled. "I wish you could see the expression on your face. It's precious."

"What did you say? I heard memory and then sperm." He made a motion with his hands as if to say: how do the two connect?

"Just wanted to see if you were paying attention."

"Did you ever think of performing with music?"

♥See ABC Directory, *Marathon Man.*

"And have to worry about a page turner?"

"I'll be your page turner. But the trouble with me is that when I look down and see your breasts. I'll get carried away and instead of being a page turner I'll be a—"

"Nipple flipper," she said.

That frightened her most of all—that blanking out in front of an audience. The sheer terror of it could not be described. It was like dying. And dying again and again. When it happened to her she felt like throwing away the cello and giving up playing altogether. Even as a kid, she remembered, she would hide comic books behind her music to goof off. "Who needs this stress?" she asked Guido. "How come others can do it? I'm not any more stupid than any other cellist."

"Who said so?" Guido snapped. "I'll fight any man who disagrees."

When she stopped laughing, she said, "I'll just have to practice more. If only I had a little protrusion on my chair, I'd spend more time there. And then again, what's the point of it all, anyway? . . . So . . . what?" Both words accented, large space between the words. She said she won't give public solo recitals any more.

She knew this drove him up a wall. He went into a tirade.

"What's the point of any endeavor? Better to pick at a guitar or pluck a g-string and blow into a f-hole than pick your nose or flick chicken feathers or flip nipples or pluck nickels with your fingers. You still haven't gotten that question out of your system. You said that to me the first days we got to know each other, and I'm glad you did because that gave me an excuse to take you for a walk, ostensibly to talk to you about what's the point of it all, for during and after lessons there was no time to discuss this, but actually to flip your nipples . . . Man is made to create—*that's* the point of it. You might as well ask: What's the point of photography?"

"What *is* the point of photography?"

"Got me," Guido said. "You can't be a nihilist. Because then that question can be applied to anything. What's the point of anything? The point is—the challenge. To show that something creative can be done with human hands. To show that you can make music with those very hands that other people use to kill and maim. To bring beauty and joy into the world. With those discrete little movements of your hands and fingers you can move hearts, bring to life melodies that someone conceived of hundreds of years ago. That's the point of it. I'll say it again. The person who says What's the point of it? can also say it in reference to relationships and bounce from one to another. You don't have to shake worlds or become a Casals. You just have to become Aviva. And do with those hands what you were destined for, by training, by practice, by genes and inclination. In other words—stroke me."

"I love when you say my name. You don't often call me by name. Your voice sounds so beautiful when you say my name."

He rolled his eyes. "Methinks I'm talking to the wall."

She just couldn't get it together, runs through her mind. Practicing. Teaching. Housework. Some time with the children. The house was entirely neglected. But she'd rather neglect the house than her children. Anyway, whom was she going to clean for? Him? Who threw food he didn't like across the room, the animal! But Guido's house impressed her.

"Wow. I wish I could keep my place like this. I mean, this is Mr. Kleen. Spic and span. You should see my bathroom. On any given morning, give or take a few items, on the floor there'll be three sneakers, a crumpled plastic cup, some dirty socks; a couple of wet washrags, wrappers from soap and other beauty items. It's disgusting."

"So what do you do? Clean it up?"

"No, I use the downstairs bathroom."

"My wife is a neatness fanatic. A cleanup bug." And Guido told her that he had this vision of her as a queenly, elegant, regal woman who would never lift a finger to clean, cook, dust, and shop. He just couldn't imagine her doing laundry or mopping. "Laundry," she said, grimacing. "It piles up and up, until one day I have to face up to it. And there were mice too," she confessed. She could smell the droppings. "You mean to tell me you can identify mice droppings?" "Yes," she said. "I walk into the garage or basement, take one whiff and know it's mice."

"You could become a consultant," he said. "Another item for your resume."

Mice droppings! Where the hell did she get *that* from with all her *tsoress*? The present was problematic, the future cloudy. Only the past was secure. And how she reveled in the memories of those first days when he came for lessons. But even then, at the beginning, there were problems.

Although she'd been lusting for him, longing for him, loving him for weeks, after the first lovemaking she lost all feeling. She withdrew, had a splitting headache, held her head with both hands, was near tears. She couldn't stand her husband, but she had never been unfaithful, despite his idiotic false accusations over the years. The second time she visited Guido she told him she was upset, turned upside down, inside out. She didn't know if she'd come back any more. She'd have to think it over. Then why did you start? he raged. Offer one taste? Hold out your promise and then slam the door? She'd have to think it over, she repeated. She'd call him tomorrow.

But the next day instead of calling, she returned, smiling shyly as he opened the door to her knocking. He told her he knew she'd come back. How'd you know? I just knew, he said, kissing her. She pressed so close to him she thought she'd take his breath away, like he'd taken hers away for months. That day of squabbling and hesitation, he said, summed up an entire lifetime within twenty-four hours: courtship, canopy, divorce, and reconciliation. And she told him: After she'd left him the other day she was tingling for an hour. She had never spoken like this to any man, she admitted. It took her most of the day to calm down. "At night I undressed you in my thoughts," she said. "You're a magician. No wonder I came back today."♥

You're vulnerable, she hears a voice telling her. Doesn't know if it's her own voice or Guido's imagined call. But it comes to her like a vatic warning. Yes, she had always felt vulnerable. Especially when younger. Old Dr. Gelbauer, the tiny psychiatrist with the yellow polka-dot bowtie, had told her years ago; the Indian shrink had never said it but made her feel that way; and her current counselor also suggested it. She always felt apologetic. When a situation went wrong, it was her fault. And on the contrary, she never took credit for good things happening. She couldn't tell if a man responded to her because of her attractiveness or out of politesse. Early on, she gave the impression of being aloof and untouchable; only later did she become more extroverted, dared to open her mouth and crack a joke.

And when she married the Arab, and he told her she was the best, it didn't add up. She couldn't take the compliment—because it came from him. She thought: something is wrong here. He claimed he had had lots of women with lots more experience, but she was the best. When she told this to Guido, thinking it would raise her up a notch in his estimation, he merely snapped: "Shows you what poor taste he has"—putting them both down with one crack. Now if Guido had said that—that would be something. But she had never become a sophisticated lover. Never. Some women spend their lives with sex. She didn't. They prepare for evenings, they devote a large percentage of each day thinking of sexual activities at night. She didn't. She didn't think about sex that much at all. And never thought of herself as being energetic sexually. So why the phony compliment?

She had always maintained that nothing ever comes knocking at your door. You gotta go out and search for it. But with Guido it happened. He just knocked on her door and good luck came into her life. Her first lucky experience with the cello. And she felt lucky with him—well, at least half of him. The good half, she laughed to herself. In the past she never knew if her feelings would be reciprocated. She would think: this is the guy I was always looking for. Then another voice would say: How do you know? And that feeling of emptiness and loss spread through all her bones like a venom.

And when she shared some of these thoughts with Guido, he said:

"You had a certain power, didn't you? Not everyone who wanted to lay you could, but everyone you wanted to screw you did."

He had a point there, she thought, but had never considered it. Sexual politics was beyond her.

♥See ABC Directory, *Brat, growing.*

Her mother's Be a good girl, and that *A* for Adorable, for Andermann, for her mother Abigail, and least of all, for Aviva, that *A* that had adorned her sweater and which other kids in class read as Adulteress and she as Anguish, shaped her attitude for years. Her mother even got into her hair.

To wit:

A year after she returned from Florence, she spent three weeks in Europe with a girlfriend. In Paris, on her way to a Monmartre café, she passed a beauty parlor. Through the window they saw two men, the master and his assistant, cutting the long blonde locks of a stunning girl. So slowly, it seemed hair by hair. Just then the master turned and looked straight at Aviva. He gaped at her and then dashed outside. He started babbling in French amid many gestures, which included pointing at her prim upswept hair. When she told him she didn't understand French, that her three years of high school French had not prepared her for this, the hairdresser switched to English.

"Mon Dieu! Your air. Eet look like your grandmere's. Old-fashioned. Come. Weeth zat face! Mon Dieu! Nevair. Nevair. Nevair!" And he took her by the hand and led her into the shop. "I undo your air. Now. Zees minute. Eet must be long. Down. Fall like, ow you call, waterplunge. Down, down, down."

She had wanted to do that for months, but her mother didn't let her. Her mother said it would make her look like a wanton. She wanted Aviva's hair to be up, to look prim and proper, proper and prim. Aviva wanted it down, free, cascading, but didn't have the nerve to contravene her mother. But now, three thousand miles away, the master beautician did it, with swift, ballet-like movements, to the applause of Aviva's girlfriend and the French blonde. He cut, shaped, and created the auburn waterplanche, waterplaige, waterplunge.

Yes, for years, in one way or another, her mother had sculpted, molded, shaped her attitudes. The instinctual expressions of feelings had to be muted. She thought noises during lovemaking vulgar and, worse, in bed with the Arab she felt she was just a receptacle. As she admitted this to Guido, he wondered aloud if she was fickle, if she could last with anyone more than a year. Maybe she grew bored quickly, he said. The guys didn't satisfy her any more. Not so, she said, but she had often told him that her life had been humdrum and unsatisfying. The only exception had been her contact with the Indian psychiatrist. He treated her like a woman, an adult. He gave her a spiritual lift when she was stuck in that virginous marriage with Paul. He gave her advice. He told her to stop wearing bobby sox like a kid. But she was still a kid, she felt. A good girl. Not till many years later did she become a woman. Then Guido asked, if with all the affection the Indian displayed didn't he have hot pants for her? She replied that he never showed it. Sexual excitement changes, Guido said, from a first meeting with a woman. In the beginning there is anticipation. It's intense. There is a higher pitch of sexuality in the air. Sometimes it's unexpected. Its aura is overwhelming; it can be compared to nothing else. Maybe only to itself. It's not a gradual acclimation to something expected. At first you have a crazy feeling of being overwhelmed by the surprise of it—then later you get used to it.

And she *was* overwhelmed, Aviva remembers, no doubt about it. It took a few times to get used to Guido; new curves, new bones, new skin. Like playing a different cello. But once they got the hang of it, she was hooked. Guido was a Strad.

Once, after a great session of lovemaking,♥ she looked at him and said: "I'll bet plenty of women would give half their bosom to be made love to like this."

"So when are you gonna start giving? Or were they much larger and you've already given at the office?"

Then with a suddenness that surprised her, she asked:

"Why'd you take up with me? I still don't know. Was there something wrong in your life that made you do it?"

"No."

But she didn't believe him. There had to be something wrong. A man just doesn't start a relationship with a woman after fifteen years of marriage just for the fun of it, she thought.

But Guido himself couldn't tell her why. He felt a pull, he said. "Only photography can explain it. Something from the world of the surreal, like the pictures of Moholy-Nagy. I felt I was the negative and you my positive print. Or put it in cosmic terms. We were two stars and there was a gravitational pull between us. I couldn't resist. Didn't want to resist. You were made for me eons before me met. That's why Tammy became acquainted with our ex-neighbor, Janey Altman. So that when she fell ill, she'd call me to bring her daughter to you."

"It all sounds very nice, but it still doesn't click. Something is missing."

"But you took up with me too, right?"

"Because things weren't going smoothly for me, and I had the impression that you were looking . . . So the hope was—that something permanent would come of it."

"But you knew I was married. Why'd you stick with me so long?"

"You know," she said slowly, musically, singing it like a lament.

"I don't know," he said, rather harshly.

"Because I love you . . . Because you showed me Casals' magic garden."

And because she loved him she wanted to find out all about him. She could ask questions too, right? How he slept. Which side. Which way he faced. Did he toss and turn? Fall asleep with ease?

"And when someone sleeps with you, how . . ."

♥See ABC Directory, *It, how she loves.*

"What do you mean, someone?" he interjected.

"You know what I mean," she said unsteadily. "When someone slept with you, did they press up to you? Can you sleep if someone throws a leg over you?"

"Is the leg attached?"

"Yes."

"If he puts a leg over me, I can't sleep," Guido said.

"Do you press close before you sleep?"

"What am I, a tailor? I never press clothes before I sleep."

"Stop it. Press close. Do you press close before you sleep?"

"To whom? To him who brazenly threw a leg that is neither his nor mine over me?"

She disregarded him.

"Hey, what's this? *She's* asking questions? I'm the question specialist, remember? . . . Okay, I used to, years ago, but I can't sleep that way any more."

"Do you always sleep on the right side of the bed?"

"No. Sometimes on the wrong side . . ."

"Will you answer?"

"Looking at it which way? Stage right, or stage left?"

"Standing at the foot of the bed . . . Oh, come on, like the position you're in now."

"The position I'm in now you can hardly call sleeping."

"Stop it, you nasty man, and answer my questions." She looked at an imaginary interlocutor on the ceiling and said, "For years all he does is sit in that Fidel Castro convertible like a conductor and ask me hundreds of questions and now, as usual, when I ask a couple I can't get a straight answer out of him."

"Always right side," he said crisply.

"Let's try it the other way," she said. "See what happens."

He climbed over her and lay on the left. He feigned disorientation. "Where am I? When is the boat docking? Wake me up at customs, *cara mia.*"

Laughing, she clambered over him and he shifted back to his normal position. "Ah," he said. "The security of home plate . . ."

"Do you cuddle?" she asked.

"You're testing me," he sang. "And I don't like it. But to answer unequivocally, I sometimes sleep in the middle and let the other two sleep on either side of me so as to share the cuddling energy."

Aviva rolled her eyes.

Now he began to question her.

"How do, did, you sleep with the Arab?"

"I can't sleep if someone touches me," she said, "but if you and I ever spent a night together, I would fall asleep even if you pressed up against me."

"If you ever spent a night with me, you wouldn't get a wink of sleep. Not even a blink of a wink."

She tilted her head, crossed her eyes even more, and stuck out her tongue: Fucked to death! Her destiny! But what a way to go!

"Do you think our relationship is based on sex? It's not, is it?"

"Yes it is," he asserted cheerfully, unhesitantly. "Absolutely. Beyond a shadow of a doubt."

She laughed, knowing he was teasing.

"And you? Do you think so?"

"Of course not," Aviva said.

"Would you be upset if I were having an affair?" Guido asked.

"What do you call this?"

"I mean another one. A real one. Would you be upset?"

"No," she said calmly. "I'd just kill you and then, snip, snip. Do to you what every mohel is tempted to do but doesn't for fear of malpractice suits." Then she laughed. "But you are having an affair . . . with your wife . . ." She paused for a while, considered the conundrum. "That's funny, isn't it? Having an affair with your own wife . . . Wait a minute? Why am I laughing?" she said, suddenly sad.

Then he changed the subject, as usual. Soon they were making love again.

"Don't you want me in you forever?"

"You know, that thought comes to me later when I'm alone—I look up, even though I'm either an agnostic or an atheist, I don't know which, and say: Thank you, God . . . Now let me ask *you* a question."♥

"Uh-oh," he said, imitating her. She knew he was wondering if she'd ask him again how many times he made love to his wife.

"What would you do if I had a genealogical problem . . . ?"

"You mean, like you discovered that three of your grandparents were males?"

She looked blankly at him for a moment and then realized. "I mean a *gynecological* problem and I couldn't make love to you for six months. Would you still love me? Would you still see me?"

"You want an honest answer."

"Of course."

"I'd wish you a speedy recovery," Guido said quickly, "and I'd pray daily to God fervently for your quick recovery during those one-hundred-eighty long and lonely and awful days that I, in order to hasten your healing, would regretfully and with heavy heart, not be able to see you . . . But the main thing," he said, assuming the quick patter delivery of a Borscht Belt comic, "is you should only be healthy between the legs . . . and speaking of health, when you're healthy you love it, don't you?"

♥See ABC Directory, *Affair, wife having an, what if.*

She nodded once, kept nodding.

"Now, for the first time in my life—imagine, after all these years?—I can say I love it. Isn't that incredible?"

"Didn't you love it before?"

"Are you kidding? Not the same way."

"So when can you say you first began to love it?"

"Not until ten years after my first marriage."

"In other words with the Arab."

"Yes," she said sadly.

"Not even with Capetown?"

"I told you it wasn't that exciting with him."

"So it was the Arab," Guido said. The disappointment was clear in his voice.

"Yes. And only then on occasion and with great reservation."

"With so many guys after your pussy they would *have* to make reservations."

She drummed her feet on the bed like a timpanist going wild.

"Stop cackling," he said, "you're waking the termites . . . So you mean it's only with me, for the first time, that you can say you really love it?"

"You know that. Yes, for the first time. I love it. I love it. Can you imagine? At fifty-four? Or am I fifty-five already?"

Screwing screwing. Sex sex. That seemed to occupy ninety percent of their time. Luckily, she didn't have those nasty days any more. But, still, once in a rare while there was a problem. Already in bed with him and fooling around, she said:

"Sorry, I can't today. I got a stomach problem."

"What?" he shrieked. "*Now* you tell me."

He pointed.

She looked at the arched sheet.

"I see. You got a problem too."

"Think we can solve it?"

"Well," she said, amenable and impressed. "Your problem is bigger than mine. So my problem is your problem."

"No," he said. "Let my problem be your solution."

And the funny part was that the stomachache went away, just like her headaches went away when she was with him.

Only the heartaches remained.

But still she tried. She tried awfully hard. If only she'd tried so hard at her playing. She wanted to give everything in her to persuade him that she should be the love of his life and make the proper moves. Because she loved him. She'd never loved anyone like that before. He was constantly on her mind. Even away from him, she smelled his skin, his hair. She felt his kisses on the back of her knee, on the rim of her ear, the palm of her hand. She felt his hands on her when his hands weren't on her. The thought of him sparked desire that began in her throat and worked its way down to her loins. She felt him filling her when he was miles away. After making love to him she was still making love to him. No one else told her what Guido told her, no one else had that magic wand with words, that fantastic way with film. True, she said, "Words words words," sarcastically to him at times, but still those words of his enchanted her. Like when at the first or second lesson he suddenly popped out with the odd request, "Teach me to make cello faces?" "Cello faces?" she remembered shrieking delightedly. "Yeah," he said, "those faces that cellists make when they play to make 'em look more professional. One guy twists his lips and nose till he looks like an early Chagall self-portrait. Another puffs out his lips till he looks like a mongoloid. Another bares his lips and gazes up at the ceiling as if he's in pain. Another keeps his eyebrows up, eyes wide open, nodding, looking like a silent movie actor who's trying to convey feelings with exaggerated motions. Can you teach me how to make faces like that?" "Just follow the recipe in your descriptions," she told him, "and you'll do very well." And then, from thinking about his words, she began thinking about his body. She thought of his strong forearms, the fine dark hairs on his hands and legs, the downy hair on his chest, his tightly muscular ass. When she dreamt of him it wasn't sexual. She just felt his presence and it fluttered on her eyelids as she awoke. She wanted to possess him so badly she sometimes felt she was embracing wind, something whose essence was there but fleeting, like cello notes fading away.

She shut her eyes and let her good feeling for him inundate her. She loved his touch, his body, his cock. She had ached for him until she got him. Now she ached some more. There was no one like him. He caused her pain, he caused her grief, he made her feel so bad. But when she was with him she wanted to never let him go. When she was with him, she didn't think of music, she could forget about her students, even her children, so mightily did his person encompass her, from his intense look to the way he held himself, the way he moved, the satiny baritone timbre of his voice that sent little sexual thrills through her. He sang in her cello everytime she touched it. Every note she sounded she played for him. He was unique. He called her *sui generis* and when he explained the Latin term to her, she bounced it back in her usual self-deprecatory fashion. No, she was a dime a dozen; he was just bamboozling her with the compliment. It was he, Guido Veneziano-Tedesco who was *sui generis*. It was he who for the first time in her life vivified that abstract concept, that simple monosyllable she'd never comprehended before.

Love.

Which she poured out like—and he told her this—a fifteen-year-old in love for the first time. Each kiss, each embrace, each gesture of love was virginal. Like someone treading on freshly fallen snow. Like they did on their first heavenly walk.♥ Each touch was new, never done before. She didn't quite understand the image. The virginal metaphor floored her. But after thinking about it, she gradually realized it was right. She'd never loved like this before. When he had once asked if she ever displayed spontaneous affection for her husband, let's say going up and kissing him or throwing her arms around him, she said she never thought about it. Then, as usual, she looked up at some spot on the ceiling and tried to remember. "An interesting question," she said, "and you know what, it never dawned on me till now." She nodded, as if trying to remember. "No, I didn't," she said. "Never. He never deserved that sort of loving. Never. I didn't do it to him, and he certainly didn't do it to me. Never a sign of affection. Only in bed, to lead up to sex, and then it's quickly over."

"Turn around and go to sleep," Guido said.

"Worse. Go into another room. But with you, affection is so natural."

"Do you love me a lot?"

"Mucho mucho," she said.

"You never say it."

"I do say I love you."

"Tell me how much."

"An awful lot. But you never say it that often to me."

"Because I'm reticent," he said.

"You don't know how reticent I was. Tongue-tied. Mute. But I tell it to you more times in one day than I said it to the one man I really loved during the few years I knew him."

"Who?"

"You know."

"Capetown?"

"Yes."

"You said you loved me an awful lot." Guido made a face. "Sounds like a bad real estate investment. Do you love me with all your heart and soul?"

"M-hmm."

"What?" He cupped his ear.

She leaned forward, lifted her chin, whispered, "Yes."

"Then say it."

"I love you with all my heart and soul."

"Good. That means you can't leave me. Ever." His eyes sparkled suddenly and she caught it.

"What? What?" She smiled, swiggled her breasts on his chest, and said softly, "What are you thinking? What's going on in that buzz buzz head of yours?"

♥See ABC Directory, *Jealous and* —.

"I read the other day that gravity is the force of attraction between two bodies . . . I guess we suffer from gravity."

"But attraction lasts only so long. Now we're young and healthy and vigorous. What happens when the private parts begin to atrophy?"

"You first," Guido said. "And then so long."

There again his subtle little dig at her age, that she was older. Sometimes she wondered what he saw in her. Why didn't this good-looking forty-two year old go and get himself a twenty-eight year old girlfriend. That's what she feared most deep down—when she'd hit sixty, he'd kiss her good-bye.

"I'm not joking ," she said. "Sometimes you have to go beyond sex. Into understanding and feeling and love. I think that love is displayed more in talking than in sex. Because in talking there is a special sense of intimacy. Whereas in sex you feel that everyone does it. At this moment maybe a thousand people are screwing. But few are talking. That's why talking is better, more enriching . . . And how come," she said without a caesura, "we always end up in bed?"

Guido made a face as it to say: Stop talking nonsense.

"I guess it *is* better than talking," she continued.

"It is," he said. "There's nothing, nothing better than this . . . Nothing."

"Um, let's see . . . Chocolate?" she teased.

"No. Nothing."

"Not even photography? Getting a cover on *Photography* magazine?"

"No. Nothing. Being in you is the best thing in the world . . . Isn't it better and better?"

She didn't answer right away. "It's not linear. It doesn't go in a straight line."

"For me it is . . . But even though there's a dip, it always keeps going up."

She grinned. "I should hope so."♥

"Okay. Now you like, you love it, but there was a period when you weren't crazy for sex."

"Right."

"But men you liked."

"Mmm."

"Well, then, let's see if we can differentiate—see, we're talking—if you didn't like sex but you liked men, what parts of the man did you like?"

"The moving parts," Aviva said.

He laughed so merrily she loved it. And it was because of him that she was so funny. He inspired her.

"When did you first realize you were sexy?" he asked her.

"I haven't realized it yet. Nowadays kids are sexy—pregnant too—in grade school. I wasn't even sexy in high school."

♥See ABC Directory, *Rooster.*

"Did you go out much then?"

"Hardly. I was unpopular, even ostracized. I'm glad I didn't meet you then. Or even at PAMA."

Aviva shook her head. "Boy, was I completely off track. In many ways. I wouldn't have had the good sense to appreciate you. I didn't know what I wanted, I didn't know how to go about getting it, and I didn't know what was good for me." She stopped, not for dramatic effect. "I was such a total fool. And I say this not in any way to deflect from my responsibility for getting into so many dead-end involvements. If I had then a fraction of the little sense I have now, I wouldn't have made the choices that I made. That nice old psychiatrist, Dr. yellow polka-dot bowtie Gelbauer . . ."

"The one that pawed you?"

"No," Aviva laughed. "Who said he pawed me?"

"I thought no doctor could keep his hands off you."

"Stop! In any case, he said, and it's so true: People are more careful about choosing a dress than a husband. That's the way I was."

So why am I choosing him? Aviva thinks. Isn't Guido as dead-ended as all the rest?

"Maybe all you were interested in is the six seven inches," she remembered him saying.

"That's cruel. Cruel and unjust." And she tapped him from head to toe, measured the full length of him with a wave of the hand. "I'm interested in the full six feet . . ." And she walked to the other side of the room and said, "If only the six seven inches interested me it would really be pitiful."

She didn't quite know how to feel about the days between visits. As time to gird strength against depression and to practice putting a distance between herself and him—or as interminable hours and days that seemed like years, full of vague, gnawing metaphysical hunger to see him again. With Guido it was stressful,♥ sweet, bitter, ecstatic, awful, bittersweet, heavenly, hell. She wished she could swallow a time pill and dream away, sleep away the stone burden of the nonproductive, non-Guido days. She lived from one Saturday or Monday to another. The days in between were empty and meaningless, yet at times she would say to herself, I survived one day without him, two days without him, it's getting better, my depression is improving, I'm learning to slowly unlove him. But when she saw him again everything melted away. And once more the next set of days that she did not see him were barriers to leap over.

She loved the way Guido paid attention and lauded her body. Of course, she loved his body too but could never bring herself to say it: I love your

♥See ABC Directory, *Pressure.*

back; your ass is so delectable; your skin so baby smooth, unlike the gruff skin men usually have. At times she'd say he was sexy. But he told her he loved her breasts, which were a little cockeyed like her, her fingers, her smooth young neck, her big gray eyes, her lips, and after each compliment he zeroed in with a barrage of kissing as if he were specializing in that particular limb or organ to the exclusion of everything else on her body. He especially went for her lips, the ones, he said, that didn't go yat-tat-tat on the telephone endlessly or tell music counselors whom she was involved with. Nobody, certainly not her husband, had ever devoted so much time to her, loved her so much. With the Arab she got so used to a lack of affection she never realized what she was missing. If you don't have something you never know what you could have had, right? Until someone comes along and gives it.

Okay, she thinks, she has it bad with the Arab. So what! On balance, if she was objective, she has it bad with Guido too. And she recalls some lines she wrote in her little diary:

"I will never again experience the ecstatic joy, the warmth and closeness and the loving I had with Guido—but if I ever find it again, and I'm sure I won't (people are lucky only once in their lifetime, not twice), I hope and pray that I won't be as tormented or so completely desolate. He is both sensitive and insensitive. A puzzle. An enigma. I can still see the tears in his eyes as he describes how his father, aware of his responsibilities as a doctor, ran into a burning building to save a child, and then collapsed and died. But for me he doesn't have any sensitivity at all."

And these disturbing sensations—taking another woman's husband, not knowing if he would ever leave his wife—affected her feelings for him; they rubbed the wrong way, like sandpaper on skin. And she knew he sensed this.

It began on a different tack.

Once, when he questioned her about her lack of orgasm, she admitted, "I don't want to get involved any deeper." "So now the true Aviva is coming out," he said. "She is giving herself only up to a certain point." "Yes," she said, for she'd have to reserve a bit of herself for herself, otherwise she'd be wiped away, kicked in the ass. And she promised herself she wouldn't be kicked in the ass any more.

"Are you so sure what your feelings will be like a year from now?" she would ask with bite. "I'm not."

But then, again, in the fire of lovemaking she'd ask him, "Is it always going to be this way?" And he always said, "Yes," until she said, "How do you know?" When she asked again, he said, "I'm not going to answer because I know what your response is going to be." Months later, he asked her, "Is it always going to be this way?" and she said, "Yes, I hope so," and he snapped, "How do you know?" There's a dose of your own medicine, she remembered telling herself.

"You're not going to get tired of me?" she asked. "When I'm old and gray . . . I mean," and she laughed, "older and grayer?"

He didn't answer.

"Will you? Hello? Anyone home?"

"Can't answer. No matter what I say, I'll get it from you. If I say yes, then I'll really get it. If no, you'll say: How do you know?"

"Are you fickle?"

"Why do you ask?"

"Because you keep mentioning other girls."

"I'm a healthy young man."

"I'll be the first witness to that," she said.

"Does the age factor disturb you?"

"Yes," she said, sad. "That and other things. How many good years do I have left?"

"About forty," he said.

She grimaced. "Maybe four. And then I'll be too old for you. You'll dump me."

He held her close. "You'll never be too old for me."

But she didn't believe him. He often complained that she didn't praise him, say sweet things like he said to her. So she said:

"You're everything rolled into one. Three men couldn't possess what you have. I'd need one man for intellect, another for fun, and another for . . ."

"Fucking."

"No, that's part of fun."

"Did you ever like or fall for a guy because of his body?"

"Never . . . You see that I liked Capetown. Because he was such a sweet man. The physical part was secondary."

"What's the third guy for?" Guido asked.

"For good conversation."

What a difference, she thought, between Capetown and the Arab!♥ And what a difference between the Arab and Guido! With Guido she'd reached godly heights. No wonder she kept calling "God God God"—her religious phase, he called it—when Guido was in her.

She wished she could tell someone about his staying power, about those ecstatic forty-minute, sixty-minute screwings, going from one position to another till she was exhausted, even more cross-eyed than she was, stumbling, walking bow-legged, turned into a just-laid cliché.

"More?" he would say.

"No . . . Please . . . I can't take any more . . . act my age . . . I mean, *at* my age." And she laughed so hard at what she said, and so did he, that he slipped out.

♥See ABC Directory, *Kids, the Arab's sudden interest in.*

But with every bit of joy came the constant, nagging doubt, like a pain that would not go away. She never knew his true intentions. There was something slippery about him. You can't trust someone who cheats on his spouse. Her instincts told her that it would not work out; the longer she stayed with him, the worse she would feel.

"Please don't ever lie to me," she pleaded. With her full lips turned down, her entire face became a mask of sadness. "You don't lie to me, do you?"

"No," he said. "Do you?"

She shook her head, "No. If you do, I'd be devastated. I'd rather you told me, I don't want to answer, or just be silent, or say something else. But please don't lie to me . . ."

"I don't," he said gently. "I won't . . . I just hope that you don't doubt the beautiful things I tell you."

"For instance?" She smiled and tilted her head in that I've-got-you-now look, her grey eyes wide open. "Give me an example of something beautiful that you tell me that might make me think you're lying."

He thought a while, "All right . . . When you come up to me and kiss my shirt, or in a spurt of love, suddenly kiss my hand, it's as meaningful to me as when I'm in you. I consider both acts of love . . . Now do you believe what I say?"

"Uh-huh."

"Say it."

"Yes . . . I guess."

"Still not sure, right? You still think that I'm making this up to please you . . ."

"I'm always doubtful . . . but that's the—"

"—way I am," he said, mocking, finishing the phrase with her.

She looked at her watch. "Oh, my goodness, I'm late. I have an appointment for a brake job in half an hour. I'll never make it."

"Screw the appointment," he said.

"I'd rather screw you," she said.

And meant it. There was nothing better in the world. Guido was right. Nothing. She knew it; he knew it; she knew that he knew that she knew it. And with this joy he got her to say things she never would have dreamt of uttering out loud.

Like:

"Say it," he told her. "I love your cock."

"Yes."

"Say it . . . Repeat after me . . . I . . ."

"Repeat after me . . . I."

"Stop it," he said, "Say it."

This time she didn't hesitate. "I love your cock."

"Me too," he said.

"Really?" she said in her usual fashion, disbelieving a compliment.

"Yes. I love my cock too."

"You would," she said.

"Now repeat after me," he commanded as he moved in her. "Come what may, I will never leave you."

"This . . . coming . . . May . . . I . . . will leave you," she said slowly and giggled. Then turned her head. She felt her left eye floating outward. "How come we're always on the cock topic? How come we never discuss social issues?"

"Such as?"

"The drug problem, for instance. I read the other day that poor people are more and more addicted to crack," she said.

"I'm addicted, and I'm not poor," Guido said.

"I don't believe you," she said. "You're addicted to crack?"

"Yes," he said, putting his hand on it. "Yours."

"See what I mean? You have a one-crack, I mean, one track mind."

"I don't, I'll gladly discuss inter-religious relations with you."

She looked skeptical. "The only relations you know are sexual."

"Trust me. Turn around."

"Why?"

"Just listen to me."

Aviva turned. "What are you going to do? If you tickle me, I'll kill you."

It would be just like him, she thought, to tickle her just when he said he wouldn't. She waited, but he merely said:

"I just wanted to see if you have a WASP ass."[♥]

She looked over her shoulder at him. "What's that?"

"A high ass. Jewish girls usually have droop tooshes."

"Is mine high?" She sounded concerned.

"I'd say that the left cheek is semi-Episcopalian. And the right, a lapsed Protestant."

That's all he thought about, the pervert: sex, body, sex. Ass, calf, pussy, an entire zoo.[♥♥]

Once she had difficulty buttoning her slacks.

"No wonder these pants were on sale," she said. "It takes half an hour to get them on."

Guido's eyes flashed. "Strange. It only took you three seconds to get them off."

Yes, there was laughter. There were highs. But every rise must have its fall. Like her mother said, "If you laugh too hard you begin to cry."

[♥]See ABC Directory, *Ass.*
[♥♥]See ABC Directory, *Zoo.*

When the lovemaking didn't go well because she was depressed at home—the Arab had been nasty to her—he sensed it and told her: "Today it wasn't good, right?"

"What's the difference?" she said in her motherly wise way. "It just goes to show how super it was last time and how great it will be the next."

After the hugging, she lay on top of him and said, "I never thought I would ever feel this way. You make me feel so safe, so happy, so fulfilled . . . Even the other night, when things were bad at home, I had a sudden need of you and felt you inside of me and that made me feel good."

She smiled at Guido and then for a millisecond her lips drooped; she felt as if a wave of old age had swept over her.

"What's the matter?" Guido asked. "You just had a sad thought."

"How did you know?"

"Because for a split second you looked older."

"Why do I get these thoughts? It isn't normal. I thought: What if someone came and took you away. . . . And the other day I daydreamed we were on a plane, and Arab terrorists highjacked the plane and we were in trouble."

"Why? Because when you find something precious, you always fear it will be taken away from you," he said. "And the Arab terrorists are just your dreamway plural for the one Arab terrorist in your life."

Then, without realizing it, she switched gears and said:

"And in your life isn't there something missing?"

"Nothing," he said. "The only thing missing in my life is you."

That felt good, she thought. But it also felt empty because he wasn't doing anything about it, wasn't hinting at making a move, would never make a move. That imbecile son of his had Guido chained.

"Something is lacking," she said. "I told you that a year ago . . . You were searching . . ."

"For you," he whispered dramatically. "Only for you."

She noticed that whenever he wanted to make a point, he whispered, as if to give it more impact. Maybe he whispered when he was lying.

A look of pain came over his face, Aviva saw. He had read her thought and it hurt him.

"No. For anyone . . . And you happened to find me."

"Dead wrong," Guido insisted. "You're so much part of me, I feel you're my wife."

"But I'm not."

"That hurts. I had thought that the make-believe became real with me and you . . . From a soul point of view, you *are* my wife . . . And didn't you say that you felt I was your husband?"

"True. And I didn't even feel that for the longest time about my first husband, and I don't know if I ever felt that with this one, the one we've called the Arab for so long that's the only way I refer to him. But then reality sets in and I go my way and you go yours. Your life is fulfilled and I'm just a little side affair . . ."

"That hurts too."

". . . a little side affair in your life. I repeat it," she said forcefully. "I'm not shy about it. I told you a long time ago I don't want to share you, and that feeling is going to get stronger, not weaker. The fact that I don't tell you this every time I see you doesn't make the feeling any less real. I resent it. And the resentment is going to grow."

But she knows too that he resented all her past affairs,♥ even though he claimed that it didn't bother him any more. Talking about them had been a stupid mistake. If only she could take it back. Now she was sorry she told him everything. That is, everything she told him. Guido was the sort of guy who wanted total possession and had said so. For him, total meant not only now and henceforth, but the past as well. He had once muttered that her arms and legs had embraced so many others, he wondered if there was room for him. Which made her wonder if he could really love her knowing what he knew. And he knew too much, dammit. Her and her big mouth. Why couldn't she have shut up? Sewn her lips. All of them. Followed her mother's advice. "It was a mistake to tell you," she said. "But it wouldn't have changed the fact," he said.

"But you wouldn't have known."

"Yes I would have. No mortal can keep a secret."

"That's what my old Dr. Gelbauer said."

"Quoting Freud."

"How do you know?"

"I know everything."

"I mean, how would you have known? About me?"

"You get to know these things. Believe me, it oozes out of every pore. It's better I found out earlier than later. This way I got used to it, digested it, forgot it, and it doesn't bother me any more."

"Sure?"

"Yes."

But she knew he wasn't sure. He probably doubted that she could love him after making love to (but not necessarily loving) so many men. She had only really loved one. Then why, he asked again and again, had she lain down with so many? She could not answer. Again and again. "Sex," he said. "Cock crazy," he accused. No. It wasn't that, ever. It was aimless circumstances, how could she explain? Hoping that one of the men would be Mr. Right. A cousin had once told her, consoled her, that somewhere in the USA, maybe in

♥See ABC Directory, *Advantage, others took of her.*

Missouri, the man perfect for Aviva existed, but she didn't know it. And now she'd found her Missouri man right next door—well, almost next door—in Long Island. He had shown her, this man from Missouri. She'd always been a blabber. That had been one of her failings. Even the things she wanted to preserve in a private corner of her memory, even that, after his cerebral, incisive, intuitive scalpel probing, even that she had revealed. He didn't leave a corner unexamined, that Sherlock. She was sure that all her lovers made him uncomfortable. He said it was jealousy, but she didn't believe him. How could a man be jealous of a woman's past of twenty, twenty-five years ago, especially since she was no longer the same person. He claimed that he began to understand the human dimension. The more she described the guys, the less ciphers and names they became, said he. They assumed the guise of real people. And he said he could commiserate how a young woman after being married for seven years to an impotent man would want seven years of fire to recompense for seven years of ice. And he quoted one of those Italian proverbs that he always had up one sleeve or another like a magician. Something about natural balance, something about how the left hand gives and the right hand takes. How did he know so much about Italian folk sayings? she always wondered. And Guido said he really understood that some of her affairs were not just adventures but a search for a more permanent relationship. But she still wasn't convinced by this. She felt that he saw many other arms surrounding her when he embraced her and saw her legs entwined around a dozen other men when he screwed her. There was no room for him, he must feel, with all of them in her. Not for nothing was his crack one day: "Wouldn't it be interesting if you had a reunion of all your former boyfriends? We could rent the Coliseum," Guido said.

When things were good, she would say to him, as she did one of the first times he made love to her and the glow within her was unlike anything she'd ever felt before, "I feel like I swallowed a light bulb,"♥ and "You're the best thing that ever happened to me." But when her feelings teetered and the scale began to tip the other way, she would say, or think: "I never thought anything good would happen to me in my lifetime." That's why she felt so scared with him. It seems too good to be true. She'd never possess him; she didn't deserve him. She had always been so self-critical. Her mother began it; she continued. "I looked in the mirror and didn't like what I saw. I sat at the cello and didn't like what I heard." And then Guido, who never could take her gloomy assessments, in his usual manner, turned everything into parody and continued:

"And you cooked food and didn't like what you tasted. You sniffed your skin and didn't like what you smelled. You ran your fingers over your arms and didn't like what you felt. Bingo. You just killed off all five senses!"

♥See ABC Director, *Lightbulb, swallowing a.*

But when things were bad and she felt gloomy, even when the trees began to bud—always for her the most beautiful part of the year; those chartreuse, almost transparent leaves gave her a Bach high—it was no longer beautiful. Instead, it was a mockery. She compared her situation to a kind of cancer. Makes no difference how verdant the outside—the inside of the patient is rotting away. No hope. So what's the point of showing him the cherry blossoms, the magnolia tree in all its mauve glory? Sure there was a difference, she consoled herself. Loving Guido is not like cancer. But it was still hopeless. There was no future in it, even though he gave hints, saying, you can never tell. If you broke off it surely was hopeless, but if she kept it up there was hope. Who knows what could/would happen with him and his wife down the line? So he said, but she didn't believe it. She loved him and was angry with him at the same time. And it wasn't good. It was awful. She'd made enough stupid mistakes in her life: Her entire life had been a mistake; her personal life, her professional life. Ladies and gentlemen, our next exhibit. The pretty lady with the long auburn hair. Please note, here's one all of whose life has been a mistake. We do not have many examples of this kind in our museum . . . Continuing now, immediately to her right, the woman in glasses in the red hat . . . It was time to take control. If not now, after fifty-plus years, then when? Still, she loved him. She adored him. She would never find another man like him. Ever. He was her dream. Her miracle man. Her marathon man. With him she had everything. You're everything I wanted, she told him over and over again.

When she was down, and foods, especially junk, jumped out at her of their own accord from containers, packages, boxes, as if animated from a cartoon; when the kids harass me, she thought, when I'm tired, when I see the treadmill my musical career is on ("Why don't you practice?" he shouted at her. "Why do you sleep till ten? Why don't you crawl out of bed when you wake up instead of staring at the ceiling in a catatonic state?"), when I see what a mess I've made of my life with these two lousy marriages and all the crab steps in between, she felt she was at the end of her world. "When I'm depressed," she told Guido, "all I want to do is sleep, step out of myself. I turn and look back and there I am, holding my problems, but I'm no longer me. I'm free. I have my magic boots on and I can be somewhere else. Or if those magic boots are unavailable ("The boots that that hypocrite Rabbi Doctor Horny Matchmaker rubbed so lovingly?" Guido said), I sleep a magic sleep and when I wake I don't shudder, yes, actually shudder, shake with fear of the coming day, but I don't shudder after that magic sleep for I wake up and find out I'm not me."

"A kind of dying," Guido said. "A craving for perpetual sleep is suicidal. A death wish."

"Yes. A long sleep. Although, curious, I don't crave naps as a kind of shutting out of the world."

"That's a good sign," he said.

"I don't know. I just don't have the time to nap . . ." she paused. "I spend most of my time with you—and you never let me sleep."

He was about to say something, but she added:

"And then there's that damn cello hanging over me like a sword. That's another stress. I just don't like to perform any more. Some people enjoy performing. I don't.♥ The problem with memorization, the tension, nervousness, and anxiety I have when I have to perform isn't worth it."

"But the audience enjoys it."

"It's not enough. Musicians perform because they love it. I just don't. It's torture for me. Can't you understand that? Torture! Why do I have to undergo weeks of stress—I actually get ill to the pit of my stomach—for something I find distasteful? It's senseless. Sometimes I feel if I died, hurray, I wouldn't have to perform."

"Cut it," he ordered.

Easy for him to say, she thought. He thinks one order can wipe away an inside stain. I'm not a Formica countertop: wipe it away, she didn't say.

"Do you want to die?" he asked her.

"Sometimes," she said softly.

"Fairy tale princesses never die," Guido said.

Aviva knew that he thought of her as a princess, a lady, a queen, but she didn't tell him about her rages, her foul mouth, which she let loose only during her marriage (credit the Arab with bringing this out in her, which she'd suppressed all these years. Two years of psychiatry couldn't undo the cork; but after seven months with the bastard, she let loose.). He saved her thousands of more dollars of analysis, the fuck. Also she found her tongue with him. A loose, street-sassy, untempered, distempered, unfettered tongue. Another attribute Guido didn't know about. She could wreck her kids' room when enraged, well, not wreck it, but tear up the bed, crumple and throw the sheets all around, open the drawers and dump the clothes, throw 'em up in the air to the four corners of the room and fling the books like missiles. Serves them right for harassing her. She could curse like a trooper, and in front of the girl too. Later, she felt bad, knew it was awful, but couldn't contain herself. She wasn't telling this to the counselor either. She refused to be stepped on any more. Years ago, a perceived insult would be swallowed and then she'd worry about it and say to herself, "What did I do wrong? How did I deserve it?" It was always her fault. But in her marriage with the Arab, she let go. Perhaps the Indian shrink would have applauded this. A sign of maturity. Coming into her own. Gone the bobby sox and pleated skirts, gone the tight-assed innocence. Should she have a reunion of all her shrinks? she mused. Town Hall, maybe?

♥See ABC Directory, *Cello, going back to.*

She wondered sometimes if she hadn't become a mirror image of her primitive husband. A Moroccan without restraints. When as a youngster she was furious with her mother for not allowing her to go somewhere or for instructing her how to hold her spoon or sit straight or not blow her nose at the table in the presence of her friends, in her rage she daydreamed of going into her mother's room and destroying it, of flinging her mom's precious china to the floor, piece by piece, tearing the lace off her precious slips. But good, well-tempered, even, behaved, polite, nice good little Jewish girls didn't do things like that, for they always bore in mind the family they came from; they remembered not to shame the family. So she waited till she was forty, forty-eight. And smashed the Arab's precious plates, his grandmother's Lalique that he claimed she had bought in France on her wedding trip and kept as an heirloom for fifty years, but which Aviva knew the Arab had bought at a Long Island garage sale, as part of the process of reinventing himself, de-Moroccanizing himself, de-Africanizing and pro-Frenchifying himself (You can take the Arab of the *mellah*, but you can't take the *mellah* out of the Arab, Guido quoted), bought along with the rest of the prestige he bought, everything with money, the honor he bought, the respect he bought, the taxis he bought, the public adulation in his synagogue with donations and Purim masks of piety and concern, buying everything with money, that crazy rotten inconsiderate Moroccan Arab bastard fuck, who took her early brief love and flung it away like a dead insect. But the only thing he couldn't buy, never in a million years, never with a million dollars, was his wife's heart.

With the Arab she never laughed, or did her constant laughter with Guido color her memory? In any case, with Guido she had endless fun.

"Do you like Snickers?" he asked, when she said she couldn't resist chocolate.

"Used to," she said. "Stopped eating it long ago."

"Good. Keep it up," he said.

"You too," she said.

And once in a park, Guido suggested, "I'll play you tennis. If you win, you have to screw me. If I win I screw you."

"Either way I win," she said.

"Either way I lose," he said.

Or the time she was thirsty and he poured her a cold drink and held it. But as usual, she couldn't resist chatting, so as she spoke he drank it and watched her watching him.

"I'm drinking it for you," Guido explained.

Then poured another glass, which she stuck her hand out for.

"This one I'll drink for myself," he said.

But she seized the glass with a laugh. "That's okay. I'll drink it for *you*."

Even serious matters, like what would happen with them, became part of the verbal game.

In the midst of the lovemaking—well, actually, during a break—she remembered saying, trying to make it sound casual:

"When you gonna come and live with me?" She said it in a softer voice than usual. Higher pitched too, as if she were parodying herself while actually saying what she meant.

Guido didn't answer.

"Come live with me," she said in a quick whisper, then louder: "When will you? And answer honestly, no evasions, Mister Evasiveness."

He was on top of her and lowered his chin to her lips. Instead, she kissed his throat. "He presents his chin to be kissed rather than answering." Aviva addressed an imaginary arbitrator up on the ceiling. "Okay, answer yes or no."

"Yes."

"I didn't starting asking yet. Now I'm beginning . . . Do you want to come and live with me?"

"Yes."

"What steps will you be taking to—stop nodding. It's not a yes or no question. Is it going to be this year?"

"No."

"Next?"

"Blip."

"What does that mean?"

"That's not a yes or no question."

"Come on. Time out. What does blip mean?"

"It means the computer can't figure it out."

"Are you going to try?"

"Blip, bleep."

She kissed him again and laughed.

"What does *that* mean?"

"Game's over. Too bad. You just forfeited the game by not asking a yes-or-no question."

"If you don't come and live with me, snip-snip you know where."

Guido laughed, rolled over. "Then I can't win. It's snip-snip in either case. I don't come to live with you, you snip-snip. I *do* come, it's she snip-snip. So I'll be ball-less in any case and two women will be crying. Maybe more. So no matter where I come I won't be able to come no more. Snip snip. Bleep bleep. I have a great career ahead of me, singing the contralto lead in *Aida*, the first Italian castrato in ninety-nine years."

Aviva sighed. She could get nowhere with him. When she asked him serious questions, he changed the subject, made her laugh, made love to her again, as if his ardor were an answer to her nagging doubts. It was the history of men and women all over again. Women want a relationship, men a fling. And if they weren't doing it, they were talking about it. Or he asking questions. Once, after his persistent queries, she decided to humor him and create a few more lovers. For instance, he was absolutely positive that she had that accountant her husband had sent her to, just as he was sure that she must have made love to Plaskow. So the next time he asked her about the accountant, she said:

"What do you want me to say? Yes? I did it? Is that what you want?"

"Yes," he said.

"Okay, I did it."

She knew that wouldn't be the end of it.

"Where?"

She thought a while. "In the Plaza."

"He could afford the Plaza?"

"Well, my husband paid for it."

"What?" Guido shrieked.

"He gave him an advance, so actually he was using my husband's money."

Guido made a face and continued. "Any others?"

And she made up stories about other guys. But she couldn't fool him. Either with yeses or nos. Son of a gun, he saw into everything. Just like a night lens.

Guido said he was sure that, though she was concocting the others, with the accountant it was indeed so because she didn't protest his questioning. Last time she even said, "You'd make a good lawyer . . . Enough already. Let's drop it."

But she did admit that after a flare-up with the Arab, she drove around the streets for a couple of hours, musing over if she should call the accountant. Finally, she did. He hinted that they go somewhere where they could be alone. She didn't recall if he said a hotel, but she suspected that's what he meant. They couldn't go to her apartment because of her mother and the baby and certainly not to his house. But, of course, she didn't take him up on it at all.

No matter how hard she tried (she guessed she didn't try hard enough), she couldn't steer Guido away from his pet subject. God! Those questions must give him some kind of sexual thrill. He even got her to consider aspects of sex she'd never thought of before. Even articulating out loud what she'd never told her eighty-two-year-old ruddy-faced Dr. Gelbauer (first name forgotten) whose bow tie she saw so often she had polka-dotted dreams. Aviva laughed to herself. Doctor's first names she forgets; lovers' last.

"Were you ever comfortable with sex?" Guido said.

"I was uncomfortable with sex for a great while," she told him. "Even into my late twenties after seven years of so-called marriage. My mother wasn't only a conservative, she was an ultraconservative. Compared to her, Reagan is a liberal. I remember once a younger boy cousin talking about a couple of girls traveling with two friends and sleeping in separate rooms and my mother saying, "Nice girls don't do things like that." So I had this sense of wrong ingrained into me since childhood. So even when I slept with a man, my conscience pricked me," she said, ticking her head forward, eyes laughing, "among other things."

" 'Tis a consummation devoutly to be wished, says Shakespeare, for one maiden to be pricked twice on the same occasion."

"Now that I think of it, that's also when I began to use the vibrator. On the one hand, it didn't prick my conscience; on the other, it made sex better."

"So it had two opposite purposes."

"I didn't think about that. I guess."

It was then that Guido asked her to stop using it.

"But you're not always available," she said.

"Do you think of me?"

"Between jolts." She laughed.

But he was not impressed.

"It selfishly accents your body, its physical needs, and its own satisfaction. Save it, save the joy, store your heat for me. Maybe you'll sensitize the rest of your body and not just your pussy. Imagine my hands all over your body, inch by inch . . ."

"Mmmm . . ."

". . . and sensitize yourself to touch and stimulation on all levels and not just rubbing the most intense spot."

Her eyes widened. "MMMM!"

But she was noncommittal. Not only did he want her when he wanted her, she thought, he wanted to deprive her of pleasure when he was away. Knowing that he would soon be off on another assignment, she told him, "You know what I'm going to do? I'm going to take Oscar and personalize him. I'll draw eyes and nose and mouth and tongue, especially a tongue on him, and play with him when you're gone."

"How disgusting," Guido said. "Why don't you go to the butcher shop and get yourself a real tongue?"

"I would. But in that state it doesn't move any more."

He said he'd love to have a photographic record of her using the vibrator, to take rapid fire still shots of her until she came.

"Yeah, sure," she said. "I'm running. It's enough you took those dozens of pictures of me in the nude,♥ claiming you'd send them to *Playboy*."

He stamped his foot. "I never said *Playboy*. I said *Modern Maturity*. I said the AARP Annual Nude Study Contest. And anyway you love when I snap

---

♥See ABC Directory, *Posing naked*.

you naked or clothed . . . You see, the relationship is very practical," he told her. "You like me because I'm your photographer man. Blowups, not blow jobs. Conversions of color slides into black and white photos. Re-doing all your old family pictures. Magically removing the Arab from all your snapshots. And I like you because of your great body."

She didn't know if he meant it or was joking. Sometimes she felt that *that* was the only *that* he was after. Otherwise, why didn't he ever make a move to disengage himself and be only with her? And that was another pressure on her. Maybe he didn't like her for herself—but just as a plaything.

She looked down at her body. Pinched her stomach. "Yuk. This gotta go. I'm getting so fat.♥ I wish I were thinner for you."

"I heard of a great diet. You want a no-fat, no-cholesterol, no calories diet with absolutely divine taste?"

"Yes, sure. What is it?"

"An Italian dish called fellatio."

"No thanks, I'm a vegetarian. I only had vegetables and an egg today and I'm starving. It's so easy to put on a pound or two and so hard to get it off. Sometimes I just want to leave this body. Did you ever want to take a vacation from yourself? To get out of your skin? I have so many pressures on me I'd like to run away. The kids are wild. They sense the tension in the house. And then there's you. You're the biggest pressure, the greatest stress is you. I feel blue and gloomy inside. If only I didn't have to deal with so many things at the same time—how come you never take your socks off?"

"So if I disappeared you'd have a personal memento . . . But just let me tell you, it will be easier for you to get out of your skin and take a vacation from yourself than for me to disappear—because I have an extra toe that I'm ashamed of."

"How come," she asked, "you switch in midsentence from one thing to another, don't you ever feel as if these blues, blahs, blehs, emptiness and hopelessness envelop you?" she asked.

"Rarely. Almost never. Maybe years ago when I was a kid and at first I couldn't make the sounds go right on the cello."

"But this blue feeling doesn't come and go on occasion?"

"No."

"You're lucky. And you always have energy."

"Yes."

"So you don't know what this despondent feeling feels like. Or what it is to have waves, periods, days of exhaustion, or inability to do anything."

"Yes . . . I mean, no. I never have that."

♥See ABC Directory, *Overweight and love.*

"You don't know how lucky you are."

"The only time this emptiness overwhelms me," he admitted, "is if I imagine you are gone."

"Aha! And how would you know? Suppose I got killed over the weekend? Let's say on Friday night. Or had to be rushed to the hospital. How would you know? How would I let you know? Would you come to visit? Or suppose something happened to you. Could I come to see you? See? That's the awful part of this relationship. The normal connections aren't there."

The bottom line, she knows, is that she's a fool. She told him she didn't want to die a fool, but she knew she would die a fool. Although she always threatened to leave him, she always relented. It was he, she knew, who would leave her. Every year she'd get older and older until one day he'd wake up and see an old woman hovering about him. She would say, No more, and mean No more, but each time she would succumb. His words, his feelings cast into words, he himself so mesmerized her she couldn't help herself. It was like with chocolate and ice cream. She could swear off—between indulgences. Why couldn't she stick to her resolve? Because of him. His eyes, his body, his presence. His magic touch. Like Guido said about her. If one could hug a smile, she would have hugged his smile. It was so heartfelt, so cozy, so wrapped around you. He embraced her with his smile that she could have hugged. He was more than the sum of his parts. He once said something so absolutely on the mark: There is a mystique in this world, a force greater than all physical laws, and its name is love. She couldn't resist him, go do her something. She hung on to the slightest spider web or promise that would permit her to change her mind. Yes, she realizes, she would die a fool.

"I'm so unlucky," she told him. "Why am I so unlucky?"

He said he couldn't believe his ears. Here was a woman who was pretty, no, not pretty, beautiful. Well formed. Great body. Auburn hair awash with womanly vibes. Talented. Great musician. Super teacher. Everything going for her. Yet claimed to be unlucky. Is this Aviva talking? he wanted to know.

"You're lucky," he said. "So lucky you don't even know it. If you only knew how much unluck people have in this world, you'd thank the God you don't believe in for the luck you do have . . ."

". . . to have you," she whispered, giving her sad smile. "I'm lucky and yet unlucky at the same time."

"You're lucky, I say. If I say you're lucky, you're lucky. You are lucky. You will be lucky. A lucky star will look over you."

"Really?" And as soon as she heard "will look over you"—she immediately transformed it to "will overlook you."

"Really," he said.

"Promise?"

"I promise. Luck will be with you. Luck will be close to you. Luck will be your second skin."

And just then, as if she'd had been hit over the head, the magic cloud that hovered over them when she was with him lifted and she saw the real world for a moment and blurted, "Only when I leave you."

To which he immediately responded, "If you do, unluck will square and cube."

He had it all planned out. She'd skid, he said. Go downhill. All the way. Repeat her actions of years back. First with this guy, then the next. Resuscitate her promiscuous ways.

"You can't help it. You won't be able to stop."

"I will. I'm not the same person I was twenty, twenty-five years ago."

"How can you help it? You go out once with a guy, let's say you have coffee."

Aviva rolled her eyes. Then told him she'd done this once with a man recently, as a way of reducing her resentment toward him.

"You have? Who?" Oh, the jealousy in Guido's voice, she loved it.

She wasn't saying. "I told you I would start going out. And if I didn't, I meant to."

"Okay. Don't tell me. I won't press you . . . Anyway, you have coffee once, twice. How much coffee can you drink? Especially if you don't drink, can't stand, coffee. Next time he'll take you dancing. He puts his arms around you, wants to kiss you, who can resist you?"

"But that doesn't mean bed."

"Okay, not the first two times. But later? It will happen."

"It won't."

"Latest survey shows that men want to get laid on the first date. You'll screw him and then you'll see that he's not really to your liking and another candidate will roll in."

"I can go with a guy for six months or more, and by then I'll know if I want him permanently."

"You'll go to bed as a rebound. Just like you did with me after the Arab."

"First of all, you were different. You were, are, my soulmate. Remember how that word just blurted out of me. Me! Me who never said anything to a guy. No. No way. There's no rebound anymore."

"You'll do it out of anger towards me," he said. "Just like when you're depressed you say you don't care, you're sorry you met me, I was a mistake, and you don't need anyone, that you'll get involved with someone just to create a wedge."

"That's only when I'm angry, and it's just talk. I won't happen, and I'll tell you why. I had much more cause to be angry with the Arab, which lasted over a period of many years, and I didn't do it. Because if you do something like that it's not against that person, it's against yourself, and I have no intentions of doing anything against myself. I've had only long-term and stable relationships. I've been in this rotten marriage for fourteen years and except for that one instance of kissing the accountant I didn't touch anyone, and before that three-and-a half years with Capetown. I mean, isn't that a sign of stability? This old flitting around had stopped long, long ago, and it won't happen again."

"But sometimes anger leads to action. Like a few months ago—after you left angry and said you were going to a wedding that night—and I drove over to your house the next morning and saw a strange car parked there and knew it was a guy you'd met at the wedding the night before and he was already in your house and your phone was off the hook and I know you do that when I'm in bed with you."

"And who was it?" Aviva laughed.

"You told me a student for a makeup lesson."

"Some bed partner."

Could she break, she wondered, that cycle of depression? Joy with him, gloom at leaving, depression at home. Was she a masochist? Why did she subject herself to this crap? One morning, when she felt particularly down and wanted to stop seeing him, for she was jealous and didn't like the idea of sharing him,♥ of him having two wives, and he cajoled, connived, convinced her to stay, she said: "I'm going to regret this," and then he pulled away and she said, "Come over here . . . You love women, don't you? . . . You always have and you always will. They don't cease to amaze you . . . You can't resist them . . . I know it. And that's why, even if you end up with me, you're going to cheat on me . . ."

"I love people . . ." he said. "Humanity."

"Yeah, sure. Fifty per cent of it."

She had mentioned this aspect of Guido to the counselor she was now seeing and wondered what to do. But these types are trained to squeeze the decisions out of you, not offer advice, which you'll eventually blame them for. But even the counselor seemed to be hinting that she cut with Guido.

"Okay," Aviva said. "Let's leave the plus, the upside, let's look at the downside for a moment. You and I have nothing in common. Our life styles are different. You fly all over the world, I like to sit still. You told me you once believed in God. Me, I'm an atheist."

"I'll convert," he reassured her. "With God's help, I'll become an atheist too."

She laughed despite herself. She swore to God she wouldn't laugh at his jokes, that it would be a way of distancing herself from him, but he made her laugh anyway. Once, when she called to tell him she wasn't coming, he told

♥See ABC Directory, *Sharing two women.*

her to come and promised he wouldn't make her laugh. "You promise?" she said. "I promise," he said, and then she heard him muffle a choked laughter.

"What's so funny?" she wanted to know.

"I promised." Now he let loose the laugh.

"You promised what?"

"I promised not to make you laugh . . . Sorry." He giggled.

"But it's you who's laughing, not me, so you're not making me laugh . . ." and she began giggling too despite herself. "Come on, tell me what's so funny."

"I think to myself," he says, "I promised not to make her laugh. I won't say a word. But when she comes I'll shove a mirror in front of her face, and there goes my promise."

And so again she laughed. She broke her promise to herself of not going to his house and he broke his promise to her of not making her laugh, saying, "Promising not to make you laugh is the biggest joke of all."

She was a fool, she knew, an absolute fool. And she was going to—her greatest fear—die a fool. A sucker. His term, not hers. For once, after she had told him that she loved his lollipop, that it was like an all-day sucker,♥ he gave her one of his cutesy responses: She'd been taken for a sucker for God knows how long; with her birth, P. T. Barnum's sagacity was confirmed. Or like Guido told her, and she believed him, that Poles genetically cannot have children, that all Poles are adopted. It was only when he said that the Polish government had passed a resolution to invite all barbers to become Poles and that when Lech Walesa was told to take a poll before elections, he asked, "Whereto?" that she realized he was joking. When, she wondered, would she wake up? She knew she was being taken for a ride. On a merry-go-round with rings just out of reach. She knew that his goal wasn't marriage. He liked her for her body. For sex. Otherwise, why was it the first thing he did when she came to him, sometimes even before a hello was exchanged, was to take off her clothes slowly one layer at a time, to which deed she'd smile her pleased sleepy cat smile, "redolent with eros and pussy," as Guido put it. True, she liked his touch, but he never told her that he loved her, well, actually, he did tell her but she didn't believe him; he never told her that he wanted to be with her, that there was some kind of always to their relationship. He didn't. But she to him—God, how often had she told him that she wanted him always to be with her. She said things to him that she never even dreamt of saying to a man, couldn't believe the words she uttered came from her, words that were translated into speech two milliseconds, no, at the very moment, the thought was born.

He didn't understand women, probably never did. He doesn't realize we're on a different time zone, she thinks. Women's now and their distant

♥See ABC Directory, *All-day sucker.*

tomorrow were fused. For her, today was just an inseparable particle of the promised tomorrow. But men would live for the separable moment. When she saw him, was with him, she saw time as a musical motif that would play itself out later in the symphony, come to some kind of beautiful finale. Every moment, every note, built phrases for the entire score. Her wanting him now was inextricably linked with her holding him years from now, attaching herself to him forever. She meant it, she mused, when she told him that had she dreamt up a man, she could not have dreamt up someone more perfect for her. For with him she had everything: fun, brains, talent, personality, and sex. Not necessarily in that order. And that sexiness of his invaded every part of his being. That guy was born sexy. But what good was it? Would she have him tomorrow? Would he be hers, or would he slip away, like magic moments slip away in fairy tales? Like magic moments of childhood bliss slip away. For deep down she was suspicious of him. In her darker moments, she sensed he was using her. To make his marriage more enticing? she wondered. To put a little spice into his life? When her mood was up, the sun shone. Vivaldi all over the place. God! Those stunning solo cello sonatas. She could isolate those blissful, ecstatic moments, like pluck- ing out beautiful phrases of one of his sonatas, and sense that they would add up, one after another, that Guido would treasure those moments and want more until he'd decide to be only with her. That was the difference between men and women. Men wanted to get laid; women—married. But when she was down—and lately this happens more and more often—her jealously of Guido having two wives knotted her stomach and poisoned her mind. She was gruff with her children, who needed not more gruffness— they had enough from their nonfather—but more affection. And she told Guido this—that when she felt down it had its effects not only on her innermost being but also on her music, the way she taught, how she related to her children. And that must not be. She would not permit that to happen. They had enough abuse and mistreatment from the Arab, she thinks. If they were to survive as balanced human beings in this world, she had to be there for them, a whole person, giving them the love they needed and deserved. But Guido didn't seem to understand. He was selfish that way, never wanting to let her go, pleading for the moment, for another six months, as if it were an extension to a terminal illness, as though that would make a difference. It was just another three or four or six months of pleasurable—there was no denying that—screwing. He was a high for her, like cocaine, but once the high of the drug wore off she was plummeted into despair that took lots of climbing to just get her chin over the edge of the precipice. She was quite open about her stress, but he, he hardly spoke of his side of the emotional turmoil. Did it roll off him like water off a duck's back? Yes, he was Mr. Enigma. He told her that once while on a train in England he saw a little girl playing with her windup music box. It played "Twinkle, Twinkle, Little Star" but it only went up to the "lit . . ." and that break in the melody, that sense of incompletion, musical and emotional irresolution, reminded him of their love.

"That's where I'm caught with you," he told her, "impaled on top of that 'lit'—yearning for that completion of melody."

"Me too."

A look of anger crossed his face, she saw, that seemed to say: Dammit, is that all she's going to do? Repeat what I'm saying? Did she really know Guido? she wondered. She hardly knew him. How quickly he got angry. He probably didn't want to show it, but his face, like the music box story, was an open book.

In her frequent down moments, Aviva thought that that was all Guido wanted—good screwing. All his whispered protestations of how much he loved her rang empty in her ears, like a cello string out of tune. Either she would have him all to herself, or she would have to give him up. She couldn't take any more the stress of a part-time boyfriend who was inaccessible, who couldn't be called when she felt lonely on Saturday night and Sunday, who appeared like some kind of guardian angel only at certain hours on certain days. It was insulting to have to live around that fucking camera shop's schedule. What kind of life was it, to come over only on the days Tammy was selling film and cameras? Damn that Tammy. Aviva had had enough. She would go. And that's final. But each time they separated he convinced her that we go through this world only once, that a miraculous coming together like theirs doesn't happen every day, that that special starlight of theirs should be preserved even at the risk of disappointment and pain, that even in separation they should see each other, even if only to be friends, for they had a relationship that went beyond friendship and had entered familial kinship. She laughed, remembering how he had once called her his aunt, his camp counselor, his sister, cousin, grandmother too. So even when they split up and she said she wasn't going to sleep with him any more ("all of sudden it's 'sleep'," he said. "Like the Venetians say: Change of heart, change of language."), he seemingly accepted it and on her living room sofa lay down next her ("we'll just be friends. Friendly like," he said and she said, "Okay.") and they hugged and he kissed her face and it felt so good to have his arms around her and his face next to hers and he held her breast and she laughed and said, "Is this friendly?" and he replied, "Very friendly," and then he lifted her sweater and undid her bra and sucked on her nipples and said, "And this is even friendlier" and he brought her hand down to his crotch and she said, "What are you doing?" and he said, "Testing the limits of friendship." And she rubbed and then he guided her hand into his pants and she held his cock and he said, "Speaking of friendship, I thought you'd like to kiss your friend hello," and she said, "Uh-uh, I'm not *that* friendly," and he said, "Just once?" and she agreed, "Okay, you devil, just once," said laughingly, "and then we'll bid him a friendly good-bye." "Au revoir," he countered and she kissed it once and peeked up at him with a shy look and said, "Is this how you act with all your friends?" and before she knew it his fingers were massaging her pussy while she was licking him, and he flicked his tongue on her clit and she said, "What's the difference between this and screwing?" and he said, "I'll show you, pal," and began to demonstrate the difference between serious fucking and friendly screwing, going in and pulling out and making comments on differences until she begged him to stop demonstrating the differences and stop stopping and just get into the serious part of it after which she hugged and kissed him and said, "You're the best friend I ever had."

It wouldn't work. It can't work, this friendship mode. There was too much fire between them. It was ecstasy while it lasted and then depression set in. Why had she done this? Was she a drug addict? A masochist? Always looking for pain. He would never be hers entirely. He would revel in that part-time love affair forever. If she had any sense, any sense at all, she would cut. Completely. Not see him. Because if she saw him he would touch her. That's all he would have to do is look at her and touch her and she'd be lost. Again in that momentary magic, that web of illusion that he spun so well that lasted no longer than a sunset. Maybe she would let him call her. He had such a beautiful voice. And she *would* want to know how he was doing. After all, as he said, they did create something unique together. But if she had any sense, she would get on with her life and sever herself from bondage. Because that's what it was. Bondage. Slavery. She was a slave, a love slave, a sucker—and she wanted to be free.

But Guido doesn't understand. He just doesn't understand what a woman wants. She didn't even want excitement, though Guido was exciting enough for three. She just longed for a little peace ("Me, too," he said, dead pan, and again she couldn't help laughing), quiet and tranquility; she yearned for a little nest without fights, stress, worries. Was this too much to ask? Was it possible in this world? Had the same God that sent Guido to her also determined that she would never find happiness in this world?

Then, when he was in Iceland—for the summit, a letter came, well, not a letter, but a letter anyway.

He said:

I miss you the minute I wake up and your image doesn't leave me until I go to sleep and then I dream of you. When I wake from a night's sleep there is a moment of space, an anxiety attack, and then, whoosh, you slip, slide, sidle into me for the rest of the day. When I'm working with the photos, I look for a picture of you, standing behind Reagan and Gorbachev for instance, and when I see in a newsphoto someone who even remotely resembles you, I montage your face onto hers and see, create, you. In my mind, I write letters to you, I write about you. When you're not with me, you're with me. You're never without me, always within me. The minute I stop embracing you, I hug you in my mind. I rehearse ways of kissing you, sitting you in a chair and telling you not to move, not to dare move your lips, don't move, I tell you, and I press my lips to yours. I rehearse positions with you and imagine you taking off your clothes and you whispering to me, "Let's go upstairs," when we've talked too much after you've come in. I imagine kissing your neck, your hair, your back, the crack in back of your shoulders, your left breast, your right breast, the one that makes you moan and arch your back and press yourself against me, and when we lie down I imagine you saying, "From the back," and I say, "Now?" and you whisper in the softest pianissimo, "Yes, yes," and in your ecstatic expectant desire you give the litany, "Yes, yes, yes," and I enter you and ask, "More?" and you keep saying, "More, more, more, please, more" and you echo me, for we are one voice, one wavelength, one heartbeat, one desire, one love, "Please more, please more," and I give you more while you give me more, always more, and I think of telling you, I love your fingers, I love your cheeks, I love your cockeyed squinty big gray eyes, I love your full lips made for kissing, your kissable smooth neck, I love you ears, I love your breasts, your belly which you always say has got to go, I love your back, I love your graspable ass, your white smooth thighs, your knees, the little wrinkle above your left knee, I love your back of the knees, which I taught you to become sensitive to, your fawn legs, I love your walk, your hair, even the two flecks of grey that are coming through that rich tawny cascade of auburn wildness, and that gray doesn't give you age but added desire, it makes your girlish look become womanly, I love your voice, I love the change in your voice from phone to in person, I love you at the cello, I love you not at the cello, I love you sitting, lying (but not untruth lying), standing, looking like a new born fawn, unsure of her legs, looking a bit discomfited and shy. I love the way you move, I love your smile. I love your radiance. Your glow, your passion, your enthusiasm for sex, your lovemaking. I love the way you love me, I love your talent, your embrace, the way you kiss me when you come in. I love your mistakes in English, your fumbling for words, your elegance with the pluperfect, in fact I consider you pluperfect, I love your tongue-tiedness, your shyness, the way you hesitate and look down before you tell me something. I love your music, the way you say, I'll do anything for and with you. From far away I recreate you, just as in the darkroom I create those magical images that float on my prints, ex nihilo from the developer. So even though I only talk to you and don't mail this to you, know that I write to you when I'm working, when I look at slides, when I look through the enlarger, talking and writing to you when I'm driving or flying, in my sleep and in my dreams.

"You're reading this," she said.

"Yes."

"I'm overwhelmed. Is it a letter?"

"Of course. But not mailed."

"That's so sweet. Calling from Iceland. You sound next door. Is it cold in Reykjavik?" she asked.

"Not anymore," he said.

"This is costing you a fortune."

"I reversed the charges."

Even if she'd planned for a year to leave him, how could she leave him after a love letter/call like that? Wouldn't anyone hesitate to put a brake/break in her determination to leave her man after hearing words like that? Or were they calculated, since he was so far away, to keep her in line and prevent her from straying?♥

Once he told her of a three-part dream he had. First he's sitting on a ledge with lions, and they spoke and said: "Don't be afraid." Next he's in the army, captured by the Germans, but he escapes and hides, then runs to a village where he sees a grocery. The grocer says: "Don't be afraid, we'll protect you." Finally, he finds himself driving along a road that hung suspended in the air.

"It's all one dream," she said, expert now in dreams, for her counselor was interpreting her dreams to her. "You're under control. You have it all under control. You are the lions. You are lucky. Someone, somewhere is protecting you."

But no one is protecting me, she thinks. If I don't look out for my own interest, who will? The Arab? One morning she looked at the mirror and saw another face. What had she been doing to herself? How much more crap would she take in this no-win situation? Besides Guido having her whenever he wanted her and she never having him whenever she wanted him, he was always putting her down. Sarcasm really hurt her, like when he told her if she had a reunion of her old boyfriends she'd have to rent the Coliseum, or was it Madison Square Garden, or like when he went into his Busoni Bassani Buitoni tirade when she didn't recognize the Italian Jewish writer's name and then mixed him up with the composer, Busoni. Here again was a perfect example of how she swallowed insults. Please, she told him, please don't be sarcastic. Please! Imagine! She pleaded. With him. What a jerk I am, she thought. I shoulda called him a conceited supercilious ass and not said, "Please," in my polite, good-Jewish-girl fashion.

The breaking point came when he returned from one of his trips and he called her; they made a date for her to visit him. He canceled once; he

♥See ABC Directory, *Dialing again.*

canceled twice. For the second he was honest, or stupid, enough to mention his wife. That was the last straw. Shit! Again she had to schedule her visits to him to accommodate his fucking wife. She'd had it. Had it with him, had it with the Arab, had it with depression, had it with having only crumbs. And once, right after she called him to say she wanted to talk to him, something happened that devastated her, an event that she tried to expunge from her mind, told her counselor about, but could not erase. It merely confirmed her instinct; he was not to be trusted. But she vowed not to say a word about this to him.

And those questions of his. There was a limit, right? They oppressed her too. But because she wanted to safeguard a measure of her privacy, she couldn't get *that* off her chest and discuss some of them with the counselor. Obviously, there were questions Guido asked that she answered that she couldn't tell anyone else. Certainly not to her counselor. Therapists don't have to know everything. And moreover, lately she'd become sensitive about her age, which she'd never been before. If she looked thirty-nine, let other guys assume she was thirty-nine. And in protecting her age, she couldn't tell that she would have wanted to have children with Guido but couldn't because that would give away her age. She couldn't tell that Guido asked if she'd been a counselor at the camp he went to as a kid. There was a time she wasn't concerned about her age or looks, but now she kept her hair long to hide even more her squint. She spent more time in front of the mirror trying various makeups to disguise the wrinkles above her lips. See how one nasty crack by a daughter prompts a change in behavior? And she couldn't tell the counselor about all the questions Guido asked about various boyfriends. How and if she missed A; what words she said to B while screwing; if C liked foreplay; if D kissed her toes and ears and puss-puss and what positions they used, and did E go for it a second and third time. There were some things one keeps to oneself, although God knows Guido did his damnedest to undo that principle. What could she do with these questions? Keep them on file, write them in a diary, or jot them down and rip them up?

And she wouldn't tell the counselor (or any future therapist) that Guido asked her if she remembered the names of all the guys she slept with and she had to tell him she couldn't. A couple of them just blanked out in my mind, she told him, just as the actual sex has always blanked out with every one of them. And I can't reveal, she thought, that Guido said that I look so young and innocent despite so many affairs and disappointments. But she was no Lady Chatterly. The only one she'd had hot pants for was Guido. And he betrayed her. Men! she muttered to herself. They're all alike. And so, it would have to end with Guido, although he had said he didn't want a movie script good-bye: It was nice knowing you, I'll always love you, but I have to think of myself. That he didn't want to hear. He wanted, he said, the fairy tale love: No matter what, my love for you surpasses all obstacles. For he had said: "When I start something, I want it to last. I don't go for shards," he said, "I go for the entire vessel."

The next time she came to see Guido her mind was set. She'd made a concrete decision. (Later, over the telephone, he sang "I've Got the Concrete Decision Blues" to her.) She told him she wanted to take him for a walk. He was surprised but agreed. She drove to the site of their first magical walk. During the ride she said nothing. "What's the matter?" he asked. "Wait," she said. "The place looks familiar," he said. "The old magic. But with a different wand." He wasn't stupid, that's for sure, she remembers thinking.

He held her hand but felt her hand limp in his, and in turn she felt his lack of enthusiasm. Even in negative energy, in minus impulses, they were attuned to each other.

At the precise spot where they first kissed, she turned to him and said: "I'm not going to see you any more. I can't. I won't."

He wanted to know if she was seeing anyone else. She told him no, but she wasn't going to tell him about the counselor. It was none of his business. She was a free agent. Guido had once given her enough of an earful regarding yat-tat-tat and women's blah-blah-blah when long ago, during the early stages of their relationship, she'd told him that she had seen a music counselor. He was so damn protective of himself. That's all he cared about. Himself. Not her.

"And no extensions. Do you want me to be miserable? Do you want me to die? Because that's what I'm going to do. Die. The way I feel now all I want is to go to sleep and not wake up any more. I want to sit in the tub and slit my wrists and bleed to death. Painlessly. Please, please, please let me be. Get out of my life. Let me get off the star and land on earth on my own two feet. I've had enough of the stars. They're making me dizzy. You want me to be in the stars and in Long Island at the same time. You want a foot here and a foot there. You don't know what you want. You want to leave a door open. You can't fool me, though you've been doing it for months, years, decades."

"What do you mean, fool? What are you talking about?" he said with all innocence.

It was at the tip of her tongue to say, I know something about you that you didn't think I knew or would discover, but she bit, she sewed her lips, yes, oh, thank you, dear Mama, she finally sewed her lips, was in full control, a stance she should have taken long ago, and said nothing. Let him stew in quandary.

"The most distant stars can't shed enough light to express the length of time you've been fooling me. And her. All the things you promised were a load of bullshit. Give me time. The boy is going to die. They have only so long a lifespan. You know what? With your luck and my luck and her luck, or unluck and his luck, he's going to live forever. But I won't. Because me too I also only have so long a lifespan. My heart, my soul, can't take it any more. Only reason I don't go into that tub and do what I said I thought of doing is that it'll harm the kids and leave them to that maniac. So I'm going to live. But I know that everything you said to me was just to string me along. For you *love* is just a word. You know what? I don't think you ever had a single feeling in your life. Not a one. Ever. Like the Arab who expressed all his love for the fender of his new taxi, polishing it with an ecstatic look in his eye—you too, all your love is poured into your f.2 lens. But it's not an ethical lens. Remember that term you used about Pablo Casals? If a person really cares, he shows it with deeds. And you haven't. Not a one. You haven't been fair to me and you know it. Or to her either. All I was good for was fucking." And she began, she didn't want to do it, she tried her best not to but couldn't help it, to cry, sobbing her heart out.

"It takes two to fuck," he said drily. "One can't do it alone."

She dug her nails into her skin and forced herself to stop crying.

"And that's the only thing you can respond to. Everything else I said doesn't matter to you. But you know why I did it? Why I kept coming back to you, even though my instincts told me not to? Because I kept deluding myself that things will work out. That's me. All my life deluding myself. Brushing crap under the rug and seeing a magic carpet." And she burst into tears again, then bit her lip. "Because I always hoped we were building to something. That something would come of that special wavelength we were on . . . I saw you as someone so special there was no one more special in the world, and I deluded myself into thinking that I was special for you too."

"You are," he said.

"Words. More words. Just words . . . Why don't you just go and leave me alone? Let me rebuild the broken pieces and become whole again, okay? Don't call me, don't see me, don't write me. Just let me be."

"Who's advising you? Who's your handler? Someone is advising you. You're seeing someone to get advice. Your inner you wouldn't split up with me like this."

"I can think for myself. Act for myself. What kind of moron do you take me for?"

"A very special one . . . I mean, a gullible one."

"I mean it. Let me be . . . You have no morality, do you? I mean, do you consider *any*thing wrong?"

He thought a while. "I don't do high jumps in front of cripples . . . But look . . ."

"No buts. You don't seem to understand me. I mean it. Let me be. Let me go. Make believe I'm dead . . . What if I were dead?"

"I'd put fresh weeds on your grave every day, I swear."

"Very funny . . . But I mean it. I mean every word. Just . . . let . . . me . . . be . . ."

He didn't say a word. Perhaps for the first time ever with her he feels guilty, she thought. He *looked* guilty. She turned to him. He didn't know what to say. What *does* one say when the end is so near one can taste it like bile in the back of the throat? I've stopped him dead in his tracks, she thought.

"I once read," she continued, "a tribute a man gave his wife. He said: She had a moral compassion. Which you do not. And no loyalty. Neither to her nor to me. Worst of all, to yourself. So, please, I beg of you. See? I'm pleading again. Please get out of my life."

"I'm loyal . . ." he said. His face was hard. His voice harsher. "You can be very tough, right?" she had once told him. "Cruel, even, right?" He had nodded.

"I'm loyal," Guido said, "to only one thing. The thing that never lets me down. Never doublecrosses me. People let you down. Men and women disappoint you. But my little thing never lets me down. That's why it's the only thing I'm loyal to."

"You bastard," she said. "Why is it my rotten luck in this world to hook up with one bastard after another?"

"Like Shakespeare said: Like to like, like."

The next evening she took good advice. When she had told Guido she'd never see him again, he slipped in that he had to fly back to Europe in a couple of days, had returned just for her, groping for a last straw of sympathy. But that bit of news cut no ice with her. That day had drained her so she took her counselor's advice to unwind and did something she hadn't done in ages: she went to the movies.

But she saw more than the film. So much for Guido's movie-script good-bye.

What she saw at the movies, during the movie, after the movie, interlaced like a woven story with the movie, was a movie itself.

And she was one of the stars.

Charlie

I was speeding and I knew it. I was speeding and there was a reason. Guido's story at the reunion had hooked me. Seeing our humdrum class of eleven, I never dreamt one of us led such an exciting life. Trips to exotic places. An affair with a beautiful woman. At first glance we're all pots with the lids on. But lift one of the lids and see what varieties of stews bubble underneath. I was quite sure that Guido was telling me the truth about his affair. But truth can be modified, stretched, or even invented. Fiction, right? What better truth is there? But unless a story is verified, one can never know the truth. I suppose that even then one can never know. Guido had bragged that Aviva loved him so much he'd never experienced anything like it. But years ago he had also said how much Ava had loved him. And look what happened. He always had had a penchant for exaggeration, for self-boosting. His stamp collection, remember? That's why I had to see for myself. That's why I was on my way to Long Island. Actually, there were two reasons for my trip to the Island. And the first made the second easier. The first was to take over for a couple of months (much longer, as it turned out) the practice of a colleague, Gad Sharoni, who had to go back to Israel for family reasons. The second is obvious: to find and meet Aviva. Although Guido was cagey, I knew I'd find her, even without a last name, either by calling the Long Island Symphony or the Long Island Music Teachers Association.

Driving along the Brooklyn Queens Expressway, I remembered a conversation with Guido. He had mentioned a promise to Aviva not to talk about the affair; still, he couldn't abide by his own proscription. So he assumed that Aviva too was dying to talk. After all, she was a woman. Once, Guido had blown up at her when she admitted she'd told her old cello coach that she was lusting for him, and the coach, a white-haired old lady with a zest for life, had said, "Go for it!" Afterwards, he had made her promise never to blab again. She promised. Guido said he trusted her. But I wasn't so sure. The thoughts that ran through me as I passed cars and trucks and watched trees whiz by me were: Aviva is dying to talk. Aviva is bursting to talk. All I have to do is find her, take the right—the clever!—approach, and

I'd have her side of the story. The lovely Aviva that Guido had created for me during his hours of chatting. Blabbing, if you will.

With no traffic, I arrived in Garden City earlier than I'd planned. I stopped at a coffee shop. My first appointment at Gad's office wasn't until late in the afternoon, but I needed time to look over the files. I had plenty of time. The day before I had called Guido at the *Long Island Post*. An editor told me he was abroad on assignment and would be away two weeks. Now that he was away a maniacal high surged through me like a spurt of adrenaline. A sexy feeling of conquest came over me, and I actually asked the editor, "Can you tell me where . . . ?" about to ask where Aviva lived before I quashed that idiotic notion. "The Hotel Majestic in Paris," he said.

But Someone answered my unfinished question soon enough. Maybe the destiny Guido so often invoked. I asked for a refill of coffee and noticed a newspaper on the counter. *The South Shore Weekly Reporter.* I flipped the pages. Typical small town stuff. But on page five I saw a picture and feature story that made my heart sink and expand at the same time. A feeling of discovery, even of uncovering, if you will. As if by accident I had peeped into a secret cave and seen what I was not supposed to see. Like the town worthies reveling in Hawthorne's "Young Goodman Brown." Or the catharsis the ancient Greeks must have felt when they watched their kingly tragedies. I kissed the phone call to the L.I. Symphony good-bye. There, on page five, was a photo of an attractive, longhaired woman in her late thirties. Her name was Aviva Esther Prinsky and she was pictured with a cello. The article told of her recent First Prize in the Newberg Cello Competition and her recital in Town Hall. At the same time, it also noted—a plug, no doubt—that she was teaching privately, giving lessons to intermediate and advanced students. And her phone number was there too. I was sure that Aviva Esther Prinsky was Guido's Aviva. The only trouble was Prinsky. That didn't sound Moroccan. But it wasn't the name that convinced me that she was Guido's Aviva. It wasn't the prize or the recital. It wasn't even the cello. It was the picture of a ripe woman that sent a message to me. I would have responded even if her name were Max. Even if she'd been pictured as a passerby in a parade, the face would have sent a message to me. The photographer—of course, it had to be Guido—had done a great job. Who else could have made a shot like that? He'd captured the allure, the womanly beauty, and the glint of sadness, all of which mingled in her face.

I looked at my watch. Still time. The luncheonette had an old-fashioned phone booth with a door that actually closed. No answer after the third ring. My heart pounded. Please, I prayed, no answering machine. In midfourth, a woman answered.

"Is this Miss or Mrs. Prinsky?"

"Yes?"

I introduced myself and said, "I just read that beautiful article about you in the *Reporter*. Congratulations on your prize and recital."

"Thank you."

"I'm calling to find out if you're accepting students."

"Depends on which level the student is at."

"What's the right answer?" I said.

She said, "And I'm only taking a limited number this year. Is it for yourself?"

"My son . . . he's been playing for four years and studied at . . . Excuse me, the phone booth is stifling . . . I'm in the area now and, if you don't mind, I'd like to discuss this with you in person. May I come over for a few minutes?"

Her two-story house with two large rather overbearing wooden columns was in a cul-de-sac with lots of trees on a small lot. The houses—three hundred fifty thou, for sure—were set apart. With a warm "Hi" she let me in. The interior appointments were a curious mix of grace and kitsch, probably reflecting the conflicting tastes of husband and wife. It was as if the couple were battling even on the walls. One could feel the pulled rope tension in the furnishings. A Magritte print next to a repro of a schmaltzy Liberman of a kerchiefed woman piously lighting Sabbath candles. A Matisse papercut next to a Jerusalem oil painted by the numbers by an Arab in Hong Kong. On a long mahogany sideboard a large painted plaster cocker spaniel sniffed at a pair of graceful mesh wire ballet dancers. On the living room floor two small burgundy Bokharas lay uncomfortably atop the smooth fur of a white wall-to-wall carpet.

Her welcoming smile lit up the entry hall. She shook my hand warmly. Did she welcome every guest like this, I wonder, or was that smile reserved only for males? Or for friends—but how could she know?—of Guido's. For a moment—confession—I felt I was Guido awash in the radiance of her special, Aviva-for-Guido smile. Her big gray doe eyes, long, wavy, reddish brown hair and Limoge china skin turned that black-and-white photo in my mind into a color video. She was even more beautiful than the photograph. No still photographer could capture the vivacity of her face.

We sat on her sofa in the living room. There was no doubt in my mind that she was Aviva. She did look like a woman in her late thirties, as Guido had said. Slim and bursting out of her tight sweater. But two things led me in another direction. Faces can fool time, even the neck and throat, but the skin on the back of the hand—that cannot fool time. The little tightening there on the skin added a couple of years, as did the barely perceptible vertical wrinkles above her upper lip.

"What level did you say your son is at?"

I looked her in the eye, about to say: Aviva, I'm the one Guido wanted to share you with. But that would have killed my plan. For that one moment of glory, to see the surprise, the astonishment, the shock in her eyes, I would have killed any future contact with her. Would never have heard her side of the story. Certainly not the truth as I wanted to hear it. Once she surmised I was Guido's friend, it would color her memory and her interpretation of events. As is there was enough self-censorship in one's memory.

"How shall I address you, Miss Prinsky, Mrs. Prinsky?"

"Call me Aviva," she said.

"And I'm Charlie Perlmutter." I stretched out my hand to shake hers again.

Then it was back to business. "What level is your son at?"

"I don't have a son."

A glint of insouciance surged in her wide open gray eyes. I now noticed for the first time the slight squint. Now I knew, and a stone fell from my heart.

"And if you *had* a son, what level would he be at?" Aviva laughed, and I saw at once why Guido had fallen for her. That flirty, mischievous demeanor that would have tempted any man.

"Probably at mine."

"So the lessons are for *you*," said the perceptive Aviva, out-psyching me. "*You're* the son . . . Why did you concoct the curious reversal?"

"Because I thought you might not accept beginners."

"I don't."

"But will you take my son?"

Aviva fell into the routine. "Only if he's advanced . . ." And began laughing again. "Do you live in town?"

"No. In New York. But I come out to visit clients."

"Are you a law . . . an attorney?"

"No. Doctor."

"I thought doctors have patients."

"Not if I'm contradicted."

Aviva shook her head. Shaking the fuzz, the cobwebs, the absurdity away. Her nostrils flared, suppressing a smile. Then it broke out and a hearty laugh cascaded. I liked her smile. Liked it for itself and because I knew it from Guido.

"I'm a doctor of the mind."

She perked up. "Psychiatrist?"

"Not quite. Industrial psychologist by training."

"What do you do, cure neurotic machines?" And she again burst into a merry laugh, moving her head forward in a little jerking motion.

"People who work neurotic machines. But I've wound down that aspect and do general consulting now."

"And you call them clients, not patients?"

"Of course. Patients. I just said that to mislead you a bit. Yes, I'm a psychologist and a lay analyst." I didn't want to watch her too closely on that one. She let it go by. In fact, for a woman with problems, she looked quite calm, not distressed at all. If I'd been involved in a torrid, adulterous affair, had just won a cello competition, done a recital at Town Hall, practiced hours daily, taught, sought to have a solo career, rehearsed with an orchestra and had a miserable marriage, I'd have had two breakdowns a day, morning and night, not counting fainting spells at noon.

BOOK FOUR

Guido

kay. First lesson," Aviva told him. He had forgotten how beautiful she was. And that one of her big gray eyes was, like his, a bit off center. He had looked at the photos he had taken of her some months back as she was teaching the little Altman girl and had only her image in his memory. So seeing her now was like seeing her for the first time. He hadn't expected her to be so serious, but she got right down to business. Chitchat, he supposed, was for small kids. This was school, not recess. "Before you begin to play," she was saying, "the first commandment is relax. Free your arms." And she waggled her elbows as if attempting to fly. "Free the arms. That's one of Casals' great contributions to cello playing. He freed the arms. Long fingers, I see you have them, are also an advantage."

He watched Aviva's face as she spoke, hoping for that patina of flirtatiousness (long fingers?) he had felt when he brought Jill Altman to her house and their verbal exchanges were touched with perfume. But he didn't sense this now. He told her he admired Casals as a humanitarian. A dreamy look came over Aviva and she said, "My cello teacher at PAMA was a student of Pablo Casals', but the old man's warmth never rubbed off on him."

Guido listened patiently as she talked about Casals' cello technique, wondering when she would finish. And as he watched her he photographed her with his eyes, clicking his mental shutter every second.

"Okay, now," Aviva was saying, "now let's see you play a scale . . ."

He took the instrument and, self-consciously, slowly began to play. "Wow! That's very good. Your fingers seem to leap naturally to the notes. It's amazing," Aviva said.

"It's been years," Guido said, "but I guess the fingers never unlearn. Like riding a bike."

"Now hold your bow like this." She showed him. "The two hands have to work together like, like . . ."

Like a couple screwing, he thought.

"Like two workers on an anvil," Aviva said. "Remember, the bow is an equal partner to the cello. In fact, cellists if given a choice of a mediocre instrument and a superior bow, or an excellent cello and a poor bow, would choose the former . . . The bow is your voice. Let it speak."

"That's nicely said. Is that your phrase?"

"No. It came down to me from Casals via my teacher. Bowing is like blowing bubbles. That's mine," she laughed shyly. "You use your instincts to determine how gently or forcefully you let air flow from your lungs to create bubbles without bursting them. It sort of exists in your imagination. You sense and feel it before it happens."

"Like making love?" he teased her.

Aviva licked her lips, gave a feline little smile.

Guido looked into her eyes. Her eyes danced at his, then she looked away. "Who was your teacher?"

"Ian Plaskow . . ."

I know him, almost popped from his mouth like a bubble uncontrolled. And Casals too. But he didn't tell her right away. No sense overwhelming her, he thought.

It wasn't too long before she lost her non-genderality at lessons. Probably fourteen minutes into the lesson and he was already thinking of her as a woman. Yes, the bow was important. But her bust was even molto importante. He tried to keep his eyes off her tight sweater. On her part, her initial reserve vanished. She smiled more readily, laughed at his comments. Within three weeks a subtle minuet was taking place during the lessons and both knew it. He teased her with his slow playing, with his occasional holding back, like a sigh, the last note of a dominant. Soon the flirtations, the tensions of their meetings, began as he rang the bell and absorbed her welcoming smile. Oh, how he wished he had taken pictures of them meeting. He pulls the screen door while she opens the main door and that delicious smile lights her face and he—already exercising proprietorship after a few lessons—hangs his jacket in her dark closet, sensing the symbolism of entering her dark closet door by himself. And then, watching her slim body, he followed her into the music room. It was all he could do to restrain himself from lifting up her reddish hair and kissing the nape of her neck. Didn't all her students kiss her at the end of a lesson?

But she wasn't perfect, he convinced himself. Her nose was shiny as if oil were constantly being produced there. Her forehead by the hairline was a bit too rounded. Like the scientist in Hawthorne's "The Birthmark," Guido looked for a defect, for no one had perfect beauty. He didn't want her to be perfect on her own. This is where he comes in. To help her, he would retouch the flaws like an old-fashioned photographer with an airbrush and make her perfect.

By the third or fourth lesson, when he saw the bird-like tilt of her head as she spoke to him—bending it a bit more than was warranted—he zeroed in: she focused on him more with one eye than the other. By God, he realized. The beauty is damaged goods. She wasn't perfect. Hurray! Like me she has an ever so slight, delightful squint.

To compensate, he saw, she wore black mascara. It helped—but still she gave a pert little turn of the head, as if favoring the left eye.

Guido remembered reading somewhere that teaching was a substitute love affair, a complex form of seduction. But who is the seducer, who the seducee? Was his teasing at the instrument any less than hers?

"Can you teach me to make cello faces?" he suddenly said during one of the lessons.

"What?" she cried with an amazed laugh, perhaps more a delightful one-note soprano screech.

"Come on. You know. Cello faces. The puss that cellists pull when playing. Teeth biting lips. Lips compressed, eyes rolling upwards like an epileptic's. Grimaces. Snorts. The quick insucks of breaths. The chin-up-Rudolf-Valentino-in-ecstasy profile look. The works. The entire repertoire. Cellists always look the most impassioned, the most anguished, the most classically romantic. Would you teach me the when and the how?"

"That's not part of the curriculum," she said. But she smiled, showing that his remarks pleased her.

When Aviva taught she usually wore a tight black stretch cotton jumpsuit that she called her studio uniform. It showed off every sinuous curve of her body and at the same time gave her room to maneuver with her elbows, wrists and forearms. The cello between her legs, the vibrating fingers, her head ticking, her long hair floating as if in slow motion—Guido considered all these extremely erotic.

Guido asked her why she wore black and she said because she was shy. She didn't want to call attention to herself, rather to her instrument. Hey, he said, that black jumpsuit calls attention to itself like a black man at a KKK convention.

And soon thereafter, as by now is well known, he took her on that magical walk.

As they drove from the park in their cars, at the point in the highway when he would turn, he glanced to his right to wave good-bye. She rounded her lips and blew him a kiss.♥

"You're sure you wouldn't have done anything if I hadn't asked you for a walk?" he asked.

She shook her head. "I left it up to you. And what would you have done had I come for Italian lessons before the walk?" Aviva asked.

"I'd have said, You know what pasta means? You'd have said, Yes. I would have said, Fine, now you know Italian. And then, like the Romans say to American girl tourists: *Bene, benissimo,* now give me a kissimo, and I'd have laid you on the couch."

♥See ABC Directory, *Airborne sign of love, another.*

"You would not have," she laughed.

"I love your grammar. Such mastery of the near pluperfect!"

You know, I'll tell you something I haven't told you all these months. You were nervous the first time, right?" Aviva asked.

"Well, it was you whose behavior was skewed. Didn't you pop out with, What am I doing here? just as I was about to enter you. Soon as I heard that—phhht, there it went!"

"But you were nervous too, right? I mean, you didn't go around bringing women up to your spare bedroom."

"Of course not," he said, then after a pause: "I take them to motels."

"Well, when I went home that day I talked to God, even though I don't believe in Him, and told Him, Her—" she laughed—"He didn't answer me, so I did all the talking, I told Him, please, no, not with him. My luck, right? Just when I was finally both hot and in love with someone he wouldn't be able to do it."

"But I did."

"And how! Wanna show me again?"

Another confession of hers enraged him so he saw her face actually turn grey with fright and contrition. She said she had spoken about him to her music counselor, whom she was seeing about memorization problems. Aviva had told her that she was lusting for a man she was teaching. And the woman advised: Go for it! And it was this sharing of their intimacy that infuriated him. He told her, There's a Roman proverb: If two know, fine; if three, the world.

How come, he wondered aloud, she didn't mention to the old lady—he kind of imagined she was an older woman—that she loved that man? Lust but not love? But the two go together, don't they? Aviva protested. He would have phrased it differently, he said. The two don't necessarily go together. But for me they do, she said. One is an expression of the other.

True, he said, lying through his forked tongue.

"I know it's different for men," Aviva said.

Dead right, he thought.

"How come you didn't tell your counselor you loved me?"

"I did."

"But first you said you lusted for me."

"I don't remember what I said first. I probably said both. For me they're connected."

"I know," he said, but he didn't know.

One twilight they took a walk in a local park and watched boys playing basketball. She really didn't like the outdoors, she said, got bitten easily, said Yuk when bugs came on her, but at least she didn't screech. They sat in the car; she stroked his legs, his arm.

"You see," she said suddenly, "how fate decides that I'm sitting here this evening and not in Kansas?"

"What do you mean?"

"Years ago, when I was in PAMA, I heard that Ian Plaskow's assistant was leaving. And since I was his star pupil, I thought he would give me that job. He could have but didn't."

"You would have become his assistant in more ways than one," Guido said.

She laughed and nodded resignedly. "And he didn't make that call for me to that college in Kansas either, where they had an opening."

"You know," Guido said. "I'm glad he didn't make it. You'd have gone to Kansas and married some wheatfield yokel. By him not making that call—see, it's fate!—you're here for me."

She smiled and nodded and stroked his arm some more.

Then he reminded her that she'd once told him that Plaskow had summoned her to dinner in New York and she said she was sorry she accepted. Why? he wondered. Did she make it with him?

She pursed her lips and shook her head. "No."

"Then why sorry?"

"When that dinner invitation was given, a boundary was crossed. When you go from being a student to being a date, that switch is like a change of geography."

She listened to him playing some passages on the cello—they hadn't had a formal lesson in months—saying "That was good" in a mechanical way, the way she might say it to a young student when she was tired and had no more strength for concentration. He caught that banal tone; she admitted she was tired. "If you're tired and don't want to listen to me, why don't you say so?" and he put the cello away. "Next time, when you're more relaxed," he said. It was her old problem. She wouldn't say anything when she was discomfited. For instance, after four or five hours of lovemaking he would ask her, "Are you hungry?" and she said she was starving. He would ask, "Why don't you say you're hungry. Why do you always wait for me to ask?" and she would either say, "I don't know" in that soft baby voice or shrug and say nothing. He wanted to tell her that Einstein too didn't eat until someone asked him if he was hungry, but he didn't want to give her a swelled head. She wouldn't complain. She wouldn't say no. She would sit there next to him at the cello and wait for him to comment on her fatigue or edginess or inability to concentrate because she'd had a difficult evening with the Arab or he'd harassed the children again, or there was some other stress. Enter Eris, exit Eros.

But she always looked like a queen, like the night he took her to the Westbury Fair concert and he saw all the men turning to look at her in her elegant dress and he told her she looked like a queen and she said, "I've been called that before." He wanted to know by whom and she said she can't remember but one of her old friends called her Queen Esther. Esther was her middle name, she said, and he decided not to call her queen anymore, tried to expunge the queenly image from his mind, recalling with a twinge that one of her boyfriends had called her Queen Esther. He also recalled how he had taught her to be a little more mobile in lovemaking and not just lie there like a PAP, a term she didn't know because he made it up on the spot, Protestant American Princess, who rumor had it would just lie there like a Nova Scotia lox during lovemaking.

He also wanted to ask her why she didn't grab him as soon as she saw him, just like he did, hinting, let's go upstairs, even before she would playfully whisper after some initial conversation "What do we do now?" which became a password between them, one created years ago when she and her little sister played together when her parents left them alone at home, when leaving two children alone for a few hours in Tel Aviv was quite normal, no sooner did Aviva put her arms around him and he embraced her slim waist than he would growl and with a leg behind hers, trip her and slowly bring her to the floor, where, barking and biting and nipping, he would kiss her all over and roll around the floor with her as she said, "You crazy delicious man you," as he kissed her lubricious thighs. He wanted to tell her he couldn't believe a man in his forties could be in love like a teenager. "I feel that you're so much mine I can do anything I want with you," and she immediately answers in that sensual, sleepy whisper, with eyes half closed and thick lips pouting, "You can, you can." He told her that love,♥ like God at the moment of creation, was creating higher and higher summits. He thought it strange that he had images of peaks, he who had spent the first few years of his life in an area so flat that he never even dreamt that mountains existed. The highest things he saw were the five-story structures in the Venetian Ghetto, the biggest residences in all of Venice, except for the huge bell tower in San Marco Square. When he was five or six, in the Scuola Cantorum Hebrew classes, Rabbi Toledano had taught him about Jacob's dream ladder with angels ascending and descending, from heaven to earth. That dream ladder and its rungs, he now realized, was Jacob's dream of love for the Rachel he hadn't yet met but was surely dreaming of. Love was that endless ladder. Always room for another rung.

At the beginning they would see each other at 1 p.m. on a Saturday when his wife was at the camera shop and he had a couple of hours before he went to work. Then once he mentioned that he'll be working nights for the next three weeks but had Monday off. But he did not invite her. But

♥See ABC Directory, *Love, how deep it is.*

since he had dropped the hint, he was hoping she would call. Monday morning at ten the phone rang:

"Can I see you for a few minutes?"

Her smile shone off the walls when she came and the few minutes turned out to be a few hours. This was now the pattern for following Mondays. Then she began analyzing why he was doing what he was doing. She assumed that it must be revenge against his wife. For Aviva, Guido thought, revenge is a model for adultery. She couldn't understand pure love. She also couldn't understand how a man could make love to two women at the same time, even the same day. That much morality she had, she said, even though she considered him more moral than herself and even though she had never committed adultery with anyone. She claimed she wasn't interested in sex or in men, but she once admitted she would rather be with men than women for the former were less catty, more vibrant, less gossipy, more interesting. Still Aviva claimed she was shy, but there was nothing demure about her once her clothes were off, flinging her bra in one direction, her panties in another, and saying, "Come *here*!"

D̲id you feel any desire for him?" he asked her.

"For whom?"

"Plaskow?"

"When?"

"At the dinner."

"No," she said. "Not then."

"When then?" Oh, he caught that "then" all right.

Trapped, exposed, Aviva gave a little guilty smile.

"I invited him up for coffee . . . Or maybe he invited himself up."

"Is that when you felt it?"

"Just for a moment. As the elevator went up, I felt it between the fifth and sixth floor. For maybe three seconds. But then it disappeared and nothing happened."

T̲he day after that first walk she came to his house, and after an abortive lovemaking, came her hysterics: "My God, what am I doing here? This isn't my house!" and then when he calmed her, just hugging her as she lay naked in his arms, she whispered:

"I love you so much, I feel you're my soulmate."♥ Her eyes were closed. "And all I want is for you to love me a little bit."

Saturday she came back, agitated. She was a wreck, she said. She couldn't take it. Couldn't sleep. Couldn't get through her lessons. Took two Valiums and something else I don't want to tell you. A few days later he pressed her

♥See ABC Directory, *Soulmate*.

and she said: Gin. You crazy? he said. That's an awful combination. I know. Just once, she said. I promise. I won't do that again. I never take medication. Her life is a mess, she said. She would not be able to continue with him. He was married, she was married—an awful combination. Thought of not coming, but wanted to tell it to him to his face. Then he asked her to sit on his lap, and he rocked her again and said, "Even if you don't want me to make love to you, just holding you like this is enough for me," and she melted.

Another time, when she was already in his house, she admitted that she'd considered not coming and was about to call him to say she won't visit him any more. But he said, Don't ever do that. Not by phone. Come in person. And she promised she would always come, not call. She would never break it off with a phone call. When she left that day she said she'd call him next morning. And he wondered, suppose she phoned and said, I've decided. This whole thing is too complicated. I can't handle it. What would he do? he wondered. The other day when he had gone to her house for a lesson, she was nervous; she couldn't concentrate on his playing, and she excused herself by saying: I'm not made out of wood, you know. I know, he said softly, and continued in the same understated tone, I've never screwed a table. At 9 a.m. he already began looking at the clock, urging it along. By 9:20 he was pacing in front of his telephone, heart beating, unable to contain himself, waiting to hear her voice. When the phone rang he picked it up but there was no one there and his heart fell. She called, he thought, and changed her mind at the last minute. Gone, finished. Vanished this special love. But as he held the phone in his hand and looked at it, just as actors in films do when they stare at the dead phone in their hands in bemusement, he heard the bell still ringing and wondered how a phone could ring when it was off the hook and then realized it was the door bell. He hung up and ran to the door. She fell into his arms and hugged and kissed him and said, "Take me up to the magic room."

There she quickly began tearing off her clothes and whispered, "You too, a little quicker."

Then commenced her ceaseless summons to heavenly deities, but despite her orisons she never came.

Very few women have orgasms, she said.

Nonsense, Guido said.

And I'll tell you a secret. Fewer like sex . . . But I had a friend who was a walking orgasm.

How so?

She would come at the slightest. For instance, listening to Brahms Second Piano Concerto made her come.

You're glowing, he said to her as she sat on the bed later. Indeed her face did glow. She told him she thanked God for him, then said, Oops, I forgot I'm an agnostic. Or am I an atheist? . . . God only knows!, for he told her not to swear to God, explaining that people who swear a lot, lie a lot. I don't lie a lot, she said, just a little. But that, he thought, that too may have been one of her little lies.

Guido couldn't put a finger on the quality that radiated out of her, until the time they heard a Casals recording and she said his playing has oxygen. He couldn't understand that. How can a performance have oxygen? Then he realized in a flash that that is precisely what Aviva had: oxygen. A vitality. An effervescence of life stuff.

At first during the lessons there was an interesting see-saw. He was truly interested in the cello, of course not unmindful of the personable instructor. The cello rode high. But with each visit the see-saw tottered more and more. During lessons one through four or five the music superseded. But gradually her face, aura, body, presence—not her smell; unlike other women, she never gave off any special odor—tipped the see-saw.

Guido knew full well that this—he didn't want to use the word "affair"; that would cheapen it, might even put a time limit on it, as if like radium it had a half-life, quarter-life, eighth-life, no-life, for affairs, common wisdom had it, ran their course in two three years—love was not a result of some hormonal imbalance, some kind of mandatory disease, spell it dis-ease, that the early forties bring, a later spring awakening that has the ineluctable force of an apple snapping off a tree and plummeting. No. And told Aviva so. He wasn't doing it because he was forty-two and itchy. He was not a text-book case. Never trod the paths of pop psychology texts nor easy predictability. I had my mid-life crisis in my twenties, he told her, and that's the last I thought about it. He had turned down several other opportunities. Women were always after him. A succession of secretaries and lab assistants had hot pants, he knew, but the most he ever did was flirt with them. And now came she, Aviva, who knocked everything cockeyed, no pun intended. Now he felt accomplished. At twenty-five, he still lived in a dream world. Had vague notions of becoming an Ansel Adams, a Steichen, a Stieglitz, of photographing the entire world. And if not that—then of becoming a great musician.

And if you talk about mid-life crisis, the middle-age syndrome, the guy who wakes up one fine morning and finds out by looking at his watch, passport, driver's license, that he's forty and gets a yearning for a younger girl, some nifty dream dame in her twenties, why then this Aviva-Guido nexus also didn't fit any preconceived pattern. Who ever heard of a guy who supposedly had mid-life crisis and was out for a fling to undo the middle-aged blahs, getting hooked on someone older? A dozen years ago, if some-one had told him he would have a fifty-four-year-old girlfriend, he'd have called him a pervert. A dirty old man.

Guido had a strange feeling every time he saw Philadelphia in the news. A little tweak of metaphysical pain. That's where the love that should have been saved for him had been squandered. But there was no withdrawing the past. Done was done. Philadelphia. That's where the involvements (her term), fucking sessions (his), call it by whatever name you will, began. The same feeling surfaced again—call it a moral hurt—when he saw mention of the upper West Side in the news. At once, he saw *her* apartment, with the well-used hi-riser, the same hi-riser she'd already used with all the guys in Philly, with her first husband (although you can't really call that using, can you?—and maybe that's why she kept that same bed throughout her career, as if to show it and herself that she wasn't doomed to be a seven-year married virgin after all), and who knows how many others. But every time he heard upper West Side, he saw the guys in her room taking her clothes off.

He wanted to know, since she'd already made four conquests, didn't another conquest, that is, her teacher, occur to her?

"No," she said. "First of all, I never made the first move with those guys. I told you that. And Plaskow was off-limits. He was my teacher. And married. At that time I was in a somewhat depressed state. Depressed and always tired."

"So what better way to undo depression than to seduce your teacher, whom you yourself say was attractive?"

"I was very timid and shy with him. I felt I could never do anything right at the lessons. I played better at home than in the studio. Playing the cello for him during lessons I felt a tension. He was a tough teacher."

"Was he ever sarcastic or angry with you?"

"Sometimes he was impatient for a while and after the lesson I would go to the bathroom and cry."

"But you wouldn't burst into tears during the lesson?"

"Are you kidding? That would be totally unprofessional. I controlled myself. But when I was alone in the bathroom I let go."

Did she cry because she liked him, he wondered, or because he hurt her? Maybe she was more sensitive because deep down she liked him.

"Look," he said, "you sat next to me for a number of lessons when you were married, and you got fired up. So why not in Philly when you were just divorced, all alone and unattached, why didn't you get fired up sitting next to him?"

"I wasn't flirty. I always had the fear of rejection. And I wasn't brave enough to initiate anything. I was always holding back, perhaps because I was always self-centered and never thought of another person's needs. That's why I couldn't love someone. You have to be able to let yourself go, give yourself up, lose control, and I couldn't do that."

"You still didn't answer the question."

"He was my teacher. It's as simple as that. I was surprised he made that move to invite me to dinner. I never gave him any indication I liked him. You won't believe this, but at that time I really believed that men had no feelings. They couldn't be hurt by a bad relationship or fired up by a good one. I thought that men were detached."

"Interesting," Guido observed. "Because you told me that at that time *you* were the one who was detached. So you're transferring your actual feelings onto the men."

But, to his relief, she never asked him. And you? Didn't you make love to a dozen, two dozen, women before you met me and never love one of them? Of course, he would have said, but men are different. No matter how liberal a woman is, those affairs weigh on her psyche, and each has its effect on other relationships.

Like numbers, like verbs, torment too had a color. If the demon of jealousy is green, all of Aviva's other guys were a faint chartreuse, but Ian Plaskow was a dark forest green.

"What happened after the dinner with Plaskow?"

"Nothing. I invited him up for coffee."

"And that's when he kissed you."

"Who said he kissed me?"

"I did . . . Didn't he?"

She lowered her head. "Yes. Just once, then I told him no more . . . What was I to do?"

"And he was satisfied with just a kiss?" Guido said angrily, as if he'd caught her now with another man. "Hardly! I wouldn't be."

"But not everyone is like you. And besides, he was my teacher. I didn't want to be impolite."

"Not spreading your legs is also being impolite."

"I didn't want to get involved," she said coldly.

But Guido knew there was more to it. With Aviva it couldn't be as simple as that. And he'd heard that phrase—"didn't want to be impolite"— from her before.

"And besides," she added, "he was married . . ."

He marveled at her sense of fidelity. Kissing a married man was okay; screwing him was sinful. "And, furthermore, I may have been involved with someone else at the time, and that's why I only kissed him and refused to go to bed with him. That's another reason I put a stop to it after he kissed me."

"But why did you kiss him if you were involved with another guy?"

"Because I felt like it."

The old capriciousness again. "Because you like to be polite."

"Yeah," she laughed.

"I can't believe it. Only kissing and stroking. Here's a man who comes up, excited, after dinner . . ."

"No stroking. And who says he was excited?"

"After paying a New York restaurant bill who *wouldn't* be excited?"

At which time Aviva shifted gears and said brightly:

"Did I ever tell you that the guy who de-virginated me I didn't have a long, drawn-out affair with? It was just a one-time event, the only time in my life that happened. And not a pleasant experience at that. Can you imagine, I wait twenty-nine years to, you know, and I get a guy with a midget-sized pecker? It's a wonder I didn't sew it up and go into a nunnery. He wasn't even enthusiastic about making love. I sort of had to cajole him, shame him into the act."

But her pathetic attempt at distracting him with Mister Mini did absolutely no good, for the next time he asked her again and she said, "My God, drop it, forget it, it was only a thirty-second encounter. I shouldn't have done it. It was a mistake to accept a dinner invitation from a teacher. But I was a nerd then."

"Maybe he was so hot for you because that other teacher, the clarinetist you'd been involved with, passed the word along: I'm screwing her."

"No. They didn't even meet. That clarinetist commuted from New York and Ian lived in Philly."

But he still didn't believe her.

"Don't you see that men consider an invite up for coffee an open lease, a kind of tease? You can't excuse your actions with an innocent, I didn't know how to handle it."

"I told you I was a nerd. I was in my late twenties but had the social graces of a ten year old."

"Argument rejected. Motion denied. You can't call yourself a nerd. You can't use today's slang as a catch-all rationale for behavior twenty years ago. You were not a blah. You were a nubile woman and you'd had men left and right."

Was it done, he wondered, without loyalty, commitment? Because he knew she had done it. There was no doubt in his mind that she'd screwed Plaskow. But was it done out of love, lust, curiosity, politesse? Or out of a feeling of emptiness? Too bad pussies don't have odometers, he mused, or counters like copying machines.

In later days came varying explanations.

Once she said she had kissed Plaskow because it was the polite thing to do and she didn't want to be unappreciative. Another time she suggested that she couldn't help it. She was a dope, a nerd. A third time she admitted she was attracted to him. And still later she told Guido that she kissed Plaskow and went no further because she didn't want to become emotionally involved.

"I didn't know how to handle it once he was upstairs. You have to be polite."

"For some girls spreading legs is also a form of politesse."

"You said that already," she said tartly. "This investigation, this inquisition, is on a merry-go-round . . ."

"And he was satisfied with just a kiss?" Guido said. But he'd asked that already. She was right. They were on an endless carousel. "How come he didn't take you to bed?"

"You'll have to ask him that."

"I will," Guido snapped. "Well? How come?"

But she didn't say.

"Not everyone is like you. So hungry. So sexy. Such a lecher. And besides, he was my teacher. So I kissed him. Out of politeness."

On the carousel, Guido thought. In retrospect, each one of those pat phrases sounded hollow. Each one was a jab. Each a lie and one lie was applied with patchwork skill atop the other. Later he realized that her first story was even more despicably capricious, bitchy, than the second version. At least the second version was forthright.

"Not everyone is like you." She pressed close to him. "No one is like you." She kissed him. "No one in the world." And she gave him her naughty girl smile and said, "You're officially my lover."

But that still didn't tamp the buzzing in his skull.

He imagined a fascinating—and frustrating—no-win situation in his obsession. The next time he saw her he would tell her that he intuited, that just as he had correctly intuited that she hadn't only been talking for weeks to the Indian psychiatrist but that they had actually been kissing, so he knew that when she invited Plaskow up to her apartment she didn't only just kiss him but screwed him too.♥ And that's why she didn't want to tell him about it, because it was either a one-time encounter or a brief affair and she knew it would upset him, especially since she knew that she knew him. Plaskow wasn't faceless like the others. And that's why she didn't go back to PAMA the following year, and that's why it was "a mistake," in her words, to have accepted a dinner invitation with him. But as he confronts her with this, she can either deny it, affirm what she had said once before, or even tell him: Stop persecuting me. Is that the only thing on your mind? Lay off!

True, he did not want her to think that that was the only thing on his mind. He would give it a rest for a while. Save it for an opportune moment.

♥See ABC Directory, *Bothered by Plaskow.*

Maybe even surprise her. Catch her off guard. By a ruse, a play, or something in between, he'd prick the conscience of the queen.

"Come," she said, taking him upstairs.

He let the riposte that almost bubbled by itself off his tongue sit there. They were completely alone. It was the first time there was an absolutely safe opportunity at her house. The Arab had gone to visit his sister—or so he claimed—in Los Angeles. David and Yaffa were in camp for a month. She couldn't believe that the Arab had agreed to send them. He didn't do it for their pleasure, she knew. He did it for himself, Aviva said. To keep them out of his hair. He's so stingy it's unbelievable. I have a great story about him concerning a penny, she said, but in the process of cuddling and inspecting all the bedrooms and listening to her, the story was forgotten and she never mentioned it again.

She showed him one bedroom.

Guido pointed a to hi-riser. "Have you been laid here?"

"No . . . I mean yes, in the bed, but no, not on *that* mattress. Wait . . . yes, on that one too." And she smiled her feline smile.

"I don't want to go to your bedroom," he said. "He's been there."

She showed him the guestroom. "That's where my hi-riser from my Philly days is." She gave an impish little grin.

He pressed his ear to the mattress.

"What are you doing?"

"Waiting for it to talk. If this mattress could talk, what tales it would tell."

She showed him another room with a sofa in it.

"Here too?"

Aviva looked contrite. "I'm afraid so. This one used to be downstairs— and the Arab, you know, slept there often."

Again he was jealous. "My God, isn't there a bed here that you haven't been screwed on?"

"Come on, I've been married fourteen years . . . there has to be some screwing."

"Some, okay—but all over the damn place? It looks like you never stopped."

"Believe me, we stopped plenty."

"To catch your breath, so you could start all over again . . . Why in heaven's name did you marry him?"

Aviva stopped in the hallway. There were silly little pictures hanging on the walls. Probably his influence, he thought.

"Look. I was desperate. I so badly wanted to have children. If only for my parents. My biological clock was running out. So I put aside all warning signals, like I usually do, and made believe they weren't there . . . Enough . . .

Look . . . Here, I'll show you my parents' room. When they came to visit this was their room."

"And he never laid you here?"

"Never." She pulled the shades down even though no one could see in and threw her arms around him.♥

Later, she said, "Now I know how a baseball team feels playing a home game."

It's an image he never expected her to use.

"You like having me here?"

"I wish I could keep you here. I feel sexier here at home."

"But what about the Arab?"

"He'll go soon. It's inevitable."

"And your children?"

"They'll grow up."

"And you?"

She laughed. "I'll grow old . . . And you never screwed your wife in all kinds of places at home? Like the upstairs bedroom we use?"

"No. Why?"

"For variety's sake."

He shook his head.

"Never?"

"I'm telling you. Never. Always in the master bedroom."

"Why?"

"Because I'm the master. So I go in the master bedroom. The mistress goes in the mistress' bedroom."

"It's too bad," Aviva said.

"What do you mean?"

"Too bad you didn't have fun."

"I didn't say that."

"I thought you said you didn't."

"That's what you wanted to hear."

He remembered the hurt look that passed like a drear wave over Aviva's face.

"Remember," he told her, "about a month after we began thump-thump-ing, you said that I do everything well . . . How did you come to that conclusion?"

"Well, by then I had already heard you play. I saw what magnificent progress you were making. Then I saw your photographs. You showed me your prize certificates. I had been listening to you talk for months. The things you know. Your sense of your humor. The way you made love."

♥See ABC Directory, *Phone rings during* . . . .

"What measuring . . ." rod he almost said, "device do you use for *that?* I mean, how do you judge a man who makes love well?"

"You do it so effortlessly . . ."

"You mean without panting, breathing, like climbing a mountain?"

She waved her hand at him. "The staying power, the length of time . . . I didn't say length, I said of time, you keep screwing."

"What's the big deal about staying power?"

"The Arab lost it very quickly . . . You know . . . use it or lose it."

He had expected her to have a certain smell. But she was absolutely without perfume. Only after lots of sex did a scent, that universal piscine fragrance, percolate out of her puss. Her skin was smooth and tight. Maybe her toosh had a bit of flab; but her body, her miraculously well-tooled body, had the elastic suppleness of a woman half her age.

Guido didn't know whether Aviva was hungry for love or for him. Nevertheless, he knew from that sort of expectant look on her face that he could summon her by a flick of his index finger, make her undress by a command or gesture. He once told her he enjoyed making love to her because he felt each lovemaking was the penultimate one. There was always the next time to look forward to. But deep in his heart he knew the possibility existed that each one would be the last. That she'd call up and say, No more. Or say, No more, as she was leaving. Or say, No more, in her heart and return no more.

"We're at the stage now, right, where you won't even look at another guy, right?"

"I won't. I won't even consider it," she said.

Maybe we shouldn't talk so loud he told her. The Arab probably bugged the house.♥

He loved hearing her say that when she met him she was breathless and that the feeling lasted a long while. Was she that way in Philly? he asked. No, Aviva said. There I felt detached. I just didn't care. I must have been depressed. I walked around the empty streets on weekends full of empty, lonely feelings.

"Was it desire to taste another man that prompted a change from one guy to another?"

"I don't know. I never did. And still don't. In view of my conservative background it was a contradiction. I guess I felt more curious about their reaction to me than mine to them. I wanted reassurance that I was attractive. Maybe, I said, this isn't right. There's something wrong here. Maybe with the next one I was looking for something that doesn't exist. Perfection doesn't exist, does it?"

♥See ABC Directory, *Bugged, her house is.*

Guido looked modestly down at the floor, a bashful little smile on his face.

"Stop it, Mr. Perfection! . . . Sex used to be a forbidden topic at home. It was avoided because it wasn't nice. This I learned from my mother. My father, of course, with his musical silence, gave me little philosophy of life, except love of music. For him music was philosophy and life combined. I once read that some guys are—" and here she pointed to her crotch— "crazy. But I wasn't," now she pointed to his, "crazy. Not at all. Despite what you said, for me the penis wasn't disassociated from the person it was attached to. In Philly, I was curious about men's passion. Just an observer with empty feelings. Dizzy. Isn't that awful?"

She was dizzy in other ways too, he thought. She didn't know how to refuse a date without hurting feelings. She thought hints were sufficient. Instead of No, she'd say, I'm busy for the next couple of weeks. She was just a girl who can't say No. She was, as the Europeans say sarcastically of loose women, a kind-hearted girl.

But he couldn't say No either. So there were two of them that couldn't say nay. He knew the elemental yearning, the untamed hunger, in his cockeyed eyes when he stared at a girl. As he grew older he was able to control it, to turn the volume down, at least in the presence of others. But like Charlie Perlmutter said, he still made U-turns to follow a looker with bouncing boobs.

Still, there was a world of differences between a girl who can't say no and a guy. Her inability to say no annoyed him. But that one date she should have refused bugged the life out of him.

You're my miracle, she said. My mirror. My little piece of Paradise, she said. My true ring of light, she said. I can't imagine any man after you, she said. But he knew her remark was nonsense. For her whole life was a string of men. She fell into relationships, sometimes not even intending to, by being perfectly innocent.

She couldn't help it, she said.

I didn't know what to do, she said.

I couldn't get out of it, she said.

I felt like it, she said.

I was curious, she said.

I didn't know how to say no, she said.

I was just being polite, she said.

Like the time she invited Plaskow up to her apartment after the dinner, really intending nothing more than coffee. But on the other hand, in that two-track scheme, where time and intentions moved at two different speeds along parallel tracks, she knew very well what that dinner invitation would lead to. That was another thing about her. Her wires were crossed. She never knew what signals she was sending. Oh, she knew, all right, he thought. All women deep down know what signals, what messages they are sending, those expert carrier pigeons!

Guido has the entire scenario photographed, just like he had snapped Randall Parker, that fuck, and Ava in action when he surprised them. Plaskow sees Aviva as an attractive, available young woman, intimidated by him, his talent, his fame. And perhaps he'd even had word from colleagues at school about her. So naturally he begins to kiss her, to which she responds. Up to a point. Guido imagines Plaskow's irritation at her sudden stopping. It smacked of cock tease.

But more irritated than Plaskow was Guido, Aviva's mirror. Being a mirror has its advantages. Disadvantages too.

Mirrors break.

What Guido didn't want was a casual love, something fallen into, something that, in her words, couldn't be helped. What *did* he want? The moon, the sun, her entire galaxy.

Even though he knew it pained her, he kept questioning her; still she always answered. She was good, kind-hearted, amenable. He had told her that in Italian when they say a woman has a kind heart it has another ring: she drops her pants too readily. Big heart, big belly, he told her, is an expression you hear in Naples.

"None of the others count," she said. "Only you."

Aviva in love.

Minutes before social security.

For the fun of it, he asked her if she had already applied for social security. But I'm not old enough, she said. I'm years away. To which Guido answered, One is always old enough to write to them and ask about the benefits they'll pay. The years go by quicker than you think. You'll soon be of age, he reminded her. I don't want to think about it, she said.

It was about at this juncture that three things happened. Happened? Guido said to himself. They tumbled over each other like clothes in a dryer.

A) Aviva said: I wish I were younger for you.

B) He went to the class reunion; reconnected with Charlie Perlmutter.

C) He befriended Teresa.

D) All of the above.

And, as usually happened in his life, his ABC's♥ were intertwined.

♥See ABC Directory, any entry.

Aviva's remark was prescient, a gift from her eternally beneficent heart. For Teresa, his new lab assistant, was a younger version of Aviva, perhaps as she might have looked during and even before the PAMA period. She'd been at the lab several weeks, but although he paid attention to her, he really didn't pay attention, despite her come-ons. At the same time, after the reunion, he renewed his old friendship with Charlie Perlmutter, giving Charlie, over a period of several weeks, many of the details of his emotional state. But now he wondered if he should have spoken. Perhaps like Aviva he too should have stitched his lips. But on the other hand, he had to speak. He couldn't wouldn't didn't tell Charlie everything, but the basics of the story he had to get off his chest. There was an inexorable push within him to spill the beans. By talking he rode the sliding point from hubris to contrition. No mortal can keep a secret, said Freud. Man gives himself away by motions and gestures.

Betrayal oozes out of every pore.

Guido didn't know what to do with Teresa. That is, he knew what to do with her, but he wanted to show himself that he could resist—to prove to himself that he wasn't an intractable libertine, an unreconstructed womanizer. But he also knew that by not succumbing to the lab assistant's pleading glances he was revving her up, increasing her desire. It was uncanny. Aviva had said she wanted to be younger for him and then went ahead and fulfilled *her* wish for him. She activated some positive hex force and found him a younger version of herself.

Maybe it was his talk in the *Long Island Post* meeting room that did it. One day at noon Guido gave an in-house presentation on war photography, giving a brief overview from the Civil War on, starting with Matthew Brady's classic photos. He never expected Teresa to come. After all, she worked with him most late afternoons and didn't have to come in at twelve. She had said good-bye the previous day, giving no indication she'd seen the poster announcing Guido's talk. And not only did she come (a bit late), she sat in the front. He tried hard to superimpose on her the classy features of Aviva, but all his mental trick photography couldn't do the trick. Maybe that was the difference between a Jewish face and a goyish one. Breeding was all. Yes. She did look like Aviva, but in a cheap, low-class sort of way. But Teresa's sex appeal had a direct, in-your-face wallop. You'd have expected a broad like that to pile on the makeup and wear cheap perfume. Neither. The latter Guido saw to. He warned her about it when she was hired, telling her that if she wore perfume to work it might interfere with his sense of smell in the darkroom. "I don't usually put on perfume," she said without a trace of huff in her voice. Was it her sitting up front that made her look different? For the first time he saw her without the loose white lab coat, which she always wore over rough denim shirts or bulky sweaters. He never did see what kind of figure she had. But today she wore a formfitting green dress with a modest white little collar. Egads, he thought, he hadn't realized what a slim waist and big delectable breasts she had. Also, he had never seen her in conjunction with other people. Sitting in a crowd gave her a human dimension, even a social complexity, which she didn't have when she worked one on one with him. Sitting here with others made her real. And, my God, he observed, she's taking notes. Wait a minute, he remembered, she didn't just come in early. Wednesday was her day off. She came in on her day off to listen to me. That gesture of hers he was able to montage onto her features; it gave her some invisible points. So this cute chick was actually interested in what he had to say.

From time to time, Guido made eye contact with her, as if addressing certain remarks to her. Seeing her reaction—were they having a secret dialogue, he wondered?—he began ad-libbing, making in-jokes, using lab techniques as metaphors, which she realized were being directed at her. I know what you're doing, said her special smile. She's inspiring me, flew through his brain.

After the lecture she stood at the edge of a cluster of people with an expression both shy and knowing, as if she'd known Guido for a long time and were waiting to greet an old friend she hadn't seen in a while. She waited until all the others were gone and she was alone with him.

"Hey, so nice of you to come." He took her hand for a moment. "And on your day off too. Don't think I didn't notice."

"I wanted to hear your talk. I loved it. Boy, you know a lot."

"You don't hear me talk enough?"

"You know what I mean. This is different."

"I'm touched. Impressed. I really am. And . . ." he looked down at her pad, " . . . taking notes too."

"Actually, I wrote them for you. Read it. I hope you don't mind."

1) I was hopeing youd be funny. You seemed to be nervous when you saw me comeing in and sitting in the first row, but then you calmed down. And you were funny, but with the nature of the subject, war and all that, I understand.

2) Your descriptions of some of the photos were so touching, I felt I had to tell you.

3) Your socks match your shirt today.

4) Are you aware that occasionally you take hold of the lecturn and tilt it forward as if it's a woman your dancing with?

5) You shaved extra special today. Your face looked so soft and smooth.

6) Who scratched your nose? And what's confabbulation?

7) Was it uncomfortable for you to have me sit in on your talk?

8) I noticed you threw a couple of remarks directed to me. Which only I could understand. They made me laugh. It was like you were giveing two lectures. One to them. One to me. It was nice of you. I liked that.

There was an intimacy to those notes, almost like a love letter. Those nose and socks comments especially changed the character of her notes. Notes, indeed. She was examining him, looking him over. Keeping a diary, for goodness sake. Working class spelling and all. Reading her notes he felt an erotic charge, which no doubt she'd wanted him to feel. And that's why she came on her day off, wearing a tight-fitting dress.

"Come with me," he said. "I want to show you something."

"What?"

"To the lab."

They walked together. He held the door open for her. She brushed against him as she entered. He shut the door and did not switch on the light. He seized her shoulders, turned her, and kissed her lips. He kissed and kissed and didn't let go. She opened her mouth so wide he thought she'd suck him into her. He almost missed that Oh that escaped her lips like a sigh as he kissed her, for she ran her hands over his face, his neck, his chest and down to his crotch. He switched on the dim safety light, carefully—not removing his gaze from her eyes—unbuttoned the top of her dress and lifted the bra. He had never seen such stunning breasts. She held them up with both hands.

"You can do anything to me except fuck me," she said.

"Oh yeah?"

"Yeah," she said with a sad musicality, as if the words of her mouth were a counterpoint to the words of her heart.

And slowly he placed his hand on her face, pressing once gently. And did the same to her head, shoulder, breasts, waist, ass, lingering long on her pussy.

"You know what I'm doing?"

"Yes."

"What?"

"I don't know." He noticed she looked so vulnerable, so lost, as if she were a wounded bird waiting for the hawk to come in for the kill.

"I'm staking out my property. What belongs to me."

"Okay," she said. And kissed him again.♥

Of all the guys she'd told him about, the kookiest was Kleingeist.

"That Kleingeist was something," Aviva said. "These religious Jewish men. They present this front of superorthodox, old-world, black-hat, bearded piety, and then when you sit next to them they show you their barroom manners."

"He must have thought you were a cinch. Boot in the crotch! It's as if he'd put his hand on your tits or your puss."

♥See ABC Directory, *Harem, delight with a.*

"And if he did put his hands on my tits, as you so delicately phrase it, perhaps he was just assessing my modesty. Look, he's a rabbi, he's not interested in things like that. He would just be checking to see if I was wearing a bra," Aviva said with a straight, placid face. Guido knew she was trying to pull his leg, reversing the mood so he would think she was criticizing Kleingeist now.

Guido was shaking his head. "I mean if you'd at least admit that Kleindong surprised you."

"He did surprise me. He said, don't worry, it won't hurt . . . No one had ever picked up my foot before."

"Because the rest of you usually followed. How naïve can you be? It was a sexual move."

"I asked him what he's doing."

"You don't ask, you don't learn, goes the Venetian saying. I suppose you didn't know what Rabbi Dr. Crotchpresser was doing. Body language is a foreign tongue to you."

"Don't be mean. You know very well what I mean . . . and anyway, I withdrew my foot right away . . . He spotted the Gucci . . . He liked my boots . . . He had good taste . . . And he was right . . ."

"About what?"

She laughed. "It didn't hurt."

"Did you consider Kleinballs sexy?"

"He aroused my curiosity," she said. "He was very interesting . . ."

"Can you recall one interesting thing he said?"

Aviva thought a while. "No."

Guido shook his head impatiently. "Priests love God, the Romans say, but they love sex more."

"Sex sex," she tsk-tsked. "That's all you think about."

"But you always liked it, right?"

"I didn't have anything against it."

He burst out laughing, banged his feet on the floor. "The understatement of the year."

"You're wrong," she said. "When a doctor once told me I couldn't have chocolate, that was more devastating than if he'd said no sex . . . I needed affection, involvement, love. That's the difference between a woman's understanding of a man and a man's understanding of a woman."

"My cock has no understanding."

"The understatement of the year," she said. "Are you an agnostic?"

He shook his head quickly, brushing the cobwebs away. Again that out-of-left-field segue.

He thought a moment and said, "I don't know if I'm an agnostic or not. But I can tell you I admire St. Augustine's prayer: 'Give me chastity and self-restraint. But not yet.' "

There were others too, he knew, Aviva was mum about. For instance, the accountant. And the Indian shrink probably stuck it to her too in his office but couldn't get very far because she still had her virgin's accoutrements.

Annoyed, he began badgering her again about former lovers. If he couldn't photograph her past, at least he'd possess the closest thing to it: her memory.

"I've already told you too much," she said. "I've got a big mouth." And again she made sewing motions with her fingers near her lips. "I have to learn to shut up."

"No," he said. "It sounds vulgar when you say that."

"Yes, I know, for your North Italian aristocratic nature I'm too low-class . . . But you yourself once said I have a big mouth."

"That's different. When I say it it's okay, because it's not true. But when you say it, it's true and I don't like it. How many men did you spread your legs for?" And he pulled out a list of questions.

She didn't reprimand him for his insulting tone. She just made a little self-deprecating face. She didn't lash out and say, "Where do you come off talking to me like that?" And she didn't walk out in a huff and snap, Screw you, I'm not talking to you! Guido knew he was being nasty, but he wanted to be nasty because he was hurt by her affairs. Aviva, head back on the easy chair, was counting.

"Spread my legs for," she mimicked and curled her lips, as if that could take the edge off his remark.

"If you run out of fingers and toes, I'll lend you some of mine."

"Do ones that couldn't make it count?"

"That's up to you," he said.

"In that case, nine, including husbands."

My God, he thought. Nine men!

She must have seen the look on his face, for she said, "You resent my past?"

Jumping on her lap he explained, "You see, I want to reverse time. I want to possess you in the past, as I do in the present. It's called sexual transubstantiation."

She seemed to like that because she gave him one of her glowing smiles.

"Okay, now close your eyes. We're going to have a little ritual."

"Ritual? What Jewish holiday is today?"

"When I see you it's always a Jewish holiday. Yes. Ritual. As the Sicilians say, let's see . . . um . . ." He thought a moment. "Ritual and wine will make her mine . . . So close your eyes and take your pants off. It won't hurt."

"I should hope not," she said. "Because I trust you, Rabbi Kleingeist."

Whenever he saw young models in fashion magazines, a model who even faintly resembled Aviva—big doe eyes, generous lips, cascading auburn hair— he immediately thought of her as she might have looked twenty, thirty years ago and how lucky were those guys to have a willing prize like Aviva in bed with them.

Which was another reason he didn't feel so bad fooling around with Teresa. She distracted him from his jealousy about Aviva's past.

"Where we goin'?" she said in the car, dropping, as usual, the *g* from all her verbs.

"Where I can photograph you privately... I have a place in Montauk—maybe we'll go there some other time—but for today it's too far."

"You gonna photograph me?"

"Uh-huh."

"How?"

"With my camera. Film. Flash. That's how they do photography nowadays."

"I meant, with clothes on or off."

"We'll see. Whichever way you look better."

She held her hand on his thigh throughout the ride.

"Why we stoppin' in the mall?"

"To get film. In that camera shop over there."

"You outa film?"

"No. I'm not outa film. I just want you to have the exercise of getting outa the car, cuttin' through all these parked cars and getting me a roll of 35mm Kodacolor ASA 400."

"I can't understand why you didn't take it from our stock."

"You don't have to understand everything. Just listen to me. Go there and I'll go into that pharmacy over there for a minute."

"Oh. I see."

"And I'll meet you. Here. By the car." He handed her a ten dollar bill. When they got back in Guido asked her, "Who served you?"

"Why? Do you know the people there?"

"Yeah. I once had a run-in with one of the salesgirls. Who served you?"

"A tall blonde woman. She was very nice."

"Think she's pretty?"

"Yeah," she said, stretching the syllables. "Looks like a classy lady."

"She's okay." Guido looked at his watch. "Come, let's get moving."

He could see the excitement peaking on Teresa's face as soon as he came back with the motel key. Because of her silence, his desire had hung in the balance for a moment. But as soon as they were in the room and he locked the door, Teresa was all over him.

Now he felt absolutely at ease with her, in full control. But the truth was that some weeks back, as soon as he saw her—personnel had sent her up for an interview—for the first time in his life a woman so confused him he couldn't think straight. He asked her—Teresa was her name—some perfunctory questions, which he didn't hear the answers to. He knew he'd give this attractive girl the job even if she couldn't tell developer from an enlarger lens. He'd train her. Yes, she was gorgeous, in a crass, low-class sort of way, sending out the uncensored, raw sexual power that low-class beauties sometimes exuded.

He pushed down once on the bed with his hand. As soon as he felt the ripples he popped a pill.

"What's that? Vitamin?"

"Nope. Dramamine. Waterbeds make me seasick."

"Then let's use the other one."

"Nah. Let's go for the ride. I could use a cruise."

He began to undress her. As he would learn later, she too was surprised at her body each time she took her clothes off. A shy look in her eye that said: I can't help it. I know it's amazing, but I can't help it. That's the way I was made. From the narrow waist down she was built like a ten-year-old boy; no tummy, flat hips, round toosh, all nicely complimented by those big bell-like breasts that she reigned in, hid, wanted to make disappear by rounded bras and loose, bulky sweaters, by droopy sweatshirts, and lab coats.

But God must have made her in two parts. On the installment plan. Slim she was yes, face and waist, but the arms and legs, wrists and fingers, were adorably round and chubby, as if the baby fat had never left her. That's why the extremities seemed at odds with her girlish torso. The bridge, but, was her bazooms. Centerfold-large, firm, and pear-shaped, they tied the two installments together in perfect counterpoint.

And afterwards, after running the rapids, plowing the deep waters, afflux, paddling up the Volga, floating the Nile, cascading down the Danube, licking all the nectars of the good ship Lollipop, and crossing the Jordan to the Promised Land—oh, my, one could go on and on scraping the barnacles of sea metaphors till rosy-fingered dawn—the floodgates opened and they came, that is, they arrived at the sweet port Paradise and lay with arms and legs entwined, looking up at the still quivering mirror.

"You fuck so goo-oo-ood," she said with a serious mien, a frown of sorts, but her upraised eyebrow accented the twinkle in her eye. "Your body makes my body feel great. God, I could do it all day with you."

"Ride 'em cowboy. Where'd you learn these tricks, you wild tiger?"

"Sex school."

"You can do anything to me except fuck me," Guido said.

"Oh, shut up," she said pleasantly. "I was in a state, then."

"Changed your mind?"

"Yes," she said. A rise, then falling pitch to that yes, her usual melody when she was pressed to admit something. "Now I want you to do nothin' but."

He pointed to the ceiling. "See that little hole up there? That's where the manager and his staff peek down at us."

Teresa quickly pulled the sheet over them which Guido just as quickly threw off.

"Only kidding," he said.

Nevertheless, they wondered if the owners had a camera or a peephole above the mirror to look down at the action below. "That's why I never choose a first floor room," he said. "Always top floor. They're not gonna lie on the roof for a little voyeuring." To which Teresa added that she had heard once that motels along the way to Florida had peepholes for the help, and one motel even had a secret video camera and when couples checked in they were able to watch on the VCR the foolin' around of previous couples. But one couple who checked in saw on channel 69 a couple they knew. Rather two half-couples. "God, was that embarrassing," she said. "But they loved every minute of it." But as Guido and Teresa watched themselves in the mirror they soon forgot about peeping Toms and enjoyed their own naked images on the ceiling. They looked good entwined, they concluded, even though the mirror was slightly distortive.

"Feel seasick?" Teresa asked.

"I felt vertigo at first. Everything spun."

"But I cured you, right?" And she kissed him.

"Right. And I felt I was free floating on a rubber raft in a calm sea. Why you looking at yourself so much?"

"I'm not lookin' at myself," she said. "I enjoy lookin' at you. I feel funny lookin' at myself."

"Me too. But when I look at you up there, I see myself too."

"We look good together." She pressed his face close to hers and watched it in the mirror.

"Imagine," he said. "Comes checkout time and instead of us leaving, they check out"—he pointed to the mirror—"and we remain. Or. We leave, but our images stay pasted up there in the mirror. It's like out of a story by Borges. You heard of Borges?"

"No."

He told her who, where, what. When he mentioned that Borges was blind she said, "From Argentina?"

"No, from jerking off. Bach did it too and *he* went blind. He never wrote in C again." And Guido began to laugh. Then she began to laugh, which prompted further gales of laughter.

"I never heard you laughin' so much," she said.

"I know. It's hilarious."

"I don't get it."

"Then why you laughin'?"

"Because you are," she said, brushing his body lightly with her fingers.

"Talk to me," Guido said. "All you girls are interested in only one thing. Sex sex sex. Talk to me. I got a mind too, not just a body."

"You wanna hear somethin' funny?" she said. "I heard about this couple who split. The guy moves in with his girlfriend and has the two kids on weekends. Then he calls up the wife to, like, try and reconcile. He takes her out, like, you know, on a date, and they have a grand time and end up in a motel with a waterbed and mirror ceiling. And they fuck like crazy. Later, the wife asks the husband where the kids are, you know, who's watchin' them? So he says his girlfriend is watchin' them. At this point, the wife decides, cheatin' on a wife is, like, bad enough, but cheatin' on your girl-friend is awful. She won't have anything to do with a guy who cheats on his girlfriend with his own wife . . ." And Teresa began laughing . . . "What's the matter? Don't you think it's funny?"

"It's hilarious. But not everything funny is ha-ha funny." He stood her up.

"What are you doin'?"

"Looking at you vertically. You've been horizontal for three hours. Horizontality needs to be verticalized." He nodded. "Yes, indeed, that is some body."

"It's a good body, but my breasts are too big. I'm so self-conscious. Maybe I should get them reduced."

"Don't. Your 36D bras are cheaper. Don't touch 'em. Don't let a plastic surgeon touch you with a ten-foot pole. Lots of girls who don't got what you got would love to have half of what you have. Don't forget, you're you. There's only one of you in this whole wide world. And if you want a second opinion, I'll give it. No plastic surgery. No way. Be proud of your body."

"Who says I'm not proud? I am proud of my body," Teresa said.

"But you hide it with those heavy denim shirts and bulky sweaters as if you're ashamed."

"Self-conscious, yes. Ashamed no. Proud," she said. "I like my body," she said. "I love it," she said slowly, lasciviously, like a porno queen and, with one shoulder up, slowly ran her hands provocatively over her breasts. "I just don't want people staring. Men always stare."

"The beasts! Do you go to the beach with that body?"

"No. Not with this one. I got another body for the beach."

He laughed. "Now *that's* funny. Very funny . . . I meant, do you wear bikinis? Or is that against the Miami anti-riot act?"

"I wear one-piecers and usually some kind of dark gauzy jacket as camouflage."

"To deflect attention."

"I don't want to reflect attention," she said. "Just the opposite. It's because I don't want people starin'."

"Because you like your body."

"Everybody likes my body."

"Including me."

"Did you ever see a girl with a body like mine?"

"Never. And you?"

"There's not too many girls with a body like mine," she said.

"Can't argue with that," he said.

"I got on the right line when they gave out bodies."

"But where were you when they gave out brains?"

"On the body line. You can't stand on two lines at the same time."

"Can't argue with that either. Getting on the body line was a smart choice. A brainy choice, even though it contradicts what Cardinal Richilieu said. You know Cardinal Richilieu?"

"Not personally . . . I don't go to church no more . . . But what did he say?"

"The Cardinal said: 'Intellect doesn't become a woman,' the accuracy of which you are the living em*bodi*ment."

"I told you I got a great body," she said. "Fuck me again."

A new wrinkle in their relationship was dancing. He put on a Bach Brandenburg Concerto and began to rock and roll. At once he told Aviva to take off her blouse. "Next item too." He never dreamt this classical cellist could or would shake her shoulders and wiggle her breasts the way she did. She lowered her head, looked up at him with a coquettish smile, shy and questioning at the same time.

"The way you move really surprises me . . . Wait, I want to photograph you."

It popped out before he even noticed it. He had never thought of photographing her before. But now as she stood naked from the waist up, moving so sensuously and giving him that loving look, he wanted to capture the moment.

"Why?" she asked.

"I want to sell them."

He ran into his study to get his little Konica, always ready with film. (He had another loaded camera in the car.)

"Won't someone know it's me?"

"Don't worry . . . I develop them myself. Just lift up your hand and stick your chest out. If this doesn't make it to the AARP Annual Nude Calendar I'll eat my filters."

She posed for him, a melancholy little smile on her face. She kept glancing out the window, as if afraid a police car or taxi would pull up.

He took one picture after another, rearranging the poses.

"Enough," she said.

"Just a few more, till the end of the roll . . . Now off with the slacks."

"If I weren't so fat, I wouldn't mind."

"Are you kidding? Who has a body like yours at your age, and at a hundred twenty pounds to boot?"

He helped her untie her shoes, then pulled her slacks and panties down. As he snapped, he felt an odd sensation of eros, of sexual victory, in having her submit to being photographed naked.

"What are you going to do with them?"

"Sell 'em to *Playboy*."

The unmarked envelope addressed to him disturbed him even before he quickly tore it open and found a Xerox copy in Hebrew and English of some verses from the Book of Proverbs. No letter, no note. The postmark was New York City. Who could have sent it? he wondered. The Arab? But how did he know him? He knew him neither by name or address. That's what comes from blabbing. Aviva's music counselor had probably spoken to someone; it got back to a taxi driver who told the Arab. But the verses hit the mark. A father's warning to a son—like Polonius to Laertes—on how to behave. Avoid the sinful woman. Consort with strange women and the path leads to death.

Saturday at 1 p.m. when Aviva came, he showed her the sheet of paper and the envelope. She began shaking her head in amazement as soon as she caught sight of the page.

"Look at this," Guido said. "Her feet go down to Death and her steps lead to the grave. 'See Chapter 2 on the forbidden woman and all of Chapter 5.' Neatly typed so as to avoid calligraphic recognition. And this: 'He will meet with disease . . .' My God, they knew about AIDS three thousand years ago?"

"Do you think it's some kind of warning?" Aviva asked.

"I'm sure it's meant to scare me. Did your music counselor blab? And it got back to a certain taxi driver . . . ?"

She laughed. "Don't be absurd. Are you on that again? I never even mentioned your name to her . . . Stop it."

"I don't know what to make of it. It's creepy. It bothers me . . . Do you think it's the Arab?"

"Absolutely not," she said.

"But the Hebrew is there . . . That's his language."

"He doesn't have a monopoly on it. It's also mine. Missionaries know Hebrew too. Anyone can request a Hebrew-English Bible and xerox some pages. It might be a missionary group sending this on a mass basis, warning against promiscuity. I once got a couple of pages from the New Testament in the mail."

"But how did they know of my situation?"

"They don't. It's you who's filling in the gaps. It's you who's interpreting it."

Guido shrugged, shook his head.

"Think it's your wife?" Aviva said.

"Abs . . . " He stopped. "Hmm," he wondered,". . . solutely not . . . Maybe it's a local Jewish zealot from the Preserve Your Wife Society."

That letter was one thing to worry about. But that was nothing. There were major things, like cornices dropping from buildings and bridges (*pace* Herbie Ginzberg) collapsing. His old classmate Herbie had been right after all. That Connecticut Turnpike bridge had indeed collapsed, and Herbie had always avoided it. In fact, he avoided Connecticut altogether. Guido wondered if he avoided dentists later in life too. You had to keep your eyes open for collapsing bridges and flooded tunnels. You had to watch out for muggings at night and daylight thugs. Computers caused miscarriages. Too many decibels made you deaf and depressed. Screwing? Passé! It would kill you quicker—or slower—than fat, smoking, breakfast cereals, water, sprays, and drunken drivers put together. Emily Dickinson was right: I died for love, she wrote, and was scarce adjusted to the tomb when I looked down and saw canker sores within my womb . . . And John Donne and his dying/ loving nexus. They all predicted AIDS.

And breathing? Forget it. Guido knew you can't breathe the polluted air from here to Mexico. Cosmetics, dangerous. Shampoos too. Too much washing. You can't swim—medical wastes, syringes filled with contaminated blood. You can't eat—too many additives. No butter. Watch the ice cream. Hold the steak. Broccoli, first it was in, then out, then back in again. Milk was irradiated. Fruits next. Quit eating—salmonella, preservatives, chemicals, carcinogenic food dyes, poisonous pesticides on produce, fish full of PCB's and mercury, madmen who lace food with cyanide. The waters of America were toxic. In the house, the walls have lead and wood furniture leaks formaldehyde vapors. From below the house, decaying uranium forms radon gas that devours your lungs. In libraries and schools, asbestos particles fill your lungs. Tobacco kills your lungs. Sunlight gives you cancer and moonlight drives you crazy. The ozone layer is cracked. So are the homeless. Acid rain is eating up our trees. Greed is destroying our rain forests. The weather is getting worse. The polar caps will melt and flood us. The only thing one can do safely is die, and today even that is a long, drawn out affair.

So nothing's left but music. Can you imagine cello sounds making you dementive!? Piano, syphilitic? A flute, blind? A piccolo, HIV positive? Imagine a quartet that stunts your growth. Or a concerto that makes you impotent. The sole safe pleasure left in this world was music.

But still humans were tra-la-la-ing along with better things. Guido read about the new micromachines smaller than the breadth of a human hair, or less than 60 microns wide. He told Aviva that one of the applications was (and she believed him) that they would soon develop a microvideo recorder which would be swallowed, or placed under the skin, and it would record dreams.

One day he got a call at his health club, around 3:00 in the afternoon, about an hour before his return to his office. He had never had calls there before. Who could it be? he wondered. But he suspected. And how did she find out? When he arrived the manager said, "You just missed a call. They said they'll call back in ten minutes."

They? he wondered. Who's the *they*?

When the call came, the manager, with a little knowing smile, wordless complicity, handed him the portable phone. He walked away with it.

"Hello," he said.

"Hi-ii . . ." That musical voice. "You're late. It's five after three."

"How did . . . Did I . . ."

She laughed heartily, a sharp, perky little giggle, as if he'd told a joke. A pleased laugh. She was proud of herself.

"Did I tell . . . ? I didn't . . ."

"Even when I'm not listenin'. I'm listenin' . . . The other day I was out of it at the lab, but still I remember you said you were goin' to work out on Wednesday around three."

"But how did you know which club . . . ? There are six in the area."

"But only two with the words New York in the name. And you told me weeks ago that you go to the New York club. So I called one, asked if Guido is there yet, they said they don't have a Guido, so I tried this one. So don't talk too friendly to me. I'm your sister Barbara."

"I don't have a sister," Guido said loudly.

She gave a delightful laugh. "Well, you got one now."

"Okay, so how's mom doing?"

"That's better. And next time, say: Hi, Teresa, sweetie, how are you? I'm so glad you called. what a pleasant surprise."

"I'm glad to hear she's feeling better."

"You know you have a sexy voice."

"She said the nursing care is very good."

"Your voice is so sexy, you must have started shavin' when you were eleven."

"Four," Guido said. "Four . . . more days."

She laughed at his ploy. "Your face is sexy, your eyes are sexy, your walk is sexy, your body is sexy. Everything about you is sexy, and you know it, don't you?"

"I know," he said, "that she'll soon get better . . ." And he walked to the other side of the room and whispered, "You can do anything to me except fuck me."

"What a way to speak to a sister!?" Teresa said.

"Are you coming to the family reunion in Montreal?" he said loudly, then dropped his voice. "I have an assignment in Montreal this weekend, and I need an assistant. Free? Wanna come?"

"Sure." Then she stopped. He sensed her hesitation.

"What's the matter?"

"Can you postpone your assignment for next weekend?"

"I think so. Why?"

"I can't make it this weekend."

"Why? Got a date."

"No."

"Then what? Tell me."

"My husband is home this weekend. But not next."

"Married?" he exploded. "Married! You never told me you were married."

"You didn't ask . . . Are you upset?"

"Yes . . . No . . . It makes it more exciting . . . What does . . . he"—Guido didn't want to say "your husband"—"do?"

"He drives a long haul big rig."

"Now I get it. That's why you said that day in the lab, you can do anything to me except fuck me."

"Yee—eesss," she sang. "I wanted to be faithful. Kind of."

"But it's not gonna be Montreal. It just starts with Mon . . . It's my place in Montauk."

"Just you and me?"

"Yes. Unless you want to bring Big Rig."

"He does have a big rig," she said slowly. "But I like your MG better."

"Yes." He swallowed. "Just you and me. And camera makes three . . ." Married, he thought. Nobody's single anymore. "So what do you do at nights when he's away?"

"Go to the movies."

"Alone?"

"Yes."

"You go a lot?"

"Three four times a week . . . I love movies . . . I'm alone, but yet there's a lot of people around me so I'm not lonely."

Guido wasn't a political person; sure, politics interested him, but he didn't go haywire over it. All "-ists" repelled him—communists, fascists, socialists, scientists—except one. He didn't know he was a pan-sexualist until—quite by accident—he ran across the word in the dictionary. Definition: The view that the sex instinct plays a part in all human thought and activity and is the chief, or only, source of energy. Bingo: Webster's had him down pat—which was the word he was looking up in the first place when he spotted pan-sexualist.

In the same dictionary he tried to find *cunt* and *pussy* without success. What an idiotic lexicographical tool! The words most used in the English language didn't seem to exist within the columns of respectable alpha-beticality. But as a pan-sexualist he gave some deep thought to the woman's pudendum, which isn't as redundant as it sounds. You can look it up!

At first glance, Guido told himself, a cunt is so unaesthetic. Come to think of it, at second and third too. Yet we can't stop glancing, he thought. If pussies alone would be the criterion for beauty, women would never make it. Was there anything beautiful, *photogenic* about a cunt? Nothing. But Teresa was an exception. She had an absolutely clean-looking rubescent little fenestra. As a professional pan-sexualist, however, he knew he should always be on the lookout for others.

How long had he known Aviva? A year-and-a-half? Two? And he still couldn't figure her out. At times she gave him such headaches he couldn't enjoy anything. The same speeches, again and again. Orbiting words sailing down from their eternal flight. Luckily, a temporary distraction came along, a breath of fresh air. Her name was Gina.

The *Post* library was generally a dull place. The librarian, Stella Wellbright, was typical of her calling: pasty-faced, with large, unattractive glasses and a hairdo that was more a hair don't. She reminded him of the spinster rare book librarian that Aviva had once described. But one day the place smelled different. Alive. Somebody somewhere was giving off sex hormones. He looked around until he found a pretty, black-haired, Spanish-looking girl sweeping. She was about twenty-one, good body, moved well. Suddenly a patina of excitement bubbled in the library. Who's the maid? he asked the librarian. The little flick of her eyes showed she didn't appreciate Guido's joke. She shrugged. Friend of a friend of the wife of the advertising manager, the librarian whispered. Guido went to the stacks where she was sweeping. She caught his glance and smiled. That smile finished him. At once Guido was off in dreamland, posing her in his living room, naked. He saw she had a cute, well-rounded bust, but because she wore thick dungarees he couldn't tell a thing about her ass. As he left, she gave him another fetching smile. Then she dropped the broom. She tried to catch it, but her movement was awkward, poorly timed; somehow it seemed very foreign to him, and girlish as well. He recalled how girls threw a ball overhand with an awkward forward shoulder movement as if they were righties throwing lefty, their coordination out of whack. She looked to the librarian with a look of trepidation, as if she were going to be reprimanded. Perhaps back home in Rio, or Bogota, or wherever she came from, the boss would have shouted at her for being a clumsy oaf. But her trying to catch the slipping broom remained fixed in his mind, a kind of off-beat, ill-synchronized, poorly syncopated gesture that, when linked to a pretty girl, was rather appealing, even sexy.

A day later, when he returned to consult some photography magazines, he saw her again. Again she gave him that shy but direct smile. He nodded and approached her.

"Where are you from?"

She laughed and looked down.

"Land? Country?"

She surprised him by saying, "Italy. Sicily." He could have sworn she was Spanish.

"Which city?" He resisted the temptation to talk Italian to her.

She didn't understand. How could she get a job here? he wondered. Probably doesn't even have a green card. He asked the librarian. I don't know, the librarian whispered. Why don't you ask her? You know Italian, right? How do you know? Well, you have an Italian name. And you have an English name, Mrs. Wellbright, do you know English? Her face fell, but when Guido gave her a big grin and tapped her on the arm, she gave a tentative smile.

Back in the lab, Guido realized he should have taken the girl's hand and drawn a map of Italy on her palm and pressed his forefinger into the city she was from. He didn't want to talk Italian to her, for he had a plan, which he didn't want to ruin.

Next time he asked her:

"How long you here?"

"America," she said.

"Family?"

"Grandmother. Husband."

No good, he thought. Not two days here and already married.

"What does he do?"

"Thank you. Fine," she said. "How you do?"

"Thank you," he said.

The next time he went to the library she wasn't there. But perhaps it was early. He planned to tell her he had to go to Rome for a couple of weeks. Would she give him Italian lessons? At his house? Did she drive? If not, he'd pay the taxi fare. He watched the door. People came and went. Not the ones he wanted to see. Then the door opened and a pretty young woman came in wearing a pink sweater dress that reached just below her thighs. Guido saw the beautifully rounded ass, the black hair, and realized it was the girl. At once she went to the closet, took out a broom, and began to work. They exchanged glances and again she smiled shyly at him. He approached and gave her a soft *Buon giorno*. She literally lit up—her face pinked three deeper shades than her dress—and she began a patter of Italian which he pretended to not understand. He went to another part of the stacks. Soon she was dusting there. The sunlight through the window lit up the shaggy wool of her short sweater dress, rounding out her tush. The wool looked especially clingy there. Then she sat down and pulled a little book out of her pocket—probably an English primer—and began reading. But sensing that Guido was watching her, she couldn't concentrate. Now was the time to ask about lessons and surprise her with his quick progress. He was sure she'd accept; it was just a matter of getting her to understand. But he would have to do it softly; he didn't want the entire library to get involved with his little adventure.

"What's your name?" he whispered.

"Gina."

"Studying English?"

"English, yes."

Her cheeks were lightly rouged; her skin smooth like a baby's. But her eyelids were shaded a garish pastel blue, which didn't go with her dark eyes nor with her clothes. Yes, a peasant from Sicily, quickly Americanized.

He pointed to the primer. "Tell me, could you . . ." he spoke slowly, ". . . give me Italian lessons?"

"Yes?" Gina said in an up-pitch tone.

"When?"

"Ten years."

Guido shook his head, more to himself than to her. If it weren't so sad, it'd be hilarious.

"When can you teach me Italian?"

"In school. Twice week."

"No. No. Not you study English. But teach . . . teach Italian . . ." He pointed to himself.

"In Wilson School. Night. Twice week."

The frumpy librarian came over. She had evidently heard, had been straining to overhear. "No, Gina. Not you study," she whispered, ". . . but teach . . . you teach . . . Italian?" She turned to Guido. "She can't do it. She doesn't understand the simplest English. Why did the boss bring her here? She sits more than she works." And she walked back to her desk.

"Where do you learn English?"

"Wilson School. Monday . . . Wednesday night."

He didn't want to ask her if she went to study with her husband. What now? he wondered. How do you keep the conversation alive? He remembered the classic advice to beginning writers: make the start of your story exciting. Example: "Get your hands off my knee!" cried the duchess. (And put it on my crotch.) Maybe he should use the international language and put his hand on her knee. He looked at her book. Plucked it out of her hands. Again, she had that open, helpless look. A slight flush on her cheeks. Excitement? Embarrassment? He opened her primer and glanced back at her. That trepidatious look flickered there as it had several days ago when she dropped the broom.

"Your English book."

"No." Gina pointed to someone who wasn't there. "Girlfriend."

He looked at the first lesson, scanned the first exercise. He moved his chair closer. "What's your family name?"

"Gina. Gina Pianti."

He nodded, as if this were very important. There seemed to be an edge of excitement in her voice. She breathed quicker. Oh, how he could take this lovely round-assed girl with the black bangs and give her English, Italian and banging lessons. But if he couldn't talk to her, what could he say? He looked into the primer, at the dictionary in the back, and began to say a few phrases. She smiled, she laughed, then understood. He forgot the word for "model" in Italian, but if she modeled for him, he was sure she'd strike some great *Playboy* poses for him. He could just see her lying on her belly amid well-placed lighting catching the rising globes of her ass. He squeezed her shoulder. "Comprende? Italian lessons for me?"

"Yes."

"How long will you study English?"

"Yes?" she said.

He shook his head, laughed. She did too, in that innocent way where joy and a flicker of fear mingled. He wanted to, but did not, roll his eyes in frustration. He squeezed her shoulder, and said, "See you, Gina."

She laughed, realizing that they were both tongue-tied. But he also knew that even if he got through to her, her husband would never agree. Deciding not to give up, he took the primer, flicked pages, looked at the glossary, nodded seriously, made notes, then told her in halting Italian. "Do you want to give me Italian lessons? I'll pay you well. Your house or mine. Here's my phone number at work. Call me."

She made an appreciative moue at his Italian and wrote out her address. He said he would come at seven. It wasn't too far from the office.

But when he rang the bell to the apartment a young man came down and growled, "Gina no home." The guy looked forbidding, a Neanderthal. He knew that Gina was home; knew that his prediction of the husband nixing it would come true.

He called immediately from the next gas station. She answered. So she was home. She recognized his voice. "My husband, sorry. No lessons. Sorry. Good-bye."

Good-bye, hell! Guido thought. There's always lunchbreaks.

Did you hear of Teresa Berganza?"

"What?"

"You didn't hear of her?"

"No."

"She was a famous Italian opera star."

"Oh."

"Do you know Joyce?"

"Joyce who?"

"Faulkner?"

"Joyce Faulkner?" She shook her head.

"Steichen? Stieglitz? Jelly-Roll Morton? King Saul? Saul Bellow? Jasper Johns? John Williams? William Safire?"

She looked blank. Then annoyed. As if to say: What do you want from me? Then she turned the tables.

"Elton John?"

"Yeah."

"Madonna?"

"Which one?" he said.

"Is there more than one?" Teresa asked.

Then he threw "Phnom Phen" at her.

"I got one for Christmas, but it leaks."

"Don't you ever pick up a book?"

"So I don't read. So what? Most people in America don't read. Most people in the world don't read. So I'm like most people. Scaasi?"

"What?"

"Do you know Scaasi?"

"No."

"Then you don't know everything either."

"Okay. My turn. Answer true or false. Balanchine."

"True."

"Solzhenitsyn."

"False."

"Winslow Homer."

"False."

"Picasso."

"Very true," she said enthusiastically.

"Casals."

"True."

"Ian Plaskow."

"False."

"You're dead right on that one. Frank Rich."

She didn't answer.

"What's up?" he wanted to know.

"I'm thinking . . . True."

"Great," he said.

"Did I do good?"

"You got one right . . . Okay, one more. Stradivarius."

"That's easy," she said. "A kind of dinosaur."

"Right," said Guido. "Old and extinct."

Are you interested in other women?" Aviva asked.

"Yes."

"Who?" She looked hurt, though she tried to control the waves of emotion of her face.

"You . . . You're the Other Woman."

"I mean, besides me."

"Are you kidding?"

"That's no answer," she said. "Answer!"

"Of course not. I'm not interested in a single woman."

"Promise?"

"Of course. You're woman enough for me. You're woman enough for ten." Then smiling, "Would you be jealous?"

"Absolutely. If you were interested in someone else, I'd be devastated."

"Only you, Aviva, What we have happens only once to a man in his lifetime. And anyway, I'm so busy—with other women—I don't even have time to *think* about other women."

"Let's go to a sex therapist," she said suddenly.

"What the hell for?"

"Not for you, silly. For me. Us. So maybe I can have an orgasm with you."

He pointed to the palm of his hand. "When hairs grow here."♥

He liked Teresa's walk. She walked head down, craning her neck as she began to pace. From behind this slim-waisted, slim-hipped slip of a girl looked like a boy. But from the front—the front was another matter. She wore loose sweaters and blouses draped with open jackets that deaccented her, as she called them, affecting an Italian accent, "big Palermo nurseries."

"You interested in other guys?" he asked her in the lab the next day. She looked dreamily up at him. Her big brown eyes grew soft. "I'm just a prisoner of your eyes," she said, hooking his with hers. That was one of her better lines, he thought.

"Do you touch other women?"

"Jealous?"

"Yes," she said in that long drawn timbre that said she didn't really want to answer but couldn't help herself.

♥See ABC Directory, *Swedish sex therapist.*

"That's a strange attitude for a mod gal who loves fucking."

"I didn't want to be jealous. I've never been before. But with you I am." And she looked sort of vulnerable standing there, not facing him squarely, but looking at him from a side, one leg forward, hand on her hip, as if soon she'd be off balance.

"Here's the answer, Terry, to your question . . . Once I went to the theater by myself. I sat between two women. The one to my right asked me: How come that lady to your left has her hand on your thigh? I said: She's on a special weight-reducing diet her doctor prescribed. But it's not working, I said. So how come your hand is on my thigh now? the woman to my right asked. Well, I said, I'm a bit on the pudgy side too, can't you see? Maybe it will work for *me*."

"And that's all?" Teresa wanted to know. "Otherwise?"

Guido folded his hands on his chest. "Otherwise! Otherwise, I keeps me hands to meself. I'm not interested. There's not a single woman I'm interested in."

She threw her arms around him and kissed his lips. Her eyes were pressed shut. He didn't kiss back.

"Don't fuck your wife tonight," she pleaded. Then she opened her eyes. The first time she even gave an indication that she knew he was married.

That was the difference between a fifty-five-year-old Jewish princess of European parents and a twenty-three-year-old shiksa, he thought. Teresa had absolutely no qualms about Anglo-Saxonisms, although she wouldn't know the term. What the dictionary called vulgar, informal, or obscene made no difference to Teresa. And Aviva it took light years before she would even utter the f-word in his presence.

Then he had a super idea. He'd tell Aviva that his wife wanted to have him make love to her and another woman. But it would have to be done in the dark, because her one condition was that she wouldn't want to see the other woman. Of course, he wouldn't tell Aviva that it wasn't his wife and one of his ground rules would be that the two women couldn't talk. To Teresa—oh, to have the two of them together in one bed!—he'd tell the same story. Now if he could only convince Tammy, he'd have a ménage a quatre . . .

But with his luck, even if it was only *a trois*, both—like in a comic film—would somehow discover at the same time who the other woman was and whisper, That's not your wife. For Teresa was secretly studying cello with guess who? Teresa would recognize her teacher's voice in that ecstatic Oh, God, God, God, and Aviva would recognize that melodic, Mmmm, I love it, I love it, I love it . . . fuck me good, fuck me good, as the voice of her new pupil.

As soon as she got in the car with him, he closed the seat belt over her, making sure to sculpt her body with his free hand. She looked like a younger Aviva, sure, but not for one moment did he think of Aviva as he made love to her. And when they were on the highway, she once again put her hand on his thigh (he was wearing shorts). Not on one spot, of course. She moved it up and down and commented on the fuzzy hairs on his legs. What a great model she'd be. Her body was even slimmer, shapelier than Aviva's—she could appear in *Playboy* with her pencil-thin waist and cantaloupe breasts and her smile was not as sadly self-conscious. In all the snaps he'd taken of Aviva naked there was this mournful smile as if she's doing something against her better nature, as if she'd be paying someday for every single pose; that an electrode reading "Future Retaliation Coming" was being activated by this sinful deed of posing naked, as if she sensed the warning signals that she was playing with fire and steel but was saying gloomily to herself: I hear them, I see the flaming scimitar bearing down on me, but I can't do anything about it. Even in a still photo of her, Guido remembered as he looked at the snapshot, with her hands at her sides, one of Aviva's hands trembled, as if fearing that something bad would befall her, that every moment of joy in her life would have to be balanced out with anguish, fulfilling her killjoy Mama's old remark, If you enjoy something too much you pay for it later. But Teresa, yeah, yeah, she was superphotogenic. She was a modern kid, even postmodernist but didn't know it, two generations removed from Aviva, a kid with no hang-ups. All body, no brains. She'd never been to the theater, the ballet, a concert. She listened to rock music and chewed bubble gum. She hadn't read a book in years. Last book she read was in high school. "I don't remember the writer," she said, "or the name of the book, but it was about a lady, I remember, who wears the letter *A* on her chest." Homer for her was baseball. But she loved fucking. Not only the act itself which she called by no other name—euphemisms like screwing were foreign to her—but the very word itself was music to her ears.

Hard rock.

Buona fortuna. Three women in one day. Aviva in the morning. Teresa in the afternoon. Adam's mommy at night. Energy ran through him like a rapids. Ate enormous amounts of food. Sang at the top of his lungs. Ran great photos at the paper. Played the cello with verve. Even composed a melody. Was nice to everyone he spoke to. Felt closer to Aviva. In my dreams she's a virgin, he thought of telling Charlie. Thus the dream part, pal, is true. God cannot unmake her past, but in dreams all things can be. Hey! he laughed to himself, weighing the words. That could be an Italian saying. Even photos can be retouched. Like a woman, he thinks. Touched and retouched and retouched again. Like Aviva. And if we are all shadows of a dream, as the Greeks averred, then I can erase all the other men, and she'll be mine alone. I'll undo that stain, I'll retouch her in my dream. And she too would gladly erase the past. He remembered her saying, What would you say if I told you all these tales of my affairs were figments of my imagination? That none happened. Guido laughed. There's no turning back. You cannot retouch the past, he told her.

He told Aviva he had to go to Chicago for a day; he told Tammy he was going to Boston for a day; he told Teresa they were going to Montauk for a day. She told her husband she was going to Philadelphia for a day. He told her he was going to Raleigh for a day.

In the Veneziano-Tedesco family cottage at Montauk they went over every inch of each other's bodies.

"I love your body, I love your skin, I love every touch of yours. I look at you and I melt. You're beautiful."

Teresa, not Guido, speaking. Since Ava he had not met anyone so happily hungry for him. Perhaps because for weeks they had stood in proximity, and he played hard to get. Every place he touched her she gasped, as though she were a dry gully waiting to be watered, a dam waiting to be opened. He touched her nose, she screamed; ran a finger up her thigh, she yipped. She would start moaning even before he came into her. He rolled his finger slowly along her spine, she sang. He feather-brushed a kiss along her arm. Ditto.

A youthful energy poured out of her. Taking hold of the posts on the bed while astride him like a bicycle, and while he held her hips, she pedaled as though out to win the Tours de France, her eyes closed, her tongue out at an odd angle on her upper lip. "I love it," she kept shouting. "It's big, I love it," again and again until she came once, twice, three times and then once again as he backpedaled in syncopation to her tight soprano screams.

"Here . . . it . . . comes . . ." he said and the explosion rang in his ears, sent chills rolling over the sides of his head.

"Do you feel it in back of your throat?" she asked later.

No, he said.

"I still feel it pulsing there," she pointed.

"But I did feel as if my head was in a vise, and then I came and released it . . . Wow! This kind of loving happens only once to a man in his lifetime," he told her.

Then they went out to the beach. But whereas Aviva and Tammy left him alone regarding his appearance, this refugee from world culture had her finger on fashion's pulse. Soon she wanted to re-do him, to take him shopping. She didn't like his trousers, his jeans, his ties, his shirts, his handkerchiefs, his sport jackets, his suits. His shoes, "they don't go" with his socks; his socks didn't go with his feet. Main thing is I'm going with you, he told her.

"For a guy who's in love with composition in pictures, why doncha compose yourself?" she said.

The sun had set. The new moon, borrowed from a Turkish flag, hung crisp like a Matisse cutout in the starred sky. It's reflection wavered in the water as if someone were waving a torch. The moon, metaphor for coolness, he thought, was on fire. It shook, shimmered. Little tongues of moonlight shot up like tiny flames. They walked past the estates section. At one of the guard booths they stopped to talk to a guard, an American Indian. He said that in his upstate reservation married women who were unfaithful had their noses slit --at this point, Guido covered Teresa's nose with his fingers—so that everyone would know what sort of women they were.

"In my time," Teresa joked, "they made 'em stand with a letter *A* on their chest."

The one and only literary reference she knows, Guido thought, and she blows it on an Indian who doesn't dig it.

"Imagine if they slit noses in New York," Guido said. "Half the population in the city would walk around with bandages." And Ava would lead the pack, he thought. Which reminded him:

"Did you ever think of keeping a diary?"

"What kind?"

"You know, like a diary of an adulterous woman?"

"Nah, I don't like to write. I like to read." And she gave him a clever little smile.

Walking back, he remembered how much she loved the movies, how often she went. "Wanna see a movie next week? When Trucko's away in Tennessee?"

"Nah, to the movies I go alone, when I'm lonely. With you I'm not lonely. With you I can think of better things to do."

Why can't you work decent hours?" Tammy complained when he came home at two in the morning. "What a way to run one's life."

"You did nothing with yours," he shot back.

"I run your shop. Normal hours."

"Our shop."

"Yours. I was trained as an interior decorator."

"But you couldn't make a go of it. They took one look at your morose face and realized *you* needed interior decorating."

"There was ample reason for a morose face, wasn't there?"

"So it's my fault, huh?" Guido said.

"I didn't say it was. I *never* said it was. All these years I never once said it. Not like you who always threw the blame at me."

The anger welled up in him. Perhaps he was thankful for the opportunity to rev his rage up against her.

"Well, what *have* you done with your life? You never had the gumption to make a move on your own. Positive or negative. Even my idiot first wife had the guts to do what she wanted to do."

"That's guts? Is that your criterion for guts? Then I pity you. That's sluts, not guts. Is that what you want me to do? Sleep with every man under the sun? Is that doing something with one's life? You're crazy! Is that what you want me to do? Take someone else's husband?"

Who would have you? he was about to say.

"The fact is that you've done nothing with your life, except —." And now he would throw the shoe back at her for her nasty accusation. He knew he was going to be cruel. He couldn't stop being cruel. Something in him—of course, his desire for Aviva, his, you could only call it magnetism, his magnetism for Teresa, his mad desire to create a break in this sterile relationship—drove him to be cruel. But he was also cruel for the sheer pleasure of it, which is why people are usually cruel, which is why he said, "except to bring a retard into the world." Then he was sorry as soon as he said it.

First her face flushed as a look of astonishment, pain, then grief waved through it. With her blonde hair and fair complexion the redness highlighted her face like a purple flame. Then the tears, uncontrollable, as he knew they would be.

"I begged you to have more children, but you refused," Guido said to somehow reduce the sting. "Just remember that. It wasn't me who said: I don't want any more children."

She sat, her face in her hands, sobbing. She rarely cried. He couldn't imagine that WASPy face of hers in tears. Blondes weren't supposed to get emotional, highstrung, stressed out. But Guido was not moved. He wasn't moved to stroke her hair, calm her, say he was sorry.

"You're not the man I married," she said between sobs. "The real you is revealed in these outbursts. Some refinement, some Italian Jewish nobility. Now I know why there were revolutions in Italy. To get rid of cruel aristocrats like you who are interested only in themselves . . . Well, you can run your own photo shop from now on."

He approached her, but she screeched, "Get away from me! Get away!" And she clenched her fists and bared her teeth as if she would hiss, strike, bite him. He knew she would change her mind by morning.

"Yes. Run it yourself. Why am I working there? For what? We don't have to save up for college."

"Adam costs more than college . . . And what would you do? Clean the Levelor blinds twice a day? Sit here nine to five?"

"No. You wouldn't talk to me anyway. You'd be in the darkroom because you love pictures more than people. *That's* your basic flaw. And you want perfection in everyone around. Except yourself. Are you so perfect?"

"You know what they say in Venice whenever someone demands perfection? Even the sun has spots."

"And so does a leopard," Tammy retorted. "But on him it looks good."

"And so does a kid with measles. But on him it looks bad."

The fight had gone out of her, he saw. She was looking for reconciliation.

"Let's not fight, huh? Isn't there enough misery in this world?" she said.

Should he draw near? One embrace would mollify her, expunge the misery, erase his nasty cracks. He felt sorry for Tammy, for Adam through her, and he put his arms around her. In bed, Tammy insisted that he sleep close to her, drape himself around her. He can't sleep that way, he said. He can't sleep facing her, and besides, her snuffling annoyed him. They tried changing positions, he on starboard, she leeward, and he slipped his arm under her. Two, three, four lugubrious minutes passed. He couldn't sleep. He climbed over her and said, "The only thing on me that fell asleep was my arm."

She laughed and felt better again.

When he saw Aviva, he asked her how she felt, for his mother had taught him that one must always ask an older woman how she's doing. Asking young folks How are you? is perfunctory. Do you hear the reply? Nah. Never. But her answer, he knew, one pays attention to. Turns out she was anxious, edgy, off balance, had had a dream.

"I dreamt I bought a pair of nice boots . . . "

"How much and where?"

"Shh . . . and before I got home, I looked into the bag and saw one boot was missing. I woke up and had this awful trembly feeling."

At first he didn't know what to make of it, but then, in the developer lixium of Guido's mind, the word *boot* brought to mind Rabbi Doctor Kleincock. Since the old matchmaker lecher had pressed one of Aviva's boots into his crotch, perhaps that was the one missing in her dream. But after thinking about it for a while he came up with a better explanation.

"I'm not like Joseph who could interpret dreams, but it seems to me that the saying 'getting the boot' became concretized into a real boot in dream language. Since I'm going away on assignment for a few weeks, you consider it the equivalent of getting the boot."

"But I didn't *get* the boot. I lost it. Lost one boot."

"You don't get it is right. If you lost two of them you still won't get it."

But Aviva came up with a different interpretation. "My view is I had lost or misplaced a boot that was already mine—I was wearing it when I entered the store. Perhaps the missing boot represents the missing part of our relationship which lacks wholeness. Two boots symbolize a couple. When one can't be found it may simply underline the true nature of our relationship:

each boot under a different roof." That's why she was off balance, she said.

Her analysis impressed him, but he didn't tell her lest it go to her head.

"You hug with two hands, the Venetians say, but it takes only one foot to give a kick."

"You've got a good head," she said.

"Not enough. Like my grandmother Sacerdote used to say: Everybody wishes he had two heads, especially the slaughtered chicken."

You have cross eyes," she said.

"No one ever tells me that," he said with an edge to his voice.

"But it's, like, on your face. For everyone to see. I mean, it's not hidden in your pants, you know."

"I just don't like people saying it to me, like."

"What're you king or somethin?"

"Last time anyone said it to me was in school when I was a kid. Like, I mean, you have to have some kind of, you know, discretion." But she paid no attention either to his mimicry or his pique.

"So what'd you do? Beat them up?"

"No. I just had them say something in Italian."

"What?"

"An old Italian proverb. I challenged them, like, to pronounce *siamo idioti* real quick a few times . . . Can you say that?"

"Sure! *Siamoidioti siamoidioti* . . . Is that good?"

"Terrific! But can you say, *Sono cretina*?"

"Sure. *Sonocretina*."

"Well said. Perfect. Like your body. The one you got on that line you stood on when they gave out bodies. Which you then gave to me," tender voice now, "on a silver platter."

She hugged him, closed her eyes, loved his compliment. A beatific look of adoration came over her. He touched her. He forgot he was mad at her; she forgot he berated her.

Later, when the singing moans were just echoes sliding off the walls, he asked her with a proud look on his face:

"Well? Was it good, like?"

"You *are* king," she said sleepily. "Or somethin' . . ." and then with a pleased feline smile, "but your eyes are still crossed."

What's your philosophy in life?" he asked her.

"Doin' good."

"How quickly?"

"When I get around to it."

He shook his head disapprovingly. "As the Latin proverb has it:

Op cit libidus addendum,
Sli pitin de pudendum."

"You speak Latin?"

"Sure. With Italian it's a cinch, since it's a cognate, not to mention cognitive, cunnilingua."

"What does it mean?"

"What what? What I just said or the Latin proverb?"

"The Latin proverb."

"It means, if you're gonna do a good deed you should go and do it and not wait too long lest the deed won't be of use anymore for the one you wanted to go and do the good deed to."

"All that in one little proverb?"

"Yes. Latin, like Swedish, is a very compressed language. That's why it's called in Latin, cunnilingua, lingua meaning tongue and cunni meaning being able to pack a lot of meaning and feeling with just a little flick of language."

Teresa frowned. She was concentrating. Then she said:

"Remember that friend of yours?"

"Which friend?"

"You know, that St. Louis Cardinal?"

He didn't laugh; he didn't know if she was joking or not. "What about him?" Guido asked.

"I was thinking. He was right. Intellect *doesn't* become a woman. Because a girl becomes a woman. Not intellect."

A few nights later as Guido and his wife lay in bed reading, he sensed that she had put her book down. The silence wasn't a library stillness but an ominous silence before a storm. He turned to her. She stared at the ceiling, her green eyes cold, her face furrowed with the sorrow that would never go away, like anguish etched into the faces of Holocaust survivors, and she said what he feared in a wild dream she would say. He turned from her before she began to speak.

"I know everything."

"What do you know?" he said louder than he intended.

"Everything."

Now he shouted. "What's this everything you know?"

"It's taken me a long time to say this," she said.

He put his book on the night table and gazed straight ahead too. Saw the print of a Degas dancer on the wall opposite their bed. He didn't look at her, but he saw the green of her eyes anyway. "Maybe a month or two," she continued. "I didn't want to say it because by not saying it I made believe it wasn't so."

"What isn't wasn't so? What did you believe? What are you talking about?" he shouted again, irritated. Her circumlocution irritated him. He knew what her face looked like this very instant without looking at it: pathetic resignation. A woman wronged and hurt, but he still did not turn to her. He wished he could photograph her face.

"Why are you shouting?" she said.

"What's this new absurdity?"

"I'm telling you," she said, "I know everything . . . I—."

He tuned out while she was speaking, thinking of clever things to say. He was the only man in the world, he thought of telling her, who was fluent in ancient Sumerian, a now lost tongue (he wished she would lose hers). but when asked to say a few words at a gathering of ancient Sumerians, he took a breath, about to begin, then withdrew, saying he can't. Sumerian is a holy tongue and it should not be used mundanely.

"How do you know?"

"I just know. By your attitude. The way you behave. Little signs so subtle you can't even tell."

"Like motions and gestures that give a man away, according to Freud? Like it oozes out of every pore of mine?"

She didn't answer.

"Someone called you? Ingrid from Stockholm maybe? Ursula from Oslo? Gina from Pisa?"

"No."

"A letter. An anonymous letter. Signed, um, Count Almaviva from Verona, or Teresa from Siena?"

"No," she said.

"Then who told you?"

"You."

"When? In my sleep? Now I'm talking in my sleep all of a sudden."

"Do you think you mentioned her in your sleep?"

"I don't know. I didn't know I talked in my sleep. Who told you?"

"I told you it was you."

"When?"

"Just now."

Guido sat up. "What are you *talking* about? Will you please tell me what you're talking about?"

"I decided simply to say: I know everything. A test."

"Why out of the blue? Would you want me to have done that to you?"

"No. Because there's no reason to."

"It's easy to turn the tables," Guido said. "I saw you flirting at the lab with a male customer."

"The best defense is always an attack, right?" she said with vehemence, a toughness that was unlike her.

"Right?" she repeated.

He heard another echo in his head.

Right? Aviva said.

"And I saw the way you stood. You had a stance, the way you positioned your body, of a woman wanting to attract a man."

"Maybe he paid attention to me."

"So I don't pay attention to you, huh?"

She didn't reply.

Then she said: "Remember, you told me, 'This happens only once to a man in his lifetime'?"

"Yes," he said. "Once. Now it unhappened."

Tammy bit her lips.

"So don't assume it's always the man who screws around. Because I can make assumptions too. I've never cast aspersions on you as to what you do here while I'm away on assignments."

"You always manage to twist things around and win, don't you?"

"It's not a matter of winning. It's a matter of being right."

"But you always want to be right."

He took a deep breath. "Tell me, I've given you reason to test me?"

"Yes. Subtle hints. Your coldness. The way you snap at me. So I gave you a test, and you—."

"Not a test. Entrapment. Like the worst aspects of the FBI. Maybe I should be held without bail as a material witness, an accessory before, during, and after the fact."

Guido saw her lips trembling and turned away. He shut the light.

"It's no use," she said. In the dark he knew the tears would—they were already coming. "When . . . one knows everything . . . one knows everything without even trying . . . you have no heart. You only have a shutter there, you bastard." She had never called him a name before.

"Have you ever seen me flirting like I saw you flirting in the shop? Surprised you, didn't I, coming in in the morning like that? But now I send in spies, like, um, Teresa from Siena, to buy film and check on you."

She said nothing, wept into her pillow. Her shoulders shook. She said some words but the pillow muffled them. It was four words, each with a single beat. She repeated them, again and again, like a little child. He strained to hear. Thought he heard her say: You broke my heart.

"You are the most absurd person in the world," Guido said softly. "I was playing along with you, you silly creature. You think a man who has a girlfriend talks about phone calls or anonymous letters. In fact, when you said, 'Do you think you mentioned her name in your sleep?' I was going to say: 'Who says it's a her?' "

"You always had your eye on younger women with a happier disposition than mine."

"I'm not seeing a single woman, I swear. Not a single one. Not one woman. So please get that absurd, weird notion out of your skull."

"You're always running all over the world. Chile, France, Finland, Alaska. I'll bet you have girlfriends in every country."

"A, not always. B, not all over the world. C, I never had the time, interest, or inclination to start affairs while I'm on assignment, so please, no tears, no tests." He shut the light, stroked her face and arms in the dark, dried his palms on the pillow. He moved closer to her, embraced her and brought her to him.

"Unbreak your heart," he whispered.

"It isn't true?" she said later in a weak voice. In the dark, her green eyes lost their tiger fire. "You're not seeing anyone?"

"It isn't true," he said. "I'm not seeing or going out with one single woman. So unbreak your heart. It's been broken too long."

He called her at home.

"Hi. It's me. Surprised?"

"Uh-huh."

"Glad to hear my voice?"

"Uh-huh."

"God, you sound so sexy . . . Okay, let's give you a little treat, some phirst class phone phucking, a genre which you invented, if you had neologistic proclivities. Ready?"

"Uh-huh."

"First, I'm going to run my fingers genitally down your spine, then kiss you from the neck down . . . Want more?"

"Uh-huh."

"Then I'm going to kiss all the other erogenous zones, specially the ones that stick out. I'm going to linger my lips on each breast that you so love to hide under loose sweaters and jackets and then make little circles around your nipples with my tongue. Like that?"

"Uh-huh."

"Love it?"

"Uh-huh."

"Would you like to fuck my brains out?"

"Uh-huh."

"Now? That's just what I want to do to you. I've got a couple of hours. Should I come over?"

She didn't say.

"Now *you* begin the phone phucking. You're better at it. What do you say?"

She didn't say.

What's with her? he wondered. He thought of asking her if she had monosyllabilitis, but she'd probably think it was some kind of disease.

"How come everything is either uh-huh or dead silence?"
She didn't say.
"Tsamatta, cat's got your tongue?"
"Uh-huh."
Oh my God, he suddenly realized. It's not the cat who's got her tongue.
"Your husband's home."
"Uh-huh."

You don't believe anything I say."
"No, I don't."
"But dammit, you got what you wanted. You wanted me not to make love to Tammy. You didn't want me to make love to two women, so I stopped . . ."
She gave him that Tell-it-to-the-Marines look.
"I swear to God I'm not making love to two women."
"That's what you claim, but you know that I know, and I know that you know that I know it isn't so. But you're not honest enough to admit it."
"No. You know that I know that you know what you know or think you know is wrong and I know that we know that both of us know it."
"Stop being cute. I'm not going to see you any more. I just can't," she said. "And I won't. It hurts me too much. I cry every night and me, who never had trouble sleeping, now I can't sleep at night. I've started to take a little bit of gin every night to calm me down. You don't want me to become an alcoholic, do you?"
He looked at his thirty-nine-year-old beauty, who was fifty-five going on seventy, withering before his eyes. No wonder men liked younger women. And he, he had to find himself an aging filly. The pun is not inadvertent, he told himself, remembering the *situ* of her early lie-down affairs.
"Compromise," he said. "Even enemy nations compromise. Politics is compromise."
"This isn't war or politics," she said. "And how come I'm always on the losing side?"
"That's the best side to be on in a modern war. Look at Germany and Japan. The Falklands and Granada. Completely rebuilt. As you will be too. Free face lift for the losers."
"I've made up my mind. No more. And that's final. I've made a concrete decision regarding our relationship."
And he at once, on the spur of the moment, re-did a blues song he'd heard on the radio and put in new words, singing and strumming on a make-believe guitar:

The Concrete Decision Blues

"I've got the concrete decision blues
Been crying all the night;
My man has said that awful phrase
and I just don't feel right.

I've got the concrete decision blues,
So long said that man of mine;
I sleep with lots of other girls
but make love to you each time.

I've got the concrete decision blues
said the lover of my life.
My guy has said, I can't no more,
I'm returning to my wife."

"Very nice," she said flatly and her lack of enthusiasm was like a slap in the face. "It still stands, what I said before."

"Can't we postpone it? Or stretch it out? I'll see you, let's say, once in two weeks."

"But it won't change anything. You're still not, you won't be mine."

"It's because you're a pessimist. If you give a concert you'll forget the score. The audience won't come. If they come they won't applaud. They'll all have one arm and will have to applaud by striking each other's palms. If tickets are sold they'll have the wrong date. When you bow your boobs will fall out. For you, in your negative world view, nothing will ever work out."

"Has it ever? Just look at my past. I'm such a failure at everything."♥

"You can always try phone sex. It's a developing global market."

"With my luck, I'll get AIDS."

"But even failure has its redeeming points. You can always serve as a poor example."

But she steamrollered on, evidently not even hearing what he had just said.

"Our separating can even have a positive effect. It's been known to happen," she said philosophically, not knowing how close she was to being smacked, "when an affair breaks up, the man usually feels closer to his wife."

"I'm not interested in your dumb *Cosmopolitan Family Circle* pop psychology," he fumed.

♥See ABC Directory, *Half a student, Aviva has.*

"But the main reason I'm stopping now is that it's not moral. It's as simple as that."

"Moral! You're really a candidate for moral perception. You fucked Plaskow when he was married. You fucked a married accountant when you and he were married. You fucked half the Philadelphia Orchestra including two bass clarinets and a bassoon and all the custodians at PAMA and you talk to *me* about morality?"

"You bastard! I never knew . . . change that, I *always* knew you had it in you. A heart as cold as ice. I've changed. You know that. Married fourteen years and I didn't even look at another man, even though, God knows, I had reason to. I knew I shouldn't have told you all about me. What I did, I did. I regret it. And now I'm going to set a new path for myself . . ."

Straight to hell, he thought.

". . . I'm going to get my act together. Set things straight. Put myself on track."

"Create new clichés."

You'll never get your act together, he thought. And the only tracks you'll put yourself on Anna Karenina already lay on, or, in your case, laid on.

"How come you don't make up with your hubby and go help him with his Yellow-bellied Arab Cab Company?" he asked.

"Yeh, I'm running." She laughed. "And it's called Speedy Taxi and Limo Service . . ."

Then, as she usually did, she suddenly switched subjects.

"I don't like myself," Aviva said. "I'm so fat now. I used to have a thin waist, remember? Now I can't button my slacks. My buttons are always fighting my buttonholes. Like you and me. What are you doing?"

"Separating the combatants. Enforcing a truce. Making peace. The UN has ordered that for a while the buttonholes and the buttons will live apart. A kind of cooling off period."

"But if you cool off too much you're dead," Aviva quipped.

"If that happens, I'll make you alive. I'll resurrect you."

"From the inside out?" And she laughed that teasing laugh.

"I could rape you right now," he said and began to paw her suddenly, touching her everywhere quickly. She screamed, yelped in delight.

"Rape! Help! . . . Police! . . . Help me! . . . Help me get my pants off!"

She kissed his nose quickly and said, "God, are you fun . . . Tell me I'm smart and pretty and that you love me . . . Tell me . . . tell me." And she hugged him.

"You're smart and pretty and lovable . . ." He pinched his nostrils with his thumb and index finger. "No, no, it's not for the garlic on your breath. It's for fibbing . . . Why you doing this to me? Now God is going to make my nose longer."

"I don't care, Pinocchio. Main thing you said it. And I love you too and I want all of you to be mine."

"Should I split myself in two?"

"Half is not enough for me," she said.

"I heard of a new machine, it's really very sophisticated, in Chicago. A cloning machine."

"Really?"

"Yes. But it's expensive. Twenty-six thousand dollars up front."

"You're pulling my leg."

"I'm not. I read about it in *Science* a couple of weeks ago. You pay half before the procedure and half afterwards, but . . ."

"But what?"

"There's a risk factor. They may kill you while they clone you."

She slapped her forehead, rolled her eyes. "God, I'm so naïve . . ."

So much for her promise not to come back. As soon as she walked through the door the next morning, she said:

"What now?"

"Upstairs?"

"So early?"

He curled his index finger at her.

"Upstairs? I thought we were going to talk," she said.

"I don't talk at eight-thirty in the morning."

"And I don't screw at eight-thirty."

"Look at your watch," he said.

"You're right. Eight-thirty-two," she said. "Let's go."♥

In bed she said, "Massage my foot."♥♥

Then he took a northerly route on her body and stopped for a picnic.♥♥♥

But afterwards she fell into a depression again and declared that that was it. Today's the last time. Her final word on the matter. She was gaining weight. Her hearing was going. What next? he thought. A hearing aid and then dentures. She was falling apart, his Miss Humpty Dumpty, whom he couldn't hump and wouldn't dump. Then he reminded her how much they loved each other, how he'd be with her in the future, how much he always missed her. Love is an endless ladder, he assured her. Always room for another rung.

"Words. Words. Words. You're great with words. But, boy, are you poor on substance and deeds. Your words change nothing."

♥See ABC Directory, *Sex all day long, thinking of.*

♥♥See ABC Directory, *Foot massage.*

♥♥♥See ABC Directory, *Boobs.*

"Of course they don't. For nothing changes. 'The world,' Goethe once said to his friend, Eckermann, the one, as you probably know, who wrote *Conversation with Goethe,* 'The world,' Goethe said, 'remains always the same. Situations are repeated. People live, love, and feel like other people. So why should anything change?' "

"I'm not coming back."

"For how long?"

"Forever."

"Try ten days," he said. "And then you'll be back. Loving me."

"But that doesn't change a thing. I'm still miserable." And then, with a sad smile, "I bet you enjoy having two girl friends."

For a moment, he felt a tweak at his heart, a sudden rush of trouble brewing, until he realized Aviva meant Tammy. She didn't know, of course, how on the mark she was. And he wondered how Aviva and Teresa would act if they ever met. He smiled and changed the subject. With Aviva it was a cinch.

He looked at her naked body.

"Isn't it amazing? You're about to go into your seventh decade and still going at it like a bunny."

She thought for a moment.

"It *is* unusual at our age. If you took a poll you'd see how little people over forty screw."

"I think little people over forty screw as much as little people under forty. What have you got against little people screwing? You'd be surprised at how much screwing there is. No matter how short or tall they are. I went to buy a new fridge the other day and the salesman, a big paunchy Italian guy in his mid-sixties with a gravelly voice told me that he and his wife— I don't know how the hell it came up in conversation—make love three times a week. And he was bragging! Three times a week, I thinks to meself. The guy has cockatitis. Only three times a week? I tell him. Well, how many times a week do you do it, wise guy? this Mafia hit man barks. So I say: Three times a day. And she doesn't walk around bow-legged? the salesman asks. So I say, What do you mean, she? To which he says, Well for Chrissakes, who are you screwing? So I say: My fridge. That's why I need a new one. I fucked my freezer to death."

She ratattated her feet on the bed in laughter.

"That's all you have on the mind is sex, sex, sex . . . Can't you think of something else?"

"Yes." He thought for a moment.

"Go ahead," she said. "Say it. I can see that sparkle in your eye that comes before one of your Italian proverbs or folk sayings. So let's hear it."

"I can't. I've lost it. I can't concoct them any more," Guido said.

"What?" she shrieked merrily. "What do you mean concoct?"

"That's just what I mean. I used to make those Italian sayings up on the spot."

"I don't believe it."

"It's so . . . I promise . . . My all-time favorite is . . . it's so crisp . . . only four words, but packs lots of wisdom . . . Big heart, big belly, remember?"

Aviva nodded. "And how about your grandmother's sayings?"

"Well maybe one or two were hers. But most are mine. I thought of what she *might* say were she here to say it."

"You mean all those, Like they say in Calabria, Like the Romans say, Like they say in Venice, are yours?"

"Yes. Every single one. I swear. Well, maybe except one: Even paving stones have eyes and ears. That I borrowed from the Talmud."

"Then you're a folk genius. I mean, they all sounded so real. So apropos."

"I know. I'm a veritable anthology of instant folklore."

She cocked her head at him. "You're amazing . . . Are you sure?"

"If I'm lying," Guido said, "like the folks in Siena say, If I'm lying may claws sprout from your fingernails and fangs from your mouth."

She looked down at once at her fingers. "I guess you're not lying . . . And you just made that one up too."

"Yeh. The spirit of invention just floated back over me. As they say in Venice, Medicine is the gondola but a woman's voice is the oars . . . I once had a girlfriend who used to yell, Stop, stop, it's too big, it's too big."

"You stop!" Aviva clapped her hands over her ears. "I don't want to hear it."

But he wanted her to hear it. "It's not sex. It's the appurtenances." What he didn't tell her was that it was Teresa who would go into orgasmic convulsions, speak in other tongues in ecstasy. She created a grammar, a vocabulary, a musical scale of her own, during her sexual flights of joy and trembling. The girl who fulfilled Aviva's wish of becoming twenty, even thirty, years younger for him.

"See what I mean?" Aviva said. "Sex sex sex."

"Okay. Now *you* talk. But not about sex."

"Fine. No more talking about sex. And," she smiled, "no more doing it." She licked her lips. "Let's see, what can we talk about that isn't sex-related . . . ? You know, it *is* hard." And she laughed again. "I mean difficult . . . Let's see . . . I'll come . . . oops! . . . up with something . . . Um . . . When I got married the first time, my mother gave me this beautiful set of European bone china for dairy."

"And the second time she gave you the meat set," Guido continued.

"Right." Aviva laughed. "Two more marriages and I would have had a complete set for Passover too. Wanna marry me? Passover is coming."

"All right. But first kiss me," he said.

"Where?" she said. Which was her downfall, for he guided her hand under the cover.

"Do I get a second choice?" she said, laughing.

"No."

At this, Will Rogers' famous saying came to mind. It fit her perfectly. She never met a man she didn't like:♥ She never met a man she didn't like to screw. Witness how when she sat with her hands on her lap, she clasped her middle right finger with her left hand. So tightly, it disappeared into the cave of her embrace. And she didn't even realize she did it. Like Freud said, people's gestures give them away. Betrayal oozes out of every pore.

And then, without even a break for station identification, typical of her untransitioned remarks,♥♥ came one of her complaints:

"You didn't offer to help me paint when I announced I was going to paint my house," she whined. "I stood on that ladder all alone and you didn't even worry if I might fall and get killed . . . and it would be your fault."

Just then the classic Talmudic apothegm floated into his mind: One sin leads to another.

Start with adultery and end with murder.

But she wasn't far removed from potential violence herself, for he remembered the snapshot she'd once shown him, revealing her ambivalence to music, the one where she stood next to the cello, holding a knife about-to-be plunged into the omphalos of her instrument.

What he couldn't understand was her schizoid apprehension of their relationship.

One day, like today, she puts a terminus to their affair. In her black mood, she avers:

"It's dead-ended. Nothing will come of this. I can't live like this. You can't imagine what I go through every time I sneak—yes, sneak—in here. Sneak in, sneak out. Looking over my shoulder to see which neighbor is looking, if my car is being followed. My heart can't take this. One day it's going to give out and I'm going to die. I know it. I won't live out my days."

"Everyone lives out his allotted days. Not one day more, not one day less."

"So if you love me, you'll let me go."

"That much I don't love you," Guido said.

"And I don't want to share you."

Yet on another day she declares:

"Don't ever leave me. Please. Don't ever leave me. Please. Please. Please, don't ever leave me. If you leave me I will die."

♥See ABC Directory, *Will Rogers.*

♥♥See ABC Directory, *Untransitioned, off the wall, out of the blue Aviva remark, another.*

"God forbid! Again dying? Dying, the Italians say, is for others, not us."
Have you ever seen such a no-win, no-win situation?
She stays with him, she dies. He leaves her, ditto.
How come love and death, he wondered, were such bosom pals?

BOOK FIVE

Charlie

1

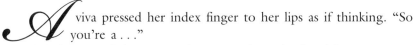 viva pressed her index finger to her lips as if thinking. "So you're a . . ."

"Uh-huh," I said, humming the assent through closed lips.

She nodded. I saw the idea bubbling.

"I don't know quite how to put this without sounding impudent, but would it . . ."

"Are you thinking perhaps." I slyly suggested, "of exchanging lessons for consultation? In fact, I've dealt with musicians before . . ."

"Do you have any friends on Long Island?" she said.

I feel as if I'm in a fairy tale and must answer the riddle right or else I'll fail the test and be turned into a frog.

"What's the right answer to this one?"

She gave a little smile but didn't reply.

"No. None. No friends here at all. Is that the right answer?"

"Yes. You say you had musicians as clients?"

"Patients . . ."

"Of course. I meant patients."

"Yes. I did. Do you have any music-related difficulties?"

She nodded slowly.

"You can't read music, you have no talent, you hate the cello. Otherwise, everything is fine."

"Right." And she laughed again. "Not bad. You got two out of three."

"Do you ever come to the city?"

"Once a week. To see my old cello coach, Marie LeClerq. Do you know her? She recently retired from the Mannes School of Music."

"You don't lug your instrument up there, do you?" I said, babbling just to extend the conversation, to look at her a little longer.

"No no no. She has an extra cello . . . All teachers do . . ."

"And prize-winners still take lessons?"

"Of course. Even great cellists like Rostropovitch still take lessons . . . Do you mean that about the exchange? Would you really be willing to exchange lessons for sessions?"

"Do you charge $75 an hour?" I asked.

"Is that your rate?"

"Yup."

"Strangely enough," Aviva laughing, "that's precisely *my* rate . . ." Then she lowered her head. Her face reddened. "Actually, it's about $40 an hour. But I could give your son an hour lesson for a half hour of your time."

"I told you I don't have a son."

"In that case, I charge only $13.95 an hour." And she gave her perky little giggle with its forward head motion. At such times, I noticed, the little squint in her eyes was more pronounced, as if the laughter freed the movement of one eye.

"Don't worry," I said. "It'll be an even exchange . . . I won't charge you a dime. When do you see your cello coach?"

"Wednesday mornings."

"Perfect. Can you come at 11?"

"Yes . . . Are you sure?"

"Sure I'm sure." I gave her my card.

"And whatever I say will be held in confidence?"

I gave her a hurt look, a reproving glance.

"I'm sorry," she said. "I just want to be sure."

I promised her she could be absolutely confident, and I congratulated her on her prize.

"It's not the Tchaikovsky," she said.

"Are you knocking your achievement?"

"I'm just being realistic. I know very well it's a small, regional prize. No one is going to break my doors down to invite me to concertize."

"How do you know?"

"Because I know a couple of the previous winners and nothing happened with them . . ."

"But it's better than not winning, Can you imagine if you'd come in fourth?"

"True."

"And there's always the chance that something good *may* come of it."

"That's true too. But anyway, no more concertizing. I'm concentrating on teaching."

I looked at my watch.

"That'll be thirty-seven fifty, please."

Again she laughed.

"Do you think that talking, words, can really help? I mean, it's just sounds in the air that dissipate."

"Isn't that a definition of music . . . And that's quite real too. And words express the psyche and the psyche is as real as the body. It's a world of its own, Jung writes, and it's governed by laws and endowed with its own expression."

She nodded in a slow, absorbed way.

We made an appointment for her to come the following week. On the way home later that evening I realized that I still didn't know her real family name. I would try to help her, I decided, but I would not consider her a patient. Because I already had my eye on her. For if she were officially a patient, I would be in violation of my professional ethics.

2

"Who are these?" Aviva asked the first time she entered my New York office. Instead of sitting down shyly as most patients do, she expressed her shyness by deflecting from herself and focusing on the pictures on my desk. But there was one she'd never see, the one I had removed before she came. Guido's beautiful portrait of Casals at JFK awaiting the arrival of his star pupil, Ian Plaskow, was one picture I couldn't keep on the wall for her to see. It was Guido's only copy of a photo autographed by the old man and he had given it to me in one of those bursts of spontaneous generosity I'd noticed in him years ago, a generosity that was one of the spokes on the axle of his self-centeredness and occasional callousness.

Aviva smiled warmly at the photos. A smile I'd get to know better as the weeks went by. A sharing smile—her *naches* smile—as if she were participating in the joy I had with the people in the picture. In one my little niece was holding a white cat.

"How cute!" Aviva purred, her voice melting with love. "I once had a cat just like that. His name was Fluffy . . . And this must be your parents." She held up the photo, looked at my father, inspected my face. "You look just like your dad. It is your dad, right?"

"Yup, they're down in Fort Lauderdale."

"Who isn't?" she said. "And who are these?" She pointed to a third picture.

"My sister and her kids. The youngest is sitting on my shoulder."

"You must love children."

I nodded, fairly sang out, "Can't deny it."

Her mouth opened, her head moved forward. She was about to ask a question, decided not to. But I would have answered, Yes, I'd love to have my own some day.

Aviva gave a pleasant little chuckle; she looked unsure of her next move. "Where shall I sit?"

"Here, on the sofa."

"And you're going to sit professionally behind your desk."

"Would you prefer that I amateurishly sat somewhere else?"

"Yes. Actually, yes, because I don't want it to be like counseling. I don't want to feel like a patient. I don't want to be called a patient."

"Precisely the way I feel," I said. "Right on the button!"

I sat at the other end of the leather sofa and faced her. I wondered why she didn't want to be called a patient. Did she fear the term? Or was it pride, since she wasn't paying for the sessions?

"Pretend it's like someone who wants to discuss music theory with you instead of taking a cello lesson. You know what?" I said. "Just call it talking. Most everyone wants to talk. Who doesn't want to talk? Just flick the dial on any radio at any time of the day. Talk talk talk. Yackety-yack. Talking about oneself is the hallmark of the twentieth century."

"Look who's talking?" And Aviva—how beautifully the name that meant "spring" fit her—laughed, pleased with her joke.

"And it's my business to listen. So keep talking." And then I laughed too. "Maybe you can start by telling me something about yourself. Where you were born, your childhood. Along those lines. Nothing formal. Just relaxed."

"Will you take notes?"

I shook my head. Folded my arms on my chest and waited for her to begin. Then remembered: if she read the pop psyche columns this could be interpreted as a hostile gesture. So instead I crossed my legs and clasped my knees. Leaned forward to her.

She began by saying:

"I was born to a musical family. My father was a younger colleague of Bronislaw Huberman, the great violinist. Both left Nazi Germany in 1934 and went to Palestine, where Huberman and my father, in 1936, organized a group of musicians into an orchestra, which eventually became the Israel Philharmonic. My father met my mother in Tel Aviv; she had fled Poland and they married there. Then, for reasons of health, many years later he came to the U.S. Maybe you heard of the cellist Gideon Andermann?"

"Yes. Indeed. So Prinsky is your married name?"

"Not quite. It's Ramati . . . I took my mother's maiden name when I went to the conservatories because I wanted to make it on my own."

"Is your husband a musician?" I asked innocently.

Aviva grimaced. "No, he's not a musician. He doesn't even like music, but that's another matter, for another time, right? He's an Israeli from North Africa named Rahamim Ramati."

She stopped. The faint smile on her lips added to the aura of gloom in the now absolute silence of the room. I could sense that she didn't know how to proceed. Just like Guido. Some people become hyper, talk all over the place to avoid essentials. But others just clam shut.

We looked at each other.

"What should I say now?"

"Something interesting."

"Am I boring you?"

I knew I'd said the wrong thing. "Not at all. I'm fascinated."

"Okay, maybe it's not interesting but unusual . . . I'm not superstitious, but the number 7 has played a role in my life. I was seven when my father started me on the cello. I studied at Hunter and the Mannes School of Music as an undergraduate and then went to the Philadelphia Academy of Musical Arts, or PAMA as it's better known, which totaled seven years, and I've been married fourteen years . . ."

"Sometimes people react even subliminally to numbers . . . Do you want to explore this further?"

"Not really." She stopped again.

"Something about your home life? Parents?"

"Okay, my mother was very nice but overprotective.♥ I felt choked at home. Although my mother didn't play an instrument, she loved music. But my father *lived* it. And so he let my mother assume most of the responsibility for raising the two girls. She spoke a lot; he was rather silent. In any case, their marriage wasn't very good. Maybe that's what happens when a German Jew marries a Polish Jew. So I myself didn't look forward to getting married. Others got married after college. Me, I went to PAMA."

"Who'd you study with?"

"Ian Plaskow,♥♥ a star pupil of Casals."

"Oh, sure. Tchaikowsky Prize."

Aviva nodded. Her eyes brightened as if in approbation of my knowledge. "And then I studied in Florence, was supposed to stay a year but I got homesick, so I returned after six months." She grimaced. "But as soon as I came home I went out to California for a month."

"But why, if you missed your parents and that's why you came home from Italy?"

"To find a job. You know how it is. You miss them in your mind and heart because in your homesickness you see perfection, and then when you get home you see reality."

"The Christmas dinner syndrome," I said. "People fall all over themselves to travel hundreds of miles to get home for Christmas and then by dinnertime they can't wait to leave."

"Exactly," Aviva laughed. "You shoulda been a psychologist."

So far she hadn't told me anything about Guido, but I wasn't going to push it. I knew that she would soon get to the subject she was dying to discuss and I was dying to listen to. In the meantime she made small talk, chit chat, trying to relax, for the next twenty or so minutes. Then she looked at her watch. "I got to go . . . Thanks so much . . . Next Wednesday?"

♥See ABC Directory, *Angry, getting.*
♥♥See ABC Directory, *Phone booth and Ian.*

"Fine with me." I escorted her to the door. Resisted shaking her hand, but I did tap, clasp for a moment, her shoulder.

3

I felt I was reliving Guido's lessons with Aviva. I couldn't wait for Wednesdays. Tuesdays were a high. Tomorrow Aviva is coming. Aviva is coming. Like in a film, I felt my image splitting and fusing. I was both Aviva and Guido, anticipating these weekly one-hour visits, which often became ninety-minute sessions. Not only because I enjoyed being with her, but also because she had such fascinating stories.

Like this one:

"As a child I had an orange dress with a Peter Pan collar. I loved that dress but stopped wearing it because my classmates—I had just transferred to the 10th grade—made fun of me. You see, my mother had embroidered a large fancy *A* on it, and I didn't know why the girls laughed at me."

"I know."

"I know you know," Aviva laughed. "They'd read *The Scarlet Letter* the term before. And, of course, I hadn't and so I was totally out of it."

I looked at her clothes. Now she was wearing chic gray slacks, a wide leather belt that accented her thin waist and a tight-fitting cranberry wool sweater. Her long slim fingers, beautifully manicured in a complementary pale mauve color, formed a little prayer pyramid as she spoke.

Aviva lowered her head and gave a shy little smile. "But the *A* wasn't for Aviva."

"Your mother's name also begins with *A?*"

"You're very perceptive. It's Abigail. Isn't it absurd? To give me a dress with her initial? At least that's what she told me. Doesn't it say something about motherly possessiveness?"

"Curiouser and curiouser. Very Byzantine," and I nodded slowly, sagely, as if by my assent her ideas had become mine and only by my agreeing was the true nature of her perceptiveness made manifest. "That may explain it. Maybe your mother felt that with her initial on your dress she could keep watch over you in some totemic, magical way."

"I never thought of that. Boy, are you good! She sure wanted to keep watch over me is right." Aviva laughed.

"Did the girls call you names?"

"No. But they laughed at me behind my back. I had no friends. I was so shy. All my life I was shy. I couldn't understand how my father played the cello *in public*. My God, what if he played a *wrong note?* Wouldn't he sink into the ground in shame? I was so painfully shy no one approached me in high school, even though I was so pretty. Pretty but aloof."

"You wore aloofness like a carapace?"

"Exactly," she said. Then a pause. "What's a carapace?"

"A kind of armor. Like a hard shell."

"Right . . . And if someone said something nasty to me, I didn't respond. My reaction was—they may be right."

I nodded slowly. "What happened to the *A*?"

"Finally, one girl told me and in a rage I tore the *A* off that orange dress at home and hid it in my closet. And even afterwards it still burned my heart like a tattoo. And my mother's maiden name didn't help much right?"

"Oh, my God!" I laughed. "Prinsky. Too much!"

"What more do you need? Aviva Esther Prinsky, heroine of Nate Hawthornsky's Jewish novel. Aviva's luck, right? I still have that dress some-where. Maybe I should resuscitate it."

"Strange you hadn't heard of *The Scarlet Letter*."

"And even if I did, do you think I knew what the *A* stood for? I was fourteen and out of it. There's that seven-year cycle again. Wait. In a minute I'll tell you an even better one. I was fourteen and had just gotten my period and hadn't the faintest notion about sex. Well, I had some idea, but it was hazy, less than knowledge. Again a seven cycle."

"You found out at twenty-one?" I joked.

"No. Seven . . . but, of course, I didn't have the foggiest notion what it was all about. We had a Polish maid at home for a while, a simple girl, big, lusty-looking, not too articulate. She'd just come over. She once told me, as I watched her ironing, that the man has a big you-know and he tries to shove it in you. Imagine telling that to a seven-year-old! I looked around at my body and wondered where he would shove it.

" 'Does it hurt?' I asked.

" 'Only the first time,' she said, 'and then it feels good.'

" 'Where's your wound?' I said. 'I was seven and I came from Mis-souri,' " Aviva giggled. " 'Show me,' was my motto.

" 'You're too young,' she said.

"I used to keep asking her to show me her wound, and she would tease me, 'Next time . . .' Then finally she said, 'I won't tell you, you'll find out later.'

"My mother saw I was hanging around the kitchen with the maid too much and so she asked me, 'How come you're always in the kitchen?' 'I like to watch her ironing, and she tells me things,' I added like a moron. My mother always did tell me to sew my lips but that craft I never did learn. She asked me. 'What things?' So I told her." Aviva laughed. "Not too bright, right? After that my mother wouldn't let me go into the kitchen any more."

"And you didn't wonder what the big you-know was?" I asked.

"I thought it was something he buys in a store."

"Nowadays, it is something women buy in a store . . . And weren't you curious? Didn't you ask the maid more questions?"

"I asked her, 'Why did you let him do this to you?'

" 'Because,' said the Polish maid, 'he bought me a scarf.'

"She must have wanted that scarf very badly, I thought to myself. And later, when I had my first boyfriend, I never got a scarf." Aviva laughed and I joined her. But I realized my laugh was hollow; there was a little hurt shaped like the hole of a bagel in that laugh.

"I can just imagine," I said, "let's say something out of a film or a novel—all life sort of works that way—that later in life a young man presents you with a scarf. Can you imagine what thoughts go through your mind?"

"Yes. Something big is on its way . . . Oooops! Shouldn't have said that." She clasped her hand to her mouth, but not before she'd laughed a naughty laugh.

"Doesn't much go with your shyness."

"I think I've gotten over much of that years ago." She gave me such an engaging smile that it took all my strength not to rush out and buy her a scarf. What kind of magic, what kind of seductive magic did that woman have? Just by talking and laughing at herself she was chipping at the professional restraint and aplomb I'd cultivated over the years—a restraint I now realized was snow thin. The merest hint of a warm smile could melt that barrier. And I'd just read a study on how many psychologists get involved with their patients.

"And all through your youth you thought that was sex. When did you really find out? From your mother?"

"Are you kidding? My mother?! She didn't even tell me about the period. My mother! Once a guy brought me home after a date. And you have to remember I didn't go out much. My mother asked me if I kissed him. I said Yes. 'Feh' she grimaced. 'I couldn't kiss a guy with lizard lips.' That's my mother." And Aviva gave a self-deprecating laugh. "She would have protected me till I was fifty."

"So when did you find out?"

She smiled and lowered her head. For all her protestations that she'd lost her shyness years ago, these little gestures indicated that her shyness was very much in place.

"I really didn't find out, but I got one step closer when I was fourteen and the girl who told me was eleven and she really lorded it over me on this one. She said babies are made like this: The man rocks the woman to sleep in bed. That's why the bed creaks. He says to her, Shh, Shhh, till she falls asleep. Once she's asleep, he hugs her and they have a baby."

"The classic contraception," I said. "If the Chinese used this method there would be no more Chinese laundries . . . What other magic sevens in your life?"

"Well." Aviva looked away from me. "I was also fourteen when I began to play with myself, but I still really knew nothing about sex. I might just as well have been scratching an itch. I was sixteen when I learned how babies are really made. Imagine! Sixteen! And I'd been having my period for about two years. Today at sixteen girls have four-year-olds. And all the girls made fun of my innocence."

"What did your friend tell you that made you rip the *A* off your dress?"

"Only that it was bad and a sign of shame. That much I understood. But why did my mother foist that dress on me in the first place? It was so thoughtless of her. She's never read Hawthorne. Too Old World. Sometimes kindness and love can be killing, right? In retrospect, I know my parents were good, but my mother's love overwhelmed me, almost suffocated me. And my father was just the opposite. Always practicing or concertizing or teaching. Withdrawn. Now you know why I didn't marry a musician. He hardly spoke to me, but once he did tell me a story I'll never forget. Because he opened up his past and because it's connected with something sweet." Aviva smiled. "My weakness. I love sweets. He told me his grandfather was too poor to buy sugar. They drank tea without sugar. But the grandfather hung a tablet of sugar on a string from the ceiling. And as they drank they looked at it."

"Wow." I said. "That sounds like something you read in a fairy tale . . . Did your father show his affection for you?"

"I can't recall that my father ever embraced or kissed me. He was quite Germanic that way. And to make up for it my mother's love was rich and heavy, like a feather quilt. Smothering, all-encompassing. She would have chewed my food for me if she could."

"There's a scene like that in a Russian novel. In Sholokhov's *And Quiet Flows the Don*."

"I don't know the book. I'm more familiar with Italian writers like Levi, Bassani."

"Anyway, in it there's an old retainer of a rich peasant in a Cossack village. He chews the food for the rich old codger who can't chew any more."

"Maybe my mother read the book." Then she giggled. "Maybe she wrote it."

I wondered when she would begin to talk about Guido. I couldn't rush it. After all, I knew nothing about the affair. But if I guided her into talking about her marriage, Guido would soon come up.

"You mentioned that your father hardly ever embraced or kissed you. Is it fair then to assume that your marriage to your husband was a search for affection?"

"Aren't all marriages? Don't you think?"

"Of course."

"Are you married?"

"Don't rub it in. I don't have to be married to have some insight on this issue."

"Sorry. I didn't mean it negatively . . . I met him at a party in my cousin's house in Tel Aviv when I went back for a visit. He wasn't a musician, so that was a plus in his favor. And he seemed so nice.♥ He came from Morocco, but that didn't bother me. It gave a touch of exotica to the relationship. He was head over heels in love with me. And he *was* affectionate, even though I assumed he was running after me for my American citizenship. I figured it would be nice marrying a man who came from the country I was born in."

"The fact that he came from a different culture didn't bother you? He wasn't educated, was he?"

"It didn't bother me. No, he wasn't educated, but bright. But we hit it off."

"Did he like music?"

"At first. He went to all the concerts with me. Seemed to love it. That too turned around after our marriage. It proved to be all show. All Mideast courtesy and grace and charm, and they can really turn it on. All of that vanished like mist. I should have seen the warning signals; they were all there. But I closed my eyes to them, made believe they weren't there. Yes, we squabbled a bit, but who doesn't? I mean, he didn't ride the donkey and have me walk in the back with the firewood on my head in typical Arab fashion, and he didn't pull out the narjillah pipe the next morning—but he did switch. Like electricity. Like current turned off. Moody. Even a bit of *arak* brandy in the house. Not enough to get drunk on. But no compunctions about lifting a hand. And accusing me of promiscuity for absolutely no reason in front of the children. And later, regrets and promises."

"For which you fell."

"Now *you're* rubbing it in, right?"

"That's your interpretation," I said. "You made up. There's a certain sweetness in making up after a fight. And then to bed."

"You turn the screw, don't you? All you men are alike."

"Again your interpretation. It's well known that there's no greater joy in sex than after a fight and reconciliation."

"You're right. It was good, but how long can you keep this up before you realize that these reconciliations are all bluff? When we came to the U.S. he got a job with old friends in the taxi business. Half the taxi drivers in New York are Israelis and three-quarters of them are North Africans. A couple of years later we bought one taxi and then, in time, a few more until he had a full-fledged business."

"We? He had money?"

"No. I did. Saved up from teaching and from my parents. But that's also another story . . . And only after a long while did this thickheaded fool who

♥See ABC Directory, *Arab, loving it with the.*

sits before you realize that all these reconciliations were for one purpose only: to get me to go to bed with him . . . Basically, I think he and all these other North Africans don't really like women. Except for one purpose.

"And my mother, whom I've accused of being overloving, to her credit she saw right through him. In the third year of our marriage, my mother fell ill. In the hospital she said to me, 'Cut away from him. As quickly as you can. Or he'll kill you.' Sick as she was she saw into his personality, which had surfaced a year earlier when our first child was born. The Arab— that's my nickname for him—didn't even want to hold her. He made a scene in the hospital because there was some difficulty in the bank. He'd forgotten to sign a withdrawal card, and he accused me and the bank of conspiring against him. Paranoid, right?"

"Right," I assented too quickly.

"You want more proof? In Israel, we went to Eilat a few days before we were married. Or maybe it was our honeymoon, believe me, I don't re-member. Isn't it strange? If things go well, doesn't a normal person remem-ber a honeymoon? But what I do remember is that we were walking . . . Wait a minute, it couldn't have been the honeymoon because we got married here . . . Anyway, we were walking along the beach and I was dying for a soda. A kid was selling cold soda and you know that the heat there is overwhelming. It can go to 120 degrees. But no, he didn't want to spend the money. So he made me walk to the public drinking fountain where the water was warm and a bit salty. Early next morning we walked from the hotel area into town. He said we'll see the part of Eilat that tourists don't see. It was nice . . . well, drudgy buildings. No character. No charm. The full heat of the day wasn't upon us yet. But on the way back, it must have been nine o'clock, I was already exhausted from the hellish heat and sug-gested we take a bus back to our hotel. But no! It cost about a dollar for the two of us, so he made me walk in the heat until I nearly collapsed. I should have seen the signals, but I closed my eyes to them.

"He was so full of charm before I married him. You don't know how he can turn on the charm. Those Moroccans with their black eyes and curly hair and self-confident macho look. He charmed my mother—at first—and he charmed me. But the day after we were married, *the day after*, I sensed an aloofness in him. It's as if once he had me, he hated me . . ."

"Do you know the biblical story of Amnon and Tamar?"

"No."

"That's what I've called the Amnon-Tamar syndrome in an article I published last year. It's the story of Kind David's son who lusts for his half-sister and after he has her he hates her . . . What kind of aloofness?"

"I couldn't put my finger on it, I thought it was me, with my usual lack of self-confidence, but I sensed as if something had changed. And I was right. Over the years it grew until he became at times a complete stranger.

He would go away by himself, sometimes for a weekend. Go out at night and return home late. But that's what you get when an American marries a North African. He would come home as if I weren't there. He pushed my food away, called it garbage."

"Why?"

"Because it *was* garbage. I'm an awful cook . . . I'm only joking," she laughed. "But I am a bad cook."

I shook my head. "And then, at night, back to bed together."

"Yes." Aviva nodded. "We made up. I always hoped it was a passing phase . . . At times I made love to my husband without any desire whatsoever. Just not to make waves. Just so he wouldn't stop talking to me for a week. Or in the hope things might get better . . . and . . ."

She stopped.

"And then?" I said, waiting.

She licked her lips; she looked as if she didn't want to say what she felt she should say.

"And then he turned right around and went to sleep," I continued for her.

"And then," Aviva said flatly, "he got up and went back to his room."

Bastard, I thought.

I wanted to ask her: You really love sex, don't you? but I changed it to: "Is it safe to say you like sex?"

"Sex sex sex. You're all alike. What are you, some kind of Freudian?"

"On the contrary. Freud reduces everything to instinctual elements. Like Jung, I'm concerned with the extremely complicated psychological contexts, so answer the question."

"No. I don't love sex. I love peace more. Tranquility. Stability. A bit of . . ." Her eyes misted. "Happiness . . . The Arab doesn't like women. I mean, he uses them to satisfy his needs. But he really doesn't consider them human beings . . . And the children—I have two, a boy and a girl—they're in his way. Creatures on which he can vent his perpetual anger . . . No matter how well they did in school he always knocked it. If they brought a B+ it was no good. If they brought an A, he recalled the previous B+. 'See? You can do it. So why you get such a rotten mark last time? When I go to school all I got is A's.' And I would tell him, in front of the children, 'In your Moroccan school they didn't even teach you how to read. All they taught you was how to count.' He got my point . . . And years later, when his mother visited, he would call me *Honey* in her presence. That was a code word. First of all, he used it only when his mama was there. Secondly, I knew it was an overture to something nasty. Honey, he said, as his mother stood there, is this the dress you said Mama looks so awful in?"

"So how come you married a man like that?"

"I was bamboozled. Bowled over. So charming. Later, I realized it was a façade. The Don Juan's politesse. My parents wanted me to marry a musician. So we could literally make music together. But I rebelled. Musicians seemed so limited. Not the generation of my father and his colleagues who were widely cultured in the old European sense. But the current one that knows only music and nothing else. But just because they wanted it, I didn't. Once, after I had graduated from Hunter and was in PAMA, I started going out with a very good-looking guy. But it turned out he liked men. Didn't consider me a woman. It was awful. And another one, though he liked me and I liked him, he couldn't . . . you know what I mean, buy me a scarf. My God, I thought, there must be something wrong with me. But that's the way I always think. That it's always my fault. So when I went back to visit Israel and met this nice-looking, dark-haired charmer, like the immature teenager that I was—I was a teenager for years because I really didn't have a normal teens—this desert chieftain bowled me over. I had on a romantic veil and I tripped on it."

"It wasn't a veil," I said. "It was a scarf. You brought your own scarf."

"Yes . . . yes . . . yes . . ." she said. "You're perceptive . . . you're good . . . but I already told you that."

She stopped. But I was fascinated. I could postpone Guido for a while and listen to how this beautiful woman could be hoodwinked. And it also made me wonder how come a good-looking woman could have such miserable luck.

"Go on."

"I don't want to go into it now. I'm ashamed to talk about it. Maybe some other time. I'll just say this. Do you know what my husband said when on a couple of occasions we would visit other couples and he saw a nice, sweet, considerate husband? That's the sort of man you should have married, he said. But I must give him credit for one thing. He sharpened my tongue. My wit. I became more verbal in response to his sarcasm."

She looked at her watch. "Got to go."

"Next time?" I asked.

Aviva nodded.

4

I watched Aviva as she spoke. She began tentatively, as people usually do when speaking with strangers. Her words vibrated with an edgy discomfort like someone playing cello for the first time. And no wonder. After all, I was still a stranger. I watched her lips, her eyes. Their color seemed to change with the intensity of her remarks. I always saw her during daylight. The sun on her face, which she occasionally backed away from, highlighted her little squint. And made her turn a tiny notch to the left or to the right when she looked at me. No wonder she wore her hair long. A great camouflage. It well deflected that tiny flaw in her good looks.

She took a deep breath. "I teach, as you know, and I have a number of adult students, but one of them," Aviva gave her little laugh, "was like no one else I ever had. And Guido came accidentally to me, bringing an ex-neighbor's daughter." She covered her lips. "Ooops, I said his name, I wanted to call him George . . . but you said you don't know anyone on the Island . . ." And she made little sewing motions around her lips. "I'm sewing 'em up, like my mother used to suggest when you talk too much."

I had given a little start which I hoped she didn't notice. It was the first time I'd heard her mention Guido's name. Now the triangle was complete. The story real. From faintly dotted lines to black magic marker. Aviva, Guido, and me.

"And that's how it began. He wanted cello lessons and I agreed. But it turned out to be less cello and more viola d'amore, if you know what I mean."

"Okay," I said. "But what's the 'it' that began? And how did it really begin? I mean, really."

"Well, I'd been giving him lessons for six or seven weeks—there's that number again," she suddenly gave a bright little laugh, "and from week to week—oh, I forgot to tell you he'd played cello as a youngster and was actually relearning—anyway, I found myself drawn more and more to him. I knew he was married, and, of course, that bothered me, but I assumed he was looking. You know, trouble at home, relationship on the downskids. But with him something happened that had never happened to me before. I was out of my mind with desire and longing. I became the teenager that I'd never been. I couldn't eat, I couldn't sleep, I lost weight. I literally couldn't breathe. I mean . . ." and she accented each word, ". . . I . . . could . . . not . . . breathe. When he left after the lesson it took me a long time to compose myself. I felt a vise around my chest. At night I fantasized. But the son of a gun didn't make a move. I assumed he knew I was married." She smiled, remembering. "When he first came he asked me if I could teach him cello faces. That was so charming, so funny, so Guido. I could have fallen in love with him for that alone. What do you mean, cello faces? I asked. He said. 'Teach me those faces, those gestures that cellists make when they play. How to whisper to the neck, how to put my lips to it. When to shake my head in passionate no-no-no motions, when how to close my eyes in ecstasy, when how to make intense faces as if I'm in pain, when how to sniff as if my breath were imploding'—I tell you I felt a poetry in those absurd words, even though he was half-facetious, but lots of it was true, very observant . . . One day, about seven weeks after we began lessons, he approached me as I was taking my cello♥ out of the case. He put both his hands on my shoulders, looked down at me, he's about six feet tall. I

♥See ABC Directory, *Cello*.

felt his touch for the first time, except maybe when he came the first time and shook my hand in that typically European fashion. He was born in Italy, you know . . . Why am I telling you all this? I should really learn to shut up . . . But that's an oxymoron for a woman, right? Anyway, although now that I think of it, that really wasn't the first time he touched me either. A week or so earlier, he had given me one of his photographs. And he loves old photographs of me.♥ He's a photographer, you see—oops, there I go blabbing again—freelance, but he's connected with one of the major newsweeklies, I mean, you know the European ones, one of the ones that comes out in Rome or Milan, I forget which. He also gave me that great photo he'd taken of Casals embracing Ian Plaskow on his triumphant return from Moscow . . . uh-oh . . . I shouldn't have told you that either. Me and my big mouth. Now you can find out who he is . . ."

"I haven't got the faintest interest, and I'm not about to hunt out old photos to discover the name of . . . Look, in this business hundreds of people speak of hundreds of others. I'd need two-and-a-half lifetimes to go discover identities. So, please relax . . ."

"Okay . . . but you see . . ." and she made sewing motions around her mouth. ". . . that's what happens when you blab . . . it's awful . . . He'd be furious . . . He'd kill me if he found out . . . Anyway, he gave me this beautiful photo. I thanked him and said it's a prize-winning picture. And spontaneously he hugged me and kissed my cheek. A sisterly kiss. And now come to think of it, I remember *another* time we touched. Boy, this type of talking is amazing. One memory triggers another. During one of the lessons, Guido was playing, elbow out, and I reached out and pushed it down, to show him how he should relax. I sensed a slight resistance, a stiffening, as if he resented the touch, which was another reason I was afraid to make a move. If only he'd welcomed that touch of mine, perhaps indeed I would have thrown my arms around him and kissed him during one of those moments of frustration that were a physical pain for me. It made me tremble when I closed the door behind him at the end of the lesson . . . I'm not making much sense, am I? I'm jumping around, putting the earlier later and later earlier. And then that day when I was removing my instrument from the case he comes up to me and puts both his hands on my shoulders and looks down at me and asked if I want to go on a nature walk with him.

"It was the walk that did it . . . That clinched it. I won't mince words. I'll be open with you. I'd been dreaming of Guido for weeks. Taking him into bed with me every night. If a woman could have wet dreams, I'd have flooded the house. But aside from being very friendly, I said and did nothing. That's my nature. I *never* make a move. When he rang the bell a zing went through me, an erotic charge, as if I'd been touched in the right

♥See ABC Directory, *Younger image of me, you're obsessed with a.*

places. He's here. At the door. Those mornings when he came I woke up early. Excited. I chose carefully what to wear to make myself more attractive, to give the appearance of looking as casual as possible. Contradictions, right? Planning and casualness. There's a woman for you! Another few hours and he'd be here. I practiced the cello but the notes blurred. So I go and do laundry. But I put the clothes in the dryer first. At breakfast I didn't hear a word the kids were saying. Mommy, where are you? I was totally flustered. Until he came. When he played for me and turned a page of the music and the page would buckle as it usually does, I would smooth the page down. And in smoothing the page down I made believe I was smoothing him down, stroking his skin. Or I'd put my left arm around the back of his chair as he played and imagined I was embracing him. You have to remember that during all those weeks there was no indication from either of us that anything would develop. Except that the mood, the atmosphere in the room was so highly charged that one could get electrocuted." Aviva pointed to herself. "You could have cut that flow of untouched, yet-to-be-born intimacy with a knife . . . And then, some weeks later, he asked me on that walk."

"What happened to the lessons after that?"

"Phhht. Out the window. Sort of." She laughed. "A few more sort of scattered. Back burner . . . But that waiting for him to make a move! Wow! What a time that was. Like a sonata building up, building up, but where is the coda? The coda wasn't there yet. Finally . . . Am I boring you with all this?"

"I'll let you know." I laughed. "On the contrary, I love your narration."

"It's interesting how that 'Am I boring you?' phrase just popped out of me. Guido used that word when he finished one of his lessons early on, lessons for beginners. I hope you're not bored, he said, doing these baby lessons. God! Bored! I was sizzling with desire, and he asked me if I'm bored. I loved every minute he spent with me. I didn't want to let him go. Viola d'amore. Viola d'amore. I tried to stretch each lesson out to an hour, an hour-and-a-half, until he had to go. Anyway, one day he finished a lesson, takes hold of my shoulders and says, 'Would you like to go for a walk with me?' and I say yes and my mouth is in my throat. But I couldn't do it the next day because of an audition, so we agreed on Monday. He gave me instructions. I jotted them down. But on Sunday night, *demazalado*, as he would say in Italian, bad mazel, there was a freak autumn snowstorm. It snowed all night, lightly but steadily. There goes our walk, I thought. I couldn't sleep that night. First of all, excited like a schoolgirl. I told you he excited me to the point where after each lesson I couldn't swallow, I couldn't breathe, I actually had to catch my breath when he left to calm down. I lost tons of weight during that period. I slimmed down. Even the Arab, who never ever complimented me on anything, even he said I looked twenty. I couldn't find my hands and feet, like a teenager. My hands shook. I tried to say his name. I couldn't speak. I was in a tizz. It took me hours to calm down. I was, as Guido put it, smitten. Hadn't felt like that in years. What am I saying, years? Ever! I'd never felt like that. At night I got warm, hot, excited. I took him to bed with me. But I already told you that."

"How did you manage that?" I asked facetiously.

"In my imagination, of course. But it wasn't even his looks or his body that attracted me.♥ It wasn't sex, although he was, is, sexy. But none of this excitation was visible while he was here. Oh, no, you'd never suspect a thing during the lesson. Great control, right? But as soon as he stepped out of the door, I grew faint, dizzy, confused. My heart beat as if I'd run a mile. I watched the snow. It just kept on and on but finally it let off. I dozed off, then awoke in the morning and saw to my delight a perfectly clear sky. My heart started hammering again. I knew it would be a great day. The walk was on. And that's where he kissed me for the first time. Do you know what it means to kiss a man you're in love with but aren't sure if his feelings are reciprocated? To kiss a man you're longing to kiss but don't know if you'll ever kiss him? What's the matter?"

Aviva saw something was wrong but didn't know, couldn't possibly know, what. I was perspiring. I was dizzy. I was ill. I was reliving every moment of Guido's good fortune in making it with this delightful woman. My old buddy, pal and nemesis. And she was giving me the blow-by-blow account of how much she loved him. I couldn't control myself. I dabbed at my forehead.

"It's hot in here," I said. "Shall I put on the air-conditioning?"

"Only if you want it," she said. "I'm fine."

She too, her face was aglow, reliving the moments with Guido. A distant, glazed look. Ecstatic.

"A day or so later I get the surprise of my life. In passing, I don't know how it came up, he said something about Yom Kippur, which had come several weeks earlier, that his wife hadn't gone in to work for the holidays. You see he also has a very distinctly Italian family name. So I didn't even know he was Jewish. After the Arab, I was frankly sick of Jewish men, sick of his Jewish hypocrisy and duplicity. Snooping in the garbage to see if I used milk chocolate after a meat meal, yet he's too cheap to buy kosher meat except when his mother comes and eating lobster and shrimp on a separate plate, for his health, as he puts it. He would stay away weekends and go on so-called business trips to Israel once every six weeks; who knows, maybe he had another wife over there, but when it came to the synagogue, he was first in line. They should know what a despicable sinner he is. So you could have knocked me over with a cello bow when Guido told me he was Jewish too."

"Didn't you know there were Italian Jews?"

♥See ABC Directory, *Silks and satins, a riddle among the.*

"Of course. I read Bassani, Primo Levi, Svevo, the others. But I didn't think of Italian Jews here in America."

"Where was he born?"

"Venice. An old Venetian family. And perhaps it wasn't a coincidence that Guido came from there. Both he and the city had that magic. That unusual quality. Like Venice, he is one of a kind. Just as enchanting. Venice is a wonder, built seemingly by angels and removed from the real world. And I feel that way about Guido. Only angels could have made him . . . When I studied in Florence, I took a trip to Venice with a girlfriend. The city had such a vitality, yes, even a sexiness, that in my room, all by myself, I got hotter than I'd ever been before. And when I told Guido this he said it was because, even though I didn't know him yet, I was already yearning for him in his hometown. And I believe that . . . But please understand, it's not a bed of roses, and that's why I'm here. The fact that he's married is an albatross on my back and often depresses me to the point of illness and he doesn't even feel guilty."♥

"You've relived the beauty of it."

"Yes. Yes. The beauty of it. The marvel of it."

"But reality overrides it."

Aviva nodded sadly.

5

As I listened to her I wanted to warn her away from Guido. I wanted to tell her he had no loyalty except to his cock and maybe, *maybe*, to his lenses. I wanted to protect her frail psyche from the guy who once parodied JFK's famous line by saying, Ask not what you can do for your country, ask what your count can do for you. But before I spoke I examined myself. An unexamined life is not worth living, said Cicero. Was it purely altruistic? Was there something else involved? Me, perhaps? Was it possible that I was extrapolating the Guido of twenty-plus years ago, the Guido who seemed to be in love with himself, the Guido who loved women, sex, the excitement of, aura of, suggestion of, whiff of, coquetry of women, with the Guido of today? True, Guido was involved in an extramarital affair, but I knew nothing of his married life, how it went, what problems inhered in it. And Aviva had not mentioned Guido's wife, except that his being married disturbed her. Tammy was probably a sore point with her. But I wouldn't ask. If I understood Aviva at all, I realized that as much as Guido was etched into her, even acting as an absentee guide to most of her actions, then no doubt some of her malaise stemmed from the fact that she saw

---

♥See ABC Directory, *Guilt as metaphysical/philosophical entity.*

Tammy there too, the obstacle, the barrier, that glass wall that prevented Aviva from reaching out and claiming Guido as her own.

So how could I warn her? Only in my thoughts. I was locked into a no-win situation. Ergo: Guido had won again. He'd formulated the plot of this drama so carefully. So well wrought was Guido's play that I couldn't even tell Aviva that I knew Guido, for that would ruin everything. Burst the balloon of my objectivity. The only thing I could do was make silent sarcastic comments when she spoke. Or perhaps trenchant observations. For there was a possibility that Guido's love for Aviva was sincere. Which meant that my jibes would have no efficacy at all.

For instance, Aviva saying:

"Sometimes I had the notion that he was just after sex. Maybe his wife didn't fulfill his enormous appetite, satisfy that incredible energy of his."

I didn't reply, but thought: Guido took only the best. If he didn't like, he didn't possess. I remember he once told me a woman stripped for him, but as soon as he saw the little fat fold on her waist he lost all desire. He said, Feh, or whatever the equivalent was in Italian and told her to get dressed. Which meant he wasn't just after sex. He was selective. What his relations were with his wife was an enigma. Maybe tepid, maybe torrid. Maybe he wanted to add to the sizzle. I wanted to console Aviva by telling her: if Guido has been with you so long, he really likes you. He's not after your body. But, of course, I could not say that.

Or her remark:

"Guido once told me this was the first time he was in love."

That's a lie, I thought. Guido can't love anyone. There's an eternal mirror before his eyes in which he sees only himself.

"And maybe because of this," she continued, "I overlook certain things, like his questions."

I looked at her.

"You should see the intimate questions he asks me."

"Do you answer them?"

"Yes."

"Why?"

"Because he always tells me these will be the last ones."

"But they never are."

"Again perceptive. Again and again." She smiled.

"At ninety-five dollars an hour I have to be."

"I thought it was seventy-five."

"Only when I'm out of chopped meat."

Now Aviva looked puzzled.

"My variation on an old Jewish joke. Actually, it's also a variation on your $13.95 an hour fee for lessons when I don't have a son. A lady goes into a kosher butcher shop and asks, How much is the chopped meat? $2.49 a pound. What? she shrieks. So much? Mr. Katz across the street charges only $1.99. So go there, says the butcher. But he's out of chopped meat. So the butcher replies, When I'm out of chopped meat I also charge $1.99."

Aviva laughed hard. Her laugh was so intimate it's a wonder she didn't have problems with men every day.

"So you see," I said, "super-perception makes the rates go up . . . Anyway, who says those will be his last questions."

"I do. I say to him—this is it. No more after this. Close the chapter. Finish. Ancient history. It gives me knots in my stomach."

"And . . ." I almost popped out with his nickname, Spaghetti. "And he?" I felt like a rat. Toward him. Toward her. Toward both. Even toward me.

"He just smiles."

"So why don't you just say: Cut. That's it. No more."

"Because each time we just start chatting, he subtly, without me even knowing it, gets onto that subject once again."

"For instance."

"For instance, we'll be discussing music. My background, my training at PAMA, and before you know it, those couple of boyfriends I had once are woven into the chatting."

"Is he sly?"

"No. Inquisitive. He claims he wants to understand me. To understand my motivation."

"Yesterday's motivation may not be today's. Or tomorrow's."

"That's exactly what I tell him. I tell him how I've changed. I'm not the same person I was. My God, those things happened more than . . . My God, years ago."

"May I ask you how old you are?"

"No." She laughed pleasantly.

"How old are you?"

"Are you asking professionally?" Still that smiley gleam to her eyes.

"Or what? Socially?"

She smiled. She must have worn braces as a child, for there was still a slight malocclusion on the front two teeth which were just subtly angled against each other. Her fetching smile did a good job of camouflaging the left eye floating just a touch away from center.

"I'll tell you some other time. Really. I have nothing to hide. I don't go for this European coyness about age. Although I must say, he never asked me, though he is nosy."

"Yes," I said. My God, I'll have to watch myself.

Aviva was quick. "What do you mean, yes?"

But I was quicker. "Yes, you're right. There is a coyness among Europeans regarding age. I once had a Polish patient . . . but never mind . . . This questions business is . . . it's very revealing," I said with a serious mien. I rubbed my cheek. Aviva bit.

"He had a list of questions, I guess if you put them one after the other the list would be as long as Leporello's list of Don Giovanni's conquests."

I looked blank.

"You don't know the image."

"I'm afraid not."

"From *Don Giovanni*, Mozart's opera. When Leporello, his servant, unfurls a megilla as long as the stage with the names of the women Don Giovanni had."

"I never liked opera," I said and wondered: how big would *your* list be? "I wasn't crazy about it because when I was bad as a kid, fresh or something, my parents would punish me and say, Okay, that's it, you're going to the opera with us. Don't laugh, it's so."

"I'm sure they were joking."

"Maybe. But why couldn't they punish me with ice cream?"

"You tell me, you're the psychologist . . . Anyway, I'm not that excited about opera either. How did we get into opera? Oh, yes, the list. Guido plied me with so many questions, it must have been hundreds . . . I kept a list of his questions."

"Like a diary?"

"Almost." She laughed. "He once told me to keep one."

"So strange asking you loads of questions."

"Loads. Lots and lots."

I tried to look as disinterested as possible. "For example?" And I nodded sagely, as if my nodding would be a musical tie to her unhesitant response.

"Like what were my favorite positions during marriage."

"Psychologically encroaching." I shook, tsk tsk, my head, commiserated with her. "And didn't these questions annoy you?"

Say yes. Say yes. Say yes.

"At first I asked him to stop, but when he did for a while, I actually began to miss those questioning sessions when he sat on his La-Z-Boy lounger with his feet up and a dry pipe in his mouth and made me think back to former times and confront my choices and actions."

Dry pipe, I thought. Since when did he begin *that* affectation?

"He asked me questions I never thought about."

"Like?"

"Like if my husband was ever tender to me—the Arab, I mean. If he ever would just sneak up behind me and kiss me."

"Did he?"

"I never realized that he didn't until Guido made me think about it. And when I thought about it I realized what a gap, a negative, there was in my life. No, the Arab didn't. He never showed me that tenderness that Guido is capable of. Tender, yes, and zany too. There is this Harpo Marx-like zaniness about him. I half-expect him to pull a lit cigar out of his pocket. We would be standing in the house talking and before I knew it, like Harpo hanging his knee over Chico's outstretched hand, Guido would press his index finger, clasp it like a Velcro snap, over my, you-know."

"Just like that?"

"Just like that."

"I mean, that's a pretty intimate gesture."

"Well, he felt absolutely at home with me."

She stopped. I waited.

"Once he even suggested that I meet a friend of his."

"Did he tell you his name?" I knew Guido meant me. He'd told me as much during our class reunion.

"Why?" She laughed that suggestive laugh of hers. "Do you want to meet him? Anyway, he said there was this very nice, smart, superintellectual man he'd like to introduce me to. I got very upset and he apologized. I asked him about it a couple of times, and he was evasive, as usual. Finally, he said, Just in the spirit of sharing. Which made me even more upset."

For some reason, that remark of Guido's on Aviva's lips was like a little aphrodisiac. In fact, the first time I heard it from Guido I felt a little rub on my skin as if a woman were lightly caressing it. But now that I'd heard it a second time from Aviva, I really felt its erotic impact. And why not? Guido was married, Aviva half, and I was free. Guido would never leave his wife. I had no one to leave. And it would serve Guido right for two-timing his wife and for beating me out when we were in college and interrupting my coitus once when we worked in a Borscht Belt hotel. But what if we made it and she continued to see Guido anyway. If she could two-time her present husband, why not her future one? But it was just a passing thought. Many troubled, good-looking women had been on this couch and I never touched them, although, of course, the thought sometimes crossed my mind. All you need is one lawsuit-minded gal and, bam, there goes your entire career. And you never know who is a put-up job, an investigator, a reporter on the make (in both senses of the term). So I kept still and calmed down.

"But I'm talking of the good old days . . . Lately, it's been downhill . . . I guess it's probably inevitable that it will end. He likes women," she said without a pause. "When I once asked him what if anything he believes in, he said, 'Like the Rostrafucians,' or something like that, 'I believe in the goodness of man and the sexiness of women.' "

After Aviva left I sat on the sofa, staring at the space she'd so recently filled. I remembered her description of the lessons and her feeling in Venice. I'm Guido at the lessons, I thought. I'm both of them in Venice.

Yearning.

6

"It's his wife," Aviva was saying. "My God, what am I going to do? If it weren't for his wife, things would be perfect. But things are never perfect, right? At least for me. I look in vain for some kind of negative comment from Guido regarding his wife. Each time I hope he'll come and say, I just had this awful fight with her. I'm splitting. But no, on the contrary, he tells me she gives him good advice. Is a pal. He tells me about a concert 'we went to,' a restaurant 'we went to,' a movie 'we went to.' "

She bit off each three-word phrase as if she were spitting gall, sending execration into the void. And I shook my head at Guido's callousness.

"Luckily," she continued, "he goes to his European assignments alone. And since he sees me smiling as he says these words, he assumes I take it graciously. But I seethe inside, am cut to pieces. I'm waiting for him to tell me he's had a blowup so he can leave her and I'll make him mine."

You can wait till the Messiah comes, I thought.

"I don't even know his value system. His morality. Don't you have a sense of morality? I ask him, and this Brooklyn Italian street-smart wise-ass quips, 'Yea, I don't do high jumps in front of cripples.' I mean, come on, give me a break! I don't know what's up there on his list of important things . . . I mean, what does he think is important in this world? . . . Sometimes I think photography is the most important thing in the world for Guido. He shows me his pictures. Peru. New Zealand. Fiji. Nepal. His business takes him everywhere. Exotic places. In one snap, which someone else has taken, he has his arm around a native girl. So I swallow my bile and say, Very nice. Beautiful. Because that's what I always do when I'm hurt. Make believe it's not there. Hurt myself more."

I couldn't hold back. "That's terribly insensitive."

"The understatement of the month . . . And then he wonders why these black moods come over me and I keep deciding not to see him any more and then he comes over and obviously I hug him and we talk, locked into each other, me on his lap, and he tells me there's no one more attractive than me, except his male friends, of course, and I burst out laughing and hug him, and the words, I love you, burst out of me in a heartfelt passion and the troubles are put on the back burner and we start all over again. He told me, 'You have darkness in you and I have light . . . I'm your light,' he told me and I couldn't help but respond, 'You *are* light,' For he is. No matter how gloomy I feel, when he's with me I feel happy. I once told him, 'With you I feel I've swallowed a light bulb.' When he tries to convince me that I shouldn't leave him, even though that's the rational thing for me to do, right?, he tells me, 'Whenever you're in a black depressed mood, come to me.' But I tell him, 'But *you're* the cause of my depression. It's you, the situation, that brings on these awful feelings and I feel my guts being wrenched out of me and the bad feeling, like a poison, spills over into everything I do: my music, my relationship with the kids, my students, *everything*. Even, my cooking," she laughed, "which is lousy to begin with . . . So he tells me, yes, the situation won't change, but I can offer you another angle of vision. Like the old half full or half empty cup of water. Another view is healthy, refreshing, he says. And I shake my head, because he's right. He's wiser than me . . ." She stopped for a moment. "I try to be smarter but I don't succeed. I've tried a few times not to come to him. To call and say I'm not coming, but each time he convinces me to come back. Each time he has a so-called plan. And as soon as I see him I get muddled, I can't resist. I succumb. He says I'm curious and he's zetetic.♥ Each time I say, next time I'll have to put my foot down. And the best way is to stop sex. Not let me get involved deeper. But once . . . is this getting monotonous . . . ?"

"No. Never. You are enchanting . . . Really . . ."

"Really? Me enchanting?"

I nodded.

"Once, when I came in, he, silently, without a word, pulled me upstairs and I said, 'I don't know if I want to go upstairs,' but he hooked his hand into mine and I followed him up. 'I want to talk to you,' he said. He did not want me to go to Chicago where I'd been invited by a divorced man I had met at a family gathering. With the children, of course. He said it would send a signal to the man that I was available . . ."

"He's right. It would be a signal." Why was I agreeing with him, for God's sakes?

"I wouldn't have gone anyway. Me he doesn't want to go, but *he* won't give up his wife. He told me if I went to Chicago he wouldn't see me any more because it would mean that I would sleep with that guy."

"Well, would you?"

"That's not the point," Aviva said angrily. "Questions, questions. You men are all alike." It was the first time I'd seen her huff up. "It's the double standard and I told him so."

"And what did he say?"

"He understood, but his old excuse was that his link was a preexistent condition."

♥See ABC Directory, *Zetetic.*

"You mean like a disease?"

Aviva laughed. "Yes, we laughed about that . . . He told me to go consult Blue Cross."

"He's very funny."

"Yes. Guido is, was. He said that's one of the reasons I couldn't leave him—because then fun and humor would go out of my life."

"Is he right?"

"I suppose."

7

Was it at this time that my professional objectivity began to crumble? It *seemed* to be intact, but when Aviva left I would see the mortar dust of that objectivity floating like motes in sunbeams. Every time she left I had this empty feeling. As if a vacuum were floating inside me. She'd used the word *negative* a number of times, each time in an apt, unusual, even groundbreaking way. Perhaps Guido's photographic influence. She once mentioned a colleague, a platonic friend, who not only didn't elicit any sexual interest for her, but he had, as she put it, a negative sexuality. I had this negative feeling too, but in a different way. Not only an emptiness. But a negative emptiness. As if a minus, a hunger there. Some invisible amoeba reaching out into a void to undo the void. The closest I'd come to this negative emptiness was during a summer in Brooklyn when I was twelve or thirteen. For some reason the kids on my block gave me the cold shoulder. How delighted they must have been to agree on it and carry it out. When I came out to play, they turned around. When I spoke, they stared right through me. All summer long I had that empty feeling, that hurtful void, that negative emptiness. It hung in there like a chronic flu. I cried at the injustice of it. I tried to take up fishing off a pier at Coney Island, but I couldn't bring myself to put a hook through a worm. Still, I had those bastards to thank for making me discover the pleasures of solitude, on my roof, listening to my portable radio and reading. That was the summer of Schubert's Symphony No. 2, and believe me, it was worth it, lying on a blanket on the roof, absolutely alone in the world, just the sun and sky and the chimneys and the occasional pigeon and maybe a stray butterfly who got blown over from a Jersey suburb, and those marvelous melodies written by a sad man, sad like me, in the sad summer of my thirteenth year. All July and August I longed for that emptiness to vanish. A feeling I never had again until I met Aviva. The feeling wasn't there when she sat in my office and spoke. Yes, there was an emptiness, but it was the reverse of a negative emptiness. How shall I describe it? An almost hunger. An almost satisfaction. The potential. A positive emptiness. But no sooner did she leave than—whoosh!— that negative emptiness soughed through me like a silent wind, and that yawning hunger, the pit of a vacuum whirled through me and settled until the next time she came.

Was it then that I admitted to myself: I like this woman? Can anyone ever pinpoint a moment in time when the window shade that eclipses light snaps up, quick flippety quicker flop flop flop, and sunlight suddenly streams? How her eyes lit up when she heard of another person's success? How she smiled her radiant smile when she held that picture of me and my nieces? Aviva absorbed other people's warmth. It reflected on her face. Even warm feelings from years ago affected her. I had plenty of examples. For instance, the way she loved her cat.

"When I was a student at PAMA," she had told me, "I had a pussycat,♥ a male called Fluffy. Remember, I mentioned him when I looked at the pictures on your desk? First time I came to your office? I loved that cat. Once, when I took him for a walk, he ran up a tree and wouldn't come down, so I called the fire department."

She calls the fire department, I thought, and tells them in her naïve way: my pussy's up a tree. How would that go over with the boys shooting pool and the breeze up in the fire department's rec room? A moment later she answered my question.

"I was so naïve then I didn't even know the other, vulgar, connotation of the word. The fireman repeated what I'd said to his colleagues, and I could hear them snickering and whooping it up. But I was used to people laughing at what I said, and I always wondered what did I say or do that was wrong?"

"Did the fireboys come for your pussycat?"

"Yes, but while I was waiting, I stood by the tree and yelled up to my cat, Fluffy, come down! Just then a man passed and said, 'Lady, if I was a cat with a name like Fluffy, I wouldn't come down from the tree either.' . . . I loved that cat. He would sit on my lap when I was practicing. I had him fixed, but for curiosity—"

"The ever curious Aviva . . ."

"I'd play with his penis, just to see where it was. In a cat, you know, it's inside, not like human males. You touch it—I was always looking for that little button to press—it would come out and then the cat would turn to me with its big green eyes and look at me. When he died, I don't know from what, I cried for months. I'm sentimental that way."

"I know what killed the cat," I said, in a high.

"You do? What?"

"Curiosity."

It took her a minute, but then she stamped her feet and laughed hysterically.

♥See ABC Directory, *Cat, feeding the.*

"I love furry little animals . . .♥ Are you sentimental that way too?" she asked me.

"Yes. But in a different way. Not pussycats affect me, but numbers move me. I remember how excited I was in school when I could write 5/5/55 on top of my notebook. When the mileage in my car reached 22,222.2 I pulled over to the side and stopped to contemplate it in awe."

"Why is that, do you think?" she asked me like a good therapist.

"Perhaps because such an event, such a configuration won't happen again. Like the baby who is one day old. That first day of life will never recur."

I looked at her smiling her warm, happy smile and wondered if I saw her through Guido's eyes. Was that why I gradually became—shall I use the word "enchanted"?—enchanted with her? Or was I seeing her through my own eyes? I had a lot of questions. Lots and lots. A whole list of them. An endless list. I guess I needed a psychologist too. And if I was seeing her with my own eyes, did Guido have something, even a smidgen, to do with it? But he *always* had something to do with it. Even when we didn't mention him, he was there. Once she told me about a cello she could have bought in Italy. "A Geselli, right?" "How did you know?" she said. I told her I knew she couldn't afford a Strad or a Guarneri, so Geselli came to mind. "And, wouldn't you know it?" she said, "Guido guessed it too." Why did she have to bring him in, as if we were competing in the same relay race?

But I could see why Guido fell in love with her. God, was the same thing happening to me? One doesn't take one's good friend's wife of another man. If the logic and syntax are mixed up, so be it. So are we all. I too became obsessed with Aviva's past. Just like Guido. But with me at least it was disguised as clinical observation. I started remembering things she had said. As if I'd taped them.

About her husband:

"I really wasn't in love with him, I now realize, but I was bowled over. It was time to get married. All my friends already had babies. My mother noodged me. I wanted stability. Permanence."

Twenty-five plus fourteen years of marriage is thirty-nine, I thought.

Or her music problem:

"I have memory lapses. If I have to introduce someone, I occasionally forget a name. Notes elude me. I blank out. What's wrong with me?"

"I'll answer by giving you a personal example. Sometimes I read papers at the Conference of American Psychologists—CAP for short. I know my stuff. But I can't remember the talk unless I read it. If I try to wing it, I forget. I blank out. I don't care what others say. So I don't know things by heart. So I help myself. Because in public I get flustered."

♥See ABC Directory, *Gerbil, her.*

"Stress. Same with me."

"So help yourself. If notes elude you, use music."

"Then I have to depend on page turners."

"Yeah, but suppose their fingers fall off."

"You're mean," she said. "A psychologist doesn't talk that way."

I smiled. "It's only because I know you for so many years."

Aviva looked down at her shoes, then looked up at me with those big gray eyes, her right eye now just a bit off center. She was flirting with me. Giving me the come-on. Her lips were dry. She wet them with her tongue. "That's . . ." she said softly. "That's what Guido used to say . . . I mean he also said something like that about fingers falling off. You guys, you all got the same sense of humor."

Again Guido. Again and again.

"I dreamt about him . . . Ready for a dream?"

So now I've become her steady Joseph, her friendly Freud.

"Let's hear it."

He and I are digging a tunnel in the sand. We're at the beach. And when our toes touched it sparked off the most enormous orgasm I ever had."

"Is that it?"

"That's it. What's it mean?"

I thought for a minute.

"You dig in the sand because you want to hide. You still must hide from public view and the sand tunnel is your private domain, all your own. Where you won't feel self-conscious. And in the oddball language imagery of dreams, instead of fingers, it's toes. The toes stand for your fingers, but again your dream, if you'll permit a pun, is playing footsie with you. The toes are hidden, the fingers on display. The fingers of your cello playing. And the orgasm is the easiest part to interpret. You unite with him, in whatever which way, and you get what every woman longs for."

Aviva nodded, then shook her head. "Imagine! That's what he used to say too. And he always boasted that he never screwed a woman who didn't get an orgasm with him. Mister Magic, right? But it's true, he did have that magic touch."♥

I liked her use of the past tense.

"He has some ego, right?"

"Right."

"Seems to me," I observed, "that he has an ego so big he can't even sit in a chair, because his ego is there already."

"That's very witty. That's pure wit."

"It's not mine," I confessed. "I heard this from a friend."

♥See ABC Directory, *Sex.*

"There aren't many people who would admit that. Most people I know arrogate others' wisdom and pass it off as their own."

"But I'm different, right?"

She didn't bite, didn't respond.

"Go ahead. Don't be shy. That's what you're thinking. That I'm different. So say it."

"You're different," she said softly. "And that dream interpretation was brilliant."

Her words were like a caress. I watched her face. It went through changes. Shadows crisscrossed it. Then she told me another dream.

"We arrive on a street corner. Guido lay down on the rear door of an open station wagon, and I sat down next to him. He began taking off my sweater and bra when suddenly a police car filled with people or children drove by. I quickly put on bra and sweater and a moment later a woman, not young, rounded the corner in a green or turquoise ski jacket. She stood near the car looking at Guido and saying. Hello, Guido, hello, Guido, and then walked back around the same corner. Guido didn't respond to her greeting. And although his face was in the shadows, I could sense a certain sadness there. I asked Guido who that woman was. I had to ask a few times before he detached himself from his thoughts and answered, 'That was –' but, imagine, I forgot what name he said. It turns out it was Guido's mother-in-law, and then he explained how his mother-in-law is not his wife's mother, or maybe . . . but it makes no difference . . . it's only a dream."

"This one's easy. Obviously, the police car is authority, something that represents the established order, and shame prompts the quick dressing. And you're projecting your guilt onto Guido, or are actually feeling *his* guilt, by introducing his mother-in-law who in the dream is not really his wife's mother. A way of ameliorating guilt by saying, it's not really his wife's mother who's there. But the presence of the police car shows you're angry . . . You're angry at him, right?" I said insidiously, although the police car represented nothing of the sort.

"Yes," she said. "And I once did something about it. Which isn't like me at all. I tend to let things slide, to assume that they're fine. Once, when I was angry at him, maybe more angry at the situation we both were in, I found some pertinent remarks in the Bible. The Book of Proverbs. I'd been looking up something for my daughter, some assignment from Hebrew school. You know, the verses about the Woman of Valor at the end of Proverbs. And as I paginated I ran across those lines about the forbidden woman being bad for you, how she can lead you to death, keep away from her house, don't drink from strange wells. I mean, it really zings it to you. And this was just the time that I was low, depressed. Guido was getting one international assignment after another, leaving me for longer and longer periods, and I wanted to leave him. That's when I sent him those pages."

"And you never told him?"

"No. He showed them to me. Was puzzled. Maybe even scared. But I told him it may have come from a missionary group, and I even concocted a story that once I'd gotten some New Testament pages in the mail that I assumed had come from a missionary outfit."

I was sitting opposite her, legs crossed. My foot itched. Without thinking of manners or propriety—after all, I wasn't in Indonesia where it's an insult to show the sole of your foot to anyone—I pushed up my cuff and scratched the skin above the sock. I saw Aviva staring. I put both feet on the floor. She smiled.

"I don't know if I ever mentioned this before—it may not be significant—but Guido always used to make love with his socks on. He never removed his socks."

"Did you ever see his feet?"

"Never."

"Maybe he had a cloven hoof," I said. "You know, according to folkbelief, demons never show their feet because of their cloven hoofs . . ."

"Maybe he *was* a demon. Only a demon could have had such a penetrating effect on me."

Good, I thought. Now I've linked him up in her mind with the devil. Almost all her remarks, I noted, pertained to sex. Despite her disclaimer that sex wasn't important, I wondered why sex was so important to her. But then she said something that showed she must have read my mind. It was uncanny, for just then she asked:

"Why is it that sex is such an important thing in life?"

"Is that a rhetorical question, or do you want to know?"

"No. Really. I want to know."

I held a finger to my cheek as if thinking, though I knew the answer well. "Because it's the driving rhythm of the universe. The urge to propagate the species. The most pleasurable act a man and woman can participate in. Besides reading, of course. It's the poor person's luxury. And in today's world, it's all around us. It invades our psyches, our beings. Open any fashion magazine and it's there, subtly or overtly. Listen to the jokes people tell. Watch the films. TV. Ask students what they think about in class. Studies have shown they think of sex 90% of the time. If food, drink, and shelter are little cars chasing us, sex is a huge Mack truck in hot pursuit. Although from a time point of view it occupies only a fraction of a person's day or night, it looms very large because of its secrecy, its hiddenness, its ecstasy. Look at the world's literature, from the Bible on. In every age, every society, you'll see love and sex playing a major role. And when it's good, it's delicious, right?"

Aviva's eyes softened. She leaned her head back against the pillow and a mellow, desirous smile suffused her face.

"Mmm," she said, then seemed to sober up, to remember where she was, with whom she was. A serious look came over her face. Over mine too. "In most marriages the sex factor is not that exciting . . ." she said. "Depends how charged up one is . . . It's like the peasant with the herring and boiled cabbage. He has that all his life, he's happy. He doesn't know there's caviar or other goodies."

But sex wasn't it, I realized. It took me all those weeks to finally understand. It wasn't so much sex she was interested in as affection. What she desired above all was the all-embracing cocoon of love and warmth. She needed it like a baby. Of course, sex came with the man. And curiosity was all. Thinking of curiosity, I thought of her cat. And just as she was leaving, I pulled a toy badge from my desk drawer and said, "You're under arrest . . . For cat abuse."

8

A few days after my last session with Aviva, I went to hear the New York Philharmonic at Avery Fisher Hall. It was the second time in a week. Now I went to see Yo Yo Ma in the Elgar Cello Concerto. Halfway through the piece, my overwrought imagination, in a kind of moral fever, overtook me and Aviva's face montaged over Yo Yo's until I saw only the long auburn hair and her gray eyes gazing now at the conductor, now out at me. At the energetic pizzicato in the first movement I saw *her* hands moving on the strings with fire and zest, and the misplaced applause at the end of the first movement was for her. I wanted her to succeed. Normally, I wouldn't have gone to see the Elgar. But the fact that it was a cello piece hooked me. I'd have gone to hear any cello soloist, no matter what screechy composition was being played.

I scanned the few women's faces in the orchestra until I found her among the first violins. I knew it couldn't be Aviva, but still I couldn't take my eyes off the woman. She had the same long tawny hair, big doe eyes and full lips with a slight downslant. The sort you sometimes see in the splashy Revlon lipstick ads. As she chatted with a colleague I saw Aviva's mischievous expression, as if she'd just told him a double entendre. The concert began. The conductor too couldn't take his eyes off her. I imagined him sending her secret signals. Even when he has to attend to the basses he looks to her in the violins. Aviva's doppelgänger too had a penchant of pressing her chin down and, eyebrows raised, looking up with a slight frown at the conductor as if peering over lenses that weren't there.

Lenses. I had my glasses on my lap and suddenly saw a vision. With the final chord the notes sank into the walls, the seats, our heads—or wherever music goes when it leaves the instruments. In my glasses I saw hundreds of little lights. When the mist cleared I realized that because of the angle, the light of the chandeliers was concentrated in my lenses, like a hologram. The tiny dots of light looked like a circular staircase, and Aviva was walking down the stairs. Then the lights became eyes, eyes made up of tiny electric dots staring at me.

People were moving all around me. It was intermission.

"What are you playing with?" I heard a woman's voice behind me.

Like an obedient schoolboy I said, "My glasses," before I even turned and saw Pam. She bent over and kissed my cheek. Good old Pam. We'd grown old, and single, together. My parents had always said that Pam's waiting for me, and I pooh-poohed that remark. But maybe they were right. As the years passed they were more and more right in lots of things. Pam and I had seen each other over the years, like loving cousins who cross beyond the taboo. Serious and not serious at the same time. We knew each other too well. We trod that thin line between platonic and sexual and dipped into both. Having our cake and eating it too. It was curious, our friendship. Very mod. Very New York. We were proud of it. We could depend on each other. Half of our old foursome, still in touch in a skewed way: she with Ava, I with Guido; she with me.

"What's with you, Charlie? You look down. It's not like you."

"Really? Do I look down?"

"Well, sad. Pensive. That effervescence is missing."

"Because you're not sitting next to me."

"I could have been if you'd called."

I nodded, acknowledge guilt. Stood. "You here alone?"

A little mirror image of my slow three little nods, a wan smile on that small pretty face.

"You're not alone now," I said.

Pam looked up at me with an almost—well, maybe it's my easily aroused fantasy—wifely intimacy. "You always manage to say the right thing at the right time."

I took her hand. "Come." We created our own breeze as we walked up the elegant aisles, me feeling suddenly, inexplicably, rich and famous, everyone staring at me. To avoid talking, to skirt around telling Pam what was on my mind, I went into a manic monologue.

"D'ya notice who's guest conducting tonight?"

"Zubin Mehta is not a guest conductor."

"Wait. He is. I'll explain. You noticed how breathless he was? His agent had him fly in from Tel Aviv where he's permanent-for-life guest conductor of the Israel Philharmonic. He was told it was a guest conducting assignment. They never even rehearse. The musicians and conductors just listen to each other's recordings. Anyway, Zubin was away from the New York Philharmonic for so long he was paid to guest conduct the orchestra he's permanent conductor of. What a mix-up. What musical chairs. They jump all over the place. Andre Previn is principal conductor of orchestras in London, Rome, and Los Angeles, and also principal guest conductor of the Chicago Symphony. Charles Dutoit of Montreal also goes by the name of Ricardo Muti, so it shouldn't seem that he overexposes himself. The music director of the Cleveland and Houston orchestras is also principal guest conductor of the Maine Chamber Orchestra and the Singapore Sinfonietta. And to supplement his income he's also conductor of the Long Island Rail Road, Westbury to New York run. Most resident conductors conduct only half the season's concerts. Other times they're all over the world guest conducting while other guest conductors come in to fill their slots. Once in Manila, because of an administrative snafu, they had two guys conducting the Manila Symphony at the same time. There's one guy who has all these coming and goings on a computer, but no one knows who he is."

I recited this monologue to Pam but imagined Aviva laughing, as I addressed it to her.

Pam, petite, with a small lovely face that hardly aged over the years except maybe around the eyes, laughed with delight. When her face lit up, she looked like a kid. Then, toning down the volume of her smile, she raised her eyebrows a bit, signaling: What is it you really wanted to say?

I didn't want to tell her everything, but I did say: "Well, it's an ethical problem. Professional peccato. I'm beginning, I think, to like a patient. Who's actually not a patient because . . ."

"Is he nice?"

I mock punched her.

"Don't worry your head over it. You won't be the first therapist to do so. Tell me about her." She looked calm, objective, understanding. At least she tried to. But I noticed a little flicker of lesser light in her eyes. Uh-oh, I thought. The questions are starting, will start. Better stop now before I put my foot in it. She's married, I'm going to say. Trouble, she'll respond. And she's seeing me because she's seeing a married man, I'll say. Worser and worser, Pam quotes Lewis Carroll. And unbeknownst to her, I continue: I know the married man she's seeing, and he's one of my friends. And you, I try to bite my tongue but it slips out anyway, know him too. Bottom, she'll say. You've hit bottom with lead shoes.

So I decided to shut up.

"Take care," Pam said, "it might be trouble."

"I will," I said, but my heart wasn't in my words.

"How come you haven't called? Is it because of that non-patient?"

She was trying a different tack. Again I didn't answer. She's hurt, I thought, and telling me. My parents, bless them, are right.

"Mea culpa for not calling. But whenever I see you time stands absolutely still. It's eerie. It's like we're in a movie together, and the same scene can be replayed years apart."

The audience was starting to drift back.

I put my finger on her cheek. "The Russian Tea Room after the concert?"

Her smile moved from her lips to her big brown eyes. She closed her eyes slowly in assent.

The next time I saw Aviva I told her that I'd seen her at Avery Fisher Hall (I omitted the chandelier vision). She made a face. At first I thought she disapproved and I felt a twinge of rejection. Then she explained that her grimace was an expression of disdain at not getting a full-time job with an orchestra.

"The New York Philharmonic, never! You might see me sometimes when I'm called to fill in with the Long Island Symphony. But even with them getting a full-time job is next to impossible. Sometime I wonder why I pursue this altogether."

She stretched her legs, about to put them on the sofa, but since I sat at the other end she sat up again. I jumped up and sat on a chair opposite her and told her to make herself comfortable. She looked at me shyly for a moment and then, with a little self-effacing frown, stretched her legs out. I wondered if she'd begin to talk about music because ostensibly that was why she had come to me. After all, I told her I had experience with musicians. She closed her eyes for a moment. I captured that face in repose and turned away, nurturing the image. So that's what she looks like when she sleeps. Perfectly relaxed.

"Why should one frustrate oneself by running fingers over taut strings, or blowing into a trumpet, for that matter? The more you play, the more you have to discipline yourself, the more difficulties there are. Learning how to bow, to angle your arm, to achieve that delicate glissando, watching, always on the lookout, that your fingers don't get hurt or nicked. To learn how to play softly yet firmly. To learn to close your eyes and let your unconscious take over. Why? Why bother?"

I was about to respond, but Aviva continued:

"It's my old line again. What's the point of it? There are so many cellists in this world, it doesn't need another one."

"But each human being," I said, "adds his own uniqueness to the world. The world may have dozens of cellists, but it doesn't have Aviva Esther Prinsky . . . And maybe it needs one. You have to have a little ego."

"Ego, you say?" She gave a shy little laugh. "That's not my bag. That's Guido's. He has enough for both of us . . . One day he says to me, Aviva, you're really lucky. I know, I said, I have you. No, Guido said, I mean it another way. You're lucky because you can see my face all the time, while I can see it only when I look in the mirror."

"But maybe he can't even look in a mirror because his ego is already there arrogating the glass."

"Maybe." Aviva gave a little snort. "Hey! Isn't that a variation of your friend's ego remark?" She turned to me, pushed her hair aside. I was aware again of that faint squint that made her look so charming and vulnerable. It brought the aloofness of her beauty back down to earth.

"Wanna hear another dream?" she asked suddenly.

As soon as she said dream, one I had about her returned. It's short; a photograph, really. It's after a concert and her hands are upraised to acknowledge applause.

"Hello?" she said. "Did you hear me?"

"Of course," I said.

"Actually, I have two dreams. In the first I'm at the cello practicing." She gave a sudden laugh. "Lately I do a lot more practicing in my dreams than in real life . . . Soon Guido comes by on skis. I tell him not to ski after a heavy meal. We start walking, his hand around my waist. He shows me beautiful mountain scenery."

"Is that it?"

"Uh-huh. What do you make of it?"

"Well, let me ask you: what do *you* make of it?"

"I don't know," she said.

"Well, let's analyze the parts. Are they ominous? Is there anything distressing in them?"

She puckered her lips and shook her head.

"Basically, it's a good dream," I said. "You're practicing. The snow is a tranquil image. You show your concern for Guido. He shows his affection for you. There is an atmosphere of peaceful acceptance. And the walk through beautiful mountain scenery is an even more positive step into happiness. It shows you want tenderness and affection."

Aviva sat, rather, jumped up. In one swoop her legs swung like a bat from a supine to a sitting position. "But the other dream isn't so pleasant . . . I see Guido eating a huge plate of veal and some kind of latkes. Then three or four pieces of veal suddenly take shape. They have eyes and faces and stare at me . . ."

My God, I thought. My chandelier vision at Avery Fisher Hall, the electric dots staring at me through my glasses.

"They got up and looked about, moved around. Then Guido began cutting the veal and eating it. I jumped up and ran away."

Aviva looked up at me.

"Obviously, not a pleasant dream. The eyes and the face are you. You are afraid of Guido cutting you up."

Suddenly she covered her face with both hands as if weeping. She shook her head as if to blow away the thought and dropped her hands. Her face was pale.

"Did you dream both dreams during one night?"

"Yes. Any significance to that?"

"Possibly. The two dreams show your mixed emotions. Happiness and gloom. Joy and fear."

"I *am* afraid of being cut up.♥ I'm so alone. I have no husband. No one I can count on. You're right. I *do* want tenderness and affection. And from my husband, except maybe before we were married, I never got it. He never said a tender word to me. And I longed for tenderness. In the early years I did my best to try to love him, to make him a comfortable home, but for him I was just another piece of furniture. He lavished more care, more affection, more tenderness, more attention on the fender of his new taxi than he did on me. I watched him through the window one day. With what love he washed and polished and buffed that car. God, there was a loving look in his eyes, almost ecstatic, as he saw his reflection in the shine—a look I'd never seen him direct at me. With one glance he was loving himself in his car."

"You're very perceptive," I said. "Amazingly so. Maybe we should change places and I should talk."

"Then I'll bill you," Aviva laughed.

"I don't mind," I said.

"Can you imagine living a life where you're always criticized? For shopping. For telephoning. For cooking. Breathing. *Living*. Always reprimands. I'd leave the faucet dripping and get bawled out. Leave the light outside for one of my students and get bawled out. Shop for clothing. Criticism. I'd put on lipstick to go shopping in the evening, and he'd accuse me—in front of the children—of running around with men. Always the same nasty, unfounded accusations, as if it gave him some sexual high to think I was having other men. But this is part of his personality flaw. His wild imagination. His fantasy life. And this bastard was given the name of Rahamim, which in Hebrew means 'compassion' . . .

"But in business he calls himself Roberto and tries to talk with an Italian accent. Roberto Ramati, the Israeli North African Italian mafioso of the taxi business. So by all this he distanced himself from me, even in moments of supposed closeness.♥♥ So there's no one close to me. Except Guido. And he has two wives, right? And enjoys it. He loves that role. I knew it, I know it, though, of course he would never admit. God, he was *never* wrong. He *loved* having two wives, just like a Biblical patriarch. Once I told him, You were born to have a harem. So he says, From your mouth to God's ears. I'm about to wollop him for that when he puts on the innocent look that can charm the pants off anyone and purrs, I can't help it if God listens to you. So Guido has his day wife and his night wife. His weekend wife and his Monday wife, although most of Saturday mornings were also mine—in

---

♥See ABC Directory, *Vulnerable, she is.*
♥♥See ABC Directory, *Distasteful, how, the Arab's screwing is.*

the afternoons I had lessons—because it was her busiest day at the place she worked. How he must have reveled in that! Once when I pressed him, he said he made love to his wife 'occasionally' but not on days he was with me. The fact never sank in. Because I'd always assumed he *never* made love to her. That there was something wrong between them. That that was the reason he came to me. That soon he would leave her. That one day he'd admit, I fooled you, I'm not married to her at all. But I'd been deluding myself. Little by little that realization that he had a wife demolished me. I couldn't stand the thought that the same hands and other attachments that stroked me so lovingly would a day later, or maybe even hours later, touch another woman. It drove me crazy. To depression. I couldn't handle it. He claimed it wasn't intimacy. Didn't I make love to the Arab, he reminded me, over the years without it being intimate? He had me on that one. And he reminded me how I'd once told him about a girlfriend who had taken a lover but could never have an orgasm with him, but only with her husband, She didn't love her husband, he was a mean bastard, she felt better with her lover, but with him she just could not have an orgasm. Sex without intimacy. So I had to agree with Guido because I had the same thing at home. And he was always complaining how it hurt him that in years past I'd had two or three lovers. He couldn't imagine how the same arms that embraced him had embraced other men. But that, I tried to explain to him, was years ago and my anger, my jealousy, pertained to now. Now. Now!"

Aviva was shouting. Acting out. Furious. There were tears in her eyes. "Can you imagine being locked into a no-win situation? He's happy when I'm with him. And I'm happy too, but troubled. I'm happy when I feel I've gotten him out of my system. Then *he* can't sleep, my poor love. *He's* unhappy. *He's* miserable."

"And aren't you miserable when you're away from him?" I asked, regretting my idiotic remark the moment it popped out.

"Yes," she said and I noticed a downspin sadness in that yes. "Very. But I know it will have to end and I've told him that—but it makes him angry and miserable and then, against my better judgment, I continued to see him."

Aviva's Dream

"Guido and I are on an elevator, and the man either running the elevator or in there with us as a passenger was ugly in a threatening way. He carried an iron object in his hand and, as I asked to see it, I took it from him. He got out next floor and Guido quickly closed the gate behind him."

"I see you dream in 1940's elevators."

"We arrived at our stop, which seemed more like a place than an elevator stop. We got out and found ourselves in the midst of crowds of well-dressed

orientals wearing yarmulkes singing Chanuka songs in a synagogue. They
weren't sitting but seemed to be arranged in standing rows, with some people
moving about freely. Guido explained to me that these people were not con-
verted Jews but full-fledged Jews like us. They merely looked oriental because of
assimilation. I felt closest to Guido there."

Interpretation:
   The elevator is a symbol for privacy, where the couple can be a couple by
themselves. The outside danger is soon peaceably gotten rid of. The oriental
synagogue expresses a desire for the comfort and tradition of Yiddishkeyt but
with a foreign flavor, as if to show a wish to be removed from the present
"normal" occidental world. There are no outside forces or threats or cops or
veal-with-eyes. But the two of you are there, free and clear, in an atmosphere
where you both can be together. No wonder you feel closest to Guido there. I
would too.
   "To whom? Me?" she asks.
   "No," I say. "To Guido."
   "You'd probably like each other," she said.

9

   I changed the subject. Purposely. To see if we could talk and not have
Guido intrude. We began to talk about books. From books to gallery
shows—she knew nothing about art; for her it was a foreign continent, a
galaxy removed, and I was itching to say: Let me take you to the Museum
of Modern Art—to automobiles (I told her I had fixed my own electronic
ignition). I must admit I enjoyed impressing her. I'll show her there was
more to this world than brilliant photography.
   "I once knew a man like you; he was older. My father's generation. That
type is gone. But you seem to know everything. Your profession, of
course . . ."
   I modestly looked down.
   "But you also know music and art and psychology and dreams and
architecture and electronics."
   "I can tune a car, can you?"
   "No."
   "Can you can a tuna?"
   "No."
   "But you can tune a tuna."
   Aviva looked puzzled.
   "Ask me how to tune a tuna."
   "How do you tune a tuna?"
   "By running up and down its scales."

"You know," she said, laughing. "I feel so deficient when I talk to you or Guido."

Again Guido. Not five minutes without him.

"Don't feel that way. It's very difficult being perfect . . . I'm only kidding . . . Music takes so much devotion and time, there's little room for anything else . . ."

She made a face, as if not fully agreeing.

"It's true that European musicians of the old school, like my father and his friends, were cultivated in many areas. Americans tend to be, you know, to have only one culture . . . I want to read more. You sometimes mention a writer, even a composer, I haven't heard of. I used to see that flicker of disapproval on Guido's face when he mentioned a writer I didn't know . . . Can you recommend some books?"

I wondered if that was a line she used on Guido.

"Sure. You like Spanish writers?"

"Okay," Aviva said.

"Start with Juarez."

She opened her pocketbook. It bulged with papers, envelopes, notes. Wrote his name.

"He wrote a great romantic novel called, *Love in the Night*."

"Mmm, sounds good. You think the library will have it?"

"As Mark Twain said about Jane Austen, 'Any library that doesn't have a book by Jane Austen is a good library.' If your library has none of the works of Celedino Juarez, it's a super library, set to win a citation from the American Library Association."

I saw her writing down *Love in the Night* and underlining it three times.

"You heard of deconstruction?"

"Is that anything like de-composing? When my students play wrong phrases, I call it decomposition."

"I like that," I said. "With deconstruction. You start with a title and work your way up from there . . ." I stopped. "I don't know what I'm talking about. I'm sorry. I was pulling your leg. There's no such author, no such book."

"You're terrible," Aviva said.

"I just wanted to show you how much I know . . . Actually, I only give the impression of knowing everything. I don't know everything."

"No!" she said sarcastically. "*You* don't know *every*thing?"

"That's right," I said. "What I don't know can fill a pamphlet."

The words "you're terrible" echoed in my mind. She said it with such flirtatiousness. And when I said I was pulling her leg, I meant it. I would've loved to pull her leg. Watching my glance rolling across the length of the sofa, that ocean space between me and her. I could easily have bent over and picked up her leg and pulled it. What was happening to me? Did I notice a change in her? And if she were showing signs of attraction, what was happening to her relationship with Guido? Could she be attracted to—and flirt with—two men at the same time?

I weighed her remarks, sifted out those that had a burnished look, golden like a freshly baked egg roll. And I reheard the words she had said the last time: I know it will have to end.

I know it will have to end were the sweetest words I'd heard Aviva say. The Guido-Aviva affair was a classic. I sensed it from the few remarks that both had confided in me. Aviva's intuition was correct. He would never leave his wife. And she had to tell someone about it. She had to talk. Then, it seemed to me, I caught the bug too. Couldn't hold it in any longer. So I decided to call my parents. I spoke to them once or twice a week. Even though discussing women with them was frustration, I did share general details of my social life with them. My father had a cynical attitude to bachelorhood; somehow it compromised his masculinity to have an unmarried son. Never mind Charlie's presumed lack of machismo, it was Sidney Perlmutter who was being lambasted. Telling my father would only elicit ironic jibes, even though underneath the old man would be happy. My mother, well, it was no use worrying her. Because in her mind, she'd create phantasmagoric weddings and imaginary guest lists, lists that had become petrified over the years, with hardly a ripple in them each time a new girl was announced as an (inevitably temporary) girlfriend.

But beneath the bantering there was a genuine interest in what I was doing. Both were on the phone. I pictured my mother in the kitchen and my father in the bedroom. They did this so they wouldn't miss a word, so they wouldn't have to depend on each other to repeat, "Charlie said . . ."

I told them I had bumped into Pam at Lincoln Center.

"Oh, yes," said my mother. "Did you propose yet?"

"Yeah, Pam. The friend of what's-her-name." My father very well knew Ava's name.

"Ava," said my mother from the kitchen.

"Yeah," said my father. "The one who set the Guinness world record for men in one month, plus the mailman for good measure."

He chuckled, though my mother didn't laugh. He always liked stories about Ava; I suspected he wanted to be the mailman himself on Ava's postal route. Because he was an energetic, live-wire man, my dad. Even at seventy-nine he was frisky and agile. When he pulled his trousers on, sitting at the edge of the bed, he would lean back on the mattress and in one jump-swoop thrust up his hips and pull his pants up and, without breaking stride, leap up on his feet, pants drawn up to his waist. I once told him I'd like to see him do that trick and come up fully zipped and he said, A gentleman never has his fly zipped. Zipped flies are the monopoly of eunuchs.

"Here's one for you, Charlie," my father says. "How does a skyscraper protect itself from getting knocked up?"

"Umm . . . I don't know . . . I give up."

"It wears a condominium." And he barks a long laugh.

Then my mother said, "There's a nice young Jewish divorceé down here. Thirty-five with a little boy."

"Next time I come down I'll take a look."

She then took another route. "So what did Pam say?"

"Oh, nothing much. We went to the Russian Tea Room afterwards."

"Expensive, expensive," said my father.

I didn't want to pursue events of that evening. It was so easy to go from Pam to Ava to Guido to Aviva.

"Seeing anyone else?"

"If he was seeing someone else," my father interrupted, "he would have told us."

"I asked him. Why don't you let him answer?" my mother said.

"Because it's costing him for the phone call as is. Let him go. He probably has things to do."

"If he would have things to do," my mother said, "he wouldn't have called us and been talking so much."

These little spats on the phone, long distance, were a standard feature of my calls. They never fought when they called.

"Hey, listen," I would say. "I didn't call to hear you argue."

"Why not?" said my father. "We want to give you a taste of home."

"Why don't you argue after my call?"

"So it's the expense, huh? Then you wouldn't have to subsidize our quarrels."

"It's not the money," I say.

"It's the principle," my father finished for me. "Charlie is right. Let's show him, Sophie, how we get along."

There was silence for a full minute. I could hear the sparrows alighting on twelve hundred miles of telephone wires from New York to Fort Lauderdale.

"You know what? It's more fun to argue."

"Stop picking your nose, Charlie," my father said.

"I'm not."

"I can tell," he says, "by the contemplative silence. Your index finger is way up there . . . You probably want to hang up, right?"

"Why don't you let Charlie decide?"

"Okay," I say, "maybe I better."

"He probably wants to go out. Go, Charlie, take a bath and a shave and have a good time," says my mother.

My father repeated the sentence with a sarcastic bite, then added: "He's only forty-two and been bathing at least for ten years. Maybe you shouldn't tell him when to take a bath."

"Don't be snippety," my mother said. "I'm still his mother no matter how old he is."

"And I'm still his father."

My mother waited a moment and then weighed in with: "Oh, yeah? How do *you* know?"

Again silence. My father says, "Well, don't you have anything to say?"

"Who are you talking to?" asks my mother. "Me or him?"

"Him."

"Yes. Dad, you're the perfect Jewish mother."

"And where does that leave me?" say my mother, offended.

"Mom," I say. "You take perfection to unimaginable heights."

That makes her happy.

Another call come and gone and I'd said absolutely nothing. I had wanted to mention Aviva—maybe not—but never got around to it.

10

On Wednesday I concocted a little surprise. The week before, en passant, I'd asked Aviva where her cello coach lived. On the Upper West Side, she said, and gave me Marie LeClerq's address. And where do you park? I asked solicitously. She said there was a parking lot on the block. I waited for the proper hour, found her car, and left an envelope on the windshield. Inside, instead of a note, I drew a picture of two cellos sitting side by side (a little closer than we sat) on a sofa.

I couldn't wait for her reaction.

She smiled as soon as she came in. "I didn't even notice it till I was on the FDR drive. You're too much."

"Notice what?"

"The envelope."

"What envelope?"

"You know. Come on."

"I don't know what you're talking about."

For a moment her face fell; she believed me. She was confused. But when I smiled her face lit up.

"First of all," I said, "I didn't write that note."

"Gotcha." She jabbed the air. "How did you know there was a note?"

"Most envelopes have notes," I said, offended. "And anyway it wasn't the paper I usually use."

That took a while to sink in.

"Anyway, it was very nice of you to do that. It was really very nice . . . Do you mind if I use your phone?"

I stood up and walked to the other side of my office. She spoke to someone and the conversation concluded with "I love you too, honey."

"Who was that?" I laughed, but there was a pinch of jealousy in my voice. "Your cello coach?"

"No, my daughter, Yaffa . . . You know what she said to me the other day. Two things. One, that I was getting old, and two, that I wasn't pretty any more."

"That's normal. Nothing to worry about. It's the daughter's jealousy . . . she's about thirteen, right?"

"Yes . . . how did you know?"

"It's the right age . . . She's feeling her oats as a teenager. By knocking mommy she's asserting her own femaleness . . . How did you handle that?"

"I told her, if I wanted guys they would line up around the corner for me."

"Wrong!" I exploded. "Bad . . . bad . . . Sorry, but that wasn't the right thing to say . . . By saying that, you reinforced your husband's false accusations against you. Going out to meet men."

"He's told them worse. But I just meant for dating."

"But Yaffa doesn't know that . . . As a teenager, especially hearing her father's accusations about your promiscuity, she assumes the worst."

"But she sees me home every night."

"That's not the point. Imagination and the big lie are more potent than reality. When you said that she assumed all kinds of lasciviousness. Sometimes silence is the best answer. If you're silent, the person is left hanging with his own last remark. The nastiness of it sinks into that person's consciousness and is reinforced by your silence. But if you reply, it's your answer that remains in her mind, not her own baiting remark. You're not obliged to respond to every remark, barb or question . . ."

Aviva nodded pensively. "And she also said something else that's curious . . . Something she said her brother told her. He said, If mom and dad get divorced, if mommy gets another husband, I want him to be young and have lots of energy, be tall and handsome and not have a gray hair in his head."

Seems to fit a description of me, I thought.

"So I said to Yaffa: Tell David I'm not twenty years old. Now I don't know if David really said it, or if she's putting her wish into her brother's mouth."

"If it's her, it sounds like she's looking for a boyfriend. If it's him, he's looking for an older brother. In any case, neither seems to be looking for a father."

"Interesting point," said Aviva. "I never thought of that. Sort of made-to-order boyfriend/brother."

Or maybe, I thought, neither of the children said it. Maybe it's Aviva's wish, a subtle suggestion to me.

Aviva's Dream

She walks with Guido in Manhattan and somehow is on 44th Street and 11th Avenue, in a bad neighborhood, and she sees her dead father. He holds a cello and is silent. He's been to a party. He walks with his cello and she follows. The cello seems weightless. It floats alongside him. She wants to introduce Guido to him. But she cannot. She wants to know what her father is doing living in this area. But he's silent, apparently ashamed to let his daughter know he is living there. She follows him into an apartment house where along a narrow corridor on each door there is a small glass showcase with some of the person's possessions: a belt, a mug, a pair of shoes, some pamphlets, a couple of spoons, a vase. There are no scores. She recognized some items of her father's and walks in.

"Why are you living here?" she asks.

But the father's voice is almost inaudible. He turns his face from her.

She wants to introduce Guido but can't.

Interpretation:

She's still afraid of her father. Fears for her father's disapproval. Not only doesn't he answer her but he turns from her. And her fear of disapproval prevents her from introducing Guido to her strict father. Also, note that besides the cello, there is no hint of anything musical. It's as though by blocking out music he has disowned her musically, spiritually.

11

It was around this time that Aviva's remarks became so personal that a new dimension was added to the priest's/confessant's relationship. The tone of her comments was so suggestive, double-entendred, maybe (in retrospect) even duplicitous, that I was in a quandary. To begin with, though Guido was in my mind during the first weeks of my sessions with Aviva (he lurked in every word and gesture of hers whether he was mentioned or not), later he gradually faded away, perhaps in direct proportion to his fading away in her comments. I felt as if Guido, Aviva, and I were on a huge chessboard. We're on a bare stage where the set designer has angled on a 17% gradient a chessboard as the only prop in the play. I'm viewing all this from the balcony as if in a dream and I see myself, Guido and Aviva onstage. We make moves that not even a chess pro can cogently explain. Meaningless, pointless moves. Sometimes we're all close in the center. At times only Aviva and Guido are there while I observe. At times Guido and I huddle like King and Queen, and Aviva is the pawn at the edge. And at times Aviva and I are King and Queen, the chessboard rises in the middle like a roof, and Guido is barely visible from his lips up beyond the downslope of the board. The colors we represent are never clear. In the dim light, black, white, and gray meld. But then, in the real world of my office, I find myself alone with Aviva—Guido almost forgotten.

An example of her personal remarks:

"My husband used to . . . I'm ashamed to say . . ."

I waited. I know when a woman says those words hesitantly, it's a prelude to confession. A kind of metaphysical Vaseline protection for the soon-to-be revealed wound.

". . . used to hit me. And as close as I was to Guido I was too ashamed to tell him. And he beats the children too, the clever bastard, in places where it isn't visible . . . Once, without his knowledge, I brought in a cleaning woman—he refuses to let me hire one—and, my luck, that day he came home early—he usually comes home very late—and he smacked me. Out of brute rage he pummeled me in the chest, the side, the side of my head. Coolly, methodically . . ."

I shook my head. Incredible.

"He's a man with a lot of anger in him. I don't know why. Maybe because I'm more cultured than him. And he has a gratuitous mean streak which he thinks is good humor. But it's fun only for him. For example, we'd walk into a shop, look around, and when the owner wasn't looking he would turn the sign on the door from OPEN to CLOSED, and after we left I'd have to run back and suffer the embarrassment of righting the sign myself. Or he'd ask prices, try on expensive coats, ask about delivery cost, and get a shopkeeper all excited about a possible sale and then leave, smiling to himself."

"And you say he beats the kids too . . . I mean, shouldn't you report this?"

"Once, I was about to call the police because of what he did to me, but I chickened out. It happened when he drove home from work during a late January snowstorm—it took him about five hours from New York, and he took it out on me. I hear him stamping his boots on the mat outside the front door, and I rush to open the door for him. I asked him how it was. What an idiotic question, he said, and when I wanted to take off his snow-covered cap dripping with water, he hit me, saying, Get your hand off me. I ran away and locked myself in the bathroom. And hour later, I'm still trembling, he said he was sorry, which was totally out of character for him. He said he struck out at me because he thought I was going to hit him. Why should I do that? I said. Because I came home late. You're sick, I said."

"What did you do?"

"Nothing."

"Did you sleep with him that night?"

Aviva looked guilty. "Yes."

"Why, dammit?"

"Because he apologized and the making up felt so good."

"Did he ever do that again?"

"Yes."

"Did you ever discuss it with members of your family?"

"No. I was too ashamed."

"And the next time he beat you, what did you do?" I bit off each word like a prosecuting attorney.

"I went to the police and they took down a report."

"Good! Did they arrest him?"

"No."

"Why?"

Aviva looked down, crestfallen. Was I being too hard on her?

She said softly, "Because I didn't, I couldn't sign the complaint."

"You're crazy," I told her.

"I didn't want to make waves," she said passionately, on the verge of tears. "I wanted, I longed for, I craved a normal life where husband and wife lived in peace. But it didn't happen. Peace didn't hold for more than two, three days. Two days of calm, then another flare-up. I was on the telephone too long. He couldn't get business calls. Install another phone, I said. No. He looked in the garbage for price tags. Complained I never bought bargains. Other husbands would say, Go out and buy yourself something nice. He said, Shopping again? . . . Do you know he used to have a fit when the roll of toilet paper was put in, according to him, the wrong way? The paper had to be pulled down from the back, not the front. And once I put a penny on the floor of the bathroom. It stayed there for weeks. He never picked it up. The guy is such a slob. He'll drink a cup of coffee and leave the spoon on the counter, grains of instant on the floor, the unwashed glass or cup in the sink. He won't even rinse the cup. He expects *someone else* to do it. And the pig doesn't even change his socks daily. For him, changing socks is putting the left one worn yesterday on the right foot today. And stinginess clings to him from the very first days we were married. I think I told you how he begrudged me a soda in the 120 degree heat in Eilat. He'd grumble when I went to the beauty parlor. Forty dollars for *that?* He made me feel like a worm. I tried my best to please his palate. But no. The soup is too salty. Ek, he'd push the plate away and leave the table. Sometimes he'd even throw the food he didn't like across the room. Or stop the kids from having double portions of meat. Eat more potatoes, he'd say. Too much meat is no good for you. Or he sees a dish is cracked. He complains. Go buy a new set, I said. We can afford it. You choose the set. Any set your choose will be fine. He refused. Told me to buy it."

"Did you?"

"No. I'm stubborn too. If I buy it, I'll never hear the end of it. What rotten taste you got and so on. This dishes business happened not too long ago, one of the rare times we've actually talked. But this pattern of nastiness began at the very beginning of our marriage, twice seven years ago. I was pregnant with Yaffa. He was so mean to me I moved out of the apartment we lived in and went back to my parents' place."

"For how long?"

She lowered her gaze and looked up.

"One day."

"He came for you?" I asked.

"He called."

"He didn't come in person?"

"No."

"One day?"

"Why am I telling you all this? All I get is criticism whenever I'm honest with anybody. All right, it was my mistake. I admit. I should have known better. I should have stayed, not gone back. I should have known this pattern would continue. I should have listened to my mother. My whole life is one long I-should-have. If I was wiser that incident would have revealed a lot to me."

"What prompted your leaving?" I said gently, by way of apologizing for my judgmental reaction.

"Who knows? Some argument or other. I don't recall. But I left for a few hours—I was in my second month and not feeling too well—and wandered around Manhattan and came back around eight. But I found that when I rang the downstairs bell he didn't answer, so I rang a neighbor's bell. I had forgotten the downstairs key and only had the apartment door key with me. I got out of the elevator and went to our door. When I tried to insert the key I found that I could turn the lock, but I couldn't budge the door. I heard him moving on the other side, but he made believe he didn't know I was there. You jerk, I shouted, and gave a great shove and pushed open the door blocked by a heavy lounge chair that he had propped against the door. When I walked into the bedroom he was in bed pretending to be asleep. I was so angry that I picked up a dishtowel and threw it at him. At that point he jumped up and, pregnant as I was, he slapped me in the face. Then I picked up a suitcase, packed it, and went to my mother's house. I was so angry at him I wanted to get an abortion, and I told my mother this. I didn't want that monster's baby in me. But she said that it's my baby too, not only his, and she talked me out of it."

Aviva took a deep breath and let out a heavy sigh.

"You know what women sometimes do when they have mean, abusive non-husbands. They get consolation elsewhere," I said.

Aviva gave a sad smile. "Guido once asked me the same question. Early on, when things were rough between the Arab and me, probably after I ran off to my mother's house, my husband sent me to an accountant. I arrived in the morning and we discussed some details about taxes and he invited me out to lunch and then asked if he could see me again. When I told Guido this he wanted to know how come I didn't get involved with him. He couldn't understand, and maybe you don't either, that you don't do these things out of spite. Why should I hurt myself and take up with anyone just to revenge myself against the Arab? Just because I'm angry I should feel like garbage? That was my way of thinking and that's why I didn't take up with anyone else, even when things got worse. And I too felt worse and worse. My mother fell ill and my father, he also had heart problems, stopped playing the cello. His left hand developed what all string players fear—a nervous tremor, maybe it's in my genes too—and he demanded more and more attention. I was in a morass everywhere I looked.

"I'll give you another example of how the Arab relates to me. You know that I had won a cello competition, not a major one, but it got me a recital at Town Hall. I was lucky, I got a wonderful review in the *New York Times*, did you see it?"

"No, congratulations, I must have missed it."

"Anyway, this prompted some offers for concerts and a small tour, but I had had enough. The stress, the pressure, was, is, too much for me. I can't take it. It actually makes me physically ill. I just want to hide in an orchestra or a small chamber group and not have everyone's attention focused on me. But, of course, I didn't tell Guido about these offers. If he'd known he would have killed me."

"How did your husband react?"

Aviva twisted her lips and nodded; her expression fused sarcasm and scorn.

"That's what I wanted to tell you . . . The Arab said cruelly, How many times you . . . and he used a vulgar word . . . the critic. Everybody knows in Hollywood how you become a star. And this is still him speaking, I'm quoting: First you must to . . . bleep . . . with the casting director. Same in music world. First, you spread your legs for cello, then for conductor, then you must to spread your legs for critic . . . That was his reaction to my little moment of musical glory."

I had felt sorry for Aviva all along. For her untenable situation with Guido. For her messy marriage. For her love/hate affair with her cello and her musical career. But her last remarks clobbered me in the solar plexus and twanged my heartstrings at once. It just wasn't fair—on many scores. First, obviously, to be beaten. And secondly, good-looking women weren't supposed to be losers. Pretty, talented women were supposed to ride to the top. They get successful husbands with roving eyes, big houses, large cars, small-numbered license plates. Light-skinned Carib housemaids. Pampered fingers decked with rings. The works. Isn't it common knowledge that talented beauties ride high in the saddle? And that the losers were the sad sacks (see news photos in papers and magazines), plain and ugly, thin or dumpy. The rejects of the world. But the pretty, the sexy, the desirable, the talented (all of which Aviva) usually made it. But not this one. This one had bounced from misery to deprivation (sex and love) to a shaky plateau (a love that didn't, couldn't last) and finally, out of desperation, back to misery again (her twice-seven year marriage). She would delude herself that misery would fade tomorrow. Procrastination was her malaise. Promises her salve. And now the beatings were revealed. It made me miserable too. It touched me to the quick. The Arab beat his wife, beat his kids. I could just imagine this chunky, darkly handsome, solidly built Moroccan (I'd seen plenty of them in New York) with lots of muscle and energy wanting an American girl for the green card he needed, charming a vulnerable and hungry Aviva. At probably 5'7" he was just about her height but three times as strong. During the rare moments he was at peace or in a good mood he was solicitous, even winning, but when in a foul funk or in a rage he would swing mercilessly at a one-hundred-fifteen-pound woman who was not only physically defenseless but, even more, psychologically naked. Physically, she may have stood on two spindly legs—she had thin, fawn-like legs, not particularly womanly or shapely—but they were two legs nevertheless. Psychologically, she stood on one. Maybe less than one.

"Do you think his mistreatment, plus my aversion for him, which built up over the years—you know, in their North African culture, almost totally Arab behavior, by them hitting a wife is like, I don't know, like having Turkish coffee in the morning. It's perfectly normal."

"So I've heard." I said. "But you didn't finish your question." In a minute I realized why.

"Do you think treatment like that, plus my negative feeling for him, can, you know, during relations, suppress . . . ?"

Her eyes widened a moment, then she looked down.

"Well," I said, "we might as well be direct about it, you mean suppress an orgasm?"

"Yes . . ." Tears formed in Aviva's eternally young eyes.♥ She opened her pocketbook.

I must confess, I must admit. Aviva touched me. I got up, pretended to consult a book on my desk, ostensibly to give her an opportunity to dab at her eyes, but really finding myself also in pain.

♥See ABC Directory, *Eyes, killing them.*

"Do you know what it's like *not* to have one? For years with the Arab. This constant riding up to a certain point but unable to get over the top?"

"No, I don't," I said.

"So you always . . ." and she wagged her finger in a little lasso motion to complete the thought.

"Are you talking from the woman's point of view?"

"Well, yes, from the woman's . . . I'm sorry for the personal turn . . ."

"It's okay." It really was. I welcomed the personal turn. I loved the gavotte, the minuet, the entire dance of this personal turn.

"From the women you've been with."

"Well, the truth is, I've never been with one who hasn't had one."

Aviva looked surprised. Maybe even envious. "Never?"

"Never. Should I sing the line from *Pinafore* and say, "Well, hardly ever!"?"

She laughed. "Lucky them . . ."

"And with Guido?"

"Oh, that's another story." She smiled appreciatively, then frowned. "He goes away so often. And often stays away a long time."

Was that an invitation? Objectively, it sounded ambiguous, evasive. But if I looked at it subjectively, that's about as clear an invitation as it could possibly be. Did my last remark stir her? Or did these few days, these compressed hours, days, of talking stir her? Her remarks stirred *me*.

Had she ceased looking at me as a counselor and begun looking at me as a man? What was I to do now? Ask her for a walk? And should she refuse me, I'd be shattered. I'd be neither counselor nor possible male friend. I should have said, It's a common problem. Many women, I should have said, don't have them. But words that are said are hard to unsay. Guido was a dream for her, but an impossible dream. The inevitability factor was approaching with the inevitability of darkness or old age.

She looked at her watch.

"I think I should start paying you," she said in a businesslike manner. "It's time. Or else you should start taking lessons."

I confess that hurt me. It dropped me from that rise of intimacy with her that I'd deluded myself into believing. But on the other hand, maybe she wanted me to come to her house.

At the door she turned, stopped. "I always suspected that he was doing the very things that he was accusing me of."

"Who? Guido or the Arab?"

"The Arab. Once, I brought his pants to the cleaners and, like I usually do, I emptied the pockets. I found two betting stubs and two tickets from Belmont Raceway. Not one, but two. He never told me he went out there, and I realized that's where he used to go on Saturday afternoons after shul;

I assumed that he went to New York to his business. He ran a cash business and who really knew what he earned or spent. He complained about me giving the kids lamb chops, yet he bet on horses. He probably had accounts I knew nothing about. And running around with women for all I knew— but I couldn't care less. I didn't consider the Arab my husband any more think about taking lessons okay?"

12

Aviva began talking even before she sat down. By now, late fall, early winter, the sun had moved. No longer did it shine right on her like a spotlight as she sat on the left side of the sofa. And I was working harder than ever. My Israeli colleague further delayed his return because of family health problems, and I was juggling his practice and mine. To tell the truth, I didn't mind. It was more convenient for Aviva to come to the Long Island office than to come to New York.

She started at the point she left off the previous time, as if only moments had elapsed.

"On the other hand, I couldn't call Guido my husband either. I didn't have the right, though I wanted him more than anyone else on earth. I'd never really wanted anyone before. He was the one I wanted, dreamt of, since I was a teenager, yet he wasn't mine. He had someone else. A wife. A gloomy, sorrow-ridden wife who drove away the pain of having a retarded child—oops, I shouldn't of said that either—by working like crazy and spending free time with the boy, which added to her gloom. So it's his wife again. Every time I think about her, his wife I mean, a little jolt of depression hits me. If only she weren't there, my life would really be a miracle. I call Guido a miracle. My meeting with him. It is a miracle, don't you think? Like Guido says, waiting years for love and finally finding it. The Italians have a saying, he says, you roam the world for what you want and find it in your yard.

"I'm sure she's a very nice lady, and I told Guido that. I can't imagine a guy like Guido not marrying a nice lady. But she's in my way. I have to share him with her, and I don't want to share him. Once she flew to Chicago for a few days to some kind of flower show convention. Well, you know what I thought? It's awful, the thought that flew—do you think the pun is accidental?—through my mind."

"I'm not a Freudian," I said.

"First comes adultery, then murder. A wish for a quick, painless death. The plane should disappear into a pink cloud and make Guido mine. That's terrible, isn't it? Hello? Are you there? Isn't it terrible, my fantasy?"

"Do you want a theological or a psychological response?"

"Dammit, stop being so professional and be a little personal."

I was taken aback. I grimaced for her to see. Just because she wasn't paying me did she have the right to be impudent?

"Well, it is a natural wish, but of course if it really happened, aside from the other one hundred ninety-nine innocent victims, you'd probably eat your heart out with guilt."

Aviva nodded slowly. "I'm caught in a classic no-win situation. I have Guido. He has her. So how can I really have him? I try to imagine when I'm with him that he's all mine, and for a while I succeed in blocking her out. But then in conversation with Guido it's always *we*. Well, not always. Sometimes he says I and sometimes he even cleverly drops the pronoun. Like: Went to a concert the other night. When I hear that my magic world crumbles. Another accidental, or not so accidental, pun. Crumbles. That's what I'm left with. Crumbs. He has the cake. On both sides of the table. And me, on the floor, I get the crumbs. I can't sleep. I get a knot in my stomach, a pain that won't go away for hours. I play the cello and as I hold it I embrace Guido, who doesn't leave my thoughts for a moment, imagine, not for a moment during the day. Why do I get so depressed, it's not normal?

"Whenever I come, he says: You are recreated for me each time I see you. Or maybe he said: reincarnated. Last time he said this I took a sudden deep breath and sighed. He noticed. I threw my arms around him and kissed him. For me you are gerontic,♥ senescent, he said, which means, he said, you smell good. Do you really love me? I ask. He said: As soon as you go, your image comes into my mind, and I hear you whisper Yes, yes, yes, now now. And as soon as I wake up, you slide into my head and you don't leave me until I fall asleep and then I start to dream about you. Me too, I told him. Everything I say and do is in relation to you. You're my guide. I wonder what will you think about this or that. Will you like the bra I bought, the new piece I'm studying, the earrings I bought at a craft shop? He said he dreams about me too but that his dreams are often ambiguous. He's not sure that I'll come back to see him, and that's why each time I come back and buzz the intercom to tell him I'm there, I'm created anew for him."

Intercom? I thought. In a private house? But perhaps she's just saying that to disguise where he lives.

"Do you believe him?" I asked.

"Yes." She paused. "Yes and no . . . There were lots of times I didn't believe him and he was furious with me. It just destroyed him. He collapsed—fell to the floor as if in a faint—when I said I didn't believe him. Now you know why I'm always depressed. It's not normal, right?"

I pressed my index finger to the edge of my lips. The classic thinking pose. To make Aviva believe that I was thinking, evaluating her problem.

♥See ABC Directory, *Gerontic*.

But I wasn't thinking about her. That is, I *was* thinking about her, but not in relation to Guido. I was thinking: I wish someone would think about me day and night. I wish someone would have me in their gut, heart, soul, mind, body like Aviva has Guido dybbuked into her. I wish someone would think about me like I'm beginning to think about Aviva, looking forward to Wednesday morning sessions with her, trying to compress the Wednesday through Tuesday in my mind, crumpling it like a huge piece of paper into a ball. I too deserve some happiness after floundering so many years. Well, don't I? Hello? Say something!

But it wasn't my thoughts that I heard. It was Aviva saying:

"I too deserve some happiness after floundering so many years. Well, don't I? Hello? Say something!"

"I'm sure you do. Of course you do."

"Do you think he'll leave his wife for me?"

"Did you ask him?"

"No. I wouldn't dare."

"Dare. You know him long enough."

"No. I won't do it. That's the way I am. The most I ever say to him is: Are we going to be together?"

"And what does he say?"

"Yes. He says yes, it's destined. But you didn't answer my question. Will he?"

"Do you want him to?"

"Another Jewish question for a question? Yes, I do. But will he?"

"I don't know him, so it's hard to say . . . But from what you've told me . . ." I stopped. The word *inevitability* popped into my head. Use it, I counseled myself, use it. "From what you've told me, given the circumstances of his family life, I doubt it. There is a certain inevitability here. Best you can get is the sharing he offered you. At least, that's what I think. You yourself said that he said, Better half of me than none. And didn't you once say you'd gotten used to the situation?"

"I did. But not for long. I changed my mind. It's not enough. I can't live this way. It's not enough for me. Now I want everything."

"Or nothing," I coaxed her.

"Right. Or nothing. I can't live like this any longer. It's killing me. I once asked him if he would look at another woman once we're together. He said, No. But I'm not so sure. I wouldn't want done to me what he's doing to his wife. And if he does that to her, maybe he'll do it too me to."

I nodded emphatically. "It's quite possible. People hardly ever change. There's an inevitability there too."

And perhaps Guido had done this to his wife before he even met Aviva, and maybe he's even two-timing *her*. How do I know? Pam told me. She told me that one day Ava dropped in on Guido—a fact which Guido had once mentioned en passant without elaborating. Ava's purpose was to see if she could still attract him, seduce him, and as Pam heard it from Ava, she did. Which proved what? That Guido was still a skirtchaser? That he had pity on his former wife? That he had no scruples? Or that Ava was a liar? After all, the story was told from her perspective.

"Do you miss him when he goes away?"

Aviva nodded as if answering a question she had asked herself.

"You know, that's a good question. It's interesting, I often enjoy missing Guido more than when I'm with him. Because when I'm with him I feel like garbage when I leave him. When I don't see him, I experience him mentally and spiritually, which doesn't cause me inner turmoil and depression. You know, before I was married, I had a boyfriend who would read poetry to me over the phone, and I'd be more stirred up than when I was with him."

"The aloneness syndrome," I said, gloating, feeling that inch by inch I'm moving forward. "It seems to me that, judging by your reactions to him, a breakup is inevitable."

Inevitable-shmevitable! I still never knew (unless she explicitly told me that he was away) if she came to me directly after being screwed by Guido.

I closed my eyes.

"Hello?" she said softly.

"Excuse me, are you okay?" she said again.

Then she tapped my hand.

"Yes," I said through closed eyes. "I'm awake, Shh! I'm thinking . . . putting myself into your soul. Into your shoes. I'm filtering all your feelings into me . . . You're right. Even though you love deeply, I can feel how painful, disorienting, depressing it is to keep coming into someone else's house. To have to leave at a certain time. Never to stay over. Limited to certain hours and days. Never able to call when you want. To be startled at every sound in the house. I can feel how it hurts to have to live like that. One wonders if the joy really outweighs the pain and frustration."

"Exactly," she said. "You do put yourself into my shoes. That's precisely the way I feel. Now why can't Guido understand that? He's never been able to picture my situation . . . No, that's not true. Once, about six months ago, he told me that one evening he exchanged souls with me and felt my depression and couldn't sleep all night."

She paused. Her jowls drooped. Her mouth was slack. She looked old again. "It's wrong, isn't it? All of this is just *wrong*, right?"

"On whose part? Does it *feel* wrong for *you* doing this constantly? Or do you mean it's wrong on his part to insist that you keep loving him and coming to him under these circumstances?"

"What would you do if you were I?"

"Me."

"Yes, that's what I mean."

"No. I'm just correcting the grammar. What would you do if you were *me*? Let me think."

And I really had to think. I had to remove myself from myself and from my history. But how could a human being do that? Could I erase the past and the subtle tensions, the chess game that had developed over the years between Guido and myself? And what kind of ethics was it, if my suggestion, advice, whatever, to the impressionable and thirsty-for-guidance and even more thirsty-for-love Aviva—Aviva hungering like a little lamb waiting to be cuddled, hungering for love that was true, free, unencumbered, open in every way—was based upon my feelings? Feelings that had been building over the weeks that I got to know her. And what kind of ethics and morality guidepost to my behavior was I using if Guido had no ethics or morality to his wife and maybe even to Aviva and Aviva was committing adultery against her husband? I replayed the last thought and saw how muddled was my inner speech. I couldn't think straight any more. Would she do the same for me—now?—if I were to make the right move? If now, *now*, I would stand and take her in my arms and kiss those naturally red, generous lips, would she too, once I had caressed her, would she say to me, Are we going to make love? Those magic words that Guido had been lucky enough to hear?

I watched her as she spoke. It was years since I'd savored that sexual chemistry and glow that a woman subtly sends off. And Aviva emitted it. I could have taken that essence and filled perfume bottles with it. That sexual radiance, that eternal femaleness poured out of her with every gesture, every smile, every time she changed position. Her very shyness invoked sensuality. And I had to listen to how she loved Guido and how Guido loved her.

How much spiritual flailing can one human being take? But yet, I swear, Aviva wasn't sexy. Now I understood her own observation that she wasn't sexy. She didn't have cliché TV or movie or center-fold sexiness which sixteen-year-olds learn. She didn't throw her body or hair around. She did it with words, smiles, and eyes that devastated you.

But it was time to answer. Aviva's silence demanded answer.

"All I can think of is that powerful word you once used and which I've echoed a number of times today. Inevitability. You said it was inevitable that you break up."

"So that's what you would do."

I spoke slowly. I made a dam to hold back the torrent of words.

"It's always difficult to make decisions for another person. But I think, yes, yes, that's what I would feel. Inevitability. It doesn't look hopeful." And I tried to look as commiserating as possible.

"That's exactly the way I feel. I'm glad you see it that way too . . . You know, you're more than a psychologist. You're a good friend. A pal any chance of seeing you on Friday?"

"For you, anytime," I said, and we set an hour. "And . . . oh, yeh . . . by the way, remember you once said you'll show me someday a list of questions he used to ask."

She blinked slowly, in assent. "Fine. I'll bring them Friday."

When she left, a thought flooded my mind like a supernova exploding light. When I was a child I would sometimes lie in bed and think to myself what existed before God made the world. And the vacuum, the emptiness, the void, the not knowing drove me wild. I had nearly the same feeling thinking that Aviva might not come to my office any more. That one day, although she'd said, See you next time, there would be no next time because she'd changed her mind, conquered by whim and caprice. And I would never see her again.

Aviva's Dream

This dream is absolutely the most disjointed one I've had. I dream I'm about 30% fatter and sunbathing outside with a bra on. Guido tells me not to. In the house, lots of students are milling around. All of them have cellos, which are also about 30% fatter. Guido picks up one of these cellos, then drops it. He tells me he's leaving. Come see me later, he says, but I say no. Then I see a woman taking books from the house without permission. I see this entire dream projected onto the ceiling as if from an overhead projector.

Interpretation:

This is perhaps the most difficult dream so far. What is clear is the self-dissatisfaction made manifest by the excessive weight—both you and the instruments are about one-third fatter. You appear inappropriately dressed in public, which annoys Guido, especially since your students are all around. He picks up, then accidentally drops, a cello, whose 30% weight gain is interestingly the same as yours. In dream and symbolic language you and the cello are one. Guido dropping the cello is Guido dropping you. He leaves, perhaps in a huff, and you, similarly disgruntled, refuse to visit him. The women taking books without permission is dream language reversal for taking a woman—you—without permission. And the dream within a dream accents the dream nature of your dream, as if you're very aware that you're dreaming while you're dreaming. There's lots of forbiddenness here. You exposing yourself; the taking of books, or a woman, without permission; the dropping of a musical instrument, which one just doesn't do. The dream shows your fear of being dropped, of looking fat, but you fight it in two ways: one—you say no to a visit to Guido, and two— even in your dream you reassure yourself that it's only a dream.

13

So now only Thursday was empty. Aviva on Wednesday. Aviva on Friday. Frankly, I thought she'd come empty handed and say: I forgot. But, bless her, she showed up with it. Three pages long. Without any preliminaries, she said:

"Here's some of the questions he asked me. Now isn't he crazy? He said he asked because he wanted to recreate in his mind the me from years ago. But the most important reason came to him in the middle of the night. It's as if I wanted to make up for all the years I didn't know you, he said. That really killed me. But lately I've put a stop to it, and he doesn't ask any more."

I was silent. He's got her by the balls, nice and tight, I think to myself. She's caught.

"Guido says it's good for me to talk," Aviva continued. "I get to understand myself better. He's right, isn't he? . . . Hello! Hello? Are you there? . . . Isn't he?"

I snapped out—she snapped me out of it.

"Talking is always good. Better than keeping it in."

"But he doesn't like me to reveal things about us . . . I feel like I'm betraying him."

"People with ego," I said, "usually like privacy and probably would resent other people talking about them."

"You're sharp as a . . . well, whatever the image is. You hit the nail right on the head." And she gave an enchanting smile. "Is that a better image? I know I shouldn't talk. But it's bursting at the seams in me. I must or I'll explode. He has this terrific intuition. One day he told me he had this sudden wave of knowing that I'd spoken about us to my sister, and I blurted out that it wasn't my sister but my music coach."

"I suppose he was angry . . ." I led her on.

"Angry? Furious! He stamped his foot and shouted, I knew it. I knew it. I got the vibes. I knew you spoke and I knew it was to a woman. I just got the person wrong. But I didn't mention your name, I told Guido. He didn't want to listen. You killed it, he said. You promised you wouldn't tell anyone. But it's not anyone we know, I said. Makes no difference. You see! he raged. I knew it. I got the signals. But the reception wasn't clear. Not sister but coach . . . Then he made me swear, made me lift up my right hand and swear that I'd never tell a soul . . . Do you have a soul?" Aviva giggled slyly.

I rolled the next remark over my tongue a while, then decided to chance it.

"And you're breaking your oath." But I smiled as I said it.

She smiled too. That naughty, lovable, almost teasing smile—that full-toothed grin that is shaped to hook you.

"No, I'm not," she said. "I had my left hand behind my back with my fingers crossed when I promised. But the moment I swore, I meant it. I really did. And that's the most important thing."

"Has *he* spoken to anyone?"

"Yes . . . He told me he had to. Just once. Briefly. To a friend from far away. To sort of balance out, he said, me telling my cello coach that I was madly in love with a married man. But for goodness sake, I revealed nothing else."

"And you he forbade to talk!"

"Forbade? Not at all. He just made me swear not to talk . . . The old double standard, right?"

I had the list of questions in my hand all along but avoided looking at it, saving it for last. Now I scanned the questions. Maybe Guido *was* crazy, but I wouldn't have told Aviva that.

"Seems to me he's interested in all aspects of you."

"Mostly sexual."

"Isn't that an aspect?"

"I suppose."

"Secondly, he's trying to penetrate your essence."

She laughed. It was a laugh that bordered on raucousness; it was bawdy, almost licentious.

Aviva read my mind. "I'm too loud, aren't I?"

I didn't comment. The hell with grammar. I looked down at the questions again. It wasn't his handwriting.

Is this his handwriting?"

"No. I sort of reconstructed the list."

My first thought was: perhaps she edited it or emended it, or added questions of her own. Memory is a funny thing. Research has shown that childhood memories can be absolute fantasies. So why not the same for adults?

I admit that looking at her I too would have wanted the answers myself, perhaps asked even more questions. How can one describe the tease, the allure of sexuality that come from the hints, descriptions, adornments around sex, which envelops us like an amoeba its prey? Even credit card ads have a patina of sexuality with a purring-voiced woman flirting under the restaurant table using her throaty sex laugh, come-on voice with a guy from the next table she doesn't know who is helping her look for dropped change. All you think of when you hear that ad is running out not for a credit card application but zooming out to make it with her under the table before she dives under another table with another guy. It reminded me of a patient I once had, a woman whose husband had run off with another woman. Or another man. I forget which. In any case, this wasn't your usual husband-leaving wife scenario. There was a fascinating twist. The wife herself had triggered it. How? For years she had worked in a lingerie shop and would always come home from work and tell her mild-mannered wimpo about the luscious women with the big boobs who had come into the store. One day she raved about a mid-thirties beauty. "You've never see perfect boobs like this one . . . She had everyone google-eyed. Even Mr. Martin, the boss, came out from the office to ogle. She was a naïve one, I think she came from Poland, and Mr. Martin said he would personally supervise the measurements in the dressing room." Finally, the husband couldn't take this teasing any more. Something popped in him. He was in the insurance business and, pretending to work on a claim audit, called Mr. Martin and got the woman's address. The name of her town he'd gotten from his wife the day before. She said she came all the way from Queens to the Bare It All Lingerie Boutique. He called and started seeing her. Why do I bring this up? Because here too the list was an element of tease, and Aviva herself is the wife in the story (or maybe the naïve woman with the perfect boobs). Aviva herself with her combination of shyness and frankness began casting a net of allure over me, so I, poor fish, I was no longer an objective observer.

I looked at some of the questions and read aloud:

"If you saw someone on the street would you take him to bed in your thoughts? . . . Did you ever think of yourself as a nympho just because you had three affairs? . . . Are there different types of desire?"

"This one I answered," she said. "I told him there are different types of attraction but not desire. Desire is desire . . . The biological longing is the same. But frequency may change level of desire."

I nodded. "You could write a book."

"Or a diary," she laughed. "The *Diary of an Adulterous Woman*."

I continued. "Are bookish people less interested in sex?"

"I liked that question. I told him that even though I know it's nonsense, an idea has taken root that people who are bookish are indeed less interested in sex."

"It *is* nonsense," I said, "because it's a well-known fact that even books copulate. You should see the rare book room at night . . ."

Aviva laughed. "He also asked me if I ever had sex fantasies during marriage?"

"Well, did you?"

"Not of a real man. An abstract one, only during screwing. I certainly didn't picture the Arab. I thought of what color to do the bathroom."

"You must know the joke about the Jewish woman."

She shook her head, but her eyes glinted in anticipation.

"How do you know when a Jewish woman has had an orgasm?"

Aviva shrugged.

"She drops her nail file."

Aviva laughed, but I could see she was puzzling over the mechanics of it.

"And Guido also asked me if I ever used a vibrator. I told him, you should have seen our electric bill."

"Would you screw me every day if we were together? . . . This is Guido talking, not me," I said, feeling the color rising to my face.

"I told him that desire is irregular. Like music, sometimes it's high-pitched, sometimes low."

I read aloud from Guido's—or her—list.

"When did such and such an affair begin? When did it end? Did the guys assume you had protection? Did they ask you if you were on the pill? Did you ever go to bed with someone because you felt sorry for him or because you thought he wanted it so much? . . . Well, did you?"

She smiled. "What am I, crazy? A martyr? A saint? You got to be kidding . . ." Then she added, "Yes, sometimes."

"That means you had more than three affairs . . ."

Aviva shook her head. "I meant, once I was already with the guy. And he also asked me if I went to a singles weekend and if I slept with someone the first night and what thoughts went through my mind when I made love, questions like that. I could give you another list."

"Please," I said.

"You're holding it," she gave out a merry, deep-throated shriek.

I looked at her. How right Guido was. She *is* lovable. Maybe she doesn't do it purposely. But she radiated a kind of passive force that made men want to touch her, hold her, want her. They put their doggy noses in the air and sniffed; their male sense told them: an available woman.

What kind of charm did this woman possess, I wondered, that made men fall in love or lust for her? Was it that smile? Those big, gray, sloe eyes, innocent as fawns, timid as doves? That puckish, irrepressible sense of humor with its occasional patina of libido?

Or was it that helplessness that she exuded? Help me, help me! cried the rabbit.

For she didn't send sex signals, at least as far I could see. In fact, she was restrained in her body motions. She'd once told me that when Guido had commented on her lovely fawn legs, she said she walked like a duck. I wouldn't quite say that, but there was a certain restraint in her tush-out walk. She didn't wiggle, didn't stick out her breasts. Still, sex seemed to flow out of her. I don't doubt that many men who saw her, despite the plug that she put on her sexuality, still undressed her quickly in their minds.

"I was never sexy," she said, reading my mind. "I never thought of myself as sexy."

"Still, men couldn't keep their hands off you. You must have something that says, touch me, kiss me, screw me."

Aviva smiled. It was a sad kind of smile. "When Guido and I first became intimate, he told me: You know, when I looked at you, your face, your being, your entire essence didn't say screw me. It said: Love me."

I bit my lip and nodded. For a moment there was nothing to say. Aviva had stopped talking. She sat holding her bag, a kind of astonished look on her face. Expectant. As if waiting for me to say or do something. Her nose twitched. And all I could think of saying was what my doctor had told me a week before.

"I went to my doctor a week ago for something, a cold, a cough. He's a talkative chap, always reminiscing about his days in med school. He said, 'Men go through three stages. At twenty all they think about is sex . . . At forty . . .' And I couldn't hear what he said next, for the sex part still reverberated in me, and then he continued, 'and at sixty, all they think about is a good bowel movement.' So I told him that I'm still stuck in the twenty-year-old category because I don't think about anything else."

"Really?" Aviva said admiringly. The anecdote had made her perk up. That little sadness, that touch of age on her face vanished, and she was an alert, vital young woman gain. "Is that what you really told him, or what you wished you'd told him."

"I swear! That's exactly what I said."

"You're sure your left fingers weren't crossed behind your back?"

I wanted to try to deflect her from talking about Guido. But maybe by talking she was getting him out of her system, so there would be room for me. But before I could change the subject, she was at it again:

"Once as he lay stretched out next to me he kept saying: Do I love you! Do I love you! Do I love you! He repeated this maybe a dozen times. I didn't say anything. I was in my withdrawing, my distancing mood. Finally, he said, Well, answer me! And I burst out laughing. I loved that comic switch from confession to mock question. That Answer me!—are you following?—deflated his declaration of love into a silly question."

I wasn't about to analyze Guido's cleverness. What concerned me was, "Why, if you were in a distancing mood, why were you stretched out next to him?"

"Guido was a nudnick. He wouldn't let go. I had made up my mind several times to stop, to say good-bye once and for all and then I backtrack. Why do I keep doing this?" she asked. "Saying I'm leaving him, that's it, no more! And then letting him convince me, one more time, an extension, a new plan. Just the other day he promised me he'll divorce his kid and put his wife up for adoption."

I stared at her. "Did you hear what you just said?"

"Yes. I said he's going to divorce his wife and put his kid up for adoption."

"That's not what you said. You reversed it. He'd divorce his kid and put his wife up for adoption."

She covered her mouth and laughed. "Is that what I said? That's hilarious. See how confused I am? Everything is mixed up. I always thought that life with him was like music. A perpetual Vivaldi cello sonata. But now it's dissonance. Jarring music. It's like that Venetian saying he once quoted to me: Happiness is a soap bubble. The bubble bursts and you get soap in the eye. That's what I've got. And knots in my stomach too."

"But if you had been adamant, you could have resisted. You know . . ." then I stopped. Should I tell her this? I thought, then decided—yes. "One of Picasso's friends once wrote about him. Picasso loves passionately, but he kills what he loves . . . You get the picture? It's like too much chocolate can make you sick. That's why I say, you could have resisted. How do you know you'll be able to resist his importuning next time?"

"I will . . ." she said, hesitated. "What does *importuning* mean?"

I told her. "Was it solely his nudnistry, his power of convincing, that made you do that? I presume you kissed and so on . . ."

Aviva shook her head as if berating herself. "He even told me to wear skirts, not slacks during our so-called friendly, platonic period . . . Yes, he felt—and he told me so—so at home with me, as if I were his. He always told me he couldn't stop kissing me."

"And could you?"

"I suppose . . . But once he started it was hard to resist. Guido had a tremendous energy. I envied his drive. He kissed my fingers, wrists, elbows, the insides of my hands."♥ She closed her eyes for a moment, as if savoring a remembered ecstasy. Her left eye, the one that floated ever so slightly away from the bridge of her nose, picked up speed as the eyelids shut out the light. It was a gentle closing, feathered with a smile. "No wonder I was crazy for him, right?"

"Right," I said, but I no longer knew what I was saying. I was crazy too, listening to this blow-by-blow. *I* was nuts. Loony. Demented. Off the wall. Ready for apoplexy. So I tuned out. Why was she doing this? Was she really naïve? Did some segment of her babyness still remain, and did she really have no concept what a narration like this could do to a man, even if he was a professional? Or was she calculating? Was it overt, unabashed signals that shy Aviva was sending me, giving me a game plan for the very things I could—indeed, should—do to make her feel good? The modern woman's message to the cloistered counselor.

Again a force within me told to change the subject. But it came out as: "You mentioned a diary before. Did you ever consider keeping a diary of your love life?"

"It couldn't fill a tiny address book. But I'll tell you who could have. One of my neighbors in Queens where my parents lived could have. What

♥See ABC Directory, *God's creation*.

a sexy apartment! She had a constant stream of visitors. Maybe she was even in business. Her diary would've been a sizzler. That's the authentic *Diary of an Adulterous Woman*."

"Well, you could write one like that too."

"With that title?"

"Well, you've mentioned it twice so I guess it's yours. But it's up to you. Author has first rights to choice of title."

Aviva looked serious. When she looked serious the lines on her face settled in. A wrinkle appeared above the lip. Even the squint lost its panache. Aviva serious was no beauty. It was only when she smiled, looked mischievous, that she looked smashing.

"Well, I guess I am an adulteress. Technically." And she burst into a merry laugh. "Maybe I should dig up that old orange dress my mother made me years ago, embroidered with a big *A*. Technically an adulteress, yes. But not morally. Oh, no. Morally, I don't. For I don't consider myself married. And since I don't consider the Arab my husband, I'm neither deceiving nor betraying him."

She looked down, then up at me. "But I have kept a little diary mostly recording the differences I've had with my husband over the years."

"Well hidden I hope."

"Among my old cello scores." She laughed. "He'd never look there."

I noticed that no matter what I said to her she didn't react. Call her an adulteress, she took it with equanimity. It melded with her old assessment of herself: when people said something to her, she thought perhaps they were right and it was not appropriate to be indignant.

And she continued talking . . .

No, no, I thought. Stop. At first I wanted to ask her loads of questions, yes, to penetrate her essence, but then I thought, Stop. I don't want to hear any more. You're mine, I thought. You're at the peak of ripeness. You glow. You're going to be the mother of my child. Mine. No one else's. Don't tell me any more. And as I thought thus, I blocked out what she was saying and missed what she said. What kind of psychologist am I, becoming so involved? I'm a fraud, I'm afraid, not a Freud, not a psychologist, taking a liking to—No, not a liking. Obsessed. In love. Yes. I admit. Moonstruck.

Smitten.

Loony in love.

On the other hand, I thought, according to the Ethics Committee of the American Psychologists Association, becoming involved socially with a patient is a violation of professional ethics and standards. But on the third hand, when it comes to live-saving or life-threatening situations, ethics goes out the window. And someone's life *is* at stake.

Mine.

I remembered a survey that showed 10–20% of therapists did become involved socially and sexually with former patients. With current patients they didn't even mention. And to be absolutely meticulous about the facts, Aviva was definitely not a patient. She'd come for advice, to chat, to talk things over. I never even filled out a chart for her. Never took a penny from her. It was I, in fact, who had sought her out in an attempt to confirm Guido's story. Also curiosity. That couldn't be denied. So she really couldn't be considered a patient, and hence ethics considerations were moot. That was my judicious, objective judgment.

In fact, the survey showed that more than half the therapists became friends with former patients. So even if Aviva were a patient, I could declare the sessions ended, go out with her, and not be any different than a majority of my colleagues. In fact, the report showed (assuming interviewees were honest) that 75% of them had hugged their patients, 83% of them had been sexually attracted to them, and nearly 30% had kissed them. And if that high a number admitted, think of those that did it but didn't admit.

But only 11% had become sexually involved. That means that 20% of those who kissed patients weren't attractive enough to the patients to have sex. That's a bad sign. It showed how sexless were my colleagues. (Or perhaps the patients?) The sexlessness of my colleagues was especially brought home if 75% of them hugged a patient. And if only 30% of them kissed that also meant a rejection factor of about two out of three. After hugging, they couldn't even get to first base.

Shmucks!

I looked at Aviva. She was downcast. She looked so sad. Was it Poe who said there was nothing more beautiful than a pretty woman in tears? But for Aviva this seemed now to be a permanent state. If I was twinning with Guido then she was becoming a morose Tammy.

"You're not happy," I told her.

"I don't even know what that sensation feels like any more . . . I thought I was happy when I was with Guido but—" and she trailed off and blinked. To suppress tears? "When I was younger I had a friend who married young, and she told me that every day when she wakes up, happiness comes over her and she thanks God for her husband. I wondered if that would ever happen to me." Aviva smiled sadly. "Now I wake up every day and say, Why? How? How did I get into this? What have I done wrong to be so unhappy? There was a time when I could and did say to Guido: The only happy spark in my life is you. When I'm with you I'm happy. When I think of you I'm happy. You're the best thing that ever happened to me. But I can't say that any more. I always dreamt that happiness would come to me. But it never did."

It will with me, I thought. When I have you, you'll wake up with me every morning and you'll be happy.

Then the remark burst out of me. I didn't think. If I'd have thought I never would have said it. I never would've had the nerve to say: "Are you happy with me?"

Aviva didn't flinch. "I enjoy talking to you," she said diplomatically.

I dreamt, I wished, I dream-predicted she'd say something else.

"Even unhappiness takes time to sink in. It takes me a long time to realize something is wrong. I sweep it under the rug. When you lack courage to make a decision, you have to make a much harder one later on."

These words cheered me a bit.

"Would you like to come Monday morning?" I said. "Are you free?"

This time she didn't even look into her pocketbook.

"Sure . . . At nine-thirty?"

"Super," I said.

14

On Monday Aviva came in, sat down, looked shyly at me and then down at her lap.

"When I was about twelve or thirteen, I was called *di sheyne malka*, the beautiful queen in Yiddish, by a favorite aunt, because of the way I held myself . . ."

"Sheyne malka, huh? Unbelievable. I sensed deep down that there might be links between us. That's what *my* grandmother was called. Is your aunt in her seventies, good looking, nice features, high cheekbones, high color?"

"Yes."

That gave me the excuse I needed. I jumped up, embraced her, and kissed her cheek.

"Tante Aviva," I said. "Your aunt is my grandmother. That means you're *my* aunt."

She laughed. "I was only fooling."

"So was I," I said. "I had no grandmother. All my great-grandparents were childless."

Aviva stretched her legs out, went into hysterical laughter, and drummed her feet on the floor a dozen times. "You're too much."

"No joke," I said. "That's what my grandmother was called. Sheyne Malka. And because of that she came to America."

"On account of that name?"

"Yup. Wanna hear the story?"

"Sure."

I looked at my watch. There was time. I had the next hour free. "This isn't on your time," I said. As if I would collect from her anyway! "Once, in the old country, when my grandmother was fifteen, a letter came into the shtetl addressed to Sheyne Malka. The semi-literate postman, knowing that my grandmother was called by that name, made no further inquiries but gave the letter to her. In it was a $14 ticket for a ship passage to America. The family didn't know who sent it but decided not to miss the opportunity. She sailed, arrived in New York, and reported to the unknown benefactor who had sent her the ticket. He took one look at her and said, 'My God, you're not the one!' But he was nice and fixed her up with a job. The only condition was that she had to save up enough money to buy a ticket for the real Sheyne Malka, which she soon did."

"Did she ever meet the other woman?"

"I asked her the same question when she told me the story. The answer: yes."

That kiss on the cheek reverberated in me. It trembled on my skin. Not so much the kiss itself as the little intimacy, friendliness, of me going to embrace and kiss her. I'd crossed, if only for a moment, a little invisible border. Guido giving her the Stockholm photo.

I recorded in my mind the way she lifted her chin to accept my kiss. Like a baby. A child. Here was a woman who gave off an aura of purity, of innocence. Even her naïveté, her lack of self-confidence, her unsureness about things pointed to that innocence.

I didn't want any more casual affairs. I sensed her affair with Guido was winding down. At least she wanted it to. It *was* inevitable that it would end. She herself had uttered the fateful word, and I had heard it. After meeting her I was ready. She would be the mother to our child. At thirty-eight or so, with two adolescent kids, she had married not too long after college and hadn't run around very much. More sinned against than sinning.

I wondered if Aviva realized that she'd never called me by name. Never. And I'd never called her Aviva.

"You're not gay, are you?" she once asked me.

How shall I prove to her that I wasn't? Tell her me and Guido had screwed the same girls? Except one?

"Not gay. Happy. But shy."

"Shy," she said. "That's why straight guys don't marry. Me too. That's why I was so aloof. As a protective coating. That's why I too never really married. I married but I wasn't *married*, if you know what I mean. But you, what about you, come on, answer a question for a change. How come you're not married?"

"Good question." I felt like lying down on my back on a sofa and having Aviva behind me, prodding my memory. "I figured, what's the sense of it? You marry and after a while another man will come along and take your wife away or she'd willingly give herself to another man for the fun of it, either because she's bored, or angry, or experimenting, or wants to be in fashion. Almost 75% of married American women screw around nowadays after five years of marriage . . . Or maybe *I* would get tired after three or four years, who knows? In fact . . ." and then I ran out of words.

"But the real truth is?" Aviva said with an upbeat flourish, waiting for me to fill in the blank.

I curled my lower lip out and nodded. As if to say, Aviva, psychologist, clairvoyant, lip reader, mind reader, ESPnik extraordinaire, bingo, you hit it right on the head.

"The real truth is," you tea-leaf-reading seductive gypsy, the real truth is I've waited for you, "that I hadn't met anyone I wanted to spend the rest of my life with."

And I wondered if she got the significance of that pluperfect usage. I didn't say "never"—I said "hadn't." Up to just recently I hadn't met a woman I could love.

"I often wondered," I told her, "how people could stay married for *twenty, thirty* years. Together with the same human being for so many decades? Letting a perfect stranger into the house with you for a quarter of a century or more? And people actually celebrate these milestones! I wouldn't celebrate. I'd sit down on a low stool, take off my leather shoes, and cover the mirrors with sheets. And you sometimes even hear of people getting testimonial dinners for being married fifty, sixty, even seventy-five years. I hear that I cringe. Instead of being honored, they should be, well, not actually shot, but at least put in the pillory. What jerks! Listening to snores for a century? If I had my way, marriages would last maximum ten, fifteen years."

"That's more than enough," Aviva laughed. "In fact, fourteen is tops. And I suppose you speak from vast experience."

I let the sarcasm pass. After all, I'd told her that not every remark need be answered.

"And I have a theory about children too. Children should be born serrated down the middle like those paper pads kids use in college so that they can be evenly divided when the parents separate."

"I suppose you're a great expert on children too," she said, but this time she wasn't laughing. "Are you . . . well, let me rephrase this. I read recently that many people go into counseling because they themselves are troubled, even disturbed . . . Are *you* troubled in any way?"

"Hey, wait a minute. Turning the tables on me?"

"Uh-huh . . . Well, are you?"

This came as a surprise. Shall I say that my mouth fell open? Never, never, never before had a patient asked me that question. I was totally unprepared for this role reversal, for this intimate probing of my being. Was I troubled? Of course. Would I tell her? Of course not. A feeling of discomfort, a nagging pain in my gut that spread up to my throat and constricted it—it was a kind of fear, anxiety, I guess, a trapped animal sensing death—I didn't want to confess to her.

"No, not in any special way. No, I can't say I am." But the voice that spoke I didn't recognize. The only thing that really troubled me was the existence of this lovely woman, so close to me and separated by a partition called Guido.

"One more question. When do you want to begin cello lessons?"

Well, at least that one was a relief. Still I stalled her by saying, "I'm still looking for a cello." I really didn't want cello lessons. I had no intentions of riding out to the North Shore for lessons. The cello was Guido's forte. Mine was singing in tunnels or humming string quartets. So I kept putting her off.

But she said, "Nonsense. I have another cello. Always do, for students rarely lug their own."

"It's okay. I've been busy with two practices. And I'll need one at home to practice on. I'll let you know."

"Because I'm feeling uncomfortable having these sessions with you and giving nothing in return."

On my lips was the phrase, You've given me a lot already.

"Don't worry about it, please," I said. "My pleasure." Without wanting to I echoed her phrase to Guido when he once thanked her for her wonderful lessons.

Aviva looked more relaxed today than she had in a long time. Even the way she sat was relaxed. As I looked at her she laughed suddenly.

"I once went to a boring family party in Great Neck and remembered I had a friend who lived in town. So I called her. She looks like she could step out of the pages of *Vogue* magazine. Slim, beautiful, flaming long red hair."

"How old?" I asked with exaggerated crispness to make it sound professional.

"Late thirties." And she shook her head as if recalling something absurd. "She showed me a huge Picasso etching that her husband had given her as a birthday gift, but I sensed something wrong. Her eyes looked lifeless. The eyes on the etching had more life than hers . . . Within five minutes she told me everything."

"How long hadn't you seen her?"

"Five or six years."

"And within five minutes—all her problems?"

"All . . . In fact, I asked her, why tell me? Because, she said, I know you so well . . . You see, she has no children. She wanted them but her husband never wanted any. She pleaded with him. So he said to her, If you agree to a cocker spaniel, we'll have a baby . . . But since she's mortally afraid of dogs, it was no-go."

I shook my head. "*He's* a dog. A son of a bitch. And even if she agreed . . ."

Aviva finished for me. "Right you are. It shows he's incapable of being a father to a child . . . But that's not what I'm getting to. It turns out she had an affair with . . ." she hesitated, lowered her head, and smiled into her chest. "You'll laugh . . ."

"What's her number?"

Aviva raised an eyebrow.

"I mean, maybe she needs professional help."

"Yes . . . She'd probably like you . . ."

"Finish your sentence . . . I won't laugh."

"She had an affair with her psychologist."

I laughed.

"I told you you'd laugh."

"I didn't."

"You did."

"I know when I laugh. It was a cough. A cough-laugh in Jungian lingo . . . Is it still going on?"

"No. She broke off a year ago. I sort of told you about her affair once in passing, in general terms. But the interesting thing is she could never have an orgasm with him—only with her husband . . . Maybe she held back . . . Maybe she felt guilty," Aviva mused. "Anyway, she felt the need to speak to someone. But I told her to be discreet. You never know who might report this back to your husband . . . But she said she was telling this only to me, because she knew me so well."

"Bullshit, it's all over town."

"I agree . . . How did we get sidetracked? I was going to talk about Guido."

I wondered what prompted Aviva to talk about her friend. Obviously, she wanted to let me know the woman had had an affair with her psychologist. Was this some kind of hidden wish of hers? Some kind of transference?

"You know, you have an innate sense of psychology. You'd make a good psychologist yourself."

"I wish I could make a good psychologist," she said and laughed that mischievous laugh of hers. Her nose crinkled and she showed all her teeth. "How come you never married?"

"I once told you. Honestly. Like you, I'm also shy."

"You, shy? A psychologist? Whom plenty of willing women come to daily?"

"There's all kinds of coming."

"Don't be sarcastic."

"I'm not sarcastic. I'm being professional."

"There's all kinds of help, you know."

I weighed that remark. It sounded neutral enough. I looked for the glint in her eye. None there. It reminded me of a dream I had. I was at customs at a small foreign country, and the officer demanded money for my suitcase. Since when is there duty on a suitcase? I wanted to know. It's made out of leather, he replied. Our country imposes duty on all leather goods. I have no more money, I said. Then give me the glint in your eye, he said. Okay, I said, and I opened my eyes wide and winked at him. He blinked a few times, rather tightly, as if a ray of blinding light had entered his eyes. He turned away and I walked through with my bag.

Aviva was still sitting calmly in her chair, while I was in turmoil from her neutral-sounding remark. And then there was that not-so-neutral response to my rather innocent, "You'd make a good psychologist," to which she in her typical double entendre fashion said she wished *she* could make a good psychologist. Meaning me. Just like her redheaded friend had done. Followed by, why I wasn't married.

I see myself repeating Aviva's history. Guido's history. Each time there's a discussion with Aviva I want to get up and kiss her. I see her as married and not married at the same time. She sees me as her red-haired friend's doctor who made, perhaps will make, a pass at her. She thinks she's her redheaded friend and I'm the friend's shrink. I get up and kiss her, catch her unaware.

So I weighed the remarks. I weighed the rapport that had developed between us. I weighed the glint in our eyes. I weighed the weight of the wavelength. I weighed her animadversion for the Arab and the distancing between Guido and her. Her old bugaboo of inevitability. Her yearning for stability. Security. Solidity. For lovely Aviva love was something special. But she couldn't live on it. She needed Guido. For herself. Totally. Of course, Guido wouldn't dump his wife. He knew that. She knew that. I knew that. But what Guido did not know was Practicality's real name. He missed the snake in the garden because he'd assumed all along it was only a garter. And deep down he knew Aviva's flightiness, caprices, weakness, and was afraid of them. Weighing all this, I decided I would tell Aviva, Would you like to take a walk? And never mind the resonances, the echoes, the imitation, the spinning roulette wheel of history. It was time for *me* to make a move. The hints were there. The signals too. But vague. Slippery. Subject to various interpretations. I'd been waiting for a clear signal for so long but hadn't received it. I knew they were out there. Perhaps I was too thick to read them.

Go figure how a woman's mind works. For just then Guido's shadowy stamp collection popped into my head. How he'd fooled me for years. And how he never invited me to his naked girl photographing sessions—talk about photo opportunities! And how he stole Ava from me and tried to explain it away with a seeming tongue-in-cheek quote: King Henry II said to Thomas à Becket when he took his girl away—I am the King. This is my hour!

There were so many unanswered questions about Guido. And about Ava too. Was Ava that way before she got married, or did some demon get into her? She didn't appear to be so insatiable when I knew her. Can a woman become a nympho after marriage? Was it something that Guido had done to her? And why did he marry Ava in the first place? Because he won her away from me? I wouldn't have married her anyway. Guido was the sort of guy who was suited for a higher class girl, more noble, with more prestige and elan. A woman like Tammy, who looked like she had class. So why Ava?

"There's all kinds of help, you know," Aviva said.

Her remark could also refer to the personal help that the psychologist had been giving to Aviva's beautiful redheaded friend. That too was a kind of help. Who knows? I still remembered that friendly little kiss I'd given her, oh, was it an hour or weeks ago? Did she remember, savor it? Or was it one of countless, meaningless kisses she'd gotten from countless, meaningless men? So, instead of asking her for a walk, I rose from my chair, strode to where she was sitting and, not asking her like my poetic, romantic friend Guido if we were on the same wavelength, not concocting some cockamamie cock-and-bull story to get hold of a luscious woman's upper lips so's to get at the eternally luscious lower ones, I simply went up to her and quickly bent down and kissed her on the lips. I didn't say, Are we on the same wavelength? I didn't say I wanted to ask you a question. I didn't imitate, I had no intentions whatsoever of imitating Guido. I didn't even say, though I could have, though it might have been a cute gambit, a neat, seamless follow-up to her remark, I didn't say, How's this for help?

Then waited for the reaction, head bent over her. She wasn't passive when I kissed her, although I remembered her telling me she wasn't particularly crazy about kissing.

I guess she was waiting for the second kiss.

Now I took her hand and lifted her up. This time I did say: "How's this for help?" when I kissed her and she threw her arms around my shoulders and kissed me with fervor; with eyes closed she kissed me with her almond-milk lips.

She opened her eyes and I saw there the tracks of previous lovers, the taste of other men who'd touched Aviva's lips.

"I'm so confused," she said. "I don't know who I love."

A surge, I swear, for the first time in my life, a surge of such candle-glow feelings, of such all-enveloping warmth, perhaps akin to right after birth when the baby nuzzles his mother's breast, that's what I felt hearing that word *love* passing through love-starved Aviva's luscious lips, that it took all the restraint I had not to smother her face, her hands, her entire body with kisses.

Aviva fanned her face with her fingers.

"Whew! I'm all stirred up."

Now what was that supposed to mean? Stop, I'm confused? Let's not proceed? Or was that another hint that she was ready? Had been longing for me for weeks?

I spread my hands to envelop her, but just then the phone rang and broke the spell.

Aviva's dream

I doze off, reading, and have a dream. No, not a dream, less a dream than a message from the unconscious, which tells me: if you miss an opportunity it never comes again.

Interpretation:
Since this isn't a dream, there is no other voice here, there's nothing for me to interpret except to say it's indeed a good message. Do not miss an opportunity.

15

I picked up the phone, said "Hello?" and put the caller on hold for a moment. Aviva stood and waved good-bye. "See you next week," she mouthed as she went out the door. She saw my consternation and said, "I can't this week, okay?" I made a circle with my thumb and index finger. Her kiss still lingered on my lips.

"Sorry to keep you waiting. May I help you?"

"Doctor Sharoni's office?" said a voice with a foreign accent.

"Yes, this is Dr. Sharoni's office. I'm Doctor Perlmutter, taking over his practice while he's away in Israel."

"Ata medaber ivrit?"

I understood his question but didn't want to get drawn into a Hebrew conversation. "Excuse me?"

"You don't speak Hebrew?"

"No. I'm sorry, I don't." Certainly not enough to conduct a professional dialogue. "Do you speak English?"

"Of course, what you think, eh?" the man said belligerently. "I'm a American citizen. You not a Israeli?" His voice dropped sadly.

"No . . . Must you have an Israeli?"

"No, no. Not necessary. I called Israeli because of he's my countryman and Jewish. But you are Jewish, yes?"

"With a name like Perlmutter how can I not be?"

"So you understand why I ask to not have appointment on *shabbat*, on Saturday."

"Yes. Of course. I don't even have office hours here on Saturday."

"Good. Good. You see it's for Jewish religious reasons."

"I understand."

"You have night office?"

"I have Wednesday evening appointments."

"This Wednesday you canned to have a opening?"

I looked at my calendar. "Yes. At seven. By the way, have you been referred to me?"

"No. I look in Yellow Pages under psychologists . . ." he pronounced the *ps* . . . "for Israeli name so I could be comfortable with Israeli, a Jew."

"I've counseled many of Dr. Sharoni's patients, so I'm sure you will feel comfortable with me."

"Can I bring my children? They want talk too to you."

"Indeed you can. I'll leave the seven to eight p.m. slot open for you. But may I have your name? I still don't know who I'm talking to."

"My name is Ramiti. Rahamim Ramati. For the goyim it's Roberto."

I almost dropped the phone. Although I fantasized it might be him from the moment I heard the Israeli accent, I couldn't be sure until I heard his name. Another slice of destiny. I'd always thought that piddling around with destiny was Guido's slant on life and I'd kidded him for it, but I was beginning to come around. Look at the evidence, from Guido's hooking Ava from me and marrying her and finding her in bed with her piano teacher, to him telling me about his affair with Aviva, to me finding Aviva, serendipity, via the local newspaper, and her husband finding me because he wanted an Israeli and because Gad Sharoni had his own family problems in Tel Aviv and to help out a buddy I'd taken over his practice—my God, it's been months and months—until his return. Now if that isn't Guido's kabbalistic convergence, or the fortuitous meeting of characters on the Trans-Siberian Express in the grand nineteenth-century Russian novels, I don't know what is. And wasn't it also predetermined that the Arab would spot the only Israeli-sounding name in Garden City in the Yellow Pages and that's how I would get to meet him, for never in a million years would I have met the Arab on my own? And was it not predetermined too that I would get a crush on Aviva, I who was available and free, while her romance with Guido was foundering because he was not available and free, having tied himself down to a girl who had been mine but who he made his? But wait, it wasn't Ava to whom he was marrried now. I'm eliding time. I kissed her lips, Ramati, a.k.a. the Arab. I kissed her lips, merciful Rahamin, and she kissed mine. A moment before you called.

Ramati came into the office from the waiting room with two timid-looking children, a boy and a girl. The girl was thirteen, as Aviva had said, and the boy about eleven, both beautiful but nervous-looking children, as if an invisible cord were tied around them. Both looked like Aviva, espe-cially the girl. Ramati, wearing a yarmulke, was a darkly handsome man with black curly hair and deep black eyes, typical of the North African men I'd met in Israel during my one visit there, or the ones I'd seen, yes, driving taxis or managing Mideast restaurants. He was on the short side—obviously Aviva was taller—and chunky. They way he moved gave off an aura of great physical strength. His rather swarthy face exuded a toughness that he tried to mitigate by frequent—and here, I confess, I editorialize subjectively— oleaginous smiles. His low forehead gave him a somewhat Neanderthal look, but he was well groomed; an expensive suit and high-gloss, black Italian shoes. I suppose he wanted to show he could afford the consulta-tion. (On the phone he hadn't even asked what my fees were.) The children were dressed in jeans and sneakers.

"Tell doctor your names," he said.

"David."

"Yaffa."

Then he said something to them in Hebrew and added, "Be polite. Go shake doctor's hand."

They stood and came to me.

"I'm glad to meet you all," I said. I looked Ramati in the eye. I kissed your wife. I was delighted to send him the message. I kissed her luscious lips. "Please sit down."

After a few pleasantries to break the ice—I didn't even get a smile out of the children and I marked that phenomenon—the Arab began to talk.

"I soon must to be starting the *protzedura* of to divorce my wife to much regret because always the dear children they suffer from a step like such, but one of the big prob*lem*as is—how they say?—terrible influence my wife she has on the children. Because of her behavior and the children, right?" Here he nodded toward them and they both nodded earnestly at me, "the on them influence is, Oh God should save us, the way she behaves is . . ." and he began to shake his head from side to side slowly . . . "is very very very bad."

I was about to say something but he lifted a finger like a man who is used to being obeyed and said:

"First, I tell you something about myself so you the doctor to be know-ing the sort of a man what is talking to you. You see the yarmulke I wear," Ramati pointed to it and moved to the edge of the seat, "I carry it with me always. Because I ma-Jew. And for good luck. And always to prepare for min*yan*. In case, let's say I'm passing a bet knesset and they must to have a, you know they need to finish to the nine one more man for min*yan*. How can I say no? Especially if a Jew he have to say Kadd*ish*. It's the best mit*sva* a Jewish human being he can make. That is how my parents, you know, my father and mother, they brought me up. A mother a father's good teaching it sticks with you for whole your life. I saying this to you because a man's religion that's his character what teaches me to be patient and good. This I get," and he rolled his eyes upward. "From my sainty father and grandfather, rest in peace, all religious Jews, everyone respect them in the synagogue, even the king of Morocco's father, Hassan the First, *alav ha-shalom*, that means in Hebrew, rest in peace, he knew my sainty grandfather. In the synagogue I do little mitzvot, because the holy Pirke Avot, every Jew know it, it's in the Siddur, it teaches us that we don't know for what mitzvot we get reward, for big or little, so there, in the holy synagogue, I do hidden mitzvot what no one knows about like making straight pages, you know, I bend back the bent corners what people bent down from the pages in the holy prayerbook. Or when on wall plaster crack I go to doing it, secrety, of course, myself. For that you get no credit no testamentimonial dinners with the honors and the speeches and the tuxedos and the band playing, but what I care for that? Main thing it's the good deed. Main thing the holy God above in heaven He should know, right my darlings?"

The children, pale and sitting close together, nodded again.

"Now maybe you understanding why I wanted a fellow Israeli man to talk to, which you is not but no no don't feel bad I don't blaming you it's not your fault you not Israeli except if you make aliya to Israel you become automatic a Israeli. That's why I wear what you Ashkenazim call yarmulke and us Sepharadim a *kippa*, so I wanted someone not to go to on *shabbat*. The trouble is, I'm like—do you knowing the Bible?" But he continued quickly. "I'm like the prophet Hosea who married a whore, but I didn't do it because God He giving me the order like He did gave a command to Hosea in the holy Bible, me, I married her without command. My bad luck. To marry a woman who behaves so bad, so evil."

"For example," I said, my heart—I admit it—racing.

Ramati stood; he jingled coins in his pocket.

"She is cello player and teacher. Medium talent but ego lots, like a king. Fools herself to say I'm best. No one better. But I'm sad to saying this about my own wife, I a religious Jew who preserves the *shabbat* and care about my synagogue should have to saying this to a stranger, a doctor, in front my own children they shouldn't be knowing this because of their youngness but it's time they knowing it because the world out there it's cruel and they learned the bitter like Passover horseradish lesson I have to mention to a doctor like you that my wife, the kids' mother, make more her living by taking men in the house, up to her bedroom while I'm not home, then from cello music, which she hardly don't earn a penny from. In front her own, my own children, my wife she is not being ashamed. I am so hurt my children seen this and my little girl and my boy too who for life will carry my name they both have even a statement, a letter they wrote, I must to show you in a minute on what they seen."

I was uncomfortable with Ramati talking this way in front of the children. The psychological damage that can ensue from such remarks is profound. Who knows what he has already done to them?

"Children," I said, "would you mind waiting outside? I'd like to talk to your father alone."

"No, no," Ramati said. "They big kids. They know everything. Let them stay."

"I'm sorry. That's my policy. First, on an individual basis then, if you wish, together . . . So, please," I walked to the door. "David and Yaffa, wait outside until I call you in."

By the time I'd escorted them out to the waiting room, given them some magazines and told them I'd like to talk to them alone later, Ramati had pulled out a packet of Rothman's and lit a cigarette. Only after he'd leaned back and puffed a big ring of smoke into the air, looking very clubby and relaxed, did he offer me a cigarette and say:

"You mind I smoke?"

"Yes. There are no ashtrays."

But he either misunderstood or pretended.

"I use the palm of my hand, I smoke, see, only Jewish cigarettes. Rothman's from England. Why should I give to the goyim my money? Jewish music too. Only Goldberg Variations."

"Many of my patients are sensitive to smoke, so I have a strict no smoking policy. And I," I added without blinking, "have terrible asthma."

"Excuse," He rubbed the cigarette on the sole of his shoe and replaced it in the pack.

"Doctor, I smoke because I nervous to my stomach. Doctor." His face took on a tragic mien. "Dear, dear doctor, I married a whore . . . here, look at the paper my little darling kids write about their mother."

He handed me the paper and again jangled the coins in his pocket.

I read the one-page report on Aviva's promiscuity, how their mother took men upstairs almost every day, and I couldn't believe my eyes.

"What are you doing?" Ramati shouted as I moved behind my desk and xeroxed the page. Kissing your wife, I didn't say. The dear, dear doctor is kissing your dear, dear wife.

"Making a copy for my files . . . If you show me a document and want my professional evaluation, I must have a copy of everything . . . Here, I'm returning the original to you."

Ramati's face stiffened. He was seething. His hand went to his jacket pocket for the cigarettes, then went limp. He played with the coins for a moment. He rose and paced and again rattled the coins. I wondered if he would just stalk out in a rage. But no. He needed me. I saw before my eyes the page written in a nervous, slanting hand by one of the children. Aviva a prostitute? A talented musician and teacher a whore? It didn't go with the personality, the shy, hesitant, unsure woman. It just didn't jibe. And in this day and age? With sexually transmitted diseases and AIDS? Nevertheless, I'd learned that human beings are full of surprises. Aviva too was full of surprises. And information withheld.

"You see? You see what innocent little childrens says about their mother? And like a ole-fashion doctor, she makes also house calls. Then comes home seven eight o'clock. No supper. Everybody hungry. She comes home, the slut, from her business calls, flushed from the lovings. Her eyes, they sparkle. She looks like twenty, twenty-one, I swear, and I could of . . ." He made two fists and contorted his face. At that moment he looked bestial. He banged his fist on the armrest of the sofa. Dust rose. "Cheeks rosy. The blood the last man she had he made rise on her face still there. On her cheeks. She doesn't even bother to washing it off. And she afraid to come near me. Because she had a different smell. I know that smell from the women I been with. Not now. Before I marry, of course. And that look in her eyes. Half-sleepy look. As if she not been in bed working all day, God forbid, now she looks sleepy like she wants to stretch out in bed again and sleep it off. Like a drunk. Only she not drunk. Maybe with love. Sex. That sleepy, satisfied look. Very happy. With me I didn't never noticed that happy look. And she can't wipe it off from her face when she comes home, the whore. Just to tease me. She don't want to hide it. She wants *me* to see it, the slut. *Zonah*, whore what she is. To rub my face in it. I should seeing the happiness she has. That satisfied look. That happiness."

You fool, you're describing her love glow after seeing Guido, I thought.

"It drove me to wildness. I could take a knife and cut her heart out. It heated me up like fire. I looked at her face and seen the faceless face of the man fucking her, excuse me the bad language, and it made me hot for her. The woman I couldn't have because even if I have having her I didn't having her, you know what I meaning? I wanted to fuck her brains out. I'm sorry, but she my wife and a husband he got his rights, no? Fact she was just laid did something to me. That and that special glowing on her face I could slapped off with both my hands till either my hands or her slut face be bleeding cause I love her so much. I get one more proof she unfaithful and I swear, no mercy."

"What did you say?" I remembered Aviva telling me that long ago her mother had warned her to leave him for he would kill her.

"I said," the Arab fairly shouted, "I get one more proof she unfaithful to me, that another man has her nakedness which belong by law to me alone, where I come from a husband he got his rights, I swear I kill her with no mercy. She betray me long enough. Even years ago she done this, always with excuse." And here Ramati lapsed into a falsetto, " 'I going shopping with my girl friends . . .' Here in this country slut wives get off easy. Back home in Morocco we fix them good. They steps outside after the fixing and everyone sees what they guilty of.

"Doctor, this is a doctor office and from a doctor my darling mama she taught me is nothing to be ashamed. My wife, how you call it in English, is a nymphosexmaniac. All a man got to do is touch her and a minute later he can pull her pants down. She always running around. I can telling she goes out by the way she puts on the lipstick. I never caught her, she too careful, like a snake. If I caught her . . ." and he made a couple of slapping motions, one hand sort of applauding the other. "Who knows how many men she already had and disease she spread and gave me? No wonder I always itching. Another way I can tell she a sex nympho because when she mad at me and I pretty sure she didn't want to make screw screw, even when she turned her back on me in bed at night, no, no, she wouldn't dare go sleep in another bed by herself, oh, no, I never permit that, even then. Where am I? What saying? Oh, yes, even when mad with me, all I got to do is reach over a give her, you know, a couple of love touches and right away, like lightning her angerness feeling disappears and she be ready to go for it, like a bunny. All that 'Stop, I don't want it. Please, I don't want it, I don't want to . . .' " He was imitating her again in falsetto, ". . . is just so much talk. Oh, she want it. Bad. She crazy for sex. I never met a girl who loves fucking, excuse language please, so much. She can't live without it. She climb walls when she don't got it regular. So, imagine, when she angry with me, and normal girls don't even want to fuck their husbands when they so mad, but she, she did with me, that nympho, that slut. It was so easy. All you got to do is reach out and touch her pussy, can you imagine how she loved doing it with strangers? All they got to do was touch her, anywhere, and she melts. Jeezus, how many mens she cheated with while I married to her, the whore, the *zonah*, the good God in heaven only He knows."

"Then why did you stay married to her all these years?"

"Because in the holy Bible even the great prophet Hosea he supposed to stick with his wife. To show."

"To show what?"

"People of Israel they sinning."

"But you're not a prophet, or are you?" But my sarcasm went right past him.

"That's why now I'm making preparingness. I'm through with her. And I want you, doctor, your documents to show what whore she is. Not to be fitting to be a mother to my darling childrens. Still, like a Jew, I'm a optimist. Every day I pray to God that my wife loves me a just a little bit. In bet knesset, in addition to shalom to Israel and Jews all over the world, that's what I praying for." His voice broke. He took out a handkerchief, held it for a moment. I thought he would blow his nose, but he dabbed his eyes instead. "Because the God knows I love her so much . . ."—he punched his heart like a Jew beating his breast on Yom Kippur, punched it with a vehemence—"it hurts."

Then he rose and paced in the room. He went for a cigarette that wasn't there. Played with the coins again.

"Sometimes she make me so angry the way she yell at the poor little childrens and her face becomes, there gets on it when she get nervous with the children and mad on them which is a lots of times, a special hated look that I wish, I'm ashamed to say but I got to be honest before the dear God, I wish, I pray sometimes she not come home—because you should see, you should see how like a ugly witch her face it become when she yell at the kids that they so frightened I could die with mercy on them, it hurts me so much how she scares them to death. I could get a stroke alone from her screeching, like a taxi brakes. Talk of abuse, mental, physical cruelty. That's what I meaning when I say I wish sometime she not come home again. Do I wish she should be crushed, run over, rammed by a Mack truck? The God forbid! But just, you know, a light, a tiny little death. That something not too hurtful happens to her she disappears. Poof. That I don't see her again. Not, you see, I don't wish her hurt, oh, no, the God forbid, but I only wish I don't have to see her ugly mask face no more for the sake of the children, like the God would be so kind to me like He always been and just take her away without suffering, like suddenly go to sleep, or maybe a painless car accident, it would make me very happy. What am I saying, make me very happy? Of course, I would be very very sad, but under the circumstances like that and, of course, you know what I mean, I would feel sorry for the orphans, her, my, childrens, but must to understand," he clenched his fists and jaw, "sometime she make me so mad I boil over, the way she abuse my children, but it's only, you understand me," here he allowed a smile, "when I'm mad on her and she has that crazy look and behaving on her what make me feel these feelings that I got, otherwise, thank the God, she is fine."

I nodded slowly, rhythmically, urging him with my eyes to continue talking.

"Doctor, maybe I talking too much, but you got to know, you must to know the situation. It's not the big things that, the God forbid, that causing the troubles between me and my darling wife. It's them little things, Mister Doctor, like, Do me a favor, so much and so many time I ask you, shut the fucking faucet, excuse please terrible language, it shouldn't drip drip drip into the night—but no, go talk to the wall of China, for me she can't do that. She purposely leave the drip drip faucet all night so when I get up in the early early morning, you should excuse the expression, to pee, I hear that goddamn drip drip it drive me crazy. So believe me, Mister Doctor, it's them little things that adds up, like drip drip drops makes a gallon of wasted water before you know."

I nodded sagely.

"Mr. Ramati, I'd like to ask you something else about your life, if you don't mind."

"I don't minding at all." He sat again, leaned forward at the edge of the chair as if on the potty.

"Do you participate in extracurricular activities?"

"I don't know from these activities."

"You mean you don't know the English term?"

He flushed, angry. He tapped his foot down hard on the floor. He gave a little smile of suppressed rage. How he would have loved to stamp his foot.

"I told you I American now, a citizen. English I understanding perfect. Just these activities."

"I mean outside activities, away from home."

"You kidding?" He wagged his finger. "That's *her* department, with the extra activities. Me, I'm a one-woman man. I got plenty opportunity in my business, the ladies they sees a handsome man they think is Italian. You see, they hear Ramati, they think I'm Italian and they get excited. But no, sir, not me."

"I didn't mean that at all. I mean things like sports, going to auctions. I mean after work fun."

"Listen, Mister Doctor. I work hard. Long hours in New York and come right home. Fun for me is to coming home. Fun I have at home. With my," he smiled at the door behind which were his children, "darling family."

"No basketball games? No hockey? Horse races? None of these interest you?"

Ramati's eyes flickered. A little tic there at the mention of the races. But he shook his head. "Not cultured. For Americans. Not for Europeans, Israelis like us. Maybe to a art museum or music concerts. But home is where when the day's work it is done is where I wanting to go. Are you through with me now, doctor?"

"Well, counseling is not a begin-finish affair, but I do want to ask you, Mr. Ramati, about the relations between you."

"We have lots of relations. But they don't come between us. Except maybe her crazy sister, which is most of time in Israel."

I tried to keep a straight face and coughed into my fist. "I mean—" I used both my hands—"How you interact, you and . . ." I almost blurted out, Aviva. ". . . Mrs. Ramati. That kind of relations. You and your wife."

"Ah, ah, ah," he said. "Now I understand, doctor. The relations are all along very good between me and my wife.♥ To give an example, very often she call me Honey. Now can you imagine a wife calling her husband Honey

♥See ABC Directory, *Forgot, the penny and the Arab story that Aviva.*

and relations no good? But I don't know what happened to her. Example. We keep kosher house. But she makes mistakes. On purpose. Now she born in Israel too so she should knowing better. But does it on purpose. Comes from a very fancy family what don't care about kosher. Just like her sister who sometime I go see in Tel Aviv when I visit my family. But they all alike, these women. Like wife, like sister. Want same thing. But we not talking about that. We must to talking how small Jewish they is. You know, high-class German Jews what is more German, less Jewish. She bakes a cake when my mother and sister come visit from Israel and uses milk chocolate for a meat meal, the wrapper I found when I looked by accident in the garbage in big letters Milk Chocolate only a moron couldn't see. And after a chicken supper! I was so ashamed from my mother, she did it to hurt her and my sister. I like things simple. Economical. Been brought up such way. But she, she wastes money right and left. The phone calls she piles up. Is on the phone day and night. Women, they can't help themselves. Or I give you a example. A recipe it calls for one ounce expensive liquor. So she doesn't use Chivas Regal, big deal. Think guests know difference if it's cheap rum or Chivas? But no, she goes out and buys a $32 bottle. We got whole liquor cabinet collection just from her one-ounce recipes. Or almonds. A cake needs a bit of it. So she goes to buying a one-pound package shell nuts and never uses it again. It make me crazy. Listen, Mister Doctor, between you and I, a woman she must to take care of, feed a family. Tofu is food? She's a health nut. Normal kids—in France where I been raised, is a land of chocolate—can having a little chocolate, ne c'est pas? But she, she gives em carob-coated soy nuts. No wonder the kids are off the walls. Too much carob and tofu it makes you crazy. And she never do the laundry. The dirt clothes they pile up like garbage, you breathe in, excuse the expression, the stink. At twelve one o'clock at night when I sometime come home from my hard work business meeting I got to do laundry so to have clean underwear. Music music music. Her head is in music but she leave dishes in sink piled for days. You see, I come from Paris, I am used to neatness. But she's a, how you say, a slob. Once I left a penny purposely on the bathroom floor. For weeks it stood there. She never cleaned it up. The rooms is a mess. Clothing from Wednesday is riding on clothing from Tuesday what is on top of Monday and Sunday wardrobe. To bring in business associates I'm ashame because of the house. So I must to entertaining them in New York and after hard day work come home late at night. And then do laundry and she asks *me* where I was running, *me* who does it because of filth in my own home. I give her cleaning service but she fires them because she thinks I make them spy on her. And is no wonder she so busy because of her business. Where I come from, my tradition, wife keeps the home you could eat from the floor. Like a museum. If not, husband take her gentle aside and softly ask, Please keep house clean and in order.

If *I* tries eating from floor, I get sick to my stomach, you should excuse the expression. And she drinks. I put a little sign. A tiny piece tape on the gin bottle. She keeps on with the drinking. Is this the sort mother my beautiful childrens they should have, that sort?

"One story I must to tell. Very important. If you talk relations. From it you understand what possibly happen. My grandmother she gave me—actually, my mother, she brought it from Israel, because *her* mother gave to her to giving it to me, and me to giving it to my wife, a beautiful set Parisian glasses. Very rare. Nineteenth century. You can buy, the firm is still existing in Paris, Lalique. *Now* you can buy it sure, but the new is nothing, oh, no, nothing like the old. And she, my wife, my darling wife, the mother of these lovely childrens, she took these precious glasses, a from heart gift from my grandmother to her and after a dinner when my friends they are here, she purposely brokes, she smashed it angry because she said during whole meal I didn't once spoke to her. First of all, it's a big lie. I did spoke to her. But you think I got angry on her, you think I losted my temper and breaked her teeth with one good punch to the mouth like normal husband do? Nothing. Not a word. I swear. Maza*l*tov, I sang out, because you know in the Jewish tradition at a wedding a glass it is smashed, the heel of the groom he steps on the glass, so Jews when something breaks, even at home, they all yell maza*l*tov. You ask yourself, probably, how come he saying maza*l*tov when I say *ma*zeltov, because us Sepharadim say ma*zal* for luck, and not like Yiddish people like you *ma*zel. But all Jews are brothers like our holy prayers say, not so? Oh, my God, speaking of pray, I completely forgot. I must to talk to my rabbi. Must to call him. Can I using your phone?"

"Sure."

He dialed. "Is this the rabbi? Oh, sorry." He hung up. "Wrong number." And dialed again.

"Rabbi? Shalom. This is Rahamim Ramati. About the thousand dollars I said I would donated . . . Yes . . ." The Arab smiled, looked at me. "I forgot to telling you . . . yes, to reminding you, the donation it is honoring my father, *alav hashalom*, and the plaque it should mention that." He covered the receiver for a moment. "Do you want to talking to my rabbi? He tell you all about me."

"No . . . no . . . no," I said. "Not necessary."

"Well, rabbi, shalom and *kol toov* . . . Best regards. I'll see you Friday night . . . Well, thank you, very kind of you. It will be nice. Big honor." He hung up. "He wants me at Friday night pray service to lead as cantor. Because of my good voice." He stopped, then added: "Now you have all the information you must to have?"

"Mr. Ramati, in order to make a full evaluation, I must to talk to children. Alone." I found myself unwittingly imitating his manner of speaking. "So if you not mind, I ask you to stepping out into the waiting room."

"No, no. They little kids. Nervous from doctor. No good for them."

"It's all right. I have lots of experience. It would be better."

As I opened the first of the double doors, Ramati leaned close to me. "Watch out. They got habit to lying. They can't help it. Caught it from her, their mother."

The children stood when he appeared in the waiting room.

"The doctor he wants to speak to you." Then he said something to them flatly and quickly in Hebrew. But there was one word, repeated twice, that I remembered from Hebrew school, when we studied the Torah, the story of Moses and the Egyptian he had killed and hidden in the sand. Twice the Arab repeated the word *aharog*—"I will kill." The children replied, "*Kane, kane*"—yes, yes.

"I see the children know Hebrew."

"Yes. Very smart kids. Beautiful childrens. Speak many languages."

I put my hands on their shoulders and invited them in. I closed and locked the double doors and switched on the music to the waiting room.

"The double doors, see, I locked them, to ensure absolute sound-proofing. And the waiting room is now full of music. Not one word said here can be heard outside."

The brother and sister exchanged glances. Their faces were still tense.

"I heard from your father, and now it's very important that I hear from you. The paper you signed is a very serious accusation against your mother. If your parents get divorced and the court believes that paper, the judge will send you to be with your father. They won't trust your mother to care for you. So let me hear your side of the story. You can say what you want and don't be afraid. If you want to tell me something, anything, do it. You have to be brave . . . David, would you like to begin?"

He shook his head. I looked to Yaffa. She stared down at the floor. They both looked at the door. I got up, stood by the double door and said in a normal speaking voice:

"Mr. Ramati, I'd like to speak to you." Then I repeated it loudly.

Of course, he couldn't hear me.

"You see, children, he can't hear me even if I stand by the door and speak loudly. You can say anything you want. There's no need to be afraid. I think I know what your father has done, but it's important that you tell me in your own words. You don't want to hurt your mother, do you?"

They both shook their heads. I could see tears in the boy's eyes. "Come here." They approached me. I took their hands and held them for a while before speaking. "Don't be afraid, children," I said gently. I held their hands as if holding Aviva's "Do you think you can do it?"

Yaffa took a deep breath, more like a sigh than a breath. She nodded slowly.

"David, and you?"

"I'll try."

"So would you like to start?"

"Yaffa knows it. She can talk."

"Fine, she will speak, but I do want to hear from you too. Just a little bit. Yaffa, what do you say about your father's story?"

"Mommy is not like that. I never saw a man in her room. I never saw another man go upstairs. There are some young men who come for cello lessons, but we are always doing homework in the kitchen. They take a lesson and go."

"But that's not what you say in your signed statement."

"He beat us," Yaffa said softly, looking at the door. "He punched David and me in the back till we wrote it." She pointed to her lower back above the hip. "He dictated the letter and made us sign that mommy is a *zonah* and takes men to bed."

"He hit me here too," David pulled up his shirt and turned to show me where he'd been beaten. "He hit me in the kidneys till we did what he told us."

"Tell him to show the letter to you," Yaffa said. "You'll see by the slanty handwriting—we were crying when I wrote it and signed it—our hands were shaking."

"I saw it. Your father showed it to me. I saw the slanty handwriting."

David stood and came close to me. "He doesn't let us call her Mommy. When we speak about her we have to say *zonah*."

" 'We went shopping with the *zonah* today,' we had to say," Yaffa interjected.

"What does that mean?"

Yaffa glanced down at her shoes.

"It's a terrible word in Hebrew," said David.

"But it's important for someone who doesn't know what it means to know the translation," I said gently.

"It's the Hebrew word for 'prostitute,' 'whore,' " Yaffa said.

"How long has this been going on?"

"Maybe six months," David said. "While he dictated to us what to write, he asked me, 'How much do you think the *zonah* charges?' I said I don't know. So he said, 'Five hundred dollars. Do you know how rich she is?' "

"Does you mother care for you?" I asked. "Cook? Take you to school? Go places with you?"

"Of course," Yaffa answered.

"Does she have supper prepared always?"

"Always. Even when she has a concert or a rehearsal she prepares it and we heat it up."

"And do you like being with your father?"

"He never played with us," David said. "He was always busy with his business. Most of the time he comes home after we're asleep. When he does come home in time, he eats by himself and goes straight to the TV room . . . Should we tell him about the fruit, Yaffa?"

Yaffa was in a quandary. I noticed a slight disapproval in her face. But realist that she was, once her brother had made the suggestion, she couldn't say no.

"Go ahead. Tell him."

"There was a time," David said, "when my father's business was bad, he said. He said we can't have luxuries. No more fruits. We can't afford it. Too much money. One day, we went up to the attic to get an old game, and there on a little table were all kinds of good fruits. He was buying them for himself. And eating them himself."

"What did you do?" I asked.

Both children smiled.

"I told my mother and Yaffa and me ate them all up."

"And left the pits on the little table." Yaffa smiled. "And he couldn't say a word. We had him cornered."

I smiled at their trick. "And he never takes you out?"

"He doesn't usually," Yaffa continued. "Tonight he told Mommy we were going bowling."

"But he's all dressed up."

"He changed in the car. The suit was hanging there. He took off his sneakers and exercise pants."

"Do you love your mother?"

"Yes, very much," both children said at once.

"And your father?"

"He's a liar . . . It's very sad," said David.

"About everything he lies," the sister continued. "He wants to destroy Mommy."

"He told me he's a religious Jew."

Yaffa rolled her eyes. "It's a game with him. It's true, he goes to the synagogue on Friday night and Saturday morning. He loves the respect there. But then after lunch he drives into New York for business and stays there all day. Sometimes he doesn't come home till Sunday night . . . He's not religious at all."

"But he's wearing a yarmulke."

"Just here. For you. He never wears it . . . But please, doctor," Yaffa pleaded, "please don't tell him what we told you."

"Don't worry," I said. "And do you keep a kosher home?"

"Only when our grandmother came. She visited us twice from Israel. Then he buys kosher meat. Then she died, here."

"And other times?"

"No. He says kosher meat is too expensive," Yaffa said.

"But we don't mix milk and meat," David added. "But my father has to eat shrimp and lobster. He says he needs it for a vitamin deficiency . . ." and he smiled for the first time. But the smile vanished when he said: "We're hurting him, right?"

"You don't want to hurt him."

"He's our father," Yaffa said.

"Even though he hurt you," I said.

"But still this will hurt him, right?" David asked.

And in that tone of voice and in the big-eyed innocent look I saw Aviva in that little boy. I could have lifted him and kissed him too.

"I think you have to counterbalance it with the hurt that he caused and will cause you and your mommy."

"You won't tell him what we said, right?"

"No. But I must tell you that the truth will have to come out some day. You'll just have to be brave. Come, let's go out now."

David stopped just before the door. "Mister Perlmutter, I want to tell you something."

Yaffa pinched him surreptitiously.

"What?" he said, irritated.

"It's Doctor Perlmutter, silly."

"That's all right," I said. "What would you like to say?"

"And my father makes me pee sitting down like a girl so the pee doesn't drip on the floor."

"Oh, David, don't be gross," Yaffa said.

"But whenever I come in and find the seat up, it means he's been there, and it's wet on the floor . . . And he hits Yaffa when she's on the phone too long."

I nodded and patted him on the back. "Thank you, Yaffa and David. Thank you very much." I put my arms around both their shoulders and hugged them once. At that moment I felt I was embracing Aviva, split in two. Then I opened the double doors.

Ramati stood in the waiting room facing the wall, swaying slightly in prayer. "Just a moment, I am finishing the *Maariv* service."

As I watched him I thought about a story Guido had told me. His Grandmother Sacerdote in Venice knew of a Jew who had turned pious. He did not have a pleasant personality and in business was known as a swine. He grew a beard, wore a yarmulke, but in the synagogue on Sabbath would still discuss money matters, make rude jokes, and behave like a low-class boor. He was a fat, tall man and the beard made his face rounder and piggier. To which Grandmother Sacerdote commented, "Even if you put a beard and a skullcap on a pig, he'll still remain a *treifa* swine."

Ramati concluded with a loud *Amen* and said, "You interview them a long time. What you think?"

"I will write a report once I finish my evaluation . . . Would you mind filling out this billing card? This hour session will be $75."

Ramati looked at his watch, an expensive gold Patik Phillipe. It was 8:20. I'd given him another third of an hour without charge.

"So much? No discount for Israeli? Maybe $60? Please send bill."

"For the first session Dr. Sharoni would like to have immediate payment. I cannot compromise on his rates; it wouldn't be fair."

"So you don't trust me?"

"Mr. Ramati, I trusted you by giving you more than an hour of my professional time. This entire profession is based on trust . . . What business are you in?"

"Taxi."

"Do you ask for payment when a customer comes in to your taxi?"

He looked insulted. "Doctor, you think me a shmuck, low-class taxi driver? I own a business."

"Very nice," I said dryly. "But do you collect when a person enters?"

"No."

"So you trust."

"Yes."

"Same here. But like a taxi, you pays not when you enters but when you leaves. And what it says on the meter and not a penny less."

He wrote out a check. Only his name was on it.

"Childrens," he said. "Sit at other side of the room." Then he dropped his voice to a whisper and added. "They shouldn't hearing this but I think this very important. My boy he told me you won't believe how pervert is my wife. Once two years ago she gives him a bath and asks him to come to bed with her. Did he tell you about that?"

I rubbed my cheek, said nothing, looked Ramati straight in the eye. "Call your son over and let him tell me."

"The God forbid! Dear dear doctor, you the psychologist but I didn't study so much, I'm not so educated, just a businessman who like culture and educated intellectual people, but I think to reminding him would be a big hurt for the little boy. But what you think of my wife's pervert behaving?"

"I've learned in my practice," I said, "that human beings are capable of sinking lower than beasts."

Then I bade him good-bye, went back to my office, and shut the tape recorder in my jacket pocket.

16

As soon as they left—I could hardly wait for the door to close—I called Aviva. She recognized my voice at once. This was the first time I had called her at home, and I could tell she was surprised. No, not surprised. Astonished. We must be precise, even meticulous, with words. Doctor Johnson drew Boswell's attention to the distinction between the two words when Boswell caught his pal with Boswell's wife. Doctor Johnson, said Boswell, I am surprised. No, replied the iconoclastic lexicographer, You are astonished. *I* am surprised. So, then, I could tell Aviva was astonished. But I was to astonish (surprise, according to Bos) her even more.

"You'll never guess who's been here. And just left my Garden City office."

"Guido?"

"I told you you'll never guess. Try again."

"My cello coach."

"Uh-uh. How could she possibly be in Long Island?"

She paused, then—"Oh, no! I don't believe it! How? Why?"

"Looking for an Israeli psychologist. And found *me*! He brought your kids."

"What did they say?"

"The truth. They're lovely children . . . Luckily, they look like you. Troubled, but surprisingly in control."

"I don't believe it. They said they were going bowling. That bowled *me* over. Him taking them out! What did they tell you?"

"I'd rather tell you in person. Don't worry, it's all right. But I want you to do me a favor. Remember, you once referred to a diary you kept that contains your reactions to the Arab. Can you bring it?"

"I don't know. It's so personal."

"It can be very important. Crucial. Think it over. I'll be in my Manhattan office tomorrow."

"Tomorrow's Thursday. Let's see. I'm so busy this week. That's why I couldn't see you. Do you have a lunch hour free?"

"I always keep 12 to 1 free for emergencies."

"Good. It's an emergency. I'll see you at noon."

Now that I'd met the Arab, the double triangle (six pointed Jewish star?) was really complete. Guido, Aviva, me. Aviva, Arab, me. I imagined the scene in 3-D in living color: Aviva walks through the door, we embrace and kiss, a natural concomitant to last time. For me numbers go in sequential order. If you're at 4 one day, you're at 5 the next.

But Aviva didn't count that way. For her numbers went in some madcap way, maybe alphabetically. Entering my office, she gave me a shy smile as if discovered doing something naughty and handed me a black little diary. But nothing more radiated out of her. A light turned off. As if the other day never was. As if an aberration. A figment of both our fantasies. On the other hand—so cogitates the psychologist—maybe she was just too excited now to feel anything.

"What happened? What did he say?"

I pointed to the tape recorder. "I got it all down, You'll listen and I'll read."

"You recorded him!" she said admiringly. "You're really something . . . This diary isn't the whole thing," Aviva explained. "I'm just too embarrassed to show them all. They're just jottings of what happened. Nothing ordered and nothing profound . . . But please, don't read after page twenty, where the yellow bookmark is."

I gave her an earplug and started the tape. I opened her little book. "It's no *Diary of an Adulterous Woman*," she joked. And in a moment we were both absorbed in material we'd never heard or seen before.

April 17

He goes around the house shutting lights. I walk down the hall and boom, the lights are off. I put the upstairs hallway light on for company late in the afternoon and one guest went to the bathroom. Before she comes out that fool of a Moroccan, whose grandfather didn't even know what electricity was, goes and shuts the light. Or the other Sunday I switched on the outside floodlights for a student who was coming for the first time and didn't know the house. When my back was turned he switched them off.

April 30

In the morning he keeps listening by the toilet when one of the kids is in there to make sure they flush at the first plop. If there's too long a silence he bangs on the door and yells, Flush it, flush it, and open the window.

The other day Y and D fought, but he doesn't try to stop them. He enjoys them beating each other. It saves him a task; for him it kills two birds with one stone. I saw a nasty little half smile on his face as he watched them fighting. The smirk of a sadist. At such moments—and at others too—I say to myself: Too bad they have half the genetic makeup of that rotten human being.

May 4

Today he stopped talking to me again. Maybe it was the burnt cake of three days ago. Who knows his system of account-keeping? It reminds me of what happened when we took a vacation in Florida when the kids were small. By the pool of the hotel I bumped into the brother of a girlfriend. I'd left the dining room alone for some reason—maybe I wanted to get some suntan lotion, I forgot—and when I met Gary I began talking to him. R joined me in our room a few minutes later. I say something to him, he doesn't answer. He just stopped talking to me, for no apparent reason. I began crying. Only a day later, when the "punishment" was over, he explained that he had called to me by the pool and I didn't even turn around I was so busy flirting with that guy. That's why he stopped talking to me. I told R that I didn't hear him. The kids were in the kiddie pool and there was lots of noise. If I'd heard him I surely would have turned and introduced Gary, my girlfriend's brother. But he was jealous that I was talking to another man. That's the way he is. He punishes with silence for any presumed lapse or fault on my part. He stops talking to me for days, or when he does speak he curses at me in Arabic under his breath.

May 10

I rarely go out. Not to movies, not to theater. Maybe an occasional concert. Alone. He most always comes home late. And I don't like going with
him. I used to, with his friends, but he'd make fun of me and insult me and
they would laugh and make comments in Arabic and French. As soon as I'd
sit down in the car the criticisms would begin. The traffic is heavy. Why do
we have to go to a play? I can't stand the theater. We won't get there in time.
We'll be late. Can't you put on that stupid makeup earlier? A summary of my
life: from daydream to nightmare.

May 15

R is a slob at home—he leaves apple cores on the sofa and his underwear
is strewn all over the bedroom—but for certain things he flies into rage. He
loves his new white refrigerator to be spotless. Maybe it reminds him of his
car. This evening he found finger marks on the fridge door and had a fit.
"Whose fingers these?" he roared. "Call Sherlock Holmes," I cracked. But R
either didn't appreciate my humor or, more likely, didn't know Sherlock
Holmes. He slammed his fist on the table, hurting himself (good!) and yelled,
"Goddammit, why don't you taking a damp cloth and clean?"

I interrupted Aviva's listening. She was shaking her head.

"Excuse me," I said. She stopped the tape, "I just read the part where
the Arab tells you to clean the fridge. Did you say anything?"

She looked out toward the window and nodded. "Yes. I told him if it's
so simple, take a damp cloth and clean it up. You live here too, don't you?
And I told him, for insignificant things don't bring anger and dissension
into the house when there's no need for it."

"By the way," I said. "That's a very apt phrase: from daydream to nightmare. Could be the title of a book."

June 8

Today he went away on a business trip—thank God there will be peace for
a few days—and he left me a note on the bed. It didn't say, I'll miss you. It
said: Miss me, and he placed his belt around the note in the shape of a heart.
The son of a gun knew what he was doing. It was a kind of warning. For it's
the same belt he once hit me with and used on the children. Miss me, my
foot. He doesn't miss anyone, except himself. He never carries a picture of
anyone in the family. Not even his children. But he did carry one of himself
so he could look at himself when there was no mirror around.

I watched Aviva. Her face was pained. She was still listening to the Arab.
But later, when the children came on, the entire geography of her face
metamorphosed. A magical transformation, listening to how they loved her.
I thought this lovely, delicious woman needs a man like me. How come she

ended up with a brute? Don't sensitive, talented, beautiful women meet their equals?

July 1

How come I never hear a word of praise from him? The room looks beautiful. That cello sonata sounds great. Your hair looks nice. You look pretty today. The cake was delicious. Nothing. Either he eats the cake in silence or in the presence of the children demonstratively takes a bite and pushes it away, muttering an Arabic curse word. Never has he made me feel beautiful, outside or inside. All my life I've been dying for affection and I never got it. And along comes V who is all affection. I had to bite my lips from singing out to him: You are lovely. He said to me: If you were with me I'd tell you all day long how beautiful you are. I've lived in a world bounded by the reality of laundry, shopping, cleaning, cooking, but at the edge of this world was a larger circle of imagination and hope. The reality part roots you into this world. But when I dropped the reality part and relied only on imagination and hope I almost went crazy. And when I lived only for music, I got depressed. My whole life has been a fuzzy dream that hovers between reality and deep sleep.

I heard the click of the tape recorder.

"I'm lucky to have the kids I have," Aviva said when I showed her the children's confession. "What that bastard did is criminal. I hope he rots in jail."

"I don't know about that," I said, "but if there is ever a divorce, he'll never get the children, that's for sure . . ." And I waved that "confession" before her.

"I hope not. He'll kill them, spiritually and physically. Did you hear his threat?"

"Of course. Did you notice how I asked him to repeat what he said?"
Aviva laughed. "So you did hear what he said."

"Sure. I just wanted to make sure the machine heard." I gave her a big-eyed look, a little sign of conspiracy between us. "By the way, did you ever use any terms of endearment with your husband?"

"The honey business, huh? I was the honey and he was the bee," she laughed. "Yes, I did call him *hon*."

"Like in Atilla the Hun?"

Aviva laughed that delightful, flirtatious, slightly deep-throated laugh of hers. "Hon as short for honey. Which I called him when I forgot his name. No joke. It happened twice. So to cover up I called him hon."

"That's amazing," I said. "Because there's a famous Freud anecdote where Freud and a woman are walking in Vienna. The woman, recently married, spots her husband across the street and wants to call to him but she forgets his name. Freud thinks to himself that the woman will soon be divorced. And indeed she was. Forgetting a husband's name was a sign to Freud that the marriage was on the rocks."

"I'm not a Freudian," Aviva said with a twinkle, replaying my line to her, "but this time he's probably right. I wonder what he'd say about the Lalique affair. They weren't heirlooms. He bought those glasses at a garage sale. I know he did, just before his mother came to visit, and then he had her present it to me as an heirloom from *her* mother who, according to him, came from Marseilles. But it was a lie. All these Arab Jews claim they come either from Marseilles or Barcelona. They're ashamed to say they come from Morocco because Moroccans are on the low end of the totem pole in Israel. But his grandma came from the backward area of Morocco, the Atlas Mountains. Years ago I broke one glass. It was an accident, what can I do? You should have seen the rage he got into. He stamped his foot, tore his hair, shook me till my teeth rattled. I had black and blue marks on my arms from his claws. He screamed how little I respected his family, how little I cared about him and his mother's gift and his grandmother's possessions. He cursed me in Arabic and French, that's the only part of the language he knows perfectly. He brags that he speaks a few languages, but he can't even speak one correctly. And when I told him, Don't curse at me, he yelled, Don't tell me what to do, and slapped me in the face. I ran away, crying. He never apologized.

"After that, whenever I set up the glasses and brought them back to the kitchen, I would see him later, when I'd finished the dishes, he never helped me, I'd see him scanning the drying glasses to make sure none was missing. That God forbid I'd broken one behind his back and thrown the broken pieces away. He always looked in the garbage. The Sherlock Holmes of refuse. I'll tell you the truth. Often when I was angry at him, I felt like taking those glasses and smashing them all one by one in front of him. Especially when he turned off the communication and just made believe I wasn't there."

"Why didn't you?"

"Afraid of his temper. Once the accountant he'd sent me to, the guy had taken a liking to me, called me at home. I was in the kitchen and the Arab was there. Boy, was I in a pickle! I couldn't let either of them know the other was there. But the Arab sensed it and when I was done he asked me who it was. A girlfriend, I said. He didn't believe me and slowly, methodically kept pushing me back to the family room and then snapped his finger above his head, I looked up, and he punched me in the bread basket. I collapsed on the floor . . . 'This is just a overture . . . Don't fool around with other mens,' he said."

I just kept shaking my head.

"What you just read is the tip of the iceberg," Aviva continued. "There were always little things. A continual cycle of little things. Not major disagreements . . . If it only weren't for the little things . . . Dozens of them . . ." She stared off into a dreamy distance. "It could have been good but it wasn't."

"That's your mistake!" This time I shouted at her. "From what I see it could *never* have been good. The guy's abused you and the children. How could it ever have been good? You're deluding yourself."

"Maybe. All my life I wanted things to be good and perhaps by wanting them so much I put a coating of good over the awful."

"Now listen to this," I said. "Listen to the trick Ramati pulled. At one point during our one-to-one talk he asked to use the phone to call his rabbi. He dialed twice. Although I turned to my bookshelf, ostensibly to give him privacy, I listened carefully. For the first call he purposely futzed around with a wrong number. Then he dialed again, spoke to the rabbi about a big donation . . ."

"Yea, I heard . . . I was wondering about that."

"Okay, but he never spoke to him."

"What?" Aviva all but screamed.

"It was a bluff. The second time he called he dialed only six numbers. I'm the Sherlock Holmes of the telephone."

Aviva laughed and shook her head. "Just like him to do that."

"When he asked me if I wanted to talk to the rabbi, I should have called his bluff."

"He would have told you the rabbi just hung up, sorry."

I tapped the diary pages I'd finished reading. Up to the yellow book-mark. I tucked the little piece of paper in the book. Waved the little black book like a warning flag and returned it to her. "Here's the answer to your self-delusion. In your own words. This silent treatment. What a bizarre weapon! What an odd form of mental cruelty!"

Aviva pursed her lips. Little wrinkles converged there.

"For no reason at all he'd stop talking to me. At least no reason any normal person could think of." She shook her head and sighed. "Here's an example. In Israel he got to love chips—thought it the best food. Now, I don't particularly care for fried anything, it's not healthy, but to please him I fried potatoes. Once the chips came out a bit on the burnt side. He pushed the dish away, left the table, and didn't talk to me for two days. Now isn't that absurd?"

And she laughed that shy, self-deprecating laugh, a sad laugh, exhaled through her nose.

"I don't know," I said with a smile. "There is a scale of silence. Burnt toast, two hours. Burnt chips, two days. Burnt cake, three. At least there's a method to his madness. It has to be in proportion to the cooking time. Luckily you didn't burn a steak. That would be a week."

She snorted her helpless little laugh again. "There were times when he didn't speak to me for two weeks. And sleep in another room."

"Two whole weeks? Twice seven days. You must have burned the garage."
She threw her head back and laughed delightedly.

"Who knows? He always had some reason. Or no reason. And then after
a week *he'd* be the one to come back to me and make love."

"And you would agree."

"Yes. You know. To keep peace. And then the cycle would start all over
again . . . I was so stupid. I should have seen at the outset the signs of his
warped personality. That tyrannical Arab mentality of subjugating a woman,
of thinking of her as dirt, except for one thing . . . What a mess, huh? Why
is that men always have their way? Why is that men prevail? Why do men
rule the world?"

"Why? I'll tell you why and I'll be blunt. Not because of power. But the
penis. The power of the penis. Penis Power. PP. Call it a third leg or a sixth
finger, but it's that extra appendage that gives em power. If women would
have them, why then *they'd* rule the world."

"But then they'd be the men," Aviva protested, then added with a
grimace: "Once, to make light of his not talking to me, I told him with a
laugh, Research has shown that the average husband spends four minutes
a day talking to his wife. That much? he said, and wondered what a man
could possibly talk about to his wife for four full minutes. That's about 240
seconds. I told him it doesn't include bawling out the children, complaining to the wife, asking the kids to shut lights, take out the garbage, bring
him his robe, get off the phone, shouting at them not to bother him,
scream, or throw things. The next day he was actually talking to me. My
God, I thought. It's made an impression. Wow! It sank in. He's actually
sharing something with me. Then suddenly he looked at his watch and
stopped talking. In mid-sentence. Your four minutes are up."

"It shows," I said, "that he's not totally devoid of humor."

"Yeah, and so's a rattlesnake. A couple of days later he got into a longer
talk with me. Again I couldn't believe it. He'd been after some kind of
official position as an aide to someone on the New York City Taxi Commission. Of course it would help him financially, right? And for some reason
he was talking animatedly to me for twenty minutes. I thought, my God,
I was wrong, he has reformed. Then he realized what he'd been doing. So
he didn't talk to me the next five days."

I wanted to laugh but was afraid to.

Aviva shook her head. "I can't believe I fell for a madman like that. Why
do these things always happen to me? In retrospect, all the pieces now fit
together. My mother was right. She had better insight than me. She saw
early on what I was blind to. You know when the break came? I used to,
for the fun of it, at the very beginning, put our toothbrushes in the holder
face-to-face. Then he took his, put it in the last hole, and faced it the

opposite way. Just like he was turning away from me in bed and facing the wall."

Aviva fell silent, a resigned little smile on her face. At that moment, with Aviva looking helpless, a lost little butterfly in a garden of trampled flowers, at that moment I felt I was Guido and that Aviva was mine. I was overwhelmed with compassion for her. My whole life, she wrote, has been a fuzzy dream that hovers between reality and deep sleep. Or: from daydream to nightmare. No. I didn't feel I was Guido. I felt I was me and that Aviva was mine. I wanted to kiss her, to decorate her with warm kisses, to dip her body in kisses like sprinkles on a cone. I looked at her hands. Her long, slim, well-tended fingers were lightly pressed together. I could kiss her hands forever, I said to myself, those talented hands that make such beautiful music. I looked at her as she gazed, lost in thought, out the window. A woman ripe in her late-thirties beauty. The sort of loveliness that cannot be matched by any girl in her teens or twenties. Ripe, attractive, not only radiating but pulsating sexuality. Wanting, wanting. Still able for another three or four years of child bearing to bear the child I so longed for. And why not? Why should the line end with me? Should such a terrific gene bank, so carefully nurtured since Adam, end with me? I'm single. She's single-to-be. Why not? If she could love Guido with all her heart and disattach herself, why couldn't she love me?

Aviva sat comfortably on the sofa, not like the Arab nervously at the edge, ready to spring like a tiger, pounce like a beast of prey. I wondered if to keep the peace she too would make love to me, but first we'd have to quarrel and make up. In my mind's eye I saw my arms spreading wide like an angel's wings, like a huge, warm, furry cloak in which I'd enwrap her until the warm cloak surrounded both of us. I wanted to make the best of her dreams come true. Along with mine.

I approached, raised her by the hand, and embraced her. She put her arms not around me but on my chest as if in prayer. They felt like a barrier between us. Where she placed her hands made the inside of my heart feel cold. She demurely pressed her cheek into my shoulder.

"Oh, Charlie, I'm more confused than ever."

"Do you know," I said cheerfully, "that this is the first time you've ever call me by my name?"

"Really? And you've never called me Aviva."

"Aviva," I said.

Three Dreams

Dream one:

She holds photos of herself and can't recognize herself. "That's not me. They look better than me," she says.

Interpretation:

 Because of poor self-image—no pun intended—you can't recognize yourself. You think you are worse than the pictures, or that the pictures don't represent the real you.

Dream two:

 Aviva is a bride dressed in what seems to be a crystal wedding gown. Her nakedness is seen but at three spots the crystal is etched and it fuzzed the nakedness underneath. When asked what type of gown she's wearing, her response is: It's not crystal but ice. And she waits for the hot groom to prick through the ice and melt it.

Interpretation:

 The old fear of being seen naked in public is evident here, combined with a longing to be a true warm flesh-and-blood bride, not an ice princess.

Dream Three:

 She comes to Guido and says:
 "I'm special."
 "No, I'm special," he says.
 She then says, "I'm specialier."
 To which Guido responds: "Okay, do you have one of these?"
 And he proceeds to display his cuke.
 "Sure," she says and starts looking for one in her pants. Then she begins to cry. "I had one just a while ago . . . now I can't find it . . . you stole mine."

Interpretation:

 That she thinks she's special and even "specialer" is a positive thought; but she subsumes herself to the male, the old Freudian penis envy by looking for a cock, which only in the dreamworld can she presume to have. She mourns her loss of specialness by crying, but strangely her specialness is linked to a cock, perhaps his, which she's crazy for. The tension in the relationship can be seen by the fact that she accuses him of taking away that specialness. And the paradox is that her specialness is indeed what makes him what he is. Maybe she wants his cock so that he can't use it elsewhere, or maybe to keep at least a part of him for herself while he is away.

And then I told her about an original thought I had had about dreams, a thought that flashed just before I was about to doze off one night. All dreams have two legs and two hands, and then I woke up and the semi-sleep eidetic image vanished. I would have loved for it to continue. What did it mean? And then I thought—and Aviva loved my interpretation—that sometimes the hands lift you up, sometimes the legs give you a boot in the ass.

17

Usually Aviva came in beautifully dressed. For me or for her cello coach, I don't know. This time too. But there was something amiss. The garb didn't fit the demeanor. She wore a low-cut white jacket—linen, it seemed— and an off-white skirt of a different material. A simple gold necklace adorned her neck. But her makeup wasn't carefully applied. It detracted from her queenly looks. She looked awful, like a withered December leaf. Upset. She'd aged during the week. Other times she'd sort of gently lower herself onto the sofa; sort of float down. Today she sank.

"What's up?"

"You can tell?"

"Of course."

"Trouble."

"More than usual?"

She nodded.

"Why is the world so rotten? Why can't things be perfect?"

I gave her a sad smile. "The world was created imperfect, say Paracelsus, a medieval Swiss physician and alchemist, and God put man into it in order to perfect it."

"He's sure doing a lousy job," Aviva said.

"I agree."

She sighed. "I got a letter." She waved her hand as if to drive the thought away. "Oh, it's so damn complicated. He's so complicated, so manipulative, dammit. That inevitability word is now my beacon."

Shine, shine, I thought, Shine, beacon, shine.

I waited. Here was a turn. I just raised my chin a mite to indicate: go ahead.

"You remember I told you I'd studied for a couple of years with the cellist Ian Plaskow?"

"Yes, of course."

"Well, after I told Guido that I'd once had dinner with Plaskow, Guido kept badgering me to tell him all about my romantic links with him. I told him there were none. But he kept asking and asking and insisting there had to be." She was out of breath. As if she'd run from home to get here. "So to get him off my back I concocted a very brief affair with Plaskow, lasting a couple of months, when he supposedly visited me the one time a month he came to New York."

"But in reality . . ."

"The relationship was always student and teacher. I always called him Mister Plaskow. I stood in awe of him. But that's neither here nor there. Guido kept pressing me. Admit, admit, he told me. I won't believe you till you admit. And if I admit, will you leave me alone? I said. If you admit just like that, mechanically, he said, I won't believe you. It was like out of a comedy routine. He had me both ways. Still, I figured, it'd be best to have him believe it happened than to tell the truth and say no and have him hound me." Aviva drew a deep breath again. "And don't think that this topsy-turvy scene isn't representative of our entire skewed relationship . . . Also, I knew that since Guido had photographed Plaskow—he took that famous photo of Plaskow coming off the plane after he'd won the Tchaikovsky Prize in Moscow with Casals embracing him—I knew he'd be jealous, as indeed he was."

"Ah," I said. "Now I understand the trouble. Plaskow wrote you a letter."

"You're very perceptive. But wait. It's more convoluted. It's signed Plaskow♥ but it's really by Guido. You follow?"

"No. Not at all. Even the convolutions have wrinkles."

"You see, Guido is testing me. And I don't like it. He's become like the Arab. That would have been one of *his* tricks. I despise that. Can't stand it. Guido evidently went to a Philly suburb and, making believe he was Ian, wrote asking me if I'd like to see him. He said he got my address from a mutual acquaintance at the Manhattan School of Music. He wrote that he's disengaging now, would like to renew our acquaintance, but I'd have to write to him care of a POB as P.I. Laskow."

"How did you know it was Guido? The handwriting?"

"No. He's not that stupid. He used a typewriter, but I'm attuned to tricks♥♥ like that. He must think I'm a moron."

"Did you answer the alleged Plaskow?"

"Of course."

"What did you say?"

"Let me ask you. What do you think I did?"

Aviva smiled a wicked smile. It was so unlike her, this aggressive stance, this rebutting of a question of mine with another question.

"You wrote back a short note saying Yes."

"But what upsets me most is," she said, nodding, "is that I didn't confront him with this. He's got me so bamboozled with his sweet talk and promises and touches that I'm in a different space zone when I'm with him. My trouble is I can't confront people, even if there's a smoking gun. When I got into my car to say good-bye, I was about to say something, the words almost came out of my mouth, my lips formed the words, but then I shut my mouth, sewed my lips, as my mother used to say."

"But by saying Yes to Plaskow, you risked driving Guido away."

"True, but I figured I have to get back at him. Punish him in my own way. I don't like being snooped on. I don't like entrapment. Fairy tale tests. He's not the FBI and I'm not a crooked politician."

♥See ABC Directory, *Obsessed with Ian Plaskow.*
♥♥See ABC Directory, *Case of the Typed Letter, the.*

I applauded her and shouted, "Good for you." But now I didn't know who to believe. Had she or hadn't she had an affair with Plaskow? But even if she did fifteen or sixteen years ago, Guido's trick was a low one. Why did he do such a stupid thing? Maybe Guido is nastier than I thought. Or maybe Plaskow *was* writing to her.

"You see, crooks give themselves away," Aviva said. "Guido screwed up on two scores. First, the school I went to before I enrolled in PAMA was the Mannes School of Music, not the Manhattan School of Music. He was always forgetting that. And secondly, and this Guido would not have known, Plaskow never typed. He didn't want to take a chance hurting his fingers, he once told me. All his correspondence was in longhand."

"So Guido never knew you were onto his trick."

"No."

Good, I thought.

"The full impact of his trick hit me much later—that's when I usually react to events, much later—and I was very angry. I didn't respond to that box number till about ten days later. But I will write to Guido. I want to let him know that I know."

"To his home?"

She smiled. "Oh, no. To his office."

"You've wanted to leave him for some time now."

"I know . . ." she said with a resigned voice and then the "but" popped out of her mouth, as if a dybbuk in her were speaking. "I'm confused, aren't I?"

"If you had the opportunity, would you call him and explain?"

She leaned forward, actually jerked forward, as if the same force in her that compelled her to say "but" was steering her spirit. Her lips moved, shaped an incomprehensible syllable before she uttered, "No."

Better, I almost shouted. She was angry and I'd never seen Aviva angry at all. I thought it was healthy that she expressed her rage and outrage.

"I don't like being set up for a sting operation. And, anyway, what business is it of his if I want to meet Plaskow? I'm not Guido's wife, and he has no rights over me. *He* has another woman too. Would he like it if I caught him with his wife?"

"You're right. So you definitely won't call."

"I think that's the wisest course. It's most painless this way," she said, "because each time I want to break up he convinces me to resume, don't you think?"

I nodded and tried to sound neutral. "I think you've indeed chosen the wisest course . . . So, then," I stopped and rubbed my hands, "it's not trouble after all—but relief. That he did this is a blessing in disguise."

For a moment Aviva brightened. "Yes . . . yes . . . you're right . . . not trouble. Relief! A blessing in disguise!"

Best, I crowed.

"Do you know what Guido's test shows?" I asked her.

"Yes. That he doesn't trust me."

I nodded. "And you, do you trust him?"

"Completely," she said quickly, then added, "up to a point."

"What is that supposed to mean?" I said, annoyed.

"Well, you know, photographers, editors, always on assignment. You know, you've heard, photographers always make love to their models."

"So you don't trust him."

"Well, it's a moot issue now. But I do."

"But that's a contradiction. I've never heard anything so absurd. Completely . . . up to a point."

Aviva shrugged. "I don't know," she said weakly.

We looked at each other for a moment, a neutral, noncommittal look. Then she asked:

"Excuse me for being personal again, but would you have done something like that?"

"Of course not!" I stood. Paced. "Absolutely not. Never." I enjoyed Aviva looking at me, her glance following me wherever I went in the room. "To trap someone you love? Are you kidding?"

And then that notion I'd once had, of twinning, one of Thomas Mann's favorite themes, returned. Was it possible that Guido was a kind of twin, an alter ego? And that's why we competed for the same girls when we were in school? And even—my Lord, almost a generation later, when we were grown men with gray coming in at the sides of our temples (mine, not his)—a generation later we fell in love with the same woman. And it was all capped with the Arab falling into my lap. Doesn't that say something about that mirror imaging and twinning of souls that I was now so ready to accept? That plunging, gravity-affirming verb—falling in love; falling in lap.

Then Aviva's face changed as though the light had been sucked out of it. She opened her mouth, lips twisted as if she were having an attack, but no words came out. Suddenly, but so quickly I only saw the echo of the movement in my mind rather than the movement itself, she slid to the floor, crumpled herself into a ball and cried, "Help me! Please, help me! I'm drowning . . ." she said into her knees, "I feel as if I'm in a glass, you know those wax-filled glasses they use for yorzeit candles, except that the wick and the light and the flame are gone, and I'm so small I can fit in there. The glass is filled with water not with light and I'm drowning. Please! Help me! The flame is gone. You're so big and I'm so small in that little glass in which I'm drowning. Please! Help me! Save me!"

She rocked very slowly.

I looked down at her. I stretched my hand—it was trembling—to pick her up. I touched her hair. She looked at me, said No with her eyes, with one sideways motion of her head. Her squint was more noticeable than ever.

"In the olden days," she said, "people were unhappy because they didn't have food, money, clothing. No hope of ever improving their lives. Like people during the Depression. Now people are unhappy because they're unhappy. Out of this Depression you can't buy your way out. It's like a second skin. Why are we so unhappy? Help me! Please!" And she began to sob. "I'm drowning in that little yorzeit glass from which the light has gone, the flame has gone, and I'm so small and you're a giant and I'm so unhappy I could die."

I bent down, then sat next to her. "You're in mourning for your life. That's why you're using that yorzeit glass image. Don't mourn. You're very much alive."

"My God," she said, as if waking out a trance, "in mourning for one's own life!"

"It's not my image. There's a heart-piercing line said by Masha, one of the minor characters in Chekhov's *The Seagull*: I am in mourning for my life."

I stood and stretched my hands out to her. "Come." This time she accepted and I helped her up. I pressed her to me. But I didn't kiss her. No, now that she was at the ebb of her fortune, I wouldn't take advantage of her vulnerability.

"It'll be all right," I said.

"Promise?" Her eyes were wide open, hopeful, like a baby's.

How could I promise? How could one human being reverse a decades-long slide with one word? But I nodded anyway and that made her feel better.

"You know what, why don't you treat yourself to a movie tonight? After supper, just get into your car and go see a film. It'll do you good. Okay?"

"Okay," she said. "I have a lesson tonight. But I'll do it one of these nights. I promise. I'll curl up in the safe haven of a movie and enjoy myself."

I smiled. "I'll share this with you. You'll appreciate it. My father had a cousin, a survivor of the Holocaust, who when he came into a room would look up at the ceiling. I didn't understand this till I was older, but later he told me that he always looked for an attic, an imagined trapdoor, wondering if the occasion should arise, would he have a hiding place, a safe haven, and for how many and for how long."

"I wish," said Aviva, "I could find a magic attic."

She touched my cheek before she left.

For a moment I imagined that that was *my* magic attic.

Guido

Before he came to meet Aviva that Monday Guido walked through the
streets of New York to calm down. He didn't go to his office; he didn't go
home. He had the awfulest presentiment of death. He had been in London
for two days and on the flight back for the first time he was mortally afraid.
First, he thought the plane would crash. When it took off smoothly, hit no
air pockets, and landed safely, he was surprised. In the cab from Kennedy
to the city he thought he'd be rammed by a truck. For a while a hearse
followed the cab. Was the god of traffic sending him signals? In the city he
thought he'd be mugged or hit by a bus. He felt scooped out, empty. A
vacuum soughed through him. He found himself on Sixth Avenue. The
early morning was warm. Mid-June already. Sunshine so bright it blinded
his eyes even through sunglasses. Of course, no birds sang in New York.
They had left centuries ago. He felt depressed. On a Richter scale of depression he'd record a minus ten. The flags were out. Flag Day. There were
still patriots in New York where birds no longer sang. He passed flower
shops on the street and brushed against the leaves of young, seven-foot
trees pressed together like a forest on the sidewalk. They blocked the sun
and created an aura of cool. Felt good on his skin those green caresses.
They gave him a bit of the love he needed. He turned and went by them
again. He needed that. He thought of Aviva caressing him.♥

He took a cab to the *Long Island Post* parking lot, picked up his car and
drove to the appointed site. When she didn't show he understood the
reason for his depression. His psyche had sensed it before he had. But he
wasn't going to let her off easy; she promised and she'd keep her promise.
He drove out to her house and without ceremony rang her bell. She opened
the door. No surprise on her face, but the chill of her unwelcome sent a
shiver through his back. Not even the hint of a sad smile. They stood there
silently looking at each other like strangers.

♥See ABC Director, *X-rated screwing*.

He stepped inside and shut the door, the door that had been his door, shut the door behind him. He didn't know what they spoke of for the next thirty seconds. He took off his sunglasses and set them on a little table.

The blow finally came when Aviva told him mercilessly, coldly, her face slightly puffy and old-looking: No more. She'd thought it over while he was away and to put it as simply and bluntly as possible, she no longer wanted anything to do with a married man.

"But I was married all along," was his defense. "It didn't seem to bother you then."

"It did. And I told you all along, but you didn't seem to care about my feelings. And that's another problem. You never cared about my feelings."

Immobile in the middle of her living room, their hands at their sides. His arms longed to embrace her. His arms strained, like in the old children's game when one's hand is pressed with force against a wall and then when one lets go the hand levitates seemingly of its own accord. He longed to embrace her. But Aviva stood like a mannequin. Devoid of feeling. Out of the corner of his eyes he saw her cello, and it prompted a rush of memories.

"Do you want me to go?" he asked stupidly, giving her an opening he shouldn't have. She might not have said it so directly. She was too polite. "Yes."

He had once imagined this scene in the privacy of his thoughts. Make her laugh, his will—shaped like a lifesaver—urged him, but now he couldn't think of anything funny to say. His only hope was that this scene had replayed itself a number of times and each time he had the skill, good fortune, persistence, sheer browbeat force to get her to change her mind. Once Guido had even succeeded in getting her over to his house when she had said, No more, it's easier this way over the phone . . . Once she was there, he sweet-talked her to bed. She only halfheartedly protested and laughed as he carried her up the stairs. "You'll fall . . . I'll fall . . . I'm too heavy . . . You're carrying me and my belly . . . it's too much for you . . ." "I'll leave you downstairs and take your belly with me." Upstairs, in bed, in a passionate embrace with him, she fondly recriminated, "What am I going to do with you?"—a litany that would repeat itself countless times till he once said, "I told myself that the next time I hear that I'm going to say: I'm not an object that one can do things with."

"You're not?" she said, with that innocent gaze, that purposeful flutter of her eyelids.

But now that he had propelled those idiotic words into the air, "Do you want me to go?" and she had said, "Yes," he called her bluff and went to the door, hoping she would summon him back. He closed the door, then opened it again (as he had imagined it and in his fantasy took her into his arms and without music in the background one could see the heart-palpitating double embrace of destined lovers reunited).

"No," he gave out a feral cry. "I can't do it."

But stonily she said, "You're out the door already . . . and cut the melo-drama. It doesn't impress me."

The look on her face said he could do nothing more with her. He closed the door. Closed the chapter, the book, the epic known as Aviva-Guido. He couldn't believe it. Gone the destined ecstasy. In the car he put his hand on the seat for his sunglasses. Realized he'd forgotten them in the house. He rang; she opened. No smile on her face as in those sunny days when he came for lessons and that shy, radiant smile suffused her face.

"I forgot my sunglasses."

She gave them to him.

"And something else," he said.

"What?"

He looked for a sprig of tenderness in that *What* of hers, that *What* that he would often hear as a loving whisper in reply to his *Aviva*.

"My heart."

"You can have it back," she said.

She didn't say it slowly, savoring it. She snapped it out, a gut reaction.

"No," he said. "It's yours," and without enthusiasm took her in his arms. She stood stiffly. Did nothing. Said nothing. As if she were dead. As if all the years of loving and cries from the heart were wiped away.

"Don't cut me up this way," he said as he slammed the door shut behind him. In a flash he saw her face, slightly pudgy, hair awry, eyes puffy, skin darkish. She could have posed for a photo of an Ozark woman standing alone and forlorn in the doorway of her shack during the Depression.

Her "You can have it back" cut him like a knife. As if she didn't give a damn for all that had passed between them. A spurt of bile ran through him. He felt its quick passage like a speedboat in the river of his guts. Maybe she already had someone else. The rebound factor. She'd done it before. She herself admitted it. The ungrateful slut. She didn't deserve him. In his mind he'd made her a princess and she turned out to be a chamber-maid in an eighteenth-century English roadside tavern. Ready to hitch up her skirts and tumble with the next comer. Ready to go back to Ian. Son of a bitch! But he wasn't going to tell her he wrote that letter. Let her wait for him. Until Kingdom Come.

"So it wasn't love," he'd asked her before he left.

"Maybe it wasn't."

"And maybe it was just sex . . ."

"Maybe," she said.

What was wrong with him? Why was he feeding her those self-defeating lines?

"Your Arab didn't satisfy you . . . so you found yourself another stud."

The bitch. Still longing for new thrills at fifty-five. Who knows? Maybe older. He'd never seen her passport or driver's license. No matter how old they were their pussy still longed for cock. Her pubic hairs were turning white; she had old age hairs sprouting on her cheeks but her nether zone didn't watch calendar or clock. Menopause had reduced her estrogen but she still liked to fuck. But no longer with him, the slut.

"I may not have been the first," he told her once, "but I'm going to be the last." And later: "Can you imagine yourself making love with anyone else?"

"I never thought of that," she'd said. "I guess not."

"To a man, I mean," he said, and she laughed.

And again he told her, "This happens to a man only once in his lifetime."

But now she was ready for another man, and who knows, maybe she had him already, which may account for her stiff reaction to his embrace, the callousness of her remarks, the ease with which she was able to wipe away their loving past. The trouble with Aviva was she couldn't take a man for more than two years. That was her maximum.

"And maybe it was *only* sex?" he said, standing by the door.

"Yes," she said. "That's what it was."

Was. Was. She and her past tense. She used grammar as a political tool. She and her was. So she was tired of him. And he was no less tired of her. The zing was gone; it was getting boring. He didn't want to admit it. It came bubbling up in his veins and he suppressed it. Usually, men who screw their wives think of their girlfriends. But he, dope that he was, lately he'd begun thinking of Tammy while screwing Aviva. Now didn't that show, he thought, how off balance things were? When such an oddball thought passes through a lover's mind, Guido realized, things were definitely no good. What an absurd—fantasizing about one's own wife! He'd been with Aviva too long. In fact, research had shown that affairs last on the average eighteen months. The eighteen months were long up. And he *was* getting tired. Tired of her incessant, When are you going to be with me? Tired of her repetitive Really? whenever he told her how much he loved her. She was fifty-five now—God, how she'd aged the past year—in five years she'd be sixty. Yuk! Maybe even sooner. For after forty, women age quicker. It's no longer cross-country skiing but a downhill plunge. She'd be withering and he'd be at the height of his vigor. She would be old and wrinkled. Her breasts would sag; her belly droop. Like in the old high school science experiment where iron filings arrange themselves like fine wrinkles on a piece of paper above a magnet, so would her face look. Crows' feet would march down from her eyes seeking mates on her neck.

"Sex, huh?"

"Yeah, sex." But she wasn't so sure this time. Later she'd say she just said it in anger. Didn't mean it. How could she mean it if she loved him?

Yes, that's what it was. Was, was.

"I'm leaving for Italy in a couple of days," hoping he'd salvage something from the sentimentality of a journey. "I flew in from London just for you. I didn't go home. I didn't even go to my office."

"That's nice," she said flatly.

She didn't even say, Have a nice trip, he thought sadly. Did you miss me? she would always say when he returned. Did you miss me?

He also noticed that he didn't push the days as quickly between visits as much as he used to. He would tear the days off from a phantasmagoric paper calendar, unable to wait to the end of the day when he would rip, rip it off so the next day could come quicker. Now that too was gone. He didn't prod the mule-stubborn hours on to rush to their destination. And he'd long promised himself that he would be the one to cut. And on his terms. These women were all alike. In fact, who knows what sad Tammy did when he was abroad? She always looked so innocent, but maybe her passion-driven body couldn't wait for two or three weeks while he was gone. Women, they were all the same. The minute the guy's back was turned, bam bang, the clit had to be rubbed. It was good he was going abroad soon. No more complications.

Yes. That's what it was.

Well, then screw you, Aviva!

"You can be mean and rough, can't you?" she'd once told him.

"When I'm rubbed the wrong way." He smiled at her.

"Then I'll rub you the right way," she said, rubbing him the right way.

But now she rubbed him the wrong way. She wanted to see Ian Plaskow. She didn't want him any more. Which meant he was through with her.

From a convenience store a few blocks from Aviva's house he called Teresa.

"Hello?"

"Hi," he said.

"Hi-ii! . . . You calling me again from London?" Oh, that bright, perky, devoted voice.

"Alone?"

"Yeah. Do you miss me?"

"That's why I'm calling . . . I wish I could see you . . . I miss you so much."

"Me too . . . That's so sweet of you to call . . . You okay?"

She was running out of things to say, he felt.

"Sure I'm okay . . . Miss me?"

"I'm so horny for you," she said. "Wanna phone phuck me?"

"Yeah . . . wait . . . just a minute. Excuse me. I've just been handed a fax . . . Will you be home in an hour?"

"Yeah."

"Stay there. Don't move . . . Hubby away?"

"Yeah."

"Where?"

"North Carolina somewhere."

"Okay, gotta go. Bye, talk to you soon."

He bought her a dozen yellow roses, would have clipped them from his back yard but it was out of the way, and drove to Teresa's place. When hub goes trucking, he thought, then begins the fucking. When out zooms the rig thing, in slips the big thing. Oh, he could go on rhyming two-timing for hours. Mr. Big Mack was roaring toward Raleigh you bet, so they'll spend the morning moaning in Teresa's little working-class house working up a sweat.

He rang her bell, pictured the surprised look on her face.

She opened without asking, Who's there?

"You're here," she said.

"Uh-uh, I'm not."

"What are you doing here?" she said happily. She looked around to see if any neighbors were looking.

"You'll see in a minute, Miss Cliché, if you let me in."

He stepped in and kissed her as soon as she closed and locked the door.

"I can't believe it. And I'm thinking, How sweet, he calls from London again."

"You liked that London call?"

"Ye-e-ess."

"You'd rather phone phuck?"

"No-ooo," she sang a down pitch tune. "I like the real thing better."

He still held the flowers.

"You brought me flowers." she said, burying her nose in them.

She put the roses in a vase then threw her arms around him and, eyes closed, kissed him. He picked her up and carried her to her bed.

"I flew back just for you."

"You did?"

"I went crazy those two days without you. The further away I'm from you the more I miss you. I had to go to Rome but I wangled a trip back for a couple of days . . . I didn't even go home."

"You must be exhausted."

"Yeah, I wanna lie down."

She giggled.

"So I'm gonna phone phuck you in person."

She undressed with exaggerated slowness, not taking her eyes from his, and threw each item of clothing in a different direction.

"Now you," she said.

"This happens to a man only once in a lifetime," he said.

In gratitude, she pressed up to him, kissed his lips and everything else as well.

"Tell me," she said, "what happens if you die while screwing?"

"What a morbid thought? What a way to go! You think I'm that old?"

"All my boyfriends were twenty-two, twenty-three, twenty-seven. I've never gone out with anyone older than twenty-eight."

"Me neither," he said.

"You're *thirty-seven*. That's old. Who knows what exertion can do to you."

"The great Dutch philosopher, Ian Plaskow—you heard of him, of course."

"No-ooo," she stretched the syllable shyly.

"One of his theories is that love makes you live longer. So with you I'll live and fuck forever."

"Still. What happens if you die here in bed? . . . I'll be so embarrassed."

"That's all you think about is your embarrassment . . . How do you think I'll feel?"

"How can you feel anything if you're dead?"

He looked at her. Could never tell if she was joking or just ingenuous in her simplicity.

"Dead is dead," she said. "It's the living who suffer the embarrassment."

"If it happens, just walk me out the door to my car and write me a suicide note."

"And what happens if you fuck my brains out?"

"No chance of that," he said.

"I mean if you, remember you once said you're gonna fuck me to death. Well, what if you do? What would you do, like, if today you fucked me to death?"

"Take the flowers back."

"Will you say, what's that prayer Jews say to the dead?"

"*For* the dead. You mean Kaddish?"

"Yeah, Will you say Kaddish for me?"

"Sure."

"Promise."

"Yes."

She gave a blissful little smile, as if already she'd been imbued with a halo of sanctity.

"Why you so hung up on death and dying?"

"It's part of my life . . . Because my husband drives a rig . . . I don't know," she whined. "Fuck me again. I didn't have enough. This happens to a girl only once in her lifetime." And she stuck her tongue in her cheek and cocked her head at him with a glint in her eyes.

Charlie

A few days had passed since I'd last seen Aviva. I was in the Garden City office with a patient. He'd asked me a question and I stood and walked about my office. I glanced out the window. A big American flag, fluttering, hung out for Flag Day, blocked my view, but it didn't prevent me from seeing Aviva emerging from her station wagon across the street. I excused myself and went into the waiting room. She opened the door, obviously distraught.

"I saw you from the window . . . Is something wrong? I'm with a patient . . ."

"It's an emergency," she said. "Please."

"Why didn't you call?"

"I just got in the car and drove . . ."

I took her into a side room, an alcove really, where records and files were kept. The tears magnified Aviva's big gray eyes. "I'll be right back."

Inside, I told the patient that I had an emergency. Amid apologies, I said I would cancel the fee for this visit and would not charge him for the next one. I escorted the pleased man out and brought Aviva into the office.

"I'm through with him," she said. "Finished. I was supposed to have seen him one last time in the parking lot, but I decided against it. He came to the house. The atmosphere was icy. He asked me if he should go. He thought I'd say no, like I always did. But I told him yes. It's all over. And I feel much better."

She looked up at me. "There's no point in dragging this out any longer. These ups and downs are destroying me. I have enough problems at home. I can't get that letter test out of my mind, even though I didn't mention it to him. Let him think I didn't suspect. And he can't keep his eyes off other women. Last time we were together in the car we almost crashed because he turned his head to follow a pretty girl. He didn't even care I was sitting next to him."

Guido hasn't changed, I thought. Not a bit in twenty years.

"He's flying to Italy in a couple of days. I didn't even wish him a safe trip."

I nodded slowly, sympathetically, as if to counsel her: Don't worry about it.

"But you never know with him. We split and then he returns. Recently, when we separated, God knows, for the sixth or umpteenth time, he returned a videotape of a Casals festival I'd lent him. He comes to the house. We don't say a word to each other. Just stared at each other. Then he said to me, 'There's that look in your eye.' 'What look?' 'I see it,' he said. 'It's glowing on your face. Your eyes are misting.' And in truth they were. I was crying over what could have been. 'It's no good,' he said. 'You can put a wall between us, you can put time between us to make believe you're going to forget me, but you won't forget me. That magic is there like a presence, a star, a light that won't go away. Whenever you see me or think of me, that light, a light a photographer would love, that light, like the light your eyes are shedding right now,' and I covered my eyes with my hands so he shouldn't see the light, but he continued, 'that light is going to shine from your eyes because I'm the switch and you're the flash bulb and a bulb ain't no good without a switch and a switch is useless without a bulb.' He voodooed me, right? Jinxed, hexed, put the pizzazz on me."

"He did *not* put a spell on you," I said emphatically. "You're not a primitive, are you? Who's in control?"

"I am," Aviva said weakly but she straightened up. "Me. I'm in control of my life. My destiny. Me me me."

"That's the spirit," I said. I put both my hands, brotherly, on her shoulders. "I'm proud of you."

At this point I gave her a manila envelope I'd prepared for her, which she opened with a little cry of surprise.

"You forgot it here. I just found it this morning between the cushions."

"Thanks," and she grimaced at her carelessness. "And I thought I misplaced it somewhere at home . . . I could have sworn I took it with me . . . You didn't . . . I mean . . . you know . . ." she faltered.

"Would I do such a thing? I didn't go beyond the yellow bookmark."

"No. I guess not." And she looked up at me warmly. "And I'm proud of you . . . For everything."

And then Aviva said what she said, and it must have taken all the will at her command to say it. She who never made a move on her own but let herself be the moved object in the vortex of the storm, she who never initiated, but reacted to the invitation of others, she, vulnerable now, spoke.

She said, "Do you want me?" "Do you want me?" I heard. "Do you want me?" she said.

Like chocolate on the cake, I wanted to savor the best for last. In fact, I persuaded myself that I didn't really understand the full import of her words, that they did not mean what they were supposed to mean but meant more like, "Do you want me to wait?"

"Well?" she said. But she didn't repeat the question.

So quickly to bounce from one man to the next? I thought. But I did want to make sure I'd heard correctly.

"Did you say: Do you want me?"

"Yes," she said, looking directly at me.

"Do you love me?" I countered, even though I wanted, oh, how I wanted to tell her that I'm dying for her.

"Yes. It's the old story. Pupils fall in love with their teachers, and patients with their therapists. And I've been falling in love with you in Wednesday increments," she said with a mischievous smile. That Aviva smile. "And then when Mondays and other days were added, the increments increased . . . oh, there's a good word for it that slips my mind now."

"Exponentially?"

"That's it. Exponentially. And do you love *me?*"

"So you love me too?" I said. I meant, of course, that she loved me as much as I loved her, but it must have come out wrong, for she assumed that I meant that she loved me in addition to Guido.

"You all know how to drive the hammered nails deeper," she said bitterly. "And turn them into screws."

Instead of explaining, my pride burst out like a Nijinksy leap and I snapped:

"Screws are your specialty . . . No, I withdraw that. I'm sorry." Guido had once quoted an old Italian saying: You can put potatoes back in a sack but not words that have left the mouth. I held my hands out to her. "I don't mean that." Then why did I say that? Confirming precisely her analysis of men. Just at the moment I should have displayed my tenderness I showed her my scorn. What was wrong with me? Did I fit into her presumption of what all men were like? Why did I snap at her? Did I, like Guido, want virgin oil in a crystal flask? Or was I like a confused little boy who, not quite knowing how to handle love, gives tweaks for hugs? None of the above. I was annoyed that she had loved Guido. That's what bugged me, I realized.

"You bastard! So you believed the Arab's accusations? And I had high hopes for you to be different than all the rest. But you're all alike! All all alike!" She wheeled and headed for the door.

I thought she'd go out the door and I thought that my arm would shoot out and I thought that I'd stop her and I thought that I'd seize her arm and I thought that I'd pull her to me and kiss her and affirm my feelings for her that had been welling up over the weeks, not by increments and then exponentially but by exponential increments, feelings I knew were growing in her too. Because Aviva had a practical nature. And I was available and Guido not. But I didn't want to be loved for practical feelings. I didn't want to be wanted because I was available, and I certainly didn't want to be wanted because Guido was not. But I didn't have to stop her. The football maneuver I had planned, a tackle that wouldn't hurt, was no longer necessary. Aviva got to the door and then her will, like a rag doll, collapsed. Her show was over. She couldn't pull off the dramatic exit and slam the door, the *Doll's House* Nora door bang that would be heard around the world. She sank down in a chair, eyes glazed, broken, defeated. With all her talent, with all her brilliance, her youthfulness, her beauty, poor Aviva was a lost soul. A billiard ball without a pocket. And now she wanted me to be her cue.

Years ago my ancestor Adam had tasted from the Tree of Knowledge, and so had I. And what good had it done me? For all my brains I was still a dope. Tasting of the knowledge tree didn't kill me—but I wasn't smart enough to take a bite out of the Tree of Life. So I didn't get death, but I didn't get life either. I was still waiting for something. Aviva. I saw her as my chance for life. To really—finally, finally—taste from the Tree of Life. For what good was knowledge without life? There's a beautiful Negro spiritual that goes: *Sit down servant*, and the servant says, *Can't sit down! My soul's so happy, I can't sit down!* Well, my soul's so happy because my eyes have seen the Tree of Life and I want to take a bite and taste of life. Yes, I saw her as the Tree of Life. Literally. I once had a dream where I saw her standing tall and proud, arms upraised, acknowledging the cheers of the crowd after a performance. And as she stood there in my dream her body became a trunk, her upraised arms branches. And goodly fruit dangled from her branches, fruit that offered life. So stand up, servant, and taste the tree. My soul so happy that I feel free.

I bent down before her on my haunches. "I'm sorry for what I said. Truly. Truly. I'm sorry, Aviva, I'm so sorry." I thought I'd bury my head in her head in her lap and have her stroke my head. I thought to lift her chin and kiss her eyes. What was I to do? I was on the exact middle of the seesaw. Could tilt either way. When she asked me if I loved her, why didn't I tell her the truth straight out? Why couldn't I say "yes, yes," with the passion and expectancy that Aviva had revealed to Guido? Or, better, with the passion I knew was in me. Would *my* psychologist say I was afraid of love and collapsed it like a wax paper cup when the crunch came? Why couldn't I take my heart in my own hands and show it the way? Why, as Aviva said about herself—or was it Guido who had said it?—did I consciously reject or destroy the very things that could be my salvation?

Aviva sensed my equivocation.

"What shall I do now? Stand in the center of town with an adorned letter *A*? Take poison? Or throw myself on the railroad track?"

Those three literary allusions, one after the other, wowed me. Hawthorne, Flaubert, Tolstoy, all in one sentence. Never thought of Aviva thinking that way. Perhaps another book, her *Diary of an Adulterous Woman,* could be her guide.

"Each generation finds its own way to suicide," I said.

"Quote of the day," she snapped. "Did you pull that out of your sleeve? Or is that a stock response of yours for a patient in deep distress?"

I didn't say a word.

"You too have changed overnight. Just like the Arab . . . Did anyone ever tell you you need a good psychologist?"

"I hope your rates are cheaper than mine," I said. "Only madmen go into this field." I dropped my voice. "You know what?" I tried to smile. To bring back the magic.

"What?" she said softly.

"Let's call a truce for a moment. Tell me what happened with Guido."

"No sense going over it again. I told you. It's finished."

"Really?" I coughed to hide my enthusiasm, cleared my throat and said diffidently. "Over? Are you absolutely sure?"

"Yes. Finally. He left in a rage."

"I'm going to ask you a question I never asked before."

"Yes? yes?" and she began comically to pant quickly like a puppy.

I smiled. "Did you enjoy making love to Guido?"

A flicker of disappointment passed like a moving thought before her eyes.

"I thought I told you I did. He made me so full of desire; I've never had a feeling like that before. But it's all gone now."

Then Aviva laughed. "You know, the Gnostics believed that the only way to avoid sin was to commit it and be rid of it."

"Again and again and again. My, my. You impress me more and more." I remember Guido saying that to me. So Guido's been teaching her other things too, I thought. "First, three authors in one breath and now ancient philosophers. Well, that's one sin you want to keep getting rid of. Like in one of Boccaccio's stories, where the priest tells a nubile fourteen-year-old about putting the devil into hell and she gets to love it so much that she wants him to keep putting that devil of his into her hell all the time."

"I want to talk about more important things," Aviva said. And she gave a little shrug. With one shoulder. It drove me wild. Blood swirled through my head. All this talk about her affair with Guido, it was as if she gradually, teasingly, were taking her clothes off before me, week after week. Should I put my arms around her? . . . But before I finished the thought, I had my arms around her shoulders. She tenderly touched my face with both hands and kissed me. In one quick motion I lifted her sweater and bra and kissed her breasts. We tumbled to the floor, kissing. She lifted her hips and I undid her slacks. It was so easy. We rolled over. She kissed my lips and face as I tugged at my belt, fly, pants.

"God, you're beautiful," I said. "You remind me of a movie star."

"Oh, God. I've been . . . wait . . . ing . . . for you . . . for . . . weeks . . . You're so kind. So loving. I felt the love flowing . . . out . . . of . . . you . . . for . . . weeks. Oh, God God God, oh God . . . God!" she screamed one long, high scream that broke into smaller ones like a flaming ember in a fireplace breaking into bits of fiery wood. Then she collapsed with a sigh and said, "I love you I love you I love you . . . I had one . . . You did it . . . I love you . . ."

My soul so happy I can't sit down. My soul so happy that I feel free. Amen. Singing Amen. My soul so happy and I feel free. My soul so happy I can't sit down. Hallelujah, my soul so happy I feel the tree. My soul so happy, my soul so free. My soul so happy I taste the tree.

When she opened her eyes I could only say, "Well, here we are."

My soul sang poetry, my lips dripped dross.

And Aviva said, "Wow. Wow . . . You do love me!"

Am I better than Guido, the words bubbled like fermentation on my tongue? Or will you say, Different? Will you say, Different, Aviva?

"A new chapter," I said. I was floating. Happy. Ecstatic. I'd won her, wooed her, wowed her. "I do love you, Aviva. I love you with all my being."

Wednesday morning?" I said. "Or at lunch break?"

"Can't. I have rehearsals. Is Thursday at four okay?"

"Fine. But it's a long time to wait . . . So you see, something good did come out of your Newberg Prize. If you hadn't won, there wouldn't have been an article in the *South Shore Weekly Reporter,* and I wouldn't have read it and I wouldn't have met you. That's destiny."

She smiled a glowing smile, a happy smile. "I love people who have a positive outlook on this world. Yes, destiny."

"Did you treat yourself to that cinema yet, my movie star?"

"I haven't forgotten . . . Today's been too hectic. Tomorrow's the night. You're not hinting that you want to go with me are you?"

"Yes."

"I'd like it, but I'm afraid. Especially after hearing the tape. It wouldn't be a good idea for us to be seen in a local movie, right?"

"Right," I said. "For who knows where the Arab prowls? . . . But the time will come."

Aviva nodded.

I don't know why, but that nod put the crowning flower on my blossoming tree of life.

Guido

He was addicted and he knew it. Just once more, he decided. He came to her house in the morning, knocked, no response, rang, heard the opening notes of Beethoven's *Ode to Joy*, remembered the times he rang and a moment later a glowing Aviva with a shy smile welcomed him to another lesson, another world, now rang again, no response, no movement behind the door, her smile settling in a postage stamp-size corner of his memory, heart pounding quicker, no sounds within, rang again, jabbing the button this time, once and once again. He waited a minute, two, pounded three times in anger at the door, half expected a dog to bark, then turned and left. He can't explain what prompted him to do it, but he looked up to the second story to the window he'd looked out of so many times and for a flick of a second sees in shutter speed the stir of a curtain, slight as exhalation, as if she'd been standing there all along watching him. When the wave of fury, of animal rage, surged through him he could not tell. Was it the moment his eye photographed that white curtain in motion, or was it after it hung still and the thought floated and popped that all through his ringing, his memories, his impatience, she'd been peeking down at him, immobile in her grim stubbornness not to let him in? In his body and soul he felt a great nervous jolt, and suddenly, without transition, he detested her. But a moment later, remembering the special intimacy she'd had in his life, his great rage crumbled like earth clods, melted like a color slide too close to the projection bulb, and left only regret and feelings of desolation. A frisson of surprise and *de ja vu* ran through him, for as he recalled these shifts of feelings he didn't know whether they were triggered by something he'd read—Maupassant, Conrad—or whether he truly felt them. But then the jolt returned. She'd betrayed him. Had no sense of loyalty, fidelity, trust. And the rage and detestation surged like a rapids, a waterfall. He wouldn't let her get away with it, he decided.

Years back, he had let Ava get away with it for betraying him, but not this one. Oh, no, not Aviva! For she'd lied to him all along. She was still carrying the torch for that teacher of hers. And the things that he had learned from Plaskow when he had gone to see him at PAMA recently, ostensibly to give him a photograph of Casals embracing the young cellist! According to Plaskow, Aviva had had every male at PAMA. On the other hand, it could have been sour grapes speaking. Still, it fit in with her entire sexual history. Guido's thoughts scattered. Scenes tumbled in his mind, free-floating like astronauts in space. Then he saw the solution to his anger. In a brilliant burst of gall. Like an image suddenly appearing in the developer. On display. As if in a gallery show of his photos. Who can explain the genesis of a bright idea!? Any creative thought that meshes many things in one. No matter how skewed or perverse. Was it revenge that sparks it? Rage? Or a quest for justice? That hunger to get even for an unjust hurt? What an idea! His quid pro quo to her for giving back his heart, for taking his love and making it disappear. How brilliant! How neat! How fitting!

Aviva

Finally, that evening, she took Charlie's advice and went to the movies to relax, unwind. The film was good enough, a light romance; it wasn't so much good for itself but for the never-never land it created. It let her escape and at the same time permitted her to bring up beneficent images of Charlie. Then, in one scene, the lead actor whispered to his girlfriend. "This happens to a man only once in his lifetime." It was Guido's phrase; they stole it from him; and without realizing it, she blurted out, "That's what he always says to me."

"Excuse me," she heard, and turned to a young woman sitting next to her.

"Oh, it's nothing," she smiled. "It's just what my boyfriend always says."

"I thought you said that. So does mine."

Aviva looked at her. Her neighbor gazed back. Even in the dark, the ghostly light of the screen lit up both their faces. Smiles faded. Even in the dark, Aviva could see the resemblance. A fear came over her, a cognition from another cosmos. Oh, my God, she thought. I don't feel well. Without a word, without planning it, they both rose and walked out. The initial feeling of not knowing whether to laugh, cry, or claw each other's eyes out gave way to a feeling of, yes, that phrase that Guido had once used, linking her and this other girl in sisterly commiseration. Now there was no enmity between them but the grace of kinship, the understanding of twins.

"So he was your boyfriend too," Aviva half said, half asked in trepidation.

"Depends who you're talking about," the other girl said cagily.

"My God, you even look like me when I was younger. I always told him, I wish I could be younger for you and of all my wishes this one has to come true."

"Shit!" the dark-haired girl said. "Go trust a man."

Aviva stared at her and wondered what Guido saw in her. She was pretty, yes, in a cheap sort of way, and short. I'll bet she has no neck, she thought. From that hangy jacket and thick denim shirt she didn't seem to have too much of a body either.

Does he tell you Italian sayings too? Aviva was about to ask and imagined, like in the movies, their shared feelings would overwhelm them and they would fall on each other's shoulders and weep.

Streams of people now filled the lobby. Another film was about to begin. She looked at her younger self and wondered what she was thinking. Why didn't she tell Aviva her name? Her face was an absolute blank. But in her eyes her anger sizzled.

"Excuse me," she said. "I'll be right back."

The stress is pressing against her bladder, Aviva thought, watching the girl go to the bathroom. She didn't believe it; couldn't. There always were errors, coincidences. She wanted to believe that. It's just a line composed of English words: "This happens to a man only once in his lifetime." Like Guido says: "There's just a limited amount of emotions in this world and just a few ways to say them." Then, when her younger lookalike was a few yards away, she half turned and threw over her shoulder, "And he always wears his socks."

The fist came at her breadbasket. She felt herself doubling over, even though she wasn't doubled over. The sun had never shone much in her life, but now, whatever sun there was, was gone. And in her soul clouds of darkness, negative light, grew and spread until they enveloped her like a black shroud.

Aviva waited and waited but the girl never returned. Was it all an illusion? Stood up by a rival too, she mused, and in a fog she went to her car and wondered what would be the next scene in the bizarre film that was her life. Starring in my own film. My movie star, she recalled Charlie's words. Some movie star! She had wanted to ask the girl how long Guido had known her, where they met, what her name was, where she worked, was she married. She wanted to ask a long list of questions.

She wasn't as furious as she thought she'd be. On the contrary, a calm coursed through her like a beneficent breeze. Maybe, deep down, she expected this, and it made the exit easy for her. Like not answering the door two days ago when that stubborn mule who couldn't take no for an answer came knocking. She recalled Charlie's remark: blessing in disguise. But she never expected such blessing to come in the guise of her lookalike. Okay, one cheats on one's own wife—but on one's girlfriend?

She sat in her car trying to calm down. She looked up at the full moon. She wanted to get even with Guido, her betrayer, but it wasn't within her to take revenge. Oh, she knew, she could have lifted up the phone, just like Plaskow's wife had done years back when she tried to call Aviva while she was in Europe. One call to Tammy would do it. But she couldn't. Wouldn't do it. But she would write a note to Guido, telling him what she knew.

I had plenty of reasons, she wrote, for not wanting to continue with you and now, just a few minutes ago, I made a discovery which showed me how right I was about you. You're a worm. You're faithless, a double betrayer. I was at the movies last night and . . .

Really? she imagined him saying. I don't think of you as going off to the movies by yourself. How odd! What did you see? he'd ask, slyly trying to change the subject as usual.

Never mind. Some films one forgets, some films stay pasted in your memory forever, would be her reply.

. . . and guess who I met there? she continued writing. I trusted you and you betrayed me. We made unprotected love in this high-risk era and without your telling me you made me become high-risk. That's the ultimate betraying of a sacred trust. Who knows what death you planted in me with your adventures with other women? Two weren't enough for you? You needed three? And who knows, maybe more. I could have made a scene, confronted you when you come back from Italy, but it's not my nature to do things like that. But I also want you to know, you sly s.o.b. that I know it was you who wrote that phony Ian letter and that's why I said yes to his (your) note and I had enough self-control not to mention it to you last time we met. Can you imagine my lip-sewing discipline in not saying a word about this to you, not savoring that delicious righteous indignation, not shouting it out as I left you, Thank you for your letter, Mr. P. I. Laskow, and slamming the door in a huff? How would you have squirmed out of that one? But there is a silver lining. A blessing in disguise. I'm free now. Absolutely unencumbered. You have revealed your true self to me, and I'm glad I cut with you before it was too late.

She delivered the note, unsigned, to the *Long Island Post*, asked for an envelope at the receptionist's desk, and labeled it, Urgent, Please forward at once to Guido Veneziano-Tedesco in Rome.

And she drove home quickly, hoping to get home before her husband.

And he acted on his brilliant idea.

In his darkroom that evening, he enlarged the pictures. The next morning, on his way to the airport, he would mail two envelopes (in case one got lost) marked Personal to the Arab's business address, for he had learned the real name of Ramati's firm from Aviva after he had jokingly called the Arab's cab service the Yellow-bellied Arab Cab Company.

At the mailbox, his thumb and forefinger refused to let go, as if warning the rest of him what he was doing. Then his mind pried open his fingers, and the envelopes slid down into the box.

At that moment, as he posted the pictures of Aviva, a memory slid into his mind, he doesn't know why. Seeing a homeless man shivering in the alley in Brooklyn outside the concert hall, that night he and Charlie double-dated Ava and Pam, he takes off his jacket and gives it to the man. That's the thought that slid into his mind as the pictures took their ineluctable slide downward.

On the plane he had another momentary qualm of regret, but it was too late to do anything about it. Done was done. Now he would concentrate on Teresa. Oh, the connubial bliss with that thin-waisted, big-breasted, porcelain-skinned girl. And there was Jamaican Jennifer he'd sent the reunion snapshots to. He had called her and she was amenable to posing for him. Her words smiled. Female vibes lilted over the phone, and in a steel drum beat too. Willingness, a welcome, dripped all over the phone lines. And he would try his luck with Gina as well.

But the Arab was also speeding home from Manhattan, going through red lights, having just picked up his mail after spending the entire day on a trip away from his office, speeding home that mid-June night, the rage red and bursting in his neck and head, rage as red as the dozen red roses he found in his living room one day, given to that whore by one of her lovers no doubt, the rage a red coif around his skull.

fermata

When Charlie saw the story splashed on the front page of the *Long Island Post*, the *New York Post*, and the *Daily News*, he felt chills on his skin. Now he understood why Aviva hadn't shown up for her appointment. For a moment he blanked out, then saw the hair on his arms bristling. As the blood sank from his head, bringing vertigo, he felt so lost, so alone, he thought he was going to die. Oh, my God, he said, and put his hands to his eyes. He didn't know if he was sitting or standing. In Manhattan or Long Island. He didn't know he was weeping. And when he learned her age, he felt cold again.

He read the story in the *Long Island Post* but didn't absorb the details. His eyes read, his mind rejected. What kept repeating in his mind was the husband's remark, She deserved it, and the fact that the police reported stemware and dishes smashed all over the kitchen, as if the man's rage were first directed at the objects the woman loved and then at the woman herself. But Charlie never did see the follow-up story the next day which revealed that in a thorough search of the house the police found something unusual and revealing. When they turned the victim's cello around from its standing position against the wall, they saw that a knife had been plunged deep into its tawny, gleaming back. The detective's assumption was that the husband had first demonstrated what he would do on his wife's instrument.

The night before Charlie had looked at the moon and thought of Aviva, thought he saw her there, smiling at him, the lovely woman in the moon, until a cloud came and covered her face.

The sun sets and rises. The moon goes down, comes up once more. But the heart, once the heart has set, it doesn't rise again.

ABC Directory

A modest but revealing alphabetical directory, with index,
wherein one may learn, *inter alia*, more about Guido, Aviva,
and others who intersect their lives, from A to Z,

along with delectable glancing references to:

Bach, Bartok, Ingrid Bergman, Casals, Casanova, Chaucer,
Einstein, Feynman, Hawthorne, Haydn, Joan of Arc,
Gene Krupa, Golda Meir, Pascal, Petrarch,
Piatagorsky, Popeye, Pushkin, Rimbaud,
Will Rogers, Rostropovich, King Saul,
Schubert, Schumann, Shakespeare,
Stieglitz, the Talmud, Turgenev,
da Vinci, Vivaldi, Whistler,
and Rip van Winkle

$\mathcal{ABC}$ $\mathcal{Index}$

- Aah time, once upon
- Absurd, imagining the
  Achieve, super-orgasm, how
    to. *See* Secret of life
- Adultery, rules of
- Advantage, others took of her
- Affair, how it began
- Affair, wife having an, what if
- Affairs, her
- Afterglow, lessons in
  Age, Aviva. *See* Feeling like a
    kid in her presence
- Age, her
- Age and marrying
  Aging. *See* License plate
  AIDS, fear of. *See* Rubbers
- Airborne sign of love, another
  Aladdin's lamp. *See* Mermaid
  All-day sucker. *See* Lollipop
  Alone, going it. *See* Orgasm
- Always disapproves, the Arab
  Angry, getting. *See* Smacked,
    getting
  Applause. *See* Hand, giving a
  Appreciating Guido. *See* Arab,
    loving it with the

- Arab, loving it with the
  Argument, Aviva's and Guido's
    constant. *See* Enigma, the,
    that Guido is
  Ass. *See* Calf
- Atmosphere she creates
    teaching cello
- Attention!
- Ava knew Guido was at home,
    how
  Aviva's age. *See* How old is Aviva?
  Aviva unclothed. *See* Posing
    naked

- Baby, supposed
- Backwards runs time. *See also*
    Physics, laws of
- Betrayed
- Blinders is what she wore
- Bombscare
- Boobs
  Boob test. *See* Pencil test
- Born in three installments,
    Aviva was
  Boss, he likes to be. *See*
    Power, he likes

Attention: When there is a "See also" or a "Continued" note at the end of an *ABC Directory* entry, be certain to look it up first in this *ABC Index*—otherwise, you may not find the desired entry. The solid bullet identifies each entry found in the Directory.

- Emptiness, how she fills it
- Enigma, the, that Guido is
  Epitaph for Guido. *See* Will
  Rogers
- Erotic cello
  Estrogen, loss of. *See* Meno-
  pause, Guido reads about
- Eyes, killing them

- Famine
- Fantasizing, musically
- Fat she is, Aviva complains how
- Feeling close
  Feeling her. *See* Dybbuk,
  feeling a
- Feeling like a kid in her presence
  Feynman, the physicist. *See*
  Physics, laws of
  Filling her emptiness. *See*
  Emptiness, how she fills it
- Finger technique
  Flee erections. *See* Chinese
  pronunciation
  Folk saying. *See* Guido's Italian
  proverbs and folk sayings
- Foot massage
- Forgot, the penny and the
  Arab story that Aviva
- Four-word review
  Friend, girl, swiped. *See* Wife,
  taking someone else's
- Frivolous, she is
  Furious. *See* Famine
- Fuzzy legs, his

- Galoshes
- Game-playing
- Gerbil, her
  Gerontic. *See* Senescent
- Gift, birthday
- Glow on her face

God, belief in. *See* Attention!
- God's creation
- God, thanking, for Guido
  Grand Union. *See* Wakeable
  Guido. *See all entries*
  Guido pregnant? *See* Various
  alternative pregnancy
  procedures
- Guido's Italian proverbs and
  folk sayings
  Guido's possible need. *See*
  Clothing, up to pick the
  Arab comes
- Guido's son
- Guilt as metaphysical/philo-
  sophical entity
  Guys, off her, can't keep
  hands. *See* Vulnerable, she is

- Half a student, Aviva has
- Half life
- Hamster
- Hand, giving a
  Harem, delight with a. *See*
  Sharing two women
- Harem, times are over for a
- Heaven
  Heimlich maneuver. *See*
  Galoshes
- Hereafter, her parents in,
  arranged meeting
- Honeymoon
  Hot flashes, no. *See* Meno-
  pause, Aviva ecstatic over
  Hot getting. *See* Car, getting
  hot in
  How old is Aviva?. *See* Aviva's
  age
  Husband checking up on her.
  See Zap her, is her husband
  trying to?
- Hyphenated names

Massage, foot. *See* Foot
massage
- Masturbating
- Mediocre talents in screwing
- Menopause, Guido reads
about
- Menopause, Aviva ecstatic over
- Mermaid
- Mine(s)
- Minsk
Misery in her life. *See* Transat-
lantic trip
Modest. *See* Guido
- Mood shift
- Mortgage agreement

- Naïveté
- Name, origin of Guido's
- Negative
Never! *See* Daily sex?
Nightgown, beautiful, did
not work. *See* Search for
orgasm
No sex. *See* Sex, no
Nostrils. *See* Pecker
- Not, do, go out
Notes, pleated. *See* Dream,
Guido's musical
- Not remembering any of them

- Obsessed with Ian Plaskow
- Old, looking
- Older, getting
Older woman. *See* Age her
Olive oil. *See* Popeye
Oral method of teaching. *See*
Half a student, Aviva has
Organ. *See* Piano
Orgasm. *See* Vibrator, when
first used
- Orgasm, how she tingles before

- Overweight and love

- Palindrome
- Paradise
- Pascal and Pushkin
- Passion as penance
- Passive voice, her
Past, Aviva's. *See* Pictures are
reality
Past, possessing her. *See*
Questioning, his incessant
Paving stones with ears. *See*
Italian proverb
Pecker. *See* Bubble gum
Penance. *See* Passion as
penance
- Pencil test
- Pennies from heaven
Penny, story of. *See* Forgot,
the Penny and the Arab
story that Aviva
- Petcock
Petrarch's secretary. *See* Rimbaud
Philadelphia, went wild in. *See*
Photos, her, interpreted by
photographer
- Phone booth and Ian
- Phone rings during . . .
Photographs of Aviva. *See*
Posing naked
- Photography, why he was
drawn to, maybe
- Photos, her, interpreted by
photographer
- Phrenics
Physical, sex is not. *See* Sex
isn't so much
- Physics, laws of. *See also*
Backward runs time
Piano. *See* Upstairs to play?
Pickpocket. *See* Affair, wife
having an, what if

- Virgin, professional
- Voice, loves listening to her
- Voice on phone, his
- Vulnerable, she is

- Wakeable
- Walk, the first, Aviva's version
- Watch, last item removed
- Wedding picture, looking at Aviva's
- (W)hole business
- Why she loves it so much
- Wife, taking someone else's
- Wild, going, about fourteen years late
  Will Rogers. *See* Rogers, Will
- Windshield wipers, solar
- Wisdom of Solomon
- Wit, Aviva's
  Witch, Aviva is a. *See* Betrayed
  Wives, more than one. *See*
    Laws in the world, man
    makes
- Wonders of the vibrator
- Words, direction of
- Writing a book, she

Wrong numbers. *See* Zap her, is her husband trying to?

- X-rated screwing
- X-rated, that's what you are

- Yankee Stadium, how to fill it
- Yek!
- Yonder, out in the wild blue, with her vibrator
- Younger image of me, you're obsessed with a
- Yummy, the walk continues, Aviva's version

- Z, letters beyond
- Zap her, is her husband trying to?
- Zetetic
- Zing! the fifth force in physics just discovered
- Zone, mystical time
  Zoo. *See* Lamb; Lion; Tiger
- Zzzing went the strings of her heart!

$\mathcal{ABC}\,\mathcal{D}irectory$

A

Aah time, once upon

Once upon a time there was a tall and handsome photographer, forty-two, forty-three, witty, wise and warm, with a wife named Tammy, who made it with a beautiful, curvy, auburn-haired cellist name Aviva, who had a husband whose name is better forgotten, but whom Guido named the Arab. Guido took cello lessons with her, fell in what he thought was love. They had problems. Some usual, some not. She didn't want to share him; he didn't want to give her up.

Read on.

Absurd, imagining the

"Imagine," he told Aviva, "you come in to my house. The door is open. You walk in. See someone else sitting in the easy chair, reading a newspaper, which is held up in front of him. He lowers the paper and it's not me."

"Oh, my God, then who is it?" she asked.

"I don't know. Maybe the Arab."

Adultery, rules of

"Even adultery has its rules," Guido advised. "And the first rule of the house: the lover cannot be jealous of the other lover's spouse."

Advantage, others took of her

Aviva said:

"On the one hand, you listen objectively, hear what I have to say, calmly ask questions as if you're not concerned, and on the other, I get the feeling that you're more and more distressed about my adventures."

"No. I'm not," Guido lied, but to a degree he sympathized with her. All her life she'd been taken advantage of, he thought, and she didn't know it. Her measuring rod was niceness. As long as the guy was nice, it was okay. It could have been a front—nice-guyness was an easy pose for a guy out for a lay—but she couldn't see through it. All her life she'd been longing for love, affection, warmth, and would do anything for it. But it eluded her. She didn't get it from her musician father who directed all his love toward his cello; she didn't get it from the husband, whom they call the Arab, who directed all his love into his taxi till it shone with his reflected image. Aviva was like a pussycat longing to be cuddled, not for just a day, not for just a year, but always. And she constantly hoped that her temporary liaisons would be the always connection. But they never were because she always found fault.

Affair, how it began

"Did I know what would happen after the walk in the snow?" she repeated Guido's question about the walk he'd invited her to after the sixth lesson. "No, I didn't. But I did know we would cross a border."

"Did you expect me to kiss you?"

"I didn't know what to expect. I felt, I knew, that we would hold hands. I really didn't know what to expect. But I knew things wouldn't be the same after the walk. We'd gone for the first time into neutral territory and that was liberating us from the constraints of the cello lessons."

"Did you love me then, even before the walk?"

"Of course," she said.

Affair, wife having an, what if

"How would you react if you found out your wife was having an affair?"

"It's a moot question," Guido said smugly.

"Impossible. Huh?"

"Absolutely. She just wouldn't do such a thing. And anyway, she doesn't have the time."

"You're absolutely sure."

"Yes."

"Just as she is," Aviva hit home, "sure about you."

"Q.E.D.," said Guido. "Well, reverse it. How would you feel?"

"If the Arab had, is having, an affair, I couldn't care less."

"I'm talking, let's say, at the very beginning."

"Then I would've been upset."

"Me too. Here's the analogy. As they say in the Naples underworld, a pickpocket picks pockets, gladly. But when *he's* pickpocketed, he explodes, madly."

Affairs, her

Hawthorne's "The Birthmark" was not far from Guido's mind as he tried to recreate her in his image. In other words, perfection. As seen by him. Like retouching a negative to make a better print. He knew the danger of closely exploring, exfoliating, and even implicitly criticizing her past, while his own past went unquestioned. She was either naïve, or a saint, to be asked for names, dates, length of relationship, sexual details. She took it for weeks as he subtly probed, like silver nitrate digging into photographic paper, innocently asked a question here and there, inter-larding it, like a good medieval tale, with other by-the-way comments and questions. And he kept asking about her affairs until one day, with a force that surprised him, she said, "Let's drop it, okay?" But there was a question in her voice, as if she waited for his assent to her request, rather than asserting the finality of her own demand. And he realized that that "okay" was her Achilles heel; that in the very act of protesting she was giving him an opening to decline. Poor, self-defeating Aviva. "You have a judgmental tone," she said, a word he never thought she'd use. "I'm a different person now," she said. "I probably made some mistakes, which I wouldn't do again. But they happened and I can't do anything about them now. They happened twenty, twenty-five years ago. Enough! And what if I were to ask you, What's worse? Isn't what you're doing unconscionable?" He knew it was, but wouldn't admit it to her. But he was still jealous, he told her, of everyone who touched her. "I'm just an old-fashioned guy," he said, "I want to possess your past."

"And I can't even possess your present," she said.

Of course there was danger, as she herself later realized, and said eloquently, that if you go on picking all you'll have left is broken pieces. But he couldn't resist. And anyway it was her fault. She only gave a piece of the story and, like a true artist, revealed another element with each subsequent telling, or probing. And the more she told, the more he wanted to hear. She told him ABC. Then he wanted to know A^1, B^1, and C^1, and so on. He made little charts of her affairs and the years she had them, as if he himself couldn't believe them, hoping they wouldn't add up to as many as he feared they would, then broke them down into months, even weeks. As though he himself had had the affairs, wanted to have them with her. That was it. He wanted to have them with her; he wanted to possess her when she was young, shapely, and beautiful, and wipe away those nothings who were foot passengers in the revolving door of her life.

Of chronology, who where when, she hadn't the faintest idea, until he came along. Her historian. And she didn't even realize that there were that many until she started adding them up. Then, in her apologetic way, she asked sadly, "That's a lot, isn't it?" Looking, as usual, for approval—or disapproval.

Afterglow, lessons in

Down came her slacks, but she was still sheathed in pantyhose. Them he pulled halfway down until they were taut about six inches below her crotch. He tickled the nylon pad at the very epicenter of the hose and even though he only touched cloth, she began moaning and singing.

Later, she asked, "Do you still feel it under your tongue, on the roof of your mouth, tingling in the bottom of your feet, between your legs?"

"Not quite that way," he said.

"You don't know how to enjoy it," she said. "You need lessons in afterglow."

Age, her

When he figured out how old Aviva was, he panicked. God, he didn't want to have an old lady friend. He'd have to help her across the street, carry her bundles, fill out her Medicare forms, give up his seat in the bus for her. She's over the hill.

"I know where I know you from," he told her. "You were my counselor in camp, and we used to call you Auntie Aviva."

You know how you can tell how old a woman is? he thought. It's the hands. The skin on the back of the hands that dries up and in the light looks like finely dried leather. Most of the other aging spots can be disguised by fancy cosmetics. But not the skin on the hands. Your face made you look years younger than me, but your hands were the rings on the tree trunk.

Age and marrying

"A guy shouldn't marry a woman his age. You look around and you see couples the same age and the woman invariably looks like the guy's mother. Take couples I've seen where they're in their late forties or mid-fifties. The wife looks like a grandma and the husband looks like a young duke. Women get older quicker, so if a guy is forty-five and his wife is forty-five, she usually looks ten years older than he does. Luckily, I married a woman five years younger than me. If I had married a woman my age I'd have run away from her twelve years ago."

"If you'd married a woman your age," Aviva said, "she'd have five more years experience in shutting faucets."

Well said, he thought, for he'd often criticized her, after washing up, for never shutting the faucet properly, and it would drip drip drip until he shut it.

Airborne sign of love, another

Months later, after their first walk, again in two cars, and again just before their cars would go off in two different directions, she speeded up until she rode alongside him. He pointed to himself, drew a heart in the air and pointed it at her. At once, and with an alacrity that amazed him, she drew two ditto marks in the air.

Always disapproves, the Arab

"Everything in the Arab, a.k.a. my husband, was disapproval. Disapproval was his middle, no, his first name. He disapproved of the way I spoke, dressed, lived, breathed. He disapproved of the way I played cello. He said, Why waste your time? Nothing will come of it. He disapproved of the way I shopped. Everything I bought was too expensive. He inspected the garbage to see if food was being thrown out. He would listen to my phone calls and tap his foot impatiently when I spoke too long and make scissors motions to cut my yakking. He would tell the kids to get off the phone. He would disapprove of my children's friends and bad-mouth them after they left the house. When friends were there he wouldn't even say hello to them or make them feel welcome. He criticized the kid's report cards but would never encourage them with their studies or help them. If the grades were poor he'd rant: Why such low marks? If high, the teachers were too lenient; there was no competition. He would tell the kids to wash the dishes but never lifted a finger himself. He told them to wash not to help me but to keep them busy, for the sake of discipline. He would never say a dress I chose was pretty. Never. Always disapprove. Only a couple of times did he buy me nice things. With my money. The inheritance from my father. Most of which he took, and like a jerk I was too naïve and said nothing. His friends he would go to see but never mine. When the kids left the light on in their rooms when they weren't there he would snarl at them, and he would curse at drivers who didn't move fast enough when the light changed. He never ever said I look pretty, and never said, I love you."

"How can you live with a man like that?"

She didn't seem to hear the question.

"He was mercurial. When I criticized him he changed for a while. A day or two. And then, you know me, I got passive, let things slide. Hoped they'd get better. Didn't want to make waves. Had two kids to think of . . . He'd get furious if I misplaced my keys but laughed it off when he lost his. Fly into a rage if the door wasn't double-locked at night and carry on about loss of insurance coverage, which was a lie. When he courted me he was sweet and charming and then right after we got married a change, like a sudden switch of key, came over him. My mother taught me to buy the best. It was always cheaper in the long run. So I bought the best. Like in canned foods. And he used to run and exchange them at night for the Shop Rite brand. Cheaper, of course. And lousy quality. Not that we couldn't afford it, for God's sake. At that time he owned three taxis in New York. One he drove, the other two he hired drivers for and even leased out his and then he came home in his own car at night. So he had the money. When it came to his imported Swiss chocolates he didn't stint. And it wasn't even 100% meanness. That probably I wouldn't have been able to take. But there was this yo-yo syndrome. For a week he was sweet as honey. Went on a buying binge for the kids. Said nothing about the use of air-conditioning for a few days. And then, as if a mania got hold of him, he refused to come down when we had guests. Or he shouted at the kids when guests were present, embarrassing them, the guests, and me. He ranted about phone bills, doctor bills, electric bills. Left the children little notes with Xerox copies of the bills underlined in red. Reduced their allowance . . ."

Arab, loving it with the

"Could you say, when it comes to sex any time previous in your life—I loved it?"

"Occasionally, with—believe it or not—and only at the beginning, with the Arab."

"And not during earlier times, with the other guys?"

"No. You have to understand, I'm not the same person I was fifteen years ago, or even five years ago. First of all, I feel much better. There is no constant. There are always variables. For instance, I don't think I would have appreciated you twenty years ago, and you probably wouldn't have appreciated me."

"But I would have fucked your brains out."

"There wasn't too much then to—"

"Go ahead, say it."

"No," she said. "I can't."

"Say it."

She whispered it softly and covered her face.

Atmosphere she creates teaching cello

"I liked to create a happy and pleasant atmosphere during lessons. Isn't that good for students?"

"What would happen, for instance, if a student had three hands. Would you let him, to keep him happy, clasp one on your bosom, while he played with the other two?"

"It depends what he was playing with the other two."

Attention!

"Do you believe in God?"

"No," he said.

"But are you religious?"

"From the waist up."

"Stop it! Don't you believe in any of the commonly held values?"

"Yes. Respect for elders. You're older, so I respect you. Rising before the whory head as a mark of respect. It's in the Bible. So like a student in an Italian high school, that little thingie down there always stands at attention when you come into the room."

Ava knew Guido was at home, how

To make sure Guido was at home alone, she first called the *Long Island Post* and gave them a cock-and-bull story that she was a photographer at the *Washington Post* and had to talk to Guido Veneziano-Tedesco.

The secretary at the photography department said he wasn't in and probably was at home.

"Do you have his number?" the secretary asked Ava.

"Yes," she said. "Guido gave it to me. . .Just a minute. . .No, I don't have my address book with me."

As soon as she gave Ava his number, she dialed and, faking a southern accent, asked to speak to Mrs. Veneziano-Tedesco.

"Sorry," Guido said, "she's not at home now . . . Who is this?"

"Veronica Gibson, I'm an old college friend, and I want to tell her about a reunion . . . Is there anywhere I can reach her now?"

Guido gave her the number of the shop.

"I have to catch a train now. Can I call her later?"

"She'll be there till five this afternoon."

That was all the info Ava needed. She'd have him to herself all day long.

B

Baby, supposed

Lying in bed with him, she asked:

"Suppose we'd had a baby. Suppose I'd gotten pregnant. I'd love to have a baby with you."

"But I thought you were in menopause."

"But I recently read that a woman can become pregnant even one year, maybe two, after menopause."

"That would have been rough. Passing off our child as the Arab's."

"Worse, Suppose I hadn't been sleeping with him."

"Then, I guess we. . ."

Her face fell. "No, you wouldn't have . . . not our baby."

"No, I guess not . . . But the squint would have given it away."

"Not at all. My kids don't have my squint."

"But two parents with squint. That baby would never have looked at the Arab. No matter where little Guidissimo was playing he'd be looking my way."

See also **Desire and pregnancy**

Backward runs time

He told her:

"In physics, when you get to infinitesimally small sizes, time can either stand still, move backwards, or move in two directions. In that case, the world of dream and reality elide, and certain events can take on a magic patina. We stand on a time zone that floats above the real world and time stands still for us."

See also **Physics, laws of**

Betrayed

Aviva said she had heard a sad story and immediately began to laugh.

"I don't know why I'm laughing, because basically it's a sad story. Barry Walters, a fellow cellist I know from the Long Island Symphony, went to see an old friend of his in New York and came back depressed." And she began to laugh again.

"His friend died while he was visiting," Guido offered.

"Not quite," Aviva said, and began giggling again. "But his friend, Marco, is married to a woman eighteen years younger."

Guido, nodding, saw the whole scenario at once. He saw the young woman, imagined boyfriends. He zipped through the three-hundred-page novel in a minute.

"The slut," he said.

Aviva grimaced and nodded too.

"But what's worse, she flaunts it. The kids know about it too."

"That's disgusting."

"It *is* disgusting." Aviva said and began to laugh uncontrollably again.

"Anyone with manners, anyone with decency in his or her heart," Guido said, "anyone with the slightest pretensions to ethics and morality knows that an affair should be kept secret. As a wise man once said, "Not more than two should know about it. Not 2.2 or 2.1.""

Aviva said, "You quote yourself very nicely," and continued laughing.

"You're a witch."

"I'm a witch," she said.

"It's a side of you I haven't seen before," he said, thinking that the transformation from *W* to *B* can be swift.

Blinders is what she wore

"If I didn't want to believe it, I would chuck it, discount it, color it. Assume it was meant in jest. It's like going through life with blinders on. For instance, if the Arab said he once hit a girlfriend for not being cooperative, I laughed. Disbelieved it. I would fit round pegs into square holes to make it comfortable in my imagination."

Bombscare

They'd been having a bomb scare every couple of weeks. Perhaps because of the PLO exposé series that the *Long Island Post* was running. Once there was a knock at the door of Guido's lab at the paper. Two cops stuck their heads in. They already knew him.

"Mr. Veneziano . . . we'd like to speak to you for a moment." He drew close. "We've just gotten word that. . ."

His heart began palpitating. He couldn't hear the rest of their sentence. Oh, my God, he said, Aviva ratted on me. She called the *Post* and they called the police. There goes my life, my career.

". . . there's a bomb scare in the building. If you want you can leave, but I know some of you guys have deadlines, so it's not mandatory."

"Thank you, officers," Guido said with elation and couldn't wait to tell Aviva the story.

"Aviva I had an unpleasant surprise . . ."

Continued, see **Cops knock on the lab door**

Boobs

"Boobs are very important to you, right?"

"Typo!" he cried. "You mean books."

"No. I mean boobs. Like the things I got."

"Boobs and books are etymologically related. You draw sustenance from both and both have little jackets to protect them from dirty hands and inclement weather. Or is it dirty weather and inclement hands?"

See also **Mermaid**

Born in three installments, Aviva was

He said she was born in three installments. First, when she broke through her mommy's womb; second, when the doctor cut her hymen after seven years of marriage; and third, when she met him.

Bothered by Plaskow

Guido wondered why the affair that he suspected Aviva had had with her cello teacher Ian Plaskow bothered him so much. Was it because he'd met, photographed, and had spoken with the cellist and imagined him stroking and kissing and fucking Aviva every time she saw him? And suppose he had known her other lovers, would he have been upset? Probably not. Then what was it that upset him? Because it was so casual? Because Plaskow was world-famous and he suspected that Aviva still had a little bit of hots for him? No. Not that either. Then it hit him one day. It's because Plaskow was married. Aviva was disgusting. She was absolutely sans morals.

Box, Aviva's suggestion

"I can't get enough of you." Guido said. "What am I going to do?"
"Want a suggestion? Can I drop it in the suggestion box?" she said.
"Drop it in yours." he said, tapping it.
"That takes only one kind of suggestion."

Brat, growing

"My goodness, already so big . . . Hi, there, I knew you back when,"
Aviva said, "when you were a little brat, about a minute ago, when you
weren't a great big lech like you are now," and she bent down and gave
the big brat a loving kiss.

Breasts, shape and geography of, her

When she sat up or stood, her breasts were rather far apart, the nips
aiming out at different directions, as if mimicking her eyes. But when she
lay down the spread really became apparent, as if they were off and
running onto two opposite paths. Once, looking at her far-spread boobs
while lying next to her, Guido said, "Wow, what a long march it would
be for an ant to make a trip from this nip," touching it, and marching
his fingers slowly to the other side of her rib cage, "to this one."

"If you do that crazy insect routine once more," she warned, "it's
going to be an even longer April."

Bugged, her house is

Aviva thought it absurd that her house had been bugged by the Arab,
but since that is what Guido thought, she went along. They agreed they
wouldn't say anything that might be compromising, but Guido discovered that by written notes, a cute charade could be played. Even double
entendres. At the cello, after the first selection, he said calmly, "This is
a lovely piece. One of the loveliest I've played," and he turned to her and
stroked her thigh, belly and breasts. After a series of scales, he pulled
from his pocket the first of several notes (he even had them numbered
so they shouldn't get mixed up). "Guess who missed whom very much?"
She pointed to him and then herself and he shook no and she laughed.
Then he pointed to her emphatically with a stabbing index finger and
then, as emphatically, to himself and she laughed again. He played a
short piece and pulled out another note which said: "Will what's-his-
name have a long list of questions prepared sitting in his Lazy-boy re-
cliner?" And then he told her out loud that she hadn't made any comments
on how relaxed his hands were, whether his touch was light, if his wrists
were relaxed or stiff. "I rather prefer it stiff," she said and he clasped his
hands over her mouth. When he left she asked, "Do you feel you're in
the American Embassy in Moscow?"

"This place is so bugged it needs pest control," he said.

"But when a certain someone leaves," she said, "the pest goes too."

C

Capetown, Aviva's response to

"The only time I really responded sexually to him was over the phone. I remember that more than anything. But that was years ago—before I married the Arab."

Again that aloneness syndrome, he thought. For her sex is better alone, at a remove from men, who may be threatening, and whom she feels uncomfortable with.

"I would have liked for it to have been more exciting and passionate with Capetown. But I can't separate sexuality from other qualities. Response to a person is based on many factors."

"That's fascinating," he said.

"What?"

"Your command of the pluperfect in all its subjunctive subtleties. I would have liked for it to have been . . . Only a foreigner like me can have such a native appreciation of the nuances of such finely tuned grammar."

See also **Passive voice, her**

Car, getting hot in the

Riding in the car with him she got so hot, hotter than she ever had been in bed with him. Didn't it happen, he wondered, because nothing could be done in a moving vehicle? Or was it, as Guido once said, that in the car there was a gradual buildup, the tease of stroking and touching, which awakened the senses and stirred them up?

"You know what?" Aviva said. "Screw me and then your analysis."

Casanova, what he said

"Casanova once said that one does not desire what one possesses. But he's dead wrong. I desire you, I possess you."

"Do you consider yourself Casanova?"

The secret wish of every post-nineteenth century male, he thought. Of course, he crowed. Wouldn't you, if you were a man?

"No," he said. "But I'm your private Casanova."

Case of the Typed Letter, the

Aviva remembers a story she didn't tell Guido:

I was once engaged to a goy. When I came back from Italy, all of my girlfriends were already mothers and my poor mom had two spinster daughters. It was at that time that she made arrangements with the Renaissance man: Rabbi Gershon Kleingeist, psychologist, columnist, counselor, con man, shadchan, sex charlatan, boot-and-foot fetishist, and all-around holy man. The guys he fixed me up with didn't click. Maybe he purposely set me up with duds so I'd keep going back to him. That's when I met the gentile. I was living in New York in a big apartment house and like out of the movies the goy comes to borrow a cup of sugar. We got to talking and so on. We went out a few times. Then he would accompany me on visits to my parents in Queens. Of course they were upset that I was with a goy. But I got to like him, started going out seriously, got engaged, perhaps to break my mother's heart. One day I got a letter from his girlfriend. She pleaded with me to stop seeing Jimmy. They'd been in love. He was the love of her life. Then I came in the picture and he dumped her. Same thing may happen to you once he meets the next one, she warned. She was despondent, contemplating suicide. Her blood was on my conscience. If I had any human compassion whatsoever, I would break off with Jimmy and permit them to resume their normal, destined course in life. Okay. Nice, neat, pathetic letter. I was truly touched. Then I read it again. The more I read it the fishier it sounded. Then I knew why. The typeface bugged me. It looked familiar. The year before I had helped out in my aunt's office and done some typing. I used her old, beaten up Underwood manual which occasionally skipped a space after the "h." Exactly what was happening in Jimmy's girlfriend's letter. So, I went to my aunt's office, on the pretext of visiting her, compared and—voila!—I was right on the button. Why did you do it? I asked my aunt. After hemming and hawing, she admitted that she and my mother had made machinations to break up the engagement with the goy. They didn't want me to marry him. And they got their wish. But not because of the letter. Once, at a party, Jimmy let slip a nasty remark about Israel, a pro-Palestinian statement. He probably didn't know I was standing nearby. Then I realized what I'd be getting into, and I broke off with him.

Cat, feeding the

Aviva realized late one night in Guido's house (of course, no one was home in either place; the Arab was away, the children sleeping over at a friend's, Tammy out at a pops concert with a girlfriend) that she forgot to feed the cat and let him out. Otherwise he'd pee all over the house. "Should I go?" she asked. She wrinkled her brow. "I don't want to go . . ." They talked some more, pros and cons, till he counseled her to go.

"Go . . . and then you'll have the joy of coming back."

"Maybe I'll call him," she said.

"Good idea," he said. "Call. And if a pussy answers, hang up."

See also **Petcock**

Cello, going back to

"What prompted your return to the cello?"

"It was after the Arab had driven me to a near breakdown with his harassment, it was then that I just sat down, a kind of spontaneous self-therapy, and began to play."

"Was he encouraging?"

"Are you kidding? Just the opposite."

"And you continued in spite of him."

"Yes. And to spite him. My biggest revenge against him was winning that competition. Once, after attending one of my concerts, and he rarely came, he told me in the car—and he knows as much about music as I do about air conditioning—that my playing wasn't anything special. I burst into tears. And swore that I'd never let him go to any of my concerts any more, and I didn't. And I also swore he'd never make me cry again, and I kept my oath. I never again gave him the satisfaction of letting him bring me to tears."

"But crying is good," Guido said. "As an internal release and also to soften the heart of a cruel man . . . Did you know that the human species is the only living thing that can cry out of feelings?"

"Crying is good when you're dealing with a human being who has normal sensitivities."

"And I thought you have good taste," Guido couldn't resist saying.

She rolled her eyes in a self-deprecatory gesture. "I sure pick winners, don't I?"

Cello, sexiness of the

The cello has a deep and visceral appeal. In other words, it's sexy. Even more, erotic. It reaches our emotions, like love, on a deep and profound level. It talks to the innermost in-ness in us.

See also **Erotic cello**

Cellos are like people

Guido to Aviva:

"You see various cellos in a chamber orchestra. They all look alike. Yet one could be a thousand-dollar cello and the other a Strad. All people have ears and eyes, yet their sensitivities, their *tones*, are different."

Cemetery, visiting the

"My parents would have loved you," she told him one day. "They simply would have adored you. Eaten you up."

"Have you visited the cemetery lately?"

"No," she said with a guilty look. "I really should. They're buried here on Long Island."

The next time she came, he told her, "We're going to visit your parents."

She was taken by surprise but immediately agreed. Her eyes shone as they walked to his car. That glow in her eyes bespoke of another notch in the ever-rising intensity of her love.

In the cemetery they walked among the stones until they came to a double tombstone in the shape of the tablets of the law. He read the inscriptions. There were tears in Aviva's eyes.

"Mom, Dad, this is Guido. The love of my life. The love of my life," and she clutched his left arm with both her hands and pressed her forehead to his shoulder. "This reminds me of another cemetery story, but what a difference!"

In the car she told him . . .

Continued, see **Dread of the dead, the Arab's**

Children, Guido not having

He didn't miss having children until he saw pictures, read books, watched films, heard others talking. Not having children was bad enough, but having and not having a child was worse. When he saw photos of a father playing ball with a child or a father walking hand in hand with his son, he felt a twinge of pain, an emptiness blowing through him, a sad chill wind. All his parents and ancestors had had normal children; why did it have to stop with him? He would never be able to play baseball with his son. Never go swimming or skiing with him. Never show off for him. *Never* was an awful word.

"You mean you never visit him?" Aviva asked. She couldn't understand.

"I used to, but it was painful."

"For you, or him," she said cruelly.

"Touché. Believe me, if it would do him good, I'd go."

"How do you know it doesn't do any good? You read about autistic kids being brought back by treatment, by constant touch and stimulation."

"He's not autistic. He's retarded."

Still, he didn't like her subtle indictment. She must think I'm a hard-hearted bastard, he thought. But she had normal kids, so she didn't, couldn't know the anguish of having something and yet not having it. Like water slipping through your fingers. It was like having a canister of what you know were superb shots lost in the mail. If only they weren't taken, the loss wouldn't be so great.

Clothes she wore, the

Loose sweaters, monochrome. Darkish slacks. Never wore bright colors. Maybe they would deflect from her face. Like pretty girls befriend mediocrities so they wouldn't deflect attention to themselves. But once, at a lesson, she wore a tight white T-shirt, with colorful decorations. Her son's. To tease him. To see how many mistakes he would make keeping one eye on her tits, the other on the music.

Clothing, up to pick the Arab comes

"Once, I actually kicked him out. Years ago. But, unfortunately, it lasted only one week. I broke down. You know, the old story. His promises to reform. He came to pick up his things, and there was a moment of pain, of tears. Maybe there's something wrong with me. I felt sorry for him seeing him picking up his stuff. But I tightened my will. Became hard as nails. He wanted to take some old appliances. I said, that stays here. He was only allowed to take underwear, pants, sport jacket, suit, socks—things like that."

"You shouldn't have let him take the sport jacket."

"Why?"

"I might want it someday."

Condoms for midgets

"I passed the pharmacy. . ."

"Congratulations," Guido said.

". . . and I went in and asked if they have little protectors for fingers. . ."

"So you don't knock yourself up while masturbating. . .?"

"Stop it," she said. "So my callused fingers can heal. The druggist gave me a box of little rubber caps and I kept it on my music table near the cello. . ." She stopped. "You're not going to like what I said. You'll disapprove, you prude."

"*You* stop it. What happened?"

Aviva laughed to herself. "One of my students came in, a woman, and she saw the box. I saw her looking at it. She was about to say something then she stopped. 'Go ahead, ask,' 'I told her. So she said, "I wanted to ask you what those things were but then decided not to. Well, what are they?' So I told her: 'Condoms for midget students.'"

Guido burst out laughing. "That's hilarious! Why should I disapprove? But you wouldn't have said that to a guy, right?"

"No, no, of course not."

"That's very good. I like that. And I think it's very a responsible thing to do. Because some of your midget students may indeed be carriers. Even midget AIDS is dangerous."

Congressional Medal of Honor

"For someone who said she didn't feel well, you moved like a can-can dancer. You deserve a Congressional Medal of Honor."

"Yeah? Where is it?"

"In you."

Cops knock on lab door

"Aviva, I had an unpleasant surprise at the lab this morning."

"What happened?" she asked, concerned.

"Cops. They knocked on the door, poked their heads in, and said they'd like to speak to me for a moment. Uh-oh, I thought. We've just gotten word that . . . and I couldn't hear the rest because of some noise down the hall. I think they said, Did you? And I thought it best to confess and said, Yes, yes, I molested the cellist. I took her. I confess . . . Where do I sign?"

Aviva was laughing, but she still wasn't sure it was a joke.

"And the cops said, You sure are a card, Mr. Veneziano. It's a bomb scare, but you don't really have to leave the lab if you don't want to. You can stay right here."

"Why?"

"BECAUSE WE DON'T LIKE YOUR PICTURES, they said in unison, the boys in blue."

Crazy about his cock

As soon as Aviva came through the door, before she even had a chance to say hello—the glowing smile was already there—he told her. "Take off your clothes!" And before she could respond, zhwoop!—off came her sleeveless black sweater. Her back was sweaty from the August heat. He unloosened the bra. "Help, rape." She said good-naturedly. He fanned her breast with a folded *Il Progresso.*

"What a way to learn Italian," she said, "Ah, that's cool . . . I mean, hot."

He sat her on his lap as if she was a chair and kissed her back.

"You still love my cock?"

"No." She turned to him, pursed her lips and gave a little victorious nod, as if proudly asserting her independence.

"Say it."

"But I don't like it."

"Liar."

"Talk to me. Say something else."

For moment he was silent. He knocked on her back as if it were a door.

"Yes?" Again she turned her head.

"Crazy about my cock?"

"I'm crazy. . ." she hesitated, "about your rooster, your calf, your ass, your entire zoo . . ."

"Close. But not close enough. Let's hear it in the bleachers, folks!"

"I'm crazy," she said slowly. "About your cock," she began a dependent clause and stopped.

"Aren't you crazy about it?"

"Well, maybe a little bit."

"I thought you didn't like it."

"I don't but—"

Continued, see **Paradise**

Curse, her first husband's

"My first husband put a 'curse' on me when I walked out on him. Paul said, 'No one is going to love you the way I do.' And no one did," Aviva said.

"No one else ever loved you?" Guido asked, surprised. "I thought you told me that every man you knew fell in love with you."

"Well, that was Paul's estimation of things. And maybe no one *did* love me the way he did."

"But if there was no communication, how could there be love?"

"Maybe the lack of communication started growing from the time of his frustration. Perhaps initially he did love me. And as far as the other guys are concerned, nothing good ever came out of *any* of my involvements."

"Even the one with Capetown?"

"Well, you see the result of that one. So maybe Paul was right. It was all downhill for me from that point. Perhaps I'd still be married to him if not for that impotency problem of his."

"Don't say that he put a curse on you. How can you live with that black blanket over your head? And perhaps there is another man who loves you 1.24 times as much as he did."

Aviva's face softened.

D

Daily sex?

She had never had sex on a daily basis. With anyone. Not even with her husband. At first, perhaps three times a week. But never more. How about when she visited Capetown? Again, no. Guido couldn't believe it.

"If I had you for a week, or three weeks, I wouldn't get out of bed. I'd just stay in bed and ring for the concierge."

"You'd want him too, you pervert?"

"No, silly. To bring up the chambermaid."

"For him?"

"For you."

She rolled her eyes. "Yuk."

"You once mentioned that after the beginning of your Arab marriage, sex and love went downhill . . . Did you ever think of anyone else when you were screwing him?"

She gave that naughty smile that came before she was about to reveal something.

"There were times when I thought of an imaginary man while the Arab made love to me, and I didn't realize how bad, how wrong it was until much later."

"Then why did you screw?"

"To keep the peace."

"You had a regular peacekeeping force, didn't you? Out to win the Nobel Peace Prize, eh? And there was never any real person you imagined? Someone from the past?" Like Ian Plaskow, for instance? he didn't ask.

"Once or twice I imagined it was Capetown. But basically, it was an imaginary someone. Someone else . . . But I really shouldn't have felt bad thinking this because he really didn't love me. I think deep down he doesn't like women. He likes them for only one thing, and that's what he used me for."

Da Vinci and music

"In an Italian Renaissance colloquium I had at Columbia, I learned something fascinating about da Vinci from a recently discovered notebook of a contemporary. Da Vinci was well off and when he painted he hired musicians to play merry music to drive away melancholy—maybe he read the Bible and remembered that King Saul had done that by having David play the harp for him to ward off bouts of depression. Da Vinci did this because his portraits were all having a gloomy cast. The faces looked morose. But with the musicians there, Mona Lisa got a smile, an enigmatic one, true, but still a smile."

Aviva looked at him. She loved listening to him. She'd told him that. But this time she was puzzled.

"What's going on in that never-ending machine up there?"

"I knew you'd ask. I didn't say this to show off any erudition. I said it because I too am going to hire musicians to make you smile more. To make you happy."

He knew she'd lunge forward to hug him, to pour out that boundless affection and appreciation she had for him for saying the right thing at the right time.

By making love to her everything would be cured, he thought. But for her it was both cure and malaise, and he could never know which way the seesaw would turn. As they made love—she on top—for a moment that hurt, frightened, depressed look surfaces on her face. Her lips drooped, her face became momentarily grey. She looked like an old woman. But when she smiled again, twenty years rolled off her face. Would she be a yo-yo again—you're so sexy, it's so good, she said—and say as she went to the door, "I'm not coming back"? Or would she simply not come back and, like last time, call to say that she wasn't feeling well and ask for a postponement?

Decomposition

When Guido made a mistake at the cello, Aviva said, "You're decomposing."

Desire and pregnancy

"No," she said, "I never felt this overwhelming desire before. Years ago, I used to feel it in my head. Do you know what I mean? It wasn't directed at anyone. And now I feel desire for you, not in my head but in my blood, in my body. I feel so hot for you I actually have an itch for you."

He whispered something in her ear.

"What?" she said. "I'm blind in one ear," and then cracked up, realizing what she'd said.

"You're also nuts in one head," he said.

"What would have happened if I'd gotten pregnant? You also read that piece in the *Times* that a woman can get pregnant two years after menopause?"

"Yes. What would have happened?"

"I don't know. I guess all three of us would have had to come to the bris."

"Three?"

"Of course. The presumed father, the real father, and the presumed mother . . . I would have carried the child," she said sadly. "I never would have an abortion."

"Because of the over-fifty risk?"

"No, stupid. Because it's yours. Imagine destroying a child who you're the father of? That baby would be a gem. My brains, my talent, my wit, and your socks. What a combo."

Dialing again

Guido hung up and dialed again.

"Hello?" That tentative baby voice.

"Hi!"

She gave a little screech of surprise.

"You recognized my voice from one Hi?"

"Of course." Her tone dropped to contralto.

"Where are you?"

"Guess."

"You're not calling from Iceland, are you?"

"Which city?"

"I can't pronounce it . . . You really calling from so far?" A pause. "Did you fuck Mrs. Gorbachev?"

"Not yet. You miss me?"

"Of course. You miss *me?*"

"Yes. Especially that empty little space."

"Between my legs?"

"No. Between your ears."

"I can't believe you're calling from Iceland."

"Because I miss you."

"You really miss me? I mean, all of me?"

"Listen. I miss you the minute I wake up," he read. "Your image doesn't leave me till I go to sleep, and then I dream of you. When I'm working with the photos I look for a picture of you, like when I stand in front of Reagan and Gorbachev and when I see a newsphoto of someone who even remotely resembles you, I montage your face onto hers and see, create you. I rehearse ways of kissing you, rehearse positions with you, imagine you saying to me, fuck me good, fuck me hard. I miss your fingers, I miss your cheeks, I miss your tits, your thin little waist, your puss, the way you move, the way you hug me, the way you say, More, more, please more."

"Fuck me over the phone," she says. "Now. Start. Now. I'm waiting. Start. And when you come back and everyone is out to lunch, I'm going to fuck you in the lab."

Discovering how old she is

The only time she stopped looking young was when she was upset, depressed, or taken aback by Guido's anger. ("Don't ever be angry with me," she pleaded.) Then her face fell. Jowls materialized. The slight fuzz on her cheeks and above her lips grew more pronounced, like bristles. And incipient vertical wrinkles like a picket fence compressed, the wickets pulling close for protection, surfaced above her lip. Then she looked sixty. All her beauty vanished. But otherwise, with her slim frame, light step, erect posture, straight neck, especially when she gave forth her radiant smile, she looked thirty-six or thirty-eight.

When she told him she was fifty plus, he almost fainted. What? Me, with an older woman? He thought. When she told him he didn't need protection, he thought it was that time of the month but she said it wouldn't ever be necessary. Then there were a couple of seconds he couldn't account for. He probably did faint.

"What? Me with a fifty-three-year-old woman? Now I remember. You were my counselor in Camp Wackowack. Auntie Aviva we used to call you. Remember, I used to come into your bed after I peed in and you would hug me and abuse me but I wouldn't snitch?"

She hugged him.

"Fifty-three? And I thought forty was old for a woman."

"Isn't your wife forty?"

"No, she's thirty-five."

"And you?"

"I'll tell you some other time. I can't believe you're over fifty. First of all, I thought girls stopped screwing at forty. But fifty-four! You're a wildcat. You're going to be the red hot momma of the senior citizens center. Fifty-five! You're pulling my leg. If you're fifty-six, I'm going to start believing all the singles ads in the *Village Voice*. 'Sexy, 45-year-old. Looks 25. Wants a man. Quick. No photos needed . . .' Fifty-seven? You're going to be the only woman in Medicare with a diaphragm."

"I told you I don't need that any more."

"If I told my friends that I'm consorting with a fifty-eight year old gal/woman, they won't see a frisky, perky, girlish, sizzling sexbomb with long red hair, slim waist, lovely breasts and luscious red lips that look painted but are as natural as uncolored cherries. Do you know what they'll see if I say you're fifty-nine? They'll see an old, lumbering, heavy, gray-faced, hump-necked hag who has been left by her fifty-two-year-old husband who took up with his luscious *Playboy*-breasted twenty-three-year-old secretary."

She said her mother had always taught her to walk straight. And collect social security early. Very early.

See also **Age, her**

Distasteful, how, the Arab's screwing is

"You told me once, in the form of a complaint, that in the old days you played with the Arab to stimulate him. But yet your hands always go down to play with me and no complaints."

"With you it's different. With you there's never a problem."

"And the Arab needed stimulation?"

"He had a fear of impotence. He couldn't sustain an erection. You know how it is, you worry about it and worrying makes it worse."

"Like you mean he would put it in and it would wither?"

"He wouldn't even be able to get it in."

"And you didn't bend down to the little mamzer and kiss it to make it grow."

Aviva laughed. "No. Because it was attached to a bigger mamzer."

Diversionary tactics

The next day, after the pain of screwing up while performing at Hempstead County College had subsided, she asked:

"Did you notice my belly?" And he grabbed a handful of her stomach.

"Is *that* what you're worried about?"

"I just thought of it after the concert—that my stomach was sticking out."

"What a mind! Only a woman can think of such things. You looked elegant. Regal. Like a queen. I'm sure no one noticed your belly."

"Of course not. The lousy playing diverted their attention."

Dog, fixed

"Once, when I was into the second or third year of my static virginous first marriage," said Aviva, "I stood on the balcony—we faced a rear courtyard—of my garden apartment. There were two dogs in the yard. A female was barking and yipping and dancing around the male. She nuzzled up to him, licked him, swirled around, broke out in high-pitched screams. Standing up there on the balcony, looking down, I could feel her excitement. But the other dog wasn't moved. He just stood there unimpressed. Again the female dog went into a frenzy of barking and screaming. She sniffed the other dog's balls, licked him, sprawled on the ground, thrashing her legs with excitement and yelping for all she was worth. But the other dog, the male, was fixed. It didn't move. Couldn't care less. I really felt sorry for the bitch."

Double standard

"Double standard," she said. "Double double standard. You want me to have been faithful to you in the past, and yet you want me to look the other way when you go home to sleep with your wife. I won't buy the story that you can't stop because it would look suspicious. And another double standard—you've had more girlfriends than I've had boyfriends. It doesn't bother me."

"But it bothers me. A woman should be more selective."

Dread of the dead, the Arab's

This happened a few years ago, when for a while things weren't too bad with us, she was saying. When people, my relatives for instance, assumed we were fine. But as you know, the Arab did things without rhyme or reason.

Like stop talking to you for a week or two.

Yes.

With or without burnt French fries.

Aviva laughed.

This time, it was a cousin's Bar Mitzva. This entire family was gathering in a hotel in Rockaway. But he announced he wasn't coming and that was that. I told him that it would be very embarrassing for me. Everyone in my family was coming. Everyone would ask, How come

Rahamim isn't here? Tell them what you want. Tell them I couldn't make it. But I told him, I'm not going to lie. Why all of a sudden you stopped lying when it comes to me? he says. You lie so much, lie a little more. I begged him. I pleaded with him. I cried. I lost my temper, gritted my teeth, pounded my fists in frustration on the bed, but he wouldn't budge. A heart of stone. I should have seen it coming; a heart of stone never changes. I could tell by his look that he enjoyed the scene. I'm going to complain, I threatened.

Yeh? Maybe the police?

He knew I couldn't bring this complaint to anyone. But in truth I could and I pressed forward.

I will. I can. And my complaint will be heard.

By the changing color in his face, I knew that he knew what I was driving at. If it's one thing these primitive North Africans are in dread of, it's the dead. He knew what I had in mind.

Yes. I will be heard. Because my complaint is justified. She'll hear me. I'll be heard. And I'll get satisfaction. I'm going to go to the cemetery like Jewish women have done over the centuries, and I'm going to weep at the grave of a woman who gave birth to a monster and I'm going to tell her, Your son is mistreating me. I'm going to tell her everything and I'm going to demand justice. That there must be justice in this world and that I if gave and gave and gave in to everything you wanted, that every time you had business associates over I fed them and washed their linen and entertained them year after year even though they were uncouth, rowdy North Africans who got drunk and embarrassed me. So I have it coming to me. I am going to collect my chits. I have it coming to me. I have the right to demand a little reciprocation. I *am* going to the cemetery and plead at your mother's grave.

But the monster was asleep before I even finished. The next morning he got up early, that superstitious animal, and I know where he went. Because his hat was missing from the closet shelf. He went early in the morning, before he went to work, like a good Jew with his hat on, to speak to his mother in the cemetery, to tell her lies about me, to warn her not to listen to me, to counteract the truth I would tell her. Because if he didn't, he knew that something bad would happen. Perhaps she would haunt him in his dreams. Because these Moroccan Jews are very superstitious. The dead, the cemetery, gravestones, amulets, all that stuff means more to them than life itself.

Dream, Guido's musical

I dreamt I was taking a lesson with you. I carried my music and on the outside of the book the notes were attached to the book accordion-like and pleated.

Dybbuk, feeling a

He said to Aviva:

"Did you think of me at eleven last tonight? All of a sudden I felt what a dybbuk was. I felt you in my skull. I felt your face on my face, your breasts on my chest, your belly on mine, your puss puss on my pecker. I felt you totally envelop me. There's a hole in my day when I don't see you and, what a paradox, when I do."

Dybbuk, her, invading him

She came to him in various visions. Once, he felt her like a dybbuk invading him, filling him slowly from skull to toe. Another time, at the cello, he smelled her smell. Not that she had one, but whatever faint whiff she did possess came over him, mildly perfumed, a mixture of skin and soap and face cream. Another time, her slightly sweet, pungent taste spread over his lips.

E

Elections, Presidential

Just before they made love he said, "Let's play 1988 elections."

"Now?"

"In a couple minutes, you'll see."

Then: "Remember the 1988 Presidential elections and who ran against whom?"

"Yes."

"Now watch. Hint. Other words for: De rooster is in the hedge." And he pumped into her.

"I don't get it."

"De rooster is in the hedge. Think of synonyms. Other words."

Aviva shook her head.

"Cara Aviva senza testa."

"Which means?"

"Which means dear Aviva can't passa de testa. Just think of the presidential candidates. De rooster is in the hedge . . . or . . . de cock is in . . ."

". . . the bush," she said and burst out laughing.

"In sexual liaisons we don't play partisan politics. We give each equal time."

Emptiness, how she fills it

When I'm away from you, I go over in my mind what we said, your jokes, and I laugh to myself. I review every nuance of your face. What we did and how you looked and that fills the emptiness of my day and night.

Enigma, the, that Guido is

"You're an enigma," she said. "If everything isn't all right between you and your wife..." But she didn't finish the sentence. "But if everything *is* all right between you, then I don't belong here." She stared up at the ceiling, hands folded behind her head.

Here we go again, he thought. The constant argument. Time never stops. Exasperated, he said, "Then why don't you go?"

Once before when he had said this, she sat up, picked up her panties and bra. But as she snapped on her bra from the back, he, still flat on his back, stuck his big toe in and hooked her, pulling her until she was flat on her back. "You're not going," he told her.

But this time she didn't move. She didn't respond to his provocation, except to say:

"Because I love you."

Erotic cello

She wedged the cello between her legs as if it were a man and as she fingered the strings her lips seemed to whisper into the wood. At particularly difficult pieces, she breathed heavily, snorted almost, through her mouth. Touching an instrument, she had once said, is a very sensual, a very erotic act. A cello is not shaped like a man, but if you put this big responsive thing between your spread legs what else can one expect but sensuous pleasure?

Now Aviva bent over it, a puppeteer speaking to her dummy. When she got excited, and played quickly, her jaws rocked, but the closer she got to the instrument, the more ethereal and passionate her face becomes. At one point it almost seemed like a dance—her body going in one direction and the cello in the other. Still, like a couple in embrace, they were one.

See also **Cello teaching**

Eyes, killing them

Once, in a coffee shop, a counterboy asked Aviva if her eyes were hurting her.

She dabbed at an eye, nothing wrong there, "No," she said, "why do you ask?"

"Because yours are killing me," he said.

F

Famine

After not seeing him for a few days, she said:

"Four days of famine . . . I missed you so much."

It was then that she blurted out that she had spoken about Guido to her music counselor, a kind of music therapist who was trying to build her musical self-confidence.

He was furious, "You crazy? I told you not to tell anyone. Ever. The only time a secret can remain secret if it's between two people. When a third person knows, the world knows, goes the Italian proverb. You broke your promise."

She turned ashen. She'd never seen him angry. Like out of Shangri-La her face fell, and she really looked like a sad sack in her late fifties, suddenly an old broken woman.

Fantasizing, musically

"How do you fantasize when you don't see me?"

Her smile trailed after her as she went to the taperecorder. He listened to a short cello selection.

"This sad little piece by Bach, played by Piatagorsky, reminds me of you."

"What's it called?"

She gave her chin-down smile. "On the Departure of My Beloved Brother."

Fat, she is, Aviva complains how

"Look at how fat I am."

"Your belly is so big you can hide a midget there."

"I do," she said, "and if you tickle him once more he's going to bite your finger off."

Feeling close

"You don't understand closeness," Tammy told him. "You never did. You never will. I feel so close to you that it seems to me that many little horizontal lines, all of them a different color, run between you and me. I can see them. They go 'bzz bzz,' humming like telegraph wires."

Feeling like a kid in her presence

Occasionally, he felt that he was a kid and she was the much older, more experienced woman, especially when she taught him and he felt he was learning his ABC's again. When he criticized her for laziness, she would purse her lips and little wrinkles above her upper lip would appear. Or, when her nose would twitch, he would feel that she was decades older than he was. No wonder she kept saying, When I get older, you'll dump me.

Finger technique

"Imagine if I'd started teaching you about bowing and I began by reading you this passage." She plucked a book from a shelf and opened to a page with a torn piece of Kleenex as a marker. She read: " 'Try moving your fingers back and forth across a smooth surface. Start with long slow strokes and build up speed and let the strokes become quicker and quicker. You will discover that as you get quicker you will automatically lighten your stroke in order to prevent the increased friction from building up and starting to burn. . .' Now what would have been your reaction had I read this to you during the first lesson?"

Guido laughed. There was a wicked gleam in his eye, which she had expected.

"Tell me . . . tell me," she purred.

"Well, first I would have asked you to demonstrate with your finger on a certain smooth surface to see how quickly you could stroke before I started to burn. And then . . . by the way, who's the pervert who wrote this?"

See also **Cellos are like people**

Foot massage

"Massage my foot," she said in bed.

"If you massage mine," he said. "Here."

"That's not your foot."

"I'll be the lexical judge, the arbiter of semantics and morphology. You claim this is your foot, which though it isn't, I accept. So you have to accept *my* definition of foot."

"The only difference is," she said, "when you massage *my* foot it doesn't grow."

Forgot, the penny and the Arab story that Aviva

She and the Arab were driving along a highway, and the gas was low. Aviva told him to fill up, but he kept putting it off because he noticed that the price in some stations was a penny cheaper. So he kept driving, hoping that at the next station it would be less. The little red indicator light came on. Aviva said, Stop it. Stop and buy gas. But no, he was stubborn. They'd make it to the next gas station. A little later, putt-putt-putt, and in the middle of the highway out conked the car. Outwardly, she was upset. Within, however, she was pleased. Pleased to see how he had to walk a mile to a gas station and lug a gallon back in a container. And he cursed the gas station for gouging. There it was a penny more.

Four-word review

I went to a recital of hers in a local high school. She played three cello sonatas by Beethoven with piano accompaniment. She hugged the instrument as if, yes, I must say it, as if it were a man. In the passion of the musical embrace she rocked forward like a man, with strength and determination, and I wondered how such a tiger at the cello could be such a lamb in life. When the sudden pianissimo and dance melodies came, she seemed to turn off the power and float ethereally, as if on a cloud.

After the concert I was among a dozen or more people in her dressing room. I didn't know what to say. I'd never been backstage before as an admirer. Photographer, yes. Professionally, yes. I heard people saying banalities like, beautiful, lovely, well done. What could I say that wouldn't go in one ear and out the other? I thought of the tiger image, of lion strength. Both animals were cats. There was a cat-like grace and energy to her playing, both strong and subtle. Then it hit me, a four-word review. She saw me approaching, gave me a warm smile. Obviously surprised to see me. But she played cool, pretended I was no one special, just a fan from the audience who came backstage to congratulate her on her performance. Even so, she sent me a secret warning; and ever so slight shake of the head. As if it were necessary! I bent closer to her, shook her hand for a moment, and whispered my four-word review into her ear: "Leonine ferocity, feline grace."

Frivolous, she is

When it would come to delineating how frivolous, impulsive, capricious, unpredictable Aviva was, he thought of a line he had read in Turgenev's *Fathers and Sons,* when the author describes a flirtatious princess whom the dilettante Kirsanov wants to seduce:

"There always seemed something that still remained mysterious and unattainable, which none could penetrate. What was hidden in that soul—God knows. It seemed as though she were under the spell of mysterious forces (in Aviva's case, as she said, moods determined by biochemical forces, hormones, et al.), incomprehensible even to herself; they seemed to play on her at will; her limited intellect could not master their caprices. Her whole behavior presented a series of inconsistencies."

Fuzzy legs, his

"I love to touch you," she said, "I love the smooth skin of your body. The fuzzy legs, the smooth belly and back. I get hot just looking at you . . . The way the light reflects on your skin is just beautiful . . . but you, my photographer husband, so involved with light and shades of light and dark, you never say that you see such things on me."

G

Galoshes

The other day he told her that if she starts screwing anyone else, she had better tell him because on account of AIDS he'd start wearing rubbers. Insulted to the core, she closed her eyes and sharply turned her head away. "Do what you think," she said. He leaned on his elbow and just stared at her. "Don't look at me that way," she said.

"Why not? I want an answer."

"I'd never do anything like that . . . I would never sleep with two guys at the same time."

Now, today, just before she began to take off her clothes, to get back at him she said, "Did you bring your galoshes?"

It sparked an idea. Next time she came, as soon as the erector set was on display, he jumped out of bed, opened a closet door, and, with his back to her, draped the right shoe of his rubbers over his cock and turned to her. She choked with laughter, blue in the face. He thought he'd have to give her artificial respiration, or at least the Heimlich maneuver to get her to catch her breath again.

Game playing

"Are you into game playing?" Aviva asked. She watched his face. "Don't give me that drop-jaw, surprised, knock-my-socks-off-look."

"You mean woman games, the sort we play?"

"I mean playing with people, with their emotions."

"Like teasing, that sort of game? Ah, now I see what you mean. I used to do that. Fool naïve people, pull their legs. Then it was pointed out to me how not nice it was to pull people's legs, and I stopped. Once I pulled a man's leg and it was made out of wood and I got splinters, so I don't do that any more."

Gerbil, her

Aviva had mentioned that her daughter bought a gerbil. "The kids love that furry little thing," she said.

Driving to her house, he laughed as he rehearsed what he would say to her.

"I want to see your gerbil," was the first thing he said as he came through the door.

She took him to her daughter's room, pointed to the little cage.

"No. Not that one. I want to see gerbil senior, the one with the real fur, the Mama Gerbil that out-gerbils all gerbils. The dead one, not the live one."

"Dead?" she shrieked. "I'll kill you. I'll have you mourning for that dead thing."

See also **Hamster**

Gift, birthday

After she gave him a camera carryall bag (he could get them cheaper wholesale but wouldn't tell her this), he said, "And for you I'm going to give the gift that keeps on giving. The best gift of all."

"What?" she said happily.

"Me."

Glow on her face

When Aviva told some fellow musicians that she'd won the cello competition, they said: "We could tell that something good happened to you. You're glowing!"

"That's not the reason," she said, but they didn't ask her, and she, of course, didn't volunteer because long ago Guido had told her, "If you want this to continue, you cannot blab. Not to friends, relatives, or father confessor. Only two people should know, me and you. Not 2.2 souls. Not even 2.1. Is that understood?"

"Okay," she said.

Months later she said, "That's another reason I didn't think you were Jewish. Because besides your Italian name you used the term *father confessor.*"

"But that's just a metaphor," Guido said, "for Chrissakes!"

God's creation

The best "I love you" Guido ever heard was Aviva's remark as she stared adoringly at him after kissing his neck: "Only God could have made you," she said, "and this from someone who doesn't believe in God."

He let the glow of the remark sink in and then, wanting to resist the bon mot, but unable to, began to smile.

"What's on your mind? Come on, by the expression on your face I know there is something running through that analytic computer of yours."

"Just repeat what you said."

"Only God could have made you."

He smiled again, then began laughing.

"Okay," she said. "Let's hear it."

"I wish I could say the same about you."

She gave him a puzzled look, sort of turned her head and looked up, trying to see the point of it. Then her eyes brightened and she began laughing. "You nasty man, you. That stuff never seems to leave your mind . . . But if he did, I'd be Madonna. . ."

"And go on tour, make records and films and I'd never see you again."

God, thanking, for Guido

"You know what I think when you're screwing me?" she said, he head pressed to his.

"Making love," he corrected.

"Making love," she repeated. "You know what I think of?"

"You mean when I'm fucking you?"

"Yes."

"What?"

"I say to God: 'Thank you, thank you . . .' But that's blasphemous, right?"

"Not if He's a voyeur."

Guido's Italian proverbs and folk sayings

Only three things don't lie—the looking glass, the camera, and your mother-in-law.	(Italian)
The only constant is change.	(Rome)
Words are like pasta. They stick to each other. [Re when you garble your thoughts]	(Naples)
Forget my name, but don't forget my face.	(Naples)
You have to begin to begin. [Re making a decision to start something]	(Venice)
Only a dead man says no to eating.	(Venice)
A new year, a new start.	(Italian)
One is always smarter after one falls off the ladder.	(Italian)
Open your mouth wide enough and the donkey within is seen. [Said of someone who makes an ass of himself]	(Sicily)
She really loves that short leg. [Re a women who loves sex]	(Venice)
She has ears like fig leaves, big and useless. [Said of someone who is tone deaf]	(Calabria)
One can shut a light with eyes, but ears don't have lids, alas. [Re protecting oneself against a loudmouth woman]	(Rome)
Even a windmill has to catch its breath. [Re a garrulous woman]	(Grandmother Sacerdote)
Take away the name and no man's the same. [A name makes a person]	(Rome)
It never rains when you're in love.	(Tuscany)
You can't whip a woman with pasta.	(Sicily)

Non c'e musica como la andatura della bella ragazza.
(There is no music like the walk of a beautiful girl.) (Rome)
Savor the honey, but watch out for the bee. (Italian)
A man knows his walking stick better than his wife. (Tuscany)
Only sleep goes smoothly, and even sleep doesn't
go smoothly. [Re things not going smoothly] (Sicily)
Once the [mud] slide begins, even God himself can't
help. (Alpine valley)
A broken watch doesn't stop the seasons. [Re time
moves on no matter what] (Italian farmers)
The world is under your tongue. [Re when you
know what to say] (Venice)
Too good is also no good. (Italian)
A belt has two functions: to keep your pants up and
your wife down. (Sicily)
If looks could kill, only animals would roam the earth. (Sicily)
When a man is married, his wife also becomes his
mother-in-law. (Siena)
The left hand gives and the right hand takes.
[Re natural balance] (Italian)
Change of heart, change of language. [When people
are angry] (Venice)
We only remember the sweets; the bitter is ground away. (Sicily)
Bene, benissimo, now give me a kissimo. [Romans to
American girls] (Rome)
If two know, fine—if three, the world. [Re keeping a secret] (Rome)
He'd show who held the whip and who was the ass.
[Re showing strength] (Abruzzo)
The guy in the next stall pees like a horse. Yours
is brief and to the point. [Showing how others people's
faults are intolerable; only yours are okay] (Italian)
Farming is bitter, but making babies is sweet. (Calabria)
Big heart, big belly. [Re a compliant woman] (Naples)
Eat well, laugh well. (Venice)
You don't ask, you don't learn. (Venice)
Priests love God, but they love sex more. (Rome)
Sex without joy is like wine without alcohol. (Naples)
One girl in a gondola is nectar, two is heaven. (Venice)
You hug with two hands, but it takes only one foot
to give a kick. (Venice)
Everyone wishes he had two heads. Especially the
slaughtered chicken. (Grandmother Sacerdote)

A dog knows when to stop barking, but asses bray on
and on. (Italian)
Even the sun has spots. [When someone demands perfection] (Venice)
Seeing is not necessarily believing. (Venice)
Women in love always find fault. (Italian)
Ritual and wine will make her mine. (Sicily)
On saints' days even whores become madonnas. (Venice)
Close your eyes and the world disappears. (Venice)
Happiness is a soap bubble. The bubble bursts and you
get soap in your eyes. (Venice)
Dying is for others, not us. (Italian)
If I'm lying, may claws sprout from your fingernails and
fangs from your mouth. (Sienna)
Medicine is the gondola, but a woman's voice is the oars. (Venice)
The more you confront the monster the smaller he becomes. (Venice)
A pickpocket picks pockets, gladly. But when *he's*
pickpocketed he explodes, madly. (Naples underworld)
When a third person knows, the world knows. (Italian)
Old age jumped on him like a rider on a horse. (Italian)
If a pecker had nostrils no babies would be made. (Sicily)
As a person is, so he speaks. (Italian)
If tears would be sweet, people would be crying all the time. (Italian)
You roam the world for what you want and find it in
your yard. (Italian)
You can put potatoes back in a sack, but not words that
have left the mouth. (Italian)

Guido's son

Once, early, on, she asked if he had children. He replied laconically, "A son, but I don't want to talk about it now." She assumed he was off in boarding school. Another time, she asked again, "How come you never talk about your son?" asking when both of them were—

(Oh, Lord, his poor son, whose allotted time span, as predicted by researchers and doctors would soon be up, a boy who would never read or write but live his pathetic life out in a cotton-engulfed mist. Guido remembered pictures taken of Adam when he was younger, before he was placed in a home, the boy smiling, the picture giving the illusion that he was like all other boys, but fooling no one who saw it, because all who saw it knew the reality. That was another of the illusion-shattering aspects of photography. You look at the picture and see what you hope to see, while knowing the hope was a myth, for though Adam smiled he would only cause more furrows, more worry lines, more defeat for his mother whose otherwise pretty face in the early days had become hardened as if a new rough-edge skin had been pulled taut like a robber's ski mask over her face, who took this living loss more personally than he did. You could never tell there was sorrow in his personal life by looking at Guido, but the telltale heartache was on Tammy's face, anguish like reddish talc on her skin that would never go away).

—naked, she still sitting on him after love. He refused to discuss his son while betraying the boy's mother; he refused to talk about his retarded child while naked. There was something sacrilegious about it.

But this early reticence melted in time, and as the months went by he found himself talking about everything and everyone, even his distinguished physician grandfather, whom the King had made a count, who was a member of the Italian Senate from the Veneto region, whose top hat and cravat and mustache would have turned to ash had he known under what circumstances his grandson Guido was discussing him. As Guido analyzed this change of attitude, in a lightning quick thought, perhaps a negative mood, he mused: Eve and the serpent, the serpent Eve, has seduced me once again; I've taken another bite of the forbidden bitter fruit.

Guilt as metaphysical/philosophical entity

"And you don't feel any guilt whatsoever?" Aviva asked.

"Not until you started mentioning it."

"Come on! You don't expect me to believe that."

He looked disappointed. "Really. Once you started mentioning it, I began to feel bad."

"But you're laughing."

"Yes." He smiled. "I feel good about it. Taoism—or is Maoism?—teaches that there is good guilt and bad guilt. This is a good guilt because our relationship has the blessing of karma. Extraterrestrial. Fated."

"Everything is fated. Including my marriage with the Arab."

"True. But this is special. On a different plane. In a different cosmos."

"And if you're on a different plane," Aviva fell into his thought pattern, "then you can't feel guilty, right?"

H

Half a student, Aviva has

"Guess what? I have two new students. Now I have fourteen and a half, but don't ask me how I got half a student . . ."

A minute of silence on the phone. "Hel-lo, Guido, are you still there?"

"Of course."

"Well, why are you silent?"

"Obeying your order."

"What order?"

"Not to ask you how you got half a student . . . It takes a while not to ask, you know . . . By the way, which half do you have?"

"What do you mean?"

"The top or the bottom."

"You know me," Aviva laughed. "I like the bottom half . . . Actually, it's a woman who is only coming once every two weeks."

"That . . . is . . . *bad* . . . With a capital *B*," Guido said seriously. "Only once every two weeks. Pity! What pedagogic method are you using with her? Oral or written?"

"I don't understand."

"If you have the bottom half of a student who comes only once every two weeks, I think you should try the oral method. Then she'd probably come more often. Or invite me, and I'd have her coming daily . . ."

Half life

"With you and me," he told her, "two beautiful elements, that might have gone on existing for years giving off their half life alone unfulfilled, have combined. Two half lives make one, doesn't it?"

Hamster

Even though Aviva didn't feel well, she went at it like a bunny. Which reminded her of a story:

"My daughter got a little hamster. . ."

"You told me already. You showed me. The gerbil, remember?"

"It died. Now she got a little hamster. She loves those furry little creatures."

"So do I, says he, covering New York's entire fur district with the palm of his hand."

See also **Gerbil, her**

Hand, giving a

I once told Guido that I was repainting an antique chest of drawers outside. So he surprised me, drives by, stops, gets out, admires my work. "Want a hand?" he asked. Delighted, all smiles at his surprise visit, I say, "Sure." He applauds, gets back in the car, and drives away.

Harem, times are over for a

"The times for harems are over," she said. "No more than two or more women at the same time for the same guy."

She was in her mad mode again, he noted. When she talked this way, her face slightly distorted, a frown wrinkling her forehead and that cello concentration on her face, she looked, he told her, "like someone who'd been catapulted into old age. Like the Italians say, old age jumped on him like a rider on a horse." As if the mask of her young face had been unzipped, revealing the real face, haggard skin sagging underneath. A face-lift undone. Shangri-La abandoned.

"The times for harems are over," she repeated.

"Having a harem is the norm for humans and animals," was his rebuttal. "Look at cocks. . ."

"Mmm!" she said.

". . .deer. . .lions. . .all kinds of birds."

"I don't care. For me the times for harems are over," she said with absolute finality. "Period."

He muttered something.

"Did I hear you say they're just beginning?!"

Heaven

"What's your idea of Heaven?" Guido asked Aviva.

She responded at once without a moment's thought.

"You'n me forever . . . And yours?"

"I'm in a beautiful pit, or concavity, and an orchestra surrounds me playing Bach's Brandenburg Concertos nonstop, the Sixth most often."

"And me?" she asked, disappointed. "I'm not in it?"

"You're the pit," he said.

Hereafter, her parents in, arranged meeting

"Do you believe in the hereafter?" Aviva asked.

"Good question. I really don't know. But I do believe in the indestructibility of the soul. Why do you ask?"

"Because I've thought about it a lot. I have this picture of my parents getting together in heaven or wherever and arranging it with your father that we meet . . . Why are you making a face?"

"I'm not making a face," he said. "It's just that . . . No . . . I can't believe that . . . My father just couldn't do a thing like that. . ."

"But still, that's what I feel . . . I sense it. . ."

But Guido had also told Aviva once that their link-up was on a different time/space zone. If that was so, Tao/Mao, then he can't feel bad guilt but only good guilt. And so he reconsidered his remark. If in a world of non-Euclidian geometry parallel lines never meet (or do meet, he forgot which), his relationship with Aviva also defied the laws of gravity. If here his friendship with her was severed from the laws of morality, from time and space, then how much the more so in the other world, where these laws did not apply. And hadn't they both concluded that there was something mystical in their getting together, something encoded into their destinies like genes? They *had* to meet, just as the apple *had* to fall and the chick *had* to poke out of the egg.

Guido wasn't sure about the hereafter; still, the housing there intrigued him. For instance, what would happen up there after one hundred years when a man who had had three wives reported for residence? And each of the wives had had two husbands. The condos up there would have to make lots of interlocking accommodations.

Honeymoon

"This is like a honeymoon. We spend more time in bed than anywhere else. I'm so happy!" she said and licked an exclamation point into his neck.

"The happier you get the younger you look."

"Age is very important for you, right?"

"Why do you say that?"

"Because you keep telling me how young I look."

"Yes, I can't get over it. Some rotten thing to tell a girl, huh?"

"What's going to happen when those wrinkles get deeper?"

"I'll get cataracts," Guido said.

Hyphenated names

Aviva would only occasionally come up with absurd but (or: and) wildly imaginative remarks. Once, when speaking of a woman she had met who had a double name—Sue-Ellen or Jo-Ann—she said that the whole idea of a double name was strange to her. "How does she clean around the hyphen?" she asked.

I

Ian Plaskow looks at Aviva

"During my first interview with the famous cellist at PAMA, when I made application to study with him, he checks me out with just the quickest glance at the bulge in my sweater, seems pleased, maybe embarrassed that I caught him looking, and then continues asking questions about who I studied with. But he never does that again, at least not to my knowledge, during the more than two years I studied with him until that fateful dinner invitation."

See also **Quick review for imaginary performance**

Idiot savant

In discussing one of her former lovers, Aviva had told Guido she had no complaints on the bedroom side.

"Of course, no one is like you, but if a person is nice and sweet and you like him, then the screwing is going to be fine too."

"But a guy can be nice and sweet and still be a dud in bed."

"True. Capetown."

"On the other hand, you can be an absolute moron and screw well. You said you had a boyfriend in Italy who was boring."

"Yes, but in the other department he was an idiot savant."

"He was that good?" Guido choked, jealous again.

Aviva laughed. "Only kidding," and kissed his cheeks. "I told you many times that I don't remember the actual act. That's a complete blank in my mind."

If she would have

In the car she tells him:

"Do you realize that if I'd have stayed with Capetown, I'd never have met you?"

He didn't say anything, but he thought about it. Meanwhile, she'd fallen asleep. He looked at her, at rest, her skin soft, faint little lines around her eyes, her lips slightly at a downslant. Even in her sleep she held on to his hand, her rough palms on his. He'd thought of her as an empress with her queenly face and erect carriage. His queen with dishpan hands. Then he thought about what she'd said. He didn't ponder it to say something nice or poetic. But he mused: If you'd have stayed with Capetown, then all my life the right side of my soul would have been yearning for the left. When she woke, he told her. Tears formed in her eyes.

Ill at ease

"I could never tell people what I wanted or what I liked or disliked. Most I felt ill at ease with. Especially if I'm sick. I feel clumsy, stupid, ill at ease. Everything in my head works slowly. Can't recognize things I'm familiar with at other times. My molecules go on strike."

Impotent men, differences between

All potent men are potent in different ways. All impotent men are impotent the same way.

"Was there any difference between one man's impotence and another's?"

"No. They all had the same problem."

Impressed with Guido, how Aviva is

"I didn't know they make men like you."

He smiled.

"What are you smiling at? What wheels are turning in that head of yours?"

"I didn't know they make men like me that make women like you."

Impressions that men left on her

He had read somewhere about a congenial thirty-year-old European whore who had had hundreds of men. On her face, in her being, were stamped the remnants of every man who had penetrated her. He looked at Aviva. She hadn't even had a dozen. Perhaps less than a dozen, but he couldn't see that any of them had left an impression on her. All the men she had were for naught. None of them even made a dent in her eyelids.

Insults, examples of his

"You know, now with people being more aware of cruelty to animals and wearing fur coats is not classy any more—you could make a fortune in the fur business."

"What do you mean? How?" Aviva said.

"Well, there would be no need to slaughter the poor minks or seals. You'd stand there; the fuzzy creatures would parade before you. They give one look at you and drop dead."

It, how she loves

At first, when he would ask her, "Do you like it, do you love it?" she would nod and say, Mmm," and he would say, "What?", reprimanding her for not saying Yes, and she would bring her head closer and practically poke him with her nose and say softly, "Yes, with you," lest he think that she was crazy for sex just like that, irrespective of who her partner was. She added that, Guido was absolutely confident, because of her past lovers.

But as time went by and the loving became better and better and Aviva's screams tore the roof off the house, she herself volunteered, "I *love* it . . ." and didn't feel it was necessary to tell him that she loved it with him. But the bug of doubt that he inherited from his Italian kinsman Othello, that doubt that lingers in all male minds, set to work, and he wondered if now that he'd brought her to the heights of pleasure, perhaps she was removed, perhaps the go-it-alone syndrome which used to be her height of pleasure was in full force again. But then she added, "When I don't see you for two, three days I get an empty feeling down there. Like a vacuum. A void that wants to be filled."

Italian proverb

"You really should slip away from me like a mermaid."

"Why?"

"Because in this world something that someone wants so badly is usually inaccessible. And here you are, desirable, wanted—and accessible. And here we are in this world."

"Mmm," she said. "Isn't it wonderful how I can come to this house and no one, absolutely no one, is on the street when I come? Except my husband and your wife, that lovely couple."

"Yup," said Guido, "but an Italian proverb still rings in my ears: Even paving stones have eyes and ears."

J

Jealous and—

"What would you have done?" Guido asked Aviva, "hadn't I asked you for a walk?"

"As usual, in my inimitable way, nothing."

"Nothing? Even though you were sizzling?"

She nodded.

"And what would your reaction be if I took up with someone else? Would you be upset if I had another girlfriend?"

"Do you?" she said quickly, and then tilted her head and said, "No . . . You don't . . . Do you?"

"What a question!" he said.

"Does that mean you do or you don't?"

"Of course not," Guido said. "Do you know why I ask?"

"No."

"Because last time you said you weren't the jealous type."

"But this is different. Of course I'd be upset. Upset and hurt."

"Now reverse the question. Go ahead. Ask."

"Would you be upset if I saw another man? . . . But I couldn't. . ."

He stared at her for a while. She raised her eyebrows, waiting. A quavering smile.

"I'd be furious . . . You're mine," he whispered into her ear.

"Entirely," she said. "In every way."

"And," he added, "even if you had said you wouldn't be jealous if I saw someone else, I'd still be furious. It would upset me that you wouldn't be jealous . . . Did you notice the difference in our reactions? Yours is typical of your passive way of reacting. Hurt is passive. Fury is active. . ."

Jealousy, old

During the slow second movement of Haydn's Symphony #83, when the conductor leads the soft and gentle movement with ballet-like grace, she was smiling to herself. In the audience, he smiled too. But then he saw a violist who looked like Ian Plaskow and suddenly he saw Aviva stripping for him, taking him in her arms, and slowly fucking him. And he imagined himself under her and as he looked up at her, saw her looking down at Ian and Tom and Dick and Harry and the dozen others she screwed. What would happen, he thought, if the Long Island Symphony would invite Ian Plaskow as a soloist? Would he recognize Aviva? And if he didn't, would she come up and say hello? Another spurt of jealousy as he saw Aviva still smiling (thinking of Ian?) while he writhed with a twenty-year-old jealousy that grew like a slow tumor in him.

See also **Ian Plaskow looks at Aviva**

K

Kids, the Arab's sudden interest in

Now I understand why he suddenly took an interest in the children. The day you flew in from Alaska and surprised me, he took the kids out. I thought he was spending a day with them, but it turns out he took them bowling to butter them up and then feed his corrupt or naïve social worker with the lies. He'd been brainwashing the kids against me and making them curse me until my daughter finally broke down and told me what the Arab had been doing. He would do this bowling trick a few times until he finally dropped the pretense of bowling and went straight to the social worker complaining about me.

Knowing right from wrong

Although she had once suggested, "Let's not go upstairs today," he paid her no mind that day but took her up anyway. Today, however, he was the one to suggest that. But as they talked, she finished each sentence with, "So let's go upstairs."

"I read in the *Times* that Rostropovich is coming to New York," he said. "Would you like to go?"

"Upstairs."

"The air-conditioning isn't working. We have to . . ."

"Go upstairs," she said.

"One of my pictures made it to the finals in the International News Photo Contest, but I'm not sure . . ."

"If it's upstairs or not. So let's look—upstairs."

"No."

"Why?"

"Not today."

But he wasn't about to tell her the real reason. That he'd had a portent that he wouldn't win if he did. Because what he did with photography was

right, and what he was doing with her was wrong, and in the balance scale
the wrong would overweigh the right and he would lose.

L

Lab assistant's dream

"Mind if I told you a dream I had? Would you think bad of me?"

"Of course not! Am I in the dream?"

"You're pretty self-confident, aren't you?"

"Want to call me an egoist?"

She put her front teeth on her lower lip, as if thinking it over.

"Let's hear the dream," said Guido.

She took a deep breath and said:

"I dreamt that you were my husband-to-be. We weren't married yet
and you wanted to make love to me. But I tell you not yet. Then your
desire takes on a different form. It becomes a missile shaped like a
comma, and it swirls and flies around the earth, threatening to burst and
cause destruction. So I seize it, ride it, whisper to it to calm it down, to
not let its destructive force go. I ride it all around the world until it's
tamed."

"And you want me to interpret this?"

"Could you?"

"Of course. Your dream is telling you to invest $2500 in a leading
arms producer. Try United Technologies at 98, up a $1/4$."

Lab assistant's scream

As he screws the lab assistant and she screams to high heaven, he
remarks: You sound like you're at the dentist's.

If dentists could make women scream like that, she said, they'd be
working day and night.

Ladder

There's no end rung on this ladder of love, he thinks of telling her.
But doesn't.

Laws in this world, man makes

When Guido told Aviva about men in olden times having more than
one wife, she said, "Sure, because men made the laws." He said it was
economic necessity. She said, "According to nature, women should have
more than one husband because women can take more men than a man
can take women."

"Who made the laws, men or nature?" he asked.

"Who is more powerful?" she said.

"Men," he said. "They tried to pass a law in 1100 that men would become pregnant, but somehow it didn't work."

"See?" she said. "Again nature wins."

Liberal imagination

He felt he had a liberal imagination. Kissing his wife on the cheek, his mind's eye saw in quick succession, like a rapid action shutter: Aviva, Teresa, Gina, Jennifer from the reunion. And if there's time, maybe Ava too, like in the good old days. And the cellist who modeled—Linda? And sometimes Tammy as well, the ground bass theme to his beautiful passacaglia.

License plate

Her plate read, GOV 2233, and he kept seeing that GOV on cars all over Long Island. Once he saw it as he left her house. He made a turn onto the highway, and the car in front of him had those first three letters. It was like a message for him. But he didn't know what the message meant. *G* obviously stood for Guido. The *V* was for violoncello. Now if he only had a clue to the *O*, he'd have it all clear.

Then it came to him. The *O* stood for only. Guido's only violoncello. Who was that? Aviva, whom he played. Now what did the digits 2233 stand for? Simple, 22 plus 33 is 55—Aviva's age. And GOV, he realized, could also spell out Good Old Veneziano.

Lightbulb, swallowing a

"I feel as if I've swallowed a lightbulb," she said once after lovemaking.

"Keep talking," he said. "Listening to you is a humbling experience."

Liking sex

Now it's my turn. I'm going to ask *you* a question. You like sex, don't you?

I like sex with men, women, children, plants, and things.

And with me?

Especially with you, since you're none of the above.

Liposuction

Again Aviva clutched a fistful of belly. "Maybe I should have liposuction."

"Maybe," Guido said, sucking at her lips.

"What's liposuction?" she asked. "I heard the term but I don't know what it is."

"A type of surgery where they cut away the blubber. They just— whhshhtt—vacuum it away."

"Mmm, not a bad idea."

"But there's a problem with it."

"What?" she said anxiously.

"Fear not. It's not medical but administrative. You see, in the case of massive blubber removal, in some instances twice the body weight of the patient, the doctor doesn't know whether to bill what's left of the former fat, sometimes known as the toothpick, or to bill the vacuum cleaner where most of the patient is now located."

Lollipop

"Mmm," she said. "I love your lollipop. It's like an all-day sucker."

"You're my all-day sucker," he said.

She didn't realize the negative pun of it till much later. Yes, she thought, she *was* a sucker, but not only all day—all year.

Love, how deep it is

He tells her: Love is like skin color. It can't be wiped away.

Love and lust

"You once told me," Guido said, "that love and lust for you are connected. When did this connection first begin?"

"When I met Capetown."

"This didn't happen in Philadelphia?"

"No. In Philly I never gave thought to these things. I didn't experience lust back then. Except maybe when I was alone."

"When you cease analyzing the reasons why you went to bed with all those guys—can't one conclude that it was all for sex? That you just loved fucking?"

Aviva winced at the word. He shouldn't have used it but couldn't help himself. Then he added: "Like the girl in the novel I once quoted to you: 'I can do without liquor and drugs, but if I don't have enough sex I climb the walls.'"

"Not me. There were many long periods without it. I didn't love it. More in thoughts that actuality."

"In the past, would you go to bed with a guy without being hot?"

"Yes. Probably."

"Were you just being polite?"

"Probably. How else do you explain it?"

He had a word for it, a phrase, but he didn't want to use it again. Some people love music, some fucking, some both.

"Does one become attached to a man one screws?" Guido asked.

She had already begun undressing.

"At the time," she said, "but not later."

"Then it isn't just sex?"

"No. You don't understand that. Men don't understand that. It's not just bodies rubbing. Sex is also mental and spiritual. It's also imagination. And the emotional factor feeds into the physical."

Love builds up slowly

"You know that love builds up slowly. You know what happens when a spoonful of vinegar is put into a barrel of carefully aged wine?"

She nodded.

"Well, that's what happens when you tell me, 'You call the shots and then run off,' or when for every one of your moods you say with hard-nosed abruptness: 'That's the way I am,' as if nothing can change you. And yet you say you never changed."

"The last time I changed was when I wet my diaper," she said.

"I thought of you this morning. I just had the perfect medium-boiled egg, bought from a farmer's wagon. And it made me think of you when I ate it."

"Why?" she asked, as he knew she would. "Okay, let's hear it. I'm ready."

"Why? Because like you, the egg was laid yesterday."

Lubricated, well

He noticed over the last few months that she'd stop saying, It hurts, like she used to. She no longer said, It's dry. It's a brick wall. For months now she'd been well lubricated. He even noticed spots in the very epicenter of her panties. Whereas at the beginning she had no smell, now after lovemaking that fishy juice was smeared all over her, and she always wanted to wash up before she left.

One of my students, a little girl, told me I smelled like bubble gum. A new euphemism.

There's an old Sicilian proverb, he told her. If a pecker had nostrils, no babies would be made.

Lucky, who is?

"I'm so lucky," he said.

"And I'm not?" Aviva said.

"You're luckier."

M

Make-up, wearing

She would come into the house distressed; gloom trailed after her like a billowing, wind-blown coat. She came into the living room. As usual, there was a bit more make-up on her than he would have liked. "But it's just a little bit, just a touch . . . You don't want me to look like an old hag, do you?" The azure above her eyelids clashed with her auburn hair; the black accent near the lashes somehow always dried and flecked, and she was forever picking at those little black dots. She did this when she was nervous and sometimes picked when there was nothing there. He supposed she put that stuff on her eyes to deflect that slight squint, but she never understood how charming it was. Did he put on eye make-up, he asked her, to make his squint sexier? You're as sexy as can be, she replied. If you put on make-up and became even sexier, I wouldn't let you out on the street. People, men, women, children, pets, and things would all rape you.

Man's hands

"A man's hands are a very remarkable part of his anatomy," she said. "they're the first part of him you get to know, even before the lips."

"Did you look at my fingers?" he asked.

"Yes. Among my girlfriends we used to joke: by a man's fingers you can tell how thick his penis is."

"So that's why you looked at my fingers."

"Uh-huh."

"And did you see any correlation?"

"Uh-huh."

"How?"

"You want the details?"

"Always."

"Well, your fingers were nice and thick, and so's your thing. Your fingers are not effeminate looking. Neither is your thing."

"But my thing, as you so demurely put it, *is* effeminate looking. It's always looking for the effeminate."

Marathon Man

"You're the triple M man," Aviva said.

"Meaning what?" Guido asked.

"Meaning you're my Marathon Man," she said. "the man who can hold it in the longest, keep it up for hours, although the time passes by so quickly it seems like minutes."

"Dong size never made an impression on you."

"No, I don't remember. I told you that. With the exception of the first one, who had a mini."

"How did you know it was a mini?"

She laughed. The laugh was a combination shy and impish laugh, both self-deprecating and waggish. "Comparison shopping."

Marry her, everyone wants to

"Everyone who went out with you wanted to marry you, right?"

"I never said that, but quite a number did."

"Did that guy in Italy ever ask you?"

"No. He was more remote. He never discussed that." And then she gave that head-down smile. "But there was a kid, he was twenty-one or -two."

"And you were thirty at the time . . ."

"Shh, but he didn't know that. You know I looked nineteen."

"How could a guy ask you to marry him if he didn't touch you?"

"We kissed, but that's as far as it went."

"Why?"

"I didn't want to. And then there was that redhead."

"Oh, yes, the Iranian. But he was impotent. Then what would you have done."

Aviva arched her eyebrows and laughed. "Talked a lot I guess."

"Like we do."

"Yes," and she laughed again.

Masturbating

After she told him that she'd been masturbating since she was twelve or thirteen, he said:

Did you know that Bach was blind and had twenty-two children, and that in his old age before he went blind he wrote piano pieces for the left hand? Do you know what Johann Sebastian was doing with his right hand? Do you know how he went blind?

Mediocre talents in screwing

You'd think that after all that screwing with boyfriends, man friends, lovers, and husband, she would have picked up some on-the-job training. There's a big difference, Guido wanted to tell her, between putting out and putting oneself out. The typical WASP dame, the typical Victorian lady (when ladies, while being laid by laddies), had to lay or lie absolutely still. Aviva too hardly moved at first. She still screwed like a novice. On her back she thrashed about with arrhythmic rhythm, jagging to the beat of a phantasmagoric drummer boy that in no way melded with a musical sensibility. It took months of hands-on fucking for her to start moving. Her rhythm improved. The feckless drummer boy became Gene Krupa. She screamed like a dying swan.

Menopause, Guido reads about

If sex impulse is a matter of hormones, he read, which trigger the desire to make love, the loss of estrogen at menopause should put an end to this exercise. But it's imagination and feelings toward the man that does more to stimulate pleasure than all our glands combined.

He also read: women's drives are sometimes heightened at menopause by sudden influxes of hormones. The whore moans, Guido thought. In post-menopause, generally after age fifty-five, the vagina becomes progressively thin and dry due to diminution of hormones; intercourse can become painful, leading to frigidity and avoidance of sex.

Menopause, Aviva ecstatic over

"You read in books about women in their fifties feeling old, tired, unwanted, bitter, empty. I may have felt some of that at times, especially the last two, but not because of menopause. I certainly never felt old. Ha, that's the exact opposite of what I always felt. I never had hot flashes, got no cramps, no sudden food binges (the latter I have now, about four years after my last period, especially for kiwis and pignola nuts). Do you think I may be pregnant? All these menopausal signs seem to have passed me by. Other women mourn their menopause. I was ecstatic. Who needs it? I feel as young and vibrant and sexy with you as ever. Nothing sags on me. I read a book about women at fifty and it depressed me because there are so many pathetic fifty-plus women around. But on the other hand, it made me float on air. I'm unique. The hormones tell me I'm old, but nothing else in me does. Okay, so my boobs don't pass the pencil test, but so what? Some twenty-year-olds with good-sized breasts can't pass it either, but they're still firm and sensitive to my lover's touch and kiss. What more can I want?" Aviva stopped. "I said a mouthful there, didn't I? . . . There's plenty I want.

"All the symptoms I was supposed to feel, depression, lackadaisical attitude, all these I had before I got menopause, and all were directly tied in to my husband's erratic behavior toward me: his fights, rages, silences that drove me to a breakdown. So a woman can become menopausal given the right—or wrong!—conditions and stimuli, and yet at menopause everything can go smoothly for her."

Mermaid

You should have been a mermaid.

Why? She sounded disappointed. Knew what mermaids didn't have and couldn't get.

Because then I could have zeroed in only on your boobies.

Then what would you have done, for you know . . . ?

He shrugged.

No good, she said. I won't be a mermaid. Bad fantasy. I like good fantasies. Like your Aladdin's lamp. You rub it and all your wishes come true.

Mine(s)

"You're mine," he told her.

"But are you mine?"

"Yes," he said.

"But you have another mine. You have two mines. You have so many mines you can open up a cartel."

Minsk

"My wife is from Minsk."

Mood shift

You're more stable, more consistent than me, she would say. Your moods don't shift as much. You're more on one level. For example: she would complain that her waist had gotten at least two inches thicker. It was because of the binges she went on when she was depressed. She had no self-discipline, never had any. No self-control. He vaguely remembered her girlish waist of two years ago and was impressed at the slim waistline of someone who, in retrospect, was in her fifties. You'll love me more if I'm thinner, right? I feel sexier when I'm thinner. I love you more when I feel better. Okay, he finally agreed, I'll love you more if you lose weight. But stick to it. I will, she said. I promise. No, I won't promise. Whenever I promise, I jinx myself. I'll just try.

But the next day she reproached him with: How come you don't love me for myself? Is your love in proportion to my weight? More/less, less/more? What are you talking about? he wondered. You yourself wanted to lose weight to feel better. But you said, she argued, that you'll love me more if I'm thinner. He rolled his eyes. He wasn't going to argue with a kook. If you feel better about yourself, he said without feeling, it makes me feel better too. And you did say you feel sexier when you're thinner. She nodded dreamily.

Okay, he said, now that we got that established, take your pants off.

Mortgage agreement

Guido tells Aviva that as part of equitable distribution he'd like her to sign a note that she's giving him first mortgage on her pussy so that if, in case of a divorce, the Arab seeks half of it in equitable distribution, she can claim that it's already mortgaged and he can't have it.

Prior to showing her his draft agreement, he tells her that when sole custody is sought of children, the husband, in compensation, can claim occasional conjugal rights.

"No. You're pulling my leg. I know you."

"Honest," Guido said. "It's true, Benson v. Helena, South Dakota, and that's why I want you to sign this agreement which makes me first mortgagee and first mortgage owners get first rights, *primus nightus,* in Latin."

"But that means when the Arab comes to me for occasional conjugal rights, I'll have to send him to you."

"Well . . . I think I'll pass. It's better to give than receive . . . Here's the agreement."

AGREEMENT

I hereby mortgage 100% of my pussy to (insert name of mortgagee, first mortgagee) in return for value received, which entitles first mortgagee to first rights in any future equitable distribution agreement. This is done with clear mind and clean body and is not to be con-screwed as a ruse to deprive future ex-spouse-to-be of any inalienable, equitable distribution rights. In case spouse seeks 50% of above-named pussy as part of distribution, it's not mine any more.

Signed _____

Witness _____

Date:

N

Naïveté

She was so naïve at times that she believed anything. Like his cloning story. When she said once that she'd like to take him home with her, he replied that he had read in *Science* that there was a full cloning facility in Chicago, but it would cost a fortune and it wasn't always successful. Sometimes instead of two, there's none. "Then don't do it," she said. Around the same time she wanted to tear off an annoying pillow tag. He shouted for her to stop. "It's illegal," he said. "Read the tag! Do not remove under penalty of law."

"I didn't know," she said, sheepish and contrite, "that you weren't supposed to remove them."

Name, origin of Guido's

"How did you get your name?"

"In Europe, doctors aren't cultural boobs and nincompoops like in this country. There they are men of infinite culture. Anyway, my father loved music and so he named me after an Italian pioneer in music, but you wouldn't know him."

She looked at him for a moment, a proud and naughty little gleam in her eye. "Of Arezzo," she said.

"You know Guido of Arezzo?"

"Of course," Aviva said. "Expect me not to know him after years at Mannes and PAMA and of being the daughter of my father. I'm surprised at you. Even insulted. Guido of Arezzo invented the staff and clef system of notation, in the eleventh century, I think. In fact," and she gave that little laugh of hers, "when you hold me . . ."

"Where? Name the parts."

"Wherever . . . I think of the musical term, *Guidonian hand*. But that you don't know . . ."

"That's one of the two things in music history I don't know."

"What's the other?"

"Never mind. You don't have to know everything I don't know. What's *Guidona hand*?"

"A system of notation where each part of the finger is a different note . . . What are you doing?"

"Playing a Bach Sonata on your chest."

Negative

When I miss you, he said, I feel an anti-shape of you, something like an anti-Semite, a kind of negative image, I don't mean negative in the photographic sense or the medical sense which is really positive, but in the physics sense, a kind of absence. Let's see if I can make it clearer. As though there's a vacuum in space and a, yes, I got it now, a photographic negative shape of you, vacuous, is there. It's as though the absence of you, the non-presence of you, is there, shaped like you, but made of invisible negatrons, like wind, an anti-Aviva.

Not, do, go out

"So how was Don Snow the old lecher's party?"

"You remembered it was yesterday? I told you about it two three weeks ago."

"I marked it on my calendar . . . You were there late."

"How do you know?"

"Cause I drove by."

"What?"

"How did I get his address you want to know? Since there was a little item about him in the *Long Island Post*, I called the feature editor and got his address. I drove by three times and the blinds were drawn, couldn't see a thing. What'd you do, bed down with the old lecher? You said you wouldn't start going out till three months from now."

"No. You said that. I said right away."

"You said you'd stay with me four months."

"No. You said that. You can't control everything," Aviva said.

"When I suggested a six-month extension, you said four. I said let's compromise on three, and you said, No, you can't have it your way, let's make it seven. Then I said, fine, compromise, my three plus your seven is ten, and ten times ten is 100 which is a perfect score. Bene, shalom, peace, congratulations, mazel tov, it's settled, we kissed, shook hands, and had a deal."

She burst into laughter. "You gangster, you glib-talking, double-dealing monster. You shoulda been a lawyer."

A few days later day he called, pretending he was Snow, the old pianist she'd met, who had been written up in the *Post*. Snow had promised her that they might give piano-cello recitals together, and Aviva had mentioned several times that she would call him. But of course, in typical Aviva fashion, she put it off for another day.

"Hi, this is Donald Snow. Did you call me this morning? I just caught the last ring but it was too late."

"No. But in fact, I was just about to. You jumped the gun. But funny, you sound just like Don Snow."

"Yes, I know. People have told me that our voices are similar. Would you like to come over at 1 p.m. and we can make some music together?"

"What kind of instrument do you have?" Aviva asked.

"An organ."

She cracked up. "What kind of state is it in?"

"New York. Only on rare occasions when I'm in Long Island is my instrument in Connecticut. Except when the ferry isn't working or the fog is too thick."

Not remembering any of them

"You know I told you I have no recall of going to bed with any of them. Isn't that strange? Maybe I want to block it from my mind. But I have memories of memories."

"A beautiful phrase."

"Do you know what I mean?" she asked.

"For instance."

"That guy I met in Florence. I remember remembering his eyes."

"Cold."

"Like ice."

O

Obsessed with Ian Plaskow

Guido wondered why the obsession. Example: he read in a novel the other day about a woman who invited a man up to her apartment for coffee. Whoosh! Immediately he thought of Aviva years ago putting up coffee for Plaskow after their dinner in New York. He saw her preparing the hi-riser for him, the hi-riser which she still had and which under no circumstances would he ever lie down on with her. For him, in his mind, it was an existential moment, that screwing, Ian making it with her.

He asked her if she had made it with him and she glibly said, "No." The liar! That Aviva-Ian screwing seemed to Guido to stretch on for all eternity. In Guido's mind, Plaskow has been screwing her for decades, and maybe she was still screwing him, even now, when she and Guido made love, even though she vehemently denied even thinking about him, ever. She said that Guido was the only man she thought about, dreamt of, lusted for. Are our passions equal? he wanted to know. Her sly answer was, Can anyone put in the balance two different people's passions? She reminded him that she liked the spring; he the fall. During winter and fall her head felt woozy. She sneezed more often, consumed loads of aspirin. But was she saying all that, he wondered, to change the subject; to take his mind off Ian Plaskow?

See also **Jealousy, old**

Old, looking

Yes, on occasion she did look old. A year or two back he'd noticed that when she held her head a certain way, the creases in her neck were visible. And lately, with all the pressures she was under (real or imagined), little wrinkles materialized. But naked, when she moved, her young breasts, which pointed up, as if ready to suckle angels, made her look like a youngster.

Older, getting

Aviva claimed she got much older-looking during the year. He showed her a picture he'd taken of her on a picnic with a bathing suit on and one taken a year later when she posed for him naked.

"Can you tell the difference?" he asked.

"Yes. On the most recent one I have less clothes on . . . Don't tell me it isn't so. I see it every time I look in the mirror."

It was true, he thought; she had aged. The lines above her lips, lines that toothless old ladies had, were more pronounced.

"I don't mind getting older" she said. "It's the aging signs that bother me."

Orgasm, how she tingles before

"Oh, that was so good. I almost had one."

"Why didn't you tell me to continue?"

"Because it went up to a point, then descended."

"Are you going to have one with me?"

"I will. I know it. If I ever have one it will be with you . . . You know how I know it's coming?"

"How?"

"The soles of my feet warm up . . . Then they start to tingle."

Overweight and love

"Will you love me if I'm five pounds heavier?"

"Yes."

"Ten?"

"Yes."

"Fifteen pounds?"

"Of course."

"Twenty?"

"Yes, yes, yes."

"Thirty?"

To tease her, he hesitated, pressed his lips and slowly muttered between strained lips, "Y . . . e . . . s . . . "

P

Palindrome

"I never even told you what my birth name was. My father called me, can you imagine?, Vivalda. Imagine going to kindergarten in Israel with that name? I had a wonderful teacher whom I still remember, Hannah was her name. She told my father, 'Mr. Andermann, your daughter won't survive here with that name.' 'But I'm proud of that name,' he said in his Berlin-accented Hebrew. 'I'm sure you are, and I'm sure it's an honor being named after the composer, but you don't want the children making fun of her, do you? May I suggest Aviva—it has most of the letters of Vivaldi and it's a beautiful Hebrew name.' My father grudgingly accepted it, but he always called me Viva. And so I've been Aviva ever since."

"It's a palindrome. Probably the only Hebrew name that is one."

"What's a palindrome?"

"Something that reads same forward and backward."

"Like me." She laughed her raucous laugh. "Equally adept front and back."

Paradise

Sorry, entry "Paradise" lost in a computer glitch. Try instead "Heaven," "Hereafter," "It, how she loves," or "Petcock."

Pascal and Pushkin

"Pascal says that all our miseries stem from a single cause: we can't remain quietly in a room."

"Aren't I quiet?"

"Am I not?"

"Am I not?" she said.

"No. We move around, the result of all our pleasure, all our joy. Which contradicts what Pushkin said."

"What did Pushkin say?"

"Glad you asked. Pushkin said. There is no joy on earth, but only peace and freedom. But I say if you have peace and freedom *and* love, you have joy. So he's dead wrong."

Passion as penance

"Do you think my passion for you is a kind of penance?" he thought he heard her say. He digested her remark and then, like cud, it surfaced again. The word *penance* was turned around, analyzed, inspected like facets of a gem. Then he realized she said that because he was Jewish and her loving a Jewish man was a kind of penance for having a number of her affairs with gentiles. Some time later, with his questions at hand, he said, "You once said that your passion for me is a kind of penance? Why penance?" He knew why penance, but he wanted to hear her say it.

"Penance? You must have misheard me. I said repentance."

"Repentance for what?"

"First of all, I was only joking. Second of all, perhaps repentance because I didn't want to meet a Jewish man. Remember, I thought you were Italian, so my falling in love with you is my repentance."

Passive voice, her

She showed him a letter she'd written which contained the words, "As was pointed out to you by me," and he had a ball with it. For days he teased her about that lugubrious construction, then he recalled that some of her most complicated and sophisticated grammatical usages pertained to the passive voice. "I would have wanted to have been loved by him." And realized that she was a veritable expert on the passive voice because that's the way she saw herself. He told her there's an Italian proverb: As a person is, so he speaks. She saw herself as passive; she lets things be done to her. She doesn't control events; they streamroll over her. So once he called her from Paris and faked a French accent.

"Hello? This is Jean-Pierre Goncourt from ze French Academy? Am I being spoken to by Aviva Ramati? I had the doubtful pleasance of being met by you, I mean, of you being met by me recently—no laughingness s'i vous plait at moi long distance expense, we people from

Toulouse-Lautrec are very sensitive to fun being made of our accent. Furzermore, this is not a social call, even though I distinctly remember me being given by you, how you say in English, the come down, go down, I mean, come up, or is it come on, with your eye. To me propositions are always being given ze most deefeeculty in Eeenglish. The purpose of you being called by me eez for me to inquire of you if you would have wanted to have had lessons from my friend, Oscar. Has he come for lessons? Or does he come after lessons? During ze lessons? How often does your vibrator whom you've named Oscar come and how often does he make ze teacher come? And how come? And how often does he come to play, or does he just play to come? I am sorry, but up now eez my time. Hallo?"

And up he hung. Rather, up ze telephone was hung.

See also **Capetown, Aviva's response to**

Pencil test

"The pencil test," Aviva said, "also variously called the boob test: Place a pencil under either breast and if gravity clasps it tight you've failed the pencil test, for a young girl's bosom that stands out straight and firm will reject all invasive items like pens and pencils, hangers and broomsticks."

Pennies from heaven

She was always cold. She jumped into the bed with her winter jacket on, pulled the cover up to her nose.

"That's it!" she said in her self-mocking, humorous tone. "No more comes off. I'm freezing."

He hugged her. "Last time I hugged a coat it was in Macy's."

Later, when she stepped out of her clothes, a penny pinged to the floor. He picked it up and put it on the ledge of the bed, then grabbed her, turned her upside down, and began to shake her.

"What are you doing?"

"A penny just popped out of your puss . . . Now I'm going for quarters."

Petcock

As she was fixing her car thermostat at a service station, she noted that the antifreeze was pouring out. She asked the boy helping her what's happening. He said, "The petcock is open." Hearing this Guido asked her how she reacted to that word. She gave him a blank look. "He asked if your petcock is open, and you should have said: I left him at home. I have a petcock at home and as soon as I finish with this friggin' thermostat, I'm going home to make my pet cock happy!"

Phone booth and Ian

"Ian was always restrained," Aviva said, "Always made sure you knew who he was. Was always conscious of his self-worth. But once, when we met in New York, we were horsing around, he chased me, I ran into an outdoor phone booth and got stuck. We both were laughing. Finally, he got me out."

A couple of days later, other details emerged, as usual.

"It turned out," Aviva said, "that was the last time I saw him socially."

"Was that the time you decided to stop seeing him?"

"I think so. Now, I remember! I must have gone into that phone booth because I had told him that I can't go to my place because a friend is there. Then he told me to call her and tell her to scram. I had actually asked her to be there because I had already made up my mind: no more. Still, I was sort of hoping he would say something that would change my mind."

"What? That he would be with you forever? That he was leaving his wife?"

"I don't know. I thought he would say or do something definitive . . . I don't know. Maybe that's what I thought at the time."

"That means deep down you wanted to continue with him."

"Yes. I was hoping for something better."

"For the sake of your career?"

"Never. I never thought along those lines. If I did, I wouldn't have broken up with him just when I was graduating and needed him for a job."

Phone rings during

Smack in the middle the phone rang. "No," she said, "I'm not answering . . . Oh no," she remembered, "that must be Yaffa's teacher. He said he'd call around this time. I have to take it."

She climbed off, sat at the edge of the bed, took the phone. This was a new experience for him. At his place he never answered. Now she stood, naked, and discussed Yaffa's low grades in math. She tried to nudge the teacher into saying that Yaffa would have a chance, wouldn't she, for a B or a B+ if she improved this quarter? But Guido heard the man—he had an older, pleasant, even devoted voice—saying, No, she's doing quite poorly. But I realize she's been sick often, so I take that into consideration. In other words, he won't fail her but give her a D, Guido thought. Now he stood too and rubbed up behind her. She took his cock in her hand and stroked it, played with it, while keeping up her math patter. If she doesn't improve this quarter, I'll kill her, Aviva said. And Guido mouthed to her and pointed, You've killed this thing too.

Aviva snorted into the phone, trying to check her laughter by compressing her lips and cheeks. She cocked the receiver under her ear with her right shoulder and waved a fist at him. He cocked his cock at her. She stuck out her tongue and gave a lick in the air. He made yappety-yap motions with his thumb and first two fingers. She smiled. He wanted to make her laugh again and yap-yapped with both hands. He knows, Guido mouthed, you're talking about math and being screwed. She shook her head. Guido pointed to his detumescent, ex-priapic prick and slap-clapped his hands twice to signal the party's over. It's dead down there. I'll certainly get on her back, Aviva was saying. Me too, Guido mouthed, pointing to Aviva's back. Again she had to smother a laugh. He wondered if the teacher considered her a flirt, for she had a pleasant lilt in her voice as she spoke to him. Was this the way she spoke to everyone? No wonder everyone wanted to get his hands on her. She invited it, with her innocent friendliness. And yet she was alone. The years he knew her, she had made no attempts even to make friends with anyone. Even a female. Her old friends she had neglected, a few neighbors she knew casually, some family was close, others estranged.

When she finished talking, they began again. It was slow starting, like an old car on a wintry day, but when he was almost ready he asked her to climb on her knees. Lately she'd been getting better at screwing. She rocked back and forth and from hard he became harder and she began her prayers, mingling "Oh, God" and "Oh, Guido, Goddo, Guido"—he could never quite tell which name she was using. And when he started coming, came, she called out "Don't stop, don't stop, don't stop" and later, reflecting, commented that the back position, which she called the Orient Express, wasn't bad either.

"I thought you didn't like it that much . . . That's why I kept the locomotive in the yard for months."

"Because it used to hurt."

"Did the choo-choo hurt you now?"

"Oh, yeah. I really suffered . . . And for you, was it good?"

She gave

Continued, see **Screwing, phone rings while**

Photography, why he was drawn to, maybe

In 1894, Guido's grandfather, Moise Davide Veneziano-Tedesco, then a young physician, hosted photographer Alfred Stieglitz in Venice for several days and pointed out to him some of the off-beat photogenic sights, like the little canals with docked gondolas. In gratitude, Stieglitz sent his friend Moise a dozen prints of various scenes which grandfather handed down to his son along with stories about the great photographer. Guido's father left the prints to him and later, when photography came into its own as an art form, Guido would lend the valuable prints to museum shows.

Photos, her, interpreted by photographer

One day she brought over more pictures.

In one, at age twenty-eight—the year she went wild in Philly at PAMA—she looked like a cute, playful sixteen-year-old, wearing a white skirt and white tunic blouse. In another, taken by her virginal husband, she shields her face against the sun and smiles out at the camera. She looks innocent and playful, like a naïve high school kid. In a third, an aloof, almost formal portrait taken on the old *Queen Elizabeth,* first class, her uncle in a tux, her aunt in a gown. And then two color pictures taken about a minute apart. In one, she looks dreamily up above the camera; in the other, straight at the camera with a sort of sly, duplicitous smile. Then there's one at seventeen, at the cello, in profile, with pigtails. The photo is slightly out of focus so it looks like a painting. In fact, it resembles a portrait that Whistler could have made and called: Whistler's Sister. Guido noted that in none of the pictures is there any indication that this girl is out of touch, insecure, has negative feelings about herself, or that nothing would ever work for her. When he mentioned this to her, Aviva said that looking good was just a front, as was the aloofness. It was a mask to cover the basic insecurity. What about looking beautiful and the guys who hovered around? "So I felt good about myself for a day or two, then fell back to my old negative feelings."

Phrenics

If Guido will soon go to look it up, so can you.

Physics, laws of

"You heard of Feynman the physicist?" he asked her.

"No."

"Good. Then I can say what I want to, even though I don't know what I'm talking about, because you know even less. Feynman was one of the greatest theoretical physicists of the twentieth century, a notch below Einstein. He made a series of diagrams in which he showed that positrons can run backward in time. Do you know what positrons are?"

"No."

"Good. You'll make an excellent physicist. But I hope it's not anyone I know. But you're in good company. Feynman didn't know what positrons are either."

"Then how did he know they run backward in time?"

"Easy. He demonstrated it, gave incontrovertible proof in his diagrams. Actually, positrons are found in the nucleus of an atom along with electrons, which are negative, like the Arab, and neutrons, which are neutral, like some of your past friends, and positrons, which exude, like me, a positive electrical charge."

"So what's the point of telling me this?"

"No point. Just showing off."

"No." She pouted. "Come on. Tell me."

"Okay. The point is if physicists have shown this—a basic violation of laws of nature: something going backward in time—then anything is possible."

"What you're trying to say, you slippery eel you, is that loving two women at the same time is fine."

"Or your parents in heaven arranging our meeting upstairs."

"To which let's go," she said, taking his hands.

See also **Backward runs time**

Plastic bag, living in a

"In Philly, during my fling period, I felt as if I was living in a plastic bag."

"It's very hard to make love through a plastic bag."

"I know. But at least you can't get venereal disease."

Playing, Aviva

Once, after about four lessons, he asked her to play for him. But she said she didn't know if she could: she was too tense that day. Next time, okay? The next time she agreed. "But please don't sit too close," at which he purposely pulled his chair closer. "Sit in the next room," she said. He stood, walked to the dining room, and said, "I can also listen from the car . . . Can you play something by Bach?"

She closed her eyes and began one of Bach's Unaccompanied Cello Sonatas. Her face changed. Everything in her was poured into her face and fingers. She breathed through her nostrils, which flared; her face, he told her, had an indomitable look, tough like Golda Meir's. At times her head was so close to the music it looked as if she were kissing the score. He watched her making love to the instrument, to the music, supremely jealous that she might love her instrument more than his. Above all, he liked her breathing, snuffling through her nose, *nff nff nff,* as if during love play. At that moment he wanted to make love to her and have her breathe that way because of him and not on account of musical concentration. Weeks later she told him that music was very erotic, the touching, the plucking of strings, the rich, lush, deep sexy sounds of the cello.

"And the spread legs," he said.

"That too," she allowed.

Posing naked

The camera is ready. He tells the naked Aviva to pose, guides her. Aviva on her hands and knees. Aviva standing, hands up. Aviva in profile, with deep-breath chest out (hard pose to keep for long, she complains). Aviva lying down (should be a cinch for you, he says).

"What are you going to do with them?" she asked. "I told you I was fat. You saw pictures of me. I photograph even fatter than I am."

"Impossible. The reverse is true," Guido said.

"Come on. Tell me. What are you going to do with them?"

"A plastic surgeon liposuctionist I know asked me to provide him with a series of BEFORE pictures."

"No. Really."

"I'm photographing you for *Playboy* as the oldest sexy playmate of the century."

Power, he likes

"You like to be boss, right?" she decided to ask him one day.

"Only when it's absolutely mandatory," he said. Although she suspected he was joking, she really couldn't tell.

"I don't really like power," he continued. "Never did. I just assert control to fill a vacuum. It's the nature of politics, the ineluctable politics of physical nature, which abhors a vacuum. Because my view is that there are two ways, the other guy's and the right one."

Pressure

"I don't belong here. I'm a fifth wheel."

"If you're my fifth wheel, I'm your third leg."

"Mmm," she said, then her face fell. The lines above her lips, so faint a year back, were now quite visible, like those on an old toothless woman. "I can't take the pressure."

"I'm pressure." His voice with a slight inflection, somewhere between question and sarcastic repetition.

"Yes."

"You mispronounce, Chinese-ly. You mean to say I'm pleasure . . . You orientals," and he went into clipped syllable Chinese accent, "You always miss up *l* and *r,* like when communist Chinese plomised evelyone open and flee erections in Shanghai."

Q

Questions, questions, questions

All of which she answered like a dope.

Quickly time flies with you, how

"Is it three o'clock already? My God, I feel I just came here."

"First of all, you didn't. And second, I feel the same way. Every second I spend with you is like an hour," he whispered. "And every day is like a week . . . The minutes drag by like tar when I'm with you."

Quick review for imaginary performance

Aviva Prinsky last night performed the Schumann Cello Concerto in A under de erection of Ian Plaskow, who led the Freeport Symphony in a benefit concert.

For whose benefit?

Ian's and Aviva's.

See also **Bothered by Plaskow**

R

Reasons why he likes her, three

"Give me three reasons why you like me," she said.

"Your sneakers, the way you don't make eggs, and your honesty . . . And also," Guido added, "I like your mind."

"The one between my legs?"

"I don't mind that one either."

"What would you say if I told you I had a Ph.D. in Economics?"

"Nothing, as long as you don't take him to bed with you."

Recipe for dryness

Once, when I was dry, I said:

"It needs olive oil."

"And Popeye," Guido said.

Remembers, whom Aviva

While screwing her he hears her say something that sounds like "in-in-in" with the vocal extended somewhat to give him the impression that she's saying "Ian-Ian-Ian," which makes him stop and withdraw.

"What'd you say?"

"Nothing."

"I thought I heard you say 'Ian-Ian-Ian.' You son of a gun. So you do remember him."

"I didn't," she yelped, eyes twinkling. "I said in-in-in."

Respect is part of sex

He wouldn't stop teasing her about her remark that respect for a man was a facet of his sexiness. "So you respected a lot of guys?"

"I'm very respectful," she cracked, poking fun at herself. "Did it take you a while to get used to my body?"

"Maybe five seconds. And you?"

"It took me a while . . . And the vagina," she said, treading gingerly, "is that different?"

"God made us the way we are," he said diplomatically and, as she grimaced at this evasiveness, thought of the remark the guys on the street would say: A hole is a hole. Put a flag on her and fuck for Old Glory.

Retiring in Florida

Guido tells Aviva:

Years from now, I retire to Florida. You move there too. But you get an apartment. How do I manage to see you? You let it be known that you don't feel too well. A doctor visits you. Two three times a week a man with a little black doctor's bag appears. Later, the ladies in the neighboring apartments say to you, "Dollink, you look so good after each time the doctor visits you, maybe you can ask him if he makes house calls for us so maybe he can make us feel good with whatever medicine he gives you, knock wood, we never seen you looking so good."

I know what you're thinking now: How come he doesn't have his own bag? Why does he have to use the one owned by a little black doctor?

Reversing time

Physicists have shown that travel through time may be theoretically possible by going through cosmic wormholes. Such a time traveler might theoretically be able to change events in the past, including his own birth. Of course, by so doing the rules of causality—rigorously inflexible hitherto—would be thrown into confusion.

The possible existence of these "wormholes" is a theoretical consequence of Einstein's General Theory of Relativity. This theory also provides the theoretical basis for black holes, regions in space where the density of matter approaches infinity and where both space and time are warped in bizarre ways.

Ordinary journeys are made in three dimensions of space and one dimension of time—for instance, a worm crawling over the surface of an apple. But if the traveler can find a higher dimensional shortcut, where space is warped into a tunnel piercing the inside of the apple—or a wormhole—the journey could be shortened.

So, all of this is a prelude to my question to you: What would you do if you could travel through time and re-do your life?

I would undo all my sexual encounters and be the first for you.

My God! You'd do that for me? And he wondered why she didn't bring her parents back, counsel them to see doctors earlier.

And you?

I would make my son whole.

Rimbaud

Moody, she snapped as if from a dream:

"What am I doing here?"

"You're not the first ask that. Rimbaud also said that when he wrote home from Ethiopia . . . But at least, " Guido continued, "at least you're not like Petrarch's secretary, to whom Petrarch said: What's this strange mania for sleeping in a different bed each night?"

Rogers, Will

Will Rogers' famous line provided for Guido the jump point for a tongue-in-cheek epitaph for himself, which his pal Charlie Perlmutter—with whom he never shared it—would have loved: "I never met a woman I didn't like."

Rubbernecking

"What's the definition of rubbernecking?" he asked her, but before she had a chance to reply, he said, "Two condoms in love."

S

Screwing, phone rings while

him that questioning, vulnerable look, that little frown.

"Terrible," he said. "Awful."

"Me too," she whispered.

"It may be the bed," Guido said. "Yours seems to have more bounce, more resilience than mine. It actually sings when we rock back and forth."

"I can't hear a thing," she said. "You know I'm tone deaf."

"But you can hear me coming, can't you?"

She smiled at him, put her palm on his face, and pressed his hand to her breast.

"You know what we haven't done in a long time?" Guido looked into her eyes.

"Standing up? Me bent over? You from the back? By the mirror?" she said.

"No. A cello lesson. With all these fucking lessons, the music's gone out the window."

"Okay," she acquiesced softly.

Downstairs, he played for her.

"How about some theory?" Aviva asked.

"Mmm," he said. "We reverse the natural order. Usually theory comes before practice. Here we practice first, then go into theory."

Search for orgasm

Was it possible that she went from one man to another in search of orgasm? Possible, she said. But that's what she said to every question. Maybe. Possible. When he pressed her about these evasive answers, she replied she just wasn't sure. How could she know now, twenty-five years later, what she was thinking then? She didn't know herself that well. And also she didn't remember. But she did know that the vibrator helped her.

See also **Vibrator, when first used**

Self-stimulation

Maybe since, according to her own remarks, she'd been masturbating since she was thirteen, or fifteen, her entire sexuality was self-centered. She could only have an orgasm by self-stimulation, never with a man. So sex for her was just an extension of her self-centeredness. That was why, when being stimulated, she couldn't play with Guido, but just had to lie back and enjoy being aroused.

And because she had used the vibrator for fifteen or more years, the only area of her body that could be stimulated was her clit. Not even a touch to the vagina moved her. Run your hand over her body tenderly, touch her arms and legs—nothing. Stroke her back. Maybe at a certain point she'd stick out her chest in an automatic reaction like the doctor's hammer tap on the knee. Kiss her right nipple and she'd scream. But unlike other women who would moan and sing whenever you touched them with a kiss, with Aviva the vibrator had killed the sensitivity of most of her body and concentrated it on a half-inch piece of flesh.

Of course, she denied all this vehemently but claimed that it had made her more sensitive to the pleasures of sex; it had awakened her, she said, from a deep sleep.

But for Guido she was still a sexual Rip Van Winkle.

Senescent

Senescent—anti-definition: contra Guido, it certainly does not mean, You smell good.

Sex, not interested in

She wanted to know why he asked her so many questions.

He said: Curiosity, getting to know her, imagining being with her twenty years ago, sexual transubstantiation. Which reminds me, were you capable of having delicious sex in Philly?

You won't believe this, came her answer, but during my so-called promiscuous period I wasn't that interested in sex.

Then why did you do it?

Good question. She looked out the window, as if recalling the past. She was both young and old at the same time. The little hatchwork lines above her lips made her look old, especially if her face was drawn, but the lively gray eyes and quick movements made her look like a college girl. The hope that something would develop, she said. But enough questions, okay? It doesn't make me feel good. It's like having the flu again when you've just gotten rid of it.

Sex all day long, thinking of

"Do you think of sex with me all day long?" he asked.

Egoist that he is, he thought she'd say, Yes, straight out.

But she surprised him.

"Not during lunch," she said.

Sex books all over Guido's house

Aviva took a look at the books scattered, piled, and upended on the long table in the family room. They were on the floor too and on the TV set. She looked through the books, read the dust jackets.

"Who reads all these sexy books, you?"

"Nah, not me. My wife."

"Everywhere you look it's sex. Why?"

"Because it's the second most delicious activity known to man."

"Man?"

"Well," Guido allowed, "women too."

For a while she was silent. So ask already, Guido thought impatiently. Ask.

"So what's the first?"

"I thought you'd never ask. Are you asking?"

She came up to him. Put her lips next to his. "I'm asking," she said softly. "What's the first?"

"Fucking," he said softly too.

Sex isn't so much

"Sex isn't so much physical. It's also mental and spiritual—they feed into each other."

As he heard her say this he wondered how many and which of her past affairs had this mental and spiritual quality. The remark impressed him;

so she was a thinking person too, not just a slave to her senses and desires. But then came the wormy thought, bent like an uncinate. Maybe it's just a snow job to make him feel good. A way of saying that he wasn't just another number on her list. For didn't she say just the other day? "I love being in bed with you. I mean, I love doing everything with you, but I especially love being in bed with you. You make me feel like a woman again."

"You love me for my body, not my mind," he said.

So where did this mental and spiritual quality enter? If all her lovers had this, then what was so special about him? Did she feel that spiritual quality with those slew of guys in Philly? Or was it a state of spiritual and mental grace that she achieved with that eye-cold Italian guy just before she returned to the US after spending six months in Florence? Her pointless affair with a guy she didn't like annoyed him.

"That Italian, was he a typical Italian paisano?"

"Oh, no. He was refined, educated, and gentlemanly. But there was something steel-like, almost Germanic about him."

"Did you see him every day?"

"Maybe once a week."

"Only once a week? He may have been Germanic, that jerk, but his pecker was made in Poland."

See also **Love and lust**

Sexy, what makes a man

"Different things are sexy in a man," Aviva was saying. "Not necessarily his body. It would also be the way a person talks, his voice, what he likes, the way he moves, the values he has."

Then about two months after he got to know her, she asked him the question he knew she would someday ask. But he had the answer prepared for her.

"Do you love me?" she finally said.

"It took you a long time to come out with this, right?"

"Yes," she said.

"I am a carafe of love that pours itself into you."

Sharing two women

"You'd be delighted with a harem, right?"

He didn't say.

"Well, come on, let's hear it. It would be right up your alley."

"Hard to say. I'll comment after the fact."

"But don't you find it hard making love to two women at the same time?"

"I don't have to find it hard. It's you and she who have to do that."

With a quip he'd slipped away again from dwelling on an issue he didn't want to discuss, lest she come up again with the remark he hadn't heard in a long while: I don't want to share you.

And back home he'd be delighted to announce that he was leaving for three weeks to Mexico on assignment to prepare for the Central American Presidents Peace Conference. Which put him on the low end of the seesaw at home with Tammy. Of course, he would have loved to take Aviva with him, but there was no way she could go. Anyway, she wanted half a year, not three weeks. How many times had he heard her say: Would your wife mind if you spent six months with me? How about a half-year plan? Six months with me, six with her. "Who gets me first?" Guido asked. "Me," she said. "I'll discuss it with Tammy," he said. And with his lab assistant Teresa around he'd have to find an eighteen-month year.

Shut up, not knowing when to

"Why me?" Aviva said. "I know your wife is given to depression because of your son. But still, you claim that you're not unhappy with the woman you're living with. So why me?"

"Because," he told her, "you called to me from a different realm and said, 'Love me, love me, love me.'"

"That's nice poetry, but now tell me the real reason."

Guido jumped out of bed. Aviva followed. He was surprised at how quickly she moved, especially for an older woman, especially since she always complained that her knees were getting stiff. Should I tell her that I can't live with my wife's depression? That Aviva's quiet, insistent, sex/ love wavelength called, cajoled, tapped, trapped me?

"If you had sense," he turned to her, exasperated, mad as hell, "if you wouldn't be so stupid, you would have stopped at the phrase, 'That's nice poetry.' But you don't know when to shut up."

"It's true," she said, contrite. Her hands were at her sides. Her body looked so slim, so pathetic. Even the breasts, despite their upturn, were pathetic now. She begged to be hugged, to be embraced, to let a hug cover up her pinprick in his balloon. Remorseful, she said, "It's true, I don't know when to shut up."

Silks and satins, a riddle among the

One day he pulled her into the closet, saying he had a riddle for her. She put up no resistance and he screwed her there in the dark, between the hanging clothes. She rather liked the silk and satin—that belonged to she could imagine who—on her naked skin.

"So where's the riddle?" she laughed.

"All prepared . . . You know what I am?"

"Of course . . . A lecher?" she guessed.

"No. A closet heterosexual."

Sixty, Guido glad that Aviva is

"What would you have done if you found out that I was really sixty, and not fifty-three?"

"I'd have been glad."

"Glad?"

"Yes. Delighted. For in two years you'd be so senile, you wouldn't know if you were coming or going. And what's more, you'd get social security and you'd be so involved with counting your money you'd forget about forgetting me."

Smacked, getting

He liked the way Aviva bowed.

"Show me how again."

"You just want me to bow to you."

"You have something there, no doubt about it. Come on, show me."

She clasped her hands and bowed, without bending her knees.

"First time I bowed, I sort of hung my arms in front of me—this was at a recital when I was a student at Mannes. It looked like I was doing exercises. In retrospect. I must have looked like a gorilla. The pianist I was going with—"

"Oh, no, another one for the list!"

"No, no, he was just a date for a few times, a very nice guy, while I was separated during my first marriage . . . Anyway, he rushed backstage after the intermission and cried, 'God, you look like a duck.' It was the first time I had bowed."

"And this pianist, this so-called musician, this lecher didn't ever want to touch you?"

"No, he was too polite. We maybe kissed a few times . . ." and then Aviva gave that downtilt-of-her-head smile that adumbrated another confession.

"I lived in Brooklyn at the time, in my own apartment. And there was an elevator man. When he saw me enter the elevator with this pianist he would say, 'Good evening, Mrs . . .' What was my first husband's name again? 'And how is your husband?' It was so embarrassing."

"And you didn't tell him off the next time you saw him in private, something like: It's none of your business and keep your comments to yourself?"

"If I could have gotten angry it would have been fine, but I didn't. I was only hurt by such remarks. I always thought the fault lay with me. Even when I had fun—but I told you this long ago—and laughed a lot, it was ingrained in me that I would have to pay for it later. Maybe because my mother was always so serious. 'Stop laughing,' she'd say, 'get to work.'"

"Did she every smack you?"

"Are you kidding? I used to get smacked fives times a week. Why? I wanted to wear pink socks and my mother told me to wear blue, so I insisted on pink so I got smacked. Then I got smacked for not practicing and my father would yell, 'Don't hit her on the hand.' My father never hit me. Always my mother. 'Never on the cello fingers. Hit her on tush, but watch the hands!' And I got smacked for being fresh. For pushing the oatmeal away with a grimace. For saying I don't want so-and-so coming over. There was always a reason. Sometimes I even got smacked in advance and had a credit line for my next naughty deed."

Smile, Aviva's half

Sometimes she gave off a little half-crooked smile, her lips sensually out, as if waiting to be kissed. He noticed she did this with him— probably unconsciously—when she spoke of her past affairs, always, always looking out dreamily into the middle distance, as if by recalling she could concomitantly exorcise and erase. She also did this when she mentioned seeing other men once she would leave Guido. It was a teasing half smile, the sort of smile you wanted to kiss if you were in a good mood or wipe off with a smack if in a rotten.

Soulmate

Soulmate is beyond time, part of the molecular structure of the world.

Stick-up, this is a

He loved looking at her full breasts. Sometimes, as soon as she came in, he'd unbutton her blouse or lift up her sweater and remove her bra and just watch her, even though she complained, "I'm cold. It's cold . . . Yak . . . Your hands are ice cold."

"Put your hands up."

"No. You're going to tickle me."

"I promise, I won't."

She raised her hands.

"What is this, a stick-up?"

"Yes," he said.

"Then where's your gun?"

"I don't use a gun. I tickle my victims to death."

Strabismic

Woven into some compliments to Aviva was an unusual word.

He told her she was lovely, pretty, strabismic, funny, sexy, appealing. Really? she said and took in all the compliments. Later, during screwing, smack in the middle—he could have killed her—she asked him, "What's strabismic?"

Studied with

He imagined the prize committee administrators using Talmudic scalpels in picking apart the nuances of Aviva's résumé, especially zeroing in on the phrase, "I studied with Piatagorsky at the Mannes School of Music for one year, then under Ian Plaskow at PAMA for three years." He imagined the old profs ruminating, debating, reverberating upon two different uses of the preposition and then winking, nodding, and understanding that one slip of the typewriter, in the first verb, an extra *d* instead of an *i*, would have given the whole thing away.

Swedish sex therapist

(a spurious—possibly apocryphal—addendum, being either a fantasy of Guido's, Aviva's, or an event both of them would rather suppress)

"Guess what?" Aviva said. She was smiling, cheerful, glowing. "I made an appointment for us with a sex therapist?"

"What?" Guido yelled. "You crazy?"

She inspected the palm of his right hand. Plucked a tiny hair from it.

"Shh. Calm down. No. I want to be helped. Both for me and you. Maybe I can learn to repress depression. And maybe it will help with . . . you know. So will you come so I can?"

"Touché! Who's the lucky man?"

"A Dr. A. B. Johanssen."

"How'd you find him?"

"Where people find everything. Yellow pages."

"Yellow pages," Guido sniffed. "Did your cello-plucking, clit-fiddling fingers do the walking?"

"Come on! You don't expect me to go and blab . . ." she underlined the word, "to friends of mine to recommend one, do you?"

He wasn't convinced. "Yellow pages for a therapist. Jeez! You use yellow pages for a plumber . . . And anyway, I don't need a sex therapist."

"The doctor wants both of us to come."

"Did you speak to him?"

"No. The secretary. She told me the doctor's procedure is to first have a consultation with the couple. And the initial consult is free."

"I don't want to go. Those perverts probably want to see my organ. Maybe even watch us screwing."

"I didn't give our real names. I said we're Donna and Don Ratner." At once Guido thought of the Indian doc. First he wants to see the couple and then, of course, Aviva alone. Guido scanned out the entire scenario. The therapist sees a woman with a sexual problem and then begins to try to solve it. Personally. He has a proven method for making a woman come. Nothing doing, Guido concluded. They're all alike, these doctors, psychologists, psychiatrists, rabbi-counselor-matchmaker columnists. Waiting with open arms for a willing Aviva. Just waiting for a case like hers to come along.

"And then he breaks it into individual sessions. First you, then me."

"Yes," Aviva said.

"Then nothing doing."

"Please, Guido. I'm doing it for you. I want to have an orgasm with you. Maybe he can help. If you don't like his attitude, approach, anything, after the visit I promise we'll stop."

He kissed her, assenting.

The receptionist admitted them. The office was mod, like a TV station, something out of the movies. Doctor Johanssen must have hired a Swedish decorator. There, Guido thought, on that sofa is where he fucks them, those pathetic candidates that come to him for help.

A tall blonde in her mid-thirties stood in the room.

"Hi, I'm Dr. Johanssen." And she shook hands with both of them. Guido looked at Aviva quickly; her eyes widened and she gave a slight shrug. "But please call me Anita."

As part of the beginning, Anita said, she would ask them some personal questions. She knew they would make them ill at ease, but that's quite common. But to help she had to find out as much as possible.

Aviva looked nervous; her face stiffened; that cello performance look that made her appear older. Gone the softness. Guido wondered if the doctor was wondering what a young man like him was doing with an older woman. Looking at the two women, Guido saw for the first time how old Aviva was. Would Anita ask their ages? He watched the therapist as she spoke. Though she wore a white doctor's jacket over a black bulky sweater, he could see she had a voluptuous body. She was about 5'9" and nicely shaped. Her black stretch slacks contrasted with her blonde hair and light skin. Perhaps her broad face was a trifle mannish, but it had a vitality, a handsomeness, like Ingrid Bergman as Joan of Arc. She walked around the room as she questioned them, showing off her long legs. He suddenly thought of Ava. Anita's movements had Ava's animal grace and sexuality. Did Aviva regret coming? Was that why she looked green around the gills, sensing that beneath Guido's composed, almost stiff, exterior lurked his approbation of Anita's sexual energy. Did a bit of sorrow plummet in her heart as she saw the female sex therapist materializing out of the neuter A. B. initials?

Do you have regular sex? Do you know all the positions? Did the male partner have regular orgasms? Did you try manual stimulation? Cunnilingus? Vibrators? How many times a week? . . .

You mean a day, Guido interjected and saw the surprised look on Anita's face. On good days, three or four.

Are both partners always willing, or does one impose his will on the other?

Then she began to ask about fantasies. I don't have any, Aviva said weakly. And you? Anita turned to Guido. Do you have any sexual fantasies? Any at all? Don't be ashamed. The more you both express yourselves the more it will help you. Yes, Guido said, as soon as I saw you in the room, and I saw (here he winked quickly at Aviva to show her he was just playing along) how attractive you were, I had a sudden wish that I could make love to you. Anita nodded, as if saying, yes, that's very good. That's a very good fantasy. Very healthy.

The phone ringing suddenly broke what seemed to Guido to be a dream atmosphere. The therapist excused herself and went to a small office to talk.

Aviva looked troubled, tiny, drawn into herself.

"I'm just playing along," Guido told her softly. "It's politically correct to have the most absurd fantasies. They expect it. Wait, I'll give her another one from the books that she expects. It's like a Rorschach test. You gotta give the psychologist the answer he expects, or he won't be nice to you."

When Anita returned he told her that in addition to fantasizing screwing her, he also has Donna watching and getting turned on.

But when Anita continued asking more intimate questions, Guido felt that he'd had enough. Stop! he wanted to shout. What am I doing here in Ethiopia? he mimicked Rimbaud in his thoughts. Or is it Stockholm today? I didn't want anyone to know. Not a soul. And here we are, baring every intimate detail to a perfect stranger with a perfect body. And suppose she was one of those liberal therapists who advise that Aviva try another man to see if she could be cured. The thought alone drove him into a jealous anguish. Could Anita tell they weren't married? Was their affair written all over their foreheads? Was she discreet?

He noticed that the therapist now directed most of her questions at Aviva, who somehow seemed superfluous here, an old chaperone to the lovely young couple trying not to slip on the sparks in the room.

At the end of the session, Anita asked Guido to call her at noon the following day. On the way back to the car Aviva was silent. In the car Guido kissed her. "Surprised?" he said. Aviva laughed an uneasy, nervous laugh. "Yes. And what a good looker too. What do you think?"

"I didn't realize the questions would be so intimate."

"Should we see her again?" Aviva wondered.

"You're the one who wanted this. You tell me," Guido said.

"I dunno. Let's hear what she has to say. We can always hold off for a while."

At noon next day Guido called. A woman answered.

"May I speak to Anita Johanssen?" He purposely didn't say doctor.

"This is Anita Johanssen."

"Hi, this is Don Ratner," Guido said. "You asked me to call you at noon."

"Oh, yes, Mr. Ratner . . . May I call you Don? I've looked at my notes. I believe I can help. Of course, there's no guarantees." She stopped. Guido waited. "I think it would be very helpful if we could meet separately."

"Well, I'll tell you frankly, we haven't decided yet what course we'll take. I know it's not a quick process, and I don't know if we have the time or energy to devote. And, of course, there's the expense too." Why he said the opposite of what he wanted to say he'll never know. Maybe he should see a therapist.

"I can appreciate that. But before you commit yourselves, I would like to talk to you alone, to give you a complimentary consultation, without obligation. If you are free, you can come to my office—I have office hours this evening."

A sudden swirl of temptation—he felt it as a wind of red heat coming through him. His voice choked.

"Six?"

"Make it seven."

He didn't want to ask her if her receptionist was going to be there. Oh, God, he thought, am I going into a tertiary state of betrayal? Or is it quadruped?

Later, he told Aviva he couldn't get through to Anita and that he'd like to put the therapy on hold for a while.

At the office, at seven, the receptionist was nowhere to be seen. Anita didn't wear her white jacket but a pink, rather tight-fitting, cashmere sweater and a plain red skirt. She looked fresh and bright, as if she'd just showered. She gave him a firm handclasp and welcomed him with a broad smile. He regretted he didn't have a hidden camera.

"Donna is quite beautiful," Anita said. He noticed she didn't say your girlfriend or your wife.

Guido nodded.

"And I must say that both of you make an extremely attractive couple. Usually, when couples come and one has a problem, one of the two is rather homely. I'd like to help you."

Guido had chosen the easy chair. He noticed that Johanssen didn't sit behind her desk but paced as she spoke to him. He wondered if that three-times-a-day remark might have triggered her curiosity. She wore no ring. Her vitality reminded him of a trapped animal. The sort of compressed-spring energy that Aviva had noticed in him he now saw in Anita. What made her go into sex therapy? Was it a substitute for sex? Or an extension of it? She didn't look like she needed a substitute. The woman was gorgeous. She could have been a photographer's model. In his mind's eye Guido was posing her naked at the cello like Linda in that photo poster he'd made years ago.

"Are most people's problems the same?" he suddenly asked.

"Every one is different, but a thread, like a melody, runs through most couples. As they say in Swedish:

> Svenskom ekblatt,
> Farfar lindsatt.

"Which means?"

"Which means, When a man gets a hankering for a woman, all he's after is the hole, but, on the contrary, when a woman is pining away for a man, she wants to possess the whole."

"All that in four words?"

"It's a compressed language." And she gave him a sly smile, lowering her head and keeping her gaze steady at him.

If he asked her how she came to sex therapy, he knew he would change the parameters of the consultation. He didn't know if he could do that. He expected Aviva to be faithful to him. He'd once told her, Don't even think of looking at another man. And she hadn't—or so he assumed. Although she balked at his command, told him he didn't have the right, as far as he knew she didn't look, except for occasional threats to go out on dates. And Aviva expected him not to be tempted by anyone either. But as far as he was concerned, Tammy didn't count, because she was no temptation. And anyway, he'd made clear to Aviva at the beginning: There were rules in adultery. And the first was—you can't be jealous about your lover's spouse. So, then, Tammy didn't count. Neither did Teresa because that was Rule Number Two, which he didn't enumerate to Aviva.

"Would you like me to help you?" Anita was saying. She stood in front of him and, without waiting for his reply, said, "The first thing I prescribe is that a male patient has to learn to touch a woman. Sometimes even good-looking men are incredibly naïve about a woman's body."

Doctor Johanssen said this in a neutral, professional way, like a nurse would say, Give me your hand, to take blood pressure. He looked at her, parted his lips, hooked eyes with her. She didn't avert her gaze. Lost that pro look. Guido wondered if at that moment the equilibrium had changed, or if she'd set him up from the beginning. A flush of color rose in her cheek. He felt a powerful lust rising, a searing cloud in him. He wouldn't want Aviva to do this. But it was out of his control. Rule Number Three, he guessed. He shrugged. The below the waist had taken over. The therapist part of her vanished and only the sex remained. Aviva he hadn't wanted to screw from the outset; she didn't provoke his lust. As he sat with her during cello lessons and gazed at her lovely face and full lips, all he wanted to do was kiss her. Which showed that for Aviva it was true love. No, he wouldn't betray Aviva. With her it was pure affection. But with this woman other chemicals were at work. He felt the magnet pull of electrons lining up. No volition was needed to prompt the next step. Oh, yes, out there, the strangers, the actors, were going through their gavotte of politesse, giving out brackish sounds to oil, to coat, to protect dignity, decorum, the ways of the world. But the atoms were doing their own thing in this chemo-magnetic force. They paid no attention to arranged letters of language whose meaning was cacophony to the harmony of basic matter.

"Give me your hand."

He didn't give it, but he didn't refuse either when she took it. He thought she was going to start by running his palm slowly over her bare arm, to teach him to stroke tenderly. Instead, she lifted up her skirt and put his hands on her puss, smack in the center of her black satin bikini. Her white skin and perfect thighs blinded him.

"Learn to touch. Tenderly." She still had his hand. "You have to . . ."

But he was already playing—his hand had ducked under the satin. This is not betrayal, he told himself. It's just a lesson. No. He was not going to touch her lips; that is, the northern ones. He was not going to kiss her.

"Yes," she was saying softly. "You know where it is . . . That is good . . . You know where it is."

Slowly she sank down to her knees; Guido joined her on the floor. He pulled up her sweater and bra with one motion and kissed her nipples.

"You should have no trouble . . ." she said and carefully took off her cashmere sweater. She threw it on the arm of the sofa and took off her bra. Her breasts were large and firm. Wider than Teresa's and not pear-shaped. He had her lift her hands to have a good look. Yes, Aviva's were lovely, but they hung down already. Anita's were solid and fuller.

Soon she gave out a long scream and a few little ones and, as he continued his own yelping, she came again. That's what he missed with Aviva, flew through his mind. And when Anita screamed a third time and he began his feral cry—as he came he saw lights rivers were slanted and he sailed up the incline of the river Po seeing castles in Spain and Greek villages and red and green squares of tilled fields scudding up the plains of Nepal he saw the Himalayan peaks and lush valleys where green tea grew like fine grass and yaks he'd never seen and red pointy cars with many lights, seeing mauve mushroom structures by Gaudi on a pink background crowding on a slope and parti-colored sleighs flying through the air beneath Persian carpets with Shah Abbas pastel floral motifs. An orgasm like that he hadn't had for ages, certainly not with Aviva. And as they both screamed together he heard, Ava Ava Ava Maria by Schubert ringing in his ears and in one flash Anita and Ava and the song all fused and he forgot where he was. Perhaps for an eyeblink he had fallen asleep and dreamt. Ava, he said to himself. Screwing one's own wife, even if she's an ex- is no betrayal. Screwing for medicinal purposes, for education purposes, for charity, for recreation, is no betrayal. He did it for Aviva. To help her. And then the therapist came a fourth time, in a pitch of delirious whinnying.

"What therapy!" he said.

"I knew you'd be terrific. One look and I knew."

"You're great," he said. "I've never come before."

"Neither have I," she said.

"Liar!" they both said together.

"I thought it was Donna who couldn't come."

"We lied," Guido said. "I was too embarrassed to talk about my problem."

"Oh, shut up," she said.

He imagined her saying, She's not your wife, is she? To which he didn't respond. And: And Don, that's not your real name, is it? Don't ask me questions, he told her in his thoughts. And he didn't ask her why she became a sex therapist. And he didn't kiss her either.

Guido was a man who kept a promise.

T

Teaching each other

"Have I taught you anything?"

"Yes. Self-confidence," she said.

"And sexually speaking," he said in a high-pitched Ruth Westheimer voice:

"You taught me to feel more like a woman. A fulfilled woman . . . Now I know what love is from every aspect. And," she laughed, "angle . . . And me, have I taught you anything?"

"Yes, How to hold a cello. Lovingly. How to bow it to bring out the tender sounds. How to caress the strings and make them sing."

"Cut it—I mean, really."

"You taught me to be tolerant. Being with you has taught me that not everyone can be as energetic and bright and modest as me."

Tears, why they're salty

"There is an Italian proverb that goes like this: If tears would be sweet, people would be crying all the time," Guido said when Aviva asked: Why are tears salty?

Teasing her about her age

"When you smile," he told her, "you look at least fifty years younger." Her jaw fell.

"What I mean is—you look twenty-five when you smile."

Three and fifty

Every time she said "fifty" a wave of disbelief rilled through him and he unconsciously shook his head, incredulous. Same for fifty-four. Aviva in her sixth decade? What a joke! He had always thought of fifty as chugging over the bridge, into the Styx, moving over the unrecrossable, irreversible border into the last stop, *l'ultime stazione*, the hormone-dry horizon, the drizzle-fizzle, the terminal finality of old age. Especially for women, what with their youth craze, hair coloring, wrinkle phobia, philocosmetic, facelift culture. They even dreaded the sound forty. It had an outrageous, even obscene ring. And here was Aviva, insisting on the 2x plus five factor, twice her age in weight with a leeway of five pounds. Almost an hourglass figure. As if a cello had undone its woodness and become a woman, f-stop and all. Not an ounce of fat on her, just a bit of belly. And not a wrinkle. Except above her lips. Not a gray strand in that full head of long reddish auburn hair. The gray eyes clear as the sound of a silver spoon on a crystal glass; they'd remain that way until she was eighty. Just a tiny pouch puff under each eye which gave her a touch of sexual maturity. No ugly popping veins or capillaries on her thighs. Her figure in a bathing suit made heads turn. Aviva at fifty-four was thirty-five. So age, then, was a matter of myth. Depended who filled, no pun intended, the hour glass. And with what.

Thrilling, each new man?

It was an addiction with him, he couldn't stop it, couldn't help it, exploring her sexuality, her interest in it, her indulging, her affairs. He liked it almost as much as screwing her.

Again and again he returned to it because for him—who loved every sexual encounter, who couldn't resist a frisson of delight when a woman touched his hand—he couldn't understand how she could not love it and just die when a man was in her. But no matter how often and from what angle he approached her answer was the same.

"And wasn't it thrilling, every time a new man entered you? I can just imagine myself a girl wanting sex and having a new man. Why the thought alone would make me come."

"You. But not me."

Tongue

He went down there, kissing her source.

"Hey!" she said. "Say something."

"Can't" He surfaced. "Pussy's got my tongue."

Transatlantic trip

"I went with my aunt and uncle—him I didn't like at all . . ."

"I always thought you went only with your aunt."

"No. The uncle was there too, unfortunately . . . They badgered me. Both of them, during the trip. But he was worse. To the point where by the time we sailed into Southampton, I wanted to take a plane back to New York. If one of them would have pestered me, it would have been okay, maybe. But both of them! They didn't like the way I ate. If I picked up something with my fingers—first class, you know—my uncle would make a comment. And in the front of the waiter too. Boy, was he a phony! I was always being put down, criticized."

You poor soul, Guido thought, moved to pity by the constant misery in her life. And he vowed not to insult her for the next couple of days.

Twice in a row

Had she ever been screwed twice in a row or several times a day? he asked. Only before her second marriage, she said. With the Arab, and then only that one day, a marathon day a few months before she married that Moroccan.

"With whom was it most exciting before your marriage?"

"Capetown," she said. "In anticipation."

"But in practice."

"Disappointing. You'd think a man in his fifties would have some experience, but he had none. He was uncomfortable with it. There was a reticence in him. Once I was walking hand in hand with him in Buffalo and he met his landlady and he dropped my hand like it was a dead fish."

"What kind?"

"What kind of what?"

"What kind of fish?"

"Probably a piranha."

Two-timing Guido

"You're two-timing both of us," Aviva said.

"Not you," Guido said with a laugh. "You know about it."

"That doesn't make it less two-timing. All I know is I wouldn't want anyone doing it to me . . . Now, let me ask *you* a question. What if I got married, would *you* want to continue with me?"

Guido was silent. A morose, angry silence.

"Well, answer me."

"If he were lame, old, and couldn't get it up."

She laughed. "Could I hug him?"

"On alternate Wednesdays."

U

Union, Aviva joins carpet workers'

The features of Plaskow's large face were tight. His eyes showed he could be very hard. When he smiled, the natural order of tightness seemed momentarily to crack, as if the smile were out of bounds for the face and for the personality. But perhaps it was this very remoteness that made him appealing to her.

Aviva had once told Ian after a lesson in November that she was looking for a carpet. At the next lesson he told her he had a carpet for her, but first, since he was going to New York and so was she, why don't they have dinner together? This was the first time in the two years she'd been his student that this formal, demanding teacher had suggested a personal encounter. Yes, they had had all kinds of discussions, but these talks ceased at the elevator exit. She remembered the impression he had made on her when, nervous as a first grader, she came to PAMA to audition for him, hoping he'd take her as his pupil. When she entered the reception room, the door to his studio opened and a girl walked out and he, a big man, stood in the doorway, filling it. Not only the doorway was filled but her mind too. Also her skin. For years she retained that image of him, tall and attractive, ominous, overbearing, sharp-featured, not really smiling but his lips Mona Lisa-like, trying to look accommodating, and she, naturally shy and withdrawn, with a penchant for making herself small, hoping she could have had invisibility pills, praying that her fingers and bow arm would be under her control.

Yes, she said to the dinner invitation, although later she was sorry, for a teacher ought not to have interposed himself this way. True, she was attracted to him, but in her usual way did nothing.

Still, she accepted, even though it was less an invitation than a gentle summons. The only thing that made the summons gentlemanly was the hook of the question mark. Shall we have dinner together? What was she going to say, No? After dinner both knew what would happen, and it was not Plaskow but shy, self-conscious Aviva who invited him up for coffee. As soon as they came into the apartment—at another time, in response to Guido's biting: I suppose you asked him what type of coffee he wants, she said with a remembering smile: I don't think we even got to the coffee—she switched on the light. He saw immediately it was a one-room studio apartment, and a moment after she switched it on he shut it, seized her, kissed her, and backed her to the sofa while not removing his lips from hers for a moment.

Continued, see **Zzzing went the strings of her heart!**

Untransitioned, off-the-wall, out-of-the blue Aviva remark, another

Talking about her cello playing, once she'd gotten into the nitty-gritty of describing the phrasing, she says, "You have to be particularly agile in a Bartok piece with the bowing, is my nose too long?"

Up in the balcony

At the concert with her he once noticed that in the small hall no one was up in the balcony. Later, as they walked to his car, he told her he knew a place in New York where one could screw during a concert and no one would know. Really?, she said. Where? Up in the balcony of the hall we were just in. There was no one up there. We go to a not too popular concert, sit up in the balcony, and screw to our heart's content, but if you start singing "God God God" or the Hallelujah Chorus people would come up, watch, and maybe even give advice.

Upstairs to play?

"You wanna go upstairs to play?" Guido asked.

"You have a cello up there?"

"No, just an organ."

"The joke would be better with a piano," she said.

"Why?"

"Don't you know the old story about the guy with fifteen children who wants to stop, so he goes to the doctor who gives him a condom and tells him to place it on his organ before intercourse and nine months later he comes back and says it didn't work? So the doc asks him, Did you place it on your organ like I told you to? And the guy replies, I didn't have an organ so I put it on my piano."

"Yes," Guido said. "but I don't have a piano, so I put it on my cello. I rolled it down as far as the f-stop and then it popped."

Upswept hair, photo of Aviva with

He kept asking her for a picture. She said she didn't have any but would look. He wanted to see what she looked like years ago: she claimed she was beautiful then, really beautiful, not like now. People would turn on the street to look at her again. But now he was the only one to say she was beautiful. Even she didn't think so any more. The color photo she showed him astonished him. Somehow he had expected a black and white. She sitting demurely, three-quarters pose, facing an unknown distance with a pile of unswept hair (now her chevelure was long and loose, as though an unseen wind were blowing through it. Clever hairdresser), moderately made up, glossy lipstick, and perhaps some facial cream. But it was the expression on her face that got him: upright, self-righteous, prissy, smug. As if she didn't care about anyone in the world. She agreed with his assessment. Self-righteous, yes. "I told you I was self-centered. You wouldn't have liked me then." He looked at the picture and held it before her face. "You're more beautiful now," he said. "You're right, I don't think I would have liked this girl . . ." But he still couldn't understand how a person could change so radically, as if a skin had been sloughed off and a new one assumed.

V

Various alternative pregnancy procedures

"If you could have become pregnant?" she suddenly out of the blue asked him. "would you?"

"Only if you were the father." Guido said at once. "Did it ever dawn on you that God had to make procreation a lot of fun. Otherwise, the human race would have died out ages ago. Can you imagine if to make children you had to build a big brick wall. Or put your elbow in your husband's ear. No one would have children."

"They'd have to adopt them, like the Poles," she said.

"Yes." He remembered the tall tale he'd told her.

"And building a brick wall can't give you an orgasm, which gives you energy—"

"—to push that damn elbow out of your ear and go out and build more walls."

"Okay," she said, "but what—"

"What?" he said. "I can't hear you. There's an elbow in my ear . . . I feel nauseous . . . I think I'm in the family way."

Venice, why that urge came to her in

"It first happened when I was in my mid-thirties. That's when I got those sexual longings."

"Where and with whom?"

"One summer I was travelling, and it hit me when I was in Venice. I had this horny urge to have a man. I was taking a nap in my hotel room, an extremely hot day in July. At one point I woke up and an overwhelming sexual longing came over me. Not linked with anyone in particular. I could have had an orgasm just lying there. It was an incredible feeling. I'd never felt anything like it."

"Did you masturbate?"

"No. Because first of all, I think it would have spoiled it. It was such an usual feeling of pure sexuality—I think mere masturbating would have ruined it. And secondly, my roommate was lying in the next bed. But I had this grand feeling of need. If you talk of climbing the walls, I was ready to climb. March right up the wall of the Doge's Palace. It was like the feeling of hunger, but this hunger was much more pleasurable."

"Do you know why it happened in Venice?"

"No."

"I'll tell you."

Continued, see **Zone, mystical time**

Vibrator, when first used

She said she first had an orgasm in her early thirties, after she'd come back from a stay in Italy.

"But I had it all by myself. My friend, who was writing a sex book, gave me the tip."

"Namely?"

"I'm embarrassed. I'll tell you next time."

A week later she told him. But it came about in her usual way, hesitating, saying she was shy, until he nudged her, coaxed her, became exasperated, and only then did she finally agree to talk.

"Was it a certain position of the finger?"

"It wasn't a finger."

Oh, no, he thought, she shoved a hot dog in there.

"What then, a mechanical penis? Inserted? You're not afraid of being electrocuted? Disfigured? Maimed forever?"

"I got to give you a mirror. You should see the look on your face. It's precious. I'm not a pervert. You just hold it on the vagina above the clitoris and then . . ."

"And your maniacal friend suggested this to you?"

"I was at my wit's end. Here I was thirty-three and I've never felt what the rest of humanity felt. Everyone had had an orgasm except me."

She didn't say: Don't I too deserve to have one? But that was the implication.

"Well, it so happened that my friend told me that she and her husband—"

"Shirley and Sidney Kinsey, right?"

"Right! So I told her about my problem. She said, You want a surefire method? Use a vibrator."

"I don't believe it. I thought you were playing with your fingers." She shook her head.

"You're crazy! Using a goddamn machine!"

"It's terrific!"

"Further training for you to going it alone . . . on all levels."

"No. It heightened my awareness. My pleasure."

See also **Wonders of the vibrator**

Virgin, professional

"During my first marriage, and even before that, I was so dumb sexually, I didn't know what to do." Then she gave a girlish little giggle. "Except for one thing."

"You knew that the little thingie goes into the thingamajig, yes?"

"Yes. But I didn't know why?"

"Other than having children," Aviva added. Then frowned, sadly, remembering. "I was a constant reminder of Paul's failure. Every time he saw me he realized he couldn't perform like a man, and that's probably why he withdrew into himself, playing chess with a computer, instead of talking to me. Not because he didn't screw me—since I didn't know anything about it, I didn't miss it—but because he didn't *talk* to me. And obviously—but this I didn't understand till much later—he didn't talk to me because he felt inadequate and this colored his entire relationship with me. When we went to visit his parents, they couldn't understand why we behaved like teenagers, wrestling on the floor, tickling each other, rolling around and giggling." Aviva laughed, remembering. "He was so ticklish."

"And you never felt later on that sex was underrated."

"Never. I always felt, what's all the hoopla, the hype about. I always felt it was *over*rated."

Voice, loves listening to her

"I love listening to your voice. Just listening to you talk makes me happy," he said.

"I'll send you a tape," she said.

"And I'll send you a Xerox copy of my rooster."

"You like to be on top of a situation, don't you?"

"If you're the situation."

Voice on the phone, his

His voice on the phone, how could she describe it? It was deep, sunny, with an upbeat lilt. As sonorous as a G on the cello. There was a Yes to it. An expectation, an openness, which made her want to open herself to him. She would embrace him and his voice like she embraced her cello. She wanted to hold on to his voice. That was why when they made love she would say to him, Talk to me, talk to me, which he always misunderstood. She didn't want to let go of him or his voice. But having him and his voice doubled her pleasure. It made the time that ran by so swiftly when she was him slow down a bit.

Vulnerable, she is

He told her he'd given some thought to the fact that everyone wanted to put his hand on her.

"Not everyone, just the ones I wanted to."

"I think they did it not only because you were sexy..."

"Not sexy. But you have to remember that twenty-five, thirty years ago, even fifteen or twenty years ago I was very beautiful . . . Now I look at the mirror and see the truth. Sags, lines, chinks."

"Dead wrong. As usual, you're hypercritical, seeking to fault yourself. You were vulnerable. A man can spot this, sniff this out, at once. And perhaps vulnerability plus naïveté plus your constant curiosity paves the way for sex or start of sex . . . And that's why that rabbi with the yarmulke, the sex-starved psychologist-shadchan-columnist picked up your boot and pressed it to his crotch. He sensed there'd be little resistance."

"Boy, was I stupid!"

"Or curious, as you said. Imagine, you go to an interview with an orchestra manager where there's an opening for a cellist. As you start talking to the guy, he pulls your panties down and starts to lick your . . ."

Her tongue dropped. She rolled her eyes, threw her head back on the love seat. "That's thoroughly and absolutely disgusting! . . . Do I get the job?"

W

Wakeable

"If we were together," I asked, "could I wake you up in the middle of the night?"

"Like Grand Union," he replied, "I'm open twenty-four hours a day."
"With you screwing is a grand union."

Walk, the first, Aviva's version
It seemed like weeks since I'd been able to breathe, and eating had become just as difficult.

It had happened so quickly that I had no time to acclimate to the reality of it all. From our first meeting, the first lesson, I sensed the specialness of these vibes, and each successive lesson only confirmed that feeling. My head was filled with him and my body ached to be. Suspended in that delicious, euphoric state, I fantasized in all impossible and improbable directions. "He is perfect, he is everything I want," I thought. It's an incredible miracle and that miracle is mine!

Each week that passed brought us closer to what had seemed infinities away. I was immobilized. He would have to be the one to make it all happen, to break down all the barriers. Although I couldn't make the first move—fear of rejection, perpetual shyness, lack of self-confidence, and, perhaps most of all, suspecting he was married, I felt I didn't have the right. Still, I knew that something would happen. The sparks weren't all from my side. I could tell by the way he spoke to me, smiled at me, joked with me, that he liked me too. I sensed something would happen. I just didn't know when or how or what form it would take. But I had no doubt that this gradually building tension would explode. One week he brought me a photograph of Casals that I always loved. "For you," he said, and I liked the sound of those words: for you.

And then, finally, one day—after our sixth or seventh lesson—recalling that I had once told him that I didn't particularly excel in sports, except perhaps Ping-pong, he said casually, but with one hand on my shoulder (first time he touched me):

"You don't ski or swim, but how about a game of Ping-Pong?"

"But I don't have a Ping-Pong table."

"That's okay. We'll just stand in your dining room and I'll chase you around the table with a paddle."

I laughed, I smiled, I knew it was getting closer. He didn't remove his hand.

"Actually, the question is: you don't ski or swim, but you do walk."

"Yes, of course," was my reply.

"Would you like to take a walk with me? There's a beautiful nature trail in Eisenhauer Park."

"Yes, of course," I said again. What dumb, banal words! But I couldn't think straight again, I was so excited. "Should I wear boots? Will we go into the woods?"

The walk was planned for the following Monday morning. On Sunday there was a fluke autumn snowstorm. It snowed so heavily I wondered if destiny had changed her mind. But Monday turned out to be a clear and sunny day. We met at an appointed place and I followed him to the park where we started our historic trek through the deep snow.

It wasn't cold, rather warm, the snow crisp, and our footprints devirginated a long area of smooth snow around us. We were totally alone (who walks in a park on Monday morning?), on neutral ground now, approaching the point of no return. Unhesitantly, we took each other's hand, or maybe he took mine, and had hardly gone fifty feet when we stopped and turned to each other. That first kiss was like coming home after a long, long absence. So sweet and incredibly delicious, so long awaited. I had a canker sore on my lip, but he didn't seem to mind.

As soon as he kissed me the love part and the sex part exploded and I was dying to ask him when are we going to make love but my shyness held me back until later when it just came out without me even thinking. On other occasions we would go to parks and walk in the woods and for some reason I would lead the way and I could feel him looking at my legs which he called fawn legs because of my unsure gait and I couldn't wait for him to catch up to me and take my coat off and lie down and hold me and make love to me. I never realized that a woman past fifty could get so hot and I didn't even like the outdoors. The bugs and worms and ants always repulsed me but with him near me and me looking up into his face and seeing the sky above his head I forgot about everything.

"What a sexy man!" I whispered.

But he hadn't heard. "What?" he asked.

"Nothing," I said, too ashamed to repeat it.

I was exuberant. My heart was flying, my soul awakening from its long, deep sleep. I asked him if the sore on my lips bothered him (it bothered me!), and I heard Guido say that nothing about me bothered him.

We walked on, talking about many things, the cello lessons, how wonderfully he played, my bad students, and he—funny man—concocted a scenario about a school of retrogressive music where after ten lessons advanced students would barely be able to play "My Country Tis of Thee." I felt his hands on my cheek and in my hair. Every touch felt so right that I wanted to possess it all at once and to savor it slowly at the same time.

Continued, see **Yummy, the walk continues, Aviva's version**

Watch, last item removed

Before he made love, he took off his watch and tossed it into his shoe. Now it's official, he said. I took off my watch too and asked: If our watches get together, will it be considered two-timing?

Wedding picture, looking at Aviva's

When he saw her picture (he refused to look at the Arab, only wanted to see the Aviva half) and compared it to the other photos, he saw at once that the smile was forced. He told her he was an expert at analyzing photographic faces. He said she didn't have the glow that she had years earlier when she was a bridesmaid for a girlfriend's wedding. But to be fair, he told her that perhaps it was a retrospective analysis, imputing something he knew now into something that had taken place years ago; still, her face didn't have that happy look. She looked better in her late teens and twenties. But in that picture with the Arab she was already in a miserable state. The smile was on AM on a rainy day, and she tried to give the impression that the reception was FM, fine and clear.

(W)hole business

"Tell me," Guido said, "doesn't that hole down there prompt drafts? Like wind being sucked in there, causing colds and sniffles."

"Of course," she said. "that's why I like it plugged up. That's the whole business. Getting it plugged."

Why she loves it so much

Why do you like screwing so much?

Because I feel good when you are in me. Because it makes me feel closer to you. Because I can love you more.

Beautiful! he said.

Why? Eyes wide, innocent. The original ingenue. She felt that her answer was so natural, so true.

Because you said the word *you* in every reason. Other women might only have said, Because it makes me feel good. Because I love it. Because I need it. But you—you connected me to each of the reasons.

Wife, taking someone else's

"Did you ever do this before?"

"What? Screw a woman?"

"Don't be sarcastic."

"Then what?"

"Take someone else's wife."

"I'm not taking someone else's wife. You yourself told me that."

"I know. I mean, in the past have you taken someone else's wife?"

"Never."

"A friend's girlfriend?"

"No," Guido said. "Never . . . Well, actually, I may have taken her, but I always gave her back. With interest."

Wild, going, about fourteen years later

The boys boys boys syndrome that hit her girlfriends at fourteen and drove them wild (at sixteen she still didn't know that guys put it in to make babies) hit Aviva at twenty-eight. That's when she went wild, let loose, at twenty-eight. This was her high-school period, seeking affection and love with her body and senses, and sensing the same disappointment that her friends had felt years ago. She was always about fourteen years late. Maybe that's why at fifty-three she looked thirty-nine.

Windshield wipers, solar

"They invented a new windshield wiper without blades. The car has a solar coil that stores sunshine, and when it rains the sunshine and heat are released, evaporating the rain and creating beams of brightness for the window, which cannot compare to the beams of brightness that shine from your face," he said, assuming a beatific, lovelorn face, hesitating, then quickly adding, "when you see me."

Wisdom of Solomon

How does it feel having two wives? Tammy once asked him, referring to Ava.

Call me Abraham. But I'd rather you called me Jacob. Better yet, Solomon.

Wit, Aviva's

Hanging back in there, just below the surface, waiting to be released was the occasional spunky, Puck-like, bubbly wit, the quick comeback, the pleased-with-myself remark, all the more remarkable for someone who had always maintained that she wasn't sure of herself, didn't know she was talented, couldn't take compliments at face value. For instance, once Guido told her:

"Don't hold back. Sing out. Sing. Sing. Sing."

"Do you think I'll make the Met?" she quipped.

"Probably the entire maintenance crew."

Wonders of the vibrator

He suggested to Aviva that once they screw from the back while she used her tiny vibrator. Maybe that way she could have an orgasm while he was still in her. But the problem was that she had to find that tiny spot which stimulated her and while he was moving in her she kept losing it. But they said they would try again. He went into her and she turned the damn thing on. It made a racket like a concrete-busting drill. At once she began to moan and scream like she'd never done before when he was in her. On the one hand he was glad that she could rise to such enjoyment—now she was crying out, "Guido, Oh, Guido"—and on the other he was jealous that only that fucking electrical instrument could drive her wild. As he pumped he mused about her erotic nature that could derive more intense pleasure from *that* thing than from his thing. But these thoughts made him detumesce and he pulled out.

"Wow, was that good!" she said.

"Was it good with both of us, I mean the three of us, I mean our ménage à trois?"

"No, I threw it away right away."

He couldn't believe it. "You did? You mean those noises were for, from, me alone?"

"Yes."

"But I heard the machine."

"I know. I couldn't shut it off."

Words, direction of

"When we write, our words go from left to right. When we speak, the words have no direction. They go like arrows where we want them to go."

Writing a book, she

Once, after they made love, and he asked if she liked it, she said, "Of course. But it wasn't long enough . . . No, I don't mean that," she said, pointing, "that was long enough, I mean the time . . ."

"You should write a book about sex," he suddenly.

"Yeh. And I'll call it *Diary of an Adulterous Woman*."

"I think I've seen that title."

"No, I'll never do it. It can only be lived, not written about. Some things can never be portrayed in print—or verbalized."

X

X-rated screwing

"Wow, your screwing should be X-rated," she said.

"So should your playing."

See also **X-rated, that's what you are**

X-rated, that's what you are

When she had mentioned that she had had five lovers in one year and then five or six more over the next nine years, he kept bugging her about being oversexed.

"Am I promiscuous?" she asked, tilting her head.

"No. Just X-rated, that's what you are."

Y

Yankee Stadium, how to fill it

For her concert with the Long Island Symphony, he suggested how the audience could be enlarged. "I know how you can fill up the hall?"

"How?"

"Simple, Invite all the guys you've said no to."

"Then I wouldn't even be able to fill my kitchen."

"How about the ones you said yes to?"

"Yankee Stadium, here we come."

Yek!

"That guy in California, who was, as they say in the Restoration comedies, the first to have his will of you, the first to take his pleasure of you—"

"Yek! Some pleasure."

"You said he was strange, but still when you went out to California, you went to bed with him."

"I don't think he liked sex. Not with women anyway. What is it about me"—eyes twinkling—"that makes men hate sex so much?"

"You poor kid," Guido said. "You had to wait all these years for the real thing."

"Imagine, First finding it at fifty-three?"

"Going on sixty," Guido said, ducking.

Yonder, out in the wild blue, with her vibrator

Everything came late to her. Sex came late, some years after she should have started having it: and orgasms were not only late, they never arrived. They lost my address, she quipped. Until the vibrator. She never really enjoyed men as much as her vibrator.

"In other words," Guido said, "the men were a kind of competitor to the vibrator."

"That's an interesting way of putting it," Aviva said.

"I'm going to sue it for alienation of affection. I'm going to initiate divorce proceedings and ask for sole custody. I'm going to get a restraining order to have your fuse box destroyed."

Younger image of me, you're obsessed with a

The photographer in Guido (can we in fact separate the two entities?) became obsessed with photos of Aviva and was more involved with the image of her past (which he wants to like but dislikes) than of her present.

"You spend more time with my photos than with me," she complained. "Maybe you like the way I looked then better than now. Maybe I'm too old for you. In five or so years I'll be into my seventh decade and you'll dump me."

She waited for a verbal denial, a feral outcry, "No!"

But all she got from him was a downlip grimace.

"And you spend more time with questions of my past than with our future. You love the twenty-eight year old in me, not the fifty-five year old."

"Not true!" he declared with vehemence; but dammit, she'd hit it on the head. That's who he loved, the elusive now-gone Aviva, but he also despised the twenty-eight and thirty-year old that pingponged from bed to bed, jealous that he didn't have her then. Then he would just have screwed her and not been emotionally involved, and he told her so.

Yes, he was obsessed with her past, he knew, and no matter how many questions he asked her, he would never be able to reconstruct it. He remembered Tammy saying—but he wasn't going to tell Aviva that— "For you pictures are more important than reality."

He denied it, while knowing that her remark too was right on the button. Pictures *are* reality, he thought. Everything fades. Pictures remain. Reality captured. Compressed.

Eternalized.

Yummy, the walk continues, Aviva's version

Climbing down a wooded slope we stopped and wound in and around the bare bushes and trees. Balancing on a log, we slowly crossed a stream at the bottom of the incline, I with uncertainty and Guido, ahead, holding my hand reassuringly. We doubled back, crossing the stream again at another point and scrambled up to the top of the hill. We stopped to rest and catch our breath on level ground. We kissed again but more passionately this time. I felt the internal temperature in my body surge. Unexpectedly, Guido pulled the zipper of my jacket down. He swiftly lifted my sweater and I felt my breasts released, fondled, and kissed.

"When will we make love?" I asked breathlessly. (He always maintained that I never said the word *when*.) And he told me to come to his house tomorrow.

We trudged across the open field of snow, talking, touching and creating sparks of excitement. I knew that when it came time to say goodbye, the parting would create a void that I hadn't realized existed before. Old memories surfaced—perhaps it's better to feel nothing than to deal with disappointment.

We arrived full circle to the place of our first kiss. There was a wooden bench in a wooden gazebo that I hadn't noticed the first time. We lingered here a while, reluctant to have it end, and made plans for the next day. I felt the glow of youthful anticipation.

We drove off, he ahead of me. I saw the back of his head, happily nodding time to Dvorak's Cello Concerto on his car radio. I could see we were tuned to the same station. He always said we were on the same wavelength. When the light in the front of us turned red, he leaped out of his car and darted to my window.

"Are you glowing inside?" Guido asked.

"Mmmm, yes, I feel as if I just swallowed a light bulb," I answered. He quickly returned to his car and continued driving.

I recalled the inner turmoil I felt those days when he came for lessons. I was like a vain adolescent. Again and again I ran to the mirror before his arrival. The doorbell would ring and my heart would beat like a sledgehammer. After he departed an hour would pass before my nervous system would return to its former state. I would then enter that delicious inner world of mine, reliving every bit of conversation, every glance, every nuance. And by superimposing fantasy upon fantasy, I was able to bear the passing of another seven days. In those fantasies, at night, in my bed, we would make love in every conceivable position, and I would imagine kissing every inch of his body and he kissing mine.

I don't know if it happened the first time I saw him or the second, but it was Bam! I was hit, smitten. When I told him this, he spoke of the beautiful scene in Chaucer's *Troilus and Criseyde,* when Criseyde sees Troilus returning triumphant from war. She takes one look at him and says, "Who gave me drinke?" She meant of course, "Who's given me a love potion?" Like Criseyde, love smit me, transported me, moved me, bewitched me, enchanted me. I couldn't eat, sleep, drink, think, I couldn't breathe. When he left after the lesson, I was actually breathless for a while. Love moved me out of myself. I'd consumed something. A magic potion called *love.*

Our cars approached the intersection, the parting of ways. I pulled my car up alongside his and turned toward him. For a second, we half-smiled at each other and then I blew him a kiss that came from the very depths of my being. Later, he told me that one waits a lifetime for a kiss like that.

The ride home alone brought on a feeling of emptiness. Paradise had come and gone too quickly. But in the solitude of my room I was able to revitalize that beautiful inner glow and relive that miracle that had touched me. A half-century was not too long to wait to be among the very lucky few.

Z

Z, letters beyond

"Don't you dare break up this love," he told her. But he thought this: I feel as if space were enlarged, like spaces between letters, the letters larger and broad openings between the letters. As if a ray gun had suddenly been fired and the normal flow of electricity were suddenly intensified; a volume raised to beyond the highest level. The number just after the last number. Two letters beyond Z. The unseen rung after the ladder's highest rung. The note on the cello beyond that highest note.

I can walk between the huge letters and see vast spaces, deserts, and mountains between the colored letters. The number not yet discovered is clearly seen. The unimagined letters so clear they spell words in a language I am about to create; the note never heard clearly ringing, pure sound, on an instrument I am making.

Zap her, is her husband trying to?

Each time the phone rang and it was a wrong number or someone selling dog tags or a baby voice saying, "Can I speak to Marilyn?" Aviva became suspicious. Was her husband checking up on her? Were the wrong numbers legit?

Zetetic

Which Guido is, on occasion.

See *Webster's Unabridged.*

Zing! the fifth force in physics just discovered

Every day physicists come up with another force. Headlines in the *Times* science section. Okay, the first force we know. And I'll translate it into personal terms. Gravity. Or man's pull to a woman. Second force; electromagnetism. I'm electric. I zing. I'm charged up. And you're my magnet. Click, we unite. Third is the strong force that holds the nucleus— nicknamed nookie for short—the nucleus that holds an atom together. My strong hand holding your nookie. Fourth force is the weak force that causes some atoms to break down in radioactive decay. Okay, that's a tough one. How to translate it into human terms? Well, it refers to the occasional breakdowns of your attachment to me. Your occasional spells of unthinking weakness. No wonder it's the weak force. And the fifth that's just been discovered is believed to counteract gravity. Everyone knows what that is. Garlic! Which pulls people apart instead of clicking them together.

Zone, mystical time

"I'll tell you why that sexual urge came over you in Venice."

She had mentioned that scene in Venice a number of times and it had gone right past him. But now he understood why her lust came to her in Venice years ago, that day she felt horny for the first time, even though she'd been devirginized seven times over. He explained that it was for him she was longing.

"Where did this lust overcome you?"

"I told you," she said, "Venice."

"Right. It didn't happen in Paris, London, or Rome. This inexplicable feeling, not connected to any man, but just a cosmic sexual heat welling up in you, had to take place in *my home town*. Years in advance of meeting me, or perhaps having already met me in a mystical time zone, you desired me, you wanted your body filled with mine."

"Yes, yes," she said, her eyes glowing. "I never thought of that. Another mystical connection."

Zzzing went the strings of her heart!

In her apartment Plaskow gave her such a deep kiss, an electric shock zzzinged through her. Now he kissed her cheeks, her eyes, her ears, and with both hands massaged her ass as he pushed her to the sofa.

"Please," she said once for propriety's sake that had about as much effect as the word *coffee* in the restaurant, a *please* that could have been a plea for more. She felt his impatience. Felt he wanted to compress their two years together into one fiery encounter. She moved backward with his firm guidance, feeling . . . Feeling what? She couldn't call it love, she knew, for he did not fill her thoughts. She never thought of him or longed for him once she left the studio. Rather call it adoration. Adulation. Even, maybe, desire. The aura of a famous man. Pupil of Casals. Instant star. Plays all over the world. Super teacher. The joy of taking her teacher. Getting to know him as a man. Deep down she had hoped for some kind of emotional involvement, something that she had really never known before. But she knew it would be difficult with Ian Plaskow because he wasn't a generous man. He was centered into himself, as witness his chill blue-green eyes. And besides, he was married.

So Aviva said "please" only once before she felt herself pulled down on the sofa on top of him. At once he pulled up her blouse and bra and kissed her breasts. It was her last remark of the evening. Even though it was dark she closed her eyes as he undressed her. His kisses, his hands, were all over. Breasts. Knees. One calf, then another. This thigh, that one. Hardly had she a chance to sense one part of her body than he was swiftly elsewhere. She felt dizzy. One moan overlapped the other. She couldn't see him, saw perhaps only a faint outline of him from the city lights that filtered through the shade. Her thighs were on fire. She wanted to suck him into her. Oh, how she wanted him in her now. How delicious that moment when a man enters. With all the others it was only mechanical. She'd known them only days, perhaps a week or two. Felt some pleasure. Tried it because everyone was making love, in and outside of marriage. And she, for seven long years, had had nothing *in* marriage. Seven ludicrous years of virginity. But with Ian Plaskow it was different. Him she had known the longest, more than two years. Two years and three months. Knew him perhaps better than her husband. Certainly there was more communication with Plaskow than with Paul. With Plaskow she'd at least exchanged some thoughts. With her husband, only silence. No wonder she wanted to please him now in a different way.

As Plaskow kissed her, she told herself it would be different now. She had never felt, had only in romances read about, the stirring anticipation, the burning desire that flames in a woman in heat.

"Now? Yes?" His first words since lying down.

"Mmm," she said.

He lay on his back. "You on top."

As he entered her or she entered him, for her head was swimming as though all the music she knew was on a carousel and all of Bach revolving, and she saw images of cellos, a string symphony of cellos, the cello he played while sitting next to her, with its beautiful pinched waist, a Strad of course, which she pictured as herself, her alter ego. He was playing her, just as she had dreamed it. She was his cello and his arched bow was running across her body. With eyes closed she slid across the sheen of the instrument, sliding quicker and quicker, and as she screamed, he played in syncopation to her movements and her screams.

Higher and higher the waves of music. But still the waves don't break. She stops at the top of the wave and cannot descend. She stops to listen to the music of the carousel. Hears a crescendo of sound. A four-chord progression. But the fourth chord, the resolution, hangs in the air. Unplayed. She longs for that final chord. Which doesn't come.

Awake now, she laughed suddenly. "I like your bow."

Plaskow stopped. His hands froze. Dropped them from her hips. She felt his annoyance.

"What's the matter?"

"What's the big joke?" He wanted to know.

"I'm sorry," she said softly, and still didn't know whether to call him Ian or Mr. Plaskow and bent down to kiss his face. "I thought it was funny."

But even in the dark, from the dim half-light coming through the shade, she could see the look of distress on his tightening face. His enthusiasm flagged.

"You're supposed to be off in la-la land," he said.

"Couldn't help it," she said, apologetic. "I know I'm being silly."

Later, when it was over, she fell into his large firm embrace, and he asked her if she was okay.

"Yes," she said. She was okay, but not okay in the way he meant, but she wasn't going to tell him that. But she did feel waves. Still, though every pore tingled (was it him or the excitement of having her teacher?), she felt empty because Plaskow was a married man, because he had said not a word to her during the lovemaking, because even in his fervor, his passion, a breath of cold mingled, because once her clothes were off his ardor seemed to cool and he became impersonal.

Of course she knew he was married. But it was theoretical for her, for Mrs. Plaskow really didn't have a face. She hardly saw her face when she said hello that day that Plaskow snarled at her when she saw them in his parked car outside of PAMA. So her involvement with a married man really didn't bother her. Or did it? But he did tell her one more thing. "Remember, I said that there's an affinity between the cello and a woman? But there's one affinity I didn't mention." "What's that?" she asked. "The f-hole." And he smiled a wicked smile.

And as she rose off him he said, "You can call me Ian now . . ." And later he said, "Now you know about the carpet."

She had forgotten. "What carpet?"

"Remember you told me you're looking for a carpet, and I said I have one for you?"

She smiled, remembering. "Where?"

"You're on it."

"So now," she giggled, "I too can join the carpet workers union."

"Why?"

"I also laid a carpet."

But he, that humorless man, didn't think it was funny. Only *his* jokes were funny.

After the first lovemaking in New York, her lessons already had a different character. Ian sat most of the lesson with his arms around her chair as she played, kissing her occasionally on the back of the neck. She couldn't concentrate. She was preparing for a Master's Recital in May, and he promised to attend, though he never came to any student's recital. Over the next seven months, they met six or seven more times in her apartment (he would come in about once a month) and a few times he rode the train with her from Philly to New York, showing his affection by stroking her hands as he sat next to her, making her tingle. On the train the excitement built up. Although she didn't think of him between visits, on the days he rode with her she couldn't wait to take him upstairs and spend the night with him. But Ian never spoke of love, nor even affection. Neither did she. It was as though both knew what the other was after—physical pleasures. Her feelings were still detached, and though she longed for a deeper relationship, she knew it couldn't happen with him. She really didn't like him that much and couldn't imagine loving a basically cold, ungenerous man. In the morning, for instance, Ian would just dress and slip away without even saying good-bye. And when he left, the fleeting joy—she persuaded herself it was joy—faded, and in its stead came a feeling of emptiness. She had heard of the feeling of distress after lovemaking. Now she knew the feeling. The last time they were together she heard him stirring early in the morning and before he had a chance to dress, she swooped up his underwear, put it on and ran to the other side of the room. He chased her around the bed—come on, Aviva, I have to go—until he caught her and fell on top of her.

Why had she done this—an antic so unlike her—with him? Her recollection was that she did this to puncture the self-puffery, to make him more responsive, to bring him down a peg from his pedestal, Mister Plaskow.

The semester was ending and she knew that for Ian Plaskow she was just a passing episode, a young woman who was available for a night each time he was in the city, a good lay, no involvement, no questions asked.

In May she gave her Master's Recital with the student orchestra. She looked out at the audience. Though her vision was a bit fuzzy she did see Ian. So he had kept his promise after all. Women sat on both sides of him. She couldn't tell if he had brought his wife. As if she weren't nervous enough—she was playing Boccherini's Cello Concerto—she now had the added vexation of thinking that perhaps Ian's wife was out there too. The thought alone made her nerves jangle. The beginning went well, but in the second movement, her memory—that which would bug her, be her *bete noir* for decades—began to slip. She played mechanically, trying to salvage the piece by good faking, but she soon lost the thread. Later, she blamed it on the woman who she thought might be his wife. Why did he bring her, dammit? That's the thought that ran through her head, blocking her memory, forcing her to use tricks to fool the audience, tricks the musically sophisticated audience at PAMA would not buy.

After the concert, Plaskow came backstage, accompanied by a tall, pretty, but rather gaunt blonde Scandinavian-looking woman. One could see at once by the way she held herself that her right hand was flawed. First Ian introduced his wife—Aviva kept her hands behind her back—and then said, You looked quite beautiful out there, but not even a perfunctory compliment about her playing, which she knew was awful. Seeing the wife in the flesh, especially her partially disabled right hand made Aviva'a blood freeze. She couldn't speak. Only nod. Why did he have to bring her here? Wasn't it enough that she hexed me out there? What was the purpose of it? Was it his way of saying, See what I'm saddled with? Or, see, you might have been her replacement?

There were several replacements over the years, Aviva knew, and she realized that Plaskow had probably gotten a kick out of having both women he was screwing meet each other. Like an arsonist going back to the scene of the crime.

At the moment, when the three of them were momentarily bound— Ian knew, Aviva knew, but they exchanged not the slightest intimate glance; the only one who didn't know was the wife—Aviva decided: No more. That was it. Seeing the wife in person, seeing both together made her realize how pointless was this affair, if it could be called an affair, with no legato to it, but just several independent encounters over the past months unlinked by anything that went before or would come after. Was there really anything to build on? He was a married man. It took the gaunt blonde wife's presence to drive the point home. Yes, Aviva had seen her once before, but only fleetingly. She really didn't have a face then, so her involvement with a married man didn't bother her. Still, she felt no joy, only emptiness after each screwing. But as usual, Aviva could not, would not, call him to break the next appointment. She let the next prearranged dinner take its course but had her girlfriend, Sue, stay in the apartment. She would use her as an excuse that they couldn't sleep together in that tiny room. But things didn't quite go as planned. He didn't mind Sue's presence. When he began to kiss Aviva in front of Sue, within minutes Sue got up and left and Aviva had to tell Ian directly that she could no longer continue. But her good-bye was compounded by another problem. She had applied for a job at a college in Kansas and wanted to clinch it by having Plaskow make a call. She had discussed it with him the day after her flawed concert, when he made the next dinner date. Would the good-bye to Ian ruin her chances? How could it? They were both pros. But even in her good-bye Aviva could not be frank. She couldn't tell him that now that she had seen his wife she could no longer continue with him. She merely said, "I don't think I can see you any more."

Plaskow was astounded, his pride wounded.

"But why?"

Aviva pressed her lips and shrugged.

"Are you going to come back in September?"

"No. I can't. I have other plans. I want to get a job."

"Look," he said, "if I haven't spoken to you about love, it's not that I haven't felt it. I do. Very much. I'm sure you know there are different kinds of love. We can all love in different ways."

I don't buy that hogwash, she thought. You're so full of shit, Plaskow, it's coming out of your f-hole. And maybe she even told him that hogwash line, though in retrospect, it wasn't like her to talk like that. She was still intimidated by him, saw him still as a cold, rather unfeeling man, despite his enthusiasm for her, and she still had that empty, pointless, useless, used feeling after he had gone. They had never discussed their feelings, so why did he start now? she wondered.

As Plaskow headed for the door, she asked—or maybe she just wished she had asked—"Did you make that call for me on the Kansas job?"

At the door he said he hadn't yet but would.

Later in the week, when he called to urge her to reconsider and study with him in the fall, she said. "No." She wanted to ask him to be sure to make that call, but somehow couldn't bring herself to do it.

She knew he never made that call. When two weeks later she called the college, they told her they hadn't yet received a recommendation from Ian Plaskow. And as quickly as she was stirred up by him so quickly was that feeling severed. Now that he was gone, there was neither joy nor emptiness, but just a neutral vacuum, like the sounds left in a hall after a wrong note has been played.

Ian's last visit to her apartment was the most difficult for her. He was expecting what he'd gotten the previous six or seven times. Aviva recalled the half-naked syndrome, where good Jewish girls would go up to a certain point and no more to preserve their virginity, their frayed and tasseled respectability. Although nothing happened, since he wanted something to happen and it was denied, he must have felt like the girl who closes her legs in the face of temptation.

Did it ever occur to her that perhaps Plaskow would leave his wife for her? she imagined Guido asking her. No, she had never had such romantic notions. She didn't, in those days, presume. Suddenly, her apartment came to her, vividly, as if she were seeing it now. After one opened the door there was a long hallway with lots of closets. Then, off to a side, a right turn to a big room, the only room, with a small kitchen off on the left.

Her daybed sofa, with three bolsters, had a tailored print cover that her mother had made. On one side of the bed was an antique oak cabinet that her aunt had given her; on the other, a dresser. By the wall stood a desk with bookshelves; these came from a thrift shop and she had painted them white. Her cello and music stand stood in a corner of the room near the TV set, the phonograph and her collection of records.

When Ian first came in, she remembered, he inspected the furniture, then seized and kissed her. After that first kiss he picked her up and carried her to the daybed. She imagined Guido asking who had pulled out the bed. She really couldn't recall. But now she thought; the bed just popped open of its own accord.

"Why couldn't you just have said no to him?" Guido had asked her.

"I couldn't really say no to his invitation because it would seem like a rejection of my teacher."

"Then why not accept just the dinner invitation without inviting him upstairs?" the peeved Guido asked.

"I think he invited himself. But in any case that really would have been a rejection"

"Aviva with the good heart," Guido said sarcastically.

"No. I guess I really wanted him."

"I thought so. Thought so all along. Had a hunch. That's the first time you came out with that part of the scenario."

"It's hard for me to reconstruct every nuance of my feelings from so long ago . . . Now, you tell me, why couldn't he have made that call for me?"

"You're still upset about this after all these years?"

"I don't know if I'm upset now, but the thought of it upsets me."

"Why?" Guido said. "I'll tell you why he wouldn't make that call. Because hell hath no fury like a male lover scorned . . . But why didn't you press him? You had a kind of psychological advantage."

"I know this is going to sound like a contradiction, but *because* I was involved with him I couldn't ask him to make that call. As a student it would have been easier for me to ask him. As a girlfriend, and especially since I'd rejected him, it was more difficult . . . I really know a lot about sex and politics, don't I?"

"So why didn't you keep him on, let's say another week, until after the call."

"Because I'm not like that. I'm not a whore."

She let that sink in for a while, then added:

"But in retrospect, if I'd tried harder, I could have made it a more lasting relationship."

"How?"

"But it wasn't in me to do that."

"What *could* you have done? And how do you know he was willing?"

"I sensed it . . . I'm not sorry I didn't. Who knows how long it would have lasted?"

"Till another Aviva came along. He's on his fifth wife now, you know."

"I suppose I could have invited him more often to New York . . . I wonder what his motives really were."

Guido didn't beat around the bush. "Piece of ass."

See **Ahh time, once upon**

Curt Leviant is the author of four critically acclaimed novels, *The Yemenite Girl, Passion in the Desert, The Man Who Thought He Was Messiah,* and *Partita in Venice.* He has won the Edward Lewis Wallant Award and writing fellowships from the National Endowment for the Arts, the Rockefeller Foundation, the Jerusalem Foundation, and the New Jersey Arts Council. His short stories and novellas have appeared in *Midstream, Zoetrope, American Literary Review, Confrontation, North American Review, Ascent, Missouri Review, Tikkun,* and many other magazines and on National Public Radio. His work has also been included in *Best American Short Stories, Prize Stories: The O. Henry Awards,* and other anthologies. Mr. Leviant's first novel, *The Yemenite Girl,* has been translated into Hebrew and Spanish and was reprinted as part of the Syracuse University Press Library of Modern Jewish Literature.

Other titles in the Library of Modern Jewish Literature